TERMINATION SHOCK

NEAL STEPHENSON is the author of: *Fall or, Dodge in Hell*; *The Rise and Fall of D.O.D.O.* (with Nicole Galland); *Seveneves, Reamde, Anathem*; the three-volume historical epic The Baroque Cycle (*Quicksilver, The Confusion, and The System of the World*); *Cryptonomicon, The Diamond Age, Snow Crash* and *Zodiac*, and the groundbreaking nonfiction work *In the Beginning . . . Was the Command Line.*

Neal Stephenson

TERMINATION SHOCK

b

THE BOROUGH PRESS

The Borough Press
An imprint of HarperCollins*Publishers* Ltd
1 London Bridge Street
London SE1 9GF

www.harpercollins.co.uk

HarperCollins*Publishers*
1st Floor, Watermarque Building, Ringsend Road
Dublin 4, Ireland

First published in Great Britain by HarperCollins*Publishers* 2021
1

A catalogue record for this book is available from the British Library

HB ISBN: 978-0-00-840436-9
TPB ISBN: 978-0-00-840437-6

Printed and bound in the UK using 100% Renewable Electricity by CPI Group (UK) Ltd

MIX
Paper from
responsible sources
FSC™ C007454

To A.L.

LONDON BOROUGH OF WANDSWORTH	
9030 00007 6769 1	
Askews & Holts	
AF THR	
	WW21006863

If it keeps on rainin', levee's goin' to break

If it keeps on rainin', levee's goin' to break

And the water come in, have no place to stay . . .

I works on the levee, mama both night and day

I works on the levee, mama both night and day

I works so hard, to keep the water away

— *KANSAS JOE MCCOY AND MEMPHIS MINNIE*

TERMINATION
SHOCK

TEXAS

Houston's air was too hot to support airplanes. Oh, the queen's jet could have *landed* there, given that, during the flight from Schiphol, it had converted ten thousand kilograms of fuel into carbon dioxide and dumped it into the atmosphere. Refueled, though, it could not safely take off until the heat wave broke. And what was going to break it was a hurricane.

Under the direction of air traffic controllers, Frederika Mathilde Louisa Saskia—for that was the queen's given name—and her co-pilot, a Royal Dutch Air Force captain named Johan, began to drive the jet through a series of maneuvers that would culminate in Waco.

Now, maybe Waco was not the optimal choice for them. But there was no point in quibbling over it. The business jet, slightly crowded with seven souls aboard, flew higher and faster than air-liners. It had been slicing through the lower stratosphere at better than six hundred miles per hour, almost ready to begin its descent into Houston, when they had gotten the news about the insuffi-ciency of that city's air. A decision had to be made. It didn't have to be the best possible decision.

As she was informed by Texan voices on the radio, as well as Willem coming up to the cockpit with whatever he'd gleaned over the jet's data link, a thunderstorm had swept over Waco in the last few hours, dropping the temperature to a mere 45. Or 113 as they measured things in the States. Low enough, anyway, that they could at least look it up in the tables of important numbers that the jet's manufacturer had calculated three decades ago, when this de-sign had been certified. It had never entered those people's minds that it would get as hot as it was today in Houston, so the tables didn't go that high.

Waco's airport would give them everything they really needed.

It had two runways arranged in a V. Current winds dictated that they should land on the more westerly of those, southbound. The air traffic controllers told them what to do. They did it.

Those controllers had their hands full juggling a large number of planes—mostly airliners—that had likewise been disappointed in their hopes of landing in Houston. Most of them needed larger airports and so it didn't seem right to argue with them about whether Waco was perfect. These transmissions could be heard by anyone with a radio. They were being recorded. It was of some importance that they not make waves, not draw attention to themselves. The queen had been raised from infancy never to seem as though she were arrogating royal prerogatives. For to do so would be un-Dutch. It would merely give ammunition to anti-royalists. Lennert, her security chief, was coming around to the view that Waco would be fine. There was a hangar suitable for jets like this one. Willem had already reserved hotel rooms and worked out how to rent cars.

All she had to do was get the jet on the ground. She was good at that. Even if she weren't, Johan could do it with no help from her.

Along with royalty and wealth, she had inherited from her father this strange pastime of piloting jet airplanes. Despite being a king, he had moonlighted as an airline pilot for KLM—Koninklijke Luchtvaart Maatschappij—Royal Dutch Airlines, whose logo was actually a crown. As Papa had explained to her long ago, there was a reason he had become a pilot. It was that when he was at the controls he had not merely the opportunity but the sacred obligation to focus solely on the machine that was keeping him and his passengers alive.

There were two things about this statement that little Princess Frederika Mathilde Louisa Saskia hadn't fully understood at the time.

One (more obvious): because Mama and Papa had tried to raise her as some semblance of a normal human being, she hadn't understood until much later how many demands the crown placed on one's attention. Now she knew this very well.

Two (which had only come to her recently): "the machine that was keeping him and his passengers alive" was a metaphor for the Netherlands: an engineered contraption that would kill a lot of Dutch people if they didn't keep pushing the right buttons.

She felt a sense of freedom and clarity of mind while at the controls of an airplane during the descent and the preparations for landing. It was all a matter of operating the controls so as to keep certain numbers within certain ranges. By the time the jet was skimming the runway at Waco, its speed needed to have been reduced to a figure denoted VREF. This varied with such conditions as temperature, weight of the aircraft, and runway conditions; but anyway it could be calculated from those thirty-year-old tables and there were known procedures for getting the plane's speed down to that number.

At the same time they needed to pass vertically downward through the entire troposphere—the shell of air surrounding the earth, where weather happened—until the number on the altimeter matched whatever the altitude of Waco was. Again there were known procedures for achieving that, all of which needed to mesh with the series of turns dictated by those harried Texan air traffic controllers. The operation of the jet's controls toward the systematic achievement of those objectives, the terse, pithy, but utterly calm exchanges with Johan and with the voices on the radio, all combined to put her into a state of being that the Dutch referred to as *normal* with the accent on the second syllable. A different thing altogether from the English "NORMal."

To explain "norMAL" fully would fill a book, but the most important thing about it, if you happened to be a member of the Dutch royal family, was that "norMAL" was exactly what royals were forever under suspicion of *not* being, and so anything you could do that made you norMAL was desirable; and since that could easily be faked, it worked best if it were some activity that would get you killed if you did it wrong.

If you rode your bicycle to school, as she had famously done when she had been a little girl, haters could and would claim it was a publicity stunt and scoff at anyone naive enough to fall for it. But even the most frothing anti-royalists could not deny that the king or queen had actually landed that plane, and that, had they just been faking it, they'd have ended up dead. Moreover, it was not something a monkey could do. Even a royal could not get certified for it until she had taken in a fair bit of mathematics, physics, engineering, and meteorology. In the distant past, kings had shown the world that they meant it by strapping on a sword and riding into war, putting their lives on the line. Getting behind the controls of a plane and pointing it at a runway was as close as one could reasonably come in the modern world to the same public blood oath.

Her staff were thinking of details she wouldn't have—and ought not to, given her present responsibilities. It was a natural mistake to think of Waco as cool, simply because it wasn't as hot as Houston. But in truth the plane would become an oven the moment it touched down. Getting out of it wouldn't much improve matters; inside or outside, it was only a matter of time before they all succumbed to heatstroke. So a plan needed to be in place to get the plane and its occupants at least under shade and preferably into air-conditioning within minutes of touching down. They had earthsuits in the cargo hold, of course, charged and ready to go, but the idea of breaking them out this early felt panicky and amateurish.

She just had to land the thing, and there was no particular reason why this should be difficult. The hurricane menacing Houston was hundreds of kilometers away over the Gulf. Air was choppy in the wake of that earlier thunderstorm, but nothing she hadn't flown through many times in Dutch skies. It was broad daylight, about four in the afternoon. The spiraling oblong descent dictated by the air traffic controllers gave her a good look at the greater Waco area. It was flat and green. Not as flat as home. But this was a landscape that as far as the eye could see was uncomplicated by anything resembling a hill. The green was darker than the Netherlands' pastures and croplands—lots of forest and scrub.

Slowly her view zoomed in. They got lined up on the runway, which was still too distant to be clearly visible. Beyond the airport was the city itself, only a few buildings and towers raising their heads above what looked to be a well-tended canopy of shade trees. It had a lot of parks. The city's outskirts faded to a grayer shade— newer developments, perhaps, with less mature trees? Just to the right of their projected course was a big lake, buffered from the open greensward of the airport by a nubby carpet of vegetation so dark green it was almost black. She could tell from the lake's shape that it was artificial. Dutchwoman that she was, she couldn't help tracing its shoreline until she identified the long straight section that had to be the dam. It was a low earthen structure pierced by a spillway, not far beyond the end of the runway.

These impressions were all gathered in an almost subliminal way over the ten or so minutes it took to bring the jet down. During that time there was surprisingly little to do. She and Johan had trimmed the plane so that its weight exceeded the lift produced by its wings; in accordance with the laws of physics, this caused it to lose altitude in a steady and predictable manner. Airspeed slowly declined through two hundred knots, headed toward VREF, which today was 137 knots. Soon they would deploy the flaps. Her eyes glanced in a circuit among several key indicators. It was an old jet. Many of the controls were mechanical switches set in black Bakelite panels with embossed white letters, very old school. But the important stuff in the middle was "all glass" in pilot-speak: glorious jewel-colored screens with virtual instruments, retrofitted into the old dashboard. Her eyes knew where to find the really important data—airspeed, altitude, roll, pitch, yaw.

But looking out the windscreen at the real world was important too. A small single-engine plane landed far ahead of them and taxied out of their way. The land flashed unpredictably here and there. They saw this all the time at home. There was local flooding. Not enough to submerge vast areas but enough to strew patches of standing water, glazing the flat landscape where drainage was slow and soil saturated. When one of those puddles caught the sun, light skidded into her eye. The airport, though, seemed to be well drained—the tower would have warned them of puddles on the runways. The runway was easy to see now, dead ahead, right where it ought to be, splotched with damp but not wet. Final approach took them low over a subdivision. Most of the airport spread away to their left. To the right of the runway was just a narrow strip of grass running between the tarmac and a security fence. Immediately outside of and parallel to the fence was a two-lane road. This bordered dark forested land that extended for a kilometer or two to the lake's convoluted shore. The woods were speckled in some places with little eruptions of dark red earth and in others with blue rectangles—tarps pitched over makeshift camps.

Always fascinating to her was this slow inexorable zooming in. Twenty minutes ago she'd have found it difficult to pick out the greater Waco metropolitan area below the black-blue vault of the stratosphere, but now as they dropped through a hundred meters of altitude she could see, in the backyards of houses, blue swimming pools—a lighter tint of blue than that of the tarps in the woods. Children—presumably much better off than the ones under the tarps—were cooling off after school by jumping into them. Her thoughts strayed momentarily to her own daughter, but she put Lotte out of her mind for now and instead checked the instruments for the hundredth time. Movement to the right of the runway created a moment of anxiety until she saw it was just a pickup truck driving down the cracked and water-splotched two-laner outside the airport's perimeter fence. Its brake lights came on for some reason. No concern of hers.

They cleared the fence at the near end of the runway. Any anxiety she might have felt in the last seconds of the flight as to whether speed, altitude, angle of attack were correct was dispelled by the fact that Johan was perfectly relaxed. They were as one. It was just a matter of waiting for the moment, any second now, when the tires would touch the tarmac and the jet would become a really expensive and unwieldy car. The high placement of the windscreen, combined with the jet's slightly nose-up attitude, made it impossible to see the runway directly ahead of them. But this jet was fitted with a video camera in its belly, enabling them to see what was below on a small screen set into the panel between the pilot's and co-pilot's chairs. Normally she ignored it while landing, since it never showed anything except clean unobstructed pavement. But she was hearing shocked exclamations from people back in the cabin, on the right side of the plane, who had apparently just witnessed something incredible. Incredible and not good. She liked to leave the cockpit door open so that curious passengers could gaze up the aisle and see out the front; but now it sounded like they were seeing something she *couldn't*.

She was just beginning to wonder if they might need to abort the landing when unusual movement caught her eye on the belly camera screen.

She glanced at it just long enough to see a sort of dark churning mass of four-legged creatures directly below the plane, moving from right to left across their path.

The jet jerked powerfully rightward. The right landing gear, under the wing, had struck something that wasn't supposed to be there. They had not touched down yet and so the tires had no purchase on the ground. The nose swung hard to the right while plunging downward, smashing the front landing gear into the pavement at an awkward angle—not before it slammed into additional obstacles on the runway.

They were traveling at VREF, which as Texans measured such things was about 160 miles per hour. Pavement came up toward her. The jet was moving at least as much sideways as forward—skittering so violently that her eyes could not focus on the instruments. The belly cam screen had gone largely red, the camera's lens spattered with either blood or hydraulic fluid. Where it wasn't red it was blurred, hurtling green. No, it was the color of the sky. No, green again. She was flung forward against her safety harness. The interior of the plane was a thumping cacophony of flying luggage. Some bit of the jet—a wingtip?—must have dug into the sodden ground. There was nothing for it now but to shed those hundred and sixty miles per hour by damaging the landscape.

Pigs. It had taken her mind a few moments to identify the four-legged animals that had made a momentary appearance in the belly cam as they had boiled across the runway. They were pigs. More like wild boars than domestic farm animals. This was a now totally useless fact supplied by her brain as they tumbled and skidded diagonally across the grass and entered into a complicated relationship with the chain-link fence.

And then blessedly the jet had stopped. Hot air spread across her face; the hull of the plane had been breached. It smelled like jet fuel. This gave her a powerful incentive to unbuckle her safety harness. Gravity then caused her to end up on top of Johan, who was slower to move. Blood was running down his face and dripping from his ear. It originated from a laceration clearly visible through his reddish-blond eyebrow. That eye was closed, but the other was open and tracking, albeit drunkenly. His arms and legs were moving. Almost certainly a concussion. She undid his safety harness.

Getting out of the cockpit was diabolically hard because gravity was the wrong way. She had to think like a rock climber and find hand- and footholds. A strong hand grabbed her wrist and pulled her out of a tight spot. Lennert satisfying himself that his queen was alive. That accomplished, he turned his attention to the door, which was basically above them. Gravity again was not his friend, but braced on one side by his queen and on the other by his deputy Amelia, Lennert was able to reach the lever that was supposed to open it. She was worried that it would be too damaged to work. But the doorway, which almost cut the plane in half structurally, had to be ridiculously strong and stiff. Lennert was able to operate the lever and get the door moving with one good foot stomp. It fell open to reveal a partly cloudy blue sky. He got both hands on the door frame and pulled-pushed himself up and out, then squatted on the fuselage next to the aperture for a look around. The sun was on his face, which was suddenly wet. The human body couldn't sweat that fast—this was moisture from the air condensing on his relatively cool skin.

She was already fighting an urge to vault through that doorway. She'd have to be the last one off the plane, though. Johan was going to be slow getting out, and others in the back might have suffered even worse injuries for all she knew.

But Lennert was uncharacteristically slow to make his next move. He did not like what he saw; it was by no means clear to him that getting out of the wrecked plane was an improvement on staying in it. His right hand glided back along his belt line, then faltered. When they were walking around in public, he kept a pistol holstered at the small of his back, covered by an untucked shirt. Some instinct had led him to reach for it. But it wasn't there. "Get my bag," he said to Amelia. He meant the little shoulder bag that would contain his gun and other tools of his trade. "I'm just going to look around, *mevrouw*," he explained. "There is no sign of fire but you should be ready to get out in a hurry." He then receded from view as he tried to work out a way to let himself down the curved side of the fuselage.

Amelia was rummaging through spilled luggage for Lennert's bag. That was slow work because the door in the back, which led to the luggage hold, had broken open at some point and stuff was all over the place. For example, a blue bundle, roughly the size of a typical airline rollaway bag, was getting underfoot. This was one of the earthsuits. The queen heaved it up over her head and got it out the door and onto the fuselage. Then she did the same thing with someone's rollaway bag. Someone's knapsack. A second earthsuit. She did not see Lennert's shoulder bag, though, and neither did Amelia.

There were three others. Willem was comforting Fenna, whose job was to make it so that the queen never had to think about hair, makeup, or clothing and yet look good enough not to become the object of ridicule. Fenna was personally responsible for the fact that, in the tabloid press, Frederika Mathilde Louisa Saskia, at the age of forty-five, was from time to time described as being hotter than was actually the case. And (given that she was a widow) "eligible," whatever that was supposed to mean. So Fenna was good at her job. Being in plane crashes, however, clearly was not for her.

And finally Alastair, the one non-Dutch person here. Scottish, but based in London, where he did some kind of math-heavy risk analysis. He was seated askew toward the back of the cabin, still belted in, gazing absentmindedly out a window. What an interesting situation for a risk analyst to find himself in.

Alastair turned his head to follow some development outside, then looked about at the others. The only one who met his eye was the queen, and so he cleared his throat and said to her, matter-of-factly: "There's—"

"Pigs," she said. "I know."

"I was going to say an alligator."

"Oh!"

"Or perhaps crocodile? I don't—"

They were interrupted by Lennert making a sound somewhere between a roar and a scream, but trending toward the latter. If any words were in it, they might have been something like "Get away!" or "Get back!" in the way that humans spoke to animals. But then he howled in some combination of astonishment building to horror and pain.

Amelia had found his bag finally and got his pistol. She staggered up the canted, luggage-strewn aisle. But just as she was getting to the door, gunfire sounded from outside.

The queen, as part of her royal duties, had spent enough time around weapons to know that this was not a pistol. It had the shockingly impressive punch of a rifle and the shots came rapidly enough to indicate that it was semi-automatic. So, an assault rifle.

Amelia's family had come over from Suriname. Various of her ancestors had been African, Dutch, West Indian, and East Indian. She had been on the Dutch Olympic judo squad and had a burly physique sometimes likened to that of the American tennis player Serena Williams. She seemed to take up a lot of space in the jet's cabin. Yet she now projected herself up through the door like a twelve-year-old gymnast and found a perch on the fuselage where she could see what was going on. The pistol was in her hands and she was gazing over its sights as she swung it this way and that. But after a few moments of taking in the scene she lowered it and looked every bit as taken aback as Lennert had been before her.

A man's voice spoke at Amelia from not far away. "Y'all got a first-aid kit in there? He needs one." Then, after a brief pause, "Hang on."

Two more rifle shots sounded.

"Damn 'gators," the man said. "Damn airplane. Excuse my language. I got a score to settle with ol' Snout over there. If I was you I'd keep an eye out for any more hogs, they'll be drawn to the blood."

Frederika Mathilde Louisa Saskia, during this curious discourse, had dragged another earthsuit pack into the vacancy beneath the open door and used it as a stepping-stone so that she could at least get head and shoulders above the doorframe.

There was a lot to see. She tried to focus on what was closest. Directly below, Lennert was reclining against the airplane's fuselage, alive and conscious but probably in shock. Next to him was a dead boar—a true wild boar, probably Lennert's equal in body weight, with bloody tusks jutting from the sides of its jaw. Blood pulsed weakly from what was presumably a bullet hole in its rib cage. A lot of blood also had come out of Lennert, who had suffered a grievous wound on his inner thigh. Above which, practically in his groin, the man who had been doing the talking and the shooting was in the late stages of applying a tourniquet. From his drawling, twanging way of speaking English, she had expected him to be a white man, but he had brown skin, with dark hair and eyes. The sides of his head glinted with stubble, but salt-and-pepper dreadlocks sprouted from a wide strip running down the midline of his scalp. He had a few days' growth of beard, and he seemed hot and tired. Slung over his shoulder was an AK-47. Until recently he'd had a Bowie knife sheathed on his belt, but he'd pulled the belt off to make the tourniquet and was using the sheathed knife in lieu of a stick for tightening it. He met her eye and nodded. "I'll be back for the knife, ma'am," he said, turning away from them to survey the overall scene.

Another pig—not as large or as toothy—came oinking and snuffling around from the other side of the plane, seemingly drawn—just as this man had foretold—to the blood. The man began to unlimber his Kalashnikov but then there was a bang that made the queen go deaf in one ear. She looked up at Amelia in time to see her discharge a second round at the pig. The pig fell over and stopped moving, apart from some jerky nervous system mayhem about the legs. The man turned half around and favored Amelia with a nod. "Double tap was definitely your correct move, sister," he remarked in a world-weary but agreeable tone, and once again turned his back on them. But then noticing something off to his left he turned back again long enough to point out "Yonder engine's on fire." His easygoing way of proffering this observation, the pronunciation "fahr," somehow made it seem less alarming.

She followed his gaze and saw a disembodied jet engine with some metal origami jutting from one side. Flames were indeed coming out of it. Which might have been the most remarkable thing she'd seen all day were it not for the fact that close to it was a dead alligator twice its size.

"Fire brigade, they ain't coming," the man said. He was trudging away right down the center of the wide gutter of churned earth, aerospace technology, and dismembered swine that they had left in their wake. "'Cause they seen this, you know." He indicated the Kalashnikov. "Ambulance? Ain't coming neither. Cops, maybe. Regular cops? I don't think so. I gotta finish my business with ol' Snout 'fore the hard men show up in armored personnel carriers and all that. Look out for the scavengers! They gonna get here a lot sooner than SWAT!" He glanced back to make sure that they were paying attention to him, which they were. He then waved his arm in the direction of the forest across the road. People were coming out of it with long knives.

Snout was a cutesy name for a monster, but Adele had been a girly girl, with cute names for everything. When she had started calling him that, she of course hadn't known that one day Snout was going to eat her.

In those days, some five years ago, Snout had merely been one piglet in a herd of feral swine that came and went across the stretch of central Texas where Rufus and his lady, Mariel, were trying to make a go of it on fifty acres. Snout had been easily identifiable to little Adele because of a distinctive pattern of spots on his nose, and, later, because he was bigger than the others.

The *reason* Snout was bigger—as Rufus and Mariel found out too late—was that Adele had got in the habit of feeding him. Snout, no idiot, had got in the habit of coming around to be fed.

Rufus blamed the situation on *Charlotte's Web*, a work of fantasy literature to which Mariel—as always with the best and purest of intentions—had introduced Adele before she was ready for it. Though to be fair there was a lot of related material on YouTube tending to support the dangerous and wrong idea that swine were cute, not anthropophagous, and could be trusted. From time to time a moral panic would arise concerning the sort of online content to which unsuspecting children were being algorithmically exposed, but it was always something to do with sex, violence, or politics. All important in their way, but mostly preoccupations of city dwellers.

Things might have turned out differently if Rufus had been able to shelter Adele from juvenile pig-related content during that formative year when she had learned her ABCs and Snout had grown from a newborn piglet—basically an exposed fetus—to a monstrous boar weighing twice as much as Rufus, who had once played linebacker. Sometimes at breakfast Adele would complain that in the middle of the night she had been awakened by gunshots in the neighborhood. Rufus would lock eyes with Mariel across the table and Mariel would say "It must have been hunters," which was not technically a lie. It had been Rufus, out at three in the morning with an infrared scope, blowing away feral hogs. And if it wasn't Rufus, it was one of the neighbors doing the same thing for the same reason.

These pigs were an unstoppable plague, to the point where they were actually taking back Texas from the human race. It was sparsely populated territory to begin with; you could only wrest so many dollars out of an acre of Texas ranchland no matter how hard you worked. Anything that reduced your income made the whole proposition that much more sketchy. Rufus and Mariel had put off having a second child for money reasons, so that, in a way, was already a reduction of the human population of their fifty acres by one.

They had decided they would try to make a go of it after Rufus had got out of the service at Fort Sill, up north across the Oklahoma border, and decided that greener pastures might be found elsewhere. He had grown up in Lawton, which was the town adjoining Fort Sill, and the surrounding mosaic of 160-acre land allotments that were largely owned by Comanches. Despite having an ancestry that included Black, white, Mexican, Osage, Korean, and Comanche, he had an ID card identifying him as an official member of the Comanche tribe. For Indians in general and Comanches in particular were a lot less interested in chromosomes and such than mainstream Americans with their 23andMe.

Rufus had met Mariel when he was in the service, doing a stint at Fort Sam Houston, where she had been working as a civilian. Turned out there was this patch of land in her family, this fifty-acre plot a few hours' drive north of San Antonio, and no one was doing anything with it. The proverbial greener pasture, or so they supposed. Her uncle let them live on it provided they kept the place up and paid him enough rent to cover the taxes and such. They pulled a mobile home onto the property and began to live. There was an old infested house that Rufus tore down for the lumber, and from that he knocked together outbuildings: a tool shed, a chicken coop, later a shelter for goats.

Until then Rufus's life had followed a trajectory that was run-of-the-mill in that part of the world: grew up in a broken home, played some football in high school but not at a level that would get him a college scholarship or a wrecked brain. Joined the army. Became a mechanic. Fixed elaborate weaponry in some of the less good parts of the world. Ended up close to home at Fort Sill. Was surprised to discover that twenty years had gone by. Honorably discharged. Had a vague plan to get a college degree on the GI Bill, which was the usual way up in the world for people like him. Put that on hold to embark on this Texas ranch project with Mariel. Her family was from farther south, a classic Texas blend of German and Mexican. Various uncles and cousins and whatnot drove up from time to time to help them get started and, he suspected, to evaluate Rufus's fitness as a man. He did not in any way resent it. For all they knew, he might have been beating her. They needed to satisfy themselves that this wasn't the case. He respected them for their diligence in the matter.

There was an odd bending around in back at the extreme limits of culture and politics where back-to-the-land hippies and radical survivalists ended up being the same people, since they spent 99 percent of their lives doing the same stuff. You had to have a story you could tell yourself about why living this way made more sense than moving to the suburbs of Dallas and getting a job at Walmart. The hippies and the preppers had different stories, but in practice it didn't come up very often. Mariel tended more toward hippie but Rufus had never picked sides.

In trying to make the ranch add up as a financial proposition, he over and over found situations where putting in a heinous amount of brute physical labor might, luck permitting, increase the productivity of the land by a tiny amount. Rufus found himself, as years went by, asking whether it was worth it. Even setting aside the whole GI Bill option, he could simply get a job fixing cars anywhere but here. The cost of living would go up but at least he'd be able to get a good night's sleep instead of setting his alarm for 2:30 A.M. so that he could go out shooting feral hogs.

He left them where they fell, and other hogs ate them. This was just one of the many ways in which it all began to seem futile. Hogs ate everything, including other hogs. Grazing animals would eat grass but leave the roots in the ground; hogs tore up the ground and ate the roots. Erosion followed. Only ants could live in what the hogs left behind. Rufus couldn't kill these things fast enough, and the ones he did kill only became food for the ones he didn't. They forbade Adele feeding Snout or any other wild pig, but by then Snout had already got the head start he needed; he'd come to associate humans with food, and Rufus began to suspect that he was drawn to the sound of rifle shots in the night, as he'd worked out that it usually meant a dead cousin lying on the ground, free for the eating. So Rufus's nocturnal shooting only led to Snout's getting bigger.

A lot of that was hindsight, after what had happened had happened. Just Rufus torturing himself. He should have marked out Snout as a special threat. Should have killed one hog as bait and then lain in wait for Snout to show up. Years later he was haunted almost every night by the possibility that he might once, back in those days when he still had a daughter, have had Snout in his infrared sights, one white silhouette among many, and refrained from pulling the trigger, just because Adele had a soft spot for him and he was afraid he wouldn't be able to look her in the eye over breakfast.

More recently he had learned the trick of sticking out his tongue when the bad self-torturing thoughts began to creep into his mind. He would open his mouth wide and stick out his tongue as far as it would go, almost as if he were gagging the bad thought out, refusing to let it in, and somehow this worked and got his mind back on the track it should follow. It made people look at him funny, but he didn't spend that much time around people.

His only consolation, and a very meager consolation it was, was that the incident—which took place while he was in town picking up a load of drainpipe—had been a sudden invasion of the property by two dozen or more feral hogs. Snout was the ringleader, but he had so many accomplices that even if Rufus had been at home standing there with a loaded gun he might not have been able to save Adele.

He and Mariel broke up, and she wandered back down south to live with family. Rufus devoted his life to killing feral hogs. He literally made it his business.

Business, by that point in his life—he was forty-four—was a thing he was finally coming to grips with. In the army he'd never had to think about profit and loss. He'd assumed that duty on the farm because Mariel was so manifestly hopeless at it. Over those years he had watched, staring into his QuickBooks late at night, as the numbers had gotten worse and worse and more and more of his army pension had been siphoned off to cover the shortfalls. In all honesty it had become a hobby farm. But it was all neither here nor there since these financial signals were drowned out by the emotional side of things: the story that he and Mariel were telling themselves, and increasingly telling Adele, about why they were living here.

Once Adele was dead and Mariel gone, the story was over. Matters became very clear and decisions easy. Rufus sold what he could and sent half the money to Mariel. He drove up to Fort Sill, where, as a retiree, he still had access to the auto shop, and fixed up his truck: a dually, as people around here referred to pickups with double tires at each end of the rear axle. His grandmother and some of his cousins had gone into the RV business. From them he got a used camper trailer that he could tow behind the dually. He moved all his tools, guns, and personal effects into that. He made up signs and business cards saying FERAL SWINE MITIGATION SERVICES and he just started driving around and parking that rig, with those signs on it, in places such as livestock auctions and county fairs.

Without the army pension he might not have made it through the first six months, but slowly business picked up and Rufus found himself driving his rig along the seemingly infinite network of farm-to-market roads that like capillaries infused every part of Texas—a state with which Rufus, an Oklahoman, had a stranger-in-a-strange-land relationship. He would set up operations for a spell on this or that ranch where the owners had decided they needed some additional firepower in this one area. He was not the only person doing it. Far from it. But he was able to compete with bigger outfits on price. The competitors had mouths to feed and equipment to maintain. Some used helicopters. Others shot hogs at night from all-terrain vehicles. Flashy but expensive. Rufus worked by himself. He didn't have to make payroll, didn't have to cover medical and dental. His method was to go out by himself with a rifle on a tripod and an infrared scope and just wait for the white silhouettes to show up against the dark background and then start picking them off, starting with the biggest ones and then working his way down to the juveniles as they scurried around in a panic.

The first six months of slow to nonexistent work had got him down in the dumps, but as he later came to understand, the time had been very well spent. He would sit at the little table in his trailer, running the AC off the generator, reading websites and later books about wild pigs. This was fascinating. For starters he learned that pigs, like white people, were an invasive species from Europe. In conquistador times, the 1500s, Spaniards had brought them across the Rio Grande. Probably before the water of the river had evaporated off their bristly pelts, they had got loose. Many such "introductions" (as these events were denoted in the literature) had taken place over the half millennium since. But none of them, taken alone, could explain a Snout. For that, you had to factor in the wild boar introductions, which were more recent. Some people liked to hunt these animals. It seemed to be a particular obsession of the Germans. There were a lot of those in Texas and they had money, as well as large tracts of land on which to stock game. Apparently in Germany there was a place called the Black Forest. Stories were told of it no less harebrained than the ones that hippies and survivalists favored. What these German-Texans were convinced of was that their ancestors had, since long before and continuing long after the Romans, roamed noble and free in this Black Forest killing wild boars with lances, and that to do so was to partake of their ancient heritage, just like the Indians with their drums and their dancing. So they got hold of the biggest and meanest wild boars that could be obtained in Europe, even sending parties into the hinterlands of Russia to find unspoiled stock, and they brought these things to Texas. Usually some effort was made to fence the land, but hogs could root under fences, ford rivers, and wade across tide flats, and so the boars had got loose in the wild almost as easily as their domesticated cousins had done hundreds of years before, and got busy having sex with those.

Rufus lacked a lot of formal education but he certainly knew how to read and he had been a very good mechanic in the army largely because he had had an ability to focus on abstruse maintenance documents to a degree exceeding that of his fellow soldiers. He had a knack for zeroing in on the key fact or figure jutting from a paragraph like a snag from the murky water of a bayou. It came in handy when tackling some of the more academic wild pig literature. For example, breeders of domestic swine aimed to make them as big as possible. The words "in excess of 700 kg" jumped out at him. This had to be wrong. He did the math: it was more than fifteen hundred pounds. Wild boars were smaller by far; the biggest ever recorded was "only" half that weight. But what would happen when a wild boar, carefully selected for ferocity and cunning, hybridized in the wild with a monster domesticated specimen?

The same names kept turning up in the literature. One of them was Dr. I. Lane Rutledge of Texas A&M University. A slight amount of googling revealed that this individual was female, first name Iona. She had made a lot of headway using genetic sequencing to untangle the situation that had developed over the last five hundred years from all these different kinds of pigs having sex in Texas. She turned out to be surprisingly easy to reach on the Internet. She returned his emails. Tersely, but she did return them.

Rufus had learned that people in general were more approachable if you could offer them something and so he began sending her data: samples that she could DNA-sequence, combined with geo-tagged photos of the deceased swine that had provided those bodily fluids. That got her attention and made Rufus feel better about requesting a face-to-face meeting.

He left his trailer on a client's property about twenty miles outside of College Station and then drove into town and found his way to the campus. Google Maps was all wrong about how to get there because there was a big protest underway and a lot of streets had been blocked off. Rufus had to probe from multiple directions, then park as close as he could and walk. At first the protesters gave him mean looks for driving a huge gas-guzzling dually until they saw through the glass that he was a person of color and then they didn't know where to direct their moral indignation.

It was hot as hell in College Station despite it being November. Rufus broke a sweat immediately and hoped that Dr. Rutledge wouldn't turn out to be squeamish about such things. He wondered if in his middle age he was losing some of his tolerance for heat. He rarely ventured out of doors during daylight hours anymore. One of the very few genetic weaknesses of pigs was that they couldn't sweat, which was why they wallowed during the day and did the hard work of rooting out food at night. Rufus had accordingly become nocturnal.

As he cut across the grain of the crowd, headed for Dr. Rutledge's office, he got a good look at the signs the protesters were carrying. A lot of them had to do with the notion of humans as an invasive species, a topic that was very much on point as far as Rufus was concerned.

It would have been easy enough, and satisfying in a certain way, to make the comparison between what Rufus was trying to do to the pigs now and what the Comanches had tried to do to white people two hundred years ago. But you had to be careful. The Comanches themselves were invaders from the north who had "displaced"—a euphemism if ever there was one—the Indians who had been in Texas before them. And they'd been able to do it because they were early and enthusiastic adopters of the invasive species known as the horse.

Some of the other protest signs, he couldn't help noticing, were on the theme of extinction: a fate that all humans were facing if we didn't get a handle on climate change. So by the time Rufus finally got to the front door of the building where Dr. Rutledge worked, he was thoroughly confused. Did these kids hate humans because they were an invasive species that should be eradicated? Or did they love humans and not want them to become extinct? Imponderable questions, these, which perhaps college sophomores stayed up all night hashing out over pizza and beer while Rufus was out alone with a tripod and a rifle hunting a demon.

He noticed a few of the protesters toting, or rather wearing, odd getups that in retrospect were the early prototypes of earthsuits: garments that looked much too heavy for such a hot day, because underneath they consisted of networks of cooling tubes against the skin. Those were connected to backpack units with lithium battery packs driving a refrigeration system. Heat had to be got rid of eventually, so the backpack had a chimney projecting straight up above the wearer's head, shooting hot air that was visible from the heat waves coming off it. Those who wore them tended to be heavyset nerds.

"Something like ten thousand years ago, people, who were always on the verge of starving to death, noticed that pigs could eat things they couldn't," Dr. Rutledge said.

"They can eat *anything*," Rufus said, and then drew back, worried that he might have been too vehement.

But she was a cool cat. "Right, and my point is that humans can eat *them*. And we are just slightly smarter than they are."

"Not by much," Rufus scoffed, and he couldn't restrain himself from glancing toward her office window, through which protest chants were dimly audible. Though he had to admit that those personal refrigeration systems were pretty clever.

"They are very intelligent," she agreed, with a glance toward the window that made it somewhat ambiguous. "Anyway, that's how they—pigs—got domesticated. We have genetic data on many domesticated breeds, of course. Getting data on the Eurasian wild boar is harder, but we have plenty of that too. That's the source material. Where it gets fun is seeing all the combinations that emerge among the several million wild pigs running around Texas."

Rufus was pulled up short by her use of the word "fun" and so spent a few moments taking stock of things. He'd never before set foot on a university campus. Some of his expectations had been correct. Lots of young and startlingly attractive people with protest signs: check. But her office wasn't paneled and book-lined like professors' offices in movies. The walls were reinforced concrete, and it was small, with cables and computers all over the place.

Not a bad fit overall with Dr. Rutledge, who was a reinforced concrete kind of gal, lacking in the far-fetched adornments that

Rufus was used to seeing on females of the species *Homo sapiens*. Photographic evidence pointed to the existence of a husband and at least two children. Medium-length hair held back out of her face by a pair of laboratory safety glasses pushed up on top of her head. Middle American way of talking—either she was a transplant from out of the north, or one of those Texans who somehow grew to adulthood without picking up a Texan accent. A little prickly and short with him until he showed that he respected her. Reminded him in that way of some female army officers.

"Speaking of fun," he finally said, "the Eurasian wild boar introductions were—"

"For sport." She nodded. He felt he might have scored a point by his use of the word "introduction."

"They're more fun to hunt if they're harder to kill," Rufus said.

"I'm not a hunter but that sounds like a logical assumption to me."

"Wily, fast, vicious."

She raised her eyebrows and turned her palms up.

"A boar like that, crossed—hybridized—with a domestic variety that was bred up to be just huge—it could . . ."

He trailed off. She broke eye contact and let out a long breath she'd been gathering in as he circled closer and closer to his point.

"You're talking about the animal that killed your daughter," she said, in a tone that was quiet and sad but firm.

Of course. She would have googled him, just as he had her. It had been all over the papers.

She waited for him to nod before she went on.

"A hybrid of unusual size is plausible. Common sense really. But I would just caution you that the larger these animals get, the more food they have to consume to stay alive."

Rufus was taken aback by her use of the word "caution," which he was most accustomed to seeing on labels attached to crates of ammunition. She seemed to be warning him against falling into some kind of intellectual or ideational risk. Which would make sense, for a professor.

"So if your Hogzilla, your Moby Pig, weighs two hundred kilo-grams? I'll buy that," she continued. "Three hundred? I'm becoming skeptical. Beyond that I think you are in the realm of fantasy. Just going full Ahab. The enormous size that you are attributing to this animal is a reflection of the size of the role that it plays in your psyche. It's just not a scientific fact. Are you about to throw up?"

"Beg pardon, ma'am?"

"You stuck your tongue out. Like you were gagging."

"It's a thing I do. Because of my psyche. I'm fine."

"I want to help you," she said. "I mean, if you want to devote your life to hunting down one hog out of several million and kill-ing it, fine. It's a man-eater. Getting rid of it would be a public service. But my role, if I have one, is to keep you grounded in sci-entific reality. So, fact number one is that it probably doesn't weigh more than two hundred kilograms. Certainly not three hundred. Point being that if you're confining your search to fantastically enormous animals that you heard tell of from some cholo in a T.R. Mick's, you're just chasing folk tales and you'll never find him."

That stung a little because it was true. But Rufus was used to being stung. He shook it off and nodded. It made sense. Explained a thing or two.

"Fact number two is that, by your own reckoning, this animal is already three years old. In another three years it'll be dead of old age. She frowned at him. "You don't believe me?"

"Huh, of course I believe you. Ma'am." People were always say-ing to Rufus variations on this. It was rarely the case. This had led him to understand that his face, in its natural resting state, con-veyed a sense of skeptical disbelief. He guessed it was something to do with his forehead, which had developed prominent hori-zontal creases. "It's just how I look when I'm thinking."

She turned her palms up again. "Well, this age limit is a *good thing*. Prevents you from going full Ahab."

"You mentioned him before but—"

"Whaling captain who was obsessed with finding and killing

one sperm whale. Problem being, sperm whales live a long time. Longer than humans. So there was never a point in Ahab's life when he could say"—and here she whisked her hands together—"well, that's that, time's up, Moby-Dick must have given up the ghost by now, I can get back to—"

"Living my normal Ahab life?"

She shrugged.

"Mariel—the girl's mother—said 'This thing with Snout is ruining your life.' You know what I said?"

"I sure don't."

"It *is* my life." He stuck his tongue out.

"Well, it's none of my business," she said, regarding his tonsils with cool scientific detachment, "but do you have a plan for what your life might consist of three years from now when Snout is definitely no longer around?"

"It's not gonna take three years."

So that was the conversation that really launched his operation in what he would call its mature form. He obtained a copy of *Moby-Dick* and kept it around for occasional check-ins as to whether he had truly gone off his rocker. He got an audiobook of it too so that he could listen to it on headphones while he was sitting in the dark. Ahab didn't show up until pretty far into the book. He didn't out himself as an obsessed maniac until some little while after that. And then, of course, it was completely obvious why Dr. Rutledge had drawn a parallel between Rufus and Ahab. But, for Rufus, that analogy didn't really "take" because by that point in the novel he had already become interested in the harpooneers: the tattooed cannibal Queequeg, the "unmixed Indian" Tashtego, and the "gigantic, coal-black negro-savage" Daggoo. The most interesting thing about these characters was that they all made more money—a larger share of the ship's profits—and enjoyed higher rank and status than anyone else on the *Pequod* save Ahab and the three mates. According to Rufus's calculations, which he worked out on a spreadsheet in his trailer, Queequeg made 3.333 times as much as Ishmael, the book's narrator.

So the immediate effect of Rufus's perusal of *Moby-Dick* was a renewed emphasis on making his business more shipshape, as whaling captains such as Ahab, Peleg, and Bildad would have construed it. For all the complicated operations described in the book, the basics were as simple as could be: they rowed out in a boat so that a guy could chuck a spear into the whale. Guys who were good at chucking the spear made bank. Boat-rowers were a dime a dozen and had to supplement their measly income by going home and writing huge novels.

There is all the difference in the world between paying and being paid. Rufus heard that! He pared back, got rid of some superfluous equipment. His primary weapon was a long rifle on a beefy tripod with a fairly expensive infrared scope. Against the dark (once it had cooled off at night) backdrop of Texas, pigs flared Moby-Dick white in the optics. He was able to observe them and satisfy himself that they were swine—not livestock or, God forbid, humans—before calmly blasting them to kingdom come. When the big slugs hit home you could see the giblets flying out of them like sparks from a welder. When Big Daddy or Big Momma went down, legs jerking stiffly into the air, the herd would always panic and scatter, but he could usually pick off several more before they got out of range. The customers, viewing the carnage the next morning, didn't see how many had got away. So the big weapon accounted for 90 percent of his business. But he kept an assault rifle handy when tooling around in the open, engaging in swine killing of a more extemporaneous, short-range nature. It would give him more options should he ever find himself surrounded. In all honesty an AR-15 type of rifle would have served the same purpose and been easier to buy parts for, but the Kalashnikov was a fine conversation starter. Putting a 7.62-millimeter slug into a hog just seemed like a better idea than a 5.56. The AK's brute simplicity, its ability to keep firing after he had dropped it into a wallow, fascinated him as a mechanic. It was the feral hog of guns. ARs, on the other hand, reminded him overmuch of the army. On the civilian side of things, he had come to associate them with kids at the shooting range wearing overpriced wraparound sunglasses. Bros in tactical trousers who were evidently in it because of some story they were telling themselves.

Beyond just the guns it was pretty high tech. He was sharing Google Earth files with Dr. Rutledge and her grad students, Fed-Exing them blood swipes, checking his email all the time for anything useful they might have turned up. During the investigation of Adele's death, the sheriff had gathered what was politely called physical evidence and used DNA testing to establish that what had happened had happened. Mixed in with Adele's human DNA there was swine DNA from the perpetrator, and Rufus was able to get that information over to Dr. Rutledge. The odds of a smoking gun genetic match were minimal, but she was able to feed him some "you're getting warmer/colder" hints that shaped his peregrinations around Texas.

He got good at drones. It was a great day and age to be a retired but still healthy mechanic with no family to distract him. What with the availability of tools, YouTube videos, and Amazon lockers, he could learn how to do anything he wanted and get the stuff he needed to do it. Piloting drones through a VR headset from the air-conditioned comfort of his trailer, he followed the hogs to their wallows and guessed where they would be rooting around for food tonight, then used Google Earth to figure out where he'd set up his tripod to best advantage and how to get there without spooking them.

The business would have been sustainable anywhere in Texas—for that matter, anywhere south of the Mason-Dixon Line and east of the Pecos. So he had the freedom to direct his operation toward areas where, according to the data coming from Dr. Rutledge's lab, the pigs he was killing bore the strongest genetic resemblance to Snout. Generally speaking this seemed to be the watershed of the Brazos, south of Waco and north of where it meandered into the suburbs of Houston. Heat, he suspected, was driving hogs in general and Snout in particular toward rivers, where they could always find a way to cool off.

A big meandering river like the Brazos could be a troublesome thing to approach in a wheeled vehicle. The road network petered out as it got closer. You were always having to take the long way round so that you could find a bridge. Having crossed over, you'd inevitably find yourself wishing you were back on the other side. He needed a boat and he had never been a boat kind of man. He ended up forming a loose partnership with one Beau Boskey, a fellow from Louisiana who was to alligators what Rufus was to hogs. Beau was as boaty a man as you could ever hope to find. Rufus had met him at a conference on invasive species management. When Rufus needed boat-related help he would try to reach Beau on his cell phone, and when Beau thought Rufus might help him out with his drones and his infrared gear, he would do likewise.

It was this that brought them together in Waco during the Summer of the Great Relay Shortage.

The three factors that entered into it were pigs, gators, and fire ants. In the winter and spring, East Texas had seen an unusual pattern of weather (if anything could be considered unusual nowadays) that, to make a long story short, had apparently been perfect for fire ants. In all honesty, conditions *always* seemed perfect for fire ants, but, according to people like Dr. Rutledge who really knew their stuff, this was the best ant year ever.

The water had then got higher. Not in a single convulsive flood that would have drowned the ants in their burrows, but a little at a time. The ants had edged toward higher ground, which was where people tended to build houses. Houston was the third-largest city in North America. So the result was what Dr. Rutledge dryly called human/ant encounters on a scale never before seen, with thousands of emergency room visits not just from ant bites but collateral damage such as Texans setting fire to themselves when trying to burn ant nests with gasoline.

Fire ants answered to weird signals that humans could only guess at. One of them, apparently, was that they were drawn to the smell of ozone. Ozone could be produced in a lot of different ways, but a very common one in that area was relays in air-conditioning units. A relay was a big electrical switch with mechanical parts that actually moved—the thing that made an audible click when it came on. Most everything else now had gone to solid state, but for some reason known only to electrical engineers, relays on air-conditioning units had to have actual pieces of metal that came together to establish contact, or pulled apart to turn it off. Whenever that happened, there was a little spark that produced ozone. In this part of the world it was typical for air-conditioning units to be installed on concrete pads external to the house. Ozone-seeking ants could easily get in through the ventilation slots and seek out the relays. There, the fate that awaited them was to be electrocuted or mechanically smashed the next time the relay cycled. Remains of dead ants built up on the contacts and fouled them to the point where the relay had to be replaced. The supply chain for these relays extended back to China where one company had come to dominate the market. It could not produce and ship them at anything like the pace needed to replace the units being destroyed by fire ants in East Texas. People came up with various jury-rigged workarounds but the upshot was that over a short span of time the places where hundreds of thousands of people lived became uninhabitable. Some folks could tough out a Houston summer with window fans, but most looked for alternatives. Just for starters this meant filling every hotel room in greater Houston. RVs—already at a premium because of COVID-19, COVID-23, and COVID-27, and the general inability of Americans to travel outside of the Lower 48—spiked in price as people snapped those up and parked them in their driveways. People went full nomad and began to occupy every legal campsite they could find, and when those were full they began to park illegally. The thing was that these people had resources. They all owned houses, after all. So they were *affluent* nomads.

For Rufus, that was all just background noise, explaining why it was suddenly difficult to find a place to park his rig or to buy replacement parts for his generator. Overwhelmingly more important was the call he received from Dr. Rutledge in the middle of July.

Over time, indigestible stuff accumulated in a hog's stomach. Eventually they would vomit it up to make room. Anyone who tracked wild pigs would encounter spews from time to time: a patch of glazed ground where the liquid had dried in the sun, littered with the skulls and jawbones and hooves of lambs, kids, calves, piglets, dogs, cats, as well as dog collars, sticks, stones, chunks of plastic, and so on. Rufus never looked too closely out of a fear that he might see human remains.

A few weeks earlier, while doing a job on a property between Waco and College Station, he had come across the biggest hog spew he had ever seen. He had scraped up a sample and sent it in.

By the time the results came back and he got The Call from Dr. Rutledge, weeks had passed and he was several hundred miles away. That huge spew had been made, not just by a hog that was genetically similar to Snout, but by Snout himself. It was a perfect genetic match.

After that phone call Rufus spent an hour or so just snapping out of a profound daze. You'd think he would have become excited, but instead he actually went to sleep for a few minutes. That, he reckoned, was him prepping himself. Putting body and mind into cold shutdown, then rebooting the system for what was to come. As Ahab remarked on the last day of his epic pursuit of the White Whale: *I've sometimes thought my brain was very calm—frozen calm, this old skull cracks so, like a glass in which the contents turn to ice, and shiver it.*

He Google Earthed the location of the spew, just to remind

himself of the particulars. It was on the banks of a good-sized tributary of the Brazos, next to a wallow he had noticed there. Since that day the temperature in that area had never dropped below a hundred degrees. If Snout were as big as the spew indicated, he'd be forced to exist as a semi-aquatic mammal—he simply couldn't shed heat fast enough to stay alive. Crossing from one watershed to another over open country was unlikely. He'd use the rivers like an interstate highway system. Rufus reviewed photos he'd taken of the spew and noticed a detail that had passed him by before: a number of turtle shells. Even some fish bones. Snout lived in the water.

He called Beau Boskey, who answered on the first ring. Beau was finishing up some gator work in Sugar Land, a suburb of Houston, on the lower Brazos. He had his pontoon boat. He said he'd trailer it up to a put-in place he knew of on the Brazos south of Waco. He said he had business up in that part of Texas anyway, "on account of the mefcators." Or at least this was what Rufus thought he heard, in Beau's heavy accent, filtered through a less than ideal cell phone connection. A mispronunciation of "malefactors"? It made no sense, but he did not care; all that mattered to him was that he would soon have a whaleboat.

Rufus drove east and tried to re-visit the site of the spew, but it had been covered by rising water. Probably just as well. He had a nightmare vision of discovering a small human skull in one of those and no amount of sticking his tongue out would drive it from his mind. While he was waiting for Beau he burned a lot of gas driving up and down both banks of the river. It tended to be hemmed in by dense vegetation. Under Texas law, the river and its immediate banks were public land. Adjoining landowners had no incentive to keep them clear. On the contrary, the proverbial largeness of Texas meant that they usually had a surplus of land elsewhere on which to concentrate their brush-clearing energies. Clearing the economically worthless river frontage would just make it easier for boat riffraff to come up and trespass. So in general the banks of the Brazos were a strip jungle of overgrown scrub, perfect habitat for wild hogs who could wallow in the river to cool down, rub their bodies against tree roots to scrape off parasites, and raid adjoining farms at night. All of which activities left behind a trail of property damage, feces, spews, tracks, and enraged farmers that Rufus had learned how to monetize. The main question he had to answer was: Had Snout traveled upstream or down from that point?

By the time Beau made it up to Travis—the closest town of any size to the spew—Rufus had satisfied himself that the answer was upstream—so, generally northward in the direction of Waco. So once Beau's pontoon boat was in the water, that was the direction they moved. It was an ungainly style of travel, putt-putting a few miles at a go up the meandering river, shadowed by Beau's son-in-law Reggie driving Beau's pickup truck ten miles for every one that the boat covered. When road and river came together they would stop and Reggie would drive Rufus back to the starting place and they would move all the vehicles up and park them. It felt agonizingly slow. But all they had to do was move faster than Snout.

A few days of that got them into the heart of Waco. There the river forked in the middle of a park where a smaller tributary, the Bosque, spilled into the main channel. A few miles upstream of that confluence, right next to the airport, the Bosque had been dammed to form Lake Waco. The Brazos for its part wandered off into the heart of Texas. So this was literally a fork in the road for the Snout expedition. There were good reasons to devote some time and some care to making sure they didn't now take the wrong turn.

They had this embarrassment of huge vehicles. In open country this was fine, but in the leafy neighborhood of Waco where the river split, there was no place for them. Around the shores of Lake Waco, however, were a number of campgrounds with spaces for RVs. In any other year some of those would have been available, but now they were all full because of the problem with the fire ants and the relays. "Relayfugees" had set up unauthorized campsites along the roads that snaked through the wooded land between the lake and the airport, and they encroached on patches of open ground where those were to be found. As in every other human settlement there was good real estate and bad. Good was a legal campsite along the lakeshore, high and dry. Bad was illegal, marshy, and in the woods. With a combination of hustle, social skills, and bribery, Beau was able to secure a place that was only semi-terrible, large enough to create a little compound consisting of Rufus's dually, Rufus's trailer, Beau's pickup, and the flatbed he used to transport the pontoon. Beau's wife, Mary, flew up from Lake Charles, which was the Boskey clan's home base, and they hunkered down on the site for a couple of days while Rufus probed up both branches of the river on an inflatable that Beau usually towed behind his pontoon.

Beau was everything Rufus wasn't: comfortable on the water, interested in large reptiles, gregarious, cheerful, diurnal, and married. He and Mary had raised three kids on the edge of what most people would consider to be a swamp outside of Lake Charles. Their oldest daughter had married this Reggie, who looked to be the heir apparent to Beau's gator mitigation business. Not that Beau seemed of a mind to retire any time soon. He seemed more the type to keep going until he dropped dead from cardiovascular issues related to his diet (pretty much what you would imagine) and sedentary (sitting in boats all day) lifestyle. But he would do so cheerfully, surrounded by photographs of his grandkids. Three of those were Reggie's, and Reggie seemed like he was on the phone to them fourteen hours a day. Sometime he would aim his phone at Rufus, and Rufus would flinch as he came in view of some number of kids and the kids would call out, "Howdy, Red!" and he would be forced to answer. He could infer from what they said to him that Beau had spoken of Rufus respectfully and even affectionately. Mary, for her part, once she had shown up and taken over the operation of the compound, seemed unduly open-minded and tolerant of Rufus's determination to find and kill Snout. Rufus wondered what was considered normal where she came from.

An interesting thing about campgrounds was the way that a little temporary society would spring up, complete with the social hierarchy and attendant drama of more permanent settlements. This place was more complicated than most. Some people were towing palatial trailers behind gleaming Escalades—these tended to be your fire ant relay refugees. There was a middle class of snowbirds who had migrated away from the Mud Bowl—the vast, sodden triangle of former heartland along the Missouri and Mississippi valleys that seemed to be flooded all the time nowadays. The lower class were people of various backgrounds, but quite often Spanish-speaking, living in tents in the woods, blue tarps thrown or pitched over those to provide some additional shelter from sun and rain. Many of them seemed to have found work cooking, cleaning, and doing handyman work for the more upscale trailer dwellers. So, past the Rufus/Beau compound, there was a regular flow of foot and bicycle traffic as such people went to and fro between their camps deeper in the woods and the better-drained sites where the mega-RVs resided in a purr of generator exhaust and a nimbus of light thick with bugs.

There was an old scary story that kids had been telling one another at least since Rufus had been a little boy, the punch line to which was: "The call is coming from inside the house!" Such a moment arrived on their third day in the Lake Waco camp when Rufus figured out that Snout and his herd had been within a mile of them the whole time.

This was an unforeseen consequence of Beau's suddenly becoming interested in a very large "meth gator" rumored to be lurking around the shore of the lake. For this, and not "mefcator," was the term he had used during the cell phone conversation.

Another thing Beau was that Rufus wasn't was easily distractible. So one day it was suddenly all about this alleged meth gator. The pigs were back-burnered. Gators of that size were, in Waco, far more unusual than wild pigs and so the story had that going for it.

Beau's hypothesis was incredible to Rufus, and yet he stated it with complete sincerity. Gators lived in rivers, which were the ultimate destinations of all sewage. Modern municipalities made efforts to treat their sewage, but sooner or later it did have to go somewhere. Sewage treatment was designed to handle poo, and little else. Complicated molecules such as pharmaceuticals tended to pass through unaltered. You could find evidence of a population's usage of drugs, legal and illegal, in its sewage.

Meth cookers were notorious abusers of the sewage system. Moreover, they were infamous for bypassing sewage systems even when they were available—which in the sorts of places frequented by meth cookers, they often weren't. So, by hook or by crook, a lot of meth found its way into rivers. Gators scented it and selectively traveled up those river forks where the scent was strongest, unerringly zeroing in on meth labs. Somewhere around the shores of this lake, someone was cooking meth, and in doing so had attracted this nest of meth gators, who might, for all Beau knew, have followed the scent trail all the way up from the Gulf of Mexico.

Since the inflatable was still in the Bosque, on the downstream side of the dam, they put the pontoon boat into Lake Waco and spent an evening putt-putting around looking for the sorts of habitats that, according to Beau, would be looked on by large gators and meth cookers alike as congenial. Rufus, nervously along for the ride, could not help but see the same sites through the eyes of a herd of feral hogs. He began to feel a gnawing anxiety about what unpredictable consequences might stem from spontaneous hog/gator interactions. He had pulled the infrared scope off his rifle. After night fell over the lake he began using it to survey boggy inlets along the shore. Beau reminded him for the hundredth time that gators were not warm-blooded: a joke he never got tired of. But Rufus wasn't looking for gators.

They came around a point and into view of a tiny inlet, just a kerf in the land where some small creek probably spilled into it. On the IR, the boundary between water and land was a solid, squirming mass of white. Around its edges Rufus was able to pick out individual silhouettes with the familiar dished head shape of *Sus domesticus*. In the open rangeland of Texas this herd would have been considered large, but not astonishing. Certainly more than twenty animals but not more than thirty. Here on the lake, surrounded by houses, it seemed pretty huge. Rufus was gaping at it, beginning to doubt the evidence of his senses, trying to work out how they had reached this place and where they were getting food, when one silhouette much larger than the others hove up out of the mass and waddled to higher ground.

Rufus had seen enough of pig body language to know that this creature had been alerted by something. Most likely their scent, guessing from the direction of the breeze. The giant hog swung its head back and forth, and Rufus knew that if he were closer he'd hear it snuffling air into its nostrils. Seen in profile the head was flatter, less dished than that of *Sus domesticus*. This animal was closer to a Eurasian wild boar.

Reggie chose that particular moment to crack open a can of beer.

Snout turned to look right at them.

Even if the rifle had been mounted to that scope, Rufus would not have taken the shot. An errant round would pass right over the point of land where Snout was standing and carry for half a mile toward the campground beyond. And they were out of range for a pistol shot. "Take her in!" Rufus said to Beau, who was at the wheel. "Get on in there!" Beau shoved the throttle forward and swung the boat around, but the next time Rufus got the inlet into his sights, the swine were gone. He could see a few stragglers disappearing into the scrub farther inland, but Snout was nowhere to be seen.

This happened around midnight. Over the next sixteen hours, matters then developed in a way that a hypothetical journalist or detective might later have been able to piece together with push-pins and yarn on a wall-sized map of Lake Waco, with spread-sheets and timelines, but to Rufus at the time it was just chaos. Just things happening too fast for him to react.

Maybe the worst decision he made was to stay calm. Which seemed reasonable enough. For years he'd been hunting Snout all over Texas. Now he knew almost exactly where the creature was. It could only move so fast. He and his herd would leave in their wake a wide trail of shit and damage; it would be as easy as tracking an armored division across a golf course.

As long as Snout remained in a populated area, Rufus would have to stay cool, get close, and use a shotgun or something. He tried and failed to get some sleep during the hours of darkness that remained, then perversely fell asleep at dawn and didn't wake up until midmorning. He drove down to where he'd tied the inflatable, on the banks of the Bosque, a little ways below the dam, and ran it all the way up to the spillway. There he poked around in the woods for a few minutes until he found the place where Snout and his herd, a day or two earlier, had climbed up out of the ravine and gone up over the levee. Once they'd crested that, it was an easy traipse down the rocky slope on its lake side to reach the water, and from there they had their pick of directions. The smart way to do this would be for Rufus to use the drone.

He was squatting there at the rock-covered base of the dam on the lake side when the purple sky to the west was snapped in half by a lightning bolt. Before the rain came he had time to scramble back up and over to the grassy side and make sure the inflatable was well roped to a tree. He got plenty wet running back to his truck, but given the heat he didn't mind it so much. It turned into one of those rainfalls so intense that he wouldn't have been able to drive in it, so he just stayed put behind the wheel until the roar on the roof lessened slightly and he felt it was safe to drive up to higher ground.

When the storm finally ended it was well after noon and he

had a powerful sense that he'd blown the last twelve hours doing exactly the wrong things in the wrong places and that he was desperately far behind. All sorts of things had gone into motion in the camp. Some kid was tearing around in one of those open all-terrain vehicles that, on ranches, had basically replaced horses. Riding shotgun—*literally* wielding a shotgun—was an older man. Message traffic from the Boskey clan was all to do with alligators. Rumor in camp had it that someone's dog had gone missing and was presumed to have been eaten. Beau was trying to get people to understand that he could get the gator situation squared away if they would just settle down, but the guys in the ATV had their blood up and couldn't be managed.

Rufus, taking all this in, was distressed by the lack of attention being paid to the herd of feral hogs. If family pets really were going missing, the culprit was just as likely Snout. And tearing around on an ATV was exactly the wrong thing to be doing. People made use of just such vehicles to chase and massacre wild pigs in the open country. Some members of Snout's herd had probably been hunted by such vehicles.

Rufus ended up driving to and fro along the roads that formed the perimeter of the camp and the woods, trying to figure out who was where. One of those roads ran along the airport fence. He was driving down it at 4:06 P.M. when Snout, followed by his entire herd, burst out of the woods to his right and stormed across the road a hundred yards ahead of him.

The airport fence would stop them, you would think. But swine had a weird genius for sniffing out low places and getting under things.

At the moment during their first conversation when Dr. Rutledge had spoken the words "Moby Pig," a nagging thought—just the trace of an idea—had come up in the back of Rufus's mind. It was a little like when you were a man of a certain age and a wild hair began to trouble the inside of your nostril, subtle and sporadic at first, but only getting worse until you came to grips with it and snipped it out. This word "Moby," it seemed, had aroused some stray recollection. Not until he'd gone back to Lawton to spend time with some of his Comanche relations had he figured it out.

The Comanches were originally Shoshones who had come down out of the north speaking a language that, of course, had no word for "pig." When they had encountered this alien species in what was now Texas, they'd had to invent a new term for them. The term was *muubi pooro*. Different bands of Comanches pronounced it in slightly different ways. The first of those words meant "nose" and the second meant something like a "tool" or a "weapon."

The meaning was clear: pigs used their noses both as tools (shovels for digging) and weapons (tusks for slashing). It just so happened that "Moby" sounded a lot like "muubi." He guessed that Dr. Rutledge's phrase "Moby Pig" had gotten crosswired in the dusty electrical closet of his brain with *muubi pooro*, a term he had heard his Comanche relatives use, and created that nagging itch in his mind.

Once he had figured this all out, he'd even had cause to wonder whether the *moby* in "Moby-Dick" had somehow emerged from Indian roots. Because sperm whales, just like pigs, used their noses as weapons.

The applicability of all this to the current situation was as follows: pigs could root under just about any obstruction using their nose weapons. Just ahead of Rufus, on the left, there was a stretch of airport fence no more than twenty feet wide that had become overgrown with vines. This must be because there was water there. There must be a low soft patch of earth where some kind of underground drainage situation was happening. Pigs could smell that kind of thing from a mile away. Beneath the fence there was enough of a washout to accommodate Snout. Which meant plenty of room for any other pig in his herd. Pretty soon they were charging under the fence three or four abreast. They paused momentarily on the runway side of the fence. Then, impelled by whatever had panicked them in the first place, they bolted across open land beyond: the airport.

Rufus stopped his truck just in time to avoid hitting the alligator that was running after the pigs. He was marveling at this creature, which was long enough to block both lanes of the highway, when he heard a loud noise to the left. He looked over to see a small jet, landing gear skimming the runway. Blood erupted from a collision between it and one or more hogs, and the entire plane slewed to the right and came down wrong and hard on its front gear.

After that it was just a long tumbling skidding disaster. A whole section of fence went down. Rufus gunned his truck across it and came as close as he deemed prudent given the possibility of fire. He was half out the door when he saw the alligator run right by him. He reached back in and pulled his Kalashnikov down from the gun rack in the truck's rear window. He had carried it halfway to the plane before it occurred to him to wonder what shocked observers in the control tower would make of a brown man with an assault rifle prowling around a jet crash.

But more pressing matters than that held his attention for a few minutes. When the gator was dead and the wounded man's bleeding leg tied off, he turned his back on the scene and walked over to where Snout was lying on his side on the runway. Hind legs paralyzed, evidently. Blood coming from his anus and from his quivering nostrils.

Four hundred kilograms if he weighed an ounce. Maybe the cops would weigh him later and publish official stats.

Snout was dazed, eyes half closed. He still had that old pattern of spots on his *muubi*.

His nostrils twitched as he caught Rufus's scent. His eyes came open and he tossed his head. But Rufus was too smart to be within range of those six-inch tusks. Anyway, this gave Rufus the impetus to do what needed doing, which was to fire four 7.62 mm slugs into Snout's brain.

He was still standing there weeping when the blond woman from the jet crash walked up to him and said, "Are you all right, friend?"

Once it became clear that the people with the knives were solely interested in harvesting meat from the dead pigs and the alligator, the queen's team evacuated the plane and began to collect the luggage. Some of this had hurtled into the cabin through a broken door and the remainder had tumbled out the rear of the plane after the tail section had ruptured. Willem and Alastair helped Johan, the concussed co-pilot, get out of the cockpit and then out of the plane. Lennert got clear of the wreck by hopping on one leg. This seemed like a very bad idea for a man who had suffered such a grievous injury, but fuel had been leaking from a ruptured wing tank near where he'd been reclining, and he had been thinking about possible implications.

Not far away, a large pickup truck was parked atop a flattened section of airport fence. Its owner, the tourniquet-savvy man with the Kalashnikov, was up to something a couple of hundred meters away, back on the runway where the initial jet/pig impact had taken place. A minute earlier this man had predicted, in colloquial English, that no fire trucks would be coming to their aid because of perceived security risks. Thus far his prediction had been borne out by events, or lack thereof. Sirens were audible but none were getting louder.

The queen's top priority, now that all members of her team had got to a safe distance from the plane, was to get Lennert and Johan to a hospital. The only capable vehicle she could see nearby was this man's pickup truck. So she was going to talk to him. As she strode across churned turf in his wake, she saw a second, similar vehicle pull up and park next to his. This one had a cartoon of an alligator painted on its door. A woman got out of the driver's seat. This woman seemed primarily interested in the man with the Kalashnikov, and not in the sense that she saw him as a threat. She was looking after him.

That somehow emboldened Frederika Mathilde Louisa Saskia to walk right up to the man even after he had discharged four rounds at point-blank range into the face of a fantastically enormous boar reclining on the tarmac.

Then he carefully removed the magazine from the weapon, cycled the action once to eject the remaining round from the chamber, and threw it on the ground. He was sobbing.

In his emotional state it took him a moment to respond to her greeting. While waiting for him to settle down, she looked around and noticed that Amelia—now her acting security chief—had followed her all the way out here. She was still gripping her pistol with both hands, keeping it aimed at the ground, focusing her gaze primarily on the sobbing man but also glancing around from time to time for incoming swine, alligators, and knife-brandishing scavengers.

The queen looked over toward the pickup trucks. The woman who'd gotten out of the second truck was headed toward them, walking as briskly as she could manage given that she was of grandmotherly age and, like most Americans, overweight. "Amelia," she said, "go and ask that woman if she can take Lennert and Johan to hospital. She is friendly."

"How do you know that!?" Amelia demanded. Then, remembering her manners, added, "*Uwe Majesteit.*" Her parents had immigrated to Rotterdam from Suriname. She had grown up poor and tough, she had thrived in the military, and she was fastidious about manners and hierarchy.

"Don't address me that way here."

"What should I call you then, *mevrouw?*"

The question hung there as a new thought was occurring to the queen, which was that she and her team had just entered the country illegally.

Presumably there would be some face-saving way to patch it all up. But until the matter had been sorted out properly, it might be wisest if they did not go around advertising the fact that she was who she was. The tabloids would have a field day with this. They would never accept that the crash had been unavoidable. Instead they would make the queen out to be a foolish person, in over her head, unqualified.

And that was before they even sank their teeth into the question of why she was coming to Texas in the first place.

"Saskia."

Amelia raised her eyebrows, but reluctantly obeyed the order, leaving "Saskia" alone with the sobbing boar-killer. She holstered her pistol at the small of her back and ran toward the woman from the pickup truck. Amelia covered ground fast.

About then the man finally pulled himself together and turned toward Saskia. He pulled his T-shirt up away from his flat belly and used it to wipe tears and sweat from his face. This made Saskia want to do likewise. She was suddenly conscious of how sweaty she had become in the short time she had been out of the plane. She wasn't wearing a lot of makeup but she wondered how bad the damage would be if she were to make a similar gesture. Fenna could always fix it later, if she would only stop being such a baby about the plane crash.

The man turned his head to one side and stuck his tongue out in a way that reminded her of New Zealanders doing their haka dance. She wondered if he might be a Pacific Islander, at least in part.

Having got that out of the way, he turned toward her.

"Ma'am."

"Thank you for helping my friend. We are going to get him to hospital. We will get your knife back to you."

The man glanced past Saskia, took in the scene. "Mary's fixing to help you. Gonna be fine. Y'all need anything else?"

It seemed a remarkably generous and open-ended offer from a man in such a condition. Saskia looked sharply at him to see whether he was being sarcastic. He would not meet her gaze, but his eyes strayed briefly toward the dead boar. "I got no purpose now," he explained. "Gotta fix on something."

"Well, for example, would you know how to get us out of here?" Saskia ventured. It might have been better if she had worked in some extra phrasing such as *hypothetically* or *in principle, supposing we were to request it* but this was how it came out. "We can pay you."

"Cash?"

"If you prefer."

"Where you want to get to?"

"Houston."

"Is there some kinda legal situation I should know about?"

Saskia shrugged. "Maybe with immigration? But we can't help it." She now thought a little harder about the man's question and understood what he was getting at. "Not drugs or anything like that, if that is what you were thinking."

He hesitated, trying to get the story to add up. Not that he didn't trust her. It was all just very odd. She could see this. Key information was lacking.

"I am the Queen of the Netherlands," Saskia told him. "I am here on a secret mission to save my country."

"Rufus. Most people address me as Red. My not-so-secret mission is now accomplished." He glanced at the huge dead boar and repeated the strange gesture of sticking his tongue out.

"It's a pleasure to meet you, Red." They exchanged a sweaty handshake and began walking back toward the plane. She had to remind him not to leave his rifle on the ground. The gator-adorned pickup truck was moving toward Lennert, Amelia standing up in the back keeping an eye on the open-air hog and reptile butchery.

"The pleasure is all mine, Queen."

"No one ever says that. 'Your Majesty' is the correct wording. But please don't. Just call me by my nickname. Saskia."

"You want to hide the fact that you're here? Is that what's up?"

"This was supposed to be discreet. People weren't meant to know I was coming to Texas."

"How many in your party?"

"Five, if the wounded go to hospital. But Willem should probably go with them. So, four."

"I can have you on a boat in three minutes."

"On the lake?"

"River. The Bosque. Which runs over yonder into the Brazos."

"Brazos?" Saskia knew the Spanish meaning of the word but wasn't sure how Rufus was using it.

"Arms of God," Rufus said. "It's the big river that runs on down to Houston. Spaniards named it that. Don't know why. They were funny with their way of naming things. Sick on religion."

She liked the sound of it. "During those three minutes would we have to pass through any roadblocks or the like that emergency services might have set up?" Because an impressive line of flashing red and blue lights was thickening about a kilometer away on the other side of the airport.

"Roads ain't gonna enter into it."

"Everyone out of the plane?" Rufus inquired, before setting fire to it. This was a pretty abrupt move on his part and caused Saskia briefly to reconsider the wisdom of entrusting her party's fate to a random desperado. As they sped away, however, leaving the eruption of flames in the truck's numerous and incredibly large rearview mirrors, she perceived the wisdom of the move. Everyone on the other side of the airport would be looking at that during the few seconds it took Rufus's truck to speed clear of the crash site and disappear into the woods. The plane was a total loss anyway.

Or perhaps she was cutting Rufus too much slack here, dreaming up post hoc rationalizations for the actions of a deranged man. Anyway, he was driving the truck and their fate was in his hands.

"Heads up!" he shouted as the truck angled across the road and plunged into the woods. Saskia and Amelia were in the cab with him. Alastair and Fenna were in the open box aft. Alastair literally did put his head up but then hastily ducked down as the truck began smashing its way through foliage so dense it was not possible to see more than a few meters in any direction. Apparently this idiom "heads up" really meant its exact opposite. Branches were whipping and cracking, and Rufus swerved whenever he spied an onrushing tree that he deemed too thick to smash into the ground with the truck's front bumper. This, however, did not happen as frequently as one might expect. It was a different sort of forest from what Saskia was used to. She had grown up, and still resided, in a thing in the middle of The Hague called Huis ten Bosch, which literally meant "House in the Woods." The woods were classic fairy-tale old-growth Euro-forest with relatively sparse undergrowth. The stuff that they were driving through in Rufus's truck was nothing *but* undergrowth. She hadn't seen a single tree thicker than her wrist. As the wall of green had rushed toward them in the windscreen, she had braced for impact, because it looked so solid. But most of it went down under the front bumper like ripe wheat.

At one point they surprised a wild pig. This ran away from them, and Rufus swerved to follow it. Saskia feared for a moment that this man might actually have no purpose in life other than killing pigs, and that he was, accordingly, seeking to run this one over. But he kept hitting the brakes at moments when the gas pedal would have ended the pig's life, and Saskia understood that he was *following* the pig. Using it as a guide through the wilderness. For as dense as these woods might appear when viewed through the windscreen of a lurching truck, in the eyes of a pig sprinting for its life it apparently seemed as open and as easily navigable as the Dutch inter-city rail network.

Anyway, it worked in the sense that they broke out of those woods a minute later at one end of the long straight earthen dam that she had spotted just before the crash. They could not see over it to the right, but obviously the lake must be on that side. Before them was an open grassy slope, unnaturally regular, angling down to a stream that (as she could see as more of the scene came into view) was fed by the spillway: a concrete and steel edifice, pierced by a row of gates, that was integrated into the grass-and-earth dam a couple of hundred meters distant. Saskia, or for that matter any Dutch person, could see at a glance how all this worked. It might have green stuff growing on it and birds—(Were those *vultures*!? Like in *Westerns*!?)—soaring above it, but that natural stuff was just a tegument, like paint on a house, allowed to cling to a structure that was in fact absolutely unnatural and engineered. Manholes and standing pipes erupted from little square islands of concrete: the visible bits of a huge buried infrastructure. Every surface that met her eye had been architected by some Texan engineer who was paid to do nothing, every day of his career, except think about what water did.

Ultimately, of course, it sought the sea. The reason that this little river had been allowed to remain in existence was that it gave excess water somewhere to go besides flooding the airport or the housing developments. Right now the gates of the spillway, off to their right, were all wide open and water was coming through them as if shot from fire hoses. The river was running fast, at some risk of spilling out of its banks. But had it done so it would have flooded an area that the engineers had carefully delimited with levees and embankments, isolating it from the slightly higher plateau of the airport. And for just the same reason, no one in the airport—none of the emergency vehicles holding on the other runway, none of the ground crew, none of the people butchering hogs and alligator around the crash site—had line of sight to them right now. The only thing Saskia could see peeking above the top of the airport's protective berm was the uppermost part of the control tower, but soon enough that dropped from view and they were weirdly alone. There was an employee parking lot below the spillway complex, but no vehicles were parked there. Dam employees well knew the consequences of parking their cars in a floodplain.

Very near, the river plunged into woods. At the edge of those woods a boat had been hauled up onto formerly dry ground and made fast to a tree. Saskia identified it as a RHIB, or rigid hull inflatable boat. Its aft part, sporting a big outboard motor as well as a backup motor to one side, was awash and waggling in the flow. Rufus drove the truck as close as he could get without bogging down in the sodden ground, ten meters or so away, and they formed a line between it and the boat to transfer the luggage: Alastair in the back handing bags down to Fenna who tossed them down the line to Amelia, Saskia, and finally Rufus who made decisions about where to stow each item in the RHIB. There was not a lot of room, but there was not a lot of luggage. Two of the blue earth-suit bags made it in. Rufus locked two more inside the truck's cab and parked it up on higher ground. Then he jogged down, hopped in, and started the outboard. Saskia handled the painter, untying it from the tree and clambering in over the prow as the river's current took the boat. Amelia and Alastair grabbed her arms and made sure she was belly flopped into the middle before she was allowed to press herself up and assume a more queenly position on the prow. "Figurehead" was a mildly pejorative English word sometimes applied to modern royalty; now she was one.

They found themselves making excellent time down the Bosque. It was not a raging torrent but it was in full spate and they would have moved at a good clip even if Rufus hadn't been running the outboard at high power. The river was narrow enough that the woods on either bank nearly arched together above to form a tunnel. Looking straight up they could see the sky, combed by branches, and lowering their gaze they could glimpse bits of houses constructed up on the banks. Those banks got higher, steeper, and rockier as they went, until they were sluicing down the bottom of a gorge: a surprise to Saskia who had assessed the landscape as flat shortly before crashing the jet into it. Then suddenly the stream cornered right and emptied into a much larger and calmer river. Saskia exchanged a look with Rufus, who nodded, confirming that they were now in the Arms of God.

Saskia and her staff used a secure messaging app for all communications. Sometimes they viewed it on old-school smartphones. Other times they piped the output to glasses. Saskia had lost her sunglasses and her phone during the crash but Alastair was still online—she could tell as much by watching the movements of his eyes, which were focused on nonexistent minutiae at arm's length.

"Any news of the others?" Saskia asked him.

He nodded. "Willem has been sending updates. The woman in the alligator truck—"

"Mary," Rufus told him.

"Mary drove Lennert and Johan to an emergency department. Baylor Medical Center. Not far from the airport apparently. They took Lennert back to surgery straightaway. Giving him blood transfusions. Johan is in a waiting room. Willem is handling details."

Alastair was a Scotsman of the ultra-dry and understated style and so it could be guessed that "details" encompassed much relating not just to the medical aftermath but how to pay in 500 euro notes for medical services rendered on patients who had just mysteriously entered the country, if not quite illegally, then certainly without passing through the customary formalities. But the whole point of having Willem was to make it so that Saskia did not have to concern herself with that sort of thing.

Fenna's role similarly was to make it so that Saskia didn't have to think about how she looked. The stylist had been terribly imbalanced by the plane crash, but the wild ride through the woods had appealed to her, and being on a boat had then calmed her down and got her mind back on her business. She had been appraising Saskia. She unzipped one of the earthsuit bags. Without opening it all the way—there was no room for that—she thrust in her hand and pulled out the first thing she found, which was the under-layer. This was a white, long-sleeved spandex top with a built-in hood. It was meant to be worn under the bulkier suit that contained the plumbing. It reduced chafing and it could be separately laundered. Worn by itself it protected from sunburn and, if you had some way to keep it wet, cooled the body without the need for the full earthsuit apparatus. "Put this on," Fenna said, "quick, before we get out of this park." This was how she talked to Saskia when she was doing her job. It was more efficient than "If you please, Your Majesty, I recommend the white spandex."

The detail about the park didn't make sense to Saskia until she looked about and understood that, at least for the next few moments, they had close to absolute privacy because they were in some kind of nature preserve surrounding the confluence of the two rivers. Saskia unbuttoned the cotton shirt she had donned this morning in Huis ten Bosch and peeled it off, momentarily exposing a brassiere and a lot of skin until she was able to pull the spandex sun-shirt down over her body. While she was tugging the silky fabric up her arms, Fenna grabbed the hood from behind and pulled it forward over Saskia's head. It came down to just above her eyebrows. Some loose fabric was tickling her chin. This was a sort of mask that could be pulled up over the chin, mouth, and even the nose, leaving only an eye slit. "Does anyone have sunglasses?" Fenna asked. Because of Rufus and Alastair they would be speaking English.

Amelia was able to produce from her bag a pair of ordinary (not electronically enhanced) sunglasses with an old-school military look to them. Fenna unfolded them and slipped them onto Saskia's face, carefully guiding the ends of the bows into the tight gap between her temples and the spandex hood. The look on Fenna's face was one Saskia had seen often: she wasn't crazy about what she was seeing, but she had tried her best, and it would have to do.

"You don't want to be recognized by some random camera," Rufus guessed.

"Best not to be," Saskia said. "Until we have things sorted."

"The rest of your squad?"

"Fenna travels with me all the time," Saskia pointed out, and so now it was Fenna's turn to go through a similar transformation using the garment from the other earthsuit. Fenna was bra-less, wiry, and heavily tattooed, so any lurkers watching from the scrub along the banks would have seen more, but not for long.

Twenty years ago these garments would have done more harm than good, if the point was not to be conspicuous. But now the opposite was true. Anyone out in the open in this heat needed to have some plan for how not to die of it. Rufus looked like he'd done this before; he'd put on a broad-brimmed hat. Amelia and Alastair, however, were dressed altogether wrongly for these conditions.

They came in view of what was apparently downtown Waco: a vintage suspension bridge, the Hilton where, a couple of hours ago, Willem had reserved rooms for them, and some commercial buildings that didn't rise more than a few stories. Bigger structures loomed a little farther away. Of these, a huge stadium was the most prominent.

"Baylor University," Alastair said, following a map he could see in his glasses.

"Where Lennert and Johan went?"

"Different complex, different part of town." Alastair removed his glasses, folded them, tucked them into a case, pocketed that, excused himself, and threw up over the side of the boat. "The heat doesn't agree with me," he explained, his chin quivering.

Rufus throttled the motor down. "Jump in the river and cool you off," he said, somewhere between a suggestion and a command. "I'm a keep an eye on you. You're the canary."

Saskia looked at Rufus curiously, and he noticed it. "In the army," he said, "you leading a platoon somewhere that's cold, you pick a skinny Southern boy, a brother maybe, and when he's cold, you stop for a spell and warm up. Some place hot, you pick someone like *him*—what kinda accent is that, sir?"

"Scottish," Alastair said and spat bile into the river.

"It ain't hot where you from."

Alastair shook his head.

"You are the canary. You start throwing up, we look for ways to chill." Rufus nodded at Saskia and Fenna. "You two splash a little river water on those garments. Be good for a while." He nodded at Alastair. "Take a swim, sir." He appraised Amelia. "Where you from, ma'am?"

"Suriname. It's hot there."

Rufus had been surveying Amelia's face, maybe trying to piece together a racial profile, perhaps taking note of the broken nose and the slightly thickened ear on one side. His eyes strayed downward. Saskia clenched her teeth, thinking he was going to check out Amelia's boobs. But he was looking at her deltoids.

"Grappler?"

Amelia gave a slight nod. "Judoka."

"Brazilian?"

"Olympic."

"Military?"

Amelia nodded. That seemed good enough for Rufus. "Take care of yourself, ma'am. We'll talk later."

Conveniently, Alastair wore boxers. Rufus ended up towing him languidly past the immense football stadium on a rope attached to the RHIB's stern.

In the corner of her eye Saskia could now sense Rufus giving her a look that said, *What's it going to be, Your Majesty?* He did not strike her as impatient or restive, just curious and . . . *available*. It was the first moment since the crash when she'd not simply been reacting to events.

"This is not such a bad situation overall, yes?" she said. She said it in Dutch, which meant that she was only saying it to Amelia and Fenna.

Both of them laughed in her face.

Saskia now perceived the humor but felt a need to patiently explain. "No one died. No one identified us. Lennert and Johan are getting the best care they can. We are here on this boat with this man who seems helpful."

Amelia thought it over and shrugged. "With Lennert gone, I'm in charge of keeping you safe. This is not what we expected. For the moment, this is no more dangerous than any other random place in America. But we are not supposed to be in a random place in America. We are supposed to be at T.R. McHooligan's guesthouse in Houston."

"You should get in the habit of calling him Dr. Schmidt," Saskia pointed out.

"Yes, *mevrouw.*"

"Would that really be safer, though?" Saskia asked. "Houston is about to be hit by a hurricane. Then it will flood."

Amelia considered it and checked the screen of her watch, which was showing a little weather map.

"What do y'all want to do?" Rufus inquired.

"Eventually we have to meet someone in Houston."

"Y'all're gonna have to kill two or three days then. Hurricane's coming. Can't go in there now."

"What do you suggest? Where is a good place to 'kill' two or three days?"

"You could do worse than Beau Boskey's pontoon boat."

Of course that was what a man such as Rufus would suggest given that that was what he had access to and was used to. But try as they might, Saskia and Amelia couldn't find any reason why it was a bad idea.

Above all, they had to sleep. This was a biological reality. They could backtrack up the river, beach the RHIB at the suspension bridge, run across the street, and check in at the Hilton. But Willem was at the hospital at the other end of town with the documents and the cash. There would be a lot of details having to do with passports, payment, and so on that would be sticky given the way they had just entered the country. There would be surveillance cameras. Not that the secret police were, as a general practice, staking out the lobby of the Waco Hilton for stray European royalty. But you could never tell where those things were networked and what humans or AIs might licitly or illicitly have access to their feeds. And from the looks of things she was pretty sure that once they put another kilometer of Brazos behind them, there were not a lot of cameras.

They had entered the country illegally, yes. But there was nothing they could do about that now. Getting all that sorted in Houston—a vast international metropolis—in a couple of days would be just as good as, and maybe better than, doubling back into Waco and trying to track down the relevant officials— assuming there even were any in Waco—to stamp their passports.

The more they went on pondering these things, the farther downriver they got. The stadium and the big structures on the Baylor campus receded. They found themselves in open country. Communications from Willem suggested he had things well in hand. Not just on the medical front but also in the sense of linking up with staff back home. Last week they had prepared a cover story to explain why Saskia would not be making any public appearances this week, and it was as good now as it had been before the jet had hit the pigs.

Rufus for his part was talking to his friends. They had retrieved his truck from where he'd left it and they were said to be "mobilizing," which sounded like it involved getting "Beau's pontoon" on a trailer and other such logistics. After dark they could all meet up at a "put-in" downriver. At that point some decisions would have to be made. The first being: Where could they sleep? Because more and more that was the only thing Saskia could think about.

She sent a secure text to T.R.:

> We have been delayed in the Waco area.

He responded:

> Willem informed me.

> Are you staying in Houston, or going to the site?

> Riding the storm out here. The whole program has been pushed back.

> So we are not going to miss the event if we wait?
> Correct. Stay safe and we'll sort it out after the hurricane.
> Thank you T.R.
> Godspeed Y.M.

They ate, and then they slept, at what Rufus had called the put-in, by which he meant an earthen boat ramp accessible from a farm road. The degree of personal warmth and hospitality exhibited by the Boskeys was nearly overwhelming. The sheer quantity of food that they were able to produce on short notice had an almost slapstick effect on the Dutch guests. Anticipating Saskia's only concern, Mary assured her that what was sizzling on the grill was by no means "swamp meat" harvested from feral swine and alligators, but had been purchased at a local grocery store "with expiration dates and everything." The Boskeys were able on short notice to carpet an expanse of riverbank with pop-up canopies and other temporary structures that they produced like magicians from all their trucks and trailers. Most of those were neither bugproof nor air-conditioned. When it was time to sleep, they packed as many people as they could into the trailers and ran the air conditioners off portable generators. Rufus and Beau slept in the cabs of their trucks with the seats leaned back.

Saskia went to sleep almost instantly. She and Amelia were sharing the large bed in the back of Rufus's trailer. She then woke up at three in the morning and knew right away that getting back to sleep was out of the question. It was a combination of jet lag and vivid visual memories of things that had happened at Waco. She got up, used the tiny but clean toilet in the middle of the trailer, then stepped over Fenna, who was sleeping in the living/dining area. Alastair had gone missing. She went out the side door, closing it quietly behind her, and stepped down to the sandy ground. She had foolishly expected that it would be cool at this time of night, but it wasn't. She had also expected quiet, but in addition to the drone of the generators, some kind of creatures, evidently quite numerous, were making a pulsating racket in the scrub that came up to the river's edge everywhere but here. Some kind of insect, she assumed. Here, insects seemed a good default explanation for just about anything that might require explaining.

Fat orange and yellow extension cords coursed over the sand, obliging her to pick her feet up as she walked. One of them ran up over the tailgate of the Boskeys' pickup truck and connected to a backpack-sized unit perched atop the cab, which was humming and aglow with status lights. Saskia went over and looked down into the bed of the truck. Lying there, deeply asleep, was Alastair. Only the oval of his face was showing, and he'd veiled that under a mosquito net. The rest of him was covered by a bulky and yet form-fitting garment: stretchy fabric shot through with little tubes. These converged on an umbilical connection at his left hip, whence a bigger hose snaked up to the purring backpack. He'd put that up on the top of the cab, the better for it to blow hot exhaust into the slightly less hot atmosphere. Evidently he'd found it impossible to sleep in the confines of the trailer and so he'd gotten up at some point in the night, stolen outside, and broken out this earthsuit. It could run off its built-in battery pack, but if you were remaining in one place for any length of time it made sense to plug it in, as he'd done. Saskia envied his cool deep slumber. But it was perfectly obvious that she'd not be going back to sleep and so she did not follow his example.

Bugs in a wide range of sizes, from microscopic up to several centimeters long, had been upon her from the moment she'd stepped outside, so she moved directly to one of the pop-up canopies that had walls made of mosquito netting. She'd had all the shots recommended for travel to Texas—dengue, Zika, the latest and greatest COVID, the new malaria vaccine—but getting chewed up by bugs was no fun even if you were immune to the diseases they were trying to give you. She zipped the net shut behind her and sat down in a folding camp chair. A torn-open bale of plastic water bottles rested askew on the ground, as if it had been flung out of a helicopter. She worried one out, opened it up, and drank most of it in one long pull. She wasn't dehydrated now, but she would be soon. She heard a distant rifle shot.

One part of her was incredulous that people would live here. Could anything less sustainable be imagined? She was drinking water from a bottle made of petrochemicals. At three in the morning the temperature was still so high that humans could not sleep unless they ran air conditioners powered by generators that burned more petroleum. The generators and the air conditioners alike dumped more heat into the air. Over dinner, Rufus—speaking in an understated, deadpan, almost scholarly way—had told the story about the fire ants and the relays in the air conditioners. Over dessert, Beau talked about meth gators in a much more exuberant style.

It made Texas sound about as hospitable as the surface of Venus. But Saskia was conscious of the fact that she and her people had been living in an unsustainable country for so long that it was the only thing they knew. If the pumps that held back the North Sea were shut off, the country would be flooded in three days. There was no place they could retreat to. If anything, Texas was more sustainable than the Netherlands. It was mostly above sea level, it produced its own oil, and when that ran out, the Texans could have all the wind and solar energy they felt like collecting.

They just couldn't hold back the ocean. When it came to that, the Dutch could give them a few pointers.

To that point: it was midday in the Netherlands and so she put on a pair of glasses and checked in. The first thing she established was that there were no news headlines about the queen crashing a jet in Waco. Of course the crash was mentioned in local Waco news, but nothing was said about who was aboard. Willem had chartered it from a British leasing service known for its discretion. The kinds of people who made a habit of flying around in these things generally didn't like having their identities and their movements exposed to every plane spotter on the Internet, and so various layers of obfuscation were in place as a matter of course.

Having established that, Saskia relaxed a bit by checking Dutch news feeds and football scores, then sent a short affectionate note to Lotte, her sixteen-year-old daughter, who could be relied upon to ignore it. Not that she was a terrible person or that their relationship was bad. Just that she was sixteen and for all practical purposes dwelled on another planet.

A minute later, though, a smiley face came back, a little warm round beacon hanging there against the Texas night like an egg yolk, and that gave Saskia a warm feeling that lasted long enough for her to drift off to sleep.

The princess's real name was Charlotte Emma Sophia. But in a family where people had such rambling monikers, nicknames were a must. Lotte was a simple contraction of the first of her names.

For Frederika Mathilde Louisa Saskia, it had never been so easy. "Freddie" was out of the question. She detested "Rika." "Mathilde" could have yielded "Mattie" or "Tillie," which weren't much better. For a while she had gone by "Lou" and some of her older relatives still called her that.

The addition of "Saskia" to her string of names had been controversial, even shocking, at the time of her christening. It wasn't a proper royal name. It had a dignified enough history—Rembrandt's wife had been a Saskia—but these days it was seen as common. The name of a farmer's wife. There weren't any precedents in the royal family tree for a Saskia; the name had been added to honor a favorite aunt, a commoner who had married into the family. So it had come in through the back door, as it were. The servants' entrance.

People who actually bothered to concern themselves with the queen's fourth name took different views of it. To the most snobbish, it was an embarrassment. From time to time, on an engraved invitation, or in an introductory address, "Saskia" would be pointedly omitted. She was not above being offended when that happened, and holding grudges because of it. Because she had really loved her aunt Saskia.

Less fancy people, on the other hand, rather liked the queen's fourth name because it showed a common touch. From time to time the queen would be referred to, in some tweet or tabloid headline, as Saskia, in the same ironic way as Queen Elizabeth might be called Bess. Snobs might do it as a sly way of suggesting she wasn't royal enough. But ordinary Dutch people—at least, ones who took a basically favorable view of the monarchy—might do it to suggest that the queen was actually, when you got down to it, norMAL. The haters, of course, would call her Queen Fred.

Among a small inner circle, Saskia had become her most commonly used nickname. At the moment in Waco when Amelia had asked, "What should I call you?" Frederika Mathilde Louisa Saskia had blurted out "Saskia" without thinking. And Amelia had raised her eyebrows for a whole slew of reasons. Foremost of which was that, until that moment, Amelia would never have dared to address the queen by that name. Its use was reserved for perhaps half a dozen close friends and younger family members. Even they considered it a bit naughty. But orders were orders. So Amelia and the others had been forcing themselves to use that name, with only occasional slip-ups in which they would say *mevrouw* or even *Uwe Majesteit*. But no one here knew what those words meant.

Rufus, of course, knew her only as Saskia, and had introduced her as such to all of the Boskeys. It was a code name; but at the same time she felt in some ways that it was her true name, and she very much enjoyed being called it.

Saskia awoke hot and sweaty to the sound and aroma of yet more food being prepared. Weather was fine (if sultry) here, but the hurricane had struck the Gulf Coast overnight, passing just far enough south of Houston that it wouldn't go down in the records as a direct hit. But rainfall and storm surge had still been huge.

Caught in the periphery of the hurricane had been the part of Louisiana where the Boskeys lived. According to news coming in from their network, there'd been some flooding. But the Boskeys had shown her pictures of their homes. These were constructed on stilts as much as six meters high. As long as those stilts didn't get knocked out from under them by floating cars, trees, or houses that *hadn't* been put up on stilts, they'd be fine.

On the outskirts of Houston there were apparently places where the big radial freeways leading into and out of the metropolis were equipped with crossover lanes that could, with the flip of a switch, be shunted into a special evacuation mode. A freeway that normally had, say, five lanes going into the city and five going out would suddenly become a one-way, ten-lane behemoth, a fire hose of traffic aimed outward into the higher and dryer hinterlands. Or, given that it was Houston, maybe the correct figure was fourteen or eighteen lanes. Anyway, that switch had been thrown yesterday. So, as Saskia and her team tried to consume food as rapidly as Mary Boskey and her son-in-law Reggie were producing it, they were treated to imagery on the screen of Rufus's laptop showing a webcam feed of a vast unidirectional traffic jam in open territory some forty miles west of downtown Houston. The camera was rocking slightly in what they assumed were powerful bursts of wind. The image was frequently blurred, or blotted out, by waves of what looked like static. It was actually rain coming down with such intensity as to stop all light. When it abated they could see a galaxy of red taillights.

Where they were, of course, it was hot and sunny with barely a breeze, and just a few clouds building up in the south that looked like rain later.

"This all look real strange to you, coming from Holland?" Mary asked, taking advantage of a lull in the eating. She and the other Cajuns had worked out that Saskia's team were Dutch, but apparently Rufus hadn't divulged more than that.

Saskia mastered the urge to correct Mary on her use of the not-exactly-correct term "Holland." "Oh, you might be surprised.

There are parts of the Netherlands where people drive around in pickup trucks, and go to . . ." She was about to say "church" but wasn't sure how these people would respond once she brought up religion, so she finished, ". . . a very traditional kind of church, very conservative."

"Got your own Bible Belt, do you?" Mary answered, with a nod.

"Very much so."

"Y'all with Shell?" Reggie asked.

"Shale?" Saskia was having trouble with his accent and assumed he was talking about the oil-bearing rock.

"I think he means Royal Dutch Shell," Alastair put in, slightly amused. "Maybe you have heard of it."

Saskia's family had co-founded Royal Dutch Shell—which was why it was called Royal—and she personally owned a significant percentage of the company.

"You meet a Dutchman in Houston, that's who he generally works for," Reggie said with a wink.

"In a manner of speaking," Saskia answered, "I suppose you could say that, yes, I am connected with that company."

But, as she came to see, the Boskeys were, in a very polite and roundabout way, trying to bring the conversation around to business. Not in the sense of seeking to extract money from the Dutch castaways—that seemed to be the furthest thing from their minds—but in the sense of trying to figure out where this was all going, and what to do next. How, in other words, to properly discharge the responsibilities they had cheerfully shouldered when they had taken in the foreign castaways. Camped here on this sandbar they were not getting any closer to Houston. Nor were they getting closer to Lake Charles, which was where the rest of the clan presumably awaited their return. A general plan seemed to be coalescing that a number of Boskeys and their friends and associates might converge on Houston in a pincer maneuver, a couple of days hence, after the storm had abated, but while they could still make themselves useful assisting flood victims.

If that was the intention, they needed to get moving. For the Brazos was a convoluted river, and the number of miles they needed to cover on the water was greater by far than the straight-line distance. If they departed now and kept moving day and night, the timing would work out. Saskia and her team were welcome to come along, but they needed to understand that it would not be a mere party cruise; from this point onward they would not again stop moving for longer than it took to refuel.

Saskia discussed it with her team, but not for very long. The weather had forced their hand. They had about two days to kill no matter what. They could kill it in some nearby hotel, supposing they could find a room—but even at this distance from Houston, all the hotel rooms had been snapped up. Staying with the Boskeys would give them lodging, transportation to Houston, and privacy. Even if word somehow leaked out to the Dutch press that the queen was in Texas, they could release video of her assisting with disaster relief, which was (a) just the sort of thing queens were expected to do, and (b) relevant to the Netherlands' timeless, overriding, existential concern of not ending up underwater.

So that was the queen's decision. They helped pack up the encampment and they headed south. Rufus was part of the caravan. His trailer, when parked, could be occupied, but when it was moving no one was allowed to be in it. Likewise the pontoon could be towed down highways, but not with people in it. So for the most part the boats were used to transport people, and rarely stopped moving. The wheeled vehicles ranged ahead of them, foraging for gasoline, food, beer, and other consumables. They transferred these to the boats at places where roads came to the river's edge. More Cajuns showed up, towing additional boats, and so both the waterborne and dry-land parts of the caravan grew. Alastair and Fenna generally looked for ways to "ride shotgun" in air-conditioned vehicles. Saskia for the most part stayed on the pontoon boat and Amelia stayed with her, both resorting to the use of earthsuits during the hottest parts of the day.

An earthsuit was not so much a single garment as a toolkit of parts that could be snapped together in different ways depending on conditions. The refrigeration system couldn't work unless it could discharge heat into the environment. Normally it did that by shooting hot air straight up out of a pipe, but in circumstances like these, where a supply of water was near to hand, the air-based heat exchanger could be swapped out for a module that performed the same task by heating up water. A system of umbilicals made it possible for the hot part of it to trail in the Brazos along the flank of the pontoon boat, so long as the users didn't expect to do a lot of moving around. There was only so much moving around one *could* do in a craft of this size and so the restriction wasn't a problem.

PENTAPOTAMIA

Deep had grown up in Richmond, British Columbia. This was an island on Vancouver's south flank, bracketed by the two forks of the Fraser River, and destined to be submerged by the rising waters of the Salish Sea into which they flowed.

Deep's elementary school had once done a "project-based learning" unit about salmon, focused on rehabbing a nearby creek that had been channelized and made lifeless by the processes of suburban development. Then, as now, "physically active" and "a kinesthetic learner," young Deep had never taken well to classroom learning. But working in the rain with a shovel, and observing the movements of fish, had brought him alive.

In the summer, Chinook salmon came in from the ocean and swam up the rivers to spawn. This had had the unintended but, to his parents, desirable side effect of lengthening Deep's school year. His family operated gas stations. They'd started in the 1960s with a single one near Chilliwack, but now had thumbtacks spattered across the map of British Columbia, conjoined by a web of kinship and financial ties. Deep cross-correlated the thumbtacks with topo maps showing the courses of rivers and cajoled his father into taking him on summer expeditions. Father would drop him off by the side of some river with a net, a fishing pole, and lunch, and then go hang out in the back room of a gas station with a cousin or a brother while Deep rambled up and down the riverbank figuring out where the salmon were, and attempting to catch them. By that point in their life cycle, they did not make for very good eating. But as he got older, and these trips lengthened from day hikes to overnight camps, he ate them anyway, cooking them over smoky fires that he taught himself how to kindle in wet wood.

It was on the return leg of such a trip that his uncle Dharmender bestowed on him the nickname that stuck. Deep had come into Dharmender's gas station smelling of fish and smoke, and been dubbed "Lox." In Punjabi it was rendered "Laka" but pronounced similarly. It was a weird nickname. But he needed one, because there were a lot of people in his world named Deep Singh—three of them in his elementary school alone.

Laks's father was a pious and loving man who never quite bounced back from the realization, which came to him when Laks was about twenty, that his son was never going to get any formal education beyond the high school diploma he already had. Laks's interest in fish was not going to lead to a career as a wildlife biologist. Fisherman was more likely. He took summer jobs on commercial fishing boats up and down the coast: basically unskilled labor, perfect for a brawny and energetic teenager. At the beginning this was couched as "saving money for college." But Laks was not college material. He was an exceptional athlete, but no university would award him a scholarship for the sports in which he most excelled: snowboarding, and the martial art known as gatka.

Father hid his disappointment well, but not perfectly. It was tough for him. He'd been the first in the family to earn a degree; grandfather had sent him to school so that he could pick up the skills needed to look after the books and handle certain legal affairs for the family business. Uncle Dharmender, on the other hand, took a more pragmatic view of how a young man such as Laks might make his way in the world. Without seeming to be overly judgmental he pointed out that working on fishing boats was dangerous, exhausting, and seasonal. Might it be just the lowest rung on a ladder?

If so, a next rung was within reach. Fishing vessels, like most other commercial ships, were made of steel, or sometimes aluminum. Repairs and improvements were made by cutting metal plates to shape using an oxyacetylene torch or a plasma cutter, then welding them together.

Laks learned how to weld. Uncle Dharmender encouraged him

to take training courses and obtain the necessary certifications. By the time Laks's high school classmates had made it out of college and entered the job market, he was already pulling down a solid income. He still worked on fishing boats when that was in season, but during the rest of the year he picked up welding jobs all over British Columbia and ranging into the oil sands of Alberta. The money was good. Laks had no loans to pay off, no dependents to support. He had all the time he wanted to go snowboarding in the mountains of British Columbia and to practice his martial art.

A foundational practice of Sikhism was the operation of *langars*: kitchens where any person of any religion, or no religion at all, could obtain a free meal merely by showing up at the appointed time. A typical langar operated on a fixed schedule and was based out of a *gurdwara*—a word usually translated as "temple" or "church." From time to time, though, members of a gurdwara might set up a temporary, pop-up langar at the site of a disaster, or any place where a lot of people were going hungry for some reason.

It happened one year that a lot of people in India went hungry, not for food, but for oxygen. A variant strain of COVID was sweeping across the country. Many were dying who might have lived if only they had been able to obtain supplemental oxygen. A gray market had emerged as desperate family members sought to obtain bottled oxygen in any way they could. Some gurdwaras had set up oxygen langars. These were improvised, frequently open-air facilities where oxygen flowed from steel bottles—the same ones used in the welding industry—into regulators and thence through networks of tubes to masks where suffering patients could obtain some relief. It was not the same standard of care as prevailed in ICUs, where patients were sedated and intubated, but it was enough to make a difference for patients who only needed a little assistance with breathing and who otherwise might have overwhelmed hospitals.

Laks's father never stopped sending him links to articles about these oxygen langars—some of which were being directly supported by gurdwaras in the Vancouver area. Father was a gentle personality, a classic kid brother to Dharmender, who had effectively become the patriarch when grandfather had passed away too young. So it was sometimes difficult to make out what he was trying to say. But eventually Laks—with some prodding from his mother—put it together that he was being presented with an opportunity not just to help suffering people in India but to make his father feel better about the direction Laks had taken in life. The skills he had learned as a welder, relating to the handling of bottled gases, could be of direct use in one of these oxygen langars. He could go over there and help people; and in so doing he could re-connect with his religious faith.

He had never decisively fallen away from this, at least in his own mind, but he had cut his hair and stopped wearing a turban. Management of hair and turban had proved very inconvenient on fishing boats. Later, when he had become a welder, he had found that welding masks—whatever fine qualities they might have as industrial safety equipment—clearly had not been designed by people who put turbans on every morning. You could always figure out some way to make it work, but easier yet was just to ditch the turban altogether. Among young Sikhs he was hardly alone in adopting Western hairstyle and headgear. But he knew it hurt his father's feelings. He had tried to make amends by making his own *kara*—the bracelet, typically made of iron or steel, that Sikhs traditionally wore on the right wrist. Supposedly it was a vestige of larger arm bands formerly worn by warriors to protect their wrists from sword cuts. You'd never know it to see some of the slim elegant karas worn by modern people. Laks, who had access to a full metalworking shop, designed his own kara, cutting the shape out of 12-gauge steel plate with a CNC plasma cutter and bending it to fit around his wrist just so. It was heavy metal, both in the literal sense and in its aesthetic, which owed as much to sword and sorcery video games as it did to traditional decorative arts of the Punjab.

He knew his parents appreciated the gesture. But what they really wanted was for him to go to India and volunteer in one of these oxygen langars for at least a few weeks. If the visit stretched out to a few months, and he came back with longer hair, a turban, and maybe a girlfriend, so much the better.

So he went over to India and he did that. At the time, the new variant of COVID was burning most intensely in Delhi, so for the first few weeks he didn't venture far from the capital. He stayed in Western-style hotels and got about in taxis. He spent his days managing tanks, tubes, and regulators at three different oxygen langars that local gurdwaras—supported by financial contributions from around the world—had set up in open spaces near medical centers that were buckling under the strain of the pandemic. He avoided contact with the actual patients. This was partly to avoid contagion—he wasn't sure whether his vaccinations would protect him from this variant. It was partly because he did not speak Hindi—just some Punjabi, which was part of the same family of languages but not close enough. But it was mostly because he lacked that personality trait, essential for health care workers, of being able to relate to sick people and their families without becoming overwhelmed. So when he wasn't busy at the langar he was back at the hotel, working out in the fitness center or playing video games in his room. Despite that he came down with this new COVID, suffered a mild case, but lost his sense of smell.

He knew that this would be distressing to his mother and father, so he didn't tell them until after most of the symptoms had abated. And he sweetened it with the news that he would now be traveling to Amritsar, in the Punjab, to spend a little time in the land that was to his people what the headwaters of the Fraser River, high in the Rockies, were to Chinook salmon.

It wasn't until he got there that he learned the literal meaning of the word "Punjab": Five Rivers. Coming to India and hearing all the languages and dialects had made him aware of words in a way that no amount of classroom instruction ever could have.

This was project-based learning all over again. This time, however, the project was him trying to understand, and to make himself understood, in a place where many languages were spoken. He'd fancied his Punjabi was pretty good, but really it was just enough to get by. Native speakers in Amritsar had the disheartening habit of switching to English mid-conversation, thinking they were doing him a favor. So during the first few weeks of his sojourn in Amritsar he burned more of his savings than intended staying in Marriots, Radissons, and Wyndhams, balming his intense homesickness by watching American television and eating room service hamburgers.

But Punjabi TV was only a channel click away from American. Gradually the language wormed its way into his brain. Some words were hardly different at all. "Sant" had a meaning different, but not terribly far off, from "Saint." "Naam," which was another very important word to Sikhs, was "Name." The Punjab had been named Pentapotamia, Five Rivers, by Alexander the Great when he had tried and failed to conquer it. But the Persian "Panj" and the Greek "Pent" both meant "five" and if you followed both upstream to their origin in the lost language of the Aryans, they were the same word.

What really blew his mind, though, was his discovery—an incredibly belated discovery of what ought to have been obvious—that the same thing applied to his nickname. "Laka" in Punjabi, "Laks" in Hindi or Urdu, "Lox" in English, "Lachs" in German, and basically the same word in many other languages across Eurasia all meant exactly the same thing. The word had been coined by people who lived, before the beginning of history, in some place where catching salmon and smoking the meat was important to their survival. From there—probably around the Black Sea—they had spread out in all directions and taken the word with them.

But having a few similarities between languages was more confusing than having none at all. So it was a rocky first few weeks. More than once, while pumping away on an elliptical trainer in the fitness center of some Western-style hotel, Laks surfed to travel websites to check the price of a one-way ticket back to YVR.

Part of the difficulty was his self-consciousness whenever he stepped outside of the Western bubble. In Canada he'd been tall and muscular enough to be mistaken for a hockey or football player. Here he was a giant. More importantly, it was obvious that razor and scissors had been allowed to touch his beard and his hair. He had begun to grow them back out. But in the eyes of a random passerby on an Amritsar street he was neither fish nor fowl: a big, somewhat shaggy chap who could have originated from anywhere between Persia and the foothills of the Himalayas.

Other than that, however, he just wasn't *special* here. Well over a hundred million people—three times the population of Canada—spoke Punjabi, and most of them spoke it better than him. He'd come to a place where everyone—shopkeepers, cops, lawyers, farmers, even criminals—belonged to the same religion. In Vancouver, being the only Sikh on the fishing boat or the only Sikh welder had made him stand out, for better or worse. Not here. He needed an identity beyond just that.

One morning, he slept later than he should have, and finally twitched his curtain open to let in a blade of sunlight that would force him not to go back to sleep. The sun happened to fall on his arm band, making the burnished steel gleam—except in one place, where he noticed a faint bloom of rust. This was so superficial that he was able to rub it off using a towel. But it seemed like an omen. He had chosen to make, and to wear, the big kara in part because it said something about his connection to the traditional martial arts of his people. Now it was getting rusty! What did that say about him?

He decided to do something about it beginning that day.

LOUISIANA

Willem drove down in a rented pickup truck and rendezvoused with the caravan during a pit stop at a bend in the river near College Station. He sat down with the queen inside a screen house that the Boskeys had pitched on a sandbar. They reviewed the various large and small affairs of the House of Orange.

They began with what was urgent and nearby—chiefly the two wounded members of the group in hospital in Waco. Lennert, he reported, would be fine, though he had a few months of physical therapy ahead of him. He would be on medical leave for a while and so he would have to fly back to the Netherlands once the doctors had cleared him for travel.

Sending out a replacement bodyguard would be complicated and slow, and so Amelia would have to shoulder that responsibility alone for the time being. Security chieftains at home weren't happy about any of this and so Willem was having to devote a lot of time to calming them down. Amelia had her hands full working out backup plans to be implemented in case various contingencies arose.

Johan was going to be as fine as it was possible for a concussion victim to be, but the plane he'd been sent here to co-pilot no longer existed and so there was no point in keeping him in Texas. Tomorrow he'd be on a KLM flight back to Amsterdam.

Authorities in Waco were only just beginning the investigation of the crash. Sooner or later they'd want to interview "the pilot" but they had surprisingly little actual power. No crime had been committed; they couldn't arrest anyone, couldn't force Saskia to give information even if they knew where she was.

They then moved on to the quotidian tasks of the royal household that they would have talked about had they been at home: preparations for the Budget Day Speech in a couple of weeks, various upcoming appearances, and the never-ending flow of royal correspondence. So familiar were these tasks that it almost became possible to forget that they were not in the queen's office at Noordeinde Palace in The Hague. But then a pause in the conversation brought them back to the here and now, and they sat there quietly for a few moments hearing the cacophony of the bugs and the frogs, the soft liquid sound of the running river.

"Is there anything else?" Willem asked. For he could tell something was on the tip of her tongue.

"I've been meaning to ask you sort of an odd question."

"Ask away."

"*Brazos*," she said, looking out over the river. "Why does the name sound so familiar to me? What am I missing?"

"You've been seeing the word on financial statements ever since you became old enough to read them," Willem said.

"Bingo! So I'm not crazy."

Willem shook his head. "On the contrary."

"So my next question is . . ."

"At the place where this river empties into the Gulf of Mexico," Willem said, "south of Houston, there are some mounds—natural formations—rich in sulfur. At the beginning of the twentieth century some businessmen started a company called Brazos Sulfur to mine those deposits. There was a lot of crossover between those guys and early oilmen. This was the era when the oil industry was just going ballistic around here."

"The gushers you see in old photos."

"Spindletop and all that. The origin of Gulf and Texaco and others."

"You are a gusher of obscure industrial history, Willem!"

"You're too kind. The only reason I know any of this is that it came to light during the last few weeks when I was putting together that packet of information about Dr. Schmidt."

"How is T.R. mixed up in it?"

"His great-grandfather Karl Schmidt was one of the founders of

Brazos Sulfur. As well as an oilman. That's how T.R. got his name. Karl was an admirer of Teddy Roosevelt. Named his son—Dr. Schmidt's grandfather—after him."

"All right," Saskia said, "so I'm getting the picture of how it all started, more than a century ago. But why would I be seeing the word 'Brazos' on financial statements? I'm not aware of any investments in sulfur mines."

Willem nodded. "But you are aware, if I may make a blindingly obvious point, that your family from the very beginning were investors in Royal Dutch Shell."

"It just came up in conversation," Saskia said drily.

Willem nodded. "If you follow the history of Brazos Sulfur through the twentieth century, it expands to other domes—those sulfur-rich mounds—in the Gulf Coast and then diversifies to other minerals. Manganese, nickel, potash. Kaolin, which is a kind of fancy clay used to make paint and diarrhea medicine. So about as unglamorous as you can get."

"How is sulfur used?"

"Tires and fertilizer."

"I see your point about the glamour."

"They changed the name to Brazos Mining. They went wherever the minerals were. There's not a lot of margin in clay and potash. They ended up in places like Cuba. Congo. Indonesia."

"Ah," Saskia said, "now it's all starting to come together."

"Like a lot of other Western companies they got kicked out of former colonies during the post-war period. Castro kicked them out of Cuba and so on. But they have, I guess you could say, tendrils all over the place—interlocking boards of directors with oil companies. Connections to big establishment figures— Rockefellers, Bushes, and so on. During the 1960s, after they'd been kicked out of Cuba and the Congo, they got wind that a geologist from our country had climbed the highest mountain in New Guinea—which is on the formerly Dutch half of the island— and seen a huge mineral deposit. Mostly copper. But where there's copper there's probably gold. The scale of it was unbelievable. Just sitting there in plain sight."

"In one of the least accessible places on Earth!" Saskia protested.

Willem nodded. "And at extremely high altitude to boot. They didn't have a prayer of getting to it without local knowledge and connections. So Brazos Mining put together a joint venture with Shell—which I need hardly tell you knew everything there was to know about doing business in the Dutch East Indies—and created Brazos RoDuSh, which went on to create—"

"The world's largest open pit mine on the top of a mountain surrounded by the New Guinea jungle!" Saskia now knew exactly what Willem was talking about. The place was famous for its hugeness and infamous for political reasons.

"Exactly."

"I own part of that."

Willem nodded. "You have owned part of it since you became old enough to own things. Brazos RoDuSh has appeared somewhere on every financial statement you have ever read."

"How are they doing?" Saskia asked. She was trying to be mischievous. But it didn't come through. She winked at Willem. But maybe it just looked like she was trying to get a trickle of sweat out of her eye. She really needed to work on her ability to project puckish wit. Maybe it would help if she were actually more witty.

"I won't go over the politics, the history with you," Willem began.

"Of Indonesia and West Papua and all that."

He nodded. "But the Asian economic book created a fantastically huge demand for copper and so they quintupled their value in a short period of time. More recently as you know there has been trouble in Papua and the stock has performed less admirably."

"But . . . bringing it all back to the here and now . . . T.R. Schmidt is also an investor in Brazos RoDuSh?"

"He was *born* there."

"In New Guinea!?"

Willem nodded. "Dr. Schmidt inherited a significant interest in the company from a generation-skipping trust set up by his grandfather in the 1970s. His chain of restaurants and gas stations was funded by the windfall when copper prices went through the roof."

Saskia looked out over the river and pondered it. "And I naively imagined he was a homespun Texas oilman."

"He *is*," Willem said, "but homespun Texas oilmen really got around during the second half of the twentieth century."

"Even to mountaintops in Papua."

Willem nodded and sat back in his folding chair to signal a change of subject. "Now, speaking of Indonesia, and white people who ended up there. If it is really your intention to proceed to Houston this way—"

"It is," she confirmed. "I can always change the plan, right? Highways and hotels are only a few minutes' drive away at any point."

"The hotels are full. The highways are running in the wrong direction."

"So be it then! We are caught in the middle of a natural disaster. We can't go back home. There's nothing to do in Houston until the storm blows over."

"In that case, I feel a certain obligation to go see my father."

"Of course! But what is the weather like where he lives?"

"There was rain yesterday but it is clearing up now. I could leave immediately. Drive through the night. Be at his place for breakfast."

"I should write him a note," the queen said and reached for a sheet of the royal stationery: a ream of printer paper Willem had scored at Staples.

"Thank you, *Uwe Maj* . . ." Willem caught himself just in time, and forced himself to say, "Saskia. He will be most honored."

Willem's grandfather Johannes Castelein was a Dutch petroleum engineer who was sent over to what was then the Dutch East

Indies in 1930 to work for Shell. He was assigned to a port town in East Java. This had a large enough expat community to support a school to which most of the local Dutch and mixed-race population, as well as Chinese merchants, sent their children. He met, fell in love with, and married Greta, who was a teacher there. They had three children during the 1930s: Ruud, a boy born in 1932; Mina, a girl in 1934; and Hendrik, Willem's father, in 1937.

When the Netherlands fell to Hitler in 1940, contact between it and the Dutch East Indies was lost. The Dutch surrendered the Indies to Japan in 1942. Anyone in the military became a POW and ended up in especially bad places such as the railway project that later became the subject of *The Bridge on the River Kwai*. Adult civilians were sorted according to both gender and blood quantum. Johannes was *totok*—pure Dutch. Greta was an Indo—mixed European and Indonesian. The Japanese High Command "invited" them to place themselves under Japanese jurisdiction at "protection centers"—separate camps for adult males on the one hand, women and children on the other.

At the age of ten, Ruud, Hendrik's older brother, was classified as an adult male and sent to the same camp as Johannes. The boy died the next year of bacterial dysentery. Greta, the daughter, Mina, and Hendrik were sent to a camp where conditions were a little better, at least during the first year. As the war dragged on, however, they kept getting shuffled to worse and worse places, losing possessions at every step. By the time 1945 rolled around, eight-year-old Hendrik had acquired a specialty in climbing trees, where he would beat and shake the branches until creatures fell out of them: big ungainly birds, snakes, monkeys, insects. He would look down to see the women of the camp converging on the fresh meat to beat it to death, tear it to shreds, and fight over the shreds. He watched it with a certain detachment born of the fact that he was up there munching on tree snails, lizards, and large bugs that his mother had encouraged him to harvest and to keep for himself. Meanwhile, down on the ground, Greta and her sister Alexandra, who had ended up in the same camp, worked out a way to cook up a sort of porridge from the prodigious quantities of lice harvested from the heads and bodies of camp inmates. It was sterile, since it was thoroughly cooked, and it seemed to have some nutrients. As a result of these measures, Hendrik grew big, strong, and troublesome enough that in mid-1945 he was deemed an adult one year ahead of schedule and shipped off to a men's camp. He never saw his mother, Greta, again. Years would pass before he saw his aunt Alexandra and sister Mina.

Conditions were generally much worse at the men's camp, but some of the older men looked after him and kept him alive through the end of the war a few months later. The Japanese guards enforced a brutal disciplinary regime. The inmates had adapted to it as best they could by using a system of code words. *"Oranje boven"* (Orange on top) was a slogan that in happier times might be chanted at football matches, but here was muttered as an affirmation of continued loyalty to the House of Orange.

At war's end, during a chaotic few weeks of being shuffled from place to place, Hendrik encountered his father, alive, but sick and emaciated, as they were being loaded into boxcars. It ended somehow with the two of them finding their way back to their house in East Java. This was half burned down and stripped of all items that could be moved. They lived in the ruins for a few months trying to figure out what had become of Greta, Alexandra, and Mina. The answer turned out to be that the women had wound up in a camp in western Java, surrounded by increasingly hostile and aggressive Indonesian bravos: teenaged males who had grown their hair long and ran around in packs brandishing bamboo spears with sharp, hardened tips, and sometimes more advanced weapons that they had acquired from the Japanese. This period was named *bersiap*, meaning, roughly, "get ready" or "be prepared." What they were getting prepared for was to run all the Europeans, as well as the Europeanized Indos and the Chinese, out of the Indies for good and make it an independent country. Loudspeakers were nailed up to trees and strung together with wires so that rousing speeches by Sukarno could be broadcast everywhere. They naturally focused their attentions on the camps into which the Japanese had conveniently rounded up all the people they didn't like. At first these were still guarded by the Japanese—who had no way of getting home—and later by Gurkhas and Sikhs parachuted in by the Brits, who were supposed to be in charge of the place until further arrangements could be made. Those camps, as bad as they still were, were safer than anywhere else.

In their little enclave in East Java, across the bay from the Royal Dutch Shell petroleum docks, Johannes and Hendrik felt comparatively safe for the time being. Johannes renewed an old friendship with the Kuoks, a local Chinese family who before the war had found a niche as middlemen, buying the produce of the interior and selling it to overseas customers. Feeling threatened by the overall climate, and now effectively stateless, they wanted guns to protect themselves. Johannes knew how to get them, exploiting his privileged status, and traded some to the Kuoks for food, which they still knew how to obtain from their connections in plantations up-country.

In time they got word that Greta, Alexandra, and Mina had been evacuated by their Gurkha and Sikh protectors to a more easily defended location closer to what was then called Batavia and would soon be called Jakarta. Johannes reckoned that he would be able to reach the place via railway and, along with Hendrik, set out to do just that. The journey was halting as the train kept getting held up in provincial towns by local gangs of revolutionaries. In some places a kind of order was being maintained by what would eventually become the government of Indonesia, or by vestigial British or Dutch forces. Other places it seemed more like mob rule. As anyone who wasn't deaf could tell, the latter were communicating up and down the line by the "coconut telegraph," which was a traditional system of sending information from village to village by beating on hollow logs.

In one of those towns, all the European-looking passengers were marched off and made to run a gantlet of thrusting spears and thudding clubs into the town square. Hendrik and other children and women were separated from adult males, who could be heard screaming. The next, and last, time that Hendrik saw his father, Johannes was kneeling naked in the town square. He was blindfolded. On closer inspection, he was bandaged over the eye sockets, and the bandage was soaked and streaming with blood, because his eyes had been gouged out and tossed into a bucket along with a lot of other eyes of the wrong color. One of the young rebels had got a samurai sword and was going down the line cutting heads off. Johannes's last words were *"Leve de Koningin!"* ("Long live the Queen!").

Whatever plan their captors might have had for the women and children never came to pass as word of the situation somehow got out to better-armed and more disciplined Indonesians who released them from the crowded cells where they had been detained and sent them back whence they'd come on the next train. Thus did nine-year-old Hendrik become effectively a member of the Kuok family. They took him in and made up a Chinese name for him: Eng, which was easy for him to remember (it meant "scary" or "spooky" in Dutch) and to pronounce. Anyone could see at a glance that he was Indo and not Chinese, but there was nothing they could do about that.

As they found out later, Mother Greta, while climbing over a wall topped with broken glass, cut her hand. The wound became septic and she died. Sister Mina at that point became, for all practical purposes, the daughter of Aunt Alexandra. They made it to a better-protected site in Batavia whence the British evacuated them to a camp in Australia.

That was a much better situation than what faced the Kuok clan during the struggle for Indonesian independence, which consumed most of the second half of the 1940s. The port city where they lived became the focus of a lot of fighting, including aerial and naval bombardment. Their family compound, after being heavily damaged, was expropriated. So they moved to a plantation up in the hills where they had business dealings going back several generations. This area later became the locus of insurgent and counterinsurgent warfare. Some Dutch commandos parachuted in and used it as a base of operations for a few days until new orders came in over the wireless and they abruptly departed. Indonesian freedom fighters, who had been watching all this from only a few hundred meters away, then moved in and conducted what were known euphemistically as "reprisals." The only females who survived the reprisals were those who had the presence of mind to flee into the jungle at the first sign of trouble. Hendrik, who put his tree-climbing skills to good use, saw some of the reprisals from a distance and still refused to talk about them. He, a few girls, and "Rudy" Kuok, a relatively senior member of the clan, escaped with the clothes on their backs and eventually found their way to an enclave on the coast that was still under Dutch military control. Hendrik at this point stopped claiming to be Eng Kuok and identified himself as Hendrik Castelein, a Dutch boy, and told the whole story. They were evacuated by ship to the Dutch base at Ambon, a predominantly Christian island to the east.

In 1951, Hendrik, at the age of fourteen, was given an opportunity to be "repatriated" (though he had never been there) to the Netherlands. He seized it, bidding a fond farewell to the Kuoks (who by that point had moved on to New Guinea) and traveling alone halfway around the world. He got off the boat in Rotterdam and was greeted by volunteers who settled him in a town in the southern part of the country, Zeeland. There he became a ward of an orphanage attached to a local church. He enrolled in a trade school, where he was found to have a knack for technical drawing.

Two years later, the unlucky combination of a high tide, a low pressure system, and a big storm sent a surge of water down the North Sea. It burst through flood control works in the Netherlands, England, and other countries that had the misfortune to lie in its path. Thousands died in the floods. In the Netherlands, which suffered by far the most fatalities, the disaster had the same historical resonance as did 9/11 for Americans. It led to a vast program of flood control infrastructure-building. Hendrik, however, missed out on all that, because, in the wake of the disaster, he moved to America. A Dutch Reformed church on the southern fringes of Chicago had agreed to sponsor him. He was hired as a draftsman by a steel mill just across the border in Indiana. Once he was established, with a job and a house, he sent a telegram to a Kuok in Taiwan, which in due course made its way to New Guinea, and a year later he was married to Isabella ("Bel") Kuok, a childhood sweetheart with whom he had been maintaining a long-distance relationship. Willem was their first child. Later they had three more.

The household, in the suburban no-man's-land between the South Side of Chicago and the heavy-industrial powerhouse of northwest Indiana, was Americanized, but Willem grew up bilingual in English and Dutch. From time to time the family would make weekend forays into Chicago's Chinatown, but Bel spoke the wrong dialect and so it was a foreign place to her. Willem did learn how to read many Chinese characters, albeit in the traditional form still used in Taiwan.

He held dual Dutch and American citizenship. In high school he went to the Netherlands for what was supposed to be one semester. In effect, though, he had never returned. His great-aunt Alexandra and his aunt Mina had ended up in The Hague. They were happy to have him in their home, and he was happy to be in a place where his complicated ancestry was not considered remarkable. In The Hague, he was just another Indo. Not only that, but there was also a community of Chinese-Dutch in the area who had more in common with the Kuoks, including some mutual acquaintances and business connections in Southeast Asia. And, finally, there were openly gay people, and Willem was gay. So after that, when he went back to America, he did so not as an American coming home, but as a Dutchman crossing the sea to pay a visit to his foreign relatives. High school led to university, and that led to grad school at Oxford, and a Ph.D. in foreign relations, specializing in the intricacies of the world that the Kuoks still, to this day, lived in.

So much for the first half of Willem's life (or so he'd conceived of it in the days when he'd imagined that life was basically over at sixty). Returning to the Netherlands after a brief postdoc stint in China, he'd got caught up in politics and surprised himself by getting elected to a parliamentary post. He was a member of the center-right party that was almost always part of every governing coalition and that accounted for many cabinet members. Re-elected a few years later, he found himself with a junior cabinet position relating to defense. And this developed into a career that accounted for much of the "second half" of his life. For decades he had reliably been re-elected and served in various posts mostly related to intelligence, foreign affairs, or defense. His name had been mentioned from time to time as a possible minister of defense or even prime minister, but he had never really sought that level of responsibility. Not until 2006 had there been an openly gay cabinet minister, so there was that.

But the positions in which he *had* served had placed him in frequent contact with the reigning monarchs, who received regular briefings on the matters for which Willem was responsible. They got to know him, and to like him. The story had got round of the manner of Johannes Castelein's death, and his last words. With that in his family background, no one could be seen as more Dutch than Willem. But his multi-racialness, his childhood in America, and his sexuality made him interesting: just the embodiment of the modern Netherlands that the House of Orange would want to have around the palace as proof of relevancy and with-it-ness. So as the "second half" of his life drew to a close and he found himself as vigorous as he had been at thirty, with his faculties intact, and with absolutely no interest in retiring, he had entered their service.

He'd thought the pickup truck a quirky, ironic choice when he'd picked it out in Waco. He'd taken a selfie with it to share with Remi, his husband. Since then, though, he'd learned that it served as camouflage in these parts. No one would look twice at a white pickup. His tailored suits and polished shoes had been destroyed in the crash. He had gone on a shopping spree in the menswear section at Walmart. In those clothes, driving that vehicle, he drew very little attention as he drove across East Texas and Louisiana, making only brief stops for food, gasoline, and toilet.

Hendrik and Bel had learned very early that there was a thing called the Illinois Central Railroad that would enable them to escape the brutality of Chicago winters. Merely by purchasing affordable tickets and hopping on a train at Chicago's Union Station, they could doze off as the frozen corn stubble of Illinois glided past the windows and wake up in the nearly tropical environment of the Delta.

During the industrial boom years before the 1974 oil shock, Hendrik had climbed the ladder to management just as adroitly as he had once clambered up trees in Javanese concentration camps. And no one knew how to pinch pennies better than a survivor. They bought a piece of land outside of New Orleans, improved it (meaning that they filled in wetlands), sold half of it off at a profit, and, not long after the turn of the century, retired to the other half. Bel had come down with dementia and passed away a few years ago. Willem's youngest sister, Jenny, fleeing a bad marriage, had moved in as caretaker. Various members of the overseas Kuok clan moved in and out, pitching in on household chores while using the property as a U.S. base of operations for more or less complicated endeavors the details of which Willem made no real effort to stay abreast of. All he knew, and all he cared about, was that someone was always around to keep an eye on Hendrik and help him out of a jam, should he get into one. Which he never did.

You got to the house by driving through the suburban develop-ment that had been erected on the portion of the land that Hen-drik and Bel had sold. At the end of a curving subdivision street the trees closed in over a road that had suddenly reverted to gravel, and a slow crunching drive through a tunnel of dark green led to a gate flanked by ornamental lions. The gate wasn't locked. Willem felt the truck gaining a few all-important inches of alti-tude as things opened up and the sun illuminated stripes of orange zinnias flanking the driveway. Bel had established the tradition of planting these every year. In Indonesia before the war, Dutch colonists and loyal Indos had grown them as a symbol of national pride. In America they were a ubiquitous garden plant. The sym-bolism of the color would be lost on most people here, but Willem of all people knew what it meant.

The driveway looped around in front of an old two-story house, torn down in sections over the years and rebuilt out of cinder block because of termites. Father rarely ventured upstairs anymore, but wings had been added to the house at ground level. Willem parked his truck at the base of a flagpole flying the Dutch tricolor be-neath a larger Stars and Stripes. Before shutting off the engine he sat there for a minute, letting the A/C run, and using PanScan—one of several competing apps in the anonymized contact tracing space—to check his immunological status versus that of everyone currently in the house. Since Willem was the interloper, he was the most likely to be bringing new viral strains in to this household.

Eventually the app produced a little map of the property, show-ing icons for everyone there, color-coded based on epidemiologi-cal risk. The upshot was that Willem could get by without a mask provided he kept his distance from Hendrik. Oh, and if he ven-tured upstairs he should put a mask on because there was a Kuok in the second bedroom on the left whose recent exposure history was almost as colorful as Willem's.

Accordingly he and his father sat two meters apart in a gazebo in the snatch of mowed lawn between the house and the bank where the property plunged into the bayou. It was screened—everything here had to be—but a faint breeze moved through it and Willem made sure he was downwind of his father. Hendrik always had a walker near to hand, in case he should require it, but could easily move a few steps unassisted. He sat down at the gazebo's cast-concrete table. Jenny brought out soft drinks on a tray. Hendrik raised a sweating glass of seltzer. Willem did likewise. They pantomimed clinking them together. "To the queen!" Hendrik said.

"The queen."

They drank. Of course, they would hold the entire conversation in Dutch. "She sends this," Willem said, and slid the queen's note across the table. Hendrik somewhat laboriously fished out glasses and put them on, then unfolded the note and read it, as if it were an everyday occurrence for him to sit out in his gazebo perusing correspondence from crowned heads of Europe.

"She's here," he observed. He'd guessed as much from the date, or some other detail in what was written there.

"Yes, I came over with her yesterday."

"A secret." For Hendrik read all the Dutch news and would have known months in advance of an official visit; he'd have been at the airport with a bushel of orange zinnias balanced on the crossbar of his walker.

"Yes."

"Unusual."

"These are unusual times, Father."

"The hurricane?"

"A coincidence. An unlucky one—it fouled up all our plans! But it gave me a free day to come and see you!"

This weak effort to change the subject was batted away by Hendrik. "If it has nothing to do with the hurricane, then what causes you to speak of 'unusual times' in such a significant way? What in addition is unusual?"

Now Willem had to struggle with conflicting notions around secret-keeping.

For Willem even to preface what he was about to say with "Don't tell anyone this" or "what I'm about to tell you is sensitive information" would earn him the verbal equivalent of a spanking from his father. Its secrecy was so patently obvious that to mention it would be implicitly to suggest that Hendrik was senile.

He turned away from his father's glare and nodded toward the dark trees growing up out of the bayou. "How long before all that is underwater?" he asked.

There was a long silence, if you could call the singing of birds, the buzzing of cicadas, the stridor of frogs by that name.

"So it's about that," Hendrik said, with a *finally something is going to be done about it* air. "What is she going to do?"

"Well, it's a constitutional monarchy, father, she has strictly limited—"

"Don't give me that."

Willem actually had to suppress a teenager-like eye roll. "It *is*, Father," he insisted. "It's not as though she has secret superpowers above and beyond what is stipulated in the Grondwet."

"What's the point of having her around then?"

They had come to an impasse. Not for the first time. Willem knew where this was going. If he kept pushing back, Father would crush him by telling the story about Opa and the samurai sword. Johannes, at the end, had been loyal to the queen. Not to the elected representatives in the States General, or the words of the Grondwet—the Dutch constitution.

And it wasn't as if Hendrik were some kind of knuckle-dragging throwback. Or, come to think of it, maybe he was; but a lot of people in the Netherlands were too. So it was good in a way for Willem to be having this conversation here and now. Hendrik could serve as a stand-in for a large slice of the electorate back home.

He nodded toward the wall of trees and vines that rose up, just a few meters away, out of the more low-lying part of the property. "This is all going to be flooded. You know it."

"Of course. I may not have a Ph.D. but I understand the greenhouse effect, I see the water rising with my own eyes."

"Are you ready for it? Truly ready?"

"I'm ready to piss," Hendrik said. "While I'm doing that, go up to the attic. Come down and tell me what you see."

Hendrik only became irritated when Willem tried to assist him with his walker, so Willem left him to his own devices and went ahead of him into the house. He walked through the living room, noting with approval that it was rigged for flood conditions: the floors were tile, laid over a concrete floor slab, softened here and there with rugs that could be spirited away to higher ground when the water came. The hallway leading from there to the stairs was lined with framed mementoes: photographs, clippings, medals, pressed flowers, and so on. It all trended strongly royalist. A large part of what Queen Frederika and her predecessors did for a living was ritual commemoration of wars and tragedies. All the Dutch people who had suffered and died in camps had received letters, medals, and so on. Their remains had been collected from shallow makeshift graves where possible and put in proper cemeteries where kings and queens went and laid wreaths and gave speeches on special days. To organize such observances, to make sure they came off well and that no one was carelessly forgotten, was a part of Willem's job. He didn't handle the details personally, but he supervised the people who did. It was routine work that flowed along, day to day, like water in a canal, forgotten as soon as gone by. So it was always a little weird to visit a house like this one and see many such moments frozen in time and memorialized on someone's wall. Even—especially—when that someone was your father. Some of the yellowed newspaper clippings, inevitably, showed younger versions of Willem, when he had more hair, posing on the steps of this or that palace with members of Dutch cabinets past, or with royals. He tried not to dwell on these.

He ascended the stairs, which were water- and termite-proof concrete below but gave way to wood above the first landing. Hendrik probably came up here once a year, if that. The bedrooms changed their purpose as younger members of the clan rotated in and out. One of them had been taken over by sewing projects. Another was plastered with posters of K-Pop stars. He felt as if he were intruding on the lives and business operations of shirttail relatives he barely knew.

PanScan was nagging him to put on an N95 mask. He did so. The app had tagged an individual in the second bedroom on the left as an epidemiological risk. His curiosity had been aroused. Who here could possibly be in the same league as Willem? He advanced down the hall to the point where he could look into the open door.

His arrival was no surprise to the young woman sitting there behind a desk consisting of a door on sawhorses. She'd been tracking his approach and put on a mask herself. She stood up as he came into view and made a slight sort of bow. "Uncle Willem!" she said in Dutch. "It is good to see you! Sorry about"—and she gestured to her mask.

Willem had the awkward feeling that he should know who this young lady was. Clearly not a native Dutch speaker, and yet she'd gone to some effort to learn the language. Her accent was somewhere between English and Chinese. She'd decorated the room with maps of Southeast Asia and a fax machine—the only operational fax machine Willem had seen in maybe two decades.

"You've changed so much!" he said in English. Stalling for time. He hadn't the faintest idea who she was. "Between that and the mask, I'm afraid—"

"Beatrix," she said. "Beatrix Kuok. Great-grandniece of your mother, Bel. I guess that makes us . . ." She turned her hands up. Her eyes were smiling. Kids these days were good at emoting through masks.

"First cousins twice removed," Willem said. "Or something like that."

"Well, it's good to see you!" Beatrix said. "I only met you once before at the family reunion after your mother passed. I probably just looked like one of a hundred little kids running around."

The most prominent thing in the room was a huge map of the western half of the island of New Guinea. Even the name of which was controversial. "New Guinea" was as colonial as you could get—Europeans naming an Asian colony after an African colony! Indonesia had named it Irian Jaya. The people who were indigenous to it preferred Papua. Beatrix, he was pretty sure, was a Papua kind of gal. Yes, she'd actually taped a sheet of paper over the map's title so that it wouldn't draw unwanted notice during Zoom calls. The map was a real beauty, making use of shading and color to show altitude and topography. The mountainous spine of the island, running generally east–west, was its most conspicuous feature. To the south of that, various river valleys coursed down through dark green valleys toward the shallow sea that separated the island from the north coast of Australia. She'd stuck yellow notes and little colored arrows to it. Most of those were strung out along a particular valley. They clustered most densely at a site about halfway between the mountain crest and the sea.

"What do we hear from Tuaba?" Willem asked, nodding at it.

"Uncle Ed is hanging in there. Business is good even if the politics are a nightmare. Just keeping his head down, you know. Most of the younger generation are . . . like me, I guess you could say."

"Looking for opportunities outside of Papua."

"Yeah. Mostly in Taiwan or Oz. Me, I graduated from law school in June and I'm taking a gap year doing, I guess you could say, activism."

"My god, how can I be that old!?" Willem exclaimed, and laughed. "Where did you go to law school? Congratulations."

"U.T." Beatrix seemed abashed that she'd inadvertently caused Willem to feel old.

"Austin."

"Yes."

Another awkward pause. They could have talked for hours now. But Hendrik was waiting. And clever noises kept emanating from Beatrix's computer. Notifications and such.

"I want to give you a card of someone I work with in the Netherlands," Beatrix decided; and Willem got the impression that the decision had been an important one for her. "Just in case you ever want to, I don't know, have coffee or something. She's in The Hague." She shuffled through some papers on her door desk and came up with a document—a hard copy of a report, with a nice cover. A business card was clipped to it. She pulled that off and handed it to Willem.

"Oh, I've heard of her! Of course! And the org," Willem said.

Idil Warsame was a Dutch woman of Somalian ancestry, daughter of refugees, a relentless campaigner for human rights in formerly colonized countries. She worked for a nonprofit that had attracted a lot of money from philanthropists in the tech world.

Willem looked up at Beatrix. The mask of course made it difficult to read her face, but the eyes were alert and intent. She very much wanted to know how Willem was going to respond to the fact that Beatrix was in cahoots with Idil Warsame. For the politics were devilish. As a Black Dutchwoman, Idil was a lightning rod for issues around immigration. Hendrik himself—awaiting Willem's return down in the gazebo—took a dim view of letting such people settle in the Netherlands.

But it wasn't a straight left/right thing either. Idil had been outspoken about rights violations by postcolonial governments. Her stand against female genital mutilation in East Africa had earned her twenty-four-hour police protection against possible attempts on her life by enraged traditionalists. She had no time for woke Westerners who wanted to decolonize everything.

"Way to go," he said. "You're doing the family proud."

The look on her face told him that this was the right thing to say.

"Come to the Netherlands," he suggested. "We'll all have rijsttafel together, and talk of Papua."

"It was good to see you, Uncle Willem!"

Backing out into the hallway, Willem found his way to the place where a pull-chain dangled from a long trapdoor in the ceiling. He reached up and drew it down, half expecting a rain of dust and bat shit to fall on his face. But it was all clean. Dutch clean. An aluminum stairway unfolded. A light came on automatically, giving him a view of the rafters and plywood that made up the underside of the roof. He ascended the stairs. The temperature shot up as his head rose clear of the attic floor. About half the space was occupied by plastic storage boxes, bug- and weatherproof, old documents and clothes dimly visible through milky polyethylene. But the area right around the trapdoor had been kept open. There was a five-gallon food-grade plastic pail of potable water; a box of military rations; a small gun safe, which presumably contained a handgun; a first-aid kit; and an axe. Not a dingy old heirloom, wood-handled and rust-patinaed, but one that looked like it had been sourced from Home Depot ten minutes ago, with a handle of bright orange plastic (of course it would be orange) and acres of safety warnings and liability disclaimers.

"I'm guessing it's about the axe," he said, when he had returned from that little excursion. Hendrik was done pissing and was killing time watching a Dutch soccer game on his phone.

Hendrik, clearly disgusted by the progress of the game, put the phone down and nodded. "I never told the story because I knew it would upset Bel. But the *Watersnoodramp*" (by which he meant the disastrous flood of 1953) "came during the night, and by the time we were aware of it the downstairs was already awash. So we remained upstairs, naturally."

"Naturally."

"Because you expect the water to go away, or for someone to come and help you, and you just aren't thinking straight. But then we had to get up on the beds, because it had come up that far. Then up on top of the dressers. Finally we waded to the ladder that went to the attic, and we climbed up there, thinking we were safe. But in fact we realized we had put ourselves in terrible danger because from the attic there was no escape. No windows or trapdoors. We did not fully realize it until the water came up to the level of the attic floor. And it kept rising."

"You're right. This would have made Mother very upset if you had told her," said Willem who was breaking a sweat just listening to it.

"I swam for it," Hendrik said. "Stripped off my pajamas, dove into that cold water, felt my way to a window, smashed it out, then went through and got up to the surface where I could breathe." He held up one arm to display a scar. Of course, it had been prominent the whole time Willem had been alive, but Father had always vaguely chalked it up to his eventful youth. "I was then able to climb right up onto the roof and pry up some of the tiles to make a little hole. It didn't make a difference because that was when the water stopped rising, but"—he shrugged—"it made the people inside feel better. And it gave me something to do."

"So now you keep an axe in the attic."

"Yes. Not an original idea, by the way. Many people around here do the same. Especially since Katrina."

Willem was accustomed to his father's roundabout way of conveying important lessons through these kinds of nonverbal signals. A brainy youngster could always argue with a parental statement, especially when the kid was a native English speaker running rings around his immigrant dad. But you couldn't argue with an axe in the attic.

"All right," he said agreeably, "so you do take the threat of rising water seriously."

"As how could I not!" Hendrik scoffed. Before his father could get going on the *Watersnoodramp*, Willem nodded vigorously and stretched out his hands in surrender. "What are we going to do about it is the question."

"We, as a civilization? About global climate change?"

"I know, right? Too vague! Too much diffusion of responsibility. Too much politics."

Hendrik cursed under his breath at the mere mention of politics and inhaled as if to deliver some remarks on that topic. Willem waved him off: "Instead ask, what are *Dutch* people going to do specifically about *rising sea level* and suddenly it is simpler and clearer, no? Instead of the whole world—the United Nations and all that—it's just the Netherlands. And instead of all the detailed ramifications of greenhouse gases and climate change, we are talking of one issue that is clear and concrete: rising sea level." Willem again nodded toward the bayou. "No one can argue with that. And for us, obviously, it is life or death. We fix the problem or our country ceases to exist. So that makes it very clear."

"Not so clear that the politicians can't fuck it up," Hendrik pointed out.

"I don't work for a politician, as it turns out."

"But you just finished giving me a lecture on the limits of her power. The Grondwet and all that."

"And you responded, Father, by telling me about the non-political ways that the monarch can inspire and lead people." Unspoken, as always—because it didn't need to be said—was Johannes on his knees, blind, hearing the faint whistle of the descending blade.

"So the question we are here to explore," Willem went on, "is whether a moment has arrived when the queen can play a role in leading the nation out of grave peril—without overstepping constitutional bounds."

"It is a good question to explore, to be sure," Hendrik said, after a little pause to consider it. "But why are you exploring it in Texas?"

"Good question," Willem said. "The answer is, there's a man down in Houston who had the presence of mind, a few years ago, to put an axe in the world's attic. We are here to find out whether the moment has arrived to pick it up."

Willem was supposed to rendezvous with the others near Houston. He could have done this directly by getting on Interstate 10 and driving due west for three hundred and fifty miles. But now that he was so close he couldn't not go into New Orleans. It had been his first big city. Chicago had always been too far from their suburban home, so enormous and brutal and forbidding. But on the family's vacation trips to Louisiana, teenaged Willem, bored out of his mind, had learned how to take public transit into New Orleans, how to find the French Quarter, and, in particular, how to find the gay part of it, which was ancient and well-established. On the whole his experiences there had been pretty tame, but later, when he had ventured into the night life of Amsterdam, he had been able to do so sure-footedly.

Later in life, he'd got to know people there. Very different people: ones he'd met at conferences where inhabitants of low-lying places came together to obsess about sea level. They'd be surprised if a personal representative of the Queen of the Netherlands just turned up without any advance notice. But he had a perfect alibi: he had gone to check in on his father. So before pulling out of the driveway he sent a message to Hugh St. Vincent, a department head at Tulane, announcing his presence in the area, apologizing for the late notice, and asking if there was anything new worth seeing. Hugh would understand that Willem was *not* asking for recommendations on where to eat beignets or listen to jazz.

Then Willem pointed his truck toward New Orleans. He passed up an opportunity to jump on an interstate, preferring an old two-laner. The landscape was flat by American standards, but not by Dutch. The usual American roadside scene of convenience stores, mobile home parks, and equipment depots interspersed with wooded areas. On the map it looked like a sponge, with water coming practically up to the road, but if you didn't know that, it would just look like normal dry land, exuberantly green, with a lot of trees. His practiced eye noted that the bed of the road was elevated a couple of feet above the surrounding earth.

A few miles short of New Orleans, he came to the Bonnet Carré Spillway, which was not much to look at but was probably at the top of the list of must-see attractions for the climate change tourist. Here all the roads and railways had been funneled into the five-mile-thick isthmus separating the Mississippi's left bank from Lake Pontchartrain. Running athwart all that was a mile-wide sluice connecting the two. Or rather it was capable of doing so when it was opened. A hundred years ago they'd constructed a spillway barring its Mississippi end. This was a palisade consisting of seven thousand massive vertical timbers arranged vertically in a frame of concrete and steel, deeply anchored in the river's bank. To one side, these were scoured by the flow of the Mississippi. To the other side was what passed for dry land: a wetland stretching from there to the lake, striped with drainage ditches and speckled with puddles and ponds, passing beneath elevated highways and railroads.

The summed pressure of the Mississippi water on the vast palisade must have been huge, but the pressure on any one single timber—they were about the size of railroad ties—was modest enough that it could be pulled up to create a slit that would let some water through. Rail-mounted cranes moved along the top of the frame pulling the timbers up or pushing them down to regulate the volume of flow diverted from the river into the sluice and thence to Lake Pontchartrain, which had its own outlet to the Gulf of Mexico.

They'd built all this after the terrible flood of 1927, which had inspired the blues song "When the Levee Breaks." It was intended as a safety valve, a bypass to be opened at rare moments of dire need, when heavy rains falling upstream—which was to say anywhere between the Rocky Mountains and the Alleghenies—had swollen the river to the point where it was threatening to overtop or burst through the levees and inundate New Orleans. Several times in the ensuing ninety years it had been used just as planned. But then in 2019 they'd been forced to leave it wide open for four months because of a wet winter. Other years since had not been quite as bad as that, but 2019 had inaugurated a new pattern, which was that the spillway was partially open more often than not.

For all its immensity, you could drive right over the Bonnet Carré Spillway and not take note of it. You'd see the water under the causeway, of course. But around here there was a lot of water.

The Mississippi was about seven Rhines. When this spillway was wide open, it diverted two and a half Rhines into the lake.

Now, where Willem came from, a Rhine was sort of a big deal. A third of the Netherlands' economy passed up and down one single Rhine. They had, in effect, built a whole country around it. Here, though, people were gunning their pickup trucks over a causeway bestriding two and a half Rhines *just as a temporary diversion of a seven-Rhine river over yonder.* It was one of those insane statistics about the scale of America that had once made the United States seem like an omnipotent hyperpower and now made it seem like a beached whale.

Willem pulled off the highway onto an access road leading to the spillway, just so he could check his messages and spend a few minutes watching the cranes gliding along pulling the wooden timbers up. It had been a wet year to begin with. Now, rains in the hurricane's wake had sent huge flows coursing down the Mississippi and so they were opening the spillway full bore. He got a few curious looks from the workers, but once again the white pickup served as industrial camouflage.

Hugh was on vacation in some cooler and drier clime, but he referred Willem to Dr. Margaret Parker, a colleague in the same department at Tulane, who agreed to have coffee with him. Ten years ago they would simply have met on the campus, but her lab had been downsized in the pandemic and never re-upsized, and she worked out of her home. It was just as convenient for her to meet him at a café in the French Quarter. She knew of a place with a second-story, open-air gallery that looked out toward the river.

The Bonnet Carré Spillway, which he now put in his rearview mirror, was the upstream bulwark of The Wall, aka HSDRRS (Hurricane and Storm Damage Risk Reduction System): a system of flood defenses, largely invisible to the non-expert observer, that encircled greater New Orleans. Dutch experts had been brought in to consult, and this was how Willem had come into occasional contact with people like Hugh and Margaret.

Once he had pierced The Wall at Bonne Carré, he saw no more of it as he drove twenty miles down the road—which eventually became Tulane Street—into the center of the city. Most of what he saw out the truck's windows just looked like any other place in Outskirts, USA. After a while, though, the buildings got bigger and less commercial. He drove through the downtown campus of Tulane University. It gave way to that part of New Orleans that answered to the purposes of all big-city downtowns: high-rise hotels, convention center, stadium, casino, and a cruise ship port along the river. Willem passed through it as quickly as he could and got an impression of many tents and RVs, cars that looked inhabited, plenty of private security at doors of buildings and entrances to parking structures.

But then he was in the old part of town. The truck got him to within a block of the café, then politely suggested he get out and walk. He opened the door and stepped down to a three-hundred-year-old cobblestone street. The truck drove away as fast as it could, which around here was little better than walking pace. It would park if it found a space, or circle the block otherwise.

Margaret had sent him a token that tagged him as having a reservation, so a hostess swung the door open for him as he drew near, plucked a menu from a stack, and led him up a rickety ancient stair and down a narrow hall to the open gallery above. This had probably looked out over the Mississippi when it had been constructed. Willem guessed it was over two hundred years old, maybe pre-Revolutionary. Nowadays the picture had been complicated by other buildings, waterfront facilities, and constructs forming aspects of The Wall. Even so, once Willem had taken the proffered seat beneath a large umbrella, he was able to see brown water sliding slowly by, sparkling in the afternoon sun. For better and worse, he could now smell the French Quarter on a warm summer's afternoon in the wake of a hurricane. It took him a full minute just to take in the olfactory mise-en-scène. More than anything he'd seen or heard, this took him back, made him a sixteen-year-old boy again, loitering self-consciously outside the entrance to a gay bar, wondering what would happen if he stepped over its threshold. So Margaret found him with tears in his eyes. She gave him a moment.

They sat there on the gallery and chatted for about half an hour. It wasn't a life-changing conversation for either of them, just a pleasant enough diversion. Willem dutifully told his cover story: going to check on Dad in the wake of the near miss by the hurricane, wanted to see the sights relevant to climate change. Margaret brought him up to speed. "We have something y'all don't," she said, where "we" meant the Mississippi Delta and "y'all" meant the Netherlands. "The river is an unstoppable land-building machine, if we just let it do its work. We can't switch it off, just point it in different directions. When y'all want to build land, y'all have to lug the sand to where it's needed, and lay it down. Pros and cons: you get nothing for free—"

"But we get it exactly where we want it," Willem said.

"With us, it's like—have you ever seen what happens when a firefighter loses his grip on a fire hose?"

"No," Willem said, "but I can imagine."

"It's a chaotic behavior. The hose can't be shut off. It thrashes around like an angry snake. That's the Mississippi downstream of New Orleans. For a long time we just tried to keep it channeled between levees. We had to keep building those higher. You'll see. It couldn't break out, so its outlet stretched farther and farther into the Gulf as it kept laying down sediment. Meanwhile the Gulf went on rising, sneaking around to attack the Delta on its flanks. Created a huge system of saltwater marshes and a whole economy to go with it—oysters, shrimp, saltwater fish. But something had to change. So we created the two big diversions. That's what you'll want to see. Here, I brought you a present."

Margaret reached into her bag, favoring Willem with a mysterious smile, and pulled out a wad of bright fabric. She shook it out and held it up to reveal a reflective fluorescent green safety vest of the type worn by road crews. "Don't worry, it's been washed." She gave it a toss. It wafted across the table and he snatched it out of the air.

"Who or what is ERDD?" he asked, reading letters stenciled across the back.

"Ecological Restoration of Delta Distributaries," she said. "The name of a crowdfunded project I worked on for a while. Now defunct. Doesn't matter. South of here, no one can read." (This was dry humor.) "You wear one of these, you can walk just about anywhere down where you're going and people will think you're doing something official."

"And I have the vehicle to go with it," Willem said. "A generic white pickup."

"Oh, you can get in anywhere with that and a reflective vest!"

"Thank you!"

"You're welcome. So. What you want to see is the two big diversions. We blew holes in the levee. One on the left bank at Wills Point, just about thirty miles down from here, the other in the right bank another, oh, five miles farther along. Fresh water's pouring through, dumping silt where it hits the Gulf, and the silt's making new land—taking back some of what the Gulf stole from us. But the water isn't clean—remember where it all came from." Here Margaret swept her arm around in an arc directed generally northward, as if to encompass the whole watershed of the Missouri-Mississippi-Ohio system, all the way to Canada. "And because it's fresh, it kills the saltwater ecosystem. All those homeless people you saw on your way in? Many of them were working oystermen ten years ago."

Willem glanced toward the adjoining high-rise district, sprouting from a low clutter of RVs and tents. "You're right," he said, "that is not a choice we have to make. Oh, fisheries are always problematic in all countries. But when we build coastal defenses, as a rule, we are creating jobs. Not obliterating valuable sources of employment."

"How's that going, anyway?" she asked. "How much higher can you pile those things?" She was just being folksy, of course. She had a Ph.D. in this stuff. Willem smiled, to let her know he got the joke.

"As high as we want," he answered. "But it's not the average sea level that keeps us up at night. It's the storm surge that overtops a dike somewhere, blows a hole in the perimeter, lets the Atlantic through faster than we can pump it out."

She nodded. "Nineteen fifty-three." Then: "What's funny?"

"Not two hours ago, my father was lecturing me about 1953. You, he, and I are probably the only three people in Louisiana who understand the reference."

"He lived through it?"

"He keeps an axe in his attic."

"Everyone does," Margaret said.

Willem drove south, cutting off a long eastward hairpin of the Mississippi and rejoining it several miles south of the city. According to the map, the road ran along the river. But even though it was only a few meters distant, he could not see it, but only an earthen levee that ramped up from the road's sodden, puddle-strewn shoulder to two or three times a man's height.

At one point he noticed the superstructure of an oil tanker high above him. Because of the way the highway curved, it looked like this enormous vessel was coming down the road in the oncoming lane. As a Dutchman he prided himself on taking such prodigies in stride; why, at home there were places where canals crossed over roads on bridges consisting of water-filled concrete troughs, and you could drive under ships gliding over the top of you. But even so he could not resist going into tourist mode for a moment. He pulled over to the side of the road and got out, immediately regretting it as his feet came down in a puddle. Not rain, but Mississippi River water that had been forced through the saturated earth of the levee by the same hydrostatic pressure that was keeping that oil tanker suspended above his head.

The ground got drier as he scrambled up the levee and came out onto its crest, currently no more than half a meter above the river's surface. He could now look across the full breadth of the river, at least a kilometer. The tanker blocked much of that view. It was churning upstream, headed for some refinery complex in the interior.

All this was happening in a linear, stretched-out town that ran continuously along the bank. It waxed and waned, but it never really became open country; it was sparsely inhabited by people who thought nothing of a passing oil tanker but found it very odd that a stranger would pull over to the side of the road to hike up the levee and sightsee.

Back in his truck, he drove on and reached the diversion a few minutes later. The riverside highway vaulted over it on a new bridge. Instead of crossing it, he pulled off onto a road that ran parallel to the diversion's bank. For the first ten or so miles, this snaked through mature woods and small towns. To judge from the aureolas of rust surrounding the bullet holes in the road signs, it had been inhabited for a while. Then old pavement gave way to new, and new gave way to gravel, and signs discouraged casual motorists from going any farther.

The diversion—an artificial construct, only a few years old—

was an alternate route for the water of the Mississippi to reach the Gulf. It was aimed toward parts of Plaquemines Parish that were still shown as dry land on old maps, but that had long since ceased to exist and been stricken from cartographical databases. Hydrological engineers had sculpted the diversion so that it would carry as much silt as possible out to its very end, then dump it in shallows that had been brackish or salt water until this thing had suddenly inundated them with fresh. The cost of it was that the species that had been living there all died. The benefit was new land. Balancing that cost and that benefit was a judgment Willem was glad he had no part in making.

He parked in a big open gravel lot at the end of the road. Again his vehicle blended well with what was here, though most of these pickup trucks were older and more beat-up than his rental. Lined up along one edge of the lot were a dozen or so buses. Their paint jobs told the story that they'd been part of Louisiana's tourism industry until ten years ago, and little maintained since, now pressed into service as worker transportation. Opposite them was a row of portable toilets. Canopies had been staked down to shade rows of plastic tables where pump bottles of hand sanitizer and rolls of paper towels stood sentry. Right now apparently it was the middle of a shift and few workers were in evidence. Four bus drivers had gathered at one table to vape and play dominoes. Service workers wiped tables and sprayed insecticide.

Margaret had told him where to go, what to look for, how to explain himself. He put on his reflective vest and his earthsuit helmet, deploying its sun shade and turning up the A/C just to the point where he could feel cool dry air on his face. He slung a water bag over his shoulder and set off in the direction of the Gulf of Mexico's indistinct shore. Past the parking lot, the road dwindled and dissolved. ATVs supplanted pickup trucks as he went along. Airboats gradually replaced the ATVs, and skiffs took over from there. Trees peeled away to reveal the Gulf. He was sloshing, his Walmart shoes long since ruined. Barges were moored here and there, along what might become a shore at low tide. They were laden with plants: some just little sprouts you could pick up in your hand, others whole trees, or at least saplings. The workers were stooping in knee-deep water to plant these. These species had been chosen because they were good at filtering silt from the flow and making it come to rest and form, if not dry land, then at least a stubborn muck that might be dry land one day when the trees had put down roots and made a bulwark against storms and waves.

When he finally got back to the parking lot an hour later, Willem found tea waiting for him, courtesy of the People's Republic of China.

He'd half expected something like this; he just hadn't known when or where. The Chinese had showed up today in a rented RV, which they had parked next to his truck. They had deployed the awning bracketed to the RV's side, creating a patch of shade between the two vehicles. A folding camp table and two chairs completed the basic setup. The inevitable middle-aged Chinese functionary was seated in one of them perusing a tablet, occasionally raising it to snap pictures. He had taken the radical measure of removing his suit jacket and loosening his necktie, but drawn the line at undoing his French cuffs and rolling up his sleeves. He stood up theatrically as Willem approached and greeted him in Mandarin while making a semblance of a bow—much better than shaking hands from an epidemiology standpoint. He gestured to the available chair and summoned his assistants, who were in the RV. To judge from the purring noises emanating from its various systems, this was running on generator power and it was air-conditioned. A guy like this would always have aides; god forbid he should ever be seen carrying an object. Tea was produced and served. It was all done according to the procedures and etiquette that had surrounded such things in China since time immemorial and that Willem knew perfectly well.

"Bo," the man said, and went on in English: "Believe it or not, that is actually my family name. When I first came to the West, they told me I should pick an Anglo name to go by. Tom or Dick or Harry, you know." He shrugged expressively, playing it for laughs. "I was thinking Bob? But then I got assigned to the South. People are actually called Bo here."

"B-E-A-U?" Willem inquired. "The Cajun spelling?"

"Considered it. But outside of Louisiana it would just cause panic. B-O is common all across the South."

"Diddley," Willem said, after considering it.

"Schembechler. Jackson. So, Bo it is. And I know you are Willem. Your father is Eng Kuok. Do you have a Chinese name?"

"Not really." Bel had called him by Fuzhounese pet names, but those were totally inappropriate in this context.

"Willem it is, then."

Bo did not insult Willem's intelligence by bothering to supply an explanation of how the Chinese had come to know exactly where he was. Willem could work that out for himself later. It was probably some combination of:

(a) they had hooks into PanScan, which was supposedly anonymized but probably riddled with grievous security exploits,

(b) they were monitoring Beatrix and she had inadvertently spilled the beans, or

(c) they learned it from a Chinese grad student in Margaret's group,

. . . but it was probably something way more sophisticated than any of that, some AI beyond human understanding. The point was the Chinese government knew that he was in Louisiana, they wanted him to know that they knew, and they just wanted to discreetly and politely touch base.

Despite some suspicions to the contrary, Willem had not, in the slightest degree, been "turned" or even influenced by China. And yet they did like to stay in touch with him—perhaps just reminding him that the option was on the table. As always, he would write up a full report later and put it in the record. Bo knew as much. Willem could have gone through the rigamarole of asking Bo for his business card, learning his official title and cover story, but he didn't have the energy. The dude worked for Chinese intelligence, presumably out of the New Orleans consulate. He would have a cover identity.

Bo was wearing the flimsiest kind of blue paper mask. He reached up with the same elaborate precision as was used to handle the tea and unlooped it from one ear, letting it dangle from the other. Hard to drink tea otherwise. According to PanScan he was a cipher, a ghost. Its neural nets could discern that a human-shaped object was over there, but otherwise drew a perfect blank. Willem sighed and took his helmet off. Then he shrugged out of the reflective vest. Bo made the slightest eye-flick toward a minion, who rushed forward to assist, as if Willem were a grand duchess struggling to get out of her mink coat in the lobby of an opera house. A coat hanger was somehow conjured up and the vest ended up hanging from the awning's edge to air-dry. Bo regarded it with amused curiosity, then raised his tablet and snapped a picture of it. "ERDD," he said.

"Long story. Means nothing."

"The Americans have not been very hospitable, but we thought that the least we could do was reach out and say hi," Bo said, in Mandarin except for the "say hi."

Willem was actually pretty sure that hospitality on a pharaonic scale was planned in Texas but saw no purpose in volunteering that.

"You are too kind," Willem said. "Here, of course, they like their cold sugary beverages."

Bo made a slight roll of the eyes and puffed out his cheeks, perhaps simulating one who was about to throw up, perhaps trying to approximate the look of one who had put on a hundred pounds' Big Gulp–fueled adiposity.

"But of course that is not the true way to *beat the heat*," Willem continued. He spoke the last three words in English and then raised his teacup to his lips. Chinese people kept emerging, Keystone Kops–like, from the RV. Bo raised an antique fan from his lap, snapped it open, and fanned his face. One of his staff members knelt and plugged in a little electric fan that was aimed in Willem's direction. All these aides were brandishing objects that looked like cheap plastic simulacra of squash rackets. As soon became obvious, they were actually handheld bug zappers. The aides initially formed a defensive perimeter, but as insects were observed slipping through gaps, they broke formation and began to roam about in a sort of zone coverage, swiping their weapons through the air with the controlled grace of YouTube tai chi instructors, incinerating bugs with crisp zots and zaps while pretending not to hear a word of what Bo and Willem were saying. A brand-new thirty-two-gallon Rubbermaid Roughneck stood nearby, lined with a heavy-duty contractor bag from a fresh roll of same, already overflowing with the packaging in which all these fans, extension cords, bug zappers, and so on had, Willem guessed, been purchased from Walmart inside of the last two hours. Occasionally the burnt-hair scent of a vaporized bug would drift past Willem's nostrils, but he'd smelled worse.

Bo seemed in no great hurry to get the conversation rolling. His eyes were tracking a group of three workers who had apparently come back to the parking lot on their break to use the portable toilets and smoke cigarettes. "A hundred years ago they'd have been black. Fifty years ago, Vietnamese. Twenty, Mexican," Bo said. They were white. "Maybe this will teach them some kind of decent work ethic. What they are doing out there looks a lot like transplanting rice seedlings, no?"

He meant the ancient process by which flooded rice paddies were planted at the beginning of the growing season. It was, of course, ubiquitous across Asia. Each language and dialect had its own words for it. The term he had used was not from Mandarin. Obviously from Bo's speech and appearance he was a straight-up northern Han lifelong Mandarin speaker, but he'd strayed into the dialect of Fuzhou that was used by Willem's extended family. This could not possibly have been an accident.

"Yes," Willem agreed, "this process looks very similar but here, of course, instead of growing food, they are creating new land."

"It must be very interesting to you and the person you work for—the Dutch know more about this than anyone!" Bo proffered. The thin edge of a conversational wedge that was aimed at getting Willem to divulge more about the queen. Did the Chinese know that she was in Texas? Did they merely suspect it? Or did they know nothing?

"Oh, I don't think you give your own country due credit," Willem returned. "Earlier I was driving along the river where it runs between the levees, higher than the surrounding land. It put me in mind of the Yellow River, which as you know has looked very much the same since long before Dutch people began constructing their sad little windmills."

Bo nodded. "Both a flood control measure, and a weapon." He uttered a phrase that meant something like "water instead of soldiers."

Willem recognized it. "You might be interested to know that the Dutch used exactly the same tactic. William the Silent, Prince of Orange—yes, the ancestor of the person I have the honor of working for—opened the dikes in 1574 as a way to rout an invading Spanish army. The gambit succeeded. Every year it is celebrated with a festival in Leiden."

"Your adopted hometown," Bo added, quite unnecessarily. "So you are a student of history. You'll know that whenever those Yellow River levees broke, it was a great catastrophe. The emperor was viewed as having lost the Mandate of Heaven."

Bo said this with all due wryness, as if to emphasize that he was not some pedantic blinkered scholarly idiot. Willem chuckled. "If you are trying to draw some analogy to the person I work for, then let's keep in mind that her mandate comes from the people. In the Netherlands no one believes in heaven anymore."

"In Amsterdam, The Hague, perhaps that's true," Bo returned. "Do you ever go into the east, though?"

"You mean, the east *of the Netherlands*!?"

"Yes."

"It is a twenty-minute drive from those cities you mentioned!"

"You are busy. Twenty minutes must seem an age." Bo took a sip of his tea. "Those clodhoppers in—what's it called? Brabant?"

"North Brabant, yes."

"They are still religious, I'm told. Conservative. Even reactionary."

Willem didn't like where this was going, but there was no getting around the fact that just a few hours earlier he had been standing in the hallway of his father's house looking at a shrine, dedicated to everything Bo was alluding to.

"In my experience, people all over the world think the same way," Willem said. "If there is a disaster, it means that whoever is in power has lost the 'Mandate of Heaven' and must be gotten rid of."

Bo said, "Western historians write about this phenomenon in China in a patronizing style, because they believe that the West—"

"Has evolved beyond all that superstitious nonsense. I know."

"Don't you think that that proclivity for self-delusion makes Western leaders vulnerable?"

Willem shrugged. "You raise an interesting philosophical question of a sort that is amusing to ponder in one's free time. My job is to remind a powerless constitutional monarch to send handwritten thank-you notes to schoolchildren and to see to it that the name cards are properly arranged on the tables at state dinners."

Bo looked away, apparently thinking that what Willem had just said was so stupid that it simply couldn't be responded to without a breach in etiquette. But it would always be thus. The Chinese were either too obtuse to understand constitutional monarchy—preferring to see it as a paper-thin cover story to conceal what was really going on—or else they were so infinitely more sophisticated that they understood the realities in ways that the self-flattering

Europeans never could. Either way, the Chinese seemed to have much firmer opinions on the matter than Willem did. Willem was willing to entertain the hypothesis that Queen Frederika actually could wield serious temporal power, but it seemed too far-fetched, too at odds with the unassailable constitutional bedrock of the Grondwet to which he'd sworn himself.

"You are—what's the English word? *Underemployed.* A man of your experience and erudition—arranging place cards? Really?"

Since that sounded like the germ of a job offer—which could only lead in the direction of incalculable disaster—Willem said, "I couldn't be happier in my role."

"Then you must have other duties that are more challenging—more interesting!" Bo exclaimed, as if this were a fascinating new revelation. "But of course, it makes sense. Why else would you be *here*—looking at *this*?"

"The obvious reason. Climate change."

"Very important in this part of America," Bo said agreeably. "Louisiana. Texas too." He was watching Willem carefully. "Its relevance to Houston, for example, could hardly be more obvious. Waco, on the other hand—I don't see the connection."

"I've heard of the place," Willem allowed.

"You've rented a truck there!" Bo nodded at this rather large and undeniable piece of evidence. "Dodge Ram, license plate ZGL-4737." He raised his tablet and snapped a picture.

"This tea is excellent. You brew it at eighty degrees Celsius, if I'm not mistaken."

"It is the only proper way," Bo said, and enjoyed a sip. "Why do you think we were not invited to this thing in Texas?"

"'We' meaning China?"

"Yes."

"You're asking me to read the mind of T.R. McHooligan?"

"As a mere social secretary I thought you might have some exceptional powers in that area."

"You must have been a teenager once."

"Of course."

"When you didn't invite a girl on a date, what was she to conclude?"

Bo shrugged. "That I didn't fancy her?"

"Or that you didn't know whether she would accept the invitation. She might turn you down—with the attendant loss of face."

"So if China wishes to be invited to such events in the future, she needs to flirt with T.R. McHooligan? To make him feel more confident?"

"I am merely speculating as to the man's possible motives. I have never even met him."

"Perhaps he knows in advance that we will decline his invitation."

"Perhaps."

"And that we will do so because his plan will be bad for China, and he knows as much—so why bother inviting us in that case?"

"It means nothing to me either way if you consider T.R. to be an enemy of China, or if he feels the same way about you. Even if I were in the habit of supplying your government with intelligence, I would simply have nothing to offer in this case."

"Well said. I see why the queen likes you. She too is perhaps underemployed."

"She has a job."

"Well, I'm sure that your next few days will be extremely fascinating. I envy you that and will try not to have my feelings hurt in the manner of the jilted teenager you alluded to."

"Somehow I think that China will endure."

"Oh, yes," Bo said. "It will."

During the latter part of this conversation, Willem's phone had been vibrating with increasing frequency. Only a few people had the power to make this happen. When he had at last extricated himself from the conversation, retrieved the ERDD vest, and emptied his tea-laden bladder in a stifling portable toilet redolent of industrial perfume, he sat down in his truck, A/C blasting, and found a string of increasingly testy messages from the queen.

> What are you doing in the Gulf of Mexico?

> Your map is out of date. Where I am it is now dry land.

> The question remains.

> Another feeler from Chinese intelligence. Will write up a report.

> Do they know where I am?

> Maybe. They know something happened in Waco.

> Are you going to drive back tonight?

> Yes, immediately.

> The Cajuns have a favor to ask of you. Can you find Port Sulphur?

> LOL that sounds relevant! Hang on . . .

Willem used the truck's nav screen to find Port Sulphur. It was on the main channel of the Mississippi, about thirty miles downstream.

> Found it. Would you like for me to go there and pick up a truckload of sulfur?

> Sulfur is T.R.'s department. You're to pick up a diver.

Half an hour later, Willem was there. He was a little crestfallen to find that there was no sulfur anywhere. In fact, there was hardly anything: no port facilities at all, just a fire station and two convenience stores facing off at the base of the levee. A couple of hundred yards in back of them was a faint swelling in the land, detectable only by a Dutchman, that must be what remained of the sulfur dome where they'd established the mine.

Jules ("as in Verne") Fontaine awaited him, the only human in view. He was perched halfway up the levee on the pile of equipment cases and duffel bags that was the lot in life of a professional diver. He respectfully stood up when the white pickup truck pulled in beneath him. Debris of beer cans, Subway wrappers, and chip bags attested to the fact that Jules, by dint of youth, good genes, and an active lifestyle, could consume as many calories as he pleased with zero impact on the eminently fuckable physique on display through his tie-dyed tank top and his voluminous cargo shorts. He was neither gay nor, it seemed, particularly aware of his own fuckability—a common trait of the young. Willem had already been made aware that Jules was ex-navy. He'd been out of the service long enough to grow a shoulder-length mane of wavy strawberry-blond hair. Sun exposure had endowed this with highlights that would have cost five hundred euros to obtain in an Amsterdam salon. PanScan, unsurprisingly, pronounced him the healthiest man on the planet. Once Jules had heaved all his gear into the back of the truck, he offered to buy Willem anything—*anything*—for sale in the convenience store. Only because he did not wish to cause offense, Willem allowed as how some jerky would go down well. Jerky was a safe bet; it was hard to screw that up, and it seemed paleo.

After Jules had made his jerky run and settled into the position known hereabouts as "shotgun," Willem said, "Say, Jules, I'm as eager to get to Houston as you are, but if you don't mind I'm going to drive around town for a minute and sightsee."

Jules was politely taken aback. "It's not going to take a whole minute, sir."

"I know. Just satisfying my curiosity."

"Suit yourself!" Jules said cheerfully. "Your truck, your rules!"

So Willem drove a short distance inland from the levee and circled the former site of the mine. This was nothing but vacant land, overgrown with scrubby trees where it wasn't scarred by traces of roads. On its south side there was a tumbledown building, scarcely more than a shack, covered in unpainted plywood gone dark with age and mold. Above its front door was a sign, hand-painted on sheet metal that was now 90 percent rust. But he could make out the letters AZOS MIN. The last vestige in Port Sulphur of Brazos Mining. Recalling the queen's interest in the name, he pulled in close enough to take a snapshot of the sign.

"Okay then! Let's get this show on the road, Jules!" Willem proclaimed and gunned the pickup out onto the river road, headed back up toward the Big Easy. Jules cracked open an energy drink, leaned his seat back, and regaled Willem with the tale of how he'd washed up in Port Sulphur. Willem was paying a certain amount of attention to the nav, trying to work out the best place to rendezvous with the rest of the caravan in Texas. So he didn't catch every last detail. An ex-girlfriend was involved, naturally. An ownership dispute over a truck. A job on an oil rig that hadn't gone as planned. It all might have worked out but for the element of random misfortune embodied in the hurricane.

"What do you know about the sulfur industry?" Willem inquired, interrupting Jules's stream of consciousness about half an hour in. This story had overspilled the bounds of being a mere country song and was well on its way to becoming an album.

"Oh, there ain't no sulfur in Port Sulphur."

"I *know*," Willem said. "Hence my question."

"Used to be a mine nearby. They would dig it up. Freeze it. Sell the, what do you call 'em, huge, like, ice cubes."

"Did you say freeze it?"

"It has a real low melting point. Like, you can melt it on your stove. Like wax almost. So they would just pour it into big, like, ice cube trays, let it set up, stack 'em like blocks at the water's edge, load 'em on ships goin' to . . . wherever the hell folks need sulfur."

"Why'd it stop? Mine ran out?"

"It's cheaper nowadays to get sulfur from sour crude."

"So it's just a by-product of all these refineries."

"Used to be," Jules agreed. "Then Alberta got into the act and the bottom dropped out."

"Because . . . oil from Alberta has a lot of sulfur?"

"Sour as can be," Jules confirmed. "Or so they say. Never been. Not a lot of work for divers there."

Willem nodded. "So Port Sulphur needs to get busy diversifying its economy."

"You work for Shell?" Jules asked. Then, feeling some need to explain himself: "They said you was from Holland."

"The Netherlands," Willem corrected him. "I guess you could say I have a professional connection to Royal Dutch Shell."

"HR? Media Relations?" Jules guessed.

Willem perceived the nature of Jules's problem. Jules was trying to figure out the riddle of Willem. Not necessarily to be nosy; it's just that the two of them were going to be in the truck together for quite a few hours, and he was trying to find some basis for friendly conversation. The only conceivable reason a Dutchman would be in this part of the world would be to work for Shell. And yet Willem didn't know basic facts about sulfur and its status as a by-product of sour crude oil refinement. The only way that this could make sense was if Willem's role at Shell was something completely impractical in nature.

"I don't *actually* work for Shell," Willem explained. "It's more of an indirect connection. I'm a logistics guy, you might say. Some of my group got stranded in Waco because of the weather. Your friends have been very generous in helping us out."

"It's gonna be real interesting."

"What do you mean?"

"Houston."

"Yes. Yes. Houston is going to be interesting."

AMRITSAR

He'd been getting by with a keski, a simple house turban, such as might be worn by children or by men taking part in athletic competitions. In America it might be mistaken for a do-rag.

Now, following instructions on YouTube, he wrapped a proper turban over the keski. On his third try he ended up with something that was not completely embarrassing. He then ventured out of the hotel to take a meal at a large and well-situated gurdwara.

The word meant "door to the guru," which in some people's minds conjured up a hokey image of an old holy man sitting cross-legged and spouting pithy wisdom. But they'd given up on gurus of that type hundreds of years ago, and put everything those guys had to say into a book. The book was the guru now. "Door to the body of written material serving in place of a human spiritual leader" was a bit of a mouthful and so the word was commonly translated into English as "temple." But this conjured up all manner of wrong ideas in the minds of Westerners, who tended to imagine something more in the Hindu or Roman Catholic vein. Sikhs didn't have priests and they didn't revere idols. So most gurdwaras, though they might have a few fancy decorative bits on the exterior, had more in common, on the inside, with Methodist church basements. Dining in the langar involved sitting on the floor in a long row of fellow diners, waiting as certain prayers were said, and then eating a simple vegetarian meal heavy on starches. Not that his people were vegetarians. But they wanted Hindus and Muslims to feel welcome without having to ask all kinds of questions about what animals were being eaten and how exactly they had been slaughtered. Feeling more self-conscious than he ever had in his life, Laks kept his eyes on his plate, ignored the stares that he assumed were coming at him from all directions, and refused to speak English.

Then he came back the next day and did it again.

The whole process—which lasted no more than a week—reminded him of experiences he'd had up in the Rockies, trying to get a campfire lit on a cold day with wet wood: it persistently failed until it didn't, and then it caught fire and he wondered why it had ever seemed difficult. In short order he was volunteering at the langar. The ladies who did the cooking wouldn't let him anywhere near actual food prep, of course; they were hygiene fanatics, and Laks didn't know the procedures. But they were glad of his help unloading big sacks of flour and rice and lentils from the trunks of cars.

Once he had earned a bit of social capital that way, a bit of asking around pointed him in the direction of an akhara. Without specific directions, he'd never have found the place. It was at the end of a maze of ancient alleyways. Newer and taller buildings huddled around it, as if trying to shield it from view.

He'd heard that some of these things were quite old, but this one seemed beyond ancient. Oh, around the edges it did have accretions of new tech such as weight benches and barbells. But the core of it was a pit of loose earth, protected from rains by a roof on stilts. For it had been the practice in these parts for thousands of years that wrestlers used the earth as Western wrestlers used foam mats and Japanese used tatamis. That didn't work unless the ground was prepared just so. Over time it would get tamped down hard by the probing feet and the thudding bodies of the athletes. Then it had to be refreshed. This work was performed daily.

Laks, at least, knew better than to waltz in during broad daylight. He set his alarm for five in the morning, laced on his trainers, ran to the akhara, and found that he was much too late. The next day he set the alarm for four but was late again. Three o'clock in the morning turned out to be the right time. He reached the akhara just as some of the younger boys were wandering in. He picked up an implement that looked somewhere between a hoe and an adze, hoisted it above his head, and drove its blade into the earth between his now bare feet. Then he pried it up to loosen soil that had been packed hard yesterday. Then again. Then again. All around him boys half his weight and age were doing likewise. For the first time since he had entered India, Laks lost track of time and just did something.

An hour's hard labor sufficed to loosen all the earth. Now it was soft but uneven. The next step was to level it out and tamp it down, but not too much, by dragging weighted logs across it. The logs appeared to have been salvaged from the wreck of Noah's Ark. The weights were the smaller boys; they stood on the logs three or four abreast, hanging on to each other and giggling, as Laks served in the role of draft animal, pulling them around the floor of the akhara until the ground was level, and firm enough to afford traction to the bare feet of the wrestlers but soft enough to cushion the impact of throws and takedowns.

By that point, day was beginning to break and it was threatening to get hot. A few of the senior members of the akhara had drifted in to perform their workouts before going off to their jobs. They looked at Laks quizzically. Some were friendly, and in a laconic way showed gratitude for his efforts. Some were standoffish. A couple of them might have been hostile. But he had expected that. They would see him as a potential rival. Every gym in the world had some of that. The best he could do was show humility and presume nothing.

He was not here to work out today. He was too tired anyway. The digging had exhausted his upper body and dragging the log had done his legs in. He hobbled back to his rooming house before it got too hot—for this was spring, before the monsoon, when it could get above 45 Celsius during the afternoon—and bathed and went back to bed.

After a week of doing that every day without anyone telling him to get lost, Laks dared to touch the equipment: the joris— what Westerners would call Indian clubs—and the gadas, which were like super-sized Indian clubs, a rock the size of a bowling ball on the end of a meter-long stick. These—or at least their modern, cast-steel equivalents—he had been working with since he had been a child. He knew perfectly well what to do with them. But the men of the akhara didn't know that. So they all watched him out of the corners of their eyes, or in some cases openly glared, as he hefted them off the ground and swung them through the simplest and least hazardous movements, then reverently set them back in their places, put on his running shoes, and jogged home. The next day he did it again but he did it longer, working his way up to slightly heavier joris and gadas, and adding in some more challenging moves.

For this was Laks's one and only trick. He was not that fluent in Punjabi, no matter how much time he spent watching Punjabi soap operas on TV. He did not have an easy smile. And yet he found that if he just kept showing up, nothing bad would happen, and gradually people would stop noticing him. And that—the simple comfort of not being noticed—was all he wanted.

After six months they kicked him out. They did it politely. His Punjabi had improved to the point where he could understand, even if he did not believe, the explanation given. It made sense in a way. He had continued showing up (a little later each day as familiarity gave him a kind of seniority) and staying a little later to do more and more advanced routines with heavier and more dangerous equipment. Some of the joris were studded with nails, imposing a penalty if you swung them wrong and let them touch your body. At the invitation of one of the younger adult members, he had entered the pit and done some wrestling. At wrestling he was merely okay. His size and strength just barely compensated for a lack of skill. So it wasn't a complete wipeout.

But he sensed he was being used as an example of a big dumb guy. Every martial art had techniques for use against big dumb guys. It was difficult to practice them in earnest against a skilled wrestler of one's own size. In Laks, they now had the perfect tackling dummy against which to practice anti-big-dumb-guy moves.

So Laks ended up hitting the carefully groomed earth quite a bit and finding himself on the receiving end of various joint locks that, when they were done wrong, could hurt.

And it was not in his nature to accept this cheerfully. He was a martial artist for a reason. He had not traveled halfway around the world to the holy city of his ancestors and joined an ancient akhara just to get his ass kicked. Many were the days he limped home and watched old martial arts videos as a balm to his wounded feelings. The oldest trope of all was that the new guy had to patiently endure a period of humble apprenticeship and even outright suffering before emerging in the final reel as a transcendent ass-kicker. Of course, in movies that was all compressed into a training montage that lasted a few minutes, whereas Laks was having to actually experience it in real time, no fast-forward button available. For a while he just had to suck it up. But as time went on he began to resist, to make it a little more challenging for his training partners. If they complained, he would tell them in his gradually improving Punjabi that his only motive was to be honest, to make them better wrestlers. They could grumble, but not argue.

For a while he suffered from the heat, but finally in late June the monsoon came. He could cool off just by stepping out from under the canopy and being rained on.

So to that point no one would have dreamed of kicking him out of the akhara. He was sane, clean, humble, inoffensive, and useful. He could tow a boy-laden log across dirt like a bloody water buffalo. His social awkwardness was disarming in a way. No, the senior members of the akhara did not see anything to object to until Laks took up the stick.

He'd been swinging the *big* stick—the gada—almost from Day One. Usually translated into English as "mace," this was a rock weighing as much as a hundred pounds, but usually less, on a long frail-looking handle. Some of the ones here looked like artifacts from the Paleolithic section of a museum, others had been fabricated ten minutes ago out of rebar and concrete. There was nothing to object to in Laks's working out with these, as long as he did it safely; it was the Indian equivalent of standing in the corner of an LA Fitness doing dumbbell curls.

Gada could also be translated as something like "club" or "large stick." The diminutive form of the word, *gatka*, denoted a smaller stick, unweighted, just a piece of bamboo or rattan maybe a meter long. Maybe longer, maybe shorter—it didn't pay, in stick-based martial arts, to be pedantic about the exact length. Some thought of this as a mere stand-in or practice implement for a sword. And indeed, senior practitioners of gatka, as this martial art was called, could be seen practicing with actual swords. But at the end of the day the name of the martial art was literally "Stick" and its students spent most of their time swinging blunt bamboo, not sharp steel. While acknowledging the romance and charisma of swords, Laks had always been perfectly content with stickwork, seeing it as something that might actually be useful in a practical situation—a junkie fight in downtown Vancouver, say. He had learned gatka from a very good teacher in Richmond (though with the perspective of seven thousand miles' distance he had twigged to the fact that this man was an outlier who, here, might have been viewed as eccentric or insane—sometimes there was a reason why people emigrated—but he'd been a great teacher for Laks). As a boy he had practiced it with pine branches up in the Rockies while killing time along high tributaries of the Fraser and the Columbia, waiting for his father to show up and fetch him. He had even practiced it in his Marriott and Radisson and Wyndham rooms here in Amritsar, with curtains drawn.

So what it boiled down to was that he was already more proficient—*much* more proficient—at gatka than even the most senior men of this akhara. The graybeards told him straight out that they did not feel they had anything to teach Laks. He was barking up the wrong tree. Which he realized was a euphemistic way of saying that Laks was becoming sort of a problem. Embarrassing the senior guys. Making them look bad. Becoming a folk hero to those little boys he towed around on the log. A solution needed to be found. The people who ran the akhara were reasonable men. Not assholes. At the very least they needed to have a story they could tell to the youngsters when Laks suddenly stopped showing up.

So inquiries had been made and they had got in touch with one Ranjit, an instructor in Chandigarh, a real wizard with the stick, who would not object to having Laks around. This could be explained to Laks's junior fan club as a kind of graduation. Their budding role model was being kicked upstairs where he could be admired from a distance, and cherished in memory.

HOUSTON

Willem and Jules made their way up into New Orleans and turned west on Interstate 10. Now they were running parallel to the track of the hurricane. For a few hours, the drive went more or less as the nav system had envisioned it. Then Willem almost got them killed when he failed to notice stopped traffic on the highway ahead until it was nearly too late and had to stand on the brakes and make a controlled diversion onto the shoulder.

They swapped drivers at that point. Technically Jules wasn't supposed to drive this thing. But Willem reckoned that working something out with the rental company would be easy compared to the complications of the jet crash. Anyway, it was less risky than his continuing to drive. He leaned the passenger seat back and fell asleep to the faint accompaniment of country music from the truck's radio.

When he woke up, it was shortly before daybreak. Jules had been driving through the night in stop-and-go traffic. He had long since exited the jam-packed interstate and was feeling his way across southeast Texas on two-lane roads, following suggestions texted to him by the Boskeys' swarm of cars, trucks, RVs, and watercraft.

It took them most of the day to circumvent Greater Houston and zero in on the caravan, which had stopped near a state park along the Brazos about seventy miles west of Houston. Here the entire group meant to form up, preparing to make its push into the flooded city at first light. The hurricane had devolved into a tropical depression that had squatted over the countryside south of Houston for a couple of days and dumped close to a meter of rain on it. The Brazos watershed, which lay mostly to the north, had escaped the brunt of this, but still the river was running high.

Their first contact was with Rufus, ranging ahead of the main body, operating as usual out of his truck and trailer rig. They rendezvoused with him in a small town of old limestone buildings and followed him down a country road for some miles. He pulled over to the side of a road just short of the goal and used his drone to reconnoiter the state park. According to online maps, several roads looped through the sparsely wooded property, connecting a series of campgrounds. In normal times they might have had some chance of claiming a site there. This year, relay refugees had clogged the place up even before hundreds of thousands of hurricane evacuees had come flooding westward along Interstate 10. It had become what in other contexts would be called a shantytown. For every official campsite shown on the map, there must have been a hundred RVs, cars, and tents. They'd spilled out far beyond the simple network of park roads and colonized green space between it and the right or south bank of the Brazos. The thin strip of public land along its north bank looked from a distance like a chalk line; it was white with pleasure craft that must have come upriver from the city. Farther north, on private farmland, more clusters of RVs and tents had found purchase.

Wheeled vehicles could circumvent all that. The boats, however, had no choice but to pass right through the middle. The only question was where they might be able to pull them up on a bank and rendezvous with the land vehicles. Rufus solved that problem by making contact with one of those north bank landowners. They had set up roadblocks at the entrances to their property and were charging evacuees a fee to come in and set up camp. It was a hefty fee, but by now Rufus and other members of the caravan had got used to spending freely from the brick of emergency cash that Willem had brought with him. He had entrusted most of it to Amelia during his side trip, but kept more than enough to satisfy the rancher. So money changed hands, and, as dusk fell, the fleets of wheeled and water vehicles came together for one last time on the north bank of the river. This put them downstream of most of the camps, as they could tell just from the smell of the water. Behind them were the days when they could cool themselves off by splashing river water on their garments or—disgusting thought—jumping in and being towed behind a boat.

THE CAMP ON THE BRAZOS

Saskia, whose primary excuse for being a queen was to support philanthropy, had been frog-marched through her share of Third World shantytowns. Most felt ancient. She was fascinated to see a new one budding. For now, the RVs were clean, their tires properly inflated, ready to roll onward as soon as conditions improved. The tents were bright and new, and a festive atmosphere prevailed as most here felt the unity that comes of shared hardship. But what might it look like if people never went home? The tents would deteriorate and be mended with duct tape and blue tarps. The tires of the RVs would go flat and they'd end up on concrete blocks. Proper sewage connections would never be made. The stink would never go away; people would learn to ignore it. None of these people would have legal title to the land they lived on and so they could be evicted at any time, or pushed off by rivals with more muscle. They couldn't accumulate equity in their homes so they'd have no incentive to make improvements beyond slapdash repairs. They would not be paying taxes so there would not be schools, clinics, vaccinations, social workers. In what would seem like the blink of an eye, the shantytown would be a year old, then ten years, then a hundred. Its origins would be lost to memory, overlooked by historians. It would become something that had always been there.

She didn't actually think that would happen here. The flood-waters would recede, people would go home. The north bank landowners would evict campers by force if need be. The state police would see to it that the campground on the south bank was returned to normal. All the urine and feces and litter going into the river now would be flushed out into the Gulf of Mexico and the Brazos would go back to being as clean, or as dirty, as it had ever been. But she was willing to bet that in other places within an hour's drive of Houston, during the last few days, shantytowns—not seen as such by their occupants, of course—had taken root that would still exist generations from now, unless they were forcibly cleared in merciless pogroms. That was the way of most of the world. Texas would be no different. Which was not a judgment upon Texas. It could happen in the Netherlands too.

Lotte, her daughter, kept late hours in the Netherlands and tended to text her when it was early evening here. At that time of day, Cajuns were especially likely to be preparing food. Saskia, who enjoyed cooking, had got into a rhythm during the last couple of days where she would text, send selfies, or (using earphones) just talk on the phone to Lotte while chopping onions or whatever else needed doing.

On the first day of the adventure, distracted Saskia had been brusque with her daughter, who had been in the middle of some interminable teen freakout over a matter that struck Saskia as being of much less significance than crashing a plane and fleeing the scene of the accident while fighting a rearguard action against man-eating beasts.

Lotte had texted:

> I hope you get some vitamin D in Texas, maybe it will improve your disposition!

Saskia had replied that the weather was sunny and that she would probably get plenty of natural vitamin D, even in spite of careful application of sunscreen. This had elicited an eye-roll emoji and an LOL from Lotte.

Puzzled Saskia had even sent her a photo of the label on the sunscreen container, which was touted as a "natural" and "green" product that would not have toxic effects on aquatic life. She thought that this would please Lotte, who could not shut up about environmental politics.

But later Saskia had realized that the "D" was actually short for "dick" and that Lotte had really been suggesting that her mother ought to take advantage of this opportunity, while out of the usual press spotlight and among new friends, to get laid. And that doing so might make Saskia happier and somehow a more easygoing and approachable sort of mom.

Now, this was new. Of course, they had had the obligatory Talk some years ago. But with the usual sense of unbearable tween embarrassment on Lotte's part. She'd just barely contained her desire to fly out of the room. Since then it had never again come up, until the vitamin D remark. Lotte had never dared to bring up the topic of Saskia's [nonexistent] sex life, much less make suggestions.

So during much of the subsequent journey down the Brazos, Saskia had been pondering how to handle this overture from her daughter. Saskia had been widowed when her husband had caught COVID while doing volunteer work in a hospital. Since then she had not had sex with anyone. Tabloids were forever claiming that she was getting it on with some tech magnate or Eurotrash princeling, but it was all just fabricated clickbait. It seemed quite striking and revealing to her that her daughter, upon hearing that Mama had crashed a jet and was fleeing the scene in a flotilla of Cajun gator hunters, would—of all things—construe it primarily as an opportunity for her to engage in casual sex. Saskia sat in the boat and watched the Brazos go by, pondering what it meant for her and for Lotte.

Every so often—not in the first year or two of widowhood, but since then—she had asked herself in a theoretical way whether she would ever have sex again. There was no reason not to. Even if the story got out, the Netherlands was famously liberal about such things. Even the most hard-bitten Bible-pounders among her subjects would probably just set their jaws and look the other way. Many might even feel a sense of relief. But Saskia had written sex off as being just too complicated to be worth it. With so many other things to worry about, it was enormously simplifying for her to never think about that. It was a whole portion of her life she'd been able to push indefinitely into the future. She rather suspected that menopause had recently fired a couple of shots across her bow and it had led her to wonder how she might feel after that—whether she'd want to pursue anything romantic beyond some pro forma arrangement just for the cameras.

But it now occurred to her that prolonged celibacy might elicit *more* gossip than just having a normal sex life. She began to look at the people around her in a new light. People such as Willem and Fenna and Amelia. Of course, these weren't potential sex partners. But it did occur to her to wonder if, when they were in the back of the plane, or having a drink together after work, they speculated among themselves as to whether, at any point in the remainder of her natural life span, Saskia was going to get some. She wondered if, were she to show interest in some man, they would be horrified—which had always been her assumption—or—and here was the new idea—would they instead give huge sighs of relief.

So much for Saskia. As for Lotte: years had passed since the Talk. An eternity for someone of Lotte's age, the blink of an eye for Saskia. Lotte—who would be the next queen—had perhaps been wondering whether being a celibate nun for the Netherlands might be in the cards for *her*. Lotte most definitely was not interested in flying airplanes, or some of the more classic avocations of royals such as fancy horse riding. There was no question that she was interested in boys. As any sane person would be, Lotte was ambivalent about the prospect of becoming the queen. Saskia knew she'd looked to the example of Prince Harry and his American wife, Meghan, who had simply walked away, renounced their titles, and moved to the West Coast to live like normal humans. Lotte was perhaps wondering if the punishingly austere approach to romantic life exhibited by Saskia during her widowhood was somehow going to be the expectation for *her*.

The royal line could terminate at any point. The monarchy could fade into history. The decision might be Lotte's to make. Could it be that Saskia needed to go out and get laid as an act of self-sacrifice to perpetuate the House of Orange? Not to produce an heir (which she'd already accomplished) but to prevent that heir from bailing out?

Yes. That was the ticket. If Saskia let Lotte know that she had done someone and liked it, it would be something that she was doing not just because she was horny (though, to be honest, she was that) but out of a sense of duty to the royal line and to the office to which she had devoted her life.

Best of all, it could begin to pay dividends long before anything actually happened. Lotte's crack about getting some had been an opening on her part—a bid to connect with her mother, woman to woman. There weren't that many levels on which they could really have a relationship. Obviously they were mother and daughter and they would always have that. But in terms of things that they had in common, ways they could relate to each other, there wasn't much there. Saskia dared to convince herself that Lotte wasn't sexually active yet. She'd prefer she weren't. But girls that age had sex all the time, and so it was a thing that Saskia and Lotte could conceivably have in common and bond over. Politics was off the table—Lotte would be horrified and furious when she found out what her mother was up to in Texas—but maybe as that door was closing this other one could open.

> Relaxing day so far

she texted on the second day of the Brazos journey. Then:

> No D yet.

After several minutes' delay during which she could see that Lotte had typed and apparently decided not to send several messages, Lotte came back with

> How's the scenery?

which actually made Saskia laugh out loud.

> Looking around . . .

And she did. But there were no realistic prospects on the boat. Alastair was apparently straight and single. But she wasn't feeling anything for him and it would have been excessively complicated.

> The valley is warm and lush but . . .

she began typing, then blushed and deleted it. Lotte wanted to change the subject anyway.

> Tell the Texans that if they stopped burning so much oil maybe the hurricanes would leave them alone!

Saskia sighed, finding this so much less interesting than what they had been talking about.

It was late the following day when they made their last camp on the Brazos and were reunited with Willem. He introduced Saskia to Jules. The young man was so beautiful that Saskia almost laughed in his face. She in turn introduced Jules to the other members of her group, including Fenna, who smiled at Jules with a light in her eyes that made Saskia wonder if they'd somehow crossed paths with each other in the past and were old friends.

But that wasn't it. They were new friends. They stuck to each other like magnets that have been brought too close together. They ceased to be aware of the existence of other humans.

After night had fallen and the temperature had dropped a few degrees, they laid plans around a line of folding camp tables zip-tied together under a row of pop-up canopies. Some of the Boskeys' shirttail relatives had showed up with a vast supply of living crayfish, squirming and shifting in mesh sacks. These had been boiled and heaped up on this table a couple of hours ago, bright and steaming, and had been consumed one by one by the two dozen or so people of the caravan as well as a few neighboring campers who had wandered by to say howdy. So they were surrounded by garbage bags stuffed with empty beer bottles and crayfish shells.

Saskia by this point had overheard many of the Cajuns' conversations about where they would go and what they would do tomorrow. She'd understood less than half of what she'd heard—she continued to find the accent challenging—but she knew the gist of it. They intended to head generally south of the metropolis, into Galveston County, and use their boats to assist flood victims there.

She liked to think that, up until this point, she and the other members of her party had not been a hindrance and might—solely by dint of Willem's cash-brick—have been of some help. That would clearly stop being the case very soon. They needed to work out a plan to part ways tomorrow that would create the least inconvenience for the Cajuns. As different versions of that plan were evaluated around the table, Saskia was in touch with T.R. via secure text message.

"My friend in Houston," she announced, looking up from her phone, "proposes that he can meet us tomorrow in a place called Sugar Land if that is not too inconvenient for you all."

Alastair threw her a private grin. During their time in Texas Saskia had begun to say "you all" as the equivalent of the Dutch "jullie," but she hadn't yet begun running it together into "y'all." Saskia winked back at him.

Heads were nodding around the table. Saskia continued, "I don't know what Sugar Land is but . . ."

"It's a suburb southwest of Houston," Rufus told her. A wry grin came over his face. "They used to call it 'Hellhole on the Brazos,' but Sugar Land sounds like a sweeter investment."

"Why was it a hellhole?"

"Built by convict labor. Legal slavery, after the Civil War. Sugar plantations are so bad, you almost couldn't have sugar without slaves."

"What's there now?"

"Subdivisions. The Brazos runs right through the middle of it. We can get there direct on a boat, or we can drive."

A man with a thick accent took exception, and for a minute they talked in a way that Saskia couldn't follow. Willem had brought up a map on his laptop. He and Saskia played a guessing game of trying to match place-names with the word fragments that they managed to fish out of the verbal gumbo. Just north of Sugar Land, in the western suburbs of Houston, the map showed large bodies of water, obviously artificial given that they were neat polygons outlined by roads. They were labeled as reservoirs. And yet on satellite imagery they appeared to be forests, dotted with recreational facilities. Sometimes, it seemed, these parts of the city were wooded parkland and other times they were underwater. Rufus and the Cajuns were talking about "Energy Corridor" and "Buffalo Bayou." Willem identified these on the map as well— both ran eastward toward downtown. The former was a row of office complexes, including at least one Shell facility. The latter was a natural watercourse that apparently drained those huge park/reservoir zones.

The direction it seemed to be going was that Rufus—as the first Texan to have greeted the Dutch, and taken them under his wing, upon their startling advent in the New World—would take responsibility for getting them to their rendezvous with T.R., so that the Cajuns could go about their business farther south. After which, Rufus—having not only killed Snout but furthermore discharged his hostly obligations—would be free to join up with the Cajuns if he wanted, or to do anything else whatsoever that struck his fancy.

The easiest way to make this rendezvous in Sugar Land would be to just blast straight down the Brazos tomorrow on a proper boat—not a slow-moving pontoon—and look for a place where they could get out and hike up the riverbank to whatever passed for dry land at the moment. The alternative, supported by Rufus, was to drive. But as to that there was much disagreement. Could Sugar Land even be reached by a wheeled vehicle? Opinions differed. Saskia, unable to follow much of what was being said, had to observe it as an anthropologist or even a primatologist. It was like any other meeting, be it of European Union bureaucrats in Brussels or members of the Dutch royal household, which was to say that it was at least as much about social dominance and hierarchy as about boats and trucks. Those who didn't like to play the game excused themselves or pushed their chairs back and dissolved into the twilight world of social media. The others engaged in this contest, which was not in any way disrespectful but was nonetheless a kind of struggle that, once begun, must be resolved. Rufus, in an understated but firm way, not lacking in deadpan humor, wanted it understood that boats were not the be-all and end-all. The Cajuns—some of them, anyway—were water-craft fundamentalists. Saskia, queen of one of the world's boatiest nations, saw in it a parable of climate change. These Cajuns had come down out of French Canada and spent the next quarter of a millennium dwelling in swamps and navigating around bayous: marginal places overlooked, or looked down on, by the dryland-ers in their concrete-and-steel fastnesses. But now the water was advancing upon the dry land. Their time had come. They were just slightly annoyed with Rufus's dogged insistence that wheeled vehicles had not become a thing of the past just because of a lit-tle rain, his patient reminders that Houston was crisscrossed with immense freeways on stilts, his pointing out that he'd mounted a snorkel on his truck that made it capable of driving through chest-deep water without stalling the engine.

It all got resolved, in the end, the only way such arguments *could* be resolved without anyone's losing face: through a sort of competition. Tomorrow the four Dutch and the one Scottish visi-tor would be conveyed swiftly down the river on a boat while Ru-fus tried to keep up with them in his truck, going roughly parallel to the Brazos on Interstate 10, and carrying the baggage. Rufus's trailer would later be towed out of here behind a Boskey vehicle and they'd look for a safe place to park it near their projected the-ater of operations. Once Rufus had seen the foreigners delivered to Sugar Land, he could retrieve his trailer and then ponder what to do with the remainder of his allotted life span. It was this last detail that seemed to be of paramount concern to Mary Boskey. She and Saskia had somehow wordlessly arrived at a shared un-derstanding that someone now needed to keep an eye on Rufus and make sure that in the post-Snout phase of his life he didn't go off the deep end.

> WHO IS THE HOTTIE!?!?

Lotte wanted to know after Saskia had sent her a selfie with the mound of crayfish in the background. Saskia scrolled back and examined it and saw Jules in the background making eyes at Fenna.

> He's taken.

> Aww.

> By Fenna.

> AWESOME

Then, later, after a few more selfies:

> OMG Surinamese guy on the left. Your age.

Saskia looked at the selfie, puzzled. Then she understood.

> Not Surinamese. They don't exist here.

> He seems fit for a guy that age.

> You mean, a senior citizen like me?

An exchange of emojis followed, reflecting embarrassment and apologies accepted.

"My daughter thought you were Surinamese," she said to Rufus later. The man was obviously an introvert, not fully comfortable with the hyper-gregarious Boskeys. Saskia exchanged a glance with Mary, a few yards away, who seemed glad to see that Rufus had company.

Rufus had never heard the term.

"Like Amelia," Saskia explained. She nodded over toward her acting security chief. As usual the poor woman was on the phone, looking preoccupied and tense, with frequent glances toward Saskia. She beckoned Willem over and they huddled on the edge of the bonfire's circle of smoky, bug-strewn light.

Rufus nodded. "Something gone wrong, or is that just how her job is?"

"I don't think anything has gone wrong in particular. It's just that there are a lot of nervous people on the other end of the line. Trying to work through all the contingencies."

"Those people didn't like it that you went down the river like you did."

"They didn't like anything about this."

Rufus nodded. "So your daughter thinks I look like *her*? That's a fine compliment."

Saskia smiled. "I'm glad you think so! I consider Amelia quite beautiful even though her looks are unusual by Dutch standards."

Rufus shifted his gaze to Saskia. "Most Dutch look more like you."

"Yes."

"Well, that's not a bad way to look either."

Saskia swallowed.

"Takes all kinds," Rufus added. "The reason I look the way I do is because of my great-great-granddad Hopewell, who was an African man. He was a slave owned by Chickasaw Indians."

"Indians owned slaves?"

Rufus nodded. "Oh yes, ma'am. Lots of 'em. Chickasaws were one of the so-called Five Civilized Tribes, down in the Southeast. They lived like white people. White people had slaves. So they had slaves too. Later the Five Tribes got pushed west across the Mississippi to Oklahoma, which was called Indian Territory in those days. Took their slaves with 'em. Hopewell, he was born into slavery around about 1860. When the Civil War started, a lot of the Five Civilized Tribes supported the Confederacy, because they wanted to keep things like they was. Now, when Juneteenth came—the day the slaves were emancipated—Hopewell's family took the name Grant."

"After the general?"

Rufus smiled and nodded.

"So that's my last name. I'm Rufus Grant. Never properly introduced myself."

"Got it. Nice to properly meet you."

"Right back at you. Now, the family kept living where they were, among the Chickasaws. Which was not a good decision. Because, out of all the Five Civilized Tribes, the Chickasaws lived farthest west in what we now call Oklahoma. Which put them right up against the Comancheria. The lands of the Comanches. The most powerful and feared of all the tribes that ever was. And in those days they were still living as they always had. They would raid the farms and ranches of the white people and the Five Tribes. One day in 1868 they raided the Chickasaws, stole their horses, burned everything down. They had a policy, I guess you could say, about captives. Small children, who were more trouble than they were worth, they would just kill. Adults they would kill *slowly*. But kids in a certain range of ages, maybe seven to twelve, they would take with them and adopt them into the tribe."

"And Hopewell Grant was eight years old."

Rufus nodded. "He was eight years old and he was good with horses, which was a useful skill to the Comanches. So they took him off into captivity and later traded him to the Quahadi."

"Quahadi?"

"A different Comanche band. The most wild, fierce, and free of all of 'em. The last to surrender. But surrender they did, eventually. So in 1875, ol' Hopewell ended up at Fort Sill. Oklahoma. Not far from the Chickasaw country where he had been born. Of course his whole family had been killed off in that raid, and he had become a true Comanche by that point."

"Except for . . . the fact that he was Black," Saskia said.

Rufus shook his head. "Did not matter to the Comanches. Comanches were a movement, not a race. There were white Comanches, Mexican Comanches, Black ones, ones who used to be Caddo or Cheyenne or what have you."

"When you say he ended up at Fort Sill . . ."

"They were kept sort of as prisoners for a while. The Period of Forced Captivity. But when things settled down the Comanches ended up controlling some land in those parts. Allotments of a hundred sixty acres were given out to them. Many of 'em leased their allotments out to white ranchers, raised cattle and such. Hopewell worked as a cowboy. Married a younger woman round about 1900—we think she was half Comanche and half white. Had a son.

My great-grandfather. He grew up on the ranch and enlisted in the army in World War One. They needed men who could wrangle horses, so he did that. Came back, started a family with a woman who looked like him—we think she was Mexican, mostly—and so on and so forth. My grandpa served in World War Two. Came back in one piece, started a family around boomer times, had my dad. Anyway, you get the picture. Up until about World War II we were horse people, but when cavalry became armored cav, that changed. I was a mechanic. Fixed tanks and APCs and such." He smiled. "It's all about mobility, see."

HOUSTON

The next morning's race to Sugar Land ended up being the most benign sort of competition in that everyone had a good time and came away somewhat vindicated. In the early going it seemed to those on the boat that they were going to destroy Rufus. The Brazos was wide open—even wider, today, than normal—all the way down to Sugar Land. Their skipper, one Mitch, was uxoriously proud of his boat and the speed at which it could travel and completely unconcerned about the rate at which he was consuming gasoline. Even in these hot and humid conditions the wind blast was more than sufficient to keep them cool, and on the long straightaways between meanders, they all had to retreat behind the shelter of the windscreen—all, that is, except Alastair, who seemed fully alive for the first time since the jet crash. His hairstyle—tawny stubble with sparks of gray and scalp gleaming through—had nothing to fear from wind, and bugs could easily be picked out of it before gaining purchase and tapping into a vein. With the exception of those rare places where the river was bridged, it looked like a subtropical stream rambling free across a landscape that had never been visited or altered by humans.

This above all was the hardest thing for Saskia to grasp about Texas. She knew perfectly well that just beyond the screen of vegetation flanking both banks existed a modern landscape of farms, roads, oil refineries, and power plants. Willem could prove as much by showing her their current position on the map, which, other than the river itself, was farmland and small towns giving way, as the ride went on, to suburbs. But all they could actually see was the same general ecosystem that had hemmed them in since Waco: trees that had become trellises for climbing vines and then been overwhelmed by mats of ivy so thick that from a distance it looked like emerald felt draped over furniture. That was the case everywhere except on the steepest and most exposed parts of the banks, which were bare adobe-red clay. As they rounded one bend followed by another and the little arrowhead on Willem's map crept closer to Sugar Land, the queen kept waiting for the moment when this foliage would peel back from the river and they would find themselves in an urban environment. But it never happened.

Mitch, tending closely to his own electronic map, cut the motor and nosed the boat over to the right bank. This was somewhat indistinct, as high water had inundated the trees above it. He pressed a button that caused the huge outboard to angle up and forward, getting its propeller safely out of the water, and then went back and started a much smaller "kicker" motor for maneuvering through places where water was shallow and obstructions numerous.

A few minutes' poking around in the flooded woods brought them suddenly in view of Rufus, just standing there, pretending to look at an imaginary wristwatch. He was up to his knees in the water, cargo pants rolled up but wet anyway. He caught a painter tossed to him by Amelia, put it over his shoulder, and towed the boat a few meters to a place where the ground finally made up its mind and rose out of the water. Saskia and the rest had long since got in the habit of wearing footgear suited for wading, so they hopped over the side and sloshed the last few steps onto what could euphemistically be called dry land.

They'd forgotten to properly thank and say goodbye to Mitch, which they now tried to redress by a lot of waving and blowing of kisses. He clambered up onto the front deck, pulled off his baseball cap, and bowed deeply, causing Saskia a moment's concern that he had figured out who she was. But it was probably just him being courtly. Rufus nearly turned it into a comic pratfall by shoving the boat back. Mitch recovered his balance well for a man carrying a substantial beer belly, and he bid Rufus adieu with some kind of complicated high five (high for Rufus anyway, low for Mitch) and finger-snapping and -pointing exchange. Then he turned his back on them and went back to see to the needs of his "kicker."

It was late morning by this point, the weather system had cleared off, the sun was high, and they had all become miserably hot and sweaty during the few minutes it had taken to get off the boat and say goodbye. Rufus strode past them and led them into the woods. Saskia was steeling herself for a long hot hike. For, anticipating that they'd end up in some air-conditioned building in Houston, they had packed up the earthsuits and worn normal, non-refrigerated clothes.

But the hike was literally no more than ten strides long. That was all the distance they needed to cover before the trees and the vines and the ivy fell away and they found themselves in a suburb. Oh, it was a part of the suburb that had been set aside as a park, but the first row of nearly identical tract homes was only a few hundred meters distant. Rufus's truck was idling a few steps away on a gravel access road. Alastair and Amelia vaulted into the back and sat on luggage while Willem and Fenna got into the rear row of seats. Saskia "rode shotgun."

"They're waiting for you," Rufus said as he put it into gear. He drove for no more than thirty seconds along the gravel road before it descended slightly into a flooded parking lot. Beyond, parked on a right-of-way just above the flood, was an immaculate black SUV the size of four typical Dutch cars welded together. Condensation beading up and trickling down its windows spoke of ice-cold air-conditioning within.

The difference in elevation between the flooded parking lot, across which Rufus's truck made a spreading V-shaped wake, and the road was probably more than one meter and less than two. Less than the height of a man. And yet it was everything. The placement of the road—more generally, the engineering of the levee along which the road ran—was all quite deliberate. People above the water drove around in clean vehicles and might live their whole lives unaware that the sea, globally, was coming for them. Those who found themselves just the height of a man closer to the earth's center found themselves inundated from time to time, according to the weather's whims, and either had to stew in shantytowns or, like the Cajuns, become masters of an amphibious lifestyle.

The occupants of the SUV—an African American driver and a Latino in the shotgun seat—did not take the rash step of opening the doors until Rufus had parked next to them and set his parking brake. Both of the men had the physique of soccer players. Both wore loose khakis with untucked shirts. Saskia had seen enough discreetly armed security personnel in her day to recognize the type. Amelia, their direct counterpart, exchanged credentials with them. They set about transferring the baggage into the back of the SUV. The driver came round to the side of the truck, opened Saskia's door, and extended a hand to help her down off the wet running board. "Dr. Schmidt welcomes you to his hometown, Your Majesty."

Saskia was at a loss for words. From the moment she had entered the cockpit of the jet in the Netherlands, she had not been a queen. She had largely forgotten about it. But the world hadn't forgotten about her.

"It is good to be here" was the best she could manage.

"Dr. Schmidt apologizes for not being here in person, but he thought you and your party might want a few moments to freshen up after your adventure."

Saskia looked down at her grubby feet, thrust into a pair of flip-flops Willem had scored at a Walmart. "That is most considerate of T.R.," she said. For Theodore Roosevelt Schmidt, Ph.D., was the real name of the man who appeared in television commercials and billboards, across the South, as T.R. McHooligan, quasi-fictitious founder and proprietor of a vastly successful regional chain of family restaurants-cum-mega-truck-stops.

"My instructions are to convey Your Majesty and her party to his estate, unless you express a different preference."

"That will be fine, thank you."

"And—so that I can make sure all is in readiness—the size of your party is five?"

She thought about it. "Six," she decided.

He looked slightly befuddled and checked a list on the screen of a tablet. "Your Majesty, Willem Castelein, Fenna Enkhuis, Captain Amelia Leeflang, Dr. Alastair Thomson, and—?" His eyes strayed toward the only one here who could bring the total up to six.

"Rufus," Saskia said, nodding at him. "Mr. Rufus Grant, Esquire. He probably has a military rank. I forgot to take down that information."

The driver nodded, taking in Rufus.

"I imagine he'll drive his own vehicle. With him, it's all about mobility."

"Yes, ma'am."

The first part of the drive took them through mile after mile of classically American strip development landscape. They got on an elevated highway that was the largest she'd seen outside of China and drove east for a while past a district of mid- and high-rise office buildings, many of which bore the names of oil companies. This wasn't downtown, though; much larger buildings loomed in the distance. Her internal GPS, calibrated for the Low Countries, told her that they were driving from Amsterdam to Rotterdam, or Rotterdam to Antwerp, but of course nothing of the sort was happening—they were just moving around between different parts of Houston, a metropolitan area the size of Belgium.

A few miles short of the downtown high-rise district, the caravan ducked off the freeway and dropped into the valley of a river that snaked right through the middle of the city. It was canopied with big mature trees beneath which sheltered expensive homes. Buffalo Bayou, as this watercourse was called, was of course flooded. Many of the streets were blocked, so the caravan had to take a circuitous route through the neighborhood. Saskia didn't mind, since she enjoyed seeing some of the fine homes that wealthy Texas families had built here.

The destination was a hotel and spa complex that had been created by merging a few adjoining properties. The hotel proper had been the mansion of some great Texas dynasty. To this a pair of wings had been discreetly added, reaching back into the woods, adding capacity without altering the look.

T.R.'s residence was so nearby as to seem almost an extension of the same complex, and indeed one of her hosts mentioned that, were it not for the flood, one could travel between the two properties by walking along a cool path through the forest. Today, you'd need a canoe.

Of the four "distinguished guests" whom T.R. had invited, Frederika Mathilde Louisa Saskia had the highest social rank, as such things were calibrated in books of old-school etiquette. She would be lodged in his home as a personal guest, while others were relegated to the hotel. Alastair and Rufus, as less essential staff, got off at the hotel, while Saskia, Willem, Fenna, and Amelia stayed in the car for a sixty-second drive to T.R.'s place. En route the vehicle passed through deep fords of running floodwater. It was the first time, in Saskia's experience, that Americans' absurd attachment for gigantic, high-off-the-ground SUVs had actually served any useful purpose.

T.R.'s residential compound rose above the waters of Buffalo Bayou on a sort of artificial mesa; he had jacked the buildings up off their original foundations, put new supports under them, then filled it all in with water-resistant soil called levee clay. There was a mansion in Tudor Revival style, and, out back of it, a guesthouse with seven bedrooms and as many baths. This was where Saskia and the others finally came to rest after a journey from Huis ten Bosch that had ended up taking the better part of a week.

And given some of what had happened en route, one might have thought it perfectly reasonable to lock oneself in and do nothing but recuperate for the *next* week. Their hosts had the good taste to leave them alone; both T.R. and his wife, Veronica Schmidt, sent their handwritten regrets that they couldn't be there to say hello in person and left them in the hands of staff members who clearly knew that being unobtrusive was part of the job description. Yet, perhaps because of that hands-off policy, Saskia found that after she had spent twenty minutes drowsing in a bathtub, washing away the Brazos grime and taking inventory of her bug bites, she was of a mind to put on some clean clothes and go back to the hotel for a drink. Some kind of optional social hour was listed on the schedule.

About half of her luggage had been salvaged from the jet crash. Willem and Fenna had made arrangements for more clothes to be plucked from her wardrobe at home and express-shipped here. She called Fenna, rousing her from what sounded like deep slumber— no surprise given the nature of her activities last night with Jules. Wrapped in a huge plush terry robe monogrammed with T.R.'s family crest, she glided into Saskia's suite like a somnambulating figure skater, profoundly relaxed and satisfied. Quite obviously Jules had been the cure for the case of jitters she had picked up in the jet crash. "One, I think," Saskia said. Fenna opened up the cosmetics case and applied Face One, a scheme that went well with the outfit Saskia had picked out: blue jeans with a nice blouse and vest, chosen to disarm people who might have inflated expectations of what a queen would look and act like, but with enough fancy bits that it wouldn't seem downright insulting. In truth Saskia could do Face One without assistance, but her hair had sustained some damage and needed a bit of chemical and mechanical help. Before long, Fenna was able to pad back to her room and fall into bed to have sweet dreams of Jules while Saskia, looking every inch the modern, norMAL, unpretentious monarch, met Amelia and Willem in the foyer for the quick drive back to the hotel and its capacious bar.

This was doing brisk business. T.R. had bought the whole place out and thrown a security cordon around it, so everyone here was somehow involved in the project, had signed all the NDAs, was in on the joke, as it were. The drinks were free. A table had been reserved and made ready for them. They plunged down into vast chairs and sofas for which many Texas longhorns had sacrificed their lives and their hides. The skull of one such looked down on them from above a fireplace large enough that it could have done double duty as a parking space for one of those SUVs. Amelia ordered club soda, Willem a Manhattan, Saskia a glass of red wine. She enjoyed her first sip and took in the scene.

Twenty-four hours ago, on the bank of the Brazos, they'd been in the world where things made of microchips and petrochemicals cost basically nothing, and a whole city could be summoned into being in a few hours out of tarps, zip ties, and garbage bags. It wasn't a fancy city, but it wasn't terrible. Gumbo might be featured on the bar menu here in this hotel lobby, but Saskia deemed it unlikely that it would be any better than what they'd made last night over camp stoves and consumed in the open air in plastic bowls.

This place, however, was about permanence. Permanence, and uniqueness. Every detail custom-built of polished old wood, wrought iron, sculpted marble. Original works of art wherever some decoration was wanted, living flowers arranged by human hands. That human effort immanent in every detail. Napkins folded just so, drinks hand-shaken and served with origami twists of citrus rind.

People were expensive; the way to display, or to enjoy, great wealth was to build an environment that could only have been wrought, and could only be sustained from one hour to the next, by unceasing human effort. Saskia, with her staff, was as guilty of it as anyone, but she tended to forget about it until some event such as the journey down the Brazos reset her thinking.

Woven through the preparations had been a series of tests, administered to all the invited guests, for contagious diseases. Everyone who'd made it as far as this hotel lobby had passed that screening, and so they were all in a shared bubble now, with no masks or social distancing required. The accents in the lobby—other than the obvious Texan—tended to be British, Italian, and Chinese. Though in truth many of the Asian-looking people spoke indistinguishably from well-educated Brits. Saskia assumed they were from Hong Kong until Willem somehow inferred from reading a couple of name tags that they had to be from Singapore. As for the Italians, she guessed that they were from the northern part of that country; there were no visual clues to distinguish them from any other Europeans other than, perhaps, great attention to detail in matters of appearance. As usual Saskia drew a lot of glances and even some indiscreet stares once people understood who she was. T.R.'s staff had been extraordinarily tight-lipped about the guest list; Saskia didn't know who the other honored guests were, and so it stood to reason that her presence came as a surprise to them.

Rufus and Alastair, the unlikeliest of couples, wandered in and looked shyly in her direction. Saskia sent Willem to corral them and make it clear they were welcome at her table. He did so and they came over, looking somewhat relieved. Neither of them was one for cocktail party banter.

"This is all I got that's clean," Rufus said, plucking at his T-shirt and then looking around at the other guests in their tailored suits.

"I'm a queen," Saskia said. "I don't think about it every minute of every day, and I try not to make a big deal about it. I try to be norMAL. I don't 'pull rank' as you say. But in cases like this I am a tyrant. *You're with me*, Red. Your T-shirt is fine. I said so."

Rufus enjoyed hearing that and came closer to smiling than usual. Willem had gone missing. On his way back from rounding up these two strays, he had been buttonholed by one of the Singaporeans. Saskia heard the man hailing him in some variant of Chinese. Willem glanced her way, she nodded, and he proceeded to return the greeting and to enter into conversation.

Amelia had stood to make room for Rufus and Alastair. They noticed this, felt bad about it, and made room for her, but she wanted to prowl around. There wasn't much for her to do. T.R. was providing security and so her main role was to stay in sync with her opposite numbers on his and the other staffs. These were standing around the periphery of the room, identifiable mostly from the fact that they never engaged in anything like normal social interaction. A Brit detached himself from the Brit squad, approached Amelia, and introduced himself. Saskia couldn't hear, but the man fit the profile of one of those ex-military guys who filled the ranks of British security details.

Both of them turned their heads to look at a man and a woman entering from one of the adjoining spaces. It took Saskia a few moments to realize that the man was T.R. and the woman presumably his wife, Veronica. Compared to his YouTube persona, T.R. McHooligan, he was (of course) older, smaller, and more dignified. A little of the same impish energy still came through. Veronica was a full-time helpmeet to T.R., a society lady who had been doing this her whole life. Early in his advance through the bar, T.R. got brought up short by a staff member and so Veronica peeled away without breaking stride and came for Frederika Mathilde Louisa Saskia like a border collie homing in on a Frisbee. Saskia stood up and there was the usual society-lady greeting, an activity Saskia had been born and bred for and that largely consisted of defusing any awkwardness or self-consciousness that the other might be experiencing without getting too informal too fast.

Veronica obviously knew her business and so it came off without a hitch. She understood the message Saskia was sending, for example, by wearing blue jeans. She'd done something similar that involved a pair of shockingly exquisite cowboy boots. It was entirely within the realm of possibility that she'd checked out Saskia on one of the video cameras that were presumably ubiquitous on her property and the hotel's, and only then chosen her outfit.

A minute or two into that procedure, T.R. sidled up to his wife, who unfastened her gaze from Saskia long enough to make the introduction—which seemed like an afterthought. So that was finally out of the way. Protocol dictated that the host and hostess move on to greet other guests before too much time passed, and Saskia gave them an opening to do so after introducing her team. Veronica, much to her credit, didn't so much as blink when introduced to T-shirted Rufus "Red" Grant, who had to transfer his beer to his other hand and wipe his hand on his pants in order to shake hers. T.R. even managed to work in a "thank you for your service." This meant that in the approximately six hours since Saskia had abruptly and impulsively added Rufus to her entourage, T.R.'s people had run a background check on him and unearthed his military record and communicated all that to T.R.

"You and I gotta talk pigs later," T.R. added as a parting shot. "Got a real problem on my Cotulla property!"

"Not for long," Rufus shot back.

T.R. was knocked back on the heels of his hand-tooled ostrich hide cowboy boots only for a moment, then pointed his index finger at Rufus like a six-shooter and exclaimed, "Oh. Yes. You and me."

"Yes *sir*!"

"We gonna take *care* of it!"

"I got the means!"

"I got a chopper," T.R. threw in suggestively. His wife was dragging him off. He turned back to utter some barely coherent instructions regarding which of his people Rufus needed to follow up with to arrange it. Though Rufus was a shy man, Saskia could see in his face how pleasantly surprised he was that T.R. McHooligan, of all people on this planet, knew of him and his profession. Just before being dragged out of range, T.R. shot Saskia the slightest glance to make sure she had observed all these goings-on. *My staff and I pay attention; in the Lone Star State no sparrow falls from a tree, no bug hits a windshield, no vulture lights on a road-kill armadillo without my knowing it.* Saskia for her part just suspended her incredulity for a moment to revel in the fact that there was a part of the world where two men with so little in common could derive such mutual pleasure—not feigned—from the mere prospect of being able to go out into a harsh place and shoot feral swine out of a helicopter.

The purpose of this get-together in the bar was to get introductions out of the way so that when the various attendees bumped into each other during the program slated to begin tomorrow morning, they'd simply be able to begin talking and not have to fuss with protocol. Saskia resolved to grit her teeth and just get on with it. To relieve the sheer tedium—for queens had to spend rather a lot of time in these kinds of situations—she decided that she would try to see the whole scene from Lotte's point of view as a loved one who deeply cherished the hope that Saskia might find a romantic partner. The first step in that process was to ruthlessly evaluate every straight man in the room on two independent axes: one, availability; two, a trait that Lotte, with Dutch bluntness, would probably call fuckability, but for which Saskia needed a more elevated term. The tools she had used to evaluate boys as a teenager were no longer adequate to the task. She decided to consider the whole matter as she might evaluate the lift-to-drag ratio of an airplane's wing.

T.R. was surprisingly more high lift than she'd have guessed from YouTube, but extremely high drag in that he was married. And Veronica, though impeccably bred, seemed like the type to interrupt the proceedings with a shotgun.

Alastair: low drag (available), but low lift (she didn't feel much).

Rufus: low drag and, the more she saw of him, extraordinarily high lift. But it would never cross the poor man's mind in a million years and so she would have to slip a Xanax into his Shiner Bock and then throw herself at him.

Having established that basic framework for all this afternoon's social interactions, Saskia met two of her three counterparts: the Italian and the Singaporean. As for the third—the Brit—it turned out she already knew him. He was the lord mayor of the City of London. But he'd had to excuse himself early because of pressing concerns in his world. Or maybe jet lag.

Willem reeled in the Singaporean: Dr. Sylvester Lin, a man in his fifties. Other than that slightly odd choice of Western first name, he was what you'd expect of an official dispatched by the Singaporean government to attend a hush-hush conference. He wore a black suit with a blue necktie, rimless glasses, no jewelry other than a simple wristwatch, had all the etiquette down pat. He made a carefully rehearsed allusion to "the long-standing relationship between our countries up and down the Straits." He was attended by three senior aides who happened to represent the Malaysian, Tamil, and white minorities of his country. Each of them had at least one junior assistant. Sylvester paid his respects, made the obligatory sixty seconds of polite chitchat, then excused himself—not before uttering some pleasantry in Fuzhounese to Willem and then ponderously translating it into English for Saskia's benefit. Saskia made a mental note to review the basics of Singapore's early history and how it related to the Dutch East Indies.

Verdict: Sylvester Lin: high drag, low lift.

The apparent leader of the Italian contingent was the most physically beautiful man Saskia had seen since Jules the diver. He was a self-assured man of perhaps forty with wavy blond hair that fell to his shoulders in a way that looked careless, and yet it somehow miraculously never fell across his face. He was here to represent Venice. The Venetian's name was Michiel (pronounced with a hard "k" sound like meeky-ell) and he didn't seem to have any titles that would supply clues as to his status or profession—no Ph.D., no doctor, professor, count, reverend, or any of that. She had the vague sense that she was supposed to know who he was, but she didn't. Pre-COVID he'd have kissed her hand. Instead he pantomimed a hand kiss from two meters away. Saskia responded by clasping one hand warmly with the other. "I should have anticipated that someone from your city would be here," she said.

Michiel nodded. "We built it in a swamp, as Your Majesty will know, because Huns didn't have boats. We have been building houses on stilts since Alaric the Goth." He looked around. "These people have been doing it since Hurricane Harvey."

She well knew the long rich gory gaudy brilliant history of the Venetian Republic. Her knowledge began to sputter out around the time of Napoleon, when the eleven-hundred-year-old republic had been extinguished, leading, after a few decades of subordination to Austria, to its becoming just another part of Italy. In the last decades they had famously been challenged by climate change and sea level rise, to which they were uniquely vulnerable. They had tried, and almost failed, to build a barrier . . .

"If you follow this sort of thing—which as sovereign of a country below sea level, you must—you'll have heard the ignominious story of MOSE," Michiel offered. He was good at this—feeding her the missing background and immediately broaching the awkward topic.

"Well, it's so complicated, isn't it?" Saskia returned. "All those channels and marshes. You can't just wall off the Adriatic the way we do the North Sea."

Michiel nodded. "Building a surge barrier can only buy us time. We must prevent sea level from rising, or lose the city."

Saskia raised her eyebrows and smiled as if to pass that remark off as a mere jest. It was very blunt talk by the standards of climate change cocktail party discourse. You couldn't "prevent sea level from rising" in just one place. That was the whole point of sea level. You had to change the climate of the whole world. That kind of thinking—adjust the climate of the entire planet just to make things good for Venice—might have been very typical of Venice in, say, the twelfth century but was not what one expected today.

He sensed her caution and gave a disarming shrug. "Pardon me," he said, "but that *is* what we're here to talk about, is it not?"

"Did you know who was invited?" Saskia asked.

"Not until fifteen minutes ago. London, Singapore, Venice,

the Netherlands, and of course Houston. What do they all have in common?"

"Other than the obvious? That they are all under dire threat from rising sea level?"

"But so is Bangladesh. The Marshall Islands. Why aren't they here?"

"Money," Saskia said, gazing at a beautiful set of cuff links on the wrists of one of the London contingent. His French cuffs had, of course, been tailored so that one of them was slightly larger to accommodate his massive wristwatch. A side benefit of being a queen was that you didn't even have to pretend to be impressed by that stuff.

"To join the club," Michiel said, extending one hand palm up, discreetly taking in the room, "I infer that you must be under dire threat—but you must also have the money and let's call it the technocratic mentality needed to take effective action."

Saskia made a mental note to ask Amelia to run a check on this guy and find out whether he had any fascist affiliations.

"Does Venice?" Saskia asked. As long as they were being blunt.

"Officially? No. Oh, it's under threat, to be sure. But it's just another cash-strapped modern city. Part of a country that pays lip service to climate orthodoxy. As does the Netherlands."

She didn't need to ask what Michiel meant by climate orthodoxy. Even if she weren't the head of state of a very Green country, she got an earful of it almost every day from Lotte.

"But . . . if you were here in some *official* capacity, I imagine you'd have told me a little more about yourself," she said.

"Venice doesn't have monarchs, so we have to make do," Michiel said, gesturing to himself in a self-deprecating way. "But the money, the technocratic will to power—those aren't going to come from the Italian government, as you well know."

She just looked at him expectantly. Her instinct was to say little until she got the background check back from Amelia.

"Look," Michiel said with a shrug, "someone like you will want to have an explanation of who and what I am. That is only fair and reasonable. We should get out ahead of that and not let it develop into a source of confusion. But perhaps you'll agree that this cocktail party isn't the place or time."

"I do agree and will take that as an offer for us to find some place and time that is better."

"Done. I do not have a staff per se, but am accompanied by my sister and my aunt. We shall work it out with Dr. Castelein."

"It has been a pleasure to make your acquaintance, Michiel."

"The pleasure is all mine, Your Majesty," he returned, and excused himself.

Verdict: Michiel was low drag (though it might be weird having his sister around), very high lift, but only on the condition that he wasn't some kind of fascist. The Netherlands too had its share of far-right characters, and Saskia had to be careful about even being seen talking to someone like that. So the verdict was out until Amelia (and the larger Dutch security apparatus at home) could figure out who the hell this guy was.

"Ex-footballer for AC Milan," Willem said, after Michiel was out of earshot.

"Ah. I thought he looked familiar."

"Played for a few seasons. Not a big star but had a good run. Parlayed it into some endorsements. You've seen his face on ads for fancy watches in duty-free shops. From an old Venetian family, as it turns out."

It remained only to make some sort of contact with the Brits. Saskia dispatched Alastair, who knew some of the lord mayor's entourage through City connections. He came back a few minutes later with a pair of white men in tow: a mop-topped blond (medium drag, medium lift, too young) who looked like he'd stepped right off an Oxford or Cambridge quad, and a posh and podgy sort in his fifties (probably low drag, but zero lift). This was the guy whose cuff links—made from Roman coins, it turned out—had caught her eye earlier. His name tag identified him as Mark Furlong. "Bob's knackered," he announced. "Just useless. Too much free Beaujolais on the Gulfstream."

A moment passed while Saskia re-calibrated her conversational brain for this kind of highly layered and ironic talk. In some ways it was more difficult than learning a foreign language. Which was sort of the point; you couldn't be part of this social class unless you got it. "Bob"—Robert Watts, the Right Honorable the Lord Mayor of London—was a teetotaler. He had blown up a marriage and a job by drinking too much, then sworn off the booze and put his life back together and gotten married to Daia Chand, a British journalist. The assertion by Mark Furlong—a trusted member of Bob's inner circle—that he'd been incapacitated by too much free Beaujolais on the Gulfstream was under no circumstances to be taken at face value. It was, first of all, a joke that derived its humorous payload from being so utterly outrageous in its falsity. But for the hearer to get the joke they'd have to know Bob at least well enough to know that he was—extremely unusually for a man in his role—an absolute teetotaler. Anyone so ill-informed or credulous as to actually believe this slander would be left out in the cold, operating on bad information. In due time they might work out that they'd committed the monstrous faux pas of taking at face value what had been meant as an ironic witticism and have the good grace to throw themselves in front of a Tube train at Bank. Further embroidering on all this was Mark's specification of Beaujolais as the drink in question, that being seen, by a certain class of drinker, as an inexpensive and faddish vintage for lightweights. The mention of the Gulfstream was a lovely touch. Mark was basically remarking on how absurd it was for people to travel that way. So the underlying reality was that Mark was a profoundly decent man who knew and loved Bob but couldn't bring himself to say as much.

Fine. But it simply took Saskia a few moments to get her head in that groove, so different from talking to the Sylvester Lins of the world. During that brief period of readjustment, Mark—who was evidently *not* a teetotaler—began to look just faintly queasy as it crossed his mind that Saskia might be too dim or literal-minded to get the joke. She was, after all, just a hereditary monarch. It wasn't like you had to pass an intelligence test to land that job.

"He says he knows you," Mark said, beginning to sound apologetic.

"Is Dr. Chand holding his head?"

"Perhaps. I thought she might join us." Mark looked around, then shrugged as if to say *no such luck*. "I'm afraid I'll have to do. On behalf of the Honorable the Lord Mayor, howdy and welcome to Texas! Can I grab you a beer?"

"I'm fine with this lovely glass of Beaujolais," she shot back.

For one exquisite second, she had him. Mark looked exquisitely mortified, his eyes strayed to the glass in Saskia's hand, but then he saw that it looked more like a Bordeaux. "I've heard it's quite good," he said.

Obviously discomfited by Mr. Furlong's breezy informality was the younger man, one Simon Towne by his name tag. He turned out to be a viscount. As such he probably had been brought up to behave in a certain way when in the presence of queens. So Saskia went through the requisite formalities as Mark Furlong gazed on, seeming to find it all worth watching. Mark was a City man through and through. His protégé Simon was of another recognizable type: fresh out of a posh education, sent down to the City for seasoning and to rack up some millions and find a wife who would enjoy picking out curtains in Sussex.

"Mark, you mentioned Alastair had worked for you. May I assume in that case that you too are a risk analyst?"

"We all are," Mark said.

"We meaning—?"

"Everyone in this room. Even the waiters and bus boys. *Especially* them. It's just that some of us actually have the temerity to print it on our business cards." He regarded Saskia. "Your country. Surrounded by walls. So high, but no higher. There's a risk that waves will overtop them. Boffins like Alastair understand the maths of waves." Mark winked.

"So he keeps telling me," Saskia returned, with a glance at Alastair.

Alastair reddened, and his jaw literally dropped open.

"We're joking!" she said. But she'd put him in a bad spot and he had to defend himself—if not to Mark and Saskia, who were in on the joke, then to others who were listening. "Anyone who claims to understand waves needs to be fired," he said.

He had written his dissertation on rogue waves—incredibly random events of astonishing power, thought to be responsible for sudden disappearances of ships, therefore of interest to City insurance companies, who'd hired him before the ink was dry on his Ph.D.

"I know, Alastair," Mark said calmingly. "So you told me ten years ago. Now it's how I cull the yearly crop of people like Simon."

With that it seemed that the basic purpose of the cocktail hour had been accomplished. Saskia could reasonably claim to be "knackered" herself and so she made excuses and returned to the guesthouse with Amelia, leaving Alastair to pal around with the City boys, Rufus to talk pigs with T.R., and Willem to brush up on his Fuzhounese with the Singapore crew. Lotte demanded a progress report via text message and Saskia dutifully let her know that two possibles (Rufus and Michiel) had been identified. But she drew the line at sending her daughter pictures.

They could have just done this aerial tour from the comfort of T.R.'s mansion-on-stilts along Buffalo Bayou, relaxing on leather furniture with drinks in hand and experiencing the whole thing through virtual reality, but that would not have been the Texas way and it certainly was not the T.R. way. Instead T.R., Queen Frederika, the lord mayor, Sylvester Lin, and Michiel were humming through the stifling air above the metropolis, each in their own personal drone: an air-conditioned plastic bubble with splayed arms that ramified like fingers, each finger terminated by an electric motor driving a carbon fiber propeller. Two dozen independent motors and two dozen propellers kept each vehicle in the air. In front of Saskia was a touch screen control system completely different from anything she'd ever seen in an airplane. She couldn't have piloted this thing if she'd tried. Fortunately she didn't have to. The drone was being controlled by swarm software, based on the murmurations of starlings. T.R.—presumably with a lot of assistance from an AI safety system—piloted his drone. The others—Saskia's, the three other guests', and half a dozen more drones containing aides and security personnel—flew in formation with it, basically going where T.R. went but never getting closer than a few meters to any of the others. Or to any solid object whatsoever. For the flock was smart enough to part around hazards when it came upon them and then to knit itself back together after leaving obstructions in its wake.

"I sucked at math," T.R. remarked as he piloted the flock on an obstacle course among the skyscrapers of downtown Houston. This was just a few kilometers to the east of the posh leafy neighborhood where they had lifted off a few minutes earlier. It was not, Saskia suspected, the important part of the tour. It was just T.R. getting the touristy bits ticked off the list, making sure the drones were all working.

"Or leastways, math as it was taught in the prep schools my folks sent me to. 'How do we get to AP calc?'" He chuckled. "That's what *that's* all about. I was a twenty-seven-year-old college dropout before I finally met some real mathematicians and found that those people don't even *give a shit* about calculus. My Ph.D.'s in probability and statistics. Took me ten years to get it because I was building a business and raising kids at the same time. You could say I went to grad school on the short bus."

Alastair had warned her to expect this, encouraged her to watch a few online videos of the *real* T.R. Schmidt. Ninety-nine percent of all T.R. content on the normal Internet was him twenty years ago during the business-building phase of his life, making an ass of himself in deliberately amateurish television ads for his chain of family-themed strip mall restaurants, which catered to the child birthday party market. Eventually he had hired a younger actor to slip into the role of T.R. McHooligan: a sort of goofy slapstick dad/cowboy figure, beloved of kids, relatable to men in their twenties and thirties. He was masculine enough to seem like a regular guy you could go have a beer with but not rising to the level of a potential wife-beguiler. That actor had eventually fallen into disgrace and been replaced by an animation, a change that had coincided with a rebranding and expansion of the chain into something called T.R. Mick's. The small (by Texas standards—unbelievably colossal to Europeans) standalone restaurants had been phased out, only to crop up on yet larger parcels on the edges of cities, where they served as the central anchors of truck stop/gas stations designed around the slogan "Never Less Than a Hundred!" meaning—as every motorist in Texas understood—that the *smallest* T.R. Mick's Mobility Center had a hundred fuel pumps. That did not include electric charging stations, of which there were also plenty. All sheltered from sun and rain by wide solar-power-collecting awnings and all connected into the central restaurant/entertainment plaza with moving walkways like in one of your longer airport concourses. Everyone knew and understood that this business strategy had enabled T.R. to parlay the tens of millions he had inherited from "Daddy" Schmidt into billions.

Not a whole *lot* of billions. T.R., over drinks last night, had been keen to make this understood. On a good day in the stock market he *might* be worth ten billion. He was not, he wanted it understood, one of "those tech boys" who had, as the result of an IPO, overnight come into more money than Dr. T.R. Schmidt would ever be able to accumulate simply by dint of actually growing a business. He'd made this statement matter-of-factly, in the same emotional tone he used to describe the underground plumbing that fed gasoline from central tanks out to the hundred pumps. He was not, in other words, bitter. In no way did T.R. wish to deprecate "the tech boys" who had ten times as much money as him. No, it was that the rootedness of his fortune in "steel in the ground" was somehow going to become a part of the argument he was making today.

They swung north up a downtown thoroughfare that was labeled "Main Street" on the augmented-reality overlay in the drone's bubble. In a few moments this terminated in a small plaza on the edge of a swollen brown stream. Another stream of about the same size emptied into it here. Several bridges had been thrown over these watercourses. "I promise I'm about done with the tourist shit," T.R. said. "This here, the confluence of Buffalo Bayou and White Oak Bayou, is Allen's Landing, where Houston was founded two hundred years ago. Y'all ought to be seeing a little old 3D movie playing right about now. Holler if it ain't."

The glass bubble darkened, cutting down the brightness of the incoming sunlight, and the landscape seemed to turn green. The bridges and streets were still visible, but they'd been overlaid with an artist's conception of what this place had looked like a couple of hundred years ago. Mostly it looked like the same kind of vegetation Saskia and her companions had traveled through between Waco and Sugar Land. In this fictional rendering, some sail- and oar-powered wooden vessels, including some indigenous canoes, had congregated on the south bank of Buffalo Bayou, right where the present-day historic site was located. A man in a broad-brimmed hat was standing on a platform reading from a fancy document. Basically it looked like a cut scene from one of your more expensively produced video games: close to photorealistic if you didn't zoom in too far. The actor who had recorded this dialog had done the best he could with the material that had been handed to him. But at the end of the day, the words were those of a real estate prospectus that had been written in 1836—not exactly Shakespeare.

In Saskia's headphones, much of the dialogue, or rather monologue, was drowned out by questions and remarks from some of the other guests. For all of them were sharing the same open comm channel with T.R. But Saskia was able to hear the actor declaiming, in timeless real-estate-hustler style, about the pure clean spring water, fertile soil, salubrious climate, and other fine conditions here prevailing. On that basis he ventured to guess that this settlement did "warrant the employment of at least one million dollars of capital," then paused as gasps of astonishment, followed by whoops and huzzahs, propagated through the procedurally generated, AI-driven crowd of improbably diverse Texans assembled to hear his oration. ". . . and when the rich lands of the country shall be settled, a trade will flow to it, making it, beyond all doubt, the great interior commercial emporium of Texas!"

"Blah blah blah," T.R. said, as another round of applause swept across the computer-generated crowd below. The simulation faded, the drones gained altitude, the glass bubbles undarkened. The swarm was climbing straight up, fast enough to make Saskia's ears pop. T.R. went on, "The gist of it is, there's a data point for y'all. Two hundred years ago. One million dollars. In today's money that's more like thirty million."

The boost in altitude was broadening the view to include much of Houston. Several miles east of Allen's Landing, the bayou spilled into a vast bay extending far to the south, where it was sealed off from the Gulf of Mexico by a barrier island. Much of that waterfront was dominated by industrial complexes and shipping facilities on a scale that would be impressive if you had never seen Rotterdam. Directly south was the downtown high-rise district, lodged in the center of a spiderweb of freeways. Any one of those freeways, traced outward, supported its own chain of sub-metropolises. "I'm not gonna insult y'all's intelligence by explaining compound interest," T.R. said. "The value of the real estate in greater Houston today is one point seven five trillion dollars. Big number. But it's just six percent annual interest compounded for two hundred years from that starting point. Now just stash that number in your short-term memory for a spell while we go look at some other unique exhibits."

The swarm had begun to shed altitude while tracking gradually northwest. They flew, at an altitude of maybe a hundred meters, up the incredibly wide freeway Saskia had seen from ground level yesterday. It was really a system of freeways at multiple levels, interlaced with ramps and crossed over, or under, by lesser freeways that would have been considered important in the Netherlands. It was bracketed between ground-level frontage roads, each many lanes wide and capable of carrying huge flows of traffic were they not partly underwater. "Interstates 10 and 45 combined is what you're seeing," T.R. said. "I-10 connects L.A. to Florida; 45 runs up to Dallas and connects to points north. In the other direction it's our connection to the Gulf." Presently those two roads parted ways and T.R. chose the left fork, veering onto a westerly course above 10, or the Katy Freeway as locals called it. "See, just looking at them on a map can't do these constructs the justice that they are due," he remarked, then surprised them all by swooping down and taking the swarm for a roller-coaster ride beneath the many lanes of the 10, which marched across sodden ground on reinforced concrete pillars. "And people talk about Rome and what they built," T.R. muttered.

"T.R., what do you mean 'the justice that they are due'?" Saskia asked.

"The size of it. The sheer amount of steel in the ground. The engineering. The *presence*, Your Majesty, the physical mass and reality of it. Every strand of rebar was drawn out in a steel mill. Where'd the heat come from? Burning things. The cement was produced in kilns, biggest things you ever seen. How do we keep the kilns hot? Burning things. We put the steel and the concrete together to make these things, these freeway interchanges, just so cars can run on 'em. How do we keep the cars moving? Burning things."

"Putting CO_2 into the atmosphere," Saskia said.

"Oh yes."

"It is not sustainable."

"With all due respect, Your Majesty, it is as sustainable, or as unsustainable, as your whole country. Later we can talk about how to sustain what matters to us. Now, hang on a sec, this calls for focus."

What he focused on next was slaloming his drone through the huge pillars he'd just been describing, cutting under ramps and looping through cloverleafs. Finally he pulled out into the open and swooped them up to an altitude where they could look down on the Katy Freeway skimming beneath them. It had become even wider, if such a thing were possible. "Twenty-six lanes," T.R. said, as if reading her mind.

Right now those lanes were only spattered with vehicles, as many businesses, schools, and activities had been shut down because of the hurricane. But Saskia noticed the bubble of her drone getting dark again, signaling another AR sequence about to start. "Not much going on today," T.R. remarked, "so I'm gonna take you on a little trip down memory lane. This is the same day of the year, same stretch of freeway, as it was back in 2019."

As he said it, the twenty-six lanes of the Katy Freeway suddenly filled up with cars and trucks, countless thousands of them, moving along at moderate speed—not quite a traffic jam, but still with enough brake lights igniting here and there to temper the flow. A motorcycle weaved through, going twice as fast as everyone else, using the bigger vehicles as pylons. The illusion was powerful even though the rendering had been simplified—every semi was a clone of a simple featureless semi model, and the same was true of cars, vans, pickups, and so on. But if anything that simplification made it easier to "read" the data. T.R. was showing them, in a way that was easy to grasp, exactly how much traffic had passed down this freeway at this time of day on this day of the year in 2019.

"2020," T.R. said, and the display shifted. This time traffic was sparser, and moving faster. "The first pandemic. Now, 2021." Another shift. More traffic moving more slowly—there was a traffic jam. "2022." It sped up. "2023. 2024." The lanes emptied out. "That was a hurricane year, just like this one. 2025. You'll notice a change taking hold," T.R. said, as the years ticked upward, "as self-driving cars take over. In heavy traffic, they drive closer together, almost like they join together into a train. So we can fit more vehicles onto the same stretch of pavement and those vehicles are all going faster—much greater throughput! Here, I'll flip between 2019 and 2029 and that'll make it easy to see."

He did so, and it was. The flow depicted in 2019 was gappy and spasmodic. Ten years later the cars were moving the way everyone was accustomed to nowadays, following one another closely, adapting smoothly to lane changes and merges. Saskia had lived through that transformation and was aware that it had happened but had never seen it demonstrated so vividly.

"So just when the Greens might be fixing to dance on the grave of the automobile, software crams twice as many of the little buggers onto the roads, makes the commute safer and easier for everyone. Guess what? People buy more cars! Burn more fuel. T.R. Mick's makes more money, builds more mobility centers on all the new highways getting laid down to carry all those cars."

The virtual display faded, the real world brightened. This whole time, the swarm had been humming eastward above the centerline of the Katy Freeway fast enough to overtake and pass the speediest vehicles. And yet, for all the distance they had covered, nothing had changed. The more Houston they put behind them, the more just rolled up over the western horizon to replace it. Like an infinite conveyor belt of mega-city.

"*What kind of money we talking?* That's the question my daddy and his daddy always used to ask, looking at an oil field, trying to work out how much to pay, how much to invest. What kind of money we talking?"

They'd passed over an interchange the size of central Amsterdam, where the Katy crossed one of the inner, older ring roads. Now they were looking several miles out toward another, much newer and larger interchange. Saskia began to see features she had noticed lately on maps: the tall corporate-campus buildings of Energy Corridor, and the two large regions shown on maps as bodies of water. On satellite imagery they looked like forested parks. Today they actually did look like reservoirs, albeit very untidy ones. Instead of placid open water their surfaces were grubby with trees, and instead of neatly staying within bounds they had burst their levees and invaded the suburban developments that had ill-advisedly been constructed on surrounding land.

"The maps lie," T.R. said, as they slowed, banking rightward off the freeway and approaching one of those reservoirs. "I'll show you what the maps have to say about what we're looking at right here."

Once again the AR system did its thing, this time by superimposing a plain old Google Map on the landscape. This was the bare-bones version, like something from the first decade of the twenty-first century. No satellite imagery, no traffic data, no overlays of any kind. Just roads in white, dry land in beige, and bodies of water in light blue. "Looks pretty tidy, don't it?" T.R. scoffed. "Who makes these things? Anyone who lives down there knows that ain't the real picture. Here's the real picture."

The map now began to fluctuate in a way that at first was visually jarring and difficult to follow. But as time went by Saskia understood that this was a collage that someone had assembled from aerial imagery. It was a mixture of satellite and drone photography showing the "reservoir" and its environs as they had actually looked over the last few decades. Early on, the coverage was spotty—they only had images at intervals of weeks or months, so the change from one to the next was jarring—but soon enough (as years went by and satellite coverage became ubiquitous) it smoothed out to the point where you could watch it like a movie. And what the movie showed was the reservoir throbbing like a living thing, an organic blob under a biologist's microscope. Sometimes it shrank to nothing and all you saw was trees. But then in the aftermath of a heavy rain it would form puddles in the low places that would grow explosively over a few hours or days to fill the neat boundaries circumscribed by the levees. Every so often it would break out and become an even larger body of water with houses projecting from its surface. As years went by, some of those houses disappeared. T.R. wanted them to notice that. He led the swarm toward the edge of one such neighborhood and let them see how a swath of homes had been lost to the floodwaters of Hurricane Harvey. "A hundred and twenty-five billion," T.R. said. "That was the price tag for Harvey. Second only to Katrina, which was a hundred and sixty-one. So *that's* what kind of money we're talking. Damages on the order of one or two hundred billion, inflicted on this city suddenly and at unpredictable times."

He ran the simulation forward over a couple of decades, then back, then forward again. Saskia sensed he must have his finger on a scroll bar in some UI, racking it up and down across the years. This made obvious something that might have gone unnoticed if they'd watched it more slowly, which was that the neighborhood was moving vertically upward—actually gaining altitude, here and there, in fits and starts. More precisely, the level of the ground itself stayed the same but the houses were rising into the air, new foundations being slipped under them. "We see the rise of the house-jacking industry," T.R. remarked. "Here are its fruits."

And he shut off the AR visuals and took the flock on a slow flyby of a suburban street that was on the front line of the struggle against rising water. There were a number of vacant lots, currently sporting brown puddles of floodwater shaped like the floor plans of houses that had once stood there. All the houses that hadn't been torn down were now standing proud of the water. Some were on high foundation walls of reinforced concrete, enclosing garages or storage space, currently filled with water but, it could be guessed, easy to hose out and dehumidify when the waters receded. Others—and these looked newer and nicer—stood above the water on reinforced concrete stilts, connected to the ground by ramps or stairs of welded aluminum.

"You can just *imagine* how expensive this is," T.R. remarked, pausing the swarm for a moment so that they could look at a house that had been caught in the middle of the house-jacking process when the current round of flooding had struck. The contractors had left it high and dry on stacks of crisscrossed railroad ties and evacuated their equipment. An open skiff was bumping against its front porch on the end of a rope. A man came to the window of an upper bedroom, drawn by the noise of the drone swarm, and peered back at them. He was an ordinary-looking man in his fifties, shirtless in the heat, a strap angling across his pudgy torso from a long weapon slung across his back.

"Screwed" was T.R.'s verdict, "because thirty years ago, before Harvey, he bought a nice home here in this nice new development, and it all seemed like a great idea." He took the swarm higher, effectively zooming out to remind them of just how many houses and neighborhoods were going through the same transition. "He did not understand—none of these people did—that this is *stochastic* land on the edge of a *stochastic* reservoir. They didn't understand it because those are statistical concepts. People can't think statistically. People are hardwired to think in terms of narratives. This guy's narrative was: the little missus and I want to settle down and raise a family, here's a house we like in a neighborhood full of folks like us, they can't all be wrong, let's take out a thirty-year mortgage on this thing. And now he's probably taking out a reverse mortgage or a HELOC to pay the house-jackers so he can have a prayer of being able to sell the thing. Multiply his story times all the houses you can see from here and you get an idea of what kind of money we're talking. Now, we gotta recharge."

As he had been delivering this peroration he had guided the swarm north and west and increased their speed. Saskia glanced at a gauge on her drone's panel that showed battery charge; it had turned yellow as it dropped to about one-third. She opened a private voice channel to Alastair. "Stochastic?" she asked. "I vaguely know this word but it is important in the mentality of T.R."

"From a Greek root meaning to guess at something," Alastair

said. "In maths, it just means anything that can't be calculated or positively known but that you instead have to approach statistically, probabilistically."

"Got it. Right up your alley then."

"Indeed. See you soon?"

"Looks that way."

"It's quite a spread, as they say."

Their destination, which they reached some quarter of an hour later, was a T.R. Mick's mobility center in a suburb that seemed to be above flood level for the most part. Its vast parking lots were splotched with puddles, but they were shallow. Most of the parking acreage was under hard roofs or pitched awnings, which Saskia had come to understand was a necessity in Texas; only a desperate person would park a vehicle in direct sunlight here. The roofs were tiled with photovoltaics, presumably helping feed the electric vehicle charging stations that were interspersed with gasoline and diesel pumps along the complex's splayed arms.

One of those arms, in its entirety, had been cordoned off for the private use of T.R. and his drone swarm. Buses—the very largest and newest kind of gleaming inter-city double-decker behemoths—had been parked in queues, nose to tail, to either side, apparently for no purpose other than to form temporary walls. Drivers sat in them, comfortable in the A/C, and security personnel in earthsuits paced to and fro on their roofs.

Within that cordon Saskia could see a dozen or so black SUVs that had been used to transport support staff to the location while she and the other VIPs had enjoyed the drone ride. Saskia's drone touched down in the open and she learned that its arms could be folded back so that it was small enough to roll into a parking space of the dimensions considered normal in Texas. In that configuration the drone found its way into a shaded stall next to an electric vehicle charger. A mechanical cobra reared up and sank its copper fangs into the drone's flank. The instrument panel announced that it was now charging. Three men with large umbrellas converged and opened the hatch next to her. Saskia had seen the umbrellas before. Security personnel used them to shield VIPs from the prying eyes of camera drones and long-lens paparazzi. Below the fringe of one umbrella Saskia could see a pair of ankles and sensible shoes that she recognized as Amelia's. A few moments later the Queen of the Netherlands was safely inside the T.R. Mick's without her face having once been exposed to the all-seeing sky.

The plaza—the central hub of the mobility center—was the size of a shopping mall but with fewer internal partitions. Maybe airplane hangar was a better analogy. One zone seemed to be a convenience store where travelers could buy chips and jerky. There were toilets, hyped as being unbelievably large and surgically clean. An amusement arcade, pitched mostly at kids, and a toddlers' play area and an indoor dog walk and a ventilated aquarium for smokers and a lactation suite and an urgent care facility and, one had to assume, many other amenities that she didn't have the opportunity to see since a lot of highly efficient personnel were dead set on whisking her past all that and getting her to one of several peripheral lobes that served as restaurants. Of those there were several, including an actual taco truck parked inside the building and outlets for several well-known fast-food chains. Most of those, as one would expect, were for travelers who wanted to spend as little time as possible here. But in one corner was a thing that better approximated a real sit-down restaurant. It was a barbecue, Texas style, of course. It had long rows of plank picnic tables and a counter where customers would normally order and fetch their food on big metal trays. But for today's event it had been cordoned off and fancied up. One table in the middle had been covered with a white tablecloth and set with cutlery that was real, in the sense that it was not plastic. There were wineglasses and a simple, rustic floral arrangement.

But before they could get to it, they had to be welcomed. Saskia and the other VIPs from the drones—four in total, plus T.R.—were greeted just short of the special table by a burly man with a long salt-and-pepper beard and a bright orange turban. He was introduced by Victoria Schmidt as one Mohinder Singh, the proprietor of this T.R. Mick's franchise, as well as part owner of two others farther west along the I-10 corridor. Speaking—unexpectedly to Saskia—in a perfect Texas drawl, he thanked the Schmidts for the opportunity to show the meaning of hospitality to so many honored guests. He quickly introduced his wife, who had tied a T.R. Mick's apron over an ornate traditional kurta, and several children and extended family members who had apparently converged on the site as reinforcements for the big day. Most of them were in a sort of uniform consisting of black polo shirts blazoned with a relatively dignified variant of the T.R. Mick's logo. Though as a matter of course, all the young men wore that particular style of head covering that gathered the hair into a small bun poised above the forehead.

This was the first time Saskia had come anywhere near Robert Watts, the lord mayor, who yesterday evening had been indisposed. Standing at his side was his wife, Dr. Daia Kaur Chand, smartly but not flashily attired in pants and flats well adapted to a daylong program of clambering in and out of diverse vehicles. She had the accent you'd expect of one who had been awarded degrees from Oxford and Cambridge. But she astonished and delighted their hosts by greeting them in a language that Saskia had to presume was Punjabi. Mohinder and his family didn't have a Willem on staff to do advance research on everyone they were going to encounter over the course of a day and so it was a joyous surprise to them to discover that one of their guests shared their religion and spoke their language. Whether or not it was part of Daia's plan, this broke the ice and created an opening for Mohinder to usher the five VIPs to their special table, leaving in their wake the family all now clustered around Dr. Chand.

The surrounding tables had marginally less elaborate settings for an additional three dozen or so. Saskia spied Alastair and Willem bending over to scan place cards, looking for their assigned seats. A long row of picnic tables against one wall served as an informal mess for support personnel. Of these there were too many for Saskia to readily pick out hers, but during the few minutes of social hubbub before everyone sat down, Fenna emerged from that crowd and came over to inspect Saskia's face. This was Face Two, a minor variation on Face One, geared for serious business, somewhat higher maintenance. The timing was good in the sense that T.R. had become embroiled in conversation with Mark Furlong about some kind of abstruse financial derivative that she didn't care about. The kind of thing Alastair thought about for a living. And indeed Mark threw Alastair a significant look that caused him to walk over and join the conversation.

"More than good enough for a truck stop" was the verdict of Fenna. "I was worried. That glass bubble—the sun—" She was hitting Saskia with some powder, knocking down the glare on the shiny bits. Men around them politely averted their gaze. "Lipstick or—"

"Pointless, I'm about to guzzle wine and eat something called brisket."

Fenna crinkled her nose and nodded agreement. "Can you guess what the vegetarian option is?"

"Let me think . . . fake brisket?"

"Yeah, two kinds! Grown in a vat, or simulated from plants."

"Ladies and gentlemen, if we could get started!" T.R. hollered as he dinged a wineglass.

"Later?" Fenna asked.

Saskia nodded. "When I go to the toilet—before dessert probably."

Fenna nodded and turned to go. Then she turned back. "Can Jules come with me?"

"To West Texas?"

"Yeah."

"Let's talk about it later."

"Before we get to the main course I just wanted to get the paper-shoveling out of the way," T.R. hollered. He was standing up, directly across the table from Saskia, who like all the other guests was seated. A team of energetic, well-groomed minions were pushing a cart piled with many copies of a bound document about an inch thick. These they passed out to people like Alastair and Willem, who tended to leaf through them curiously before slipping them into briefcases. "It's the boring necessary shit, also available electronically of course. Due diligence and all that."

Last night in the hotel bar, Rufus had made an observation that had left the other members of the party nonplussed. On the television an American football game had been playing. For this was September and apparently it was the season for that. Accustomed to the more fluid rhythm of what Americans called soccer, Saskia was struck by the amount of high-value, on-camera time claimed by the officials, who seemed to stop the game every ten seconds to litigate what had just happened and to mete out punishments with arcane gesticulations. Gazing at one especially stern official, Rufus glanced over at T.R.—who was holding forth at the bar with Sylvester Lin—and remarked, "If you put a zebra shirt and a black cap on *him*, gave him a whistle, man, he'd fit right in." Whereupon he nodded back at the television. It was, like many of Rufus's offhand comments, a very peculiar thing to say. And yet now sitting five feet away from T.R. and watching him address the room, Saskia could absolutely not get out of her head the image of this man in a black-and-white-striped shirt blandly but firmly twanging out judgment on a sweltering gridiron.

"I'm sure everyone wants to dig in, and no one's asking him- or herself 'I wonder when T.R.'s gonna stand up and give a great big long boring speech?' and so I will just say welcome to our honored guests from the Netherlands"—he glanced at Saskia—"the Square Mile" (Robert Watts, its lord mayor); "Singapore" (Sylvester Lin, to Saskia's left); "and Venice" (Michiel, next to T.R.). "You are not all, but you—along with me and my friends in Houston—are enough. I'll explain later. Let's eat." And he sat down to light, uncertain applause.

"My Lord Mayor," Saskia said to the man on her right. "You'll have to forgive me, I didn't recognize you without the huge ridiculous hat!"

"Not wearing it is a most effective form of disguise, Your Majesty. Please address me as Bob."

"I have been going by Saskia lately."

He made the closest approximation of a courtly bow that was possible while sitting on the bench of a picnic table.

"I, like you, am trying to do this discreetly, and so I left the huge ridiculous hat at home with the golden mace and the other bits."

"Should have guessed it was you from all the SAS types hanging around."

"Are they that obvious?"

"It's the hair. Or lack thereof." She looked across the room to see Fenna closely evaluating a very fit young Englishman, every one of whose hairs was exactly three millimeters long. Fenna quickly arrived at the conclusion that, while not lacking in potential, he was no Jules.

"Not like your chap with the dreadlock-Mohawk. Not conspicuous at all, that one."

"Well, I hope word doesn't leak out."

"About the biggest gun in the world? That will be hard to keep secret."

"No, that you are dining with a royal."

"Oh, the aldermen will forgive me. You're not one of *those* lot from Westminster."

"What the *hell*," T.R. said, "are the two of you talking about?"

Bob stifled a smile and collected himself. "As you know, T.R., I am the 699th lord mayor of the City of London."

"The Square Mile. The financial district. Limey Wall Street."

"Just think of it as O.G. London—the bit that was enclosed by the Roman wall," Bob said. "We have always run the place as suits our purposes."

"Business, shipping, finance."

Bob nodded. "Now, some centuries after the Romans cleared out, grubby hillbillies with lots of sheep and sheep-based money—"

T.R. liked that. "Ha! Like our cattlemen."

"Yes, they caused a lot of trouble for us, and to make a long story short people got tired of it and drew up the Magna Carta. Which among other things says 'hands off the bit of England that's circumscribed by the Roman wall, we know how to run that, stay out!' The King of England may not even set foot in the Square Mile unless I invite him to do so."

"Good for you!" T.R. exclaimed, but then threw a nervous glance at Saskia. She smiled to indicate she was not offended.

"So this banter between me and Her Majesty is a joke that goes back at least to 1215."

"You and the British royals are natural adversaries," T.R. said.

"There is a cultural divide between us and the, er—"

"I believe 'grubby hillbillies' was your characterization of my cousins at Buckingham Palace," Queen Frederika put in.

"With sheep and swords," T.R. added.

"Yes," Bob said. "The divide is probably invisible to foreigners, who see us all as English people with similar accents, but it is real."

Conversation went on as brisket, ribs, and red wine were brought out. Saskia stole a glance at Michiel, who was bemused by the ribs. Was one expected to pick these up with one's bare hands and bite the meat off the bones like a savage? Fifteen hundred years after the first Venetians had fled into the Lagoon to found a new city, had it really come to this? He wisely postponed committing to any one course of action, picked up knife and fork, and went after a slice of brisket.

"Not a fascist, as far as we can tell" had been Amelia's verdict at breakfast. The security crew at home had pulled an all-nighter trying to figure out Michiel. "I mean, we can't read his mind. But if he has fringe political opinions, he has kept them to himself. Hasn't associated with such people."

"Who *does* he associate with?"

"Others like him?" Amelia threw her hands up.

"Meaning—?"

"Old Venetian families with inherited wealth."

"*Is* there such a group, really?" Saskia asked. "One imagines that they all just intermarried, over the centuries, with other rich people who *weren't* Venetians."

"Still gathering data," Amelia said. "I don't think it is a large group. Maybe a few traditionalists from some of the old noble houses. His great-uncle seems to be a connector of some importance."

"He did mention he had an aunt with him. Tell me more about this great-uncle of Michiel."

"Banker—which can mean practically anything. Connections to shipping. Philanthropist."

"What kind of philanthropy?"

"Mostly related to the preservation of Venetian cultural patrimony."

"Well . . . keeping Venice above sea level would probably be important to him, then."

"We should know more soon," Amelia said. "But you *could* just ask him. Worst case, if someone posts a photo of you talking to him, and he turns out to be a nutjob, you can honestly say that nothing in his background or past associations provided any hint."

"Okay. How about Sylvester? To begin with, the name."

Amelia deferred to Willem. "Stallone," he said.

"*What!?*"

"Chinese have been giving themselves Westernized handles for a long time," Willem said. "The old-school approach is to pick something very conventional like Tom or Joe. By the time our friend 'Sylvester' was of an age to be thinking about that, it had become hip to choose cooler and more distinctive names. Sylvester Stallone was enjoying a comeback then. Lin liked the sound of it."

"I wouldn't have marked him out as a forward-leaning hipster at any phase of his life."

"Other than that, he's quite the straight arrow," Willem said.

"They speak Fuzhounese to you."

"I mostly speak English back. I remember very little of that dialect. It's hard to keep it and Mandarin in your head at the same time."

"What about this guy Bo? The Chinese operative who tracked you down in Louisiana?"

"The Chinese seem to know what T.R. is planning," Willem said. "They are—I don't know—offended? quizzical? concerned? that they were not invited. They are tending to assume, from that, that T.R.'s plan might be bad for China. That T.R. knows as much. T.R. knows China will naturally be opposed to his plan—so why would he invite them?"

"Is that actually the case?" Saskia asked.

"That it's bad for China?"

"Yes. Has T.R.'s team done any computational modeling?"

"Have *we* done any?" Amelia asked.

"We don't even know what the plan really *is*," Willem pointed out. "Look. It's not a question of good or bad, for a continental power like China. If you're like us—or Venice, or London, or Singapore—you're a speck on the map, right up against the ocean, and all you care about is sea level. Anything that puts the brakes on sea level rise is good."

"And it's rising because of the ice caps," Alastair said, just to be clear.

"Indeed. So for us it is very simple: make the climate colder.

Same goes for Venice and everyone else T.R. has invited. But if you're anyone else, you have to be asking yourself what are the knock-on effects of that? How is climate in the interior going to be affected? Is there going to be enough rain? Or too much of it? Will we be able to grow enough rice? Will our hydroelectric projects be compromised?"

"And no one knows," Alastair said. "Yet."

"The Chinese seem to assume that T.R. knows. Based on what we've seen so far, though—" and here Willem broke off.

"T.R.'s just shooting from the hip," Saskia said, completing the thought.

"We'll know more in a few hours. Some kind of document is going to be handed out at lunch."

After lunch the entire cavalcade—drones in the air, cars and buses on the ground—doubled back eastward, angling south so that the skyscrapers of downtown Houston swung across the horizon on their left. The sky was brilliant blue, interrupted here and there with huge roiling buttresses of cloud. These were blinding white where the sun shone on them, but otherwise a shade of dark gray that, to Saskia the pilot, suggested they were burdened with more moisture than they could handle. They were crowned with wreaths of lightning. She watched one such formation grope blindly for the earth with a fuzzy gray pseudopod. From miles away it looked soft and slow. It was even decoratively framed in a brilliant rainbow. But yesterday on the drive in from Sugar Land they had been caught in one of these. She knew what was going on in there. All the cars caught in it went blind. Most slowed down, some stopped. Collisions happened that would not be visible until the squall had moved on.

For the most part the drone swarm kept well clear of those things, but as they closed in on their destination they had fewer options and found themselves boxed in. "What do you say we just sit this one out?" T.R. suggested over the voice channel in his easygoing drawl. All the drones were settling in for a landing in a vacant field. As fat drops began slamming into the glass domes, their arms retracted into the drone equivalent of a fetal position. A few moments later the storm smote them with a vertical blast of what seemed to be solid water. Part of Saskia wondered if there was enough air between the drops to sustain life; was it possible to drown standing up? The glass dome couldn't shed water fast enough and it seemed to pile up into a sludding mound, centimeters thick. This at least deadened the noise, which had drowned out everything. Only the subsonic shocks of thunder could penetrate it.

She actually enjoyed the perfect isolation for as long as it lasted, which was no more than thirty seconds. Then over the course of a minute or two the storm abated, and the sun came on full blast. The vacant field had become a rectangular lake spotted all over with wads of crushed vegetation. This being Texas, it was not planted with any crop, as would have been the case in the Netherlands. And this being Houston, it bore zero similarity to nearby parcels, which hosted activities as disparate as schools, strip malls, office blocks, residential subdivisions, and oil refineries. The drone's arms swung back out, the props spun up, and it rose into the air along with the rest of the swarm. "We have the Johnson Space Center to thank for that," T.R. said. "It's just a little old parcel of vacant land they're not using for anything just now. Probably never will, since it's only a couple of meters Above."

Saskia had now spent enough time around him to know that when he said "Above" or "Below" in that portentous and knowing tone of voice he meant "above sea level" or "below sea level." In it was a kind of droll sarcasm at the very idea that there was such a thing as sea level in any useful sense. He saw it all stochastically and wouldn't be caught dead speaking of sea level with a straight face.

Parking lots and office buildings were in view to the east. Beyond those was an industrial port zone that put her in mind of Rotterdam, with open water beyond that. She spied a familiar logo on several of the nearer buildings and realized it was all NASA property. The Houston of "Houston, we have a problem." A little more altitude gave her the perspective to delineate a border fence, guarded by gates where it was pierced by roads, as well as other kinds of defenses that had been heaped up to protect vulnerable parts of the complex from floodwater. But the swarm didn't go in that direction. Instead it followed an adjacent road to a commercial development that was as close to the Johnson Space Center as it could get without encroaching on government property. Logos on some of the buildings, and signs planted near street entrances, were suggestive of aerospace.

One of these buildings sported a five-story parking ramp with a flat roof. That was where the drones all came to rest, landing one at a time, each folding up and rolling out of the way to make room for the next. There were more big umbrellas and choreographed movements that conducted Saskia and the others into one of the adjoining office buildings. They were ushered through the doors and past a range of security checkpoints into the offices of White Label Industries LLC, whose logo was a featureless white rectangle.

In the course of her official duties, Saskia had endured hundreds of tech company tours. White Label Industries was the same as all the others: people sitting in chairs and typing. Some had made the switch to augmented-reality glasses, others—generally older— hewed to the ancient practice of walling themselves in with flat-panel monitors. They were all writing code or working on CAD models, not of anything spectacular but of bolts and brackets. Usually the queen had to feign interest, but T.R. seemed to know full well how boring this was. "I just wanted you to see that this exists. Everything you'll see in West Texas was designed out of here. We needed a lot of aerospace guys. This is where it's easiest to poach 'em. They're happy working on shit that's actually getting built, even if it ain't going to Mars with some fucking billionaire. We gotta terraform Earth before we get distracted by Mars is my philosophy."

Saskia saw nothing during her sweep through the place to contradict that. These guys *did* look happy. A little older, whiter, maler, and squarer than techies in Sunnyvale or Amsterdam. Calmly, even serenely focused on what they were doing.

A small bus, like an airport shuttle, was awaiting them in a loading dock that was otherwise crammed with cargo pallets bearing machine parts. None of those had the lightweight gracile look she associated with aerospace tech. Most of it was steel, and little of that was stainless.

Once they had taken seats, the roll-up door was opened and they pulled out onto a road that, over the course of the next few minutes, took them generally east, toward Trinity Bay—the lobe of the Gulf that served as Houston's port. They passed a NASA gate but did not turn into it. The various buildings of the Johnson Space Center glided by them and Saskia realized with mild, childlike disappointment that they weren't going there to ooh and aah at big old rockets. It simply wasn't T.R.'s way. Instead they cut across a belt of subdivisions, variously hunkered down behind dikes or jacked up on stilts or abandoned and rotting. Boat-borne squatters seemed to have colonized some of the latter.

They entered into that industrial zone she'd glimpsed earlier, which made her homesick as it reminded her so much of the new parts of Rotterdam, close to the sea, where the big refinery complexes were built to process the oil coming in from Norway. Here, of course, the oil would be coming from offshore rigs in the Gulf of Mexico. But the equipment looked the same. She even spied a Shell logo in the distance. But eventually they passed through a security gate blazoned with the name of an oil company that she never would have heard of were it not for the fact that Willem had done his homework and compiled a dossier on T.R., and Saskia had read it. The company in question was a small (by Texas petrochemical industry standards) firm that had been founded by T.R.'s grandfather and that still existed as an independent legal entity, though it hadn't been doing a lot of business in the last decade.

The gate gave way into a waterfront property that seemed forgotten compared to the larger complexes that hemmed it in. It had its share of industrial buildings, clad in rust-maculated galvanized steel, but by far its most prominent feature was a perfectly conical mound of brilliant yellow powder rising to the height of a ten-story building.

Her immediate thought, fanciful as it was, was that this must be some kind of immense, spectacular art project. This was partly because of its size and its geometrical perfection, but mostly because of its outrageous color: intense, pure, powerful yellow. She wished Fenna could be here to weigh in on this yellow and what made it different from other yellows. To a Dutchwoman, the obvious comparison was to daffodils. Not the paler color at the petals' tips but the deeper hue at the base. But if you held a daffodil up against this thing, the flower would look paler, more toward the green/blue end of the spectrum. This cone of stuff, this artificial dune, tipped slightly more toward the red-orange. But it wasn't dark. It almost glowed.

It was one of those things like a Great Pyramid or a Grand Canyon that you just had to walk toward, so everyone got out of the bus and did that. It was even bigger than it looked, and so it took a little while to reach the crisp edge where the slope of it dove into the ground. Saskia turned her head from side to side and estimated the size of it as comparable to a football field. The peak was something like thirty meters above her head.

She bent down and took a pinch of the yellow powder between her fingers. It was finer than table salt, less so than flour.

Frederika Mathilde Louisa Saskia was more than normally technical-minded by the standards of European royalty, and in the defense of her country she had put a career's worth of effort into studying climate change. She had read the word "sulfur" a million times in scientific papers and conference proceedings. She knew its atomic number, its atomic weight, and its symbol. She was accustomed to the fact that Brits spelled it with a "ph" and

Yanks with an "f," and she knew its cognomens such as brimstone. Yet in all that time she had rarely seen sulfur and never touched it. A school chemistry lab might have a teaspoon of sulfur in a labeled test tube, so that children could say they had once seen it. But that was a very different experience from standing at the base of this . . . this industrial art project. As a sort of childish experiment she stood facing it and tried to position her head so that sulfur was the only thing she could see. Every rod and cone in her retinas maxed out on "yellow." She brought a pinch of it close to her nose for a sniff.

"It don't stink," said T.R., who had drawn up alongside her. "This is pure enough that you're not gonna get that rotten egg smell too bad."

"It doesn't dissolve in the rain?"

"Nope, water runs right through it," T.R. said. He took a step back, extended his arms, and gave it the full Ozymandias. "Sulfur!" he proclaimed, in the same tone that a conquistador might have said "Gold!" "The stone that burns!" Then he added, "S!," which Saskia knew was an allusion to its symbol on the periodic table. "We so rarely see or touch an actual *element*, you know. Nitrogen and oxygen in the air? Those are diatomic *molecules* and not the element itself. Aluminum, sure—but that's always an alloy. Iron, sometimes—but usually steel, another alloy. Mercury in an old thermometer, maybe. Helium in a balloon. But here's the real deal, Your Majesty. Two hundred thousand tons of an *element*. About a year's supply, for our project."

Saskia had gotten over the sheer visual power of the thing and begun to wonder about practicalities. "Did all this come from our mutual investment?"

This hauled T.R. down out of his Ozymandian reverie. He gave her a sharp look that made her glad she wasn't sitting across the table from him in a boardroom. "You're talking about Brazos RoDuSh."

"Yes, I was reminded of it the other day."

"You're not an activist investor," he said, with a diagnostic air. Then he brightened. "You don't read the annual report!" He was just kidding around now.

"I'm afraid not."

"Well, Brazos RoDuSh has been out of the sulfur business since my granddad got kicked out of Cuba in the 1960s! It's all New Guinea copper and gold nowadays." He looked around theatrically as if he were about to let her in on a fascinating secret. "Speaking of which, your man Red told me about his friends. The Boskeys."

"Rufus?"

"Yeah. So I hired the Boskeys to make a little side trip, as long as they're helping folks out down south of Sugar Land. That's the old stomping grounds of Brazos Mining, you know!"

"The sulfur domes along the coast."

"Exactly! I asked 'em if they wouldn't mind swinging by a certain location, see if any of the old relics and souvenirs was bobbin' around in the floodwater."

"That seems . . . unlikely."

"Just kidding, it's all in a storage locker. And they got divers."

Others had begun to gravitate toward them. T.R. turned to face them and raised his voice. "By-product of oil refineries," he said, using the German-influenced pronunciation of "oil" common in Texas.

They began to stroll along the base of the pile. Other members of the group fell in with them. "Old oilmen like my granddad used to taste the stuff."

"*Taste!?*" Very rarely, Saskia felt unsure in her command of the English language. Maybe this was some colloquialism?

T.R. grinned and pantomimed sticking a finger down into something and then lifting it to his mouth. "Literally taste. If the oil was sweet, it was low-sulfur. *Sour* crude, on the other hand, needs extra refining to take the sulfur out, so it sells at a discount. There's a lot of sour in the Gulf, especially down Mexico way. Anyway, I been buyin' it up."

"No kidding!"

"Plenty more to be had in Canada. Tar sands oil is sow . . . ER!" He got a look on his face as if he had just tasted some and squinted up to the sharp peak of the sulfur cone. "This pile ain't getting any bigger. That's as high as that conveyor can reach." Following his gaze, Saskia was able to see the muzzle of a long industrial conveyor reaching out over the pile from a source blocked from view on the harbor side of the operation.

Like any other port, this one had an abundance of railroad tracks, with innumerable spur lines reaching out to individual terminals. One such ran behind the sulfur pile. On its back side, as they could now see, the geometric perfection of the cone had been marred by an end loader that was chewing away at it, gouging out sulfur near ground level, touching off avalanches higher up. The end loader trundled across broken pavement for a short distance and dumped the sulfur into a hopper at ground level. Angling up from that was a conveyor that carried a thick flume of yellow powder to a height where it spewed forth into an open-top hopper car. A queue of those stood along the track, already full and ready to roll. Only one of them wasn't full of sulfur, and at the rate the loader and conveyor were going, it soon would be. "Still just purely at a demonstration, proof-of-concept scale," T.R. remarked, apparently to preempt any possible objections along the lines of *this isn't stupendously vast enough, you need to think big!*

Saskia deemed it unlikely that anyone would actually lodge such a complaint. She knew her way around epic-scale geoengineering projects and colossal port facilities better than anyone on the planet. Even by Dutch standards, T.R. was definitely running an operation to be reckoned with.

Their perambulation had brought them to a folding table that had been set up in the open by T.R.'s staff. Above it was a pop-up canopy to protect them from whichever prevailed at the moment: merciless sun or drowning torrential rain. At the moment it happened to be the former. Plastic water bottles were passed out. The table supported a propane camp stove, some laboratory glassware, and a plastic bin containing an assortment of safety goggles. Waving off a diligent aide who wanted him to don protective eyewear, T.R. grabbed a glass beaker about the size of a coffee mug, walked over to the sulfur pile, and scooped up a sample of the yellow powder. Most of that he then dumped back out so that the beaker contained no more than a finger's width of S. Meanwhile an aide was lighting a burner on the stove. T.R. carried the beaker over and set it over the pale blue flame. In just a few moments the lower part of the sample, in contact with the glass, changed its appearance, becoming liquid and smooth. T.R. turned the heat to a lower setting and picked up a pistol-grip thermometer. He aimed this down into the beaker, pulled the trigger, looked at the digital display. He gave it a little stir with a glass rod.

Within a minute's time the entire sample had melted into a reddish-yellow fluid. T.R. let them see the reading on the thermometer. It was nothing impressive. "The point of all this is just that S has a very low melting point. You can melt it at a cookie-baking temp in your oven. Handling a fluid at that temp is easy. You don't need weird science lab shit, just plain old metal pipes from Home Depot and some insulation to keep it from freezing up." He picked up a pair of tongs and used it to lift the beaker off the flame. He took a few steps away from the sulfur pile and then dumped the yellow fluid out onto bare pavement, forming a little puddle. "And behold, it burns," he said. He had fished a cigar lighter—a finger-sized blowtorch—from his pocket. He flicked it on, bent down with a grunt, and touched its flame to the edge of the yellow puddle. It readily caught fire, not with an explosive *fwump* like petrol, but more like wax or oil. "It don't burn like *crazy*, mind you, but it totally burns. Steer clear of the smoke." He'd had the presence of mind to perform this little demonstration downwind of them, so the plume of vapor boiling off the flame was moving away.

"That 'smoke' would be sulfur dioxide," Saskia said.

"Yes, Your Majesty, and as I'm sure you know it loves to get together with water to make H_2SO_4."

"Sulfuric acid."

Bob shrugged. "So if there's more rain—?"

"Think lungs," T.R. suggested.

"There's available water in your lungs," Saskia explained, "so if you inhale sulfur dioxide, next thing you know you've got sulfuric acid in a place where you really don't want it."

Bob raised one eyebrow and nodded.

"So what have we established?" T.R. asked rhetorically. "T.R. owns a fuck ton of sulfur. Sulfur can easily be made into a liquid. Sulfur burns. Does that put y'all in mind of anything?"

He had begun leading them toward a rusty galvanized steel warehouse a few dozen meters away. Parked near it were a few newish-looking cars and pickup trucks. Saskia observed parking stickers for White Label Industries LLC, and sure enough the distinctive white-rectangle logo—just a blank sheet of printer paper—was taped to a door that led into the warehouse.

She was also noticing an abundance of orange wind socks, such as were commonly seen around airports. These people very much cared which way the wind was blowing.

The building was a lot more spruce inside than its exterior would lead one to expect. Of paramount importance to them, it was air-conditioned. For all purposes it was an extension of White Label headquarters a few miles away. This, however, had more in the way of safety gear and other real-world operational features.

They were ushered into a control room separated from the building's cargo bay by a wall of windows that seemed inordinately thick. In spite of that, they were each given full-face respirators and taught how to put them on when and if a certain alarm were to sound. The previous conversation about sulfuric acid in the lungs had left little to the imagination and so all of them paid due attention. In the meantime, on the other side of the glass, workers in white bunny suits and respirators were working on a system that, to the eyes of a layperson, consisted entirely of plumbing. At the end closest to the open bay door, basically outside the building, was the object that seemed to be the point of it all, tended to by the bunny-suited priesthood on the far side of the glass. But even this was just plumbing. It was a pipe on a stand, aimed out at the world.

"Your Majesty," T.R. said, "will know more than anyone else here—with the possible exception of the Right Honorable the Lord Mayor—about the V-1 buzz bomb."

"The Farting Fury!" Bob said with surprising relish. "My granddad used to talk about them. He saw—and heard—one pass over him in Kent."

Saskia knew the term at least as well as Bob. She was slower to respond, though, since she had been trained to think hard and choose her words carefully when any topic related to the Second World War came up in conversation. "One of Hitler's advanced superweapons. The Nazis launched some of them from my country. They had some kind of a special engine. A primitive jet."

"Pulse jet, it's called," T.R. said agreeably. "The pulsing style of operation is why Bob's pawpaw referred to it as the Farting Fury. Absolutely terrible design for anything other than our exact purposes."

Technicians here in the control room had been talking to the bunny suit wearers on the other side of the glass. These had been opening valves and checking gauges. On a signal, they all vacated the bay. Some kind of extremely well-organized procedure ensued, similar in its emotional arc to a rocket launch countdown. As such it dragged on for a few minutes. T.R. killed a little time by stepping up to the window and using a laser pointer to draw their attention to some details that might otherwise have been lost in the welter of pipes and cables. First was an ordinary white plastic five-gallon bucket, sitting on the floor, half full of sulfur. "Our high-tech S transportation modality. Totally human-powered,"

T.R. explained, with the deadpan style that Saskia was coming to recognize as a hallmark of his personality. Near it was a rolling steel staircase, currently positioned so that it ran up to a platform at about head height. There was a vertical glass tube maybe a hand span in diameter and an arm's length in height, mostly full of sulfur. Its top was open, presumably so that more sulfur could be dumped in from the bucket. Its bottom was swallowed in a stainless-steel fitting. "Fuel tank." From there, things got hard to follow until T.R.'s laser dot tracked down the length of a pipe—or at least one could assume the existence of a pipe—jacketed in a tubular blanket of insulation and helpfully labeled S (MOLTEN) WARNING HOT. This led directly to the big pipe aimed out the door. "Fuel line," T.R. explained. "Liquid sulfur's flowing down it right now." The laser dot terminated its journey on the device. "To the combustion chamber."

A few sporadic thuds reached their ears, and their rib cages, through the glass, each accompanied by a burst of flame and a puff of smoke from the end of the pipe that was aimed out at Texas. After some false starts this settled into a steady rhythm. The tube looked like a fat machine gun emitting a series of muzzle flashes. Even through the glass, it was impressively loud. From miles away, such a sound could perhaps be likened to a long drawn-out fart.

The test ran for no more than fifteen seconds, then segued into a shutdown procedure that, if anything, was more elaborate than the startup. T.R., as close as he ever came to being sheepish, said, "We don't like to run it very long, 'cause of the neighbors and the EPA."

"Oh, I'm sure you can get away with murder in a place like this!" said Michiel.

"People do, in fact," T.R. said.

"To connect the dots, if I may," said Sylvester, "your engineers—drawn from the aerospace complex—have invented an engine—"

"The world's shittiest by any metric you care to apply," T.R. hastened to make clear.

"That uses sulfur—in molten form—as its fuel."

"Yes."

"And produces sulfur dioxide as its exhaust."

"That follows."

"Interesting! What's next, then?"

"More dots. More connecting. First, a choo-choo ride."

The property, though small by the standards of refinery complexes, was large enough that another short bus ride was in order. That put the huge sulfur cone and the farting fury behind them. They zigzagged around some other buildings and passed beneath cranes and conveyors used to load and unload trains. Then they emerged into an open logistics depot. Several parallel railroad tracks ran across it, connecting the waterfront to points inland. On the landward side those were funneled together into a single track. In other words, it was, among other things, a switching yard where trains could be assembled out of shorter strings of cars. The cars visible on the nearest tracks were, as one would expect, freight: mostly containers on flatbeds, some tarp-covered hoppers that presumably contained sulfur. The bus, moving gingerly over rough ground, cut behind these, bringing into view additional tracks. "Before you see what you are about to see and we part company for a couple of hours," T.R. said, "I want it understood that I don't, personally, give a shit about trains at all. I'm not gonna corner you and talk your ear off about trains. I'm not that guy. But I *do know* that guy. Long story. Old buddy. Too much money. Crazy about this stuff. Collects these things. Stores 'em on his property, fixes 'em up. Lended 'em to me. Likes to see 'em used. 'Exercised' he calls it. Good for the bearings or something. Voilà. Enjoy."

On one of the parallel tracks, blocked from view to either side by strings of freight cars on adjoining lines, sat three consecutive railway carriages of a type that, to this point in her life, Saskia had only seen in museums of transportation.

In Amsterdam's central train station, there was a special waiting room, technically for the use of Saskia or whoever was currently king or queen, but never actually used because it was so outrageously non-norMAL. It was where the kings of the *Belle Époque* would cool their heels waiting for their private trains. From there, when all was ready, they would be ushered into carriages that probably resembled the ones Saskia and the others were looking at now. They were the Victorian equivalent of today's private bizjets. In the American version, they were not for hereditary royalty but for business magnates, thundering to and fro over the Gilded Age rail network with their families and support staff, smoking cigars and dashing off telegrams as Kansas or Appalachia glided by outside the windows.

As usual, there were helpers, trim and polite, wired up with earplugs. Each of the VIP guests was escorted to a different private suite on one of these cars, encouraged to wander, and reminded that the cars might, without warning, go into movement at any time. After freshening up, Saskia strolled up and down the length of this three-car string, gawking like an unabashed railway-buff tourist. Clearly each of these cars had a long and interesting backstory. But circumstantial evidence told her that one had been owned by a St. Louis beer baron of German ancestry. Another seemed to have been the property of a resource extraction magnate from the mountain West: mostly timber, some mining. The last was fancier, but harder to suss out. She guessed someone from New York, in finance. She mentally dubbed them the Beer Car, the Tree Car, and the Money Car. Saskia's lodging was at the aft end of the Money Car and consisted of a bedchamber with en suite washroom complete with claw-footed cast-iron bathtub. A narrow passageway ran along one side of it. On the other side, big windows provided a view out of the left side of the train.

As warned, the cars had gone into motion almost as soon as the guests had stepped up into them, and since then had never stopped for long. It was a back-and-forth, inconclusive shuffling. If Saskia had been a train buff, she would have followed the details avidly. This string of three antique carriages was being made part of a longer train consisting mostly of freight cars. The view out the window became longer as neighboring tracks were cleared. The sulfur pile came back into view in the distance. But eventually the train pulled out for good and began to traverse the largely industrial landscape that ran west along Buffalo Bayou from Trinity Bay (which they had now put behind them) toward downtown Houston and the vastness of Texas beyond.

In the midst of Houston's industrial belt, only a few minutes' transit time from the sulfur pile, the train slowed and eased onto a side track in a larger switching yard. Awaiting them, pre-assembled, was a string of half a dozen Amtrak passenger coaches, plus a dining car. The fleet of buses and SUVs, which Saskia had last seen at the T.R. Mick's, had ended up here. She had to exit her suite and cross to the right side of the Money Car to see it. But looking into the windows of those coaches as they glided by, she could see faces she recognized, including some of her own staff.

Having passed all the Amtrak cars, the train slowed, stopped, reversed direction onto the side track, and backed up until it thudded into them. Saskia by now had abandoned all pretense of not finding it fascinating, and opened windows on both sides of the Money Car so that she could stick her head out and assemble a mental picture of what was going on. The Money Car had until now been the last in the train. Her compartment was in its rear. Another suite at its forward end appeared to house the lord mayor. Forward of that was the Tree Car, home to Sylvester and Michiel, and forward of that was the Beer Car, which was T.R.'s temporary residence as well as serving as a private saloon well stocked with, unsurprisingly, beer. Everything forward of the Beer Car, all the way to the locomotives, was freight: sulfur hoppers, container carriers, and the odd tank car.

What now happened was that the string of Amtrak coaches was coupled to the end of the Money Car, immediately to the rear of

Saskia's compartment. The corridor that ran along one side of her bedchamber was terminated by a door—of polished wood, naturally, with gleaming brass fittings—with a window in it, through which she watched as the train eased together and finally connected with a jolting thud. On the other side of the gap she could see Amelia's face framed in the corresponding window. They had been in touch electronically the entire day, of course, but one of Amelia's training and disposition could never quite relax until she had eyes on the person she was charged with looking after. So the relief on her face was evident even across the gap.

Making all the connections between the cars took another few minutes, but then the train pulled out onto the main line and began to pick up speed toward downtown Houston. The doors opened. Amelia and Fenna came forward, followed by a porter carrying Saskia's baggage. Willem took care of stashing it in Saskia's compartment while Fenna set up the apparatus pertaining to her trade on the tiny makeup table in the corner. Alastair and Rufus, the Odd Couple, entered and loitered awkwardly until Saskia invited them to make themselves at home in the middle part of the Money Car, which was a sort of parlor. Terribly important Englishmen stormed past them to get after Bob. A waiter emerged and took drink orders. Saskia excused herself and lay down on her bed for a nap. When she woke up, the fiery sun had reddened and cooled. She opened her curtain to behold the hill country of Texas, glowing in the flat red light of the setting sun.

CHANDIGARH

aks took the move from Amritsar to Chandigarh as an opportunity to do a little more traveling around the Land of Five Rivers. He had actually seen very little of it so far. It was at this point that the social network—no, the society—that he'd become a part of, just by sticking with it, humping the langar's lentils and digging the akhara's dirt, came into its own and he saw its full power and virtue. Sikhs were well represented among truck drivers. Pick a road out of town and everyone knew someone who would be driving a truck or a bus or even a motorbike in that direction soon. And if not soon enough, there was free food at the langar and maybe some pointers on where to find a place to sleep. So once he had established a basic fund of trust and cred, grown his beard out, learned how to dress and how to talk, then, just by virtue of being a likely young man traveling on his own he was able to move around the Punjab, if not always quickly, then at least cheaply. In a way, the less he spent, the easier it got, for people were more willing to help out a scrappy wanderer sleeping rough than they were a Canadian tourist with a fat wallet.

His objective was to go and visit all five of the eponymous rivers: from north to south, the Jhelum, the Chenab, the Ravi, the Beas, and the Sutlej. Eventually all of them flowed into the Indus, the great river that gave India its name.

He was under no particular compulsion to do this. It wasn't a ritual pilgrimage or anything like that. It just appealed somehow to his innate sense of completeness. He'd be able to say that he had really seen the Punjab.

Amritsar was right between the Ravi and the Beas, so those were easy day trips. He went to the site on the western bank of the Beas where Alexander the Great had thrown in the towel, abandoned all hope of adding Pentapotamia to his empire, and turned back toward far Macedonia with his exhausted and disgruntled troops.

The Ravi coincided, along part of its course, with the India-Pakistan border, cutting the Punjab in half—an amputation that had led to a great deal of trouble and explained in a roundabout way why Laks's family were running gas stations in Canada. Since the fateful year of 1947 the river had evinced a total lack of respect for the boundary line solemnly drawn on maps, and strayed to either side of it as floods pushed it out of its banks. By choosing a meander that looped into India, Laks was able to visit the Ravi, wade in its water, and evaluate fish habitats without having to go through the rigamarole of crossing into Pakistan. In the minds of his people, what lay on the other side was West Punjab. He'd have liked to visit it. But he had now overstayed his six-month tourist visa. He was in India illegally. He could cross over into Pakistan, but not come back in. And being stuck in Pakistan was not on his bucket list.

The Chenab and the Jhelum ran decisively through Pakistan in their middle courses. Farther north, though, closer to their mountain wellsprings, they could be reached in Kashmir. So that leg of the trip was the first time Laks had seen mountains since coming to India.

He found that he had missed mountains. In Canada they just plunged straight down into the ocean. At night in Vancouver you could see skeins of light suspended in midair high above street ends: ski areas just outside of town, illuminated for nocturnal customers. He had gone up there and snowboarded with his friends. He missed that dimensionality to the landscape.

He got into a spot of trouble when, on his way back south, he encountered a roadblock where Indian authorities were checking IDs. It all had to do with the border dispute between Pakistan and India. So he had to bail out of the truck he was riding in—no feat at all, since it was stopped dead in a five-mile-long traffic jam, and the driver had switched off the engine—and backtrack on foot.

Eventually he hitchhiked his way into the neighboring province of Himachal Pradesh and then found his way back down into East Punjab just by hiking across the border in a mountainous area where there could be no roadblocks, since there were no roads. That was his first encounter with Indian wilderness, which— obvious as it might sound—was just that. No one lived there. The landscape was natural. When he did happen upon a road, he hitchhiked back down into the lowlands, feeling he'd made a con- nection with the ancient gurus. For many had been the occasions when early Sikh leaders had been forced by martial setbacks to withdraw into these hills and lie low for months or years.

The Sutlej, by contrast, meandered across flat territory, abso- lute Breadbasket land, not as spectacular as Kashmir until you got your head around the sheer amount of food being produced in the green fields that the river watered. Then it was as impressive in its way as mountains. Apparently a lot of other people down through the centuries had shared the same view, for the area he happened to visit, around Ferozpur, was speckled with battle memorials.

He ended up in Chandigarh, which was a very different place from Amritsar. Both were cities of a little more than a million souls, but from that point the resemblances tapered off in a hurry. Chandigarh was a new, planned city that had been plunked down by government mandate post-1947, whereas Amritsar was so old that people there claimed, with apparent sincerity, that it had been founded by gods. While there were definitely a lot of Sikhs in Chandigarh, they were outnumbered six to one by Hindus.

Not that this statistic really mattered in Laks's daily life once he had found a rooming house and a gurdwara, both close enough to his new akhara that running between them was often faster than dealing with vehicles. Like everything else here, the akhara was new. They wrestled on foam mats and used weight machines. There were showers. Joris and gadas were certainly available for those who were hip to them. In the adjacent sports complex, laid out by the city's benevolent planners, were green fields where training could happen in the open. The mission of this akhara seemed a little different; they were somewhat self-consciously making an effort to inculcate youngsters in traditional ways, whereas the guys at the akhara in Amritsar were just doing it because they had always done it. Those guys didn't have a mission statement. People showed up, or they didn't. Here, though, the kids were *sent*. A lot of them were delivered to the place along Chandigarh's modern, rationally designed street plan, by the local equivalent of soccer moms or even by paid drivers. The akhara was providing a service. Oh, not in some shitty hucksterish way. Not at all. These guys couldn't have been more pure, more sincere. It was just a little different.

Anyway, they didn't really know what to do with Laks either. It didn't help that he was, to be honest, practicing a somewhat impure form of the art. It turned out that there were a lot of other people in the world besides Punjabis who knew a thing or two about fighting with the ancient and ubiquitous weapon known as the stick. Growing up in Richmond he'd had access to schools of Filipino and Malaysian martial arts up in Vancouver as well as down across the border in Seattle. So mixed in with his traditional gatka moves—which he knew how to do very well—were foreign bits. Improvements or impurities depending on your point of view. Styles of movement that looked inscrutable, or just wrong, in the akhara.

The characteristic movements of gatka were gracile. Hopping and twirling that sometimes caused Westerners to misconstrue it as mere sword dance—an artistic endeavor that might have been derived from martial roots but was now far removed from anything that would work in practice. In fact those movements all made perfect martial sense when you were on uneven ground, outnumbered, and engulfed in murderous opponents—which in a broader Sikh history context was pretty much all the time. Not just Alexander's Macedonians but Persians, Afghans, Pathans, Baluchis, Mughals, Gurkhas, Rajputs, Marathas, and British at one time or another had attempted to seize control of the Breadbasket. The list of tortures used to put prisoners of war to death was long and incredibly imaginative. So constantly moving around to see who was coming up behind you—considered a bad idea in some martial arts—made sense here.

All well and good. But what Laks had added was some additional biomechanics that had to do with landing powerful blows without big movements and obvious windups. Better suited, perhaps, for moments when the wild melee had resolved to one-on-one combat. Any martial artist of any size could amplify what physical power nature had given them by using these techniques. But when Laks had used them at full power against practice targets in Amritsar, the senior guys at the akhara had got a certain look on their faces that he had enjoyed seeing at the time, but that in retrospect was them making up their minds that the big weird Canadian had to leave.

This new akhara was a legit business. They had a logo. Because of the visa situation, they could not employ him in any capacity. Nor would it really have been ethical for Laks to accept employment of any sort. Even unloading sacks of potatoes at a langar could be seen as taking work away from people who needed it more than he did. To this was now added the possibility of landing an employer in hot water legally. The bracelet that Laks wore on his wrist was a constant reminder to do no wrong with his strong right arm, or any other part of his body for that matter. His uncle Dharmender had once explicitly stated—just in case this point had eluded him—that this included his penis. So far, he had remained chaste while in India, both because of that memorable conversation (it had happened while Uncle Dharmender was changing the brake pads in a Subaru) and because getting involved with a local girl could have incalculable consequences that were likely to be all or mostly bad.

So Laks was allowed to hang around and work out at the akhara, but he was a man apart except when he was training with

Ranjit, that being the "old" (he was maybe fifty-five) stick master who had agreed to work with him. They would go off to an out-of-the-way part of the adjoining field and train.

There was nothing precisely wrong with that, but it was anti-climactic in the sense that Ranjit told Laks after a couple of weeks that he had no special advanced techniques to teach him that would turn Laks into some exalted master. It was stick fighting. There wasn't that much to say about it. "It's like running," he said. "You can learn a few tricks that will make you run faster but basically you just have to run." Laks, Ranjit said, already knew enough that he could fly home and hang out a shingle in Richmond, or any other place with a large Sikh population, and operate a totally legitimate school. Was that what he wanted? Was that why he had come all this way? Done.

In fact, that idea had never crossed Laks's mind, and so he had to think about it. But perhaps it was already obvious to Ranjit, from the look on Laks's face, that hanging out a shingle in Canada was not the objective here.

Ranjit then got a clouded look on his face that Laks thought he had seen once or twice before in Amritsar. He could guess what it was.

Laks was a Canadian who had made the choice to leave Vancouver's affluence behind and return to the Punjab and get in touch with his roots. Fine. He'd overstayed his visa. A little troubling, but it could be overlooked as youthful enthusiasm. Now he had failed to rise to the bait of going home in triumph and becoming a suburban martial arts instructor. What, then, did this stranger really want?

Decades ago, Vancouver had been the base of operations of a cell of Sikh separatists who had wanted to pull West and East Punjab out of Pakistan and India and form an independent country called Khalistan. Long before Laks had been born, they had perfected a time bomb in the wilderness outside the city and then used it to blow up a 747 full of passengers. Since then the group had gone into eclipse as its support base in the community (to the extent that that even existed) had dried up and it had been hammered by anti-terrorist authorities in India and many other countries. The Russians had used a disinformation scheme to trick the Indian government into believing that the Sikhs were getting support from Pakistan and the CIA. Those had been bad times.

So that kind of extremism was less of a concern these days. It was just common sense really. Laks could remember a conversation with Uncle Dharmender in a gas station back office outside of Kamloops, where the geopolitics of it all had been summed up for Laks's edification using cans of oil and a chessboard. "Us," Uncle Dharmender had said, pulling a chess piece—it was a white rook—out of the box and setting it down in the middle of the board. Then, next to it, he had slammed down a quart can of 10W-40. "India. Second-largest country in the world. Nuclear bombs and space rockets." He had then slammed down a gallon of anti-freeze. "China. Biggest country. H-bombs." Then another oil can, bracketing the forlorn rook in an equilateral triangle. "You know who. Fifth largest. Plutonium and crazy men." He had looked up at Laks. "What do you think the future of this"—he had plucked out the rook and held it up—"looks like as a so-called independent nation?"

So being a separatist insurgent couldn't have been further from Laks's mind. But Ranjit was within his rights to be worried about it. For all he knew Laks might be one such. Maybe a forerunner of some new wackazoid splinter group that no one here had ever heard of. Or, perhaps worse, and more plausibly, some kind of undercover agent trolling through the community trying to gull people into admitting that they would support such activities. So Laks had to explain himself in a hurry. And it caused him to blurt something out that he'd barely realized was on his mind until now: "In all honesty, Ranjit, my future is most likely to join the military, and there to use my abilities in service of my nation." Then, for the avoidance of doubt, he specified, "Canada."

Ranjit nodded. "They allow you to have the Five Ks." He was referring to the bracelet, turban, and other religious emblems carried on the person by observant Sikhs.

"Yes. I had looked into applying for Indian citizenship, but—"

Ranjit was already shaking his head. As they both knew, dual citizenship was not allowed by India. He'd have to turn in the Canadian passport. Ranjit said, "If your goal is to serve with honor as a saint-soldier defending a country that has a lot of our brothers and sisters within its borders, do it in Canada."

He was styling this as a savvy choice for Laks, which it undoubtedly was. But once again Laks was getting that signal— polite but firm—that he should move on. And when he nodded in agreement, Ranjit's misgivings about him seemed to melt away. "I admire your choice and I think you will serve with honor and do us proud," he said. "Now, in what way may I help you realize this noble goal?"

They talked it through. If Laks actually wanted to get any better at stick fighting than he already was, the only way to do it was to actually participate in stick fights and test and hone his skills in something like real combat, where the penalty for putting your hand in harm's way was not a reprimand from the teacher, or a light rap on the knuckles, but a broken finger. To a degree you could get that in the sportified version of gatka, where contestants in modern protective gear competed on polished gymnasium floors under the eye of whistle-blowing referees. There was nothing wrong in doing that. A few victories, a trophy maybe, could burnish his credentials.

But he didn't need credentials. And it bore the same relation to the actual combat art as Olympic foil fencing did to medieval longsword combat.

And here was where Laks was waiting for the other shoe to drop: the moment when Ranjit would lean in close and, in a low voice, clue him in to the existence of a secret underground network of hard-core gatka fighters doing it for real, with real sticks and real consequences. But that was just Laks having spent too many lonely hours watching cheesy martial arts videos.

Instead Ranjit said, "Virtually no one does real full-contact gatka, and the ones that do—or that boast of it anyway—wouldn't likely do it with you, because they would be afraid for their lives. Look, it's just not ethical. If I knew people who did it, I would tell you to avoid them. I wouldn't send you to them." Ranjit seemed a bit exasperated. "You're not going to find that in the Punjab. At least, I hope not! The only people within a thousand miles doing that sort of thing are those lunatics."

He said the last two words in English. And then he nodded. The presence of a big orange turban on his head conferred additional gravity and vehemence to this slight gesture.

Laks turned in the direction indicated and saw—what?

- An artificial turf field where some boys were playing cricket. Almost certainly these were not the lunatics to which Ranjit was alluding.
- Beyond that, a busy street, lots of traffic in the customary slapstick Indian style, but nothing in particular happening— certainly no knock-down, drag-out stick fights.
- On the other side of the road, the typical Indian cityscape of five-story buildings. A higher modern skyline in the distance. This eventually faded into a low brown haze layer, which was there all the time.

But on this day the smog wasn't as bad as usual and so his gaze was suddenly captured by an impossibly high rampart of perfectly white mountains in the great distance, erupting out of the haze like clean teeth from tobacco-stained gums. Making the best the Canadian Rockies had to offer look miserable and tiny by comparison.

"Are you talking about the Himalayan fucking Mountains?"

Laks asked. The profanity was unusual. They were amazing mountains. But very definitely not the Punjab.

Ranjit seemed surprised that Laks didn't know. "You need to educate yourself," he said, "about what goes on up at the Line of Actual Control." He seemed almost to bite his tongue. "Please don't tell any of your loved ones that I suggested it."

Alastair and Rufus had staked out tables on opposite sides of the Money Car's center aisle and were just taking it easy, gazing out the windows. Of the two, Alastair was drinking and seemed in a more sociable mood. Saskia sat down across from him.

"This might sound odd," Alastair said, gazing quizzically into his Laphroaig, "but what is striking to me about all this is how cheap it is."

"Yes," Saskia answered, "that is a very odd thing for you to say, Alastair."

"Did you see the sulfur pile?"

"Saw it, touched it, watched T.R. set fire to it. Well, part of it anyway. How did you know about it?"

Alastair peered at her. "You can see it from space."

Saskia laughed. "That doesn't impress me; you can read license plates from space!"

"Well, boat tours on Trinity Bay pass by it so that tourists can take selfies."

"Okay, okay."

"Can you guess how much it's worth?"

"Some number that is surprisingly large or small. Please don't make me guess."

"Fifteen million dollars."

"That's *all*!?"

"That's all."

"You can buy that much sulfur for fifteen million dollars!?" Saskia was suddenly having to restrain an irrational urge to run out and buy a sulfur pile of her own.

"Not only that, but the price of sulfur on commodities markets has been going up during the last couple of years. So T.R. has probably made more, *simply by owning that pile*, than he could have made by investing fifteen million in an index fund."

"It cost him *nothing*, you're saying."

"Less than nothing, in a manner of speaking. The pile sits on a property he inherited. Its value too appreciates over time. Last night he rented out a luxury hotel, of which he happens to be part owner. Today we ate barbecue at a truck stop he owns. Now we are in this beautiful railway carriage that he borrowed from a friend, being pulled across Texas by the cheapest form of long-range transportation that exists: a bloody freight train."

"Granted. But you have to admit it's extremely well staffed and organized."

Alastair nodded. "That is indeed the big spend here. Almost none of these people actually works for T.R., of course. He has hired an event planning firm, a very good one."

Saskia gazed down the length of the carriage. Bob had occupied a table at the other end for an impromptu catch-up with his entourage. A waiter was taking orders and a busboy was pouring water. Nearby was a man who was obviously security, just standing there, not gazing out the window, not checking his phone. An outgoing woman of about thirty was chatting with Fenna and Amelia, working in tour guide mode, explaining the history of this carriage, showing them old photographs. *Of course* it would be crazy for T.R. to have all these people on his permanent full-time staff. Of course it was a contract job.

"So what is your point, Alastair? That it's all just smoke and mirrors?"

"Oh, no, on the contrary," he returned. "The sulfur pile is as real as it gets. The tech he showed you—?"

"An experimental engine that burns sulfur."

"Smoke then, but no mirrors," he cracked.

"Sulfur dioxide actually."

"What I'm really trying to say is that the man is really quite canny." He pronounced the word as only a Scotsman could. "He spends where he needs to. That's all."

"That sounds like an endorsement, then."

He recoiled slightly. "Of the whole program? Perhaps not. Not *yet*. But his overall conduct of the thing shows much more intelligence and sophistication than I was expecting when your staff first reached out to me about this, and I watched a lot of vintage T.R. McHooligan videos on YouTube."

Rufus was seated across the aisle from them, arms folded, just gazing out the window. Alastair had glanced at him once or twice, as if offering to draw him into the conversation, but Rufus had paid him no heed. Finally now some little shift in Rufus's body language signaled an opening.

"The land of your forebears?" Alastair asked.

"Hmm?"

"I downloaded a couple of books about the Comanches," Alastair confessed.

Rufus shook his head. "Tough ol' bastards."

Alastair's face relaxed slightly. Rufus had defused any social awkwardness that might have surrounded the Comanches' well-documented practice of torturing captives to death.

"That's putting it mildly," Alastair agreed. "Anyway, according to the maps, we're passing across the southern bit of Comancheria, am I right?"

Rufus looked at him. "We've been there the whole time."

"I suppose that is true," Alastair admitted, a little unsure. "Waco, the Brazos . . ."

"Nah, I mean in a larger sense."

Alastair exchanged a bemused look with Saskia and said, "Do tell."

Rufus had taken to rasping his stubbled chin between the thumb and index finger of one hand, as if limbering up his jaw for speech. He now used that hand to point, in a subtle, flicking way, down the length of the carriage. "That right there is a Comanche," he said.

Alastair could see the "Comanche" directly. Saskia had to turn round. The only person Rufus could possibly be referring to was the security guy stationed at the head of the car. He was dressed in what amounted to a uniform among such people. He had long sandy hair pulled back in a ponytail and a reddish beard. His eyes, which were presumably blue, were hidden by wraparound sunglasses. He was wearing a bulky vest over bulky cargo pants tucked into matte black speed-laced boots. Without an assault rifle he seemed naked. He looked straight out of an American Special Forces squad in Afghanistan circa 2002.

"Looks more Scottish," Alastair said drily.

"You been reading those books you downloaded, you already know it was never about the DNA," Rufus said.

"Indeed," Alastair said, "the Comanches were enthusiastic re- cruiters."

"Had to be, once they started dying out," Rufus said.

Saskia shot him a curious look.

"A euphemism," Alastair admitted. "They took captives on raids. Most of them . . ." He trailed off and shot an uneasy glance at Rufus.

"Were just put to death. You can say it." Rufus said. "But kids like my great-great-granddad—he was taken when he was eight— they were adopted into the tribe. Consequently there was white Comanches, Black Comanches, Mexicans, you name it." He put an index finger to his forehead. "You just had to adopt the mindset, that's all."

Alastair glanced at the Special Forces poster child down at the far end of the carriage. Rufus caught it. "How did we end up with dudes like *him* in the *military*?" Rufus asked. "Well, you got to go back to times before the Civil War, when Texas was young. Alamo times. Moby-Dick times. Regular army couldn't even come close to dealing with the Comanches. So they started the Texas Rangers.

Most of 'em just got killed. Old man Darwin having his way. The few who survived, survived because they lived and fought *exactly the same as Comanches*. That was the only way. They became Comanches to fight Comanches. Later, regular army saw those same Rangers fighting in the Mexican war, as scouts, and called 'em white savages. No uniform, bearded, long hair, undisciplined, random weapons, unconventional tactics."

"Got it," Alastair said. "And that's how we ended up with . . ."

"With dudes like him running around in Afghanistan," Rufus concurred. "Being glorified in movies and such. Don't get me wrong, the Texas Rangers of today is clean-shaven, spit and polish. But the *idea* of the old-school Ranger with the beard and the Bowie knife, traipsing around eating snakes and ambushing people . . . that stayed with us and it went viral beyond Texas into the whole United States. And any time you see one of these young white dudes at the range with the wraparounds and twenty-five different weird guns, flaunting that Ranger chic . . . that is the survival into our time of that. So, yeah. To answer your original question, Alastair. We are passing across the southern part of Comancheria. It's just you and I have different takes on what that is. To you it's a patch of Texas and Oklahoma and New Mexico that used to exist back in the old days. To me it's the whole United States of America *right now*."

"It never really died out, you're saying," Saskia put in.

"It's a pandemic," Rufus diagnosed.

"Do you think it is *spreading* now?"

"It spreads where it succeeds. Or leastways where people make believe it's succeeding. Young fellas, they're predisposed to love that shit. They want to have guns and violence and adventure. 'It is a way of driving off the spleen and regulating the circulation.' But in the regular army, none of that's to be had without *discipline*. Young fellas chafe under that. Comanches got the best of both worlds. Guns, violence, adventure, and glory with no one to boss you around. It worked out here"—Rufus waved his hand out the window—"when there was infinite buffalo and plenty of open space." He now pulled his focus back into the interior of the antique railway car. "But it don't give you all this here." He picked up a silver fork from the table. "A fork! Comanche can't make a metal fork to save his life." He tossed it back onto the table. "To get all this, they had to give up their ways. And since their ways was all that they *were*—being that there was this come one, come all philosophy as far as DNA and all that—they diminished."

Alastair glanced at the red-bearded "Comanche" at the end of the carriage. "And became America."

"Seems that way to me," Rufus answered with a diffident shrug. "Now, to be clear, you got your Mississippian woodland maize cultivators and your Plains horse tribes. Your Cherokees as well as your Comanches."

Saskia and Alastair exchanged a look across the table, each just verifying that the other had lost the thread of Rufus's discourse. Rufus got a sheepish, mischievous look. "Now we call 'em Blue States and Red States. But it's the same. The Cherokees, the Chickasaws, and others—the Five Civilized Tribes—got corn—what you call maize—from Mexico long before white people times and settled down and became farmers. West of, oh, about the meridian where we are right at this moment, corn wouldn't grow. Just grass. People can't eat grass. Bison can. So the people would eat the bison. Tough way to make a living until the Spaniards brought horses. Then it was a fine way to live. And that's where you get your Comanches. Whole different mindset there from the Five Tribes. They never reconciled. What we now call Oklahoma was split in half right down the center. Five Tribes raising crops to the east. Comanches and Kiowas ranging free to the west, raiding the Five Tribes nations for horses and slaves."

Rufus had previously told Saskia the story of his great-great-grandfather Hopewell's adoption into the Comanches and so didn't repeat it here. "But the whole Blue State/Red State thing is just that."

Saskia to this point had been mostly content to observe the conversation, but she now shifted forward, her face showing sudden curiosity. "Which side do you stand on, Rufus? When I first saw you, you were standing on the tarmac blasting away at a giant beast with a Kalashnikov. Which would seem to put you more on the west side of that meridian you spoke of."

"Well, that's just what I've been asking myself," Rufus answered with a wry look. "That's my decision, innit? I've tried both. Worked both sides. Tried to settle down and grow crops and raise a family. Look where that got me. Then, I went all 'Call me Ishmael.' But Tashtego and Daggoo are supposed to die at the end. I'm not dead. So what am I gonna do now? You tell me."

"I don't think I have the capacity to tell you," Saskia returned, "but you're obviously a very intelligent man with energy and skills . . ."

"It's not about energy and skill," Rufus said. "It's about finding a fit. Where does ol' Rufus fit? Not many places."

Saskia could think of one place where Rufus might fit perfectly. But this did not seem to be the right moment to point that out. So she crossed her legs demurely under the table and broke eye contact.

Michiel poked his head in from the Tree Car and raised his eyebrows at Saskia. *Is now a good time?* She smiled and nodded. Rufus, seeing how it was, excused himself and Alastair followed. Michiel thumbed out a message on his phone while coming down the aisle, then gestured at the seat across from her as if to say *May I?* Thus politely ensconced, he said, "I took the liberty of telling my sister and my aunt. They may be along in a little bit to pay their respects."

"I shall look forward to it," Saskia said. "This is very much a family affair, it seems."

He turned his palms up. "We are not here in any official capacity. Venice does have an official plan for sealing off the Lagoon during storm surges. We are not part of it."

"We're back on the subject of MOSE?"

He nodded. "Currently, further work on the project is blocked because it was found to be in violation of the European Directive on Birds."

"Excuse me, did you say birds?"

"Yes." Michiel gave a shy, wry smile. "That is only one such violation, to tell you the truth. Also, the construction of the MOSE sea gates disturbed aquatic life on the bottom of the Lagoon. Mussel populations were impacted across several hectares. Every time such a violation is found to have happened, it triggers the European Infraction Procedure."

"I have heard of this procedure," Saskia said drily.

She did have to tread a bit carefully. Michiel was complaining—with very good reasons—about the European Union and its regulations. It was a well-worn topic that had led to Brexit and other consequences. Many and vociferous were the Euro-skeptics in the Netherlands. The queen had to treat the pro- and anti-European Union groups evenhandedly. "Some say," she went on, "that it is not the most rapid or efficient process. Others say that such things are necessary for the protection of . . . birds."

A new voice joined the conversation: that of a younger woman who had come forward from one of the Amtrak cars and now presented herself at the head of their table. "Have you been to our beautiful Lagoon? There are birds all over the fucking place!"

"My sister, Chiara," Michiel said.

"Please, join us!" Saskia said.

Chiara sat down next to her brother. She was as enjoyable to look at as he was. It was one of those beautiful families. Some wordless communication passed between the two. She settled down. "Whatever Her Majesty might think in her heart of hearts about the European Union, she is here representing a member in good standing of the same, so let's not put her in an awkward position!" Michiel said, glancing at Saskia.

"Of course," Chiara said. "My apologies."

Saskia laughed. "If you could hear some of what my country-men have to say about European regulations, you would not be so worried about hurting my feelings on that score."

"And yet you find a way to build those colossal storm defenses!" Chiara exclaimed. "I have been to the Maeslantkering! Fantastic! But we can't even build a couple of gates."

"It's because their whole country needs it," Michiel said.

"True," Chiara admitted. "I complain of Europe, but in truth Europe is just a hammer that they use to hit us with."

"Who are 'they' and 'us'?" asked Willem, who had just showed up and taken a seat next to Saskia. He knew how to smooth things over if the conversation became difficult.

"'*They*' are the rest of Italy, who don't care about Venice, and also the local Greens. 'Us' means those who want Venice to still exist fifty years from now. 'They' can always identify a hundred infractions in any plan we come up with, and file papers in Brussels to stop any progress, and then congratulate themselves on being so virtuous." She put her hands together in the prayerful style of a little girl going to her First Communion.

Michiel sighed and exchanged a few words with his sister in Italian, then added, "To be perfectly honest there is also corruption."

"You will be shocked!" Chiara added.

"I had heard that there were problems with MOSE," Willem said sympathetically.

"To give you an idea, it was started in 1987 and the gates didn't become functional until 2020," Michiel said.

"By which time the whole system was obsolete!" Chiara said.

"The lord mayor can tell you similar stories about the Thames Barrier," Willem said. "They started talking about it after the 1953 disaster. They argued about it for twenty years. They started building it in 1974. They got it working in 1982. It is already outmoded."

Chiara shook her head and looked out the window at a phalanx of wind turbines that extended over the curve of the horizon, red lights blinking in unison. "My brother is too diplomatic," she said. "I'll say it. You can't solve such problems with local barriers. The politics are too . . ." She whirled her hand in the air, exchanged a few words with Michiel, and then settled on "intractable. A planetary solution is the only way."

"We have a unique attachment to our city," Michiel said. "It—not Italy—is our country." He shrugged. "Other Italians, in the high country of Romania or Tuscany, might look at the map of Italy and say, 'Eh, the Lagoon, it is a small bit of the map. If we lose it, Italy remains and is only a little diminished—we can move all the nice art to higher ground, we can even dismantle St. Marks and the Ducal Palace and reassemble them elsewhere.'"

"Euro Disney!" Chiara cracked.

"Scottsdale, Arizona, is now home to London Bridge," Saskia pointed out with a wink.

"Perhaps they have room for the Bridge of Sighs!" Chiara shot back.

"There are some in Venice who, sadly, agree," Michiel said. "We are not among them. We are here to represent those Venetians for whom the Lagoon *is* the map. Nothing else matters. Venice is our country—our *whole* country—and if we lose it, we are stateless."

"Do you see your country as part of Europe?"

"Venice has *never*," said yet another new voice, "been part of Europe."

They looked up to see a woman standing in the aisle nearby. She might have been anywhere between fifty and a well-preserved seventy. Making zero concessions to the informal Western style that had begun to pervade this train, she was in a long dark skirt, cashmere turtleneck, and blazer with a few well-thought-out pieces of jewelry including a big gold pin depicting the winged lion that was the ancient symbol of Venice. Saskia mastered a brief, ridiculous urge to duck her head around the edge of the table to check out this woman's shoes. No doubt they would be utterly fabulous and yet tastefully understated.

While pleased to see his aunt—for this was obviously her—Michiel was caught off guard and drew breath to make some greeting. The woman cut him off. Gazing directly at Saskia with big anthracite eyes, she said, "Every time we have made the mistake of trusting Europe we have gotten *fucked*." She was frank and firm but not quite scary, though Saskia could imagine a younger version of herself being quite intimidated by such a woman.

"Cornelia!" Michiel said. He turned to Saskia. "Your Majesty, may I introduce my aunt—"

"You're referring to events that happened during the time of the Crusades," Saskia said, somewhat amazed. It was impossible to make sense of what Cornelia had just said otherwise.

"Well, the Corsican did us no favors either, but yes, that is what I mean." Cornelia took a step closer and extended her hand. Saskia reached out and clasped it.

The newcomer showed no interest in anyone else. Chiara, until now a strong presence, had already scurried out of the way. Michiel now followed his sister into the aisle and extended a hand, unnecessarily helping Cornelia take the seat opposite Saskia. The two younger Venetians then just stood there observing, not quite anxious, but certainly alert.

Cornelia put one elbow on the table and cradled her impressive jawline on the heel of her hand, thrusting a couple of plum-colored fingernails up into jet-black hair streaked, just so, with gray. Bracelets cascaded down her forearm. She was looking directly at Saskia. Saskia looked right back at her and enjoyed doing so.

She'd had almost zero sexual interactions with women and had long ago written those off as the result of youthful "confusion." But her daughter's incessant demands had put her into a peculiar way of thinking. Every decade or so, some woman came along who seemed like a possible exception.

She wondered if others around them could sense that Saskia's thoughts were headed that way. It seemed incredibly obvious to her. A faintly wry look on Cornelia's face suggested that at least one person was having similar perceptions. But then Cornelia broke eye contact, sat back, and sighed. "The Netherlands knows what it is to be abandoned. To be hated by those who are jealous."

"But doesn't every country feel that way at one point or another?" Saskia asked. "It is how nations establish a sense of identity."

"Sometimes it is actually true, though. Venice has been hated and suspected for a long time. Even by other Italians. *Especially* by them. We are our own country. It is the only thing that has ever worked."

"If I may," Willem said. "Oh, I'm nobody," he added, when Cornelia's eyes briefly flicked his way. He was bemused, not offended, by Cornelia's utter lack of interest in niceties. "Just putting this all together: the whole city of Venice will certainly be underwater very soon. Perhaps no city in the world is as vulnerable. MOSE failed because of cumbersome European Union regulation and Italian corruption. Worse, it failed *extremely slowly.*"

The Venetians all laughed. It was the first time Cornelia had cracked a smile.

"If Venice were free to act in a decisive way, as it was famous for doing back in its golden age, it would just—"

"Solve the fucking problem, yes," Cornelia said.

"But being part of Italy, which is in turn part of the EU, makes that completely impossible."

"Completely. Good word." Cornelia shook her head sadly. "Europe," she said, in the tone of voice that might be used by the founder of a three-star Michelin restaurant talking about Velveeta.

"So, you are"—and here Willem looked also to Michiel and Chiara—"Venetian nationalists."

"Did you suppose we were fascists?"

Michiel flinched.

"Don't worry," Cornelia went on, "we hate those idiots."

Michiel smiled.

"We are more like oligarchs," his aunt concluded. Michiel turned sideways to Chiara, who smiled and put a consoling hand on his arm.

"How many people like you *are* there?" Willem asked.

"It doesn't take that many," Cornelia returned.

"You're not merely thinking about what I'll call Vexit—to leave the EU—"

"We want out of Italy. To be like those guys," Cornelia said, and turned to look back in the direction of the Tree Car.

"Singapore?"

"Yes. And Italy can serve as our Malaysia."

The same words, uttered in a Venetian coffeehouse, might have seemed a little ridiculous. But on this train rattling across the darkling plains of Central Texas, all things seemed possible.

"Why isn't she wearing a wedding ring?" Saskia asked, when she had a moment together with Willem, Amelia, and Fenna. They were in Saskia's private chamber at the back of the Money Car. Fenna was putting on Face Three, more suitable for evening. So Saskia wasn't free to look around—she had her eyes rolled up toward the ceiling so that Fenna could get at the lower lids—but even so she could sense Willem and Amelia exchanging a look.

"It's a perfectly normal question," Saskia insisted. "It doesn't mean anything."

Fenna snickered, and she knew she had protested a little too much.

"She is *so* fuckable. Definitely a top though," Fenna observed. Saskia couldn't roll her eyes without incurring Fenna's wrath, but she did heave a sigh. But then Fenna's phone buzzed and she actually stepped away to check it. Saskia was on her way to being shocked by this unprofessional behavior when she got a look at Fenna's face and saw the love light in her eyes. Jules was sending her selfies.

"It's thought that Cornelia's husband is now out of the picture," Amelia said, watching Fenna in a bemused way.

"What does that mean?" Saskia asked.

"Early onset dementia. Possibly other issues as well."

"Where is he?"

"Family palazzo on an island in the Adriatic."

"Because of course they would have one of those," Saskia said.

"One of those islands that was part of the Venetian Empire back in the day," Willem added.

"He hasn't been seen in public in two years," Amelia said, "and even then he was showing visible symptoms."

"I get the picture," Saskia said. "To repeat Willem's question: How many people like them *are* there?"

"Not many," Amelia said. "Look, our initial background check was focused on Michiel. And he does come from an old Venetian family. They were named to the nobility in 1019."

"Jesus, that *is* old!"

"No it isn't."

"It just gets better," Willem said.

"We're learning more now about Cornelia's family."

"The one she married into?"

"No, those were Greeks who came to Venice after the Fall of Constantinople."

"Recent arrivals then!" Saskia cracked.

Amelia continued, "Yeah. *Cornelia* can trace *her* personal ancestry back to one of the founding families of Venice."

"What does that even mean?"

Willem said, "Literally one of the Roman families who rowed boats out into the Lagoon to get away from Attila the Hun."

"And they were old *then*," Amelia said. "They knew Julius Caesar."

Saskia could only shake her head and laugh silently.

She finally managed to catch Fenna's eye. "Am I to go to dinner with only one eye done?"

By way of an answer, Fenna shyly turned her phone around. It was a photo of Jules in a wet suit. Enough said! Even the usually stoic Amelia gasped. He was in sunlight, in a RHIB. He'd just got out of the brown waters of the lower Brazos and was triumphantly holding up a waterlogged document in a picture frame. Mounted in its center was a large silver coin.

"It would be inappropriate for me to make any comment" was all Willem could say. He was talking about Jules, of course. Not the artifact he was holding up.

"His cousins all refer to him as the Family Jules," Fenna said. "It's a joke, you see, based on a slang expression—"

"That will do," Saskia said. "Where were we?"

"Cornelia's weird old family," Willem said, reluctantly averting his gaze. "To answer your question: there aren't many like her. But that's not the real question. You want to know about this phenomenon of well-heeled covert Venetian nationalists whipped up into a frenzy over sea level rise. It appears that there are just a few."

"But they are rich as fuck," Amelia said, "and they have their backs to the wall. I'll try to learn more."

The reason for Face Three was yet another in a series of planned social events, this one bringing together a dozen people around a dining table that had been set up in the middle of the Beer Car. Dress was more formal; T.R. wore cowboy boots that were black and shiny. Veronica was well turned out, though slightly off her game as she didn't know how to impedance-match with the likes of Cornelia. Easier to be comfortable with was Daia Chand, the wife of the lord mayor. While high-wattage in her own right (Oxford Ph.D., noted television presenter), she didn't mind slipping into the role of "plus one of prominent bigwig."

Saskia wasn't sure who her plus one ought to be. She wanted to give Willem a break; he had earned it, and he needed to be fresh tomorrow. She was tempted to ask Rufus, but she suspected he'd be miserably uncomfortable in that company. In the end she asked Alastair. As it turned out, Mark Furlong had been added to the roster to fill out the table (since the Venetians numbered three) and so he and Alastair could mind-meld about risk analysis if they wanted and leave the rest of the guests to talk about normal-people things.

> Possible third target identified.

> Who is he?

> She

Saskia texted with Lotte as she was making her way up the aisle of the Tree Car. Response was nigh instantaneous, with a demand for a picture.

> My darling, there is absolutely no way that you are getting a picture.

> Aww!

> I hope you sleep well. Going into a fancy dinner.

> I hope you don't sleep AT ALL

Lotte shot back, followed by a train of emojis that started with a wink and escalated from there. Saskia was so rattled by some of what she saw that she found herself suddenly in the middle of the party in the Beer Car, where Sylvester, uncharacteristically, was regaling (there was no other word for it) Bob, Daia, Cornelia, and T.R. with some kind of narration about sand pirates.

"It's simple maths," he insisted to a skeptical-looking lord mayor. "Just to maintain the land area we already have, we need to dump a certain amount of sand into the water to keep up with sea level rise. To create even more reclaimed land, as our friends in the Netherlands do"—this a way of welcoming Saskia into the conversation—"we must deposit more sand yet. We don't have our own sand mines, so we must buy it. There's a market for it, like any other commodity. But we found that when the price went up—because of our purchasing activities—sand piracy skyrocketed."

"How *does* one pirate sand?" Daia asked, as if she'd always wanted to know this. "I've heard of more conventional 'yo ho ho and a bottle of rum' piracy but—?"

"You pull up alongside some island with a barge and just go to work with hoses. It's like a big watery vacuum cleaner. The barge fills up and the island gets smaller."

"And these islands are where?"

"That, of course, is the problem, Dr. Chand. If the plan is to sell the sand to Singapore, why then the profits are higher the closer the island is to that market. So it started in nearby coastal areas of Malaysia and Indonesia and spread to Vietnam and the Philippines."

"I beg your pardon," said Daia Chand, "but am I to gather that there are people *living* on these islands that are being vacuumed up and barged to Singapore!?" Her face was showing the correct balance of amusement and moral outrage.

Dr. Eshma spoke up. She was Sylvester's plus one. Until now, Saskia had seen very little of her. "That would be very bold. People got wise to this quite early and drove the pirates off."

"And bully for them!"

"The pirates are a little cleverer than that," Sylvester said. "They go to uninhabited islands, take a little here, a little there. However, even this has bad consequences for fisheries that the local people depend on. So for a while it was quite a bad state of affairs, to be quite honest. But Singapore heard the complaints from these neighboring countries and instituted new purchasing schemes to confound the sand pirates."

Saskia was enjoying looking at Eshma's outfit, which she guessed was something traditionally Malaysian. Eshma was a computational modeling specialist with a raft of degrees and post-docs, and had been mousy and unobtrusive up to this point. Willem said that she was of mixed Tamil and Malaysian heritage. She had now, suddenly, gone full Cinderella. Saskia wanted to high-five her, but it wouldn't have been appropriate. Noting Saskia's interest, Eshma smiled back. Saskia gave her the full head-to-toe and winked.

But T.R. was still fixated on sand. "So if I pull up in front of Singapore tomorrow with a barge full of sand," he said, "I have to—what? Present a certificate that I got every grain fair and square?"

"In effect, yes, T.R.," Sylvester said, after seemingly running down a mental checklist of all the ways in which this was a crude oversimplification.

T.R. snorted. "I'd like to see how you enforce *that*."

"There are procedures that can make life difficult for sand pirates," Sylvester insisted. "The outcry from our neighbors has subsided. However, better yet, from our perspective, would be if the sea level were to stop rising."

"Here's to that," T.R. responded and raised his glass. The lord mayor tinked his tumbler of pure sparkling water against every cocktail within easy reach and drank to it with the others.

Saskia sat across from Bob. According to some rule book that Veronica must have pored over, the queen and the lord mayor flanked T.R. at the head of the table. Veronica presided over the opposite end, which tended more Venetian/Singaporean. Eshma—she used only a single name, according to Willem—sat on Veronica's left and Cornelia on her right. As Saskia stole the occasional coquettish glance at Cornelia, it seemed that she was happily absorbed in getting to know her counterparts from that other island-city-state-whose-emblem-was-a-lion. The menu, as foretold by elegant cards set out next to each plate, was Texas themed (Gulf prawns, mesquite-grilled bison with chile-based sauce, etc.) but with nods to the guests' home cuisines (a hilarious fish-and-chips-based amuse-bouche with a dot of curry sauce; Adriatic mussels and wine of Friuli; a spicy salad with Singaporean flavors; a selection of Dutch cheeses and the inevitable Stroopwaffel for dessert).

"I see you got your silver dollar back," Saskia said to T.R. during the opening chitchat phase of the proceedings. "At least, I assume that was yours."

"You *are* well-informed!" T.R. exclaimed. "Yep, those Boskeys got a diver down into my storage container. It's where we stashed all the odds and ends from the former HQ of Brazos Mining. That silver dollar was the first buck they ever made. I shoulda gone and moved all that stuff to higher ground a long time ago."

Bob and Daia looked mildly curious about all this, but not enough to follow up. From there the conversation moved on to light chitchat about the weather and such, interrupted by the occasional toast. But after the main course had been brought out, and everyone had tucked into it, T.R. looked at Saskia and said, "So what do you think?"

Bob looked up from his bison steak, all ears, and next to him Daia favored Saskia with a sympathetic smile.

"Why, you shall have to ask me tomorrow," Saskia answered. "Like a good Texas poker player, you don't show your hand too soon."

"You're too kind, Your Majesty. I was just asking in a more general sense about where it's all going."

"Perhaps you should have invited a philosopher! I can only represent the perspective of the Netherlands, of course."

"The Netherlands," Bob said, through a mouthful of bison, then swallowed. His face betokened just the right amount of dry amusement. "A place whose very name means 'low country.'"

"I am aware of its meaning and of its altitude, Robert," Saskia returned, with a glance at Daia who was enjoying the little jab at her husband.

"But it really is the eight-hundred-pound gorilla in all this, isn't it?" Bob asked.

"The City of London is not without a stake in the matter."

"The Romans, at least, had the good sense to build on a hill," Bob returned. "Oh, some of the property down along the river will be flooded. But it's been decades since we began moving the server rooms, the generators, all that up out of the cellars to the roofs. Slow and steady, but with very material progress. We could absorb a 1953 event rather easily. Not that we wouldn't get our hair mussed, but . . ."

"Love, I believe Her Majesty was referring to a *financial* stake," Daia put in.

Bob made the faintest suggestion of an eye roll as if to suggest that the complexities of all that were beyond him. "I worry about *sewers*," he claimed. Everyone laughed, enjoying his beleaguered tone. "Oh, I'm quite serious!" he insisted. "If you've ever walked down Farringdon on a rainy day, and inhaled the fragrance, you'll know it's all quite medieval. Because you are literally walking on the lid of a covered—"

Daia squeezed his arm.

"Sorry. It's actually somewhat fascinating. Similar to your present difficulties in Houston, T.R. We are at risk of being caught in a pincer attack between rainfall draining down out of the north, and storm surge coming up the Thames. At some point the sewers and the river have to meet and come to an understanding."

"It is the same too in Venice," Chiara offered from mid-table. "We can close the Lagoon. But many rivers empty into it."

"Just so," Bob said. "But we do strive to address these very down-to-earth matters so that the boffins can enjoy modern sanitary facilities while they think about all of—whatever it is these two have been going on about." He looked toward Alastair, who was next to Saskia, and Mark Furlong, diagonally across from him. The two had mind-melded very soon after taking their assigned seats and had not since shut up about their shared obsession with "Black Swan" events, rogue superwaves, The Mule from Asimov's Foundation series, and such. Every few minutes they would remember that there were other people at the table and make some token effort to bring them into the conversation. Chiara and Daia were sustaining most of the collateral damage, but making game efforts to lob in the occasional remark.

Alastair took in Bob's glare and faltered in the middle of a disquisition about some arcane financial product that had caused a bank in Frankfurt to go under because of a derecho that had destroyed all the corn in Iowa.

"You're boring my wife!" Bob growled.

"Not bored," Daia said, "but as a representative here—along with Dr. Eshma—of what you lot used to call the Subcontinent,

I will ask: we don't have derechos in India that I know of. But we do have disasters of our own: locusts, droughts, and so on. If you want to muck about with the climate, how do we know that it won't create more of those?"

"We've been mucking about with it *inadvertently* for two hundred years," Mark demurred. "Now we're talking about a different sort of mucking."

"All perhaps very true on a technical, scientific level," Daia said. "I get it. I do. But I'm talking about *how it is perceived*. That's what matters." She looked across at Saskia. "I'll let Her Majesty speak for herself and her country. But as for, say, the Punjab—where my family came from—if there is a drought there now, some people *already* will claim that it happened because Bill Gates or someone tampered with the weather *even though no one is actually doing any such thing yet.*"

"But that cuts both ways," T.R. pointed out.

"What do you mean?" Saskia asked.

"If folks all over the world are going to get riled up at billionaires messing with the climate *even when we are not really doing a goddamn thing*, then we got no real downside politically."

"*You* don't, perhaps," Saskia said.

"We might as well take action and save a few hundred million lives," T.R. concluded, as if it were the simplest thing in the world.

"They're going to condemn you no matter what," put in Cornelia from the far end of the table, where all had gone silent to listen to this. "So let them condemn you for something that is real and not just a made-up conspiracy theory."

"It is a bit different where I come from," Saskia said, but she didn't want to draw invidious distinctions between Punjabi farmers and Dutch coffee shop hipsters.

"Setting aside the political dimension," Daia said coolly, "what about actual, physical reality? Will geoengineering damage crop yields in Punjab? Or . . . Bangladesh? Hubei? Iowa? It can't be good for everyone, everywhere."

"I would, of course, defer to Eshma, who actually knows what she's talking about," said Mark, with a glance down to that end of the table. "But when you put it that way . . ."

"Nothing can be good for everyone, everywhere," Eshma confirmed. "The models tell us that much."

Mark continued. "And yet uncontrolled global warming will certainly kill, as T.R. points out, hundreds of millions or billions. We can't stop it from happening in any other way."

"Even if we could get China and India to stop burning shit *tomorrow*, and crash their economies for the sake of Mother Earth," T.R. said, "it wouldn't undo what we've done, as a civilization, to the atmosphere since we first worked out how to turn fossil fuel into work."

"People will ask, why not put the same amount of effort and engineering cleverness into removing that carbon from the atmosphere?" Daia said.

"And are *you* asking that, Daia? Or merely pointing out that others will?" Mark asked.

"Both, I suppose. I really am genuinely curious."

"Let's put a pin in that, I got a neat little demo," T.R. said. He thumbed a speed dial on his phone and muttered, "Yeah, could you bring in the bell jars?"

"This is only part of the demo we'll be showing to the media tomorrow," T.R. said, a few minutes later. "We are working on a bigger presentation. But I thought you might get a kick out of it."

"Could you first say more about the media?" Saskia inquired. "I was told—"

"All NDAed, all embargoed. As my people discussed with your people when we set this up," T.R. assured her. "Sooner or later, according to your man Willem, you're going to make it public that you visited the site."

"We have to," Saskia said.

"The agreement was, you can do that on your own timetable.

That agreement stands, Your Majesty. And it's up to you whether you take a pro-, anti-, or neutral position."

T.R. seemed rattled by how Saskia had just reacted, to the point where she now felt it necessary to put him at ease. "My job is an unusual one," Saskia said. "The boundary between personal and public is complicated and somewhat ambiguous. One moment I am enjoying a lovely dinner with interesting people and the next I'm having to think about media. Pardon the interruption."

"Pardon *me* for letting that dirty word out of my mouth!" T.R. answered. He glanced awkwardly at Daia (who had been a media personality) and then at the rest of the guests, who had fallen silent when one of T.R.'s aides had rolled in a stand supporting a pair of glass bell jars. Beneath one was a heap of powdered sulfur—a miniature version of the huge pile they'd seen earlier. Beneath the other was a mound of powder the same size, but black as black could be. "Two elements," T.R. said, "alike in dignity! The yellow one needs no introduction. You'll have guessed that the black one is carbon. Both alter the climate. Carbon makes it get warmer by trapping the sun's rays. Sulfur cools it by bouncing them back into space."

"We've been over this, T.R.," Bob reminded him.

"Sorry. Preacher man gotta preach. What's not so obvious is the incredible difference in leverage between these two substances. To put enough of this stuff"—he slapped the carbon bell jar, and his wedding ring made a sharp noise on the glass—"into the atmosphere to bring the temp up a couple degrees, we had to put a large part of the human race to work burning shit for two centuries. We chopped down forests, dug up peat bogs, excavated huge coal mines, emptied oil reserves the size of mountains. Hell, in Afghanistan they even burn *shit*. All that disappeared into the air. The total weight of excess carbon we put into the atmosphere is about three hundred gigatons. All those trees, all that coal, all the oil and peat and shit. Now. To reverse that change in temperature—to bring it back down by two degrees—how much sulfur do you think we need to put into the stratosphere? A comparable amount? Not even close. A smaller amount? Yes, but that don't do it justice. Because sulfur has leverage like you wouldn't believe. This amount of carbon here"—he once again did the wedding ring thwack on the bell jar full of black stuff—"could be neutralized, in terms of its effect on global temperature, by an amount of sulfur too small to be seen by the naked eye. So small that we couldn't even demo it in these bell jars unless I rolled out a microscope. Tomorrow you'll see the ratio. A boxcar of coal, and a cube of sulfur you can put in the palm of your hand."

"You're saying that removing the carbon from the atmosphere would be a much bigger project than putting sulfur into it," Saskia said.

"We would have to make a pile of carbon the size of Mount Rainier. About thirty cubic miles. Imagine a cube a mile on a side, full of this stuff." He rested his hand a little more gently on the carbon jar. "And now imagine thirty of those. To get that done in any reasonable amount of time—let's say fifty years—you have to imagine a 747 cargo freighter loaded with pure elemental carbon dumping it onto the pile *every nine seconds* for *fifty years*, 24/7/365," T.R. said. "Now, maybe someone will make that happen. But they gotta be a whole lot richer and more powerful than everyone sitting around this table put together."

"We all live in technocratic societies," Saskia said, "and we naturally think in terms of a certain style of doing things. A giant atmosphere processor that sucks in air and removes the carbon through a chemical process and loads it onto the 747s every nine seconds. But I am preparing, psychologically, to go home and talk about this with my daughter—whom you might think of as a proxy for millions of Greens. The question from them will be . . ."

"Why not plant a shitload of trees?" T.R. finished the sentence for her. "Or make algae bloom over big patches of ocean? Get plants to do the work for us."

"Exactly. Is it just that plants can't sequester enough carbon, fast enough?"

"Partly," T.R. nodded.

"If I may," said the lord mayor, "we have looked at this. Oh, England's not big enough. Canada maybe. The scale of the program would be spectacularly enormous, and it would by its very nature have to be distributed over a significant part of the earth's surface. Many jurisdictional boundaries crossed. Many nations would have to cooperate just so. And once the plants have grown and stored up all that biomass, you can't allow the carbon to find its way back into the atmosphere, or else what's the point? You basically have to chop down the forests, stack up the wood somewhere safe, make sure it never catches fire, and then start growing a whole new forest."

"I saw a video of some very angry chaps in Pakistan literally uprooting, with their bare hands, a new forest that had been planted in their district," Daia said. "Some sort of dispute over who owned the land."

Sylvester had been trying to get everyone to pay attention to Eshma. Heads turned in her direction. "There's another angle that tends not to get mentioned," Eshma said. "This one might be a bit tricky to explain to your daughter, Your Majesty."

"Let's have it!" Saskia said.

"What is the big question mark surrounding solar geoengineering?" Eshma asked, rhetorically.

"In other words, what T.R. is proposing to do," Sylvester footnoted.

"It's the fact that it will impact the climate differently in different parts of the world," Eshma said. "When I return to Singapore, my duty will be to organize the running of massive simulations to get some idea of the ramifications of what Dr. Schmidt is proposing."

"I ain't just proposing," T.R. muttered under his breath; but Eshma was at the far end of the table and didn't hear. She continued, "The thing is that growing a lot of trees, or algae, or what have you, would *also* have such knock-on effects. These of course can be simulated by the same computer models. And they would unquestionably be *different* since it is a different scheme from Dr. Schmidt's. But there is absolutely no basis for supposing that they would be globally *better*."

"Planting huge forests, or making algae bloom in the ocean, would create a drought, or catastrophic flooding, *somewhere*," Saskia said.

"It has to," T.R. said, "it can't not."

"The Greens," Saskia said, "idolize nature and will want to say that if drought or deluge happens in Mali or Nebraska or Uttar Pradesh because of their carbon-sequestering forest, why, that is nature's decree. Gaia's just verdict. We must bow to it. But try telling that to the victims."

"Or those whose land was expropriated to plant the new forests," Daia added.

Saskia sighed.

"Should make for one festive conversation with Princess Charlotte," T.R. remarked.

"It makes me tired just thinking of it," Saskia said. "Or perhaps I am simply tired. It has been quite a day."

That was the signal for everyone else at the table to say all sorts of complimentary things about the hospitality that the Schmidts had bestowed on them. The dinner broke up. A few night owls showed interest in smoking cigars and drinking single malt in the Tree Car, which had openable windows that made it quite breezy. But Saskia was suddenly feeling knackered, and very much not of a disposition to get laid even if any clear opportunity were to present itself. Which it did not. For Willem intercepted her on the way down the aisle to brief her on the day's events in the Netherlands, and to let her know that a jet was flying over tomorrow afternoon to take her and her entourage directly back to Schiphol the morning after that.

HIMACHAL PRADESH

Perhaps it was coincidence. Or perhaps there was no such thing as a coincidence. But Laks's conversation with Ranjit happened at around the same time as some other events that, like tributaries feeding into a river in the high mountains, all contributed their force to what happened next.

First of all it was September, which might seem like high summer, but it meant that the snows would begin soon, and if he wanted to get up to the Line of Actual Control, he needed to get moving.

Second: There was this family that had begun showing up at the langar attached to the gurdwara that Laks had been attending. They'd been literally starving the first time they wandered in. They would probably go back to starving if they skipped a day. They were decidedly not from around here. They were refugees who had come down out of the Himalayas on the back of a truck. But they had originated much farther north than that. They did not speak Hindi or Punjabi. Nor did they look like the kinds of people who would. Nor were they Tibetan. The group consisted of a mother, a granny, and four kids ranging from about five to fifteen years of age. The fifteen-year-old, a boy named Ilham, spoke English. Laks had seen them across the room but not bothered them, since it seemed that not starving to death might be a higher priority as far as they were concerned. He inferred that the people of the gurdwara were horrified by their plight (whatever that might be) and that they were being looked after. But word had it they'd come down out of the mountains. And Ranjit's strange remark had turned Laks's thoughts in that direction. So he went over and struck up a conversation with Ilham.

They were Uighurs from western China. After a long train of

persecutions, their father, an engineer, had been rounded up and sent to a concentration camp (Ilham's phrasing, which Laks construed as Ilham not knowing English very well until Laks learned more). The father had not been heard from in a long time. The rest of the family had fled, and—wisely—kept fleeing, until they had fallen in with some Tibetans who knew how to get across the LAC, and ended up here in Chandigarh.

That was the short version of a tale that, it could be guessed, was epic. Ilham looked willing to disgorge the longer version at minimal provocation. What prevented this was Laks's basic lack of knowledge about Uighurs, Xinjiang, Chinese policies toward same, and other foundational elements of the story. This was clearly startling to Ilham. He didn't know where to begin. "Don't you even have Internet?" was the best he could muster. A lesser man than Ilham would have been offended by how little Laks knew of these matters. Ilham was just bewildered. "SMH," he said. "SMH." Laks had to go look it up. It meant "shaking my head."

Of course Laks had Internet, but it was just slow enough to be annoying, so he went to a teahouse where it was better and spent a while getting up to speed on the Uighurs and (as it turned out) the incredibly sinister things being done to them by China. This branched into a whole additional freight train of browser tabs relating to similar persecutions of the people of Tibet. Tibetans were Buddhists and Uighurs were Muslims, but anyway they were both religious/ethnic minorities that China had decided needed to be assimilated, even to the point of telling parents what they were and weren't allowed to name their children, and what styles of beard were and were not acceptable on adult males.

These details really struck home to Laks in a way that more conventional atrocities wouldn't have. Sikhs practiced the least dogmatic, least pompous, least priest-ridden religion that could still be called a religion; but they were awfully particular about names and beards.

He remembered the oil cans on Uncle Dharmender's chessboard

in Kamloops. How small the rook seemed in comparison. Usually India and Pakistan were what his people worried about. But it had been centuries since any Muslim or Hindu government had tried to tell them how they were allowed to wear their beards. China was thought of as farther away, safely walled off by the world's largest mountain range, and basically not interested in bothering Sikhs. But yet a third collection of browser tabs testified to Laks's research on the topic of the Line of Actual Control, and this made it very clear that China was gradually, meter by meter, pushing the border south. They were claiming land that was new in the sense that, until the last few decades, it had been buried under glaciers for all of recorded history. But now every year the glaciers retreated, sometimes exposing tens of meters of bare rock over the course of a single year. And when you multiplied that by a bunch of years and by the convoluted length of the glaciers' front, you were talking about a lot of land that effectively had not existed until recently. Cold, barren land without enough oxygen, to be sure. But one side or another—India or China—had to claim it. There was an official border on the map, but it had always been meaningless. All that mattered was the Line of Actual Control.

The last factor in Laks's decision was already a foregone conclusion, even if he had not admitted it to himself until now. He was done with the Punjab, and it was done with him. He'd come here expecting a martial arts epiphany, just like in the videos. Instead he had found a system of values and a sanely ordered society, with a well-developed immune system that was gradually rejecting him. Sort of in the way that if you got a deep splinter in your flesh, and waited long enough, the body would find a way to wall it off and force it out. The graybeards had perceived things about Laks that he himself had only figured out at length by blundering up blind alleys. They had noticed in him a want of *miri piri*, which meant a coherence of the mind and the body—a physical/spiritual harmony, the development of which was the true purpose of gatka, or any other religious practice for that matter.

Once Laks had made up his mind, though, and explained his plan to Ranjit, everything magically got better and easier. He had stumbled across *miri piri*, or at least the trailhead of the path that might lead him to it. People who had been worried about him were visibly relieved. Somewhat contradicting his earlier statements, Ranjit managed to summon some young stick fighters who were pretty good at it and who were not afraid to spar at something like full contact. Not so much with the high-powered strikes Laks had borrowed from other arts. Those were best practiced against inanimate objects. More so with the pure gatka moves. Supposedly these were suited for defense against multiple attackers closing in from all sides. They were able to test that in simulated combat, and it ended up being a good news/bad news outcome. Defending against multiple attackers was really difficult even if you had learned the techniques; but a little bit of realistic practice went a long way in bettering one's odds.

The aerobic burden was impressive even at Chandigarh's altitude of a mere three hundred meters above sea level. This gave Laks fair warning that he would have to work on his cardio. Without supplying a very clear explanation as to why, he got his mother in Richmond to express-ship him a high-tech training contraption made just for this purpose: a face mask attached to a breathing tube that ran through an oxygen-absorbing apparatus on your back. It looked like something from a science fiction movie and it drew a lot of stares from the lads on the adjoining cricket oval, but it enabled him to breathe air in Chandigarh that was as oxygen-starved as that at the Line of Actual Control, which was at more than ten times the altitude.

He had come to India to help people get oxygen. Now he was learning to get along without it. The contraption turned out to be a recruiting tool. He couldn't wear it 24/7. Gopinder, one of his training partners, requested permission to try it out. Laks readily assented. If nothing else this gave him an opportunity to see what it was like fighting an opponent who didn't have enough oxygen. The answer was that he fought surprisingly well until he had an opportunity to think about it.

It turned out that Gopinder was into kabaddi. Laks had been aware of the existence of this sport for a long time, but only because his uncles were wont to keep live feeds of it running in their gas stations in the evenings, when it was morning in the Punjab. It was militarized tag, basically. There was no equipment. It was played in a field with a line drawn across the middle. Each round—which was called a "raid"—consisted of a single attacker from one team squaring off against a squad of four defenders from the opposing side. The attacker started at the midline. The defenders linked arms to form a sort of moving wall that generally stayed as deep as possible in their end of the field. At the start of the raid, the attacker advanced across the line and attempted to tag as many defenders as possible in the time available before retreating back across the line. As soon as any defender got tagged, though, they would break free from the line and try to detain the attacker by grappling with him, to prevent the attacker from returning "home" before time ran out.

In a modern implementation, time would have been kept track of by a referee with a stopwatch who would blow the whistle after sixty seconds or whatever. But kabaddi was a lot older than stopwatches, or the concept of referees for that matter, and so they kept time in a different way: the attacker was not allowed to breathe. As soon as he stepped across the line he would begin to chant "kabaddi kabaddi." As soon as he stopped, the raid was over. If he'd made it back across the line after tagging someone, points were scored, but if he'd run out of oxygen—for example because he'd got pulled into a wrestling match—the raid failed.

As with seemingly every other sport, there were leagues and age brackets and rankings and uniforms and endorsements and all the rest. Punjabi kids played it all the time, in the way that suburban West Coast kids played soccer, but it was also popular in other parts of India. Gopinder had been playing kabaddi since childhood. Indeed, this was how he'd gotten involved in gatka, for you could think of gatka and kabaddi as both belonging to a constellation of "Sikh pastimes derived from martial origins" and it was common to see sports festivals and tournaments where demonstrations of gatka alternated on the same field with rounds of kabaddi, all announced with lung-bursting enthusiasm through the same radically overdriven sound system. Anyway, Gopinder was pretty good at kabaddi and belonged to an adult league team in Chandigarh. He had invited Laks to attend some of the competitions and even to try out for the team, but this was not the right time for Laks to take up an entirely new sport.

As you would expect, people who were serious about kabaddi spent a lot of time holding their breath and were good at dealing with hypoxia. So of course Gopinder was fascinated by the breathing apparatus. During their early experiments on the field, Gopinder was, of course, better able to cope with its effects than Laks.

"Adrenaline will take you a long way!" was the verdict of a completely random boy in cricket whites who had wandered over to observe. On second glance, maybe "young man" was how most people would describe this fellow; he was a junior coach, or something. Tall and athletic enough that he felt completely unafraid to stroll over and bother the warlike Punjabis. Or maybe he felt that the cricket bat in his hand would keep him safe. He introduced himself as Ravi. Laks startled him, not necessarily in a bad way, by responding in fluent English. Once they had got through the preliminaries, Ravi just asked, straight out, "Are you training to fight up at the Line?" Laks had to admit that they were, since it seemed just idiotic to deny it. There was a certain amount of basic honesty and righteousness that went with striving toward *miri piri*. Ravi grinned and told him that it was "cool" that this was so. Laks assumed at first that Ravi was a rich boy, since he had that kind of self-assured nature, but on second thought he wouldn't be working as a junior coach if that were the case.

Ravi kept coming over as days went on. He put on the breathing apparatus and went for a jog around the cricket oval and nearly fell over dead. He asked detailed questions about stick fighting and whether any of the techniques would work with a cricket bat.

At the same time as all this, Laks was laying in a stock of good rattan. This was a better material than bamboo for actual, as opposed to simulated, fighting. It was heavier and more solid. When it broke, which was rarely (you could bend it nearly in half if you were strong enough), it split into a sort of stiff broomlike structure instead of just creasing and buckling like bamboo. It was a bit exotic—the best stuff came from Southeast Asia—but not that hard to obtain once he had put his mind to it.

He invested in a clever little camping saw, small enough to be folded up and slipped into a backpack, and some other simple woodworking necessaries: scraps of sandpaper, a little pocketknife, a whetstone. Ranjit turned out to know a leatherworker—a profession that Hindus tended to avoid but that was perfectly acceptable to persons of their faith. This fellow knew how to stitch leather coverings for the sticks. These were not absolutely necessary, but they were an improvement over naked rattan. At his suggestion needles, punches, and stout waxed thread made their way into Laks's kit.

Once he'd broken the nasty habit of splurging on Marriotts in Amritsar, he'd husbanded his money carefully. But now that a clear end to his journey was in sight he spent some on warm clothing and a few other items that might come in handy at the Roof of the World.

The time of his departure could hardly be kept secret from the community of the gurdwara, since he had accepted the offer of a ride to Shimla from Jasmit, a truck driver who happened to be headed that way, and Jasmit was nothing if not talkative. They were supposed to get underway at six o'clock in the morning. Inevitable delays and friction pushed that back to eight. The point of departure was an alleyway that ran behind the gurdwara and served, among other uses, as an informal loading dock for the kitchen. A surprising number of now familiar faces were there to see him off. Laks trudged up the alley bent under a fully loaded backpack and carrying a long bundle of rattan sticks. Or at least that was the case until the weight was lifted from his hand by one who had fallen in step beside him. He looked up in surprise to see Gopinder, his sparring partner, shouldering a duffel bag. He was dressed in what passed for warm clothing in Chandigarh but was probably a one-way ticket to hypothermic shock where Laks was going. "I can carry part of that load, brother," he said, taking the stick bundle in his free hand.

This should not have been such a total surprise. Gopinder had put himself through a lot of physical discomfort training in that breathing rig and was at least as altitude-adapted as Laks. But it caused Laks to start crying with astonishing suddenness. Blurry then was his view of the Uighur family, awaiting him by the kitchen's back door. He hadn't seen them in a couple of weeks. They'd been adopted by a local mosque that had evidently been looking after them well. They looked healthier. Ilham seemed to have grown three inches and put on fifty pounds. He was wearing a Kullu cap—a cylindrical hat of heavy wool, common where Laks was going. Laks assumed it was just a symbolic gesture until Ilham hauled a bag—smaller by far than that of Laks or Gopinder—out of the car that had brought them here and commenced a long series of farewells to his mother, granny, and siblings.

Laks was just pulling himself together when Ravi came striding up the alley. His rolling suitcase, designed for polished airport floors, kept trying to jerk his shoulder out of its socket as its cheap skateboard wheels snagged on breaks in the pavement. He had shoulder-holstered his cricket bat so that its handle projected up behind his head, making him look (as he was no doubt well aware) like a character in a movie. "I have never seen the mountains," he explained, "except from a great distance. I thought, what could be the harm in accompanying you at least part of the way?"

The truck of Jasmit was relatively small, consisting of a cab over the engine and a flatbed extending out over the rear wheels. Usually this was walled in by a steel frame to make it a sort of well-ventilated restraint system for cargo. Panels and tarps could be instated over that to protect from the elements, but they were entering the spell of clear weather after the monsoon and so none of that was necessary today. On big highways in more densely populated parts of India this would have been one of the smaller vehicles on the road. A large one, though, would have been hard pressed to negotiate the road up to Shimla. For as soon as they got out of Chandigarh's eastern suburbs, Jasmit was obliged to downshift as the engine began to labor uphill. The formerly straight road became an interminable series of zigzags, with little zigzags superimposed on big ones. They were ascending into the foothills of the Himalayas. They stayed as far to the left as they could to allow impatient cars to veer past them with tooting horns. But before long this ceased to be an issue as the whole road became packed solid with a traffic jam of mysterious origin. Roadside dhabas clung with increasing tenacity to the lips of increasingly high and sheer retaining walls. In traditional usage "dhaba" would mean a teahouse, and if you looked around in sufficiently remote places you could still find ones as rustic as this implied. Most of them, though, had evolved into convenience stores, as visually riotous as might be expected. On an open road the passengers would have been blown to tatters, shouting at each other the whole way, but here the wind of passage, when they were moving at all, was little more than a light mountain breeze.

Ilham hadn't bothered to explain himself yet, but now he did. "You have no idea what you're getting into," he said. "I am not much of a fighter. But if I learned one thing from watching the Chinese, it's that you need several people to think about logistics for every man who is carrying a weapon." His eyes strayed to

Laks's leather-covered stick. "So I thought it might help you to have at least one such person in your group—what is the word you use? San-something?"

"Oh, the word you are probably thinking of is *sangat*," Laks said. "It usually means a fellowship of *sants*. Not really the right—"

"*Sangat*. Yes, that's the word."

"It is really more of a religious connotation," Laks protested. "Sometimes, it's true, in old war stories they use that word to mean a column of saint-soldiers on the move, but it's a little inappropriate . . ."

"Like the Fellowship of the Ring," Ilham said, nodding solemnly. It wasn't his first foray into weird pop culture references. The hostels and dhabas of the high mountain trekking corridors tended to sport communal TV-watching parlors stocked with a diverse but absurdly random selection of DVDs left behind by previous guests.

"Fair enough," Laks said. "And by joining my *sangat* you are like my *bhai*, my brother, now, and the same goes for you, Gopinder, and you, Ravi."

Ilham signaled his approval by running his hand up the back of his neck and cocking his Kullu hat forward at a rakish and stylish angle. Then he squinted into the hazy sun rising above the white Himalayas.

THE CHIHUAHUAN DESERT

This was the most forbidding landscape Saskia had ever seen. The Sahara might be even bigger and more arid, but it looked soft—a world of dunes. This was a world of rocks. Rocks that had never been rounded and smoothed by water. What little rain fell on it seemed to have been sucked up by plants with no purpose other than to produce spines and serrations. She gazed out the train's window for hours without seeing a trace of surface water. Even before global warming, this landscape would kill anyone who tried to walk out of it.

"Welcome to the Flying S Ranch!" T.R. proclaimed, raising a stein, as the Beer Car crossed the property line. Here the railroad track ran side by side with a gravel road, and both passed between a pair of stone gateposts blazoned with a letter *S* bracketed between wings. Adjacent to that was a reinforced-concrete guardhouse topped with solar panels and antennas. A man in a brown cowboy hat stood in front of it, armed (disappointingly) not with a pair of six-guns but with a Glock. He unhooked a thumb from his belt and waved at people who were apparently waving at him from other windows on the train. No stranger to modern security measures, Saskia observed that the road had not just a gate, but also retractable bollards sturdy enough to stop any vehicle that might attempt to blast through.

"It's so ridiculous!" Amelia muttered in Dutch to Saskia. The two of them were at a table in the Beer Car's saloon with Rufus and Eshma, who had come over and befriended them. Amelia was sitting with arms folded, getting a load of the gate, like a student puzzling over a math problem. She caught Rufus looking at her and switched to English. "These Texas ranch gates! We have seen a number of these now. So huge and grand. But they don't *connect* to anything." She waved her hand off to the side. Each of the two massive stone gateposts was buttressed by a wing of stone wall, maybe two meters high and extending for a few meters away from the gate. There it gave way to chain-link fence, newly installed, which ran off into the desert for no more than thirty meters before giving way to standard-issue ranch fencing: strands of taut barbed wire that rose no higher than an average person's midsection.

Rufus pondered the question long enough to clue them in that they had stumbled upon some kind of major cultural/conceptual gap. "They're connected to *fences*," he pointed out, which was true.

"Yes but—" Saskia began.

"Traditionally the gate is the *weakest* point in a perimeter defense," Amelia pointed out. "Not the *strongest*. It's just basic logic. Surely as a military veteran you—"

Rufus nodded. "I got you."

"Is it all just for ostentation? Show?"

"Extetics," Rufus answered with a nod. They'd heard him use the word before. It was his pronunciation of "aesthetics."

"It's a signal too," he continued. "You're on my property now. Best respect it, or get you gone."

"That makes sense," Saskia said.

Rufus looked at Amelia. "Past that—as a military veteran, like you said—don't look at the barbed-wire fence and say it's nothing. Look at *where it is*. This is defense in depth. Maybe when we get where we're going, they'll let us go out in some ranch vehicles, some ATVs or four-wheel drives. That desert might look open and flat from out the window, but if you leave yonder road and try driving across it, you'll learn real soon it is a barrier. Even walking is hard—every footstep requires you formulate a plan."

Eshma nodded. "I've gone hiking in such terrain. It's exhausting. *Mentally* exhausting," she hastened to add. "The cognitive load of having to think about each step." Eshma tapped her forehead.

Rufus processed that and nodded with the distracted air of a man who was soon going to look up "cognitive load" on the Internet and spend an hour clicking on links. "That's why people who knew this land used horses. The horse handles the *cognitive load*. You just tell it where to go and how fast."

In case anyone had missed the entry to ranch property, event staff were now passing through the saloon handing out baseball caps, bandannas, and steel water bottles bearing the same winged S symbol they had seen on the gateposts. Only for a moment had Saskia assumed that this was the ancient name of the ranch. T.R. had rebranded the place. *Literally* rebranded, since the Flying S logo was a mark designed to be burned into the hide of a cow. The S was obviously Sulfur.

Eshma happily pulled on her baseball cap, first drawing her ponytail through the little opening in the back. The Cinderella of last night had reverted to the studious and efficient nerd girl. She was just socially awkward enough that she had walked up to their table a few minutes ago and sat down without so much as a "by your leave" and a complete absence of any of that "Your Majesty" nonsense. Saskia was pleased that she'd done so and made a mental note to ask her, later, about those computational climate models that seemed to be her stock-in-trade. She had gotten the impression from Alastair that risk analysts in the financial world were basically unable to do their jobs until they got numbers from people like Eshma. They viewed the Eshmas of the world as a cross between all-knowing supergeniuses and borderline charlatans reading the future from sheep guts. In any case, the respect with which he and Mark Furlong treated Eshma was conspicuous.

Amelia's gaze was fixed on her new baseball cap, but she wasn't really seeing it. She was still processing Rufus's defense-in-depth argument. "You could snip the wires and drive through anywhere—" she began.

"At *three miles an hour*," Rufus said, completing her sentence. "Might as well get out and walk. At least get you some exercise."

"Some vehicles could go faster."

"Tracked vehicles," Rufus nodded. "Even they would break down. Fixing them used to be my job. But I don't think ol' T.R. is planning to stop an armored brigade. If it comes to that, it means his strategy failed on a whole other level." He looked to Saskia as he said that. One of those moments, which she wished she never had to put up with, when she abruptly stopped being an ordinary participant in the conversation and was reminded that she was a queen.

The train had dropped to a deliberate speed, perhaps fifty kilometers an hour, as it felt its way across the unbelievably vast ranch—one-quarter the size of the Netherlands—on tracks that had not been built to a modern standard. If Saskia was any judge of such things, the rails themselves were in good repair—T.R. had upgraded them—but the line itself had been laid out long ago with sharp turns and steep grades. Most of the grades were uphill. Her ears popped more than once. She already knew that their destination was more than a kilometer, but less than a mile, above sea level. Not high enough that you'd really notice the thin air, but enough to buy some small advantage for the project.

They passed an airstrip. Parked there were two bizjets, three single-engine prop planes, and a helicopter. Willem had already told her that a Dutch jet would be landing there later to take them home tomorrow. So that helped her fix her location on the map. They were going southwest, directly toward the Rio Grande. The range of mountains where T.R. had built his facility was the last watershed one would cross before descending into that river's valley and reaching the U.S./Mexico border. The Flying S Ranch ran all the way to the river's bank.

"That off to the right, in the distance, is the Sierra Diablo," T.R. announced, apparently referring to some craggy mountains north of them that somehow managed to look even more forbidding than T.R.'s property. "Site of the last armed conflict between Texas Rangers and Apaches in 1881."

At the very end of the journey, the railroad track and the road became one, a strip of pavement with embedded rails, as they funneled through a short tunnel that had been blasted through a rock spur. The spur had nearly vertical sides and served as a natural barrier between the northern expanse of the Bar S, which was mostly alluvial flatland, and more broken and rugged terrain beyond that straddled the crest of the mountain range. Once they'd emerged from that tunnel—which the train passed through at no more than a brisk walking pace—they entered into a natural bowl, a few kilometers long, embraced by the primary crest of the mountains, which now loomed above them, and the smaller but more precipitous offshoot spur they'd just tunneled through. The railroad track curved round and sidled along the base of the spur before terminating. This was the end of the line. The curve enabled them all to peer forward out the windows and see that, ahead of them, the freight cars had come to a halt adjacent to various cargo handling facilities in what was apparently the main complex. This was underwhelming visually, but Saskia knew from satellite pictures that most of it was belowground. Separated from that complex by a stretch of open, uneven ground was a neat village of mobile homes, surrounded by a wall of shipping containers. It reminded Saskia of military outposts she'd visited in places such as Afghanistan.

"Welcome! We made it!" T.R. announced, and then paused for a brief round of polite applause. "You'll notice a distinct lack of luxury accommodations. Or accommodation of any sort, really. That's what this train is for! Not just to get y'all here, but to keep y'all comfy during your stay! For your staff, there's plenty of space in yonder bunkhouse." T.R. waved toward the village of mobile homes. "You are of course free to get out and walk around. Look for the individuals in the white cowboy hats! They are the good guys! And gals! You should know as much from the movies! They are here to help you and keep you safe from rattlesnakes, dehydration, hyperthermia, hypothermia, and other unique and special hazards of the Chihuahuan Desert." Saskia looked around and noticed that several of the event staff had indeed put on white cowboy hats.

"Brown hats are ranch staff—also very helpful," T.R. continued. "The guys and gals in the *black hats* are also here to keep you safe, in another sense which is perhaps hinted at by the color of their headgear. They are *bad dudes* and dudettes. They will not be bad to *y'all*, of course, but they will be bad *in your service* and *for your protection* should any issue with trespassers of the two-legged sort arise. They are, as a rule, less approachable than the white hats or the brown hats. But you may certainly approach them if you need anything. Just don't sneak up on them. They hate that."

The Biggest Gun in the World was *so* big that it had its own elevator, shoehorned into a space between two of its barrels. The elevator could only accommodate three people in comfort. So T.R. did the tour in two shifts: first Sylvester and Michiel, and, an hour later, Bob and Saskia.

Only a few buildings on the whole site rose to more than a single story aboveground. The most prominent was the head frame: a term from the mining industry referring to the aboveground machinery that bestrode a mine shaft. It was maybe ten meters high and consisted largely of open steel framing through which large reels of cable, motors, and other lifting-and-hoisting sorts of gear were visible. Pipes and cables converged on it from other parts of the complex and plunged down into the shaft.

Of course you couldn't dig a shaft without raking up the rock and dirt you were displacing. This material—"spoil"—had been distributed around the complex and used to buttress, or to completely bury, outlying facilities such as tanks, processing plants, and buildings that seemed to have a lot of expensive people in them ("command and control" in T.R.-speak). Without being terribly obvious about it, the designers had, in other words, hardened the site. Rufus, at a glance, had identified some of the spoil-piles as "revetments," obliging Saskia to look up the word. It meant a sort of blast wall built around a potential target to protect from near misses by artillery. It didn't take a military expert to know that a cruise missile could obliterate anything on the surface. But it seemed proof against small, furtive attacks such as bomb-bearing drones or mountaintop snipers. Large areas were screened by nets with strips of fabric woven through them. Their purpose wasn't entirely clear to her, but they would definitely stop drones, provide much needed shade, and make things complicated for surveillance satellites.

Projecting straight up from the top of the head frame was a neat array of six tubes. Each of these was fattened at its top by a construct that Saskia could not help likening to the flash suppressor on the muzzle of a carbine.

A white-hat drove her and the lord mayor in a small ATV to the head frame's ground-level entrance, where T.R. awaited them, sporting a huge ornate Flying S belt buckle. Looking up from this perspective it was evident that those six tubes were arranged in a radial pattern, like the barrels on a Gatling gun. They ran straight down into the mine shaft. Because the six barrels, at about one meter, were so much smaller in diameter than the shaft, which was big enough to swallow a small house, there was abundant space in between them for other stuff. The exact allocation of that space had obviously been the topic of much brain work among engineers. Through a kind of verbal osmosis, Saskia had picked up a new bit of technical jargon: "routed systems," which was engineer-speak for long skinny things like pipes and wires that had to go from one place to another. The results of the lucubrations of the routed systems engineers were summarized in a cross-sectional diagram posted near the door: a big circle with the six smaller circles of the gun barrels evenly spaced around its periphery, and everything else a fractal jigsaw puzzle of advanced industrial cramming and jamming. But the biggest single rectangle in the whole diagram was the elevator shaft. Second biggest was a circle labeled "shell hoist."

"Y'all do your homework?" T.R. asked, not the least bit seriously, as they got into the elevator. The outward-facing door was solid, but the walls were open steel mesh.

He was referring to a set of YouTube links he'd shared with them last night on the topic of how mine shafts were dug.

"I actually *did* click through," Bob admitted. "I've a toddler-like weakness for construction equipment."

Saskia shook her head. "I don't."

"Start at the top," T.R. said. "Place charges. Blow shit up. Scoop out the spoil. Repeat. The whole rig for setting the charges and scooping up the spoil gets lowered into the shaft by this"—he slapped one of the steel members of the head frame—"as you go. That's the point of this"—slap, slap—"to move stuff up and down. Line the walls with reinforced concrete a few feet at a time on your way down. Pretty simple really. Just got to keep at it."

He pulled the elevator's door shut behind them. The three of them fit into it without touching each other. Four would have been a crowd. "Anyone claustrophobic?" T.R. asked. This was merely a formal courtesy, as event planners had already asked Saskia (and presumably Bob) this question three times in the last twenty-four hours. Both she and Bob shook their heads. T.R. hit the "down" button, overhead machinery whined, and they began to descend. "We had a head start on digging this hole," T.R. continued, "because of an old abandoned coal mine that was already here. But it was only four hundred feet deep, and not wide enough."

"But you just *had* to use it anyway, I'll wager," Saskia said. "Because of the symbolism."

T.R. nodded, but didn't respond other than to get a slightly mischievous look on his face. Their surroundings were clearly observable through the lift's steel mesh walls. The shaft became more and more crammed, as per the diagrams, during the first few meters' descent, as various underground pipes, conduits, ducts, and cables sprouted through its walls and turned vertically downward. Past a certain point, though, it didn't get any more crowded, because it couldn't. Horizontal stripes and numbers had been painted on things so that you could tell you were moving. A panel on the lift's wall gave the depth belowground in meters and showed their progress on a cutaway diagram.

"Not the world's fastest elevator," T.R. remarked. "Obviously, the device is not manned when it's running. It is as automated as a zillion bucks' worth of robotics can make it. So whisking people up and down was not a priority for us."

"And if I understand the nature of your plan—" the lord mayor began to ask.

"*Our* plan, Bob. Our plan."

"It will be running all the time. Nonstop."

T.R. nodded. "The design spec is for it to run for two years with ninety percent uptime before it needs an overhaul."

Bob furrowed his brow. "How do you overhaul something like this?"

"There's always a way," T.R. answered. "But the real answer is, you probably don't. Just fill it up with dirt and build another one. Remember, in two years the world is gonna be a different place. A *cooler* place, for one thing." He looked at Saskia. "I had my eye on some of your old coal mines for a while. Down in the southeastern corner of your country. Some nice deep shafts there. Saves some digging. Great *symbolism*. Decided against it though."

"I think I know the place you mean," Saskia said. "Very close to the German border. The neighbors would complain about the noise."

T.R. nodded. "The Greens would lose their fucking minds."

"They will anyway," Bob said.

The lift slowed as it approached 215 meters below ground level. Their view was improving as, it seemed, some of the routed systems got routed elsewhere. It was now possible to see the six steel barrels of the gun arrayed around them. The lift eased to a stop. Through a window in its door they could see into a well-lit chamber beyond. It wasn't a large space but it was definitely external to the main shaft. "See, down here at the bottom we did a little more blasting and hollowed out some extra volume," T.R. said. He opened the door and led them into the side shaft. It was not much larger than the bedroom Saskia had slept in last night on the train. The walls were bare limestone, still bearing the marks of the pneumatic tools that had carved them out. The floor was a grate through which they could look straight down into another story below. No wonder she'd been warned not to wear heels. Two men and a woman stood against the back wall wearing air tanks on their backs connected to respirator masks dangling free on their chests. "Safety first!" T.R. said, waving at them. "This area has plumbing for four different gases, three of which can kill you. One, natural gas—basically methane, which we get for free from a well right here on the ranch, about ten miles away. That is the fuel we burn to power the gun. Two, air, which we use to burn the methane and which, incidentally, keeps us alive. Three, hydrogen, which is the light gas we compress to drive the projectiles up the barrels. The air in the peashooter. We obtain it by cracking natural gas in a plant upstairs. Either hydrogen or methane would cause an explosion if it were to mix with air, as the result of a leak or malfunction, and be ignited by a spark. So, four: as a backup system we have stored down here a large quantity of compressed argon, which is an inert gas that does not support combustion. Or life. Now, to be clear, the methane and hydrogen lines have been totally disconnected. We're not stupid. There's no way such a leak could happen right now. If one were to occur, it would be detected by these here doohickeys." He indicated a white box mounted to the stone ceiling that looked like a smoke detector as designed by the Pentagon. Saskia now noticed more of them all over the place, merrily blinking. "If that were to happen, an alarm would sound and argon gas would flood this whole volume and drive out the air and render the atmosphere non-combustible."

"And then we would all suffocate," Saskia said.

"Good news, bad news!" T.R. confirmed. "That's why we have

portable air supplies. Each of these fine people is wearing one and has a second one handy. If the alarm sounds, they'll do what it always says to do in those goddamned pre-flight announcements."

"Got it," Bob said. "So, if we hear a loud noise, we should wait for one of them to get after us with an air tank."

"You shouldn't have to wait long," T.R. assured them, "and the argon won't hurt you while you're waiting. It's—"

"An element," Saskia said.

"Bingo. An inert gas. A *noble* gas, Your Majesty. There will be plenty of time to ride the elevator to the top, where we will serve drinks."

"Sounds like my kind of emergency!" Bob said—a joke at his own expense.

"Any questions? Good. Having gotten the safety briefing out of the way, I propose to show you how the Biggest Gun in the World works from the bottom up, as this is the easiest way to understand it. And we are not quite at the bottom yet. This is Level Zero. I am told you both feel comfortable with ladders. Let's put that to the test by descending to Level Minus One and beyond."

A ladder was bolted to the stone wall, descending through a human-diameter hole in the grating. T.R. waited as one of the safety crew climbed down it, then followed with a certain amount of comical slapstick grunting and groaning intended to put them at ease. "Keep going!" he said to everyone. "'Til you cain't go no more!'"

Saskia and Bob took turns with the other crew members in descending to Level Minus One, then Minus Two, and so forth. At each level Saskia looked out at what was in the adjoining shaft, but after Minus One there was nothing to see except a blank wall of steel, curved to fit perfectly in the shaft. "The cylinder," T.R. said at one point, noting her curiosity.

Minus Four sported a massive round hatch, a meter in diameter, let into the wall of that cylinder. Minus Five had nothing but routed systems of the smaller and more intricate type: sensors, probably networked to computers elsewhere. At Minus Six, the ladder stopped and they bottomed out on a natural limestone floor. "This is the base of the excavation," T.R. said. "This is all the farther we dug. And this here"—he rapped a knuckle against the cylinder wall—"is the base of the cylinder, where the methane burns."

Another round hatch was let into the steel wall here, and it was ajar, with an extension cord running into it from an outlet on the wall. T.R., with help from a crew member, shoved on the hatch, which was slow to get moving but then glided serenely. It opened inward. Saskia could see that it was designed to withstand internal pressure, like a bung on a barrel. The space beyond was illuminated well, if harshly, by an ordinary work light plugged into the extension cord. T.R. bent over and stepped through, beckoning Saskia to follow.

"The wall is so thick!" she exclaimed as she was stepping over the threshold. "To withstand pressure?"

"Ain't really as thick as it looks," T.R. demurred. "It's got a cooling jacket all around it, coupla inches thick, but hollow—we pump water through it to keep it from overheating when it is bang, bang, banging away."

"That would explain the cooling tower I noticed topside," Bob said.

"Yep, and a lot of pipes and pumps along the way."

They were now in a steel-walled chamber about five meters in diameter. Its floor was concave, a flattened dome, so they had to mind their footing. Below the level of the port, at about knee height, it was ringed with an array of stainless-steel orifices. Other than that the walls were featureless to a height of about four meters above their heads, where a sturdy steel ring had been welded into place, projecting just a few centimeters inward from the wall. Directly above that was a flattish dome that completely sealed off the portion of the cylinder above it. "That thing moves. You're looking at the underside of the piston," T.R. explained. "Down here, where we are, is where we explode shit." He bent down and tapped one of the orifices. "These are coaxial. They let in compressed methane and compressed air at the same time. They let it in *fast* to keep reload time to a minimum. When we get the amount we want, we plug our ears and spark it off with these." He pointed out a tiny detail Saskia hadn't noticed before: little white ceramic knobs between the nozzles, with tiny metal parts projecting from the ends. "Plain old ordinary spark plugs from the car parts department at T.R. Mick's. Volume discount."

There wasn't much else to say. They took turns stooping down and exiting the port. T.R., the last one out, carried the work light with him and pulled the extension cord out in his wake. The crew members pulled the hatch shut and latched it while others ascended the ladder to Minus Four, where earlier they'd seen another port-and-hatch. Entering into this one—which was just the upper portion of the same cylinder—they found themselves again on sloped footing, as they were now standing on the top of the domed piston whose underside they'd been gazing up at a few minutes ago.

Once they'd all found places to stand, T.R. said, "This here upper part will be filled with hydrogen gas, which is the working fluid that actually pushes the shell up the barrel. The physics of it is beyond me, but they say that the maximum velocity of the projectile can't be any faster than the speed of sound in the gas that is doing the pushing. The speed of sound in light gases like hydrogen and helium is higher than that in air. Enough to make a difference for our purposes. We looked at helium. The world's helium supply actually comes from up Amarillo way. It's safer, but it's expensive and hard to work with. If you build one of these at the doorstep of Germany, Your Majesty, you'll want to take a hard look at helium. I can help you get some."

"Very considerate of you as always, T.R.!"

"Anyways, we settled on hydrogen. Some of it's gonna leak out and burn, but it's a desert, so who cares? It's easy to make more, on-site, from natural gas. So, at the same time the methane-air mix is filling the chamber below, we fill this volume with a certain amount of H_2. When the combustion chamber"—he pointed straight down—"goes boom, this piston we're standing on gets forced upward, compressing the hydrogen. Which only has one way out." He drew their attention to the top of the cylinder, ten meters above their heads, where it tapered inward like an upside-down funnel to an orifice in the middle about the size of a manhole. If the entire cylinder was a bottle, that was its mouth. "Let's see where it goes!" he suggested, touching off another round of extension cord wrangling, hatch closing, and ladder climbing that took them up above the top of the massive steel cylinder to Minus One.

If the lower levels had been straight twentieth-century tech with their spark plugs and pistons, Minus One was all modern robotics. Slightly below them was a massive construct that could only be the "mouth" of the "bottle"—the upside-down funnel that accepted and channeled the pulse of hydrogen gas being driven upward by the rising piston. A short distance above that were the bottoms of the six barrels, which were simply cut off at their bases, open to the room. In between those obvious and easy-to-understand elements was an elaborate, massive, rotating contraption that, if Saskia was any judge of these things, had consumed the lion's share of the engineering resources. She couldn't really puzzle it out until T.R. issued a command that caused a vertical conveyor system to go into motion. This thing—"Shell hoist" on the cross-sectional diagram—had run parallel to the elevator all the way down from ground level. It served a similar purpose to the lift, but it was smaller and it ran much faster. After it had been whirring along for a minute or so, it slowed.

A giant bullet descended into the room. The bullet was a bit longer than Saskia was tall, and somewhat fatter than a beer keg. It was machined aluminum in some places, carbon fiber in others. It had a Flying S logo and was stenciled "RETURN TO FLYING S RANCH - REWARD" in English and Spanish. It glided down past them on the hoist and was seized by a massive robot arm, which pulled it away, indexed around, and fed it point-first into the base of one of the gun barrels. Another mechanism, pushing up from below, then rammed the shell upward until it had completely disappeared into the barrel. Something went kerchunk. The robot arm retracted, but the shell did not fall out.

"Now, let's say we want to send it on its way," T.R. said. He nodded to a technician, who pressed some buttons.

The whole massive robotic platform went into motion, pirouetting around the central axis of the main shaft. Saskia couldn't help thinking of the big cylinder in a cowboy's revolver. It had a single large orifice in its top, offset to one side, matching the diameter of the gun barrels. When this was positioned below the breech of the barrel that had just been loaded, the whole thing rose upward in a swift, smooth movement until the connection was made.

"That's how the hydrogen flows to the barrel," Bob guessed.

"There's now a direct unimpeded channel between the two," T.R. confirmed. "If you were Spiderman you could go back down to Minus Four, into the same port we just used. You could climb up the cylinder wall, through that funnel we looked at, and up a short, oblique, snergly tube to where you could reach up into that barrel and touch the base of that shell we just now loaded."

"And it's all hot?" Saskia asked.

T.R. nodded. "Good point, Your Majesty. The shell was preheated above, and it's still hot now—hot enough to keep the sulfur in its molten state. For as long as it sits in that barrel waiting to be fired, it will be kept hot by electrical heaters built into the barrel walls. The space on the other side of this window is quite warm—and it's about to get warmer."

"How many of those barrels are loaded?" Bob asked.

"As of now? Six of six. All we gotta do is get out of here and turn on the gas." He checked his watch. "And then we should be ready for this month's meeting of the Flying S Ranch Employees' Model Rocketry Club!"

The elongated bowl, four thousand feet above sea level, in which this complex had been constructed, was referred to by T.R. as Pina2bo ("Pin a two bo"). Anyone familiar with the literature on climate change and geoengineering would get the joke. Pinatubo was the name of a volcano in the Philippines that had exploded in 1991. It had blasted fifteen million tons of sulfur dioxide into the stratosphere. The result had been a couple of years' beautiful sunsets and reduced global temperatures. The two phenomena were directly related. The sulfur from the volcano had eventually spread out into a veil of tiny droplets of H_2SO_4. Light from the sun hit those little spheres and bounced. Some of it bounced directly back into space—which accounted for the planet-wide cooling, as energy that never entered the troposphere in the first place couldn't contribute to the greenhouse effect. Other light caromed off those droplets, billiard-ball style, and came into the troposphere at various oblique angles. Since that was where humans lived, those who lifted their gaze saw that light as a general brightness of the sky. This was hard to notice in the daytime but quite obvious when the sun was near the horizon, the sky was generally dark, and the light was red.

Pinatubo was hardly the first volcano to explode during the time that humans had lived upon the earth. Earlier such events had been followed by cold snaps and awesome sunsets that had entered the historical record in anecdotal form. But Pinatubo was the first, and so far the only really big one, that had happened during the modern era when its results could be scientifically studied.

After a smaller eruption in the 1960s a high-altitude plane had flown through the plume and come back with a residue on its windshield that an Australian scientist had evaluated by licking it. "Painfully acid" was his verdict. He'd experienced exactly the same sensation as Texas oilmen sampling sour crude on their fingers. So there was already evidence, prior to Pinatubo, that volcanoes hurled sulfur compounds into the stratosphere. The 1991 blast found scientists ready to make more sophisticated measurements than windshield licking, and provided the basis for decades of research and modeling of so-called solar geoengineering—the term for any climate mitigation scheme that was based on bouncing part of the sun's rays back into space.

So Pina2bo was what T.R. called the complex where he planned to do basically the same thing, on a smaller scale. Pina2bo would have to operate full blast for many years to put as much SO_2 into the stratosphere as its namesake had done in a few minutes. Since the stuff began to fall out of the atmosphere after a few years, the best that Pina2bo could ever achieve was just a fraction of the real Mount Pinatubo eruption. But enough to begin making a difference. And if the first one worked, more of them could be built.

The gun complex—complete with its natural gas cracker (a sort of mini-refinery), its cooling tower, its tank farm, and its plant for loading and prepping the huge sulfur-filled bullets—was at one end of the valley. "Bunkhouse," a miniature town, was at the other end. Between was a no-man's-land, mostly open space, perhaps amounting to a square kilometer of broken ground. It seemed to be used for any purposes that didn't fit neatly into one end or the other. There was a track around its perimeter scoured by ATVs. Piles of coal that had been heaped up a hundred years ago and scantly colonized by weeds and cactus. A makeshift shooting range, with bullet-ridden pieces of junk strewn along the base of a slope. Huddles of heavy equipment parked out in the open. And a picnic area consisting of a few aluminum tables sheltered from the sun's fury by canopies and linked to Bunkhouse by a faint trail in the dirt. Though even in dim light you'd be able to follow it just by using bright red BEWARE OF RATTLESNAKES signs as a bread crumb trail. Canopies and picnic tables alike were lashed to massive concrete blocks or bolted directly to the stony ground.

The Flying S Ranch Employees' Model Rocketry Club held its meeting in the picnic area two hours after the conclusion of Bob and Saskia's tour. It was unusually well attended, and so the event planners had erected aluminum bleachers and pitched more sun canopies. About fifty meters away, on open ground, a folding table had been set up, and beyond that was a row of five contraptions with whippy vertical rods sticking up out of them to various heights, none rising to more than about three meters above the ground. Threaded onto each rod, and resting atop the contraption that served as its base, was a miniature rocket. Three of these were tiny children's toys. The last two were considerably larger. The biggest was maybe a hand span in diameter and twice the height of a man.

Yellow caution tape had been strung between orange cones to surround all this with a perimeter. A few children, presumably the offspring of Flying S staff, had been credentialed to step over—or, for younger rocket scientists, under—the tape. To judge from the nature of the paint jobs, these kids were the creators of the three smaller rockets. They were doing a creditable job of keeping extreme excitement under control. The two bigger rockets were being fussed over by adults.

Saskia had not expected such a range of ages, such small-town wholesomeness. It stood to reason that the ranch in general, and Pina2bo in particular, would have full-time staff, and that some of those would have families. Willem had shown her satellite imagery of the place. This had revealed clusters of mobile homes outside of the Pina2bo valley but within driving range. Some of the employees must commute for some distance. She'd been in Texas long enough to know that driving an hour or more was nothing to these people. So there was a sort of extended community here of—just guessing—maybe a thousand people all told? Spread thin over the vastness of the Chihuahuan Desert, they were held together by gravel roads and dusty pickup trucks and they came together for events like this one.

Inevitably T.R. came out to say a few words to the crowd on the bleachers over a PA system, which inevitably malfunctioned and obliged him to holler through cupped hands. Refreshments were being served to the crowd on the bleachers.

"Free earplugs for everyone!" was how T.R. began. He wasn't kidding; ELog people were handing them out from salad bowls. "The Rocketry Club has been holding these events every month for almost two years—rain or shine!" The rain part was apparently a joke. Saskia was slow to get it but the Texans were suitably amused. "It is a very safety-conscious organization! Lou here is the range officer. He is going to cover some important technicalities about federal regulation of airspace. First, though, let's launch some rockets!"

Lou, a cowboy-hatted engineer in his fifties, sheepishly came to the fore. The PA system had been dialed in and so he was able to speak into a microphone, which was fortunate since he lacked the stentorian YouTube-trained diction of T.R. "First, Jo Anne will launch an Estes Alpha," he announced. His complete lack of awareness that no one in the crowd knew what that meant, and that some further explanation might be in order, confirmed his status in Saskia's mind as some kind of inveterate geek—probably one of those people T.R. had poached from the Johnson Space Center. There was some mumbling and fumbling at the table as a girl of perhaps nine executed a procedure with some switches and wires. Lou held the mike in front of Jo Anne as she counted down in a thready but spirited voice from ten. Then the smallest of the rockets gave out a little hiss and leapt from its launch rod on a spurt of smoke. The engine burned for less than a second. The rocket, barely visible, coasted for a few seconds more, then separated into two pieces and deployed an orange parachute. "Congratulations, Jo Anne, on her first launch!" Lou intoned as applause died away and the Estes Alpha began drifting toward the ground. "We'll retrieve that later. For now, the range remains closed!"

Two more such rockets, each a little bigger than the last, were launched in short order by other children. "And the range is open!" Lou then announced. This was apparently the signal for the kids to run out there and find their rockets among the cacti and the rattlesnakes. While they did so, Lou delivered the promised peroration on federal airspace regulatory policy. "Those rockets y'all just saw can't go higher than fifteen hundred feet," he said. "The engines is just too small, they ain't got the impulse. Impulse is a little old scalar variable defined as the product of—" He noticed T.R. making a throat-cutting gesture and broke off before he could supply the mathematical formula. "Point is, the FAA don't care 'cause we ain't messing with their airspace! But these two big boys still on the pads here," he said, waving at the remaining rockets, "that is a different story! These have . . ." He trailed off, performing a mental calculation. "Sixteen thousand, three hundred and eighty-four times the impulse of Jo Anne's little old Estes Alpha! They can go high!" He pronounced it "hah." "So hah they could maybe hit a plane, or vice versa. So every month when we hold a meeting of the Flying S Ranch Employees Model Rocketry Club, you know what we gotta do?" It was probably meant as a rhetorical question but still elicited a smattering of "No! What?" from the bleachers. This knocked Lou off his stride but he soldiered on. "We gotta get us a permit from Uncle Sam! It ain't that hard. They're real nice about it. We fill out a little old form says we are fixing to launch a couple of high-power model rockets from the Flying S Ranch on such-and-such a day at such-and-such a time and you better spread the word to all the pilots not to fly over the area! And that's exactly what they do! Just like that, the FAA sends out a Notice to Airmen and warns all the pilots to steer clear of the area and keep that box of airspace—you can think of it as a box—empty. Now, some of these cowboys round here have pilot licenses. I guess there's Meskin drug runners too, but we don't care if we hit them. Anyhow, they don't bother reading the Notice and come flying around anyway, so we go belt-and-suspenders on it. We got watchers posted all round, watching the sky to warn us of any of them interlopers. If they tell us the sky's clear, which it usually is, we're good to go!" This seemed an obvious applause line, so the crowd made scattered "Woo!" noises while Lou conferred with a younger club member who was wearing a headset and tending to a radio—or, at any rate, a mess of cabled-together laptops and mystery boxes that seemed to answer to the same purpose as a radio. This culminated in a lot of serious nodding. "Skies are clear! Visibility is excellent! Sheng's gonna launch a high-power rocket, take some pictures of us from ten thousand feet. Say cheese! Take it away, Sheng!"

Sheng, a man of East Asian ancestry, didn't have much to say, but did show awareness of the crowd's dwindling attention span by opting for a truncated countdown that started at three. His rocket, the second largest, howled off the pad on a considerably larger stick of yellow-white fire and very rapidly disappeared from sight.

"Sheng'll go out in an ATV and try to find that thing later and post the movie it took," Lou said, as Sheng awkwardly high-fived a couple of his buddies. "But now our main event: a sounding rocket that's gonna top out at somewhere round a hundred thousand feet and send back telemetry about winds in the upper atmosphere and lower stratosphere. Helps us calculate windage on any giant bullets that might be headed up that way." He conferred with the radio guy again. To judge from their body language, the skies were still clear.

This rocket had a larger crew of important-seeming engineers, most of whom were in White Label logo-wear, others in Flying S livery. The distinction was a little blurry, since they all worked for T.R. When it launched, it roared and screamed and took slightly longer to get going, leaving an impressive column of smoke behind. A few seconds after it disappeared into the blue heaven, the valley resonated with a thunderclap. "Sonic boom," Lou explained. "Get used to it!"

Get used to it. Saskia hadn't thought seriously about the problem of sonic booms, but hearing one in the flesh focused her attention. She tapped Willem on the shoulder. "Could you pull up those images of the ranch—the whole ranch—again, please?"

A few moments later he handed her a tablet showing the view of the Flying S Ranch from space. Pina2bo was understated, largely because of the netting, which among other things served as camouflage. But once she had found it, she centered it on the screen and zoomed out until the outlying settlements—the bedroom communities, as it were—came in view. The clusters of mobile dwellings and prefabs where the employees lived. It was obvious now that these were arranged around an arc at a certain distance from Pina2bo. It was interrupted on its southwest limb by the Rio Grande—there were no settlements in Mexico. Or were there? She saw a small cluster of trailers on the Mexican side, right along the imaginary radius. "Most of these people," she concluded, "are housed outside of sonic boom range. So they can get some sleep!"

After the launch of the sounding rocket, it was all just nerds looking at computer screens and virtual displays for several minutes. Spectators drifted to the refreshment table and to a row of oven-hot portable toilets lined up nearby. Everyone seemed well hydrated and cheerful but no one knew exactly what was going on. No one, that is, except for T.R., who was using a nearby SUV as a makeshift command center. Senior engineers were jogging back and forth to it as they were summoned or dismissed, and T.R. could be seen gesticulating, talking on the phone, consulting laptops and tablets thrust in front of him by aides. Finally he emerged from the SUV and trudged over to the PA system. His body language was heavy. He had an air of resignation. So Saskia was expecting bad news. But she was wrong about that. T.R.'s body language was that of Caesar sloshing across the Rubicon.

"As long as the FAA has been so good as to clear the airspace," he said, "we're gonna launch some more stuff. Might want to plug your ears." He set the microphone down, turned his back on the crowd, and faced the complex at the other end of the valley. The crowd grew silent. An alarm klaxon could be heard in the distance. T.R. stepped carefully over the caution tape, strolled out into the open near the rocket launchers, and checked his watch.

A spark of light gleamed from the top of the head frame, then winked out. A few seconds later the valley was walloped by a sonic boom. T.R. was looking almost vertically up into the sky, but there was nothing to see. He checked his watch again, then turned back and indicated the microphone. An ELog employee snatched it from the table and ran it over to him. "Next one's in seven minutes," he said. "You'll want to come out into the open if you are hoping to see anything."

People slowly, then suddenly evacuated the bleachers and came toward T.R., stepping out of the canopies' shade and into direct sunlight. The caution tape was severed and allowed to flutter in the breeze.

"The muzzle flash'll catch your eye," T.R. said. "But if you look at that, you'll miss it. Shell's already long gone. You got to look into the space above. Next one's in 3 . . . 2 . . . 1 . . ."

Saskia just glimpsed it, moving straight up at fantastic velocity, as the muzzle flared and extinguished below.

A third barrel fired seven and a half minutes later, and this time she was able to track it for a few seconds before it became too small for the naked eye to see. Each launch was followed by another sonic boom equal to the first.

"Holy shit," said the Right Honorable the Lord Mayor.

"I know," said Daia Chand, next to him. "Even after all this, I didn't actually believe he was going to pull the trigger."

"It's happening," Alastair said. "After all this—it's actually happening. I sort of can't believe it. We are fixing the climate."

"*Changing* it, anyway," Eshma returned.

"This'll bring the temperature down?" Rufus asked.

"If he can keep firing that gun," Saskia said.

"Sounds like fixing to me," Rufus concluded.

Not far away, the three Venetians were engaging in a round robin of embracing and kissing. Sylvester was standing with his arms folded, looking dumbfounded. After the third sonic boom, he walked up to T.R. and shook his hand, grinning broadly under the brim of his borrowed cowboy hat.

The Biggest Gun in the World fired each of its barrels three times, launching a total of eighteen shells, before it fell silent. The test lasted for a couple of hours, not counting shell recovery time. Well before the end of it, Saskia had begun to feel dizzy from the heat. She and many others retreated to the air-conditioned comfort of the train cars to watch the proceedings on video screens.

"So this is what it looks like with an N of eighteen," Alastair mused over a bottle of Corona. Saskia had spent enough time with him to recognize this as statistician-speak. Launching a single shell—an N of 1—would have taught T.R. a lot. Launching two would have taught him a little more. An N of eighteen was big enough to do some statistical analysis and get a picture of the range of outcomes.

The positions of the eighteen shells were plotted and updated on a real-time map displayed on a big monitor. They were spread out like beads on a string along a trajectory that rose straight up from the Flying S Ranch and then spiraled down through Mexican airspace. They all seemed to be following the same basic flight plan, like cars in an aerial train. Each had two video cameras, one aimed forward and the other aimed back. The twin feeds from one shell were up on the video screens. They couldn't have been more different. The view forward was of a black sky above a curved horizon limned in blue. The view back was an endless series of flashes, which became so visually annoying that the pane had to be minimized. But it confirmed that the sulfur-burning pulse jet had ignited and was farting away.

At one end of the car T.R. was doing an interview with a tame journalist. With a couple of beers in him, he had become amusingly and colorfully exasperated by this person's stubborn misunderstanding of the muzzle flash. "It is *just a by-product*. We would eliminate it if we could. If we used helium, it wouldn't happen at all—and *it wouldn't matter* because the purpose of that gas is just to be like the air in a peashooter. Unavoidably, some of it leaks out of the muzzle after the shell has departed. We control that as much as we can with check valves and such. But it's safer to burn it off than to just have it drifting around god knows where." He caught the eye of an aide who seemed to specialize in media communications. "We need more animations or something to better illustrate that—it is just gonna be a chronic misunderstanding."

Another invited journalist asked a question that Saskia couldn't quite hear. T.R. nodded. "The gun just lobs the shell up to the altitude we want—the stratosphere. About eighty thousand feet. Where sulfur does no harm—and much good. Now, at that point it's just gonna fall straight back down unless we do something. We could just detonate it with an explosive charge and it would disperse the sulfur. Hopefully some of it would burn. That was actually plan A. But our aerospace engineers didn't think that was fancy enough and so they ginned up the idea for a sulfur-burning engine that can keep the shell airborne for a little while. It's got the worst performance characteristics you can imagine but *we don't care*—it gives us a few minutes for the shell to remain at altitude and disperse the SO_2 more widely where the jet stream can catch it and begin spreading it around. *Then* the shell runs out of fuel and glides to the ground and we try to catch it."

T.R. drew the journalists' attention to a feed from another camera, this one near the ground, aimed at a stretch of ranch property covered by nets stretched between poles. "This here is all there is to it," T.R. said. "Same as you see at the circus. It's a few miles from here, down toward the Rio Grande."

There followed a few minutes' futzing around with video feeds and camera angles that only gave a helter-skelter picture of what was going on. "The point," T.R. eventually said, after his frustration had reached a crescendo and then collapsed in a farrago of basically humorous cursing and hat-throwing, "is that we are recycling the goddamn shells. We catch them in the net and toss them in the back of a truck and drive them back to the reloading facility. Providing jobs, good safe jobs, on the ground. Come out here if you want to see what I mean."

Saskia and others followed as T.R. led the reporter out of the Beer Car and across a few meters of open ground to a flat area where another one of those ubiquitous pop-up sun canopies had been pitched. Beneath it, a giant bullet rested on a display stand. T.R. shooed a white hat out of the way in mid demo. "Most of the shell is hollow. Empty space. It's a container for sulfur," he said. "That being the entire point." He patted its base, which was flat. "This here is just a sabot for the hydrogen to push against while it's in the gun barrel. It falls off immediately and we retrieve it." He yanked the sabot off and chucked it on the ground. Revealed was a conical hole penetrating into the middle of the shell. "The nozzle bell where combusted sulfur dioxide shoots out of the combustion chamber." He walked around to the pointed nose of the bullet, and simply yanked it off. "Another disposable part. Falls off in the stratosphere, comes down like a badminton birdie. We find it and reuse it. Or not." Revealed under the nose cone was another tapering hole, like the intake of a jet engine. "Where the air comes in." He stepped back. By the removal of the sabot and the nose cone, the bullet had been transformed into a jet engine. "Now it can generate thrust by exhausting sulfur dioxide, which has the interesting side effect of saving millions of lives and trillions of dollars from the effects of global climate change. But from a strictly aerospace engineering point of view we have a problem, which is that it can't generate nearly enough thrust to stay aloft for long." He opened a hatch on the top of the shell to reveal a shallow but broad compartment just underneath, wrapping partway around the upper part of the shell's cylindrical body. It was full of orange fabric. "This is too unwieldy to display here, so here's a picture of what it looks like when it's deployed." He gestured toward a poster, mounted on a slab of foam core zip-tied to the canopy's frame. It depicted one of those parasailing wings often seen towed behind speedboats in seaside resorts: a curved leading edge, a wing of taut fabric behind it, and a system of shroud lines converging on, and supporting, the payload. "This object deploys and gives it some appreciable L over D," T.R. said, "which means it can stay aloft for a little while through a combination of running the engine and shedding altitude. The more sulfur it burns, the lighter it becomes. The farther it descends, the thicker the air. Both work in our favor. By the time the tank is empty, this thing is pretty damned airworthy and it can glide for a long ways. Even if it's out over Mexico somewhere it can glide back and try to hit one of those nets."

"Now I see why everything around here has nets stretched over it," Saskia said, "what with all these sabots and nose cones and shells raining down out of the sky."

"A certain kind of person would almost say God made West Texas for this," T.R. said. "We got concentric circles drawn all over the map. Circular error probables—CEPs—for all that stuff. We know where shit's gonna hit the ground. Sounding rockets give us the initial conditions. After that we track each shell to get an accurate picture of the upper-level winds. We can make stuff fall where there ain't nothing to fall on save rocks and snakes."

"It's an expensive way to kill snakes!" some wag joked.

T.R. looked at him coolly. "Not if you figure in the appreciation of my Houston real estate portfolio." His gaze shifted to Saskia. "Others can make similar calculations. Remember the figure I quoted earlier?"

"You're a figure-quoting machine, T.R., you'll have to be a bit more specific."

"Over Houston. In the drone. What kind of money we talking? Remember? Anyone? One point seven five trillion dollars. That's the value of all the real estate in greater Houston. Let's say my buddies and I—the kinds of people who live in big houses on stilts along Buffalo Bayou—own one percent of it. That's about twenty billion dollars' worth of real estate. If the value declines by ten percent, that's two billion in value that just went up in smoke. If it goes up by ten percent"—he turned and waved his arm in the general direction of the gun—"*that alone* pays for all this."

"You're altering the climate *all over the world*," Bob translated, "to make a profit on a portfolio of real estate that is limited to Houston."

"The numbers check out," T.R. confirmed. "Those of y'all who don't live in Houston may wish to make calculations of your own. 'Sea level' is the same everywhere." He checked his watch. The afternoon was getting on. "Oh. And as long as I dragged y'all out here into the heat, don't forget to collect your party favor." T.R. indicated a solitary boxcar that had been parked on a nearby side track. A canopy had been set up next to it. Beneath that was a table staffed by a highly presentable young woman whose white cowboy hat made for an incongruous combo with the earthsuit that covered everything from her jawline down to her cowboy boots. Saskia, sans earthsuit, was nearing the limit of how long she could remain outdoors, but decided to venture over.

The boxcar looked as if it had been chosen specifically to stand as a visual emblem of decrepit Industrial Revolution tech. It looked like it had traveled a million miles during its career, survived a few derailments, and finally reached the end of the line. Rust was blooming through old faded graffiti. No part of it was flat or straight. It was full to overflowing with coal, and excess coal had spilled out on the ground all around it.

As Saskia drew closer to the blessed shade of the canopy, she saw a row of bell jars on the table, similar to the ones T.R. had displayed last night at dinner. Each sat on a wooden pedestal. Each contained a golden cube that Saskia would have mistaken for half a stick of butter had she not spent so much time in the last two days looking at, and talking about, sulfur.

"Welcome, Your Majesty; would you like to take your parting gift? I can have it packed for travel and delivered to your lodgings."

"You are too kind," Saskia said. She'd now drawn near enough to read the words engraved on the brass plaque attached to the wooden pedestal:

TEXAS GOLD
THIS AMOUNT OF PURE SULFUR
neutralizes the global warming caused by
ONE BOXCAR OF PURE CARBON.
Each shell fired from Pina2bo carries 20,000 times this amount of sulfur.

"Such propaganda!" said a nearby voice. Saskia turned to see that Cornelia had followed her over. The tone of her voice was somewhere between disdain and admiration. She had admitted defeat and traded any pretense of fashionable attire for an earth-suit. But thanks to that her face looked a lot cooler than Saskia's probably did. Saskia was in Face Zero, which was what she basically used for gardening and swimming.

"He has a gift for the catchphrase," Saskia said. "One can easily imagine him hawking these on YouTube. Texas Gold."

"Jumpsuit Orange, if he's not careful."

"I have no idea as to the legalities. Do you?"

"No."

"Presumably there's not a specific law against shooting bullets straight up in the air and letting them fall back down on your own property."

"In Texas? No, there won't be any such law," Cornelia scoffed. "The feds will try to get him on the airspace violation. Something like that."

"Unless he has a permit. Which he did today."

"They'll stop issuing them!"

"And then he'll go over their heads. To Congress. To the president. And he'll take it to YouTube."

"And . . . to you, Your Majesty," Cornelia said. "What was the lord mayor's unattractive phrase? The eight-hundred-pound gorilla."

"The gorilla is hot," Saskia said, "I'm going inside."

> T.R. said something that reminded me of you.
> ???

> Lift over drag. Sorry. Private joke. Probably not funny.

The text hit Rufus's phone from an unknown number with some kind of weird area code. He was peeling the foil from a burrito in a sort of food court that occupied the middle of the area that these people called Bunkhouse.

> Who this?

> Sorry. Saskia. Are you available for a chat? Leaving for NL early tomorrow.

> Half an hour okay? Going to take a shower.

> Of course, I am taking a bath!

Rufus consumed the burrito a little more quickly than had been his original plan, then found the men's locker room, which included a row of shower stalls. Everything about this place put him in mind of the army. It was, in fact, made of army surplus housing modules that they hadn't bothered to repaint. This was what the military threw together when they needed an outpost in some place like Afghanistan. Though, to be honest, most parts of that country were more hospitable than West Texas. Nothing was fancy, but everything was okay—at least up to the standards that many enlisteds could expect in the kinds of places where they lived stateside. Rufus had walked away from that deal after he'd put in his twenty years and hadn't missed it. But it sure made it easy to find his way around the so-called Bunkhouse here at Pina2bo. He scored a toothbrush and miniature tube of toothpaste from a vending machine, found himself a shower stall, cleaned up using the liquid body wash from the dispenser on the wall—all army standard. He put on a clean Flying S swag T-shirt and, lacking a change of underwear, decided to just go commando beneath his cargo shorts. In flip-flops from the shower he walked slowly to the train, trying not to break a sweat or run afoul of any rattlesnakes or barbed plants, carrying his dirty laundry in a wad. This he stowed in the compartment they had assigned him in one of the Amtrak cars. He walked up to the fancy antique railway car where the queen and her staff usually hung out, but none of the Dutch were there except Amelia, standing at the far end of the coach. Her body language indicated that she was on duty, so he didn't bother her.

> Where should I go?

> Just come to my compartment.

Just as a routine, automatic precaution, Rufus asked himself what were the odds that following these instructions could lead to his getting shot. The person most likely to do the shooting in this particular scenario would be Amelia. She and Rufus had gotten to know each other during the past few days, having a few meals together while the bigwigs did their thing, sharing vehicles. He'd have been interested in her if he wasn't almost old enough to be her father. She wasn't going to pull her Sig out of her shoulder bag and double-tap him. And yet still it was weird. It put her—Amelia—in an awkward spot. Rufus walked up the aisle toward her. She watched impassively through dark glasses that more than likely had a built-in AR display. She was a fine-looking woman in her big-boned, broken-nosed way.

"Her Majesty has invited me to—"

"I know, Red."

"Okay." He turned his back and began retracing his steps.

"Thanks for checking in, though."

"Oh, no problem at all, Amelia."

"That shirt looks good on you."

"Think it's my color?"

"It's not our proper Dutch orange."

"I know. It's got a little Southern sunburn." He threw her a glance over his shoulder and saw evidence of a dimple forming beneath those dark glasses.

He knocked on Saskia's door. "Come in!" came the answer.

She *had* been in the bath. It was muggy and fragrant despite the best efforts of the modern A/C system that this car's owner had shoehorned into the old-fashioned cabinetwork. Saskia, in a terrycloth robe, was flapping a towel, trying to dispel steam.

"I'll leave the door open."

"No," she said.

"Might help get some air moving."

"The air will be fine."

What he had really been getting at was that people might get the wrong idea. Of course she was blind to that possibility. It was the kind of consideration her man Willem got paid to think of. Willem didn't seem to be around, though. So Rufus was trying to step into his shoes, do his job for him.

Saskia actually stepped past him, brushing by close in the small compartment, and shoved the door closed. And locked it. "Everyone wants to pay their respects to the queen," she said. "Not that many royals show up here."

"How many of these people are what you'd call royals?"

"None of them. But I understand your confusion." She smiled. In circumstances like this she could be taken for an affluent American woman of a certain class, the kind of lady you might see getting lunch with her lady friends at an upscale mall after Pilates. Not one of the snooty type, though. He'd seen her chopping celery. "'Royal' means actually a king or queen, or someone in their immediate family. I am the only such person here."

"What's up with that Cornelia?"

"She has a royal bearing and she comes from a family that is much older than mine. But Venice never had royals. They did have noble houses, self-selected, who elected a leader. That's where she comes from."

"She's got a chip on her shoulder about Venice."

"You could say that, yes." Saskia smiled at him sweetly.

"The lord mayor?"

"He's elected. You don't inherit that job. But once you win the election—which is a very strange one, very English—you become a lord. Still, quite different from being a royal."

"How so?"

"Broadly speaking, royals have tended to be like this with the nobility in most times and places." She was banging her little fists together.

"Oh, see now that's a new idea to me because I thought they were all on the same side."

"If you were a medieval peasant it would certainly seem that way. In general, however, it is not the case. But of course that is all ancient history; very little of it really applies in the modern era of constitutional monarchy."

"Speaking of which, what are you doing here? I never asked you," Rufus said. "According to Wiki it's more of a symbolic role."

"Well, for one thing, I personally own a significant percentage of Royal Dutch Shell."

"Shell? *The* Shell? The oil company?"

"Yes. So, even if I were not the Queen of the Netherlands, I could exert some influence over who sits on their board and so on."

"And Shell has a lot to answer for, global warming wise."

"Indeed we do!"

"Well, that is interesting. But you *are*."

"I am what?"

"The Queen of the Netherlands."

"Yes."

"And in that capacity—"

"I can do nothing," Saskia said, "except change my facial expression while reading an annual speech that is written for me on Budget Day."

"Whoa, you lost me there!" Rufus chuckled.

"In, let me see, about ten days," Saskia said, "the Dutch Parliament will open. It is the tradition that the king or queen goes there in a fancy carriage—"

Rufus waved her off.

"You've read about it on Wikipedia."

"Yeah. Oh, I don't mean to be rude. Just sparing you the effort.

You got to go there and sit at the front of the room, all the ladies wearing fancy hats, and you read out a speech."

"That is *exactly* what I do. The speech is written for me. It would be improper, you see, for the monarch to write his or her own speech."

"Who writes it?"

"Parliament. In the Netherlands we call it the States General."

"And who you reading it to?"

"The States General."

"So you could just be cut out of the loop and save yourself the trouble!"

"It has symbolic importance. And I get to adopt facial expressions."

"Yeah, that's where you lost me."

"Also, I can pause. Raise or lower my voice. Adopt various positions. Talk slow or fast. When I do these things it's thought that I am, perhaps, reflecting the attitudes and priorities of the Dutch people."

"Well, you must be very good at it."

"That is very kind of you, Rufus. What makes you say so?"

Rufus's face warmed as he became aware that he had stumbled into something. "Oh, I didn't mean nothing by it. Just that you have a very . . . beautiful presence that is warm and that expresses your feelings."

Saskia blushed.

He thought it might help extract him from what had become a bit of an awkward situation were he to draw a contrast: "Ol' Sylvester Lin, now, he would not be the man to give that speech."

She shook her head and smiled at the thought.

"Or maybe he *would*, but you wouldn't have a clue what the man's emotional state was!"

She nodded, still smiling, and averted her gaze. It would seem that a lot was going on in her mind.

"And you're saying," Rufus continued, "that by the power of that you can affect what happens."

"So it is said," Saskia replied. "And!" She clasped her hands together. "In that vein . . ."

"What vein?"

"Saskia letting her feelings be known."

"Oh."

"From the first moment we met in Waco, and you bravely put yourself in harm's way to assist Lennert, I have admired you, Red, and felt grateful to you. Those feelings only increased and deepened as you helped us get out of the airport and down the river to Houston. After that, T.R.'s program pulled you and me in opposite directions and so I never got around to expressing my gratitude—as well as expressing my admiration for all that is so personally attractive about you, Red. And now suddenly I find myself on the eve of departure. A summer storm is blowing up in the North Sea and forcing us to depart early in the morning so that we can get there before the winds become too high. I'm afraid that much time might go by before we cross paths again. I didn't want to let the opportunity just slip by."

"Opportunity?"

She made a face and shrugged as if to say, *Who knows?*

"For what?"

"Well," the queen said, and a thoughtful look came over her face for a moment, as if she were pondering an important phrase in her speech to the States General and wanted to be quite certain that she said it in just the right way and that the millions of Dutch people watching would feel what she was feeling. "A blow job would not be totally out of the question, but I was rather hoping to see those cargo shorts hit the floor."

Rufus had been expecting her to give him a medal or a letter of commendation. Blow job hadn't entered his mind. He got tunnel vision and felt his heart pounding in a way that hadn't happened since he had been on the runway at Waco, closing in on Snout and unslinging his Kalashnikov. He now wished that he had taken an extra minute to put on clean underwear, since his penis was getting bigger and rubbing against the rugged mil-spec stitching. "You have a problem with cargo shorts?" he asked, stalling for time.

"Only when they are in the way. I see their practicality."

"Well, I just wouldn't feel right about the first option you mentioned. It doesn't seem decent given your dignity and so on. I would feel bad."

"It was just an example." Saskia's phone buzzed and her eyes flicked to it. "My daughter," she said, "demanding a progress report."

"On the conversation you and I are having right now!?"

"On my romantic life in general. She worries about my solitude and wonders if something similar is in her future."

Saskia's face then fell as she perhaps realized that the remark was double-edged. Rufus too was solitary. But he had no Lotte to look after him. Just occasional check-ins from Mary Boskey.

"What about that Michael character?"

"You mean Michiel?"

"Yeah. I saw you checking him out."

"Did it make you jealous, Rufus?" she asked hopefully.

"Oh, I never dared have any such thoughts. There's a history here, in Texas and in the South—"

"I know."

"One of the worst lynchings was actually in Waco."

"I shouldn't have gone there. You asked about Michiel. He is obviously attractive. The sort of man that the tabloids would set me up with, if they had the power. But there isn't the connection." She pointed back and forth between herself and Rufus.

"Of what happened on the runway, you mean?"

"Partly that. But . . . both of us suffered losses some time ago and have been alone since then. That's really what I meant." Saskia's phone buzzed again. With exaggerated annoyance she picked it up and held down the button that shut it off.

Rufus made himself a little more comfortable by plucking at his shorts and leaning forward, elbows on knees.

"It *has* been a long time for me," he said. "I'm worried I forgot where everything goes."

"We can google it."

"You think Google will come up with anything?"

They both laughed.

"I ain't coming over there because of the history I alluded to," Rufus said. He looked at the chair he'd been sitting on. It was narrow, hard, old-fashioned *Antiques Roadshow* stuff. He eased down out of it and sat on the carpet, back against the wall. "Plenty of room here now, though, if you are feeling disposed to come on over my way."

Saskia glanced at the door (still locked) and the window (curtain still drawn), then padded over and sat down next to him, very close. She put her head on his shoulder. This felt so good he was stunned for a few moments. Then he summoned the presence of mind to put his arm around her.

"You have beautiful arms," she said.

"Push-ups," he explained. "Got no time for gyms. Look now, in case something happens and we get carried away, I gotta ask . . . birth control?"

"Taken care of. We have socialized medicine."

"These cargo shorts contain many things," he said, "but it's been a long time since I packed a . . ."

She reached into the pocket of her bathrobe and produced a condom in its little foil packet. "Any particular size?" she asked.

"That'll do."

Her thigh came up over his, making contact along the way with two different knives, phone, notebook, spare magazine, a couple of Sharpies, and other sundries.

"Ouch. Those really do have to come off," she announced.

ROHTANG

While arguably the areas being disputed between China and India were far from the Punjab and belonged to distant provinces, the truth was quite different once you started to think about the Five Rivers of the Punjab and their significance. For all five of them, as well as the Indus into which they all eventually flowed, originated in the Himalayas. Once you had gained control over a river's headwaters, you could put a dam there. As soon as you did that, you could control its flow, and thereby control the lives of all who lived downstream of it.

Sorting out the details of where to go and how to get there had been a somewhat bewildering process because of the convolutions and forkings of the river valleys in the mountains. But once Laks had uploaded the geography into his head, the place that leapt out as being of greatest interest was where the Chenab and the Beas originated within just a few kilometers of each other on opposite flanks of a high spine of rock spanned by a nightmare of switchbacks called the Rohtang Pass. Northeast of there was the even higher region of Ladakh, indistinctly bounded by the Line of Actual Control.

Down in the lowlands—basically everything west of Chandigarh— it was easy to move laterally from one river to the next by crossing the table-flat *doab* or Mesopotamian plateau between them. Now, though, topography made it imperative simply to choose one river and follow it up to its beginning. By far the most direct one was the Beas. It had stopped Alexander the Great. Perhaps it could stop the Chinese as well. Shimla, a city of a couple of hundred thousand that the Brits had planted up in the mountains so that they wouldn't all perish of heat stroke during the summer, was not on the Beas. But one of the least terrible ways to *get* to the upper Beas from Chandigarh was to pass through it, and anyway Jasmit was bound in that direction and avidly wished to support the quest of (until this morning) Laks and (now) the Fellowship. Halfway there, they stopped at a factory that, like all other structures here, was perched improbably on a slope, and picked up cargo, which the boys helped load, then sat on the rest of the way.

Once they had parted company with Jasmit at Shimla, Laks's *bhais* only slowed him down, since group hitchhiking was slower than solo. But before they went very much farther they entered into the valley of the Beas, which ran straight north to the destination. There were two roads running parallel to the river on opposite banks. It was impossible to get lost. So for a couple of days they split up, leapfrogging one another on various modes of transport, staying in sync with phones, reconnecting in hostels or dhabas. They were now decisively out of the Punjab, in a Sikh-minority part of the country, predominantly Hindu of course. But the farther north they went, the more strongly it was inflected by Tibetan Buddhists and Western backpackers. Of the latter, some were pure adventurers while others were pilgrims, figuratively and literally on the road to Dharamshala.

This put Laks into a funny state of mind when he found himself, as happened increasingly, among such people in hostels or bus stations. To extend Ilham's analogy, if this was the Fellowship of the Ring, Laks was Aragorn, part man and part elf, equally capable of hanging out with Lord Elrond at the high table of Imladris or slamming down pints in a tavern in Bree. When not standing next to his modern backpack he looked absolutely like a Punjabi Sikh, and so was assumed to be just that by locals and Westerners alike. When he started talking, most would peg him as American, though people in the know could guess from his articulation and certain vowel sounds that he was Canadian.

He generally kept his distance, though. The backpackers carried their own rolling soap opera with them, with an ever-shifting cast of characters and set-piece dramas: who was sleeping with whom, who was a cool kid, a user, a narc, or moocher, who was in the know, who was clueless, who had left the communal bathroom in a terrible state. None of this was going to help Laks and so he kept his mouth shut.

During the first part of the journey, the truck drivers who picked him up, all of whom were Sikhs, seemed to assume he was just a young wanderer who needed a lift somewhere. But north of about Kullu this all changed. South of there this young hitchhiker might have been bound in any direction, and the thing in his hand was just a walking stick, the kind of thing a savvy traveler might carry to fend off rabid dogs. North of there his destination and his intentions were obvious, the purpose of the stick unmistakable. His *bhais* discovered likewise. They opened up the bundle of rattan and passed out sticks even to the non-combatant Ilham. Their baggage grew heavy with food and even clothing donated to them by truck drivers and dhaba staff who knew what they were doing.

The ease with which they reached Manali—the last settlement on the Beas before you climbed up into high mountains—forced Ravi's hand. He had been waffling the whole way, claiming that he was only tagging along on the first leg of the journey so that he could see the mountains, and that he'd peel off and go home at some point in the not too distant future. But just like that they were in Manali, where you couldn't look in any direction without seeing a genuine Himalaya erupting straight up just a few miles distant. Far from running low on supplies, they had stocked up as they went. No one could claim that they had suffered any hardship. Even the most coddled traveler would think twice before whining in earshot of Ilham, who had endured shit you wouldn't believe. No obvious opportunity had, in other words, presented itself to Ravi to justify his falling away from the quest.

Manali was a curious place where a number of very different streams of humanity came together. They did not clash but sorted themselves into parallel worlds. The economy was based on tourism. Indians traditionally came here on honeymoons. Western backpackers used it as a base camp for mountain forays. The styles of accommodation for those two classes of visitor couldn't have been more different. Added to that was a less visible community of refugees from the north, who naturally collected here because it was the first place a person coming down out of the mountains would have any chance of survival. The fourth stream was military, but they occupied their own facilities and drove their own vehicles—sometimes on their own roads. A neophyte wandering into town would have burned a day or two trying to make sense of all that, but Ilham vectored them straight to a hostel, half in the woods and sufficiently down-market that it also served as a logistics base for a certain number of Tibetan and Uighur refugees camped out nearby. The Fellowship settled in there for an afternoon and a night, ate that portion of their donated food that seemed least likely to keep much longer, and then proceeded to draw attention to themselves by doing squats and push-ups and burpees in the courtyard until they were near to passing out. Manali was at two thousand meters: a mile high, basically. Nothing compared to where they were going but enough that the lungs noticed.

Two young men came over to watch. They looked South Asian but, to judge from speech and attire, were working-class Englishmen. Laks guessed—correctly as it turned out—that they were Sikhs who were non-observant, at least when it came to hair, beard, and turban. They were at least wearing bracelets. Perhaps they were now trying to remedy that by letting their beards grow, or perhaps shaving had just been inconvenient for them during the last week or so. They had walking sticks, but in no other way did they seem to have any interest in backpacking just for back-packing's sake. They introduced themselves as Sam and Jay, which Laks could guess were Anglicized variants of whatever traditional names appeared on their passports. Squinting through their own cigarette smoke, they appraised the stick-work of Laks and Gopinder with what seemed to be a discerning eye and asked questions that seemed extremely practical in nature.

Once they had all made friends to a certain point, they explained flat-out that they were hooligans. Soccer hooligans. Not just casual brawlers but members of organized bands that would travel en masse to foreign countries and use organized tactics to make war on their counterparts from Athens or Lisbon or Warsaw. They had reached an advanced age (twenty-five) where introspection and wisdom had begun to cloud their judgment. They'd heard of the war being waged with rocks and sticks at the top of the world and it had occurred to them that the skills they had acquired in combat against supporters of rival football squads could just as well be put into service holding the Chinese at bay. Sam and Jay were too dour and grudging to come right out and say *we'd like to team up with you* but thenceforth they simply behaved as if this were a done deal.

The way it worked here, as Ilham explained, was that drivers aspiring to go north tried to get as early a start as possible, to beat the traffic jam created by all the other vehicles pursuing exactly the same strategy. They had to get up so early that it basically wasn't worth going to bed. They pooled funds with Sam and Jay and hired two taxis. Luggage went in the boot or on the roof, and sticks were strapped alongside the luggage racks, which to the eyes of adventuresome males of their age looked cool. The road north out of town was already dismayingly crowded.

Until recently it had been necessary to drive all the way over Rohtang Pass, an infinity of switchbacks cresting at four thousand meters, then down an equal number of switchbacks into a hamlet on the upper Chenab at more like three thousand meters. From there the highway followed a maddeningly indirect route up into Ladakh, the water- and oxygen-starved province that bordered China. Remote and thinly populated as it was, Ladakh was connected to the rest of India in only a few places through which all traffic in and out of it was funneled. Hence all this traffic in the wee hours in what otherwise seemed like the middle of nowhere.

A few years ago the government had at last succeeded in punching a very long and deep tunnel all the way through the spur of the Himalayas separating the Beas from the Chenab, bypassing the dreaded Rohtang Pass. Several kilometers north of Manali, the road forked. A newer road ran to the left toward the entrance of the tunnel. The right fork, which led to the pass, was less traveled. It wandered through a little settlement and then struck out decisively uphill. Before too long there was snow on the ground, then banks of it plowed off to the sides, and then they were driving between vertical walls of it, as high as the taxis' windowsills. As high as the roof racks. At one point about halfway up they stopped for a bit at a little dhaba and were able to clamber up a snowbank and look down on the road they had not taken: a snake of red brake lights winding its way up a valley toward the entrance of the tunnel. They couldn't see the entrance from this angle, but could guess where it was from a nimbus of arctic cold white LED lights above a spur of rock. That—according to Ilham—was where the adventure would have ended for him and Laks had they made the mistake of going that way. For there was a reason the government had spent billions on that tunnel. And it was not to make things perfect for backpackers or to ease the lives of truck drivers conveying cigarettes and candy bars to the roadside dhabas of far Ladakh, though it did incidentally serve those purposes. It was first and foremost a defense installation, there to improve strategic communication with the China front. As had been quite obvious during today's drive, much of the traffic was military, and a lot of the cargo in ostensibly civilian vehicles—trucks laden with rebar, say—had a military application. Anyway, it was now the case that civilian vehicles were inspected and IDs checked at the tunnel entrance. Both Laks and Ilham would have had their journeys cut short there. The rest of the Fellowship probably could have made it through and waited for them on the other side, but they'd made a decision to stay together. Jay and Sam, on the "in for a penny, in for a pound" principle, had decided to stick with them. It was a good decision; they had no real fluency in anything but English, and in many other ways had no idea what they were doing.

Eventually, in mid-morning, the taxi drivers kicked them out, explaining to Ravi in Hindi that they had long since reached the point where walking would be faster. This could be inferred anyway from the fact that several other taxis had pulled over and dozens of people could be seen trudging right up the side of a mountain ridge, cutting across all the switchbacks. The fellowship got out, loaded up, and climbed over the pass, shrieking for breath the whole way. In his proper backpacking gear Laks felt a bit foolish whenever their path crossed with that of some random local who was just walking right up the mountain in street shoes and clothes, carrying his stuff in a plastic shopping bag. Also making them look ludicrously over-prepared were Sam and Jay, who had apparently made the calculation, back in England, that any clothing capable of keeping them warm through a ninety-minute soccer game in Leeds would be more than sufficient for summiting Everest.

The snow thinned as they went, for they were passing over into Ladakh, a place that was dry for the same reason that the Punjab was well watered: the mountains stopped all the moisture and converted it into rivers, just as with the Cascades in Laks's part of the world. Inland was high desert. Surrounding the hamlet at the foot of the pass was a redolent plateau where locals went out to defecate in the open. Laks was glad his sense of smell had been devastated by COVID. Stepping with great care across this, they came to a cluster of buildings and located the guesthouse where they would stay the night. There they encountered Pippa, Bella, and Sue, playing Dungeons and Dragons.

During his journey up from Shimla, Laks had crossed paths with all three of these women glancingly, enough to follow their stories at a remove. Pippa was a lanky, freckled Kiwi. Bella was Argentinean. Sue—presumably an Anglicized version of her real name—was Korean. They'd not been together at the time. But backpackers in general and women in particular formed ad hoc alliances when they discovered, in the dining room of a hostel or the lobby of a bus station, that they were going the same way. This looked to be one of those. They could watch one another's backs when they weren't huddling together for warmth.

Back in Kullu, these women might have taken one look at Laks and surmised he was going north to the Line of Actual Control. Laks, however, never would have assumed the same of them. Until, that is, he descended into the smoky guesthouse—dwellings here were quasi-subterranean—and found the three of them eating bad stew from a communal vat and rolling twenty-sided dice. They'd walked over the pass for the same reason as Laks: Bella had overstayed her visa while sampling the trippy delights of Goa and didn't want to get caught at the tunnel checkpoint. Sue had come down with altitude sickness during the hike and they had holed up here for a day as she bounced back.

Bella and Sue, as it turned out, were just in it for the usual backpackerish reasons—to have adventures and see cool parts of the world before they settled down—while Pippa had a mission. Completely self-assigned, but a mission nonetheless. She had traveled most of the way up the Beas Valley in the company of some guy from California who, it could be guessed, was one of those aspirant filmmakers who came from money and so had the freedom to do stuff like this—or to tweet that he was doing it, anyway—but not the grit to stick with it when it got hard. Which it very much did, beyond Manali. Laks knew about people like that because there was a whole sub-Hollywood in Vancouver. He had observed them in their coffeehouses and brewpubs, hatching their plans and engaging in the strangely protocol-bound interactions of their tribe. Pippa had grown up in Wellington, the capital of New Zealand's film industry, which was culturally quite different. Her objective in all this was to join up, at least for a time, with a network of streamers who were documenting the conflict that Laks intended to take part in.

Early in the conversation, Laks was inclined to keep Pippa at arm's length. What benefit could there be in joining up with these three women? But the more they talked, the more he understood that they might need Pippa more than she needed them. She kept asking questions that Laks ought to have known the answers to. Which part of the front were they aiming for? The southeastern toe of the Yak's Leg, perhaps, where the Chinese had lately encroached and needed to be pushed back? Or the "knee" farther north where Indian crews were rumored to be readying a counterattack across the high glaciers that fed the Pangong Tso? Were they going to join up with an established squad, or form their own new one? Did they intend to remain a purely stick-based unit, or were they going to team up with any rock throwers? Which langar network were they going to join up with; or did they have their own logistical train? Were they self-financed, or crowdfunded, and if the latter, which crowdfunding site were they using? And, most unnerving for Laks, how did he think his gatka was going to stack up in practice against various regional kung fu styles?

When Laks sputtered—for, sad to say, he was definitely sputtering by this point—that he thought gatka more than a match for anything mere Chinese might throw at him, Pippa had more questions. Was Laks aware that the Iron Lions Crew currently operating along the northern shore of the Pangong Tso consisted of hand-picked fighters from the elite Piguaquan schools around Cangzhou where they had perfected a simplified variant of the Crazy Demon style using asymmetrical red oak staffs? Or was he expecting to deploy along the ridge above Chushul, which was currently under pressure from a squad of Guangzhou-based fighters versed in the more classically southern, Wing Chun–derived style? Obviously different tactics would be called for in that case, given the latter's preference for extraordinarily long and whippy carbon fiber staffs being produced for them by enthusiastic supporters in Chinese aerospace factories.

It might have been different, somehow, if Pippa had asked him these questions in a hectoring and contentious style. But she just wasn't that way; her affect was unfailingly calm and pleasant. She spoke in the tone of a sweet, curious child. She wasn't trying to flaunt the amount of research she had performed. It simply had never crossed her mind that anyone would get as deeply into this as Laks already had without knowing all these things. To illustrate some of her points she took Laks outside where she could get better satellite and showed him a few of the more relevant video channels. There seemed to be dozens of these—enough that their thumbnails covered at least one screen, anyway. Each was the record that had been uploaded by one streamer—a streamer such as Pippa aspired to be—on his or her journey along the Line of Actual Control. And each had at least a few (some had dozens of) videos depicting noteworthy moments in the conflict. Some of the streamers were in the mold of documentary filmmakers who wanted to show behind-the-lines stuff. Support volunteers ladling lentils in makeshift langars, that sort of thing. But others were stone martial arts geeks obsessed with different styles of stick fighting and following specific combatants, like kids collecting Pokémon. They had titles like "DEVASTATING leg strike by Big Talib on SHOCKED Chinese fighter at Kangju Ridge" and "NSFW! NOT FOR SQUEAMISH! Chinese rocker gets COMPOUND FRACTURE in glacier battle!"

Pippa began swiping to additional screens of such material before Laks could take it all in. Before long, Chinese titles were competing with English for screen space. Beyond that it was all Chinese. She must have sorted the feeds by language. Only after several screens' worth of Chinese video channels did she turn up a few in Hindi, or in Punjabi. Most of the streamers on their side of the front were presumably using English.

Somewhat amplifying the effect of all this, Sam and Jay had wandered outside to smoke cigarettes (not that anyone cared, up here, but they were ashamed of their smoking habit and liked to do it outdoors, as a kind of penance). Since there wasn't much to look at here except rocks and turds, they drifted over to look over Pippa's shoulder and to make remarks about the various feeds flashing across her screen—remarks, the import of which was that they were familiar with a great many of these. "That's a new one from Sanjay, innit?" Sam remarked as Pippa scanned through the playlist of an especially well-subscribed Indian-Australian streamer.

"Weren't up there yesterday," Jay confirmed. "Five hundred thousand views already, must be a cracking fight."

Pippa obligingly scrolled through the new video to a slow-motion replay showing an airborne Sikh fighter's legs being swept out from under him by a Chinese fighter's thick staff. This appeared to be made from plastic water pipe. It was painted red and emblazoned with a row of Chinese characters and a corporate logo, somewhat in the manner of a race car or other corporately sponsored artifact.

The video then cut away for fifteen seconds to play a Kiwi advertisement for homeowner's insurance. "That's where your hopping up and down will fucking kill you," Sam opined during the commercial break. "All very pretty on the dance floor, but if you ain't stuck to the ground, you're fucked." Jay concurred in the strongest possible terms.

Laks felt his scalp growing hot beneath his turban. On a pure martial arts level there was a good rejoinder to be made to the objection just raised by Sam. No doubt it had already been debated at exhausting length in the comments thread dangling from the end of this video like a string of fecal material from a yak's ass hairs.

But he knew better than to read the comments. He wasn't angry so much as embarrassed. And he was embarrassed because he had come so far without doing any of the homework that these people took for granted. Pippa had taken to looking at him with an expression somewhere between mild concern and outright pity.

"Now that we have made it into Ladakh," Laks announced, "we have choices to make. Where to go and how to get there and what to do when we make it that far. Tomorrow we have to go down the valley. From there we need to look at the latest videos, the maps of where the Line is moving, and see where it all takes us." He made it clear, by look and gesture, that as far as he was concerned, "we" included Pippa and her friends.

The next morning the Fellowship, now filled out to a Tolkien-compliant head count of nine, simply walked the ten kilometers down the valley to the northern terminus of the tunnel. This was much faster than trying to find a vehicle in such a remote place big enough to carry such a large group. Though the altitude was high—thirty-two hundred meters above sea level—the way was nearly flat. They hitched rides a few more kilometers down the valley to a place where roads forked away to east and west. The east road would take them to the front. This was two hundred kilometers away as the crow flies, but the road distance was more than double that figure because of switchbacks on both a very large and very small scale. The way basically ran perpendicular to ranges of smaller mountains that filled the entire space between the Himalayas, which they'd put behind them, and the almost as formidable Karakorams. So in addition to being very long, the way was very slow. Along many stretches, bicyclists or even pedestrians would have left them in the dust.

Pippa's remark about logistics networks, which had been opaque to Laks when he'd heard it, now came into focus. She and Ilham had a lot to say to each other about this. Though, as days went on and they got closer to the front, Pippa began to focus more on videography and Bella began to go deep on teasing apart the various logistics trains extending their tendrils toward the front. Gopinder, whose Punjabi was a lot stronger than that of Laks, got into the act helping Bella make sense of it all. Sue, the Korean, had learned Mandarin as a second language and became a sort of intelligence analyst, sifting through the latest videos that had been posted from the front and mapping out the hot spots.

They crossed through four thousand meters again, and then

five thousand, before starting to lose some altitude. This was in river valleys; the bare crests of the ridges looked so much higher that they might as well have been on Mars. But eventually they dropped again to a mere thirty-three hundred meters so that they could cross the Indus River itself. This flowed northwest out of the mountains before hooking south toward the sea and collecting the waters of the Punjab's five rivers along the way. The point where they crossed it was still ninety kilometers away from the ever-fluctuating border. Nevertheless, crossing over the Indus seemed a momentous occasion for anyone with a connection to India, and so they stopped there for a night, got the whole Fellowship—which had become scattered among multiple vehicles—together in one place for a meal and a night's sleep, and then struck out together the next morning into the land beyond. They were now simply traveling in buses, all of whose passengers were people like them, going the same way for the same reason. They drove over a pass that topped out at fifty-four hundred meters, and stopped at the little village there to take selfies and inject cash into the local economy, such as it was. Then they descended to a some-what more survivable altitude of four thousand, where there was a fork in the road. This was a choke point through which all traffic had to pass to reach any part of the Line. Accordingly the Indian Army had built a logistics depot there and set up a roadblock. Military vehicles, of which there were many, were simply waved through. Vehicles containing volunteers were diverted to an open expanse of dead, rocky ground and their occupants herded into a big inflatable building. A few of the new arrivals had previously been chipped, so they were allowed to pass right through to the other side via a row of metal detectors. The others, including all members of the Fellowship, were funneled into a basketball court where, sitting on the floor, they were obliged to watch a Power-Point presentation and take a quiz.

SOUTH TEXAS

T.R., or at any rate his pilot, had the courtesy to put the chopper down at a decent remove from where Rufus had parked his trailer, and downwind. So Rufus's vehicles did not get pelted with little rocks and coated with dust, those being the two main constituents of this part of Texas: about midway between San Antonio and Laredo, five hundred miles east of the Flying S Ranch. It was 6:30 in the morning of what promised to be a clear but not excessively hot day. According to the schedule, which had been worked out to an amazing level of detail by T.R.'s staff, Rufus would have the boss's undivided attention for three hours, after which there would be something called a "hard stop." Rufus didn't know what a hard stop was, and given the way these people talked about it, he was afraid to ask. He had visions of being physically ejected from the chopper's side door at 9:30 sharp if he failed to complete the agreed-on program of activities by that instant.

So he was ready and eager to get going. But T.R. seemed to enjoy taking his time. Rufus sensed that this was, for T.R., a welcome break from whatever activities normally filled the schedule of such a man. For a minute he stood beside the chopper conversing with someone in the back seat, and Rufus's ears picked up the solid mechanical chunking and snicking of well-oiled firearms being checked out. T.R. said something indistinct to indicate how fired up he was, then turned his back on the chopper and came crunching over the hard land toward where Rufus had set up his camp last night. It was at the end of one of T.R.'s ranch roads, where it fizzled out in a dry wash. The coordinates had been sent to Rufus yesterday over the encrypted messaging application that T.R.'s staff insisted be used for everything.

Rufus had offered to provide breakfast and meant to make good on it, so he'd deployed the awning on the side of the trailer and set up a pop-up canopy as well. He had a camp stove going and was working on some huevos rancheros with red chile sauce. Coffee was ready and waiting. "Whoo! That smells good!" T.R. remarked from a distance. "We landed downwind of you."

"Noticed. Appreciate the courtesy."

"Did you find the accommodations to your liking?" T.R. asked wryly, holding up his hands and looking around. Though the creek bed was dry, there was apparently enough seasonal water to keep a sparse belt of trees going. Birds were singing in those. Life was good.

"I took the liberty of harvesting some mesquite," Rufus said, nodding at a small but aromatic campfire, which he'd surrounded with some folding chairs.

"Be my guest. Plenty more where that came from," T.R. said. "Nature's bounty." He threw Rufus a socially distant salute, which Rufus returned, and settled into one of the chairs. "Coffee's right there, help yourself but don't burn your hand," Rufus said.

"Don't mind if I do. Much obliged," T.R. said and poured himself a mug of java from a fire-blackened pot. "So we gonna kill some pigs?"

"As many as you got time for, sir. I know where they live," Rufus said. He was assembling the huevos rancheros from ingredients scattered around the burners of his stove.

"How'd you find 'em? What's your process?"

"Satellite imagery tells me about where to look. I drive around in the truck to get the feel of the place. The sight lines. I look for signs. After that it's all drones. Cameras on those nowadays is better than the naked eye. The pigs, you know, rub against trees to scrape the parasites off their bodies and that leaves damage on the bark that you can see." Rufus looked up from his work. "Now, if I were here on a solo job, I'd have gone out and done the work on foot, in the dark. But since you was coming with the chopper I got caught up on my sleep instead." He carried a tin plate over to T.R. and set it on the camp table next to him.

"Oh, mercy, that looks as good as it smells," T.R. said, tucking a napkin into the neckline of a UV-blocking khaki shirt. "I thank you."

"You're welcome," Rufus returned to the stove, shut off the burners, and collected his own plate. "Think of it as me paying rent on this here campsite."

"Say more about the drones, Red."

Rufus pondered it as he chewed his first bite of food. "They're like guns."

"What do you mean by that?"

"You go buy yourself a gun, say. It shoots bullets. Fine. Maybe you decide you want a custom grip. You buy that on the Internet. Turns out you need a special screwdriver to install the damn thing."

T.R. chuckled.

Rufus continued, "So you buy the screwdriver. Maybe you buy a whole set of them. You throw those in a drawer. Time goes by. You end up replacing every single part of the original gun with something different. Maybe you got other guns too. Drawer gets full of old parts and special tools. It's the same with drones, except worse." He nodded at his trailer. "That's my drawer."

"Mm, if these eggs wasn't so delicious I would request permission to come aboard and have a little old look round!"

"Plenty of time to finish the eggs and do that too," Rufus said, though he already felt that they were running a bit late. He settled himself down by reflecting that he had killed a lot of pigs in his time, it was nothing new to him, and so what he really ought to be concerning himself with wasn't killing even more of them, but rather satisfying whatever mysterious agenda T.R. McHooligan was pursuing. And this was a topic on which he could only speculate; but he had the sense that he was being recruited. Also, he had made love to a queen.

"Man oh man, Red, you are a label-making *machine*! You have got labels on your labels!" T.R., deeply satisfied by the huevos and the coffee, was now checking out Rufus's trailer. Over time Rufus had progressively gutted this, replacing the built-in cabinets with modular storage bins made of translucent plastic. They were sub-divided into innumerable compartments. Everything was labeled. "Blue labels is drone related. Red is for gun parts. White is miscel-laneous." Most of the labels were blue.

"How'd you get to be so *organized*, Red?"

"Army beat it into me. Then it was the business. Being on the road, you know, the starting and stopping and the bouncing over the washboarded roads will mix up all your stuff and make a mess of it unless you got everything in its own compartment. There's a chapter in *Moby-Dick* where—"

And here Rufus was all set to describe Chapter 98, "Stowing Down and Clearing Up," where they have made a huge mess of the *Pequod* butchering whales, but then they put everything back where it belongs and clean it all up spick-and-span, and it's as if nothing had ever happened.

"Read it," T.R. said, cutting him off. "I get it, this is your whal-ing ship, a place for everything and everything in its place. You the Captain Ahab of this little operation, then?"

"I prefer to think of myself as being more in the mold of the harpooneers."

"Excellent choice. More sustainable." T.R. turned around, took it all in, peered through the milky plastic bins at drone batteries, drone transceivers, drone propellers, spools of colored wire, tiny metric fasteners, jewelers' screwdrivers, heat shrink tubing, stainless-steel hemostats. A 3D printer where a microwave oven had once been installed. "Man," he exclaimed, "you are the Drone Ranger!"

They went out and got in the chopper and shot pigs. These were exactly where Rufus had predicted they would be. Shooting them in this way was like a video game set to "easy." T.R. had brought an assortment of old and new guns from what Rufus could only as-sume was an inconceivably expensive collection. T.R. made a point of handing Rufus a different firearm every few minutes. He always introduced it with some patter along the lines of "Hoo-ee! This one's got quite a kick but it gets the job done!" However, when Rufus was actually operating the weapons, T.R. watched his movements and Rufus understood that he was being evaluated both as to his attention to firearm safety and as to general familiarity with different weapon types, marksmanship, and so on. At one point late in the interview—for it was clear that this was a job interview—T.R. threw him a curve by handing him one of his antiques. It was some kind of early clip-fed rifle with a heavy military feel to it.

"I'm not familiar with the use of this weapon," Rufus said, after glancing it over. "I'd be more comfortable if you showed me how to operate it."

T.R. did so, enthusiastically. Rufus then copied his movements, looking up at him occasionally to verify that he was getting it right, and used it to drill a big sow from about fifty yards. He understood that if he had attempted to brazen it out and use the gun without requesting help, he would have failed the interview. T.R. would have tapped the pilot on the shoulder. They'd have flown back to the campsite. T.R. would have paid him for his time, cash on the barrelhead, and they would never have seen each other again. Conversely, Rufus's asking for help had sealed some kind of deal in the mind of T.R. His interest in ridding the world of more feral swine tapered off sharply. Ten minutes later they were back on the ground polishing off the coffee.

"I ain't one of those Rambo cats," Rufus cautioned him, before the conversation got too deep. "Stayed mostly on base. Took some mortar rounds, heard sniper bullets go by. Saw IEDs go off. Saw some other shit too. But I'm a mechanic. Not a snake eater."

"Ah, shit, I got plenty of snake eaters. I know where to find them. Hell, they won't leave me alone, word's got round that T.R. is hiring."

"For the Flying S?"

"That's right. Activity is ramping up there, as you saw. More people moving in. It is becoming a community. Really, Red, you could think of it as a microstate."

"Like Rhode Island?"

"I was thinking Liechtenstein."

"How's the United States gonna feel about that?"

T.R. chuckled. "Do you know what the United States did last week, after we fired those eighteen shells up into the stratosphere?"

"No, sir, I do not."

"Nothing."

"Not even a phone call?"

"I got people on the inside of the FAA. They didn't even *notice*, Red. They knew we had filed for a permit, of course. But if the shells were picked up on radar, no one was looking at the screen."

"It wouldn't move like the bogey from an airplane."

"Nah. It goes straight up! So on a radar screen it doesn't even move. Probably just looks like a dead pixel."

"What about when the shell is gliding down?"

"Moves differently then, of course. But we do that mostly over Mexican airspace. I'm working out an understanding with our friends south of the border. On final approach, after the shell has dropped below the radar, only then do we let it glide north over the Rio Grande. It re-enters U.S. airspace below the altitude where the FAA gives a shit and lands on Flying S property."

Rufus considered it. "How about military radar? They gotta know."

T.R. checked his watch and Rufus knew he'd gone somewhere he shouldn't have. "None of my business," Rufus conceded, "just working it out in my head."

"You're army. Not air force. A ground pounder. Not a flyboy. Let's talk about that."

"Okay, let's do."

"I want you to go to the Flying S Ranch—assuming I can make it worth your while, of course. I would feel better if you were there keeping an eye on things. I want you to be the Drone Ranger."

T.R. had coined that term earlier and Rufus had gotten the feeling that it might stick. He smiled. "You want ol' Red to keep an eye on, what, a couple of thousand square miles?"

"I got other resources, as you know. Imaging satellites passing over at all hours. Plenty of boots on the ground."

"Brown hats and black hats."

T.R. nodded. "Brown hats you could think of as cops. Black hats are your mercenaries—the equivalent of the military. But the Lone Ranger—he was neither fish nor fowl!"

Rufus laughed. "You want me in a white hat?"

"Wear whatever you want. The black mask and the blue jumpsuit are optional. I imagine you'll be in an earthsuit much of the time."

"What do you imagine I could do that ain't being done already with the resources you got on hand?"

"Roam around and notice anything that don't feel right. Respond to inquiries. Just keep an eye on things. It's a burden, Red, to own property."

"I farmed fifty acres," Rufus said. "I know."

"You lie awake at night wondering what the hell's going on there."

"Yup, you do."

"That's why we have caretakers. Ranch hands. Oh, sure there's always chores to keep that kinda person busy. But the *real* reason to hire people like that is so we can sleep better at night. Because then we know that there is intelligence—active intelligent minds—right there on the ground."

Rufus nodded. "Now, let's talk straight about one thing. You ain't worried about no wild pigs. Coyotes. Rattlesnakes."

T.R. managed to look as if he were glad Rufus had finally brought this topic up. "Pina2bo is going to change the world, Red. It's gonna change it for the better, overall. The people of places like Houston, Venice, Singapore—they'll feel the most benefit. It will benefit those places *unambiguously* by stopping sea level rise in its tracks. Now, there's other countries in this world that are gonna have more pros and cons to think about." T.R. set his coffee mug down so that he could make a scale pan juggling motion with empty hands. "Less coastal flooding—great! Colder winters. Not so great. But, overall"—he let one hand drop to his knee as the other floated up—"an acceptable trade. But. *But.* There is going to be a third category of country. Hopefully a small category." He reversed the positions of his hands, letting the high one drop to his knee, raising the other and turning it into a fist. "They are gonna run the numbers. By which I mean they are gonna run big computer sims to evaluate the effect that Pina2bo will have on their climate. Their economy." T.R. paused for a second and blinked. "And they are gonna be *pissed.*"

Rufus nodded. "And depending on what kind of country they are, maybe it's limited to, I don't know, filing a complaint with the United Nations."

"Which wouldn't do shit," T.R. said. "But other countries— who knows, maybe they got snake eaters of their own."

"You're worried about espionage. Maybe sabotage."

"Yup. And there's always the fucking Greens. The remote and wide-open nature of the Flying S Ranch, its location on the Rio Grande, cuts both ways. It enables us to fire giant bullets straight up into the stratosphere without anyone even noticing. But it also makes it easy to infiltrate, easy to spy on, easy to mess with."

"I'd do it with drones," Rufus said. "If I was one of the bad guys, I mean, looking for a way to fuck you up."

"Of course you would. Maybe part of what you can do is be a red team for us—heh! Think of how an adversary would use drones, anticipate their moves, develop countermeasures. Shit, I don't know!" T.R. checked his watch. The hard stop was drawing nigh. "That's kinda the point of hiring intelligent people, Red. You don't exactly know what they're gonna think of."

Rufus nodded. "Reckon I'll head over that way and have a look round."

T.R. brightened. "To the Flying S?"

Rufus nodded. "I'll be sure and put out the fire before I leave."

NEDERLAND

The last two hours of the flight to Schiphol featured some of the worst turbulence Saskia had ever experienced. She very much wished she was in the business jet's cockpit, where she would have enjoyed a better view of the horizon and some sense of being in control. The great circle route from Texas scissored across a storm that was pouring down the gap between Norway and Britain and scheduled to hit the Netherlands coast early in the morning local time. Finally they ranged out ahead of it, though, and made the final descent and landing in calm air. She was glad she'd taken the advice to advance the timing of their departure from the airstrip at Flying S.

Queen Frederika Mathilde Louisa Saskia passed through immigration formalities like anybody else inside the main terminal at Schiphol. This reminded her that they had never formally entered the United States. Had Willem somehow smoothed that over? Or was it still a dangling loose end? If so, did it really matter now that they were back on Dutch soil? These questions caused her to review in her mind all that had happened in the last week, beginning with the pigs on the runway and culminating with totally satisfactory casual sex with Rufus last night on an antique railway carriage in a high desert valley in the wilds of West Texas. Walking through Schiphol, dazed from jet lag and still queasy from turbulence, surrounded by Dutch voices and the familiar reality of her homeland, Queen Frederika found it almost impossible to believe that all that had really happened.

Within a few minutes they were in a car headed toward The Hague, and by two in the morning Saskia was back in the familiar confines of Huis ten Bosch. Lotte had already gone to sleep. On Saskia's biological clock it was early evening. Moreover, she had made the tactical error of napping on the plane. She took a stroll around the grounds. Stars and a half-moon were visible in the south, but the northern half of the sky was a dark indigo blur as clouds, invisible in the dark, swept across it in advance of the summer storm. A faint hiss, building toward a roar, reached her ears from the ancient forest all around as the tops of the great trees, thick with late summer foliage, began to seethe and toss in the rising wind. Part of Saskia just wanted to pull up a chair and sit in the open and let the weather wash over her, but finally she was beginning to feel a little drowsy. She went inside and climbed at last into her own bed.

If it made sense to speak of a typical disaster, then this sounded as if it had been one of those until about halfway through break-fast. Wind and waves had first struck Frisia in the north and then worked their way down the coast. The occasional rogue wave had overtopped a dike, but none of the coastal defenses had been breached. Here and there, trees were down, roads awash, trucks and caravans flipped on their sides. To all appearances, it looked like Saskia would be headed to wherever her presence might actually be helpful. This, however, probably meant simply waiting until tomorrow. Showing up right on the heels of an active disaster just got in the way of relief efforts and made it look like she was pandering for a photo op.

Apparently she had slept through a loud crack that had raised a minor security alarm until the cause had been identified as a large bough—itself the size of a mature tree—snapping off a big oak a hundred meters outside the security fence. Plans were being made for her to walk out there with Lotte in an hour or so and be photo-graphed marveling at it.

She was reviewing all this with Willem and other members of her staff when Lotte came down for breakfast. All the staff mem-bers broke off and quietly made themselves scarce as mother and daughter greeted each other with somewhat more than the usual amount of hugging and smooching. For the last couple of years, relations between queen and princess had been not exactly frosty, but distant and maybe even a little prickly in a way that was not really that unusual. Suddenly, somehow, the ice had been broken. Saskia knew why but none of the household staff did; they were content to slip out and finish their coffee in another room while mother and daughter caught up a little.

Once they sat down and looked at each other, Saskia saw that Lotte had put on makeup—not a huge amount—before coming down. She had mixed feelings about that. Lotte could do what she wanted with her body. But she'd put up a healthy resistance to the expectations that society placed on women in general and royals in particular and even earned a bit of a reputation as a young royal rebel-in-the-making. But now did not seem the right moment to broach that topic. Perhaps Lotte just anticipated that they would be going out in public soon to be photographed reacting to storm damage. The Haagse Bos was a public park. Anyone with a long lens could snap the occasional candid photo of a royal if they didn't have anything better to do with their time.

Lotte returned the courtesy by not asking Saskia directly about the topic that had been the subject of so many text messages during the last few days. This would have been inadvisable anyway with staff in the next room. It was a curious thing about texting and other such faceless electronic communications that they enabled people to say things and to reveal sides of their personalities they'd have avoided in person. Certainly any stranger who had read some of the texts Lotte had sent to her mother in Texas would have formulated an image in their mind that was at odds with the somewhat unconventional but basically wholesome teenager now sitting across the table from Saskia, her strawberry blond hair in a loose braid falling down over the front of a powder blue T-shirt. Saskia just sat and gazed upon the girl for a few moments, pleasantly shocked, as all parents always were, by how she had grown and changed.

"What was all that *about*!?" Lotte asked.

"Texas?"

"Yes. I know the official story was that you were making a private visit to friends overseas, and you got delayed because of the hurricane. Fine. But I'm just wondering . . . ?"

"We should talk about it at some point, you and I. It was a conference about climate change."

Lotte's face registered approval.

"I know that this topic would be important to you, darling, even if it weren't for—" And Saskia turned her hands palms up and sort of gestured in all directions. Meaning *the incredibly bizarre fact that you are a princess living in a royal palace.*

"Texas," Lotte said. "I know the oil industry is very big there."

Saskia conquered the urge to say something in a conversation-endingly didactic parental tone such as *my sweet child, it is very big everywhere, and we own a good chunk of it.* "It's certainly more *visible.* Because it's near the supply end. Where the oil comes out of the ground. Demand is all over, of course—more distributed, less obvious. Every car, every dwelling is part of it."

"The air we breathe," Lotte added. "That's the dumping ground for all of it. Did you hear the branch crack in the night?"

"No, I slept through that!"

"I was thinking about that tree, taking carbon dioxide out of the air for so many centuries, converting it into wood by the ton, until it grew so heavy it could no longer support its own weight."

"I hadn't thought of it in that light. But yes, that tree has seen a lot."

"Maybe we could cut sections from the fallen branch—to show the tree rings going back to before the Industrial Revolution." Lotte was just getting going on this idea when her phone buzzed and her eyes flicked briefly to it. Saskia, hardly for the first time, had to bridle her annoyance at the fact that this contraption was interrupting a perfectly good conversation. But Lotte was no stranger to multitasking. Her brow dimpled momentarily at whatever had come up on the phone—some kind of troubling news, apparently—and then she looked back into her mother's eyes and returned to her theme. "Maybe there's some kind of analysis that could be done in a lab. On that wood, I mean. On the different tree rings. Showing how a tree ring that was created two hundred years ago, before the Industrial Revolution, showed a lower amount of CO_2 in the air than the more recent rings."

"It's not my area of expertise," Saskia answered, "but it seems quite plausible that such an analysis could be done." She frowned and thought about it while Lotte diverted her gaze to her phone again and thumbed out a response. "Are you suggesting we send the fallen branch to such a lab for analysis? I'm not sure if it would be of any interest to scientists who do that sort of thing—"

Lotte executed a perfect teen eye roll and stuck the landing with a sigh. "Of course not, those people can get old pieces of wood anywhere. My point is that we are going to walk out there in a few minutes and get our photograph taken with that fallen branch, no? And what is the point of that? It's to show people that we are aware that there was a windstorm. Fine. But there are other things going on besides windstorms that we need to show awareness of. So I'm just saying that when we are done getting our photo taken standing next to this fucking branch, instead of letting the maintenance crew haul it away and put it in a log chipper or whatever, maybe I cut some pieces out of it and use it as a way to show that we are *also* aware of bigger issues like climate change and the damage *it* causes."

Saskia was just on the verge of saying that this was a wonderful idea when Lotte's phone buzzed again and she stood up. "I'm worried about Toon," she said. "I want to go to the beach."

"Scheveningen?"

"Just north of there."

"What's going on with Toon?" This was a schoolmate of Lotte's and a part of her social circle.

"He went surfing this morning, early. There are big waves today because of the storm. Something weird is happening—I can't make sense of these messages."

Saskia became aware that Willem was standing in a doorway. He was facing in her general direction, but she could tell from the movements of his eyes and his somewhat slack-jawed appearance that he was reading some virtual content in his glasses. "Your Majesty," he said, "sorry to interrupt, but I have to make you aware that—"

"Something weird is happening at the beach?" Saskia guessed and exchanged a look with Lotte.

"I think it is possible that we have a major disaster happening as we speak."

Saskia sat still and absorbed that for a moment.

Lotte slumped forward and put her forehead on her arms.

Sirens were sounding. Emergency vehicles passing through the Haagse Bos.

"Such as—what?" Saskia asked. "A mass shooting? A bomb? Shipwreck?"

"Something about foam."

"*What!?*"

Willem shook his head helplessly. "That's all I know."

Saskia stood up. "Get the bicycles."

Even bicycles were almost overkill. Huis ten Bosch was just a few thousand strides from the edge of the North Sea. They could have walked to it briskly in less than an hour. On bicycles, trailed by security and support staff in cars, they covered the distance in minutes.

Along this stretch of the North Sea coast, the basic shape of the land was a flat beach that grew wider or narrower according to the tides. Rising abruptly from that was a line of dunes, held together by scrubby vegetation that had found purchase in the loose sandy soil and survived the wind and spray that came off the sea almost continuously during much of the year. Inland of the dunes' crest, the ground dropped lower and was spattered with small pools embedded in marshy ground. That described the coastline in its natural state from the Hook of Holland, a few kilometers south of The Hague, north as far as Frisia. The Hague's bit of it was a popular recreational beach, serviced by a row of restaurants, bars, and so on built well back from the surf, nestled at the base of the steep bluff or strung out above along its brow. This, of course, was the high season for beachgoing. Conditions had been fine and warm until the onset of this morning's weather.

That sort of development—the touristy stuff that you could see at any beach in the world—terminated abruptly as one went north up the beach past Scheveningen. Beyond a certain point there were suddenly no businesses, and very few human traces: just a long wire fence that had something to do with maintaining the dune, and a couple of reinforced concrete bunkers that the Nazis had embedded in the sand as part of their coastal defense system. A paved bicycle path ran along the top of the dune, but you couldn't see that from below, just occasional wooden staircases linking it to the beach. Other than that, it was a nature preserve. During the winter, the place could be astonishingly deserted given that it was only a short walk from the capital of one of the most densely populated countries in the world.

An exception occurred whenever conditions of wind and sea combined to produce large waves. Then, this coastline drew surfers. They all had apps that alerted them when conditions were likely to be right. They would flock to whatever stretch of the Dutch coastline looked like it would have the biggest and best waves. Given the climate, they generally wore wet suits.

This morning, probably during the wee hours, those people had been awakened by those apps letting them know that conditions in a few hours' time were going to be ideal at Scheveningen, and that waves could be expected that might only occur once in a decade.

Therefore, as Saskia and Lotte and their entourage pedaled

westward over the landscape of dunes and potholes just inland of the beach, they were following in the footsteps and bicycle tracks of hundreds of surfers who had come the same way during the hours just before dawn, fighting their way up into the teeth of that wind. It was easy to see the traces they had left behind in the loose ground and various pieces of kit they had stashed in the lee of the dune line.

The crest of the dune—the highest prominence between them and the flat beach below—was now a ragged picket line of civilians, police, and aid workers, all looking down and out over the sea. They were strangely inactive. They had all been summoned here by some great spectacle, but having arrived, they didn't know what to do besides look at it.

Saskia and her group pulled over and got out of the way of a fire truck that was trying to reach the shore along the same indistinct path. Then they followed it up and found their way into a gap between other onlookers where they could look out over the beach.

The beach appeared to be gone.

What they saw was so strange and so contrary to what they had expected that it took several moments for them even to make sense of the plain evidence of their eyes. Directly below them, only a few meters below the brow of the dune, a flat, featureless slab of dirty-yellow stuff was butted up against the slope. It extended from there all the way out to the North Sea, which was still slamming into it with great waves. But for all their power the waves did not move it. They simply dissolved into it. Even their sound was swallowed up.

Looking to the left and the right, Saskia could see that this phenomenon extended south to the pier and Ferris wheel at Scheveningen, and northward for at least an equal distance. Several kilometers of beach had been buried to a depth of a few meters beneath a featureless and disturbingly quiet slab of what appeared to be foam.

Still finding this difficult to believe, Saskia ventured down a short distance from the lip of the dune, wanting to inspect the stuff close up. It wasn't that far below them. She could have poked it with a long stick. But the moment she broke ranks, an outcry came up. They had not even recognized her yet. She was just a random person to them. But all those who'd arrived earlier, all the police and aid workers, wanted her to know that under no circumstances should she descend one step farther.

"But it's just . . . normal sea foam? Natural foam?" she asked.

"This is what the experts are saying," Willem said. "You see it on the beach all the time, of course."

"Of course! But just little puffs of it. Ropes of it along the surf line."

"This is the same. Just . . . more of it. All concentrated along this stretch where the surf was strongest. It piled up on the beach faster than it could dissipate. It was trapped against the base of the dune. So it just piled up higher and higher. Faster than people could get away."

Saskia was finally, only now, observing the nature of the rescue activities. A coast guard chopper, painted a vivid shade of yellow, was inbound over the sea. A couple of huge orange RHIBs were moving around offshore, carrying rescue divers, but it looked like they were largely preoccupied just managing their relationship to the incoming waves—trying not to become surfboards. Red fire trucks were continuing to show up along the paved bicycle path that ran along the top of the dune. One of them had been used to anchor ropes that had been tossed down into the foam. A fireman in full face respirator, with an air tank on his back, was trudging up out of it. He looked like someone who had been tarred and feathered. Every square inch of him was flocked with white foam. When he reached a safe altitude he unsnapped himself from the rope and made a gesture to colleagues above, who began to haul on the rope. After a few moments a body in a wet suit emerged from the foam. When it was safely up on dry ground, medics converged on it.

Other victims—many in wet suits—were lying supine on gurneys, or just on the ground. Rescue workers were forcing air into their lungs by squeezing rubber bags. Or at least that was the case for some of them. Others were just lying motionless. They were being zipped into body bags.

The fire truck deployed a hose and began to spray water down into the foam, easily carving a trench into it. This they widened by playing it from side to side. Soon they uncovered a still human form sprawled partway up the slope of the dune.

"You can't breathe in that stuff," Willem said. "It gets in your lungs. Nor can you swim out of it. You can only run, or rather wade, to some place where you might be able to breathe. But of course you can't see where you're going. A few of them made it to the top of the dune. A few went back down, trying to rescue the others."

"How many?" Saskia asked, watching dully as the fire hose exposed another body, and another, within the space of a few meters.

"At least a hundred," Willem said.

Willem's job in such a situation was to be cold-blooded. This wasn't necessarily in his nature. He was as shocked by all this as anyone else. It wasn't completely unprecedented. There had been isolated cases of drowning in sea foam during the last few years. It had come up on the emergency services' radar as something that would become more likely as the temperature of the sea rose and algae—which apparently had something to do with the formation of sea foam—flourished. But a mass casualty event of this type was completely astonishing.

That astonishment was over and above the natural feelings of grief that anyone would experience upon seeing so many lives lost. Only for a few minutes did Willem remain in that catatonic state. Then Princess Charlotte became very emotional as it became obvious to her that one or more of her friends might be lying dead on this beach somewhere. She ran off in the direction of a cluster of aid workers who were pulling body bags out of crates that had begun to arrive in police vans. The princess got a few meters' head start before Queen Frederika lit out after her.

Amelia, who'd been on duty continuously for the last week, had a well-earned day off. But other members of the security team had swapped in for her. They jogged along roughly parallel to the royals. These people dressed specifically to blend in and not seem like armed goons, so they just seemed like extraordinarily fit and clean-cut citizens moving in a strangely intentional and coordinated fashion around two women, a mother pursuing a distraught teenager toward a row of wet-suited corpses.

So Willem's job—again—was not to do as normal human emotion might dictate (plenty of people were doing that) or to see to the immediate physical security of the royals (that was already sorted) but to look a few hours or days ahead.

Obviously, today's planned slate of activities was toast. He saw to that with a quick message thumbed out on his phone.

He did not follow the others but remained at the high vantage point on the dune, trying to assemble a picture of what was happening.

It was now obvious that they had arrived quite early to an event that was only starting to ramp up, and that would go on doing so for much of the day. This was Sunday morning and few people would be at work. As word spread, they would flock here to gawk or volunteer. Random circumstances—the extreme proximity to Huis ten Bosch, the messages on Lotte's friend network—had caused the royals to arrive only minutes after the event (or during it? For he had the horrible thought that people might be down there *now* struggling for air).

Anyway, traffic to the beach was building rapidly. Twice as many were here now as had been when they arrived, and police were turning their attention to the problem of crowd control— since all who came here would have the same instinct to get up to the top of the dune. Some would inevitably blunder down into the foam as the result of clumsiness, curiosity, or ill-advised rescue attempts. So police vehicles were now arriving in numbers and they were setting up a cordon along the dune-top bicycle path.

The yellow search and rescue helicopter came in closer and settled low, trying to use its rotor wash to dispel the foam. A good idea on someone's part. The down blast began to dig a bowl in the foam, exposing a circle of beach sand. The excavated foam flew outward in a myriad of small flecks that caught in the wind and filled the air like a blizzard.

All well and good but Willem still wasn't doing his job. He turned his back on the sea and looked down the back slope of the dune to the little cluster of emergency vehicles where Princess Charlotte and Queen Frederika had stopped. The two of them were together. Charlotte was holding on to Frederika's arm and resting her head on her mother's shoulder—sweet, but awkward now that she was a few centimeters taller! The queen stood there stolidly and with perfect posture nodding as she was briefed by a young woman wearing a reflective vest. Everything about the body language told him with certainty that their brief spell of anonymity had come to an end. The queen had been recognized. Those around her had changed their behavior accordingly. She was getting a little status report from an emergency worker. Not because she'd asked for one. She would never do that. But because when you were a first responder at a disaster and suddenly you noticed the queen was standing right there, you delivered a status report.

A police officer was headed right toward him unreeling a roll of yellow crowd control tape and giving him the stink eye. Willem dodged out of his way. Then he reached into the breast pocket of his suit jacket—he was no longer dressing like a random Texan—and pulled out a laminated security credential with an orange lanyard, which he slipped around his neck. No one was actually going to inspect it, but merely being a man of a certain age in a suit and an overcoat with a badge on a lanyard would afford him respect and access in whatever order was going to be imposed upon this chaos.

Press, as such, were only beginning to arrive. At first they would focus on documenting the tragedy and the efforts of the first responders. Inevitably there would be photographs of the queen and the princess. Random people on social media would post pictures of their own. What would those pictures show? A self-absorbed, out-of-touch monarch getting in the way of rescue operations? Or a woman of the people doing what any norMAL person would do in the wake of a disaster?

What was *needed*? Where was this operation understaffed?

Willem's eye was drawn to a flatbed truck with military markings, cruising at a walking pace down a track in the lee of the dune. Soldiers were rolling boxes over the tailgate, depositing them on the sand every few meters. Willem had no idea what was in them.

A few moments later Willem was down below with the queen. She'd had the good sense to back off a few paces and let the first responders do the melancholy—and quite physically demanding—work of wrestling dead surfers into body bags. He said to her, "We need to get you away from the dead people. How about opening some boxes?"

"Yes," she said, "set it up. Something that is actually helpful, please. We are going to try to find Lotte's friend."

He turned away and sent a two-word message:

> Need Fenna.

Then he went back to his official role of being as cold-blooded as was humanly possible.

He went and looked at the boxes that had been dumped out of the truck. They were labeled and barcoded in a way that was opaque to him.

Not far away, three people in reflective vests were standing around one of the boxes talking and pointing. He walked right up to them. Probably because of the suit and the lanyard, they stopped talking and looked at him. They were sipping coffee from go cups, in the manner of persons who had only just now showed up for work. "What is all this stuff and why is it here?" Willem asked. Anywhere else this might have come across as gruff, but it was how Dutch people communicated.

"Pop-up shelters, folding chairs and tables, emergency blankets, plastic ponchos, snacks," said the oldest of the group, an Indo woman with graying hair in a ponytail.

Willem guessed, "Planned response to mass casualty events."

"Yes. Lots of people are going to show up here in the next few hours. It's going to rain. We need to keep those people sheltered but out of the way of the rescue operation. Workers need to be fed, to use the toilet, wash their hands. Victims need to re-connect with families."

Willem nodded. "Do you need volunteers to help set this stuff up?"

Sizing him up, the woman replied using an Indonesian idiom that, roughly translated into English, meant *fuck yes*. The other two confirmed it with nods and expressions of relief.

Willem found Queen Frederika and Princess Charlotte a short distance from where he'd last seen them, in the lee of the dune. The princess was on her knees in the sand, hugging a boy in a wet suit who was seated on the ground looking stunned. Her friend Toon, apparently. He was flecked with foam, looking like a penguin chick covered with down. To borrow a phrase Willem had recently heard from Rufus, Toon looked like he'd seen some shit. The queen went over, bent down, and clasped the boy's hand. People were taking pictures that would no doubt be up on social media within moments. That was fine. She looked a bit of a mess but no one would hold it against her.

After a decent amount of time had been spent on this project of letting the wayward Toon know how happy they were to see him alive, Willem got the royals moving in the direction of where volunteers were wanted. The security team naturally came along with them. This triggered a sort of herd instinct among those onlookers who were just milling around anyway, since they had been ejected from the top of the dune by the police. Space available for random citizens was shrinking, as lanes were staked out for heavy equipment trundling in from the city: red trucks with long multi-jointed cherry pickers that could reach down into the foam, ambulances, and so on. The royals might be doing the aid workers a favor just by drawing a few people away toward the rear. Which was the message Willem would put out later today on every social media outlet he had access to when anti-royalist cranks began slinging their mud at Queen Frederika. His phone was already buzzing with alerts. He piped the feed to his glasses. As he strolled along in the rearguard of this growing crew of volunteers, he scrolled through freshly posted images of the queen clasping Toon's hand.

Someone slapped him on the ass. Fenna, blowing past him on her bicycle, cosmetics case lodged in the basket on its handlebars. Behind him a random old Dutchman, having observed this, made a quizzical/bawdy remark.

The volunteers got to work. Willem just stood off at a remove, watching it play on social media. He could sense some of the people looking askance at this weird old Indo, just standing there with his hands in the pockets of his thousand-euro overcoat while good ordinary citizens bent to the task of doing what they could in the face of this disaster. There was almost a level at which he relished being the asshole in cases like this.

He took the opportunity to skim through the last twenty-four hours' work-related message traffic. Until half an hour ago, the biggest concern on his mind had been how to manage a wave of speculation and gossip that was starting to build around the whereabouts and activities of the queen during the last week. Going out to look at the fallen branch would have served the same purpose as displaying a photograph of a kidnapping victim holding up today's newspaper. What the queen was doing right now was much better than that. They were going to win this news cycle. The livid royal-haters and creepy royal-stans flourished when nothing was happening and they had nothing to latch on to besides their own obsessions. This would silence them for perhaps three days, long enough for Queen Frederika's weeklong Texas absence to be washed out of the nation's attention span. Then Willem would have to think up something else. It would be comparatively easy since the queen's Budget Day speech to the States General was coming up soon. This was a lot of work but was something of a self-licking ice cream cone by this point. There would be a lot of articles about the fancy hats that ladies would wear to the event. There would be a stink about the queen's horse-drawn carriage, which was decorated with ancient, stereotypical paintings of colonized people.

So in a lot of ways Willem's tasks were clearly plotted out for the next week and a half.

But. There was this looming question of how and when to come clean about the trip to Texas. T.R.'s staff had done a shockingly effective job of preventing word from getting out, so far. And the fact that he had fired the gun eighteen times in a day without anyone noticing was simply mind-blowing. But tomorrow—now that the White Label geeks had finished crunching the numbers on that first salvo—the big gun at Pina2bo would go into action again, firing shells into the stratosphere around the clock. Even if no one connected Queen Frederika to the Pina2bo trip, she'd eventually be asked her opinion of solar geoengineering. Willem already had press releases cued up that he would fire off if word started to leak. But for now, the official story seemed to be holding up: She had taken a bit of time off for a personal visit to a friend in the Houston area (most people would make the obvious assumption that it was someone connected with Royal Dutch Shell) and had been detained for a few extra days because of disruptions related to the hurricane. While there, she had visited some locations related to climate change and sea level rise.

Which was all true.

Back to the here and now. A moment was going to come when it was time to extract the royals and get them back to Huis ten

Bosch. A little of this kind of thing went a long way. All the good pictures had already been taken. He knew what the front pages of the newspapers were going to show tomorrow and it would be fantastic. Staying here for hours wouldn't make it any better. They might draw crowds that would impede rescue operations.

He saw a gray-haired man pull up on a bicycle, go halfway up the dune, and turn around with a pair of binoculars. No interest in the tragedy just on the other side of the dune. He'd come here just to get a look at the queen. There would be others like him; they just hadn't gotten here yet.

Willem noted with approval that the security team had relocated the cars to within a few meters of where the queen was at work spraying disinfectant on plastic tables. They could extract her on a few moments' notice at any point.

It was up to her, of course. She could leave whenever she wanted. But Willem's job was to keep an eye on the overall scene, notice things that she wouldn't, and make discreet suggestions. The time was not now. She'd only just got to work. Leaving too soon would make this seem too much like a cynical photo op. She ducked into one of the cars with Fenna for a routine upgrade, then spelled the princess while she got the same. Willem checked his watch. Maybe another half hour of this would make sense. By then the rescue workers would have found as many bodies as they were going to find, the scale of the disaster would be known. The queen could make a statement on camera and then go back to Huis ten Bosch for a hot lunch and an afternoon nap.

An expensive car was admitted through the security cordon and rolled up to the base of the dune. Out stepped Ruud Vlietstra, the prime minister. He drew attention for a few minutes as he went up to the top of the dune for a look-see and a briefing. The interior minister showed up minutes later on an electric bicycle. All these people had flats practically within walking distance, and most such people were likely to be in The Hague now during the run-up to Budget Day.

Bodies kept coming over the top of the dune. The relentless gradualness of it was a special kind of horror. He kept waiting for the moment when some kind of all clear would be sounded. But it just never stopped. He found a bird's-eye video feed on the Internet and watched it in his glasses. The fucking beach was still covered in foam! The sea was vomiting it up as fast as it could be removed. Its overall level seemed to be subsiding, though.

Photos of mostly young, healthy-looking surfers began to cover a portable whiteboard that had been set up under a canopy. The friends and family members collected in a waiting area where they milled about hugging each other or sat on folding chairs staring into the distance and sipping hot tea. From time to time a rescue worker would descend from the triage area up on the dune and call out a name. The name of a dead person. One or two or five people would converge on them and hear a few low solemn words and then break out in sobbing and wailing.

It was just utterly, fantastically awful and it went on and on and on.

Queen Frederika had finished doing setup work and was now just roaming through the waiting area clasping people's hands, admiring the photos they'd brought of their missing sons and daughters, muttering words of comfort. Most people had the decency not to take pictures.

Willem stationed himself in the queen's eye line and just stood there. Gradually in a two steps forward, one step back cadence she drew closer. There was a wordless understanding that as soon as she reached him they would leave. Willem communicated that fact to the security team. Finally the moment arrived. The queen wound up her last, sad, hand-clasping conversation with a ruined surfer mom, accepted a curtsy (Mom was all in for old-school royalist etiquette), and turned around into a horseshoe of aides and security, centered on Willem. This became a loose flying wedge that got her out into a light drizzling rain and into the car. The bicycles had presumably been seen to.

In the moments before the cars pulled away, Willem had an opportunity to survey the crowd that had gathered on the outside of the cordon. The inevitable flower mound had begun to accumulate. Candles, tricky in this weather, were also being attempted. People were waving Dutch flags and holding up rain-streaked hard copies of surfers' selfies. And there were just a few complete assholes—there were always these people, the feral swine of the political ecosystem—who could not see this tragedy as anything other than an opportunity to show up in public and wave their fucking idiotic signs around. Since the royal house was, in theory, above politics, such persons were usually more of an annoyance or curiosity than a central concern. However, some were insanely pro- or anti-royal and so it behooved Willem to pay attention. Not wanting to be obvious, he activated a feature in his glasses that turned them into a camera, then quickly scanned the crowd, silently snapping a picture whenever he saw a sign being thrust into the air. Then he got into the back seat of the car that was waiting for him.

The drive back to Huis ten Bosch took all of about three minutes. Willem spent most of it holding Fenna's hand and trying to get her settled down. She was more freaked out than at any time since the plane crash. She didn't know any of the surfers but the whole scene had really upset her, perhaps because the victims reminded her of her darling Jules in Louisiana.

When they were back at the royal residence, though, and Willem had a moment to himself in his little office there, he reviewed the photos he had captured just before getting into the car. One detail was bothering him, to the point where he was questioning his own memory.

It was a woman of perhaps forty holding up a hastily hand-lettered sign reading

ERDD A FALSE IDOL

and adorned in the corners with crosses and Stars of David.

Typical religious wack job stuff in every way. But ERDD? He had never heard of ERDD. Or rather he had, of course. But in a very different context. Just last week. Ecological Restoration of Delta Distributaries was a defunct crowdfunded nonprofit that Dr. Margaret Parker had told him about over coffee in New Orleans. Its initials had been stenciled across the back of the reflective vest she'd loaned him. He still had the vest, folded up in his luggage. He meant to send it back to her with a thank-you note once he'd had a chance to launder it.

All the Germanic languages had words like "Erda," meaning Earth, or (in a mythological context, which was presumably the mindset of the sign brandisher) a deity personifying the earth. Mother Earth, basically. Willem did a bit of googling and satisfied himself that there was no language in any branch of the Germanic family tree in which "Erdd" was an accepted spelling.

The "false idol" reference, the crosses and the stars, made it plain that the sign maker was using ERDD in some religious way. To the extent he could peer inside this woman's mind, she seemed to be suggesting that people who worshipped the false idol of Earth—Greens, presumably?—were committing a kind of heresy and that the foam disaster was an omen, a punishment.

Willem did a few more searches, this time linking the word to religious terms, and began to land some hits. They were intermingled with old references to Margaret's group in Louisiana, as well as to other entities that used that acronym. This muddied the waters until he hit on the idea of limiting the search to pages that had been changed within the last year. Then he found a number of ERDD references that seemed to align with whatever was going on in the brain of the sign-holding lady. Most of them were in Dutch. They were cropping up on message threads and social media groups of a decidedly political nature: anti-Greens and anti–lots of other things.

He had already spent more time on this than it was likely to be worth, but he couldn't stop clicking. It was a lot of right-wing types becoming frothingly enraged because they had been tagged, with surgical precision, in postings on a few Green, tree-huggerish feeds that were all about ERDD as a kind of synthetic umbrella deity for everything related to environmentalism. These Greens were making no bones about it. They weren't claiming to have rediscovered a lost religion. They were cheerfully admitting right up front that they'd just made it all up, like dungeon masters prepping for an all-night Dungeons and Dragons session. There was one feed where the people who were boosting this idea were stating their case and tagging exactly the kinds of right-wingers who could most be relied upon to respond furiously as all their cultural and religious buttons were mashed to a point that had basically driven them mad.

Now, as T.R. would have put it, this was not Willem's first rodeo. So as he surveyed the ERDD feeds, he saw all sorts of clues that made it obvious to him that it was all fake. No one actually believed in ERDD. The sole purpose of this stuff was to induce a backlash.

He had been sifting through all this for at least half an hour when it finally occurred to him to start looking at the dates when it had been posted. Those were, of course, perfectly easy to see; he just hadn't been paying attention to them.

But now he scrolled back through all his open tabs and discovered that every bit of this stuff had gone up within the last five days.

He went back and compared it against his calendar, allowing for time zones. Not a trace of it had existed anywhere prior to his visit to the Mississippi Delta, his tour of the diversion, and his conversation with Bo.

During which Bo had snapped a picture of the ERDD vest drying out on a coat hanger.

Now, there were certain things that Willem would only discuss with the queen. Others he would without hesitation bring to the attention of the security team, the police, or Dutch intelligence. Matters of a more personal and informal nature he might chat about with Fenna. But there were certain things you could only talk about with your husband. This was one of those.

Willem excused himself for the day and took the train up to Leiden, fifteen kilometers north. He walked to the flat that he shared with Remigio. Typically for this area, it was in a post-war building, but constructed at a pre-war scale, so that it blended reasonably well with those older buildings that had survived. It looked out over a canal and it was conveniently located with respect to the university buildings where Remigio pursued his career as a history professor.

Last night Willem had just thrown his stuff down. His bag was still sitting on the floor with Walmart clothes and Flying S swag spilling out of it. He rooted through it and found the ERDD vest. He unfolded it, put it on the back of a chair, and photographed it, just to prove he wasn't out of his mind.

Then he pulled on his new cowboy boots and walked to the pub.

Remigio was Portuguese. He was a decade younger than Willem but looked even younger than that thanks to lucky genes and assiduous skin care. He'd come up to Leiden to do Ph.D. research on the migration of expulsed Sephardic Jews from the Iberian Peninsula to the Low Countries in the sixteenth century. They'd liked him well enough that they'd offered him a job, and he'd liked the Amsterdam nightlife well enough that he'd accepted it. After a decade of that he'd "settled down" in Leiden, which was where he and Willem had met. They had a happy and stable life together.

The battery of viral tests that Willem had gone through at Schiphol had come back with generally favorable results that had been duly piped into PanScan, which had deemed it acceptable for him to sit under an umbrella at a canal-side pub, provided it wasn't too crowded, and have a beer with his husband.

But he just couldn't bring himself to tell Remi about ERDD.

The sudden intimacy of being back with him, the norMALness of the pub, the canal traffic gliding to and fro—the very smallness and neatness of this old Dutch town—just made it inconceivable. To mention this insane Internet stuff would be like tossing garbage into the canal.

"This thing in Texas, Remi. It is all about geoengineering. You are going to hear about it eventually."

"Sounds as if I'm hearing about it now!" Remigio quipped.

"I mean, on the news. Internet."

"I know what you mean, Wim."

"What does that make you think of?"

"What, geoengineering?"

"Yes."

"Are you using me as a focus group?" This was an old joke between them. Willem ignored it and let the question dangle. Remigio gazed out over the canal, took a sip of beer, then grimaced and cocked his head from side to side in an *on the one hand . . . on the other hand* way. "I recoil."

"How so?"

"I feel like the Greens are going to give me an earful about how terrible it is." With comically exaggerated paranoia, Remi looked around to see whether any university folk were in earshot. "It is terrible, right?" His eyebrows were raised in mock horror.

"It cools things down, but it doesn't fix ocean acidification, which is a real problem. People don't approve of even talking about it."

"Ahh, I've lost track of all the things I can get in trouble for even talking about."

"Exactly, so it creates a bubble. One goes for years without hearing it mentioned. Because it is such a strict taboo. But then, one goes to *Texas* and . . ." Willem pointed both index fingers up in the air and pretended to fire six-guns with abandon, à la Yosemite Sam, while making "Kew! Kew!" sound effects.

Remigio nodded. "Texas. Nice boots, by the way."

"Thank you. Yes. You've never been there, have you?"

"No."

"It is this whole vast country-within-a-country where some people don't have the slightest compunction about . . ."

"Discussing the forbidden topic?"

"*Fuck* discussing it, they're actually *doing* it. Actual geoengineering. It's happening. The queen and I saw it."

"These Texans want her to support it?"

"I don't exactly know. They're not stupid. They understand that her role is ceremonial."

Remigio considered that. "All right, let's consider the alternative. These Texans could have pored over the Grondwet and then invited the minister of climate policy. Or the prime minister, even."

Willem shook his head. "Impossible. The committees that would have gotten involved . . . the leaks . . . the politics . . . just unthinkable."

"So," Remi said, "when politics reaches that point where so many things are unthinkable . . . impossible . . . taboo . . . does, maybe, the queen begin to have real power again?"

"Yes. That's the simple answer. Yes. But she *shouldn't*."

"Because *Saskia* is such a terrible and irresponsible tyrant?" Remi asked. Just teasing him.

"Of course not. Nor will Princess Charlotte be when it's her turn. It's just that this is not how it's supposed to work."

"And yet," Remigio said, "we have a queen. And she has your loyalty."

THE LINE OF ACTUAL CONTROL

Laks had at least done enough research by this point to expect the PowerPoint deck, so that was no surprise. And Ravi had found online crib sheets for the quiz, which looked pretty easy once you knew how to spot the trick questions.

The deck, making no effort to put a cheerful face on the business, opened with old stock footage of mushroom clouds rising from nuclear detonations. The voiceover was in English with Hindi and Punjabi subtitles. Dates and words were superimposed on the fireballs: USA 1945, USSR 1949, China 1964, India 1974. "Nuclear bombs have existed for the better part of a century, and yet they have only been used in battle twice, at the very beginning of the atomic age, at Hiroshima and Nagasaki." Pictures now of devastated Japanese cities and maimed civilians. "It is extraordinary in all of human history for man to have developed a weapon but then voluntarily refrained from its use. Why? Because it was understood that the consequences were undesirable." Pretty dry understatement there, as they were now watching clips of old sci-fi movies showing grisly post-nuke effects and horror-show makeup.

The next slide was an abrupt transition to a series of images depicting guns of various kinds down through the ages, starting with Chinese hand cannons and fast-forwarding through Western flintlocks, six-shooters, and twentieth-century military rifles to culminate in Kalashnikov and Armalite variants. "Much less powerful than nuclear bombs, but responsible for far more deaths, are conventional firearms."

Now a map of Asia, with China in red and India in blue, zooming in slowly on the border region between them in the Tibetan plateau. As it got closer, Laks was able to pick out the bent Chinese salient that had come to be known as the Yak's Leg, crossing over the long boomerang-shaped lake of Pangong Tso (right now they were only a short distance west of the "knee" in the leg, above the lake's northern tip). A simple animation showed the border moving this way and that, like a sail luffing in the wind. Old grainy footage of Chinese and Indian military units trudging through snow and shooting rifles completed the picture. Shooty and explody sound effects echoed harshly from the hard floor of the room. But then suddenly it went silent, except for an old-time trumpet fanfare. In huge black numerals, "1962" covered the map. The red/blue frontier froze. An animated line snaked along the boundary and a label appeared: LINE OF ACTUAL CONTROL. "The cease-fire of 1962 put an end to armed conflict between India and China along their shared border—which remains disputed to this day. A peace agreement signed by Zhou Enlai and Jawaharlal Nehru referred not to the border but to the Line of Actual Control—a diplomatic phrasing that enabled the cease-fire to be formalized without either party acknowledging the other's territorial claims." This bit was helpfully illustrated by stock footage of the respective leaders inking documents. "Since 1962 the position of the Line of Actual Control has shifted this way and that. However, the cease-fire itself—the mutual agreement not to use firearms—has remained as perfectly unbroken as mankind's collective agreement not to use nuclear weapons. Three-quarters of a century has passed without a bullet disturbing the high mountain border zone. This in spite of the fact that it is heavily militarized on both sides by units of the Indian and Chinese military. This does not, however, mean that no conflict has taken place in the area—only that no firearms have been used. Occasionally, patrolling units of the two opposing sides have come into direct contact in areas where the exact position of the Line is not precisely charted. Indian military has respected the Line but Chinese have taken advantage to make small invasions of Indian territory. Added up over time, if allowed to endure, these move the Line, causing major loss of strategic high ground to our aggressive neighbor to the north. How to punish the invaders and move them firmly back to where they belong, while still preserving cease-fire? With sticks and stones, and, if need be, fists. Incidents of this type, once rare, became common in first decades of the twenty-first century. It is not known when volunteer units first began to arrive at the front. Now it is commonplace on both sides. By stepping out yonder door you are entering a zone of low-intensity but very real warfare that can become a hot shooting war at any moment should a combatant on either side discharge even a single bullet from a firearm. We, the men and women of the Indian Army, welcome volunteers from all over our great country, and indeed the world, who come to this place to push back the invaders and stabilize the Line in its rightful spot. However, we must always be on the alert for hotheads who do not respect the rules, or foreign spies who would seek to infiltrate volunteer ranks in the role of agent provocateur. Hence the procedures enacted in this facility. Thank you and good luck in your adventures at the front!"

The deck concluded with an image of two strapping Indian men—one Sikh, the other not—striking heroic poses atop a glacier, crossing their sticks in a big X against the dark blue sky.

The lights came up and a woman wearing an ankle-length puffy coat over a sari came in, followed by a uniformed soldier pushing a cart laden with sticks and stones. The lady gave a talk, much more interesting to Laks than any PowerPoint, about what was and wasn't acceptable. People were always trying to bend the rules. Sticks could be as big and heavy as you liked, but they could not have any metal attachments or anything whatsoever grafted onto them that could make a penetrating or cutting wound. Any sort of wood was allowable provided it was not liable to break off in a way as to form a sharp point. She held up a cheap pinewood closet pole such as you might buy at a home improvement store. It had fractured along an angled grain boundary to become a sharp spear. Other exhibits—baseball bats with protruding nails, cricket bats with attached blades, sword canes—were more blatantly against the rules, but fun to look at.

Less information needed to be imparted to the rock throwers ("rockers") since there was only so much you could say about rocks. They did actually need to *be* rocks, locally sourced. Some mischief-makers had tried to smuggle in eggs made of lead. You were not allowed to use slings or atlatl-like arm extenders. You had to throw the rock from your hand with a normal baseball- or cricket-like motion. As a way of driving the point home, the soldier took up a position about ten meters away from a sheet of plywood, very much the worse for wear, and used a sling to hurl a lead egg at it. The egg punched a neat hole right through the plywood. "Of course the rules apply on both sides of the Line," the lecturer said, "and that is where you, our intrepid streamers, have your role to play. Keep a sharp eye on our adversaries! If you collect any footage of Chinese volunteers transgressing these strict rules, upload it at once, timestamped and geotagged, to our server."

There followed the quiz, which was not all that difficult, and then a strip search and collection of blood and saliva samples. They were strangely uninterested in seeing anyone's official papers. Bella, a couple of days ago, had suddenly looked up from a screen and remarked, "It's like the French Foreign Legion." Laks hadn't known what she'd meant by that. But now he got the gist. They didn't care who you were or where you came from. They just wanted the biometric data and then to shoot a chip into your arm.

In due course Laks was reunited with his clothing and personal effects. He'd removed everything except his patka—the base layer of a proper turban. Many days he didn't bother to wear anything more than that on his head. But he was aware that he was being shunted into a separate lane, as it were, for Sikhs. So he pulled a long piece of fabric out of his bag and devoted a few minutes to wrapping his head in a full dhamala, which was a style of turban associated with going into battle. Down low it was close to the sides of the head, but a lot of material was piled up above, making it flare wider as it rose above the top of his skull. It added a couple of inches to his height.

Once he was fully dressed, he and other observant Sikhs were taken aside and given a stern talking-to by an officer about their kirpans: the daggers worn by all Sikhs as emblems of their faith and of their status as saint-soldiers. All other knives had been confiscated, but Sikhs could carry their kirpans under a religious exemption on the condition they never draw them from their sheaths—no, not even in a fight.

Their luggage was waiting for them on the other side of all these barriers, and it was clear that it had been rifled by clinically paranoid officials. Vehicles were not allowed to cross over—it would have been too difficult to inspect those for concealed weapons—and so once they had repacked their bags they found themselves wandering around an open-air bus bazaar where scores of vehicles ranging from motorized rickshaws up to full-sized buses were competing for passengers.

But Sue had already identified a place along the south shore of the Pangong Tso where a new unit of Chinese volunteers calling themselves the Bonking Heads had been posting high-spirited videos within the last twenty-four hours. While their visual flair was undeniable, they were far from the most impressive such group. For that reason, though, they seemed a wise choice for a Fellowship untried in combat. Ravi had arranged a ride on a specific minibus. All they had to do was walk to it and climb on board.

The bus worked its way down the inevitable switchbacks, and after an hour made contact with the dirt track that ran parallel to the southern shore of the lake. From there it was reasonably easy going on a flat road. Laks was actually able to just look out the window and observe the scenery. The Pangong Tso reminded him of some of the long, deep glacier-gouged lakes in the Selkirk Range of British Columbia, such as Kootenay. The key difference was that the latter was surrounded by hills green and rich in wildlife, because its altitude was all of about five hundred meters. Whereas Pangong Tso—a bit high at the moment because the glaciers feeding it were succumbing to global warming—was at 4,250. And it was salt water, because it had no outlet and so was just a big evaporation basin. The upshot was that it was as lifeless as the moon. Neither the rocky slopes rising from its shores nor the transparent blue water itself supported any kind of plant or animal that Laks could see. Every few kilometers they would pass a military supply depot (neat grids of tents and shipping containers) or a volunteer logistics hub (smoking, steaming chaos of tarps and vehicles) but humans, supported by long supply chains, were the only life-forms up here.

He forgot where he was and dozed off. But suddenly the bus had stopped. "There!" said the driver in English, pointing out the window on the other end of the dashboard. But the salt-rimed glass was impossible to see through with late-afternoon sun crashing into it. Laks got up, pulled his bag and his stick down from the overhead luggage rack, and walked down the bus's side stairway until his feet were on solid ground: bouldery dirt, streaked with white salt.

A rock about the size of an egg came bouncing and tumbling across the ground toward him, as if in greeting, and came to rest a couple of meters away from his foot. Odd. Laks turned in the direction from which it had flown and looked across fifty meters of open ground into the People's Republic of China.

The Bonking Heads were standing there, drawn up in a sort of battle line, flanked by their goggle-wearing, drone-piloting streamers, picking up rocks and desultorily throwing them. But the bus driver had been wise enough to stop just out of range, to spare his windows.

In homage to a late-twentieth-century rock group, the Bonking Heads wore black dress suits over their voluminous down-stuffed under-layers. The suits were tailored after normal business attire but comically oversized to make room for all that insulation. They were neatly accessorized with white shirts and narrow black neckties. Having perceived the futility of throwing rocks from this distance, they were now just brandishing sticks and shouting imprecations. Some of them were striking wide-based martial stances that Laks vaguely recognized as characteristic of northern kung fu styles. They would be able to develop a lot of power, but their legs were vulnerable. Others of the Bonking Heads seemed to have noticed his turban, for they had begun prancing around in what was apparently meant as a cruel parody of gatka footwork. At a glance, he thought there were maybe four of those preening stick fighters, flanked by a total of half a dozen or so rockers.

Buzzing, whining noises to either side made Laks aware that he was being filmed in high-resolution video from two different camera angles. But Pippa wasn't even out of the bus yet. Their abrupt arrival had caught them all flat-footed. These were drones that had been sent out by the Bonking Heads to capture B-roll of their opponents. They seemed to have two streamers, flanked way out to the sides and a little behind the line, as if to emphasize their non-combatant status.

And what were these streamers seeing in the feeds in their goggles? Laks, in a motley collection of observant Sikh and granola-munching backpacker togs. Sam and Jay, looking a bit more pulled together in their football supporters' regalia—the closest that anyone in the Fellowship had to a snazzy uniform, yet sadly downmarket compared to the Bonking Heads'. Ravi came sleepily and clumsily out of the bus unlimbering his cricket bat, wearing a hideous purple sweater that his mother had knitted for him.

Still transfixed by that, Laks heard shouting, and turned to see Sam and Jay sprinting directly toward the Bonking Heads, sticks held high.

While not a good idea tactically, the frontal assault of the Englishmen did have the good effect of causing the remainder of the Fellowship to pile out of the bus as if it were on fire. The usually even-tempered Pippa was spitting nails over having been caught unprepared. She was already filming with her phone as she rattled down the bus's stair. Once she got clear and established her bearings, she reached into her coat pocket, pulled out a video drone, and tossed it straight up into the air. It turned itself on, unfolded its rotors, and hovered in place. Bella came out of the bus pulling what looked like ski goggles down over her eyes, then stuffed her bare hands into warm pockets where it could be guessed control devices were to be found. The drone, reacting to her touch, began to dart this way and that. She got a vacant look on the portion of her face that was still visible and began to turn her head to focus on things no one else could see. Either she was having a schizophrenic break or the goggles had established a three-dimensional video link to the drone.

Laks turned around to see how Sam and Jay were getting on. They weren't. They were just kneeling on the ground, hunched forward, rib cages heaving. They'd made it perhaps two-thirds of the distance to the Bonking Heads' position before it had occurred to them that they had no oxygen. Stopped in the open, gasping for breath, they had become target practice for the rockers, and pretty easy targets at that.

"We must go help them!" Gopinder exclaimed, and took a step forward, but Laks reached out and put a restraining hand on his arm. "We'll end up just like them." He looked around and picked out his bag and Gopinder's, lying on the ground where the bus driver had just flung them. The bus's rear wheels spat rocks as it pulled forward and veered off. "Get your *dhal*. Move slow and breathe fast, *bhai*."

The dhal was a traditional shield, basically identical to what in Europe would be called a buckler, about the size and shape of a dinner plate. It was a staple of gatka and so both Gopinder and Laks had cheap but rugged injection-molded ones that they used in training. They kept them carabinered to the outsides of their bags. Both men now unsnapped their dhals and gripped them in their left hands. A knuckle pad on the back, under the handle, cushioned the grip. The fingers were still free to grab a short stick as well. In his right hand each man was holding his full-length staff.

During all this fumbling around with gear Laks was painfully aware that Sam and Jay were exposed and under fire. But at some point he began to hear a strangely familiar voice shouting in Mandarin. He looked up to see Ilham walking alone and unarmed directly toward the Bonking Heads, but angling in on a different vector. A stream of verbiage was coming from the lad's mouth, directed at the opponents, who had all turned to look at him. His voice was thready but perfectly clear in the cold thin air. As far as could be discerned from body language at this distance, the Bonking Heads were shocked at first, then indignant.

"What's he saying?" Pippa asked Sue.

Sue could only shake her head. "Most terrible things," she answered, "I cannot even explain."

"Well, if his objective is to have rocks thrown at him, it is quite successful!" Ravi said.

To this point in his life Laks had never struck anyone in anger, aside from a few playground scuffles in primary school. Though the Sikhs were perceived by outsiders as a martial race, their religion laid down clear boundaries as to when it was acceptable to resort to the use of violence. Those boundaries were actually quite restrictive. You could fight back when attacked, basically, or when you needed to intervene in a situation where someone else was being victimized. All of which was a good fit with Laks's personality. One of the only concerns he'd had during his long journey to the front was that when he finally arrived he might not have it in him to just walk right up to a Chinese counterpart and hit him with a stick. That might speak well of his basically peaceful nature, but it would render the entire journey somewhat pointless.

The hasty, and so far disastrous, attack mounted by Sam and Jay, and Ilham's verbal assaults, were all completely useless from one point of view. But they did serve the unintended purpose of forcing Laks to take action. All his misgivings on that front had been swept away.

"Keep breathing," Laks said to Gopinder, and he began to trudge across the flat but treacherously rock-strewn battlefield. He heard another drone get into the act and guessed that Sue was piloting this one. Pippa was bringing up the rear, filming handheld. She had lugged a motorcycle helmet all the way from Wellington and now had finally put it on. A few hundred meters behind her, the bus had pulled up to a safer remove and was awaiting the outcome. In the center, Laks was taking point, flanked on his right by Gopinder and on his left by Ravi. Ravi didn't have a dhal, but he was having some early success using his cricket bat to smack away incoming rocks. For, having chucked a few at Ilham, the rockers were now zeroing in on what they perceived as the real threat. Ilham, having succeeded in giving Sam and Jay a few minutes' respite, was now backing away from the front. "Earbuds!" he shouted as they came abreast of him. Then he ducked around behind them.

Keeping his dhal aloft, Laks stopped, leaned his big stick against his shoulder, and rummaged in his pocket until he'd found those. He used his thumbs—tingling from a combination of cold, adrenaline, and hyperventilation—to stuff those into his ears. Gopinder and Ravi were doing likewise.

"We will draw fire from the rockers," Laks explained, "so that Sam and Jay can get up." During the interlude provided by Ilham's stream of profanity, the two Englishmen had flattened themselves against the ground to present smaller targets, but as soon as they tried to get up they'd be sitting ducks. "We'll swing wide right around them," Laks continued. "Ravi, get right of Gopinder." Ravi, who had been on the left, cut behind Laks and Gopinder as instructed. "Stay wide, so you don't accidentally hit Gopinder with your follow-through."

They were definitely succeeding in drawing fire. Laks took a direct hit to the top of his head, but that was where the dhamala's fabric was piled thickest, and so it bounced off harmlessly. No wonder his forefathers had used this style in combat! But it was a lesson to keep his dhal at the ready. Rocks, it turned out, were small, fast, and hard to see coming.

"Watch the throwers," Ravi advised, batting away an incoming missile. "Not the rocks."

This was terrific advice. There were only so many rockers, and their throwing motions were obvious even if the rocks themselves were hard to see in flight. To avoid being flanked by Laks, Gopinder, and Ravi, the rockers who'd formerly been on the Indians' left flank—shifted one at a time to the Indians' right. Laks risked taking his eye off them long enough to glance left at Sam and Jay, now almost abreast of him. He got a rock in the rib cage for his trouble but saw Sam roll over onto his back and give a thumbs-up. Jay was up on his elbows pressing a soccer scarf against a laceration above his eye. "If you can, tuck in behind us," Laks said.

"Roger that," Sam responded. The mere fact that he could talk suggested he had got his wind back. As Laks moved past them, the Englishmen planted their sticks in the ground and used them to get up to their feet, then swung in behind. "You're going to be my left wing when we get closer," Laks said. "Make sure we don't get flanked on that side."

"Yes SIR!" Jay responded. Military style. Not sarcastic.

"Ilham. The stick guys. What's that on their faces?" They'd now drawn close enough to see that the Bonking Heads stick fighters—who, to this point, had done nothing but make fun of them—had some kind of weird objects stuck to their noses.

Ilham, who was now trailing a safe distance in their wake, had access to all three video feeds, as well as image-stabilized binoculars. "Little cups strapped to their noses. Tubes coming out of them."

Laks had heard of them, but never seen one, while working in the oxygen langars. "Nasal masks," he said. "Like a mini oxygen mask, but it doesn't cover the mouth. They're on supplemental oxygen."

"Explains why they won't fucking shut it," Jay remarked. He and Sam had belatedly got their earbuds in and joined the feed.

Laks asked, "Sue or Bella, can you get line of sight to the source?"

"On it," Bella announced. Laks heard a drone bank and veer.

"Nice, Bella!" Ilham said a few moments later. "It's a big oxygen tank, like welders use, lying flat on the ground behind them."

"Gopinder and Ravi. When we engage, draw them away from the tank," Laks said. "Don't make it easy for them. At some point they'll have to lose the masks. Sam and Jay, which of you is in better shape?"

"I'm going to say that's me," Sam answered. "Jay's got blood in his eyes."

"Sam, wing me on my left," Laks said. "Jay, after we engage, see if you can cut around their flank and cut the oxygen lines."

"Rockers are pulling back," Ilham reported. "They'll stand off and throw from a distance when they have a clear shot."

"Jay!" Laks called and tossed Jay his dhal.

"Thanks, mate!"

But Laks did not hear it because at this moment—having not moved at anything faster than a geriatric mall-walker's pace since exiting the bus—he pivoted toward the Bonking Heads' position, sprang forward, and came at their foremost stick fighter—obviously their best guy, their ringleader—full speed, in exactly the same light-footed prancing style that this asshole liked to make fun of. Which worked great, actually, on a boulder field. At the same time Laks was whirling his stick up to a velocity where it almost disappeared. He was pleased to note that, at this altitude, air resistance was less of a factor. Despite the speed and suddenness of Laks's advance, this guy was good enough that he reacted just in time, drawing back instinctively, rear weighted, front leg poised out in front of him. Laks performed a move he had been practicing against heavy bags in the gym since he'd been eight years old, letting his stick hand pass behind him for a moment and then bringing it out so that his entire body, from the soles of his feet up through his legs and torso and arm, cracked like a bullwhip. The end of the whip was the stick, whose last six inches impacted the shin of his opponent just below the knee with a crack whose rever- berations were probably detectable on seismographs in Pakistan.

Nowhere near as loud, though, as the scream that followed a moment later. Enraged, the man moved forward to take a swing at Laks. But Laks was already drawing back, forcing him to over- commit. All his weight came forward onto the injured leg, which buckled. As the man staggered forward in an effort to remain up- right, his oxygen tube snapped taut behind him, his head reared back, and the little mask popped off his nose and bounced in the dust. All these distractions ruined him, leaving him wide open for Lak's follow-up, which was a simple pool-cue strike into the liver.

Another stick guy was trying to come around from the left, but Sam held the line on that flank. The Englishman made no effort to match the attacker's kung fu rocket science but just barreled in close, stuffing and stifling the other's moves, forcing him to back up on the terrible ankle-spraining ground. Sam had a walk- ing stick that he gripped in its middle, tucked along the bone of his forearm so that he could either block attacks while protecting his arm, or else deliver short elbow strikes intensified by the knob on the stick's end.

When they and half a million of their closest friends watched the videos later, after Pippa had had time to cut it all together, it was clear that the fight was already over at this point. Gopinder engaged another Bonking Head and gave as good as he got. At one point he got the tip of his short stick, in his left hand, under the guy's oxygen tube and flicked it off.

Ravi pretty much got his ass kicked. He didn't land a single good blow. He was forced to retreat. His opponent advanced to the end of his oxygen tube and faltered. This guy had put his outfit on *after* donning the nasal mask, so the tube was running under his clothes. He couldn't just pull the thing off his face to get free.

Meanwhile, on the left flank, Sam had given his opponent a real gusher of a bloody nose by landing an elbow shot. The guy had retreated and sat down to go into shock.

He *had* to have been in shock not to see what Jay was doing right next to him. Jay during all of this had crept around to the oxygen tank. This began to peal like some exotic Tibetan gong as rocks struck it. For the rockers, standing off at a distance, had begun to zero in on his position. Jay used the dhal in his left hand to protect his bloody head. At the top of the oxygen tank was a round valve wheel—the main shutoff. Angling off to one side of that was a regulator with two dials. Sprouting from the low-pressure side of the regulator, then, was a Rube Goldbergian tangle of tees and wyes that had been kludged onto it so that it would feed something like a dozen separate oxygen tubes.

In a classic I'm-just-going-to-cut-this-fucking-Gordian-knot moment, Jay noticed that he was sitting on a big rock, flat and sort of triangular, like an arrowhead the size of a tabloid newspaper and a good six inches thick. It was heavy. He dropped the dhal, stood up, got his back into it, then his legs, and heaved it up off the ground. He cleaned and jerked the thing, got it above his head for one glorious moment, and then brought it down on the regulator.

On the video, Jay then disappeared in a huge cloud of oxygen-rich dust produced as high-pressure gas shrieked out of a crevice in the metal. That cloud moved away from him, though, as the cylinder began spinning and skidding across the moonscape like a pinwheel firework. The regulator and the tree of fittings were still hanging on. The tube attached to the guy who'd been fighting Ravi went tight, pulled him back onto his ass, and dragged him a short distance before his suit gave way at the seams and was stripped off his body.

The Bonking Heads retreated in disarray. The Fellowship advanced, reclaiming about a hundred meters of territory for India, but stopped and held their ground when other Chinese volunteer units began to converge. It might have gone badly for them then, but Indian crews, who'd seen this all happen from a distance, rushed forward to camp out along the new position of the Line of Actual Control.

Rufus dug the silence of it. Oh, the sonic booms still crackled over the mountains every eight minutes. You had to get used to that. But the recovery was as peaceful as you could imagine. Suspended from their paragliders, the shells came gliding in over the Rio Grande. They didn't cross the river until they were just a few hundred feet above the ground. By that point each was aiming for a specific net. There were four nets operational when Rufus first arrived, with four more getting their finishing touches. They were spaced up and down the length of a new road running along the top of a mesa that rose a few hundred feet above the river.

Each net was square, about half the size of a football field. It was suspended at each of its four corners from a steel pole that projected to a height of maybe fifty feet from a concrete footing in the ground. The setup couldn't have been much simpler: At the top of each pole was a pulley with a steel cable running over it. One end of that cable was carabinered to a corner of the net. The other end ran down the pole to ground level where it disappeared into a winch. When all four cables were winched tight, the net stretched overhead like a roof, sagging a bit in the middle, but nowhere less than about thirty feet above the ground.

The empty shells coasted in from their sojourn in Mexican airspace, each vectored to a particular net. If the wind wasn't blowing and you listened carefully, you might just be able to hear a faint flutter in the parasail, or singing in the shroud lines. When the shell sensed it was over the middle of the net it would actuate a mechanism that detached it from the parasail with a faintly audible mechanical snick, and it would drop, bounce once or twice, and come to rest at the bottom of a mesh funnel, so close to the ground you could almost touch it. The parasail would crumple and glide away on the wind like a puff of smoke. There was a team called sail chasers who would follow it across the mesa on ATVs until it came to earth, then wrestle it into a stuff sack. Meanwhile another team called net runners would unreel one or two of the winch lines, lowering the net. When the shell was on the ground, they would simply walk out, pushing a four-wheeled dolly, and pick it up. At this point in its duty cycle, after it had jettisoned its sabot, nose cone, and parasail, and burned its load of sulfur, the shell was light enough that a crew of two could lift it off the ground and deposit it on the dolly.

It took hours for these things to spiral down from the stratosphere. During that time the shell had cooled off and purged any lingering fumes of SO_2. The net runners would push the dolly over to a waiting trailer and hoist it into a cradle. Then they'd use the winches to reinstate the net. Downtime for a given net was rarely more than a few minutes. When a trailer got full of spent shells, a truck would drive up, hitch on, and tow it north to one of the installations that had been built along the arc road around Pina2bo. There each shell would be inspected and refurbished and sent empty to Pina2bo itself, where it would sit in the queue awaiting its next flight. Only at the last minute was the hot liquid sulfur piped into its tank.

Meanwhile a steady flow of parasail stuff sacks was accumulating in another trailer. When full, these were driven off the ranch and down the interstate to El Paso and across the bridge to Juarez, where they were unloaded in an air-conditioned *maquiladora*. Rufus hadn't visited that place, but they'd showed him videos. Employees in white coveralls pulled out the crumpled parasails, spread them across huge clean tables, inspected them for scorpions, plucked out cactus spines, mended rips, and then carefully re-packed them so that they would deploy correctly the next time they were used. In due course they were trucked back to Flying S and installed in refurbished shells.

Sabot catchers and cone hunters were two other categories of employee. Their jobs were similar in some ways, different in others. The sabot enclosed the base of the shell during its passage up the gun barrel and fell off immediately afterward. It was made of some foamy ceramic, heat-resistant but lightweight and reasonably hardy. Most of them tumbled to the ground within a couple of hundred meters of the gun. Much of that area was under suspended nets with ribbons of fabric woven through them, which performed multiple roles: casting shade, providing some privacy, stopping any unwelcome low-flying drones. And, of course, catching sabots. As such, much of the sabot catchers' work had to do with those nets. If wind was steady, the sabots all fell in the same general area. As a rule the sabot catchers never ranged as much as half a mile from the gun.

The nose cones were jettisoned at much higher altitude. Depending on wind, they could land practically anywhere on the ranch. Many were simply lost. Supposedly they were biodegradable, though in the Chihuahuan Desert there wasn't a whole lot of bio to do the degrading. They sent out radio pings until the batteries died. Their bright orange color made it easy to see them from drones, and some of the propellerheads at White Label had ginned up a machine-learning program that could scan through aerial images and identify possible strays. That information was piped through to HUDs in the cone hunters' earthsuits, to make their work more efficient.

On the nominal firing cadence of one shell every seven and a half minutes, Pina2bo launched 192 shells a day, and so that was the number of nose cones that, on average, fell to earth every twenty-four hours. Most of the cone hunters were Mexican American and many had worked in agricultural settings where they would be paid by the number of apples picked or heads of cauliflower harvested. Gunning ATVs across the desert "harvesting" strewn nose cones was in some ways similar, though both more fun and more dangerous. The best of them, working in two-person teams, recovered twenty cones a day, though that number was slowly trending upward as they learned the tricks of this new trade.

Rufus—who spent his first week on the ranch simply driving around and observing all this—had it in mind to sit down and spreadsheet it and figure out the size of the operation. At the mesa above the Rio Grande, typically they had two pairs of net runners, leapfrogging from net to net depending on where the next shell was coming in, and three pairs of sail chasers. One or two truck drivers seemed to be on call to ferry the loaded trailers and bring back empties. The sabot-catching could be handled by one person. Maybe eight pairs of cone hunters worked during the daylight hours. He had no idea how many chute packers worked in Juarez.

At Pina2bo proper there were the kinds of jobs typical of the oil business and of the chemical industry downstream of it. Unloading bulk sulfur from hopper cars and melting it was child's play, mostly automated. Natural gas came in via pipeline from wells elsewhere on the ranch and was either shunted directly to the guns, or diverted to the cracking facility, where hydrogen gas— along with a concomitant amount of carbon black—was produced. This was a significant piece of infrastructure, but being a new facility it too was mostly automated, and controlled by engineers from the same bunker where they operated the gun. Likewise, the process of prepping the shells and slapping on the nose cone and sabot, mating it with the pre-packed parasail, running pre-launch checks on the electronics, filling it with hot sulfur, and putting it on the shell hoist—that was all done by robots. So one of the surprises for Rufus during these early days of wandering around and getting to know the operation was just how lightly staffed the actual gun complex was.

That—plus a few mission control types keeping an eye on things in Houston—was the operational side of Pina2bo. Everything else was classed as support. The ranch was so remote and the conditions so inhospitable that it might as well have been on Mars.

So "support" had to include things like: Where could employees get food? How could they put gasoline or diesel in the tanks of their vehicles? What would they do if they had a medical problem? In that way it was different from an urban company where the city would just supply all that. It was, though, perfectly familiar to the oil business, where it was common for workers to live on offshore rigs or other remote installations for months at a time. So that stuff was all subbed out to companies that simply did that kind of thing. Roughly speaking, Rufus guessed that there was one support worker for every one on the operational side. With the exception, that is, of security, which was technically under Support but for various good reasons was a whole department unto itself.

By and large, the ranch as a whole felt like a fracking operation out in the Permian Basin or North Dakota or some such, which was a way of saying that the employees tended to be young single males who lived in trailers and got around in pickup trucks. The trailers were clustered in residential compounds spaced along the Arc, which was what they called the approximately circular road that ran around Pina2bo from about nine o'clock in the west to about four o'clock in the southeast, at a radius that kept the sonic booms from being too obnoxious. The missing southern part of the Arc, from four around to nine, was unlikely ever to be completed because of mountain ranges and the Rio Grande. Anyway there were three of these residential compounds. Two of them were 100 percent bachelor. They were called simply Nine and Four, and they were at the ends of the Arc. At the third, women and families were part of the mix as well. That one was called High Noon, or just Noon, and it lay along the main road-and-railroad artery leading from the ranch gate down to Pina2bo.

Spread over all this as a separate world unto itself was Security, which seemed opaque to Rufus, and was probably meant to be. There was an over-arching contract with a big international private firm that, he had to assume, kept tabs on threats from a distance just by monitoring the Internet, looking at remote imaging data, and conducting private investigations. Another firm basically did what rent-a-cops did on corporate campuses: performed routine patrols, checked credentials at gates, investigated calls. Basically they handled the 99 percent of security-related activities that did not require a lot of training, decision-making, or acceptance of physical risk. Their job was to be visible and call for help. They wore brown hats.

The other 1 percent of such situations were handled by a collection of individuals who were all employed by a company T.R. had set up called Black Hat Practical Operations and who by and large were some combination of weird, dangerous, and expensive. Rufus was one of those. As far as he could make out, this operation was more French Foreign Legion than SEAL Team Six. It was motley and international. Of course, there were American ex–Special Forces types, but he heard plenty of accents that were not of this continent. He was not an expert judge of such things but he was pretty sure some South Africans were in the mix—at one point he heard one of them talking on the phone in a language that sounded a lot like what Saskia and Willem and Amelia spoke, and he guessed that what he was hearing was Afrikaans. But they were by no means all white English speakers.

The overall boss of the Black Hats was an American man of about sixty (albeit the type of sixty-year-old who seemed to spend half of his waking hours doing push-ups) named Colonel Tatum. He was not, of course, actually in the military and so the "Colonel" was more of an honorific nickname. He was an Anglo Texan, but apparently not the sort who hated nonwhite folk—or if he was, he did a good job of hiding it during his interview with Rufus. Obviously T.R. had briefed Colonel Tatum and everyone understood each other.

They conducted the interview in Tatum's office at the Black Hat ops center, a reinforced concrete structure half buried in the ground near the intersection of the Arc and the main ranch road. It would not have been wrong to describe it as a bunker. But a lot of ranch architecture was massive, half buried, and made of concrete, so the line between bunker and any other kind of structure was a little blurry.

Tatum, like others in his unit, was dressed in an outfit that you could think of as the inner layers of an earthsuit. Hanging on a rack in the corner of his office were other components, plugged in to keep them all charged up and ready to go. Next to that was a long steel box that was obviously a gun safe. The portions of the earthsuit that Tatum was wearing right now just looked like normal, albeit military, clothes for the most part. You could buy this stuff in various styles and patterns. All the people in Tatum's unit had, reasonably enough, opted for desert camo. Tatum was no exception. So this scene looked and felt like interviews Rufus had experienced in the service when he'd been deployed to locations in the Middle East.

"You're not in my chain of command. You and a couple of other consultants report to T.R. But you are in my department and I don't want you getting shot because of some fuckup, so we are gonna have a talk about how it all works," Tatum said after he and Rufus had exchanged the briefest of pleasantries.

How it all worked was that they had purchased and installed some kind of high-tech system that used cameras and machine vision to notice human-shaped objects moving around on the property, and then attempted to perform "IFF" on them. Rufus knew from the military that this meant "Identification Friend or Foe." If the imagery was good enough, facial recognition would do the trick, but lots of times it wasn't, and in any case people frequently wore earthsuits that got in the way of the optical path. So everyone was encouraged to wear a little device called an "iffy," which seemed to be a cross between an ID badge and the kind of transponder typically installed on aircraft so that air traffic controllers could tell one blip from another. The iffy, which was about the size of a phone, was apparently complicated and expensive. So you could get along without one if you were just working inside a building that had the usual security barrier at the entrance. But anyone roaming around the property at large needed to have an iffy that was up and running. When the high-tech system noticed a free-ranging humanoid life-form on the property who was not so equipped, drones would head that way with Black Hats in hot pursuit. Naturally all the net runners, sail chasers, et cetera had iffies as a matter of course.

What applied to humans applied to drones as well. Rufus was welcome to fly his drones around but they had to be registered and he would have to install transponders on them. "T.R. has spoken to me with great admiration of your skill with drones," Tatum said drily.

Rufus nodded. He had to suppress a smile as he imagined what that conversation must have been like.

"He refers to you as . . ."

"The Drone Ranger. I know, sir."

"Well, that being the case, I'll leave it to you to interface with your tech staff about making the necessary modifications to your equipment."

"Yes, sir."

"T.R. says you are self-sufficient in your trailer. You can park it anywhere you like."

"You mean Nine or Four or Noon?"

"I mean *anywhere you like*. Obviously, the places you mentioned have more conveniences."

"Yes, sir."

"What kind of weapons you packing?"

"My job until recently has been killing feral swine. To a first approximation, those are similar to humans," Rufus pointed out.

This phrase "to a first approximation" he had picked up from Alastair, and he liked it.

"So," Rufus continued, "by and large . . ."

"You are equipped with firearms designed for killing humans. In other words, military. I get it."

"Yes, sir. Simplifies the decision-making process by a good deal."

"All right then."

"But only three pieces. An AK. A bolt-action with infrared scope. And a plain old nine mil Glock."

"Nothing weird. Nothing full auto."

"Oh, no sir."

Tatum nodded. "We'll set you up with a two-way radio that works on an encrypted channel. But to be honest, phones work almost everywhere on the property and they usually work better."

Tatum's sensible attitude around "weird" firearms now emboldened Rufus to bring up a topic that had been somewhat on his mind. The drive from Cotulla to the Flying S Ranch had been long enough that the old mental hobgoblins had been able to get some purchase in Rufus's brain. He'd called Carlos Nooma, a half-Mexican, half-Comanche lawyer in Dallas whom Rufus had met in the army when Carlos had been working off his student loans in the JAG. Now he was part of a firm. He'd helped Rufus over a few of the humps associated with his separation from Mariel and starting his business. Once he and Carlos had spent a few minutes catching up and shooting the breeze, Rufus had explained the nature of what was happening at the Flying S Ranch, and of his proposed role.

Carlos gave Rufus due credit for never having a dull moment in his life and promised to look into it. This had taken a little longer than expected because Carlos had had to reach out to attorneys in his firm who knew about things like the Federal Aviation Administration. But yesterday Carlos had called him back and briefed him.

"Legality-wise," Rufus began.

"A contract should come through with your name on it," Tatum said with a shrug. "Not my department."

"Of, of course not, sir, that's understood."

"Then what is your question?" Tatum asked.

Rufus stuck his tongue out briefly, then remembered his manners and pulled it back in. "In terms of T.R.'s overall strategy here—which has a bearing on our jobs, yours and mine—as I understand it . . ." And at this point all he could do was repeat what Carlos Nooma had told him over the phone. "There's no actual law against what T.R. is doing here."

"If you have ever met a legislator in the flesh . . ." Tatum began.

"I have not had that honor."

"Let's just say it is not in their nature to even conceive of something like Pina2bo. Much less concoct a law making it illegal."

"Right. Understood," Rufus said. Again quoting Carlos Nooma: "And if they did? It would be a bill of attainder."

"I have no idea what that means, Red."

"According to my lawyer friend, Congress can't just pass a law targeted specifically at one person. That's called a bill of attainder and it's unconstitutional. They'd have to pass a *general* law against certain activities. And even then, T.R. could argue that it's just a thinly veiled bill of attainder."

Tatum made his hand into a blade and whooshed it past his head, indicating total lack of comprehension and total lack of fucks. "Sounds great. What are you worried about?"

"Well, but T.R. is violating FAA regulations on airspace and whatnot."

"He actually did apply for a permit, believe it or not."

"Like with the model rocket club launches."

"Yes, and the FAA granted it."

"Because they didn't know what he was actually going to do," Rufus said. "But now that they know . . ."

"It's probably just a matter of time before they cancel the permit," Tatum agreed. "After that, further operation of the Pina2bo facility will constitute a violation of FAA regulations."

"Understood, sir. But according to my lawyer friend—who was looking into it—the FAA enforces those rules by imposing fines."

"What I have been told," Tatum said, "is that they—the FAA— have no boots on the ground capability whatsoever. They can bring an enforcement action through the courts, and levy a fine if that is successful. There are limits on how high the fine can go. And my understanding is that T.R. has got lawyers who have been keeping their powder dry for this eventuality. They have got ways to slow the process down and drag it out in the courts for years. If the fine gets upheld in the court, T.R. could simply write a check for the full amount."

"Just part of the cost of doing business."

Tatum nodded. "But by that point Pina2bo will have been up and running for a couple of years and its beneficial effects will be known."

"And the bullets ain't gonna hit no planes because—"

"Because the gun don't move. What pilot in his right mind would fly over the muzzle of that thing? The FAA will just put out a warning—declare it a no-fly zone."

Rufus nodded, momentarily distracted by the thought of what one of those shells would do to an airplane. "So as far as our duties are concerned—"

"First of all, everything you and I are gonna do is strictly legal," Tatum said, "in case that's what you are worried about. We're not pulling the trigger on the Pina2bo gun. We are just securing a piece of private property. Second, the worst-case scenario is that the feds levy a huge fine against T.R. and he goes bankrupt a few years from now and stops paying us. We go out and get other jobs. And the thing is, Red . . ." Tatum held his hands out, palms up.

"Shit happens," Rufus said.

"Exactly."

During the first week, Rufus kept his trailer parked at Bunkhouse, near the gun, but slept in a sound-insulated berth that happened to be available inside. This left him free to drive anywhere on the ranch where his truck was capable of going. Ranch roads—some barely discernible—ran all over the place. The only way you could follow some of them was by shifting into first gear, proceeding at about pedestrian speed, and keeping a close eye on the nav system, which kept insisting that you were on a road even when all evidence was to the contrary. But then you'd come up out the other side of a dry wash or top a stony ridge and see it before you, like a giant had dragged a sharp stick across the desert six months ago.

Such was Old Marble Mine Road, which he followed up into the mountains between Pina2bo and the river one day, for no other reason than he liked the sound of its name. According to the nav system it would eventually terminate in a sort of box canyon just below the crest of the range. Without the nav, Rufus never would have been able to follow it, or even known that it was there. The overall direction of movement was a little west of due south, but along the way it managed to veer through every other point of the compass.

He was penetrating a valley between two spurs flung out from the northern slope of the mountains. Lower down it was chockablock with breadloaf-sized rocks that had washed down out of the higher places. The tires of his truck just had to feel their way over those. But beyond a certain point he was driving on smoother terrain that just consisted of exposed bedrock. He passed into the shade of the spur on his right, or west. Sun still shone on the opposite face of the canyon, making the sedimentary layers obvious. One of those layers was white. At first it was high above him, but over the next few miles he gained altitude and rose up to its level. That was where the road ended, in a shady cul-de-sac with a flat floor strewn with rusty old hulks of mining equipment: most notably a rock crusher. The surrounding wall consisted entirely of that white stratum of rock, and the obvious assumption was that it was marble. You could keep driving beyond that point but you'd be driving into the mountain. A hole in the rock face, obviously man-made, served as the mine's entrance.

The map claimed that another road joined up at the same place. Rufus could see it clearly, headed down a distinct watershed in the next valley off to the west. Such a road would have to exist for this mine ever to have been viable; heavy equipment wouldn't be able to come up the way he'd just done. Inevitably this was labeled as New Marble Mine Road. Tire tracks indicated that someone had been here within the last few months. On the peak that loomed over the mine entrance, perhaps a hundred feet above, was a new steel tower with solar panels and electronics enclosures. That was probably why.

Rufus got out of his truck and was pleased to discover that it wasn't hellishly hot. The altitude was something like a mile above sea level and this box canyon almost never received direct sunlight. After making sure that his iffy was working, he strolled a few yards into the mine. It was not one of your narrow claustrophobic tunnels. He could easily have driven his truck into the place for some distance. There was bat shit—there was always bat shit—but not that much of it; this wasn't one of those guano-choked holes housing millions of bats like you saw in East Texas. Stood to reason; there weren't enough bugs for them to subsist on. The whiteness of the natural stone made it seem clean. Rufus knew very little of mining, but it was plain to see the structural logic at work: to keep the ceiling from falling in, they had to give it a domed roof, and they had to bolster that with pillars of stone. These were as fat as they were high. They were simply carved out of the rock. So the pillars didn't just dive into the ground but funneled broadly outward as they merged without any clear seam into the floor or the ceiling. The whole thing sloped generally downward.

He hit on the idea of bringing his trailer up here. From the looks of it, New Marble Mine Road would be good enough, if he took it easy. Because of the cell tower, he was getting five bars on his phone. Obviously there were no utilities beyond that. But he could fetch gas for his generator and water to put in the trailer's tank. Getting rid of sewage would be an inconvenience, but he could manage it. And Tatum *had* said *anywhere*.

So the next day Rufus towed his trailer up New Marble Mine Road and parked it just outside the mine entrance. In the shady space just inside, he set up a camp table and chairs. This area was largely bug-free and comfortable for much of the day, but sunlight bouncing in from the canyon walls made it bright enough to read and work. He got busy upgrading his drones with the transponders that had been supplied to him by Black Hat.

He had been on the ranch for about a week when Tatum sent him a little follow-up message stating that if Rufus really wanted to make a positive contribution to the overall security of the ranch, it would be a good thing if he could get himself squared away and his equipment up and running "before the shit hits the fan geopolitically."

Rufus roger-wilcoed him right back, as soldiers did. But in fact he had no idea what Tatum was talking about.

The next morning he got his computer on the Internet, using his phone as a hot spot, and went to a video site and set it playing videos about Pina2bo while he spread out his tools and drone parts on the folding table. During the first half hour or so, he had a disconcerting feeling that he had got way behind on current events in the world. A week ago, when he'd driven his truck through the ranch gate, T.R.'s project had still been pretty much secret. People had figured out that he was building something big in the desert—that much was obvious just from satellite photos—but they could only speculate as to what it was or when it would become operational. Rufus's arrival had roughly coincided with the moment when the gun had been "brought up," meaning that the whole system had gone into operation, and it hadn't stopped since. During that time he hadn't left the ranch and had paid no attention at all to news feeds. So he was taken aback by the sheer volume of Internet traffic that had come into existence concerning T.R.'s project while he had been unaware.

So much of this was flat-out wrong, though, that it put him back on his heels for a little while. His confidence began to bounce back a little as he realized how much better informed he was than everyone else. T.R.'s staff had released explanatory videos presenting the facts, and a few nerds had found those and then released videos of their own that seemed credible enough, but for each of those there were twenty more that were just crazy talk. Official news outlets had done stories about it, but all they wanted to talk about was how people felt about climate change, and what a wacky dude T.R. McHooligan was in his old videos. Even more highbrow sites couldn't get off the mentality of what the political repercussions were going to be, who was for it and who was against it, and so on. It was difficult to connect any of this with Tatum's reference to the geopolitical shit hitting the fan.

So he called Alastair. They'd stayed in touch, sending occasional texts and pictures back and forth. Alastair didn't pick up right away, but a minute later he called back. "Sorry," he said, "I was inside flagging down the barkeep, didn't hear you."

The scene that now completely filled the screen of Rufus's laptop was a curious through-the-looking-glass inversion of Rufus's situation. Rufus was at the head of a box canyon, one of whose walls was in shade, the other lit by the morning sun. Alastair was standing at an outdoor table on the sidewalk of a dead-end street in London. The buildings on one side of it were lit up by the evening sun. There were a couple of parked cars in view, but the whole street was monopolized by people on foot. Apparently he was right outside a pub. A pint glass of something caramel-colored accounted for much of the screen real estate. He was wearing a dark blue suit, white shirt, open collar, no tie. The same was true of many visible in the background. There was some variation in the darkness and color of the suits, and the same could be said of the contents of their pint glasses. There were some women and they looked quite confident and well put together. They were all being extremely sociable.

Rufus understood that it must be quitting time in London. This must be the City that Alastair had alluded to, the part of it that was run by that guy Bob, the lord mayor. Even though Alastair was out of doors, the roar of conversation around him was such that he had to fish out headphones and put them on before he showed signs of being able to really hear what Rufus was saying.

"Looks like a very pleasant afternoon where you are."

"It's been filthy hot until yesterday. More like Spain. This is a little more like it."

"Maybe Pina2bo is doing its job."

"That is exactly the joke that is going around! Not thirty seconds ago people were raising pints to T.R. McHooligan."

"*Is* it a joke?" Rufus asked. "I mean, could it be having an effect?"

"Not here. Too soon. However, coincidentally or not, it's been cooler in East Texas the last couple of days. As you may be aware."

"I was not."

"Where the hell are you? I see your trailer behind you but—"

A sonic boom sounded, and the user interface on the video-conference indicated that Alastair's audio feed had been silenced in favor of the overwhelmingly louder signal from Rufus's microphone. Alastair looked confused and astonished and made efforts to say something, but the sonic boom continued to echo for a few moments off the canyon walls and so Rufus could only see his lips moving.

"Was that what I think it was!?" he finally said, after he had got audio back. His eyes darted from side to side as if he'd just been let in on a delicious secret.

"Yup."

"You're *there*!?"

"A few miles away. Found a good place to set up."

From the bemused way that Alastair looked around, Rufus got the idea that he was thinking *If only these people knew that I was talking to someone who is right there!*

"So people are talking about it, I guess," Rufus prompted him.

"Oh, yes. Biggest news story of the year to date, I'd say."

"What are they saying?"

"Too early to know, really. It was such a surprise. People have talked for decades about doing this."

"Putting sulfur into the stratosphere."

"Yes. And almost from the moment it was first mentioned, the idea was loathed by Greens. Just anathematized. To the point where you couldn't even really talk about it in public or you'd get canceled. So in general I would say that the Greens were like—" Alasdair released his grip on his pint long enough to whisk the palms of his hands together.

Rufus understood the gesture and nodded.

"We've put paid to that nonsense," Alastair said, "no need to concern ourselves with it any more, let's move along to the *real* program of, as T.R. puts it—"

"Getting China and India to stop burning shit."

"Exactly. Which somehow hasn't worked," Alastair said, deadpan. Then he continued, "So I would say that the chattering classes, who live in that sort of bubble, were knocked off balance quite badly and are still having a hard time believing it's real. Even I, who've *seen* it . . ." Alastair shook his head and took a swallow. "That's why I reacted as I did when I heard the sonic boom just now. Had this mad impulse to turn my phone around and show everyone in the pub."

"Have you been in touch with the Dutch?" Rufus asked. He was going to say "Saskia" or "the queen" but, just as Alastair had difficulty believing that Pina2bo was real despite having seen it with his own eyes, Rufus couldn't believe that he'd done what he'd done with certain other parts of his body.

"Just touching base, status updates. I'm to have a chat tomorrow with some of her staff. Possibly her as well. She has to go lay a wreath or something. Foam disaster. Might run late."

"What are you actually doing for them?"

"I'm to write a report on what it all means for the Netherlands."

"Doesn't the Dutch government have . . . I don't know . . ."

"Commissions and experts and so on? All very much in the bubble. Everyone already knows what those lot are going to say."

"What are *you* gonna say?"

Alastair grinned. "Remember Eshma?"

"Gal from Singapore. Seemed nice."

"She's in charge of climate modeling for their government. Chatted with her the other day. And you know what? She can't get instances."

"Beg pardon?"

"It's a cloud computing term. When you need a virtual machine in the cloud, or a whole cluster of them, you go on Amazon Web Services or one of its competitors and spin up an 'instance.'" Alastair used air quotes. "There's all different sorts—you literally choose the one you want from a menu, and then clone as many as you need. If you are running a computational model of the climate—which is what Eshma does for a living—there's a particular model, a piece of software, that most in that discipline have standardized on. And it runs best if you set up a cluster, in the cloud, consisting of a particular item on that menu—one sort of instance that the model has been optimized for. So when she got back from that little junket to Pina2bo, she got busy doing exactly that."

"Running the computer model on a bunch of instances to see what the effect of Pina2bo was going to be. On Singapore," Rufus said, just to be sure he was following.

"Singapore yes, obviously, but because that is such a small nation-state, they need to know how it will affect China. India. Australia."

"Because of the geopolitics of it," Rufus said.

"Of course. And what Eshma told me was that this was all proceeding normally enough until about a week ago when Pina2bo went live. And after that—do you remember, Rufus, when COVID-19 hit, and for a few weeks you couldn't buy toilet paper?"

"Sure do!"

"It's the same way right now with these instances."

"The particular ones Eshma needs to run the model. Make the predictions."

"Yes. It's an open market. Supply and demand. There are only so many of these instances that can be spun up at a given time. And right now, the shelves are bare, as it were. The price has sky-rocketed."

"Because Eshma's not the only one in the game."

"We can reasonably assume," Alastair said, "that Eshma's counterparts in Beijing, Delhi, and many other places are subsisting on late-night pizza delivery. Or whatever they eat in those places. No one wants to be the last to figure out what this all means."

"Assuming it keeps going," Rufus said.

"Do you know of any reason why it wouldn't?" Alastair asked sharply.

"Oh, I didn't mean anything by it. It's a smooth-running machine. I haven't noticed it go down at any point."

"Supply lines still clear?"

"A trainload of sulfur every day. Parasails are repacked off-site in Juarez, but I guess that could be moved here if there was a problem." Rufus checked himself for a moment now, wary of divulging information he shouldn't. But Alastair had signed the NDA. He'd been to the ranch. And he worked for someone whom T.R. apparently hoped to enlist as an ally.

"What does T.R. want from her?" Rufus asked.

"From the person I work for?"

"Yeah."

"If I had to read his mind—terrifying thought, that—he's hoping that he can keep that gun running for a few weeks, perhaps months, before anyone tries to shut him down."

"He can do that," Rufus confirmed. "They're building up a nice big pile of sulfur at the end of the line, just near the gun. Food, water, fuel are all stockpiled."

"Not even the air force can shoot down a bullet in flight,"

Alastair said. "And from what I hear, the descent happens in Mexican airspace."

"Confirmed."

"And the Mexican government officials are signaling that they are fine with it," Alastair said. "The State of Texas has something to say about it . . . but if this spell of cool weather continues, it makes everyone downwind . . ."

"Austin, San Antonio, Houston," Rufus said. "A few voters live there."

". . . feel that T.R. has done Texas a favor."

"He's one of them," Rufus nodded. "Native son. Built a huge gun. Thumbed his nose at the environmentalists. They'll go full Alamo for him."

"So it comes down to what's left of the United States government, and what they might do. And that can be delayed in committees and court filings for a long, long time. Long enough that the specter of termination shock enters the conversation."

"What's termination shock?"

"A bogeyman—to be fair, a legitimate concern—that always comes up when people debate geoengineering," Alastair said. "It boils down to asking what the consequences might be of shutting the system off after it's been running for a while."

Rufus considered it. "In this case—the sulfur's up there bouncing back the sunlight—cooling things off . . ."

"If the government intervenes—if they suddenly shut it down, might there be a disastrous snapback? More destructive than letting Pina2bo keep operating?"

"Does anyone know the answer?"

"No," Alastair said. "Nor will they, until—"

"Toilet paper's back on the shelves," Rufus said. Alastair looked completely nonplussed. "Eshma can get instances," Rufus explained.

"Yes. But to answer your question, Red, I'd guess T.R. wants allies. People who can vouch for what he's doing. And who can support him, when the time comes, by raising the specter of termination shock and what it might do to their countries."

"And Saskia might be one of those."

"Perhaps. Her support would only be symbolic. But it could influence the people . . . and the people elect the States General."

"Who *doesn't* like it?" Rufus asked. "Other than folks who hate geoengineering on principle?"

Alastair shrugged. "Any country whose ox is gored by the knock-on effects."

"When I talked to T.R. last week he said 'some people are gonna be *pissed*.' He meant what you mean," Rufus said. "Countries who run the model like Eshma and look at the results and say, 'Oh, shit!'"

"Years ago some people ran models to predict the effect of aerosols—sulfur, basically—being injected into the atmosphere from different parts of the world. What happens if we do it from Europe? North America? China? India? The outcomes were surprisingly different. It *really matters* where you do it. And it then affects each part of the world differently. But if I had to place a bet right here, right now, in this pub, based on what I've seen, I'd say it's going to come down to China versus India."

Another sonic boom sounded and shut off Alastair's audio. Rufus signaled as much by sticking his fingers in his ears and looking up into the sky for a few moments.

"I heard you say China versus India."

"Frequently, in these forecasts, what's good for one is bad for the other. Monsoons, very important."

"But you didn't say who will be on which side. Whose ox is gonna get gored?"

"Ask me in a week. Or—belay that—don't bother. Watch the news."

Rufus nodded. He didn't say what he was thinking, which was that he and the other people living at Flying S Ranch might end up *being* the news.

BIG FISH

Pippa cut it all together on her laptop during the bus ride back to the nearest volunteer base camp and uploaded it while they were eating their lentil and potato curry. The camp was centered on a little compound of stone walls and stone huts above the lake. Faded signs indicated it had once been a hostel for backpackers and extremely adventuresome Indian motorists. When their bellies were full and their wounds seen to, the Fellowship found an unclaimed patch of ground, kicked rocks out of the way, and just managed to get tents and tarps pitched before darkness fell.

Laks awoke with a need to pee and a fragrance in his nostrils. Which was unusual, for him. Since COVID, most of what he smelled was bad. His doctor had explained to him that COVID damaged the nerve cells in the linings of your nostrils—the ones that intermediated between the olfactory receptors themselves and whatever nerves ran back into your brain. Or something like that. Once the body had defeated the infection, those nerve cells tried to grow back, with varying success depending on how badly they'd been damaged. Sometimes they never grew back at all. Sometimes they got completely better. In between, though, it was like the body was trying to nail down its most survival-relevant capabilities first. And the most important thing your sense of smell could do for you in the way of keeping you alive was to warn you of things that could actually kill you: smoke, gas leaks, rotten meat. And so for some patients those were the smells that came back first. And they got crosswired to the olfactory receptors in crazy ways. So you might put your nose up to a rose or a garlic clove, give it a sniff, but instead smell something dangerous. Laks had never got past that phase. He could smell certain things correctly. Mostly dangerous things. Not so much good things.

What he was smelling right now was a blend of dangerous and

good, though. It was definitely smoke. But not the smoke of burning wood or coal, which was what you normally smelled in this part of the world. This smoke had an herbal, almost perfumed aroma.

He was not the first to wake up. He could hear Pippa, Bella, and Sue talking in their tent, quite cheerfully and with outbursts of laughter and of delighted surprise.

It sounded and smelled like someone had re-stoked their little campfire; but where had they obtained that much wood?

Laks extracted himself from his sleeping bag and stumbled out into the Fellowship's mini-compound to find an officer of the Indian Army sitting there in a low-slung camp chair next to the campfire, which was blazing. He was sipping something hot from a thermos, swiping his finger across a tablet, and somehow—as if he were one of those many-armed Hindu deities—managing, at the same time, to smoke a pipe. *He was smoking a pipe.* This was a thing Laks had seen in black-and-white movies but this was the first time in his life that he had actually seen a man smoking a real pipe! This, then, was the source of that nice aroma. They must put extra stuff in the tobacco to make it smell good.

The officer looked up over his reading glasses at Laks. Fortunately Laks, anticipating a need to get up in the middle of the night, had slept fully clothed and with his keski on his head.

"Major Raju," said the visitor in English. "I'd get up, but it's hard to clamber out of this thing once one is settled in." His accent was spiffy. "Do I have the honor of addressing Big Fish?"

"Huh?"

"You may know yourself as Laks, or Deep Singh. Big Fish is what you're called now. On the Internet. Someone took the liberty of translating your nickname into a proper nom de guerre. All the cool kids have them. The man you absolutely destroyed yesterday? That was Thunder Stick. Can't remember how to say it in Mandarin. Not his real name, I'd imagine." Major Raju, gripping the bowl of his pipe in one hand, used its stem to point at features in what must have been an imaginary spreadsheet hanging in space. "Thunder Stick's fall in the MRLB has been . . . precipitous."

"MRLB?"

"Oh, Meta-Ranking Leader Board. Many who drafted Thunder Stick into their fantasy squads are gnashing their teeth this morning!" Major Raju sipped from his thermos and added, "I expect you need to urinate! Don't let me stop you."

Laks needed to do more than just that. When he got back some little while later, he found that Pippa had emerged from the ladies' tent. She, Bella, and Sue, who had been so chatty when Laks had awakened, had all suddenly gone silent when they'd heard the voice of Major Raju. By the time Laks got back, though, Pippa was squatting comfortably on her haunches, long shanks doubled in front of her face, drinking tea and having what sounded like a very professional sort of conversation with the major. She probably was not one who needed to have MRLB spelled out for her. Laks had been puzzled by the lavish expenditure of firewood, but he now saw that Major Raju had been conveyed here in an army truck. He'd actually brought his own firewood with him. His driver was awaiting the major's return in the comfort of its heated cab.

As he neared, Pippa turned to look at him with a bemused smile. "Big Fish!"

"So I'm told."

"You're number one on the Force To Be Reckoned With metapoll, and you've broken the top 25 overall."

"Vegas is going bananas," Major Raju put in. "Macao less so, but what would you expect from those people?"

"Oh, because . . . China?"

"Have you signed anything yet?" the major inquired.

Laks's confusion must have been obvious because Pippa said, "He means deals with sponsors or agents."

"While I was taking a shit in the rocks? No."

"Good. Don't. Sign anything, I mean," Raju said. "Classic mistake for one in your position."

"Sir, why are you . . . here?" Laks asked.

"What you did yesterday added five point seven hectares of territory to India and subtracted an equal amount from China. It was the largest single shift that has occurred on this front in the last three weeks. If bookies in Vegas are interested in you, why, you can assume that the Indian Army is much more so. I work for the Indian Army."

"And when you say interested, that means . . ."

"He knows you're Canadian," Pippa said.

"It will hardly surprise you to know that the volunteer units on both sides of the Line are supported, under a thin veneer of plausible deniability, by their respective military establishments," Major Raju said, with a glance down at the generous stack of firewood. "Thunder Stick didn't bring his now world-famous oxygen tank with him from Hebei; it was supplied when he got up here and discovered he couldn't breathe. Any crew on our side that can turn in your kind of results with no support at all . . . well, it merits . . . some support. So I am here to ask you, Big Fish, what you need? Other than an agent, a manager, and a lawyer, that is."

"Rock throwers who can take orders."

"Done."

"And—I hate to say uniforms, but—"

"A look?" Pippa suggested.

"We understand each other," Major Raju said.

THE HAGUE

A curious thing about Frederika Mathilde Louisa Saskia was that, once she had got accustomed to being in a new setting—which never took more than a couple of hours—it was as if she'd never been anywhere else. When she'd been in Texas, answering to "Saskia" and floating down the Brazos, or tucking into some brisket at T.R.'s mega gas station in the suburbs of Houston, it had taken mere moments for her to forget about the fact that she was the scion of a royal family that went back many generations and lived in palaces in a faraway country. She was fully immersed in the moment of chopping the celery with Mary Boskey or screwing Rufus on the train, and that was that. She could have kept riding that train forever.

By the same token, however, when she got back home it was as if none of that stuff in Texas had ever happened. Once the bug bites had stopped itching, it was as if she'd never left the familiar confines of Huis ten Bosch. She actually wondered if this feature of her personality qualified her as some kind of sociopath. It wasn't as if she had no family at home. Her family was vast, and today—the third Tuesday in September—she was going to see most of them. And yet the only connecting thread that had remained intact while she'd been in Texas had been the exchange of messages between her and Lotte.

There was only one exception to this weird ability to feel at home in random places: Noordeinde Palace, the official "working palace" of the Dutch monarchy. She could never get used to this place. It was in The Hague, really just a few minutes' walk from Huis ten Bosch, but surrounded by streets instead of trees. Rooms of enormous size with doors and windows of enormous dimensions connected by enormous hallways lined with vast old paintings, all seeming even more comically enormous in contrast to the overall small tidiness of the Netherlands. The palace did not just have a vestibule. It did not just have two. It had three consecutive vestibules. This might have been quite useful back in the days when affairs of state required the receiving of dignitaries according to elaborate protocols while making sure they didn't freeze to death. The English idiom "cooling one's heels" might have been coined by a British diplomat awaiting an audience with some past king of the Netherlands in the days before central heating. The overall decoration scheme was blindingly white and glacially stark. The past couple of monarchs had made efforts to enliven it with colorful modern touches, but these felt stuck on, and only emphasized the glabrous obduracy of the underlying structure. This had probably worked back in the era when men and women both wore much fancier clothing. Nowadays, it just added to the overall chilly alienation.

Today—the late morning of Third Tuesday—it was as lively as it would ever be. The protocol was that various members of the royal household would emerge from a certain door and, in full view of television cameras and a throng of (mostly happy, royal-loving) onlookers safely cordoned on the other side of a massive wrought-iron fence, climb into antique horse-drawn carriages for a journey of less than a mile to the Binnenhof, which was the seat of the Dutch government. The last to leave the palace and to arrive at the Binnenhof would be the queen, who upon her arrival (in a fairy-tale golden carriage) would be escorted into a big room called the Ridderzaal—literally, the Knight's Hall—and read out a speech that the prime minister had written for her. Or rather the Council of Ministers and their aides had contributed bits and the PM had pulled it all together.

Anyway, as far as the overall scene in Nordeinde Palace was concerned: Saskia's immediate family might be tiny, as it consisted of just her and Lotte, but the extended family was quite vast, as Saskia's siblings, cousins, aunts, uncles, and so on seemed to know all about the birds and the bees. They didn't all get together that often, but when they did, there were enough of them to make even Noordeinde Palace seem lively. Not all of them would make the journey through the streets of The Hague to the Binnenhof—there weren't enough seats in the Ridderzaal, and anyway it was supposed to be a serious occasion of state. But they were all here. And the few notables who were going to be walking down that short stretch of red carpet and clambering into those carriages were all wearing the fanciest clothes, hair, and makeup one could get away with nowadays. So a lot of fuss and bother was happening in connection with that—enough to spill over into some of those vestibules and salons that otherwise rarely saw much use.

To judge from the sounds of laughter and happy exclamations ricocheting like musket balls up the punishingly hard flat surfaces of the palace's grand staircase, everyone else was having a good time. But today was all about Queen Frederika. It was a truism that, at your own wedding, you never actually got to have a real conversation with all the dear friends and family who had gathered to celebrate it. Likewise, her job this morning would be to descend that staircase on cue, air-kiss a lot of cousins, climb into the golden carriage without falling off her heels, jump out at the Ridderzaal, and read the damned speech. Unlike a lot of those family members, who were dressed as if for the Academy Awards, she was in a pretty sensible outfit. Not that she didn't like dressing up. But the point of the exercise, at the end of the day, was to open Parliament so they could get cracking on budget negotiations. To amaze the world with a fashion-forward frock was a goal that could maybe be postponed for some other occasion. So she was in a long dress, deep blue, with bits of orange that flashed out of darts and pleats and linings as she moved around. The designer had insisted that it was inspired by military uniforms. Saskia didn't see the resemblance at all, but she wasn't a fashion designer.

She had been getting prepped in one of the vast echoing rooms at the top of the stairs. Fenna, and the fashion designer responsible for the dress, had established their respective base camps at one end of this space. At the other, Saskia was having an unexpected last-minute check-in with Ruud.

Ruud was the prime minister. Technically speaking, he was *her* prime minister. He'd popped in through the back door with an emended copy of the speech.

"We did not expect," Ruud said, "that this thing was actually going to go into operation."

He did not even need to specify that "this thing" was the Biggest Gun in the World.

Saskia sighed. "We didn't expect a *lot* of things." She was referring to the pigs. This had been much on her mind of late. Everyone who knew about the plane crash was still waiting for the other shoe to drop. But apparently in Texas you could just crash jet airplanes, shoot it out with giant predators on the tarmac, set fire to the wreckage, and flee, and no one would get particularly excited about it. The story had simply disappeared. No one cared. The government of the Netherlands, eight thousand kilometers away, was the closest thing to adult supervision in the matter. They had taken the action of grounding Saskia pending the completion of what was promised to be a discreet, yet thorough, investigation.

They had the power to do this. To ground Saskia, that is. She couldn't blame them really. The deal was that the monarch was personally above reproach, but the PM was *responsible*. She could go out and murder someone and the prime minister would take the heat. Oh, he wouldn't go to jail, but he'd have to resign and the government would fall along with him. So her very inviolability created a peculiar co-dependency with the PM. Whenever they felt like it, the Dutch government could cut the budget and curtail the powers—what was left of them, anyway—of the royals. Saskia— the whole monarchy, really—served at their pleasure. If she behaved in a way that created serious inconvenience for them— forcing PMs to fall on their swords and governments to collapse— consequences would follow. She and Ruud had daggers at each other's throats. Not because they were dagger-to-the-throat kinds of people—Ruud was the very definition of a Euro-technocrat—but because that's how the Grondwet had been written.

Ruud was a few years older than her, but other than a few lines in his face, seemed to have stopped aging at thirty-nine. If his hair was graying, he hid it by shaving his head. His rimless glasses were nearly invisible and didn't seem to actually *do* anything—what sort of prescription was that, anyway? A strict one-beer-a-day policy combined with intermittent fasting and lots of bicycling made things very easy for whatever tailor was putting together his wardrobe of black, navy blue, and charcoal suits.

"Are you talking about the plane?" he said. "Last I heard, the insurance company—"

"They are no longer claiming that feral swine are an act of God. They will pay for the plane. If they don't, I will just liquidate some of my Shell stock and pay for it out of pocket, just to make this go away. They won't have to sue Waco for not properly maintaining the fence."

"Fence?"

Saskia tried to suppress a sigh. Usually, Ruud was better prepared. "*The fence that the pigs went under.* To get on the runway and crash the plane."

Ruud was momentarily torn between the fascinating and distracting topic of the jet/pig/alligator thing in Waco, and why he was actually here. He looked vaguely out a volleyball-court-sized window into a sea of orange-clad Dutch royalists. One could sense the prime ministerial superego calling to him faintly, as if from a great distance: *Ruud! Ruud! Come back to me! It is Budget Day!*

And then he was back. "I'm talking about—"

"I know what you're talking about."

"We thought we were being very clever. What we expected was that you, in your capacity as a private citizen, would accept this invitation to go to some dinners and parties in Texas and view this experimental curiosity that T.R. was fooling around with on his farm."

"Ranch."

"Whatever. Then you would come back and we would talk about it and I would decide, in consultation with the Council of Ministers of course, what position we ought to adopt."

"It did actually seem like a reasonable plan a month ago," Saskia said.

"We did *not* expect," Ruud said, slapping the palm of one hand with the revised draft of the speech, "that it would go into operation. *Full* round-the-clock operation! Actually re-engineering the climate of the whole planet!"

"Of course we didn't."

"And now there are rumors and leaks. People are connecting the dots."

"That I was there?"

"Yes. Which is all right, provided we get out ahead of it and make a statement." Ruud had the habit, which now that Saskia had noticed it was beginning to get on her nerves, of lapsing into English mid-sentence when he wanted to drop in buzz phrases, like "connecting the dots" or "get out ahead of it." Though, come to think of it, maybe that was preferable to letting that kind of talk seep into the Dutch language and clutter it up with faddish garbage.

"You want me to talk about this, specifically, half an hour from now!?"

Ruud shook his head. "Not Texas *specifically*. It would be a distraction, as you know. But to avoid confusion—if the whole story does come out—we can preempt it by issuing a policy statement against geoengineering." He shook the papers. "Which I have inserted into this new draft. I just wanted to mention it to you so you won't be surprised by the new wording when you come across it." He paused and gave a little shrug. "I don't know if you rehearse the speech—try to commit portions of it to memory—"

"I don't. But I very much appreciate the consideration you have shown me by ducking in to give me this 'heads-up.'" There. Now she'd done it too. But it triggered a memory of Rufus using that phrase in his dually, after the plane crash, and Alastair nearly being decapitated by a branch. Now she had to suppress a smile at the memory of that moment of slapstick.

Ruud noticed this and didn't know what to make of it. He was now regarding her with just a trace of concern. "The least I could do," he said. "Are you all right with this?"

On one level—the Grondwet level—this was a purely rhetorical question. It didn't matter whether she was all right with it. Her job was to read the bloody speech. But it did actually matter.

"Is this the first time," Saskia asked, "that the government has issued such a sweeping, blanket condemnation of geoengineering?"

"To my knowledge, yes."

"Do you actually consider that to be a coherent policy? For a country such as ours that is, to a large extent, below sea level and kept in existence solely through, dare I say it, geoengineering?"

Ruud got a faintly disappointed look on his face and checked his watch, as if to say *There isn't time for me to explain these basic realities to you.* There was an upwelling of crowd noise from outside. A horse-drawn carriage, not quite as magnificent as the queen's but still richly encrusted with gold leaf, was entering the gates of the palace courtyard to collect the first members of the household. Horseshoes and iron wheel rims clattered on the paving stones as it swept round in a wide curve—the turning radius of these things was atrocious—that took it up to the door below. Nearby, a military band struck up a patriotic song.

"Let me guess," Saskia said, "you're about to tell me that it's not about what you, or your party, actually think is the best policy. It's about politics."

Ruud now looked slightly less disappointed. He blinked and waited, eyes darting once or twice to the scene below, which looked not much different from how it would have during the days of Napoleon. But with jarring modern touches: the grenadiers in their red uniforms and tall bearskin caps shouldered NATO M16s, not muskets.

Ruud was the leader of the center-right party that in general got the most votes and anchored the ruling coalition. But there always had to be a coalition of *some* sort; in this country, it never happened that one party got enough votes to form a government all by itself. Ruud's party had to form that coalition with parties that were either to the right or to the left of it. It had been the case for the last few years that Ruud was able to get almost all the votes he needed from a party that was more conservative. It was not quite a fringe party. It did, however, include a fair number of climate change skeptics. New elections were coming up next year and the big center-left party was predicted to make a strong showing. By forming a coalition with single-issue parties on the far left they might be able to wrest the government away from Ruud's party.

So Ruud was guarding his left flank here. Throwing a bone— blanket condemnation of geoengineering schemes—to the Greens, to blunt the force of the opposition's campaign next year. He had probably been up all night hitting "refresh" on numerous browser tabs, watching his political foes "connect the dots" on Saskia's trip to Texas and the Pina2bo bombshell. This made him potentially responsible—according to the letter of the Grondwet— for any fallout. Inserting this language into the queen's speech would serve a dual purpose of protecting not just Ruud but Saskia as well from the repercussions of T.R.'s actions in Texas.

Saskia had pulled the speech from Ruud's hand. She allowed him to meditate over the weird cosplay scene below while she flipped through the pages looking for the section about the *klimaat nood*, the climate emergency. This over the last few Third Tuesdays had been working its way steadily up the agenda and occupying more space on the page. Pocking hooves and grinding wheel rims announced the departure of that first carriage.

She found it and read it under her breath. In her peripheral vision she could see Fenna sneaking up on her in the comically exaggerated mincing tiptoe gait, owing a lot to vintage Warner Brothers cartoons, that she used when she was well aware that she was annoying Saskia in the middle of more important duties. The dressmaker was drafting along behind Fenna, like a bike racer allowing a stronger rider to break the wind. Moments later she could feel deft hands messing with her hair and her skirts.

"I realize that you wrote this ten minutes ago . . ." Saskia said.

"More like an hour. Traffic was unbearable."

"But taken literally it would mean we are going to turn off the pumps. Allow the dikes to melt away. Decommission the Maeslantkering. That's the literal meaning of what you've written here. Which I know is not what you mean. But you are just handing the right wing an opportunity to make fun of you. 'Look, he's just virtue signaling, he doesn't actually mean a word of this.' So . . . perhaps here?" She placed a recently manicured fingernail, still redolent of volatile organic solvents, on a phrase in the text.

Ruud took it from her, tilted it toward the light, read it, and nodded. Fenna swung in between them like a basketball player boxing out a defender and had a last go with a makeup brush. The Golden Coach was approaching.

Saskia heard a faint metallic snick as Ruud drew a pen—she couldn't see it, but it would be some tour de force of minimalist industrial design, made of metals from the far reaches of the Periodic Table—from his breast pocket. "I'll add a few words," he said, "just so you-know-who doesn't jump down our throats." He referred to Martijn Van Dyck, the charismatic leader of the far-right party, who could be relied upon to notice what Saskia had noticed, and to point it out, if the Queen of the Netherlands came out in opposition to dikes and windmills. "See you there, Your Majesty."

Willem just walked. It was the easiest thing to do, and it felt good to stretch his legs. It wasn't much more than a kilometer from his office in Noordeinde Palace to the Binnenhof, and the authorities had cleared the way by lining the route with crowd control barriers. A few royal superfans had begun showing up last night to stake out the best viewing spots. For their efforts they were now reaping the reward of standing with their bellies to the barricades where their predominantly orange clothing and accessories were on glorious display. Many had brought banners that they had zip-tied to the barricades themselves. As long as these were handmade and in reasonably good taste they were allowed to remain.

Not everyone was willing to sleep rough on the streets of The Hague just to get a glimpse of the queen's hand waving in the window of the golden carriage. For those slackers, bleachers had been set up, well back of the barricades, so that they could sit in reasonable comfort and view the procession from a higher, more distant vantage point. The whole route was lined with police in dark uniforms with high-vis stripes across the chest. These stood closest to the barricades, backs turned to the procession, facing the crowd. They were reinforced by an inner layer of security consisting of military, in modern uniforms, backs to the crowd, facing the queen as she rolled by.

The procession that moved through all this was a historical mishmash. Many of the soldiers flanking the carriages, and the officers and dignitaries walking, or riding horses, alongside of it, were dressed as their forebears might have been two hundred years ago when the Dutch monarchy in its modern form had been instituted, post-Napoleon. So, a lot of knee breeches, white stockings, gold braid, and the kinds of hats usually seen on the heads of admirals in old movies. But many who walked in the procession—for it never moved at anything more than an easy walking pace—simply wore modern, albeit very formal, clothes. This included Willem who was in his blackest suit. He had not spoken to Queen Frederika today, nor would he have expected or wanted to. This would have meant that something had not gone according to plan. He had personally seen to the hasty arrangements for Ruud's last-minute check-in. This was unusual but hardly unheard of, and was, in the end, really just the system working as it was supposed to.

He knew what it was that was on Ruud's mind, since it had been on Willem's mind too, and he very much liked Ruud's solution. As a matter of fact, he liked it so much that it had, paradoxically, ratcheted up his own anxiety level. They had a fix worked out for the whole situation with T.R. and Pina2bo and all that. It only required the queen reading certain words from a piece of paper. That accomplished, people might then still criticize her for having gone to Texas at all. But she could dissociate herself, and by extension the government, from what T.R. was up to, by saying that she had only gone there on a fact-finding mission; and having acquainted herself with the facts, wholeheartedly concurred with the government's position. Then this whole thing would be behind them.

All this would happen in less than half an hour's time. But it seemed half a year to Willem, who, now that a solution was within his grasp, felt impatient with the slowness of horse-drawn transport. He longed in a strange way for the days of COVID when they had eschewed the antique carriage and the horses in favor of gray Audis. He bridled his impatience and tried to enjoy the walk. It was a nice enough day, though too hot. Not as hot as Texas, thank god. The crowds who turned up for this thing were overwhelmingly pro-royal, and so just walking among them and listening to their cheering and singing was a balm to his soul, torched as it was by late-night encounters with trolls, lunatics, and nefarious bot networks on the Internet.

During the foam disaster at Scheveningen, a photo had gone viral of the queen in a tent scrubbing down a plastic folding table with a rag and a spray bottle. This had become iconic, probably because it was an apt callout to the old stereotype of Dutch women scrubbing steps, sidewalks, and anything else that was not able to run away from their hygienic fervor. But at the same time it was modern, and nicely re-contextualized into this sudden and astonishing disaster. It was Frederika Mathilde Louisa Saskia manifesting in her Saskia avatar: the farmer's wife. So people had printed up large copies of that picture to put on signs and banners, and some had even laminated the full-body life-sized image onto foam core so that, from place to place along the route, it looked as if "Saskia" were standing there scrubbing the galvanized steel railings of the barricades. Garlands of orange flowers and cardboard crowns adorned some of these.

It would have been a little weird, a little wrong, if 100 percent of the spectators had been pro-royal and pro-government, and so protest banners were interspersed with the fan art. Up on the highest rows of the bleachers, signs in a more deprecatory vein could be seen thrust into the air. Some took issue with specific policies of Ruud's government. Others denounced the whole idea of having a monarch. Others yet were just incomprehensible.

All perfectly normal. But Willem took care to read them and to take discreet pictures. The great majority reflected positions of minority parties or pressure groups with which he was already familiar. But he didn't want to be blindsided by anything new.

As the procession came around a bend, entering the home stretch for the Binnenhof, he spied a row of protesters—or at least he assumed they were protesting something—who had staked out a few meters of space on the uppermost tier of a bleacher and deployed a banner made from a couple of bedsheets joined together. It read, simply, ZGL. Next to that was a crude cartoon—some sort of animal. Primitive heraldry.

Willem had never heard of the ZGL, though something about it did stir a faint memory. The "Z" immediately made him worry that it stood for "Zionist" something or other, and fringe groups obsessed with Zionism always went straight to the top of his list of nutjobs to worry about. So he snapped a picture.

As they got into the immediate district of the Binnenhof, the crowds peeled away and the procession trundled over a canal bridge and squeezed through a couple of narrow, ancient gates.

Then it disassembled itself in a highly programmed way. There was music, if fifes and drums qualified. The whole point of all this was for Queen Frederika to enter the Ridderzaal, and it was of the essence that she go in last. Willem pulled his credentials out of his pocket and used these to enter through a side door. He found his seat in the Ridderzaal while the band was playing and the ceremonial stuff was happening out front. He'd thereby skipped a lot of preparatory ceremony. While they'd been hoofing it through the streets, the president of the Senate had banged his gavel and opened Parliament with a little speech in which he'd introduced the various cabinet members in attendance as well as representatives of Aruba, Curaçao, and St. Maarten—remnants of the Dutch Empire that still looked to Frederika as their head of state.

Moments after Willem arrived, the doors opened, the queen was announced, and everyone stood up. A brass fanfare played and she was escorted in by the Speaker of the House. She made her way up the aisle, nodding to various notables she recognized along the way. She climbed a few steps up a rostrum to the actual throne. This was just an inordinately large, slabby chair with an overhanging canopy of carved Gothic stuff. Everyone sat down, the room got quiet, and she read the speech, word for word.

It started with a moment of silence for the victims of the recent foam disaster: eighty-nine in all.

Traditionally the speech began with a summary of major events during the past year, especially insofar as those might bear on the budget. This one was no exception. It would have seemed odd to open with a mention of the Scheveningen disaster and then pivot away from climate change, and so that was the first general topic covered in the speech.

As everyone in the room knew perfectly well, there were no new moves that could really be made in the political dance around climate change. All the parties in the governing coalition, and most of those in the States General, agreed that the climate was changing and sea level rising and that humans had something to do with it. The farther right one stood, the more likely one was to insist that the danger was overblown, and to resist any proposed actions that the government might take in the way of emissions reduction, carbon capture, and so forth. This was a losing battle, and had been for a long time, but it gave the right-wing fringe parties political currency that they could spend elsewhere. Their bitter denunciations of governments' heavy-handed meddling in free markets got them nowhere when it came to actually influencing public policy, but it raked in votes from conservative citizens and money from like-minded donors, which they could take advantage of in other areas, such as clamping down on immigration and making everything perfect for the Netherlands' twenty-five remaining farmers. All the major parties, in and out of the coalition, agreed that man-made climate change was real and that its significance was huge, especially for the Netherlands. They differed only in their estimation of how extreme the government's response to it should be.

But geoengineering per se had, by consensus, been so far off the table that it had rarely if ever been mentioned in the Binnenhof. The right-wing fringe, according to its own doctrine, didn't take climate change seriously, and so to them such measures were completely unnecessary. All the other parties just considered it anathema. So it had never before even been mentioned in the monarch's Third Tuesday speech.

But today Queen Frederika—reading words written in the wee hours by Ruud—did mention it. At the conclusion of the paragraph about climate change, she said: "There are those who say that efforts to change our ways and reduce the emission of greenhouse gases are too little, too late, and that we must instead turn to geoengineering schemes of various descriptions as a stopgap solution—like the old story of the boy putting his finger in the hole in the dike until help could be summoned. We reject this tempting, but shortsighted and dangerous approach. New geoengineering schemes are to be opposed." The word "new" had been inserted by Ruud during his last-minute edit session. It was just written on the page in fountain pen. He'd snapped a photo of this, and the following edit, and sent it to his office, which had duly altered the official text of the speech that was at this moment being released on the Internet. The queen read it all correctly. But her cadence changed. She had to slow down, pause, scan the emended page, make sure she was reading Ruud's handwritten insertion letter-perfect. "It will be pointed out by many who are familiar with our country's history that we have been pursuing a kind of geoengineering for many hundreds of years—that the Netherlands would not exist, in anything like its current form, without it, and that cessation of those efforts currently underway would lead to the inundation of our country. We specifically exclude *existing measures* from the policy just stated. Our defense of our shoreline and the lands sheltered behind it remain our chief priority." And then onward to much more conventional Budget Day talk about the amount of money that needed to be spent this year on those defenses. Then education, pension, public transit, and all the usual stuff. She wound it up, as usual, with a faint, non-denominational invocation of God's blessing. The crowd in the Ridderzaal stood up on cue and shouted "Lebende Konigin!" followed by "Hoora! Hoora! Hoora!" And then the entire procession reversed itself and took the queen back to her palace.

Not generally a day drinker, Willem poured himself a scotch when he got back to his private office in Noordeinde Palace, and put his feet up. He let video news feed run on the old-school flat-panel television screen bolted to the wall as he scrolled through social media feeds in his glasses and on a tablet and reviewed photos he'd taken during the procession.

Nothing on the television seemed worth turning the sound up for. In the courtyard of the Binnenhof, crews from three different Dutch networks had staked out positions where they could interview members of the States General, or anyone else who seemed newsworthy, with the building as backdrop. By changing the channel you could hop from one such feed to another, each showing a different talking head with basically the same background. This made it seem that each of these persons was standing there alone, when in fact they were part of an assembly-line operation, standing close enough to each other that faint crosstalk could be heard on the audio feeds. Willem found a feed from a streamer who was just aiming their camera down the row, with one MP in the foreground but two others visible farther away. He pinned that on his screen just to keep track of who was speaking, or about to go live, on each of the networks. He had a pretty good idea of the sorts of things they'd be saying. Anyway Remi was at home watching all this and sending wry text messages from time to time, letting Willem know when he should tune in to this or that feed.

Meanwhile, scrolling through his photos, he came across that ZGL banner and decided to figure out what that was about. A few possible candidates popped up on a quick search. As he'd apprehended, some related to Zionism. Fortunately, though, that turned out to be a red herring. The Z stood for Zeelandsche, "Zealandish." Zeeland was the southwesternmost province of the Netherlands, along the North Sea coast, between the Rhine to the north and the Belgian border to the south. It was flat and low even by Dutch standards, and sparsely populated, basically consisting of a series of finger-like islands reaching out toward the sea. Much of it was reclaimed land. It had been hit hard by the 1953 disaster—it was where Willem's father had nearly drowned in his attic—and it was now protected from such events, at least in theory, by a long dike with a road running over the top of it, spanning the gaps between the tips of the "fingers." On maps, this looked impossibly spindly, but when you drove over it you appreciated the mass and solidity of the sand and stones that had been carefully arranged to seal off Zeeland from the ocean.

The G and the L apparently stood for "Geotechnisch Liga" or "Geotechnical" (a synonym for geoengineering?) League. Kind of a weird name in Dutch. "Liga" came from Spanish and was normally used in a football context. But naming oddities aside, ZGL was a real organization apparently. And it had been around for a while. The founder had a brief but plausible-seeming Wikipedia entry stating that he'd been born in 1937 and had founded the organization after the 1953 disaster as a community service group to shore up dikes and aid people in disaster planning. Since then he'd passed away, but the charter of the ZGL was worded in such a way that it would support not just dike-building but any other "geotechnisch" measures that might help protect Zeeland from the ravages of the North Sea. What that added up to, in today's milieu, was that they were pro-geoengineering and—according to posts and updates from the last week—quite fond of T.R.'s Pina2bo project.

> The twat is up!

said a text from Remi.

Willem turned his attention to the video stream and saw that Martijn Van Dyck was getting into position to be interviewed by one of the networks. He changed the channel on his television until he found the right one.

There were two parties of any real significance that could be called truly far right in the sense of being quite open about their disdain for immigrants as well as espousing certain other positions that were well outside the Overton window of the politics of the day. One of these was older, headed by a senior politician who'd had a long career as a gadfly in Parliament. Then there was the party of Martijn, who was younger, more polished. He presented much the same ideas in a more palatable guise and was considered a man to watch.

The first thing Willem noticed about him was that he was sporting a ZGL button in his lapel. It was adorned with the heraldry of Zeeland: a lion emerging from waves representing the sea.

His surprise over that detail distracted him, at first, from what

Martijn was actually saying. Which on any other day wouldn't have been much of an issue, since his statements were utterly predictable. People mostly watched him for his wit and style. And Willem was tired of Martijn's wit and style. He drifted back to reading about the ZGL as Martijn started talking. The group's website included some nice old black-and-white photos of the members in the 1950s repairing dikes, and of the founder giving a speech in front of a Parliamentary committee.

> !!!

came in from Remi and so Willem turned his attention back to Martijn and turned up the volume.

"Yes," Martijn was insisting to the shocked TV journalist, "our stance on this has in fact changed. We are in the middle of re-drafting the party platform." He paused, took a deep breath, and showed emotion that even the interviewer knew better than to interrupt. "I lost a friend at Scheveningen the other day," he announced. "At his funeral, his mother came up to me and implored me to step back and re-examine my party's position on the *klimaat nood*."

Climate emergency. Martijn Van Dyck, until this moment, had never allowed the phrase to pass his lips, and he openly mocked those who used it.

"Recent research has made it undeniable that man-made climate change is real and that it poses the greatest threat to our country since Hitler."

Willem laughed out loud and slapped his desk. This was like hearing the leader of the Greens come out in favor of clubbing baby seals.

The interviewer couldn't believe her ears. "That is stunning news," she said. "Does this mean you'll be joining up with the Greens?"

Martijn looked quizzical, verging on offended. "The Greens!? Oh, no. We need real solutions to this problem. *Effective* solutions. Vague promises to cut back on carbon emissions at some point in the distant future are too little, too late. 'Decarbonization' is nothing more than a 1940-style capitulation. No, the only way out of this emergency is geoengineering. Such as what we are seeing at the Pina2bo site in Texas. I stand with Her Majesty the Queen in supporting such realistic, hardheaded practical solutions."

"Fuuuuuck!" Willem shouted.

"The queen?" asked the interviewer.

"Yes. As we just saw from the throne."

"The queen said the opposite."

"Ah, in the official text—which she, of course, didn't write—that's what it claims. But you have to read between the lines in these things. The way she hesitated—the look on her face as she rattled off those lines that were put in her mouth by the prime minister—there's no mistaking what it all means."

"But the words are what they are!" insisted the interviewer, who, to her credit, was having none of it.

"Very well, let's look at the words then!" Martijn said agreeably. He just happened to have a hard copy of the official text in the breast pocket of his perfectly tailored suit, and it just happened to be folded back to the relevant section. "*New* geoengineering schemes are to be opposed," he read, in a singsong voice as if this could all hardly be simpler. "We specifically exclude *existing measures* from the policy just stated." He looked up. "There you have it." He jammed the document back in his pocket as if there'd be no further need of it.

"She's talking about the dikes. The pumps."

"She didn't say dikes and pumps, she said *existing* as opposed to *new*. I have seen the videos from Pina2bo. I'd say it *exists*. Would you disagree?"

The interviewer was dumbstruck.

"The language spoken by our queen clearly supports Pina2bo—a site she has, I believe, personally visited—and my party stands alongside her," Martijn announced, placing his hand over his heart.

Willem just sat there for a minute with the blood raging in his ears. Texts were pelting in from Remi and others but he wasn't really seeing them.

He had to focus on the immediate. What did *he* need to do *now*?

As little as possible, was the answer. This was Ruud's problem. Ruud had written the speech. He, not fucking Martijn, was the arbiter of what the words actually meant. Once Ruud got wind of Martijn's shenanigans he'd be standing in front of one of those cameras stating in no uncertain terms that Pina2bo was *not* included in the category of "existing" geoengineering schemes and that the speech meant the opposite of what Martijn had just claimed.

But Martijn *had* announced a very real change in his party's policy.

Reactions were coming in from all over, on different feeds. Martijn had clearly triumphed in today's news cycle. The leader of the older far-right party made an announcement that they, too, had altered their position and now stood in favor of the use of geoengineering to address the grave threat posed by rising sea level to the very existence of the Netherlands.

> Snaparound!

This single word in English scrolled up his notifications. It was from Alastair. Willem didn't know what it signified.

The ZGL website refreshed itself. Superimposed on the pre-existing landing page were fresh headshots of Martijn and Ruud making their announcements. Above and between them was a smaller photo of the queen sitting on the throne earlier today. Willem wondered whether he should go find her and make her aware of all these goings-on. She was taking the rest of the day off from official duties, enjoying what amounted to a family reunion of the House of Orange. Technically this was none of her concern. She was above it. There was no action she could or should take.

For an eccentric local nonprofit dating back to the 1950s, ZGL seemed suspiciously web-savvy. Willem couldn't shake the vague idea he'd heard of them before.

He hit on the idea of searching through his old emails for any reference to this group. Several hits came back, but they were obviously false positives. The license plate of the pickup truck he had rented in Waco had been ZGL-4737. This had been cited on the rental contract and other paperwork, which had been automatically emailed to him. So any search for "ZGL" in an email just brought up those PDFs. But nothing else. And his email archive went back decades.

If it had not been for the recent weirdness concerning ERDD, he'd have shrugged it off as a coincidence. But he remembered, now, sitting there outside of the RV that Bo's staff had parked next to the rented pickup truck in Louisiana. Bo had snapped a photo of the ERDD vest hanging up to dry. But he had *also*—Willem now remembered this—quoted the license plate number of the truck from memory.

He went back and took a closer look at the ZGL website. Some of the pages had creation dates going back to the 1990s, but those could be faked.

Featured on the landing page but now overshadowed by the recent additions—now including a live chat pane auto-scrolling at dizzying speed—was a black-and-white photo of the group's alleged founder. Willem had previously clicked on this and skimmed it. He rooted it up out of his browsing history and read it again. The bio page was headed up by a larger copy of the same photo, the founder's name, and his birth and death dates.

The birth date was 4 July 1937. 4/7/37 as everyone outside of America wrote dates.

He compared it against the PDF from the car rental agency. ZGL-4737 had been the truck's license plate.

He started typing in the URL of the Internet Archive's Wayback Machine, which would show him any old archived versions of the ZGL site. This would, he suspected, provide evidence that the site, though it purported to be decades old, had not existed until a couple of weeks ago.

Then he stopped. Why should he even bother? He already knew what he would find.

He took his glasses off, sat back, closed his eyes, folded his arms, and tried to think.

His phone buzzed a couple of times. Only a few people in the world had the privilege of making his phone buzz. He checked, just to see if it might be Queen Frederika requesting an urgent meeting. But it was his father in Louisiana.

> THANK GOD. FINALLY!

A few texts farther up the screen was Alastair's enigmatic "Snaparound!"

Willem texted him back.

> Are we still on for tomorrow?

> Yes. As discussed. Unless you have your hands full?

> I'll meet you at the train station. Safe travels.

The Hague's train station was within easy walking distance of both palaces. Willem got there in plenty of time to meet Alastair's train from Amsterdam, so he bought a coffee. Most of the seats in the café were spoken for. At one table, a man in casual attire was reading a newspaper—an actual newspaper consisting of large pieces of paper with ink on them, which blocked his face from view. The front page inevitably featured a color photo of the queen seated on her throne yesterday. Down below was a picture of Martijn Van Dyck over a headline "Climate Bombshell from the Far Right."

As Willem carried his coffee away from the bar, the man reading the newspaper put one of his shoes up on the edge of a chair and shoved it out into Willem's path. Then he lowered the paper.

It was Bo.

It took Willem a moment to place him, so out of context, so out of costume. Over his T-shirt he was wearing a garland of fake plastic flowers. Orange, of course. Detritus from yesterday's parade. Pinned to the shirt was a ZGL button.

Willem sighed. "I only have a few minutes."

"Nine and a half," Bo answered, glancing up at a clock on an arrivals screen. "I admire your punctuality, sir. Always ten minutes early."

"It's very clever, what you're doing," Willem said, taking the seat. "And you do it very well. Someday I'd love to tour the facility."

"Facility?" Bo asked.

"I imagine a large, new, stylish, high-tech building in Beijing, brilliant hackers showing up every morning to engineer these sites, manipulate the social media feeds, track the metrics—"

"You're making it out to be much more difficult than it is," Bo protested. "We don't need brilliant hackers in flashy buildings. Macedonian teenagers in their parents' basements are more than sufficient. We use brilliant hackers for other things."

"Such as . . . running climate models?"

"That would be one example."

"What are those climate models telling you?"

Bo glanced at the station clock. "Ask Alastair. To judge from that man's LinkedIn, his models will show very similar results."

"Why are you fucking with me personally? Why ERDD, ZGL, and all that?"

"Leverage. You have some."

"With a powerless constitutional monarch. Who had her one yearly moment on the political stage yesterday."

Bo shrugged. "PMs and governments come and go. Your queen is young and healthy. If she stops crashing planes, she'll be around for decades. She seems a more stable long-term investment."

"You can't invest in her. She is not for sale."

"I chose my words poorly," Bo said, with the faintest suggestion of a bow. "Please accept my apologies. I meant to say it was a supportive relationship that we are investing in."

"How do you imagine that these activities are supportive?"

Bo put the paper down, folded it neatly while he collected his thoughts. "It is a very curious thing about the West. This inability, this unwillingness to talk about realities. Basic facts that are obvious to everyone not in your bubble. *Your country is below sea level,* for god's sake!"

"Actually we talk about that all the time, Bo."

"You have to do something about the fact that sea level is rising!"

"The last time we talked," Willem said, "you were miffed."

"Miffed?"

"Offended by the fact that T.R. had not invited you to his party."

"Oh, I remember," Bo said. "You said I needed to flirt with him more. To show interest." He smiled.

Willem was struck by the momentary, horrid thought that Bo's recent activities around ERDD, ZGL, and all that had been him taking Willem up on his suggestion. That Willem had started that ball rolling with a careless witticism in Louisiana.

But he was pretty sure China didn't operate on that basis.

"That was right before I went to Pina2bo," Willem said, "and saw that it was real. Now, you and I both know a lot more."

"That's for sure," Bo said.

"Why are you here *today?*" Willem asked. "Why bother coming to the Netherlands?"

"Observation. Fact-finding," Bo said. "Among other things it is an opportunity to see how your country responds to a once-in-a-lifetime storm."

Willem didn't catch the reference. "You mean what happened at Scheveningen?"

Bo seemed nonplussed. "No, I'm talking about the one in three weeks."

"We can't forecast three weeks out!"

"We can." Bo's gaze strayed down to Willem's feet. "Nice cowboy boots."

Alastair said exactly the same words a few minutes later when he stepped off the train from Amsterdam.

"I debated whether to wear them today."

Alastair blinked. "Because it might be noticed and read as an implicit show of support for T.R.?"

Willem nodded, falling into step beside Alastair. "Then I saw it was forecast to rain later, and I said, to hell with it, I'm wearing the boots."

The two men weaved around each other as they turned into the heavy flow of pedestrian traffic along the station's central artery. "Listen," Willem said, "can you—by which I mean, anyone—forecast a major storm three weeks in the future?"

A message buzzed in from his contact in Dutch intelligence: a response from an urgent query he'd fired off minutes earlier, just after parting ways with Bo. It stated that, according to immigration records, Bo had entered the country a week ago.

"Make that four weeks," he added.

"You're speaking of a hypothetical storm three weeks from today? Or four weeks?"

"Three weeks from today."

"Well, there's going to be an exceptionally high tide then, I can tell you that much."

"You just happen to know that!?"

"Consider what I do for a living—when I'm not doing weird projects for the Queen of the Netherlands, that is," Alastair said. "An exceptionally high tide makes it more likely that the Thames Barrier will be raised to protect London. This impedes shipping."

"It makes sense," Willem allowed. "Still, I'm impressed you just know the tide tables three weeks out."

"I'm just fucking with you," Alastair admitted. "My family have a cottage on Skye. I'm going there in three weeks, for a last visit before winter closes in. Was checking the ferry timetables yesterday. It's got high tide warnings posted for those dates."

"Well played," Willem said. "Coffee?" For they were near the café where the strange conversation with Bo had happened just a few minutes ago. Bo was gone. An older woman had seized his newspaper and opened it to a lavish photo spread showing the hats and frocks that had been on display yesterday at the Ridderzaal.

"No, thank you," Alastair said. "Anyway, storms are obviously more difficult to predict than tides. Oh, we know what such a storm would *look* like. It would look like 1953. A low pressure system of unusual intensity forming up near Iceland and coming down the chute between Scotland and Norway, pushing a surge ahead of it. Lots of rain just adds gasoline to the fire, if I can mix my metaphors."

"How far in advance could you predict the formation of that low pressure system?"

"Ten days? A couple of weeks?"

"Not three weeks? Four?"

"There might be some really cutting-edge models that would run that far out. With big error bars though."

Willem nodded. They exited the station and came out into a continuation of yesterday's hot weather. Scattered clouds hinted at a change later. Willem led Alastair around some construction barricades and got them pointed toward Noordeinde.

"I thought I was here to predict climate, though. Not weather. For weather you want a different sort of chap." He was just being playful.

"I got a hot tip that there would be a once-in-a-lifetime storm in three weeks," Willem explained, "and I'm trying to figure out whether it should be taken seriously."

"Does the tipster have connections to well-funded boffins with very advanced computational modeling capabilities?"

"Yes."

"Then we're fucked. Keep an eye on the North Atlantic!" Alastair said. "I'll do likewise, now that you've aroused my curiosity. Perhaps my trip to Skye shall have to be postponed."

"Oh, I've got another question," Willem said. "What did you mean by snaparound?"

"Sorry to be enigmatic. It's a thing Greens have been fretting about for years. They have always harbored a suspicion that one day their opponents—oil companies, basically—would suddenly reverse their position on climate change."

"As Martijn Van Dyck did yesterday."

"Yes. But then, instead of falling in line with what the Greens want, those people would say, 'Och, too late, the damage has been done, water under the bridge, the only answer is geoengineering.'"

"So from the Green point of view," Willem said, "they—the Greens—are steadfastly holding to the position they've held all along. But their opponents have snapped way around from one extreme to another."

Alastair nodded. "I got excited and sent you that text because, as I mentioned, Greens have been worrying about this forever. A lot of their political strategy in the climate debate is predicated on fear of snaparound. But this was the first time in all these years I'd ever watched it happen in real time!"

"Do you expect there'll be more of it?"

"I expect," Alastair said, "that T.R. has many observant friends in boardrooms up and down the length of Houston's Energy Corridor." He slowed for a moment and took an appraising look at Noordeinde Palace. "Including . . ."

"Royal Dutch Shell," Willem said.

The queen brought her daughter to the meeting. By the letter of the law, Princess Charlotte ought to be in school. But she'd reached an age when classes were less regimented, and independent study was encouraged. As long as the princess wasn't falling behind in her schoolwork, she was allowed a certain number of absences. It wouldn't have been appropriate to invite her to the weekly one-on-one with the prime minister, for example. But on occasions when there was legitimate educational value, and especially when it might help prepare Charlotte for her future duties as sovereign, she was allowed to skip school and sit in. Quietly.

Many of the old grand rooms in Noordeinde had too much historical value to be kitted out with modern office gear, but one room had been brought reasonably up to the standards prevailing in the early twenty-first century and so Alastair plugged his gear into that. Like every other state-of-the-art conference room AV system in the history of the world, it failed to work on the first go and so it was necessary to summon someone who understood how it worked; and like all such persons he could not be found.

Willem decided to make some practical use of the resultant delay. "Now that we have finally gotten past Budget Day and all that," he said, "I have been taking a look at your schedule for the next few weeks."

"And what do you think?" the queen asked.

"Well, it's a bit sparse. Just because we've been too distracted to pack in a lot of events. Nothing wrong with that, of course. Alastair did remark that there is an unusually high tide coming up three weeks from now. Could cause problems if it happened to coincide with bad weather. If you aren't averse to adding some new items to your schedule, then I'd suggest we emphasize disaster preparedness."

She smiled. "No one can ever criticize the queen for taking a bold stance in favor of disaster preparedness."

Charlotte produced an eye roll. The target, however, was not her mother. "They will criticize you for *anything*. You should see—"

Frederika gave her daughter an appraising look. "Been reading the comments, have we?"

Charlotte looked as if she'd been caught red-handed in the liquor cabinet.

"We've talked about this," Frederika said.

"I know. Reading the Internet will drive me crazy."

"People will make fun of me for being a predictable Goody Two-Shoes if I advocate for disaster preparedness," the queen agreed. "But it is a natural segue from the Scheveningen disaster. And it will flush Texas and Pina2bo and Martijn Van Dyck out of the news cycle." She turned her gaze toward Willem as she said this and gave him a nod.

"Very well, I'll begin looking for such opportunities," Willem said. "Given the usual lag, it might take a couple of weeks before this gets into full swing."

Suddenly the AV system sprang to life and the coat of arms of the House of Orange appeared on the royal flat-screen. Frederika Mathilde Louisa Saskia's breeding took over as she found a way to compliment the technician on his brilliance without making him look bad for not having had the thing ready in the first place.

Three-dimensional augmented-reality globes might actually have been useful in this case, but the software Alastair had been using was no-nonsense academic research code that liked to plot simple flat rectangular maps. So that was what they were going to be looking at. He'd made hard copies too, which he distributed to Willem and the queen. He hadn't known Princess Charlotte was coming, so she had to share her mother's copy.

"I'll get right to it," he said. "If Pina2bo continues to operate as planned, it's good for the Netherlands. That is the most salient information I can give you during this meeting."

The queen, who'd been leafing through the handout, crossed her arms and looked at him. Lotte looked like she'd been biting her tongue. She drew the handout toward herself and perused it as Alastair went on:

"Many of the negative effects and heightened risks that climate change has inflicted on your country—and mine, as it happens—in recent decades will tend to be reversed. In some cases the speed of that reversal will be dramatic. Temperatures will drop noticeably. The amount of evaporation from the ocean's surface will be reduced and so we won't see as much torrential rainfall. Ice caps will stop melting. This reduces the possibility of a sudden change in the North Atlantic Current, which truly would be a catastrophe for all of Europe."

"That's the thing that would make us like Siberia if it happened?" Charlotte asked.

"Yes, Your Royal Highness." In Texas Alastair had gradually lapsed into the habit of addressing "Saskia" informally. But a couple of weeks' re-immersion in Britain, combined with the grandeur of Noordeinde Palace, had put him back on his best behavior. "It would give us the climate we, in a sense, deserve for living so far north. Not the much more moderate one that we have enjoyed for all of recorded history. You appear to be familiar with the concept already, so I won't—"

"Mansplain it?" the queen put in.

"Yes, but since the princess brought the topic up: it is hard to overstate what a nightmare that would be for all Europe. The melting of Greenland makes it more likely, Pina2bo makes it less so. Anyway—setting all that aside—page 4 shows predicted effects on polar ice. Because the melting of the ice caps would be slowed, sea level rise would eventually stop."

"And weather would get colder?"

"Yes. Not in the devastating way that the princess just alluded to, but it would get your country back toward—" He held up his hands. "I guess you could call it Hans Brinker conditions."

The queen enjoyed the joke. "We can look forward to skating on the canals again."

"Yes. Your farmers would have to adapt in small ways—shifting toward different varieties of seeds, changing their planting schedules. But it's either that or end up under ten feet of salt water."

"Now, this all disregards the fact that there would still be far too much CO_2 in the atmosphere," the queen pointed out.

"Indeed, Your Majesty. And as we discussed in Texas, the upper layers of the ocean absorb that from the air and become more acidic. It has devastating effects on coral reefs. But if I may be altogether cold-blooded for a moment—" Alastair let it hang there.

"The Netherlands doesn't have coral reefs," Willem said, so that no one else would have to.

The princess was visibly distressed.

"It is a thing we must say out loud," said Willem, "because others—like Martijn Van Dyck—are going to be saying it in front of cameras and microphones. It doesn't mean we don't care about coral reefs. But the queen must be ready to hear from those of her citizens who will take such stances."

"There are other techniques that might be used to address the problem of ocean acidification," Alastair said. "They are outside of my remit for this job."

"Some will say," Willem added, "it's just more geoengineering to fix a problem left over from the first round of geoengineering."

"Alastair, hold on a moment," the queen said. "All these changes you're talking about—am I to understand that T.R. is creating all these global effects single-handedly just by operating Pina2bo?"

Alastair nodded. "That is the incredible leverage of SO_2 in the stratosphere. It's why people like T.R. are drawn to it."

Saskia just blinked and shook her head.

"At its rated capacity, Pina2bo is at the lower end of the size needed to effect these changes. If there were two or three or four Pina2bos all going at once, then the changes described in my report would take place rapidly. Dramatically."

"You mean, if he builds more guns at the Flying S Ranch? Or fires the one he has more frequently?" the queen asked. "Or . . . you're perhaps talking about other such facilities in other parts of the world?"

"Now you ask an interesting question, *mevrouw*. In a way, it is *the* question. What happens in these models when we break things out regionally? Both as to *cause* and *effect*? *Cause* meaning: What if T.R. had built the gun in Alberta or Ecuador instead of West

Texas? *Effect* meaning: How will different parts of the world be affected by Pina2bo?"

"I'll bet the answer is complicated," the queen said.

"If all you care about is the Netherlands, no. It's absolutely a win for the Netherlands. Another country it's good for is China. A clear, unambiguous win for China on multiple levels."

Willem felt his face getting warm.

"What's an example of a country it's bad for?" Charlotte asked in a small voice.

"Possibly India," Alastair said without hesitation. "Oh, their neighbors in Bangladesh will love it. It's going to save that country. And those parts of eastern India that have similar problems to Bangladesh will also enjoy a net benefit. Western and southern India may see . . . how shall I put this . . . *alteration* in the monsoons."

"Oh, my god!" Saskia exclaimed and splayed one hand out on her chest.

Alastair paused for a few moments to let the queen process this. They had all understood, from the very beginning of the conversation with T.R., that solar geoengineering was "controversial" and might have "side effects requiring further study" but that verbiage was the stuff of PowerPoint decks in Brussels. Narrowing the impact to one specific region suddenly made it very concrete and perhaps caused the queen to envision what kind of fallout—perhaps *literal* fallout—could result from the Netherlands openly backing any one such scheme.

The princess seemed to be more taken aback by her mother's reaction than by what Alastair had said, but she was already googling "monsoon" and so she'd understand the significance soon enough.

When Saskia met his eye again, Alastair continued: "I'm not saying that the monsoon would *stop*. It never stopped in the 1990s after the Pinatubo eruption. It is a dizzyingly complicated interaction having to do with where the sun is in the sky, the topography of the Himalayas, the albedo of the land, jet streams, Coriolis effect, ocean currents, and so on. El Niño even enters into it. Lately, it has been drier than the historical norm, even while the rest of the planet has been much wetter. When the monsoon rains are heavy, they cause regional flooding that can lead to more death and destruction than a dry spell. So this is not a simple matter."

The queen had pulled the handout from Charlotte's grasp and begun nervously shuffling through it. "Page 23 is probably what you're looking for," Alastair said, putting the graphic up on the room's big screen. It was a flat rectangular map of the world, with continents and countries outlined in black. Covering that was an overlay of color ranging from blue to red. Much of the world was tinted by a wash of pastel pink or baby blue, indicating relatively small predicted change in annual rainfall, but there were localized areas of more saturated color. Many of these were in places like the Sahara, the Himalayas, or Greenland that were relatively unpopulated. The Indian subcontinent, taken as a whole, didn't look terrible. But there was a worrisome red blotch in the northwest, between the Himalayas to the east and Pakistan to the west. "The Punjab," Alastair said, highlighting it with a red laser pointer. "The Breadbasket. Generally the last place the monsoon reaches as it spreads up from Sri Lanka in the late spring and early summer. And the first place from which it recedes, a few months later."

"So, more vulnerable to changes in the monsoon than other areas," said Willem, filling in the blanks.

"Yes. And it borders on some areas that are geopolitically complicated." In this company Alastair didn't need to go into much detail about India's endless border disputes with Pakistan and with China, or to belabor the fact that all three of those countries were nuclear powers.

The queen looked for a few moments at Charlotte, perhaps having second thoughts about having invited her. Oblivious, the princess was spawning Punjab-related browser tabs and slamming away at "subscribe" buttons.

"What can you say about the actual probability of drought or famine? The possible toll?" Saskia asked.

"Very little really," Alastair said. "But what I can say with some confidence is that maps similar to this one are probably being looked at by people in Delhi right now. As well as Beijing and other places."

"It doesn't matter anyway," Willem said. "I'm sorry to be so cynical, but once people have seen a map like this one, the scientific, on-the-ground reality no longer actually matters."

Saskia nodded. "We discussed this on the train. It's about how everything is perceived."

"Yes. People *already* believed that the weather was being manipulated even when it *wasn't*. Now that T.R. actually *is* doing something, any perceived change whatsoever will be credited to, or blamed on, him."

"Or anyone seen as supporting him," Saskia added, nodding. She nudged Lotte. No point in inviting her to these things if she wasn't going to learn anything. "How about it, darling? Now that you are an instant expert on the Punjab, what's the mood there? Are people furious at T.R. McHooligan?"

"A few of them," Lotte said, "but no, mostly they are too excited about Big Fish to pay any attention to geoengineering."

"Who or what is that?"

By way of an answer, Lotte clicked on a browser tab and rotated the screen toward her. Bracketed between luridly colored headlines in what Saskia assumed to be Punjabi script was a photo of a magnificently ripped young man posing on a peak of some impossibly high mountain brandishing a stick. "Behold," Lotte said.

Saskia gave him a good long look. The picture seemed to have been taken someplace cold. Atop Big Fish's massive pecs, brown nipples jutted out like Himalayan pinnacles.

"What does he do other than look like that?"

"Beats the hell out of Chinese bastards with a stick."

Despite being a reasonably mature woman with serious responsibilities, Saskia found it difficult to get her mind back on track, and the way Lotte was speed-scanning through Big Fish

Pinterest boards didn't help. What had they been talking about a minute ago? How it was all perceived.

"We didn't hire Alastair to set official government policy," Willem said. "That's Ruud's problem. The only thing we need to concern ourselves with is what if any stance the royal house needs to adopt about these matters."

He lapsed into Dutch at some point during all that. Alastair tuned out. But his body language said he had something to add: "Earlier I mentioned that there was a *cause* side as well as an *effect* side, when it comes to how these things are situated around the planet. There are plenty of studies showing that *where* a volcano erupts—or a geoengineering project is sited—has a very significant impact on how these effects play out around the world. It has been known for a while, for example, that volcanic eruptions in the Southern Hemisphere lead to wetter monsoons, whereas Northern Hemisphere volcanoes produce the opposite effect."

"So if T.R. had put the gun in Argentina . . ." Willem said.

"The consequences for China and India might very well be the other way round," Alastair confirmed.

Saskia had been following this even more keenly than usual. "How about—" she began, then stopped herself and met Lotte's eye.

"I know what that look means!" Lotte said and stood up. Willem and Alastair, still on their best behavior, stood up also.

"The lesson in climate geopolitics has been, I should say, even more informative than expected!" Saskia said. "Go back to your room, young lady, and pursue your studies of Big Fish."

"Oh, I very much intend to, Mother. By the time you see me next—"

"That will do." She gave her daughter a kiss on the cheek. Willem and Alastair were too embarrassed to bid Lotte goodbye. The princess left the room.

"You'll remember our Venetian friends," Saskia began.

Willem and Alastair were both a little taken aback at this unexpected turn. For Willem's part, he had never expected to see or to hear from the Venetians again. They'd been a fascinating historical curiosity, nothing more.

"I think I'm going to sit down!" Alastair joked, and did. So did Willem.

"I have remained in occasional contact with Cornelia since Texas," Saskia said. "Just friendly text messages back and forth, that sort of thing. She's been on vacation the whole time. Or so I assumed—until recently—based on the selfies she was sending me. Is there a way I can put pictures from my phone on the screen?"

It turned out that there was. And for once, it actually turned out to be simple enough that between the three of them they were able to sort it out without having to bring in a Ph.D.

Cornelia was almost unrecognizable in the first because she was in casual touristy garb very different from the kind of elegant look they'd come to expect from her on the train. A big straw hat, large sunglasses, a white sun shirt over a tank top. She was on a boat. They could see very little of this, just enough to surmise that it was a yacht. In the background was an island in a blue sea, and in the greater distance, muddled by haze, was a much bigger landform, presumably the mainland. Both were mountainous and rocky. One might think the Aegean, except that the forest was denser and darker than the islands of Greece and Turkey. "Black Sea?" Alastair guessed. Willem thought Corsica.

Saskia advanced through several more photos. Some were selfies, but Cornelia wasn't in all of them. They told a little story. The yacht docked at a pier on the island. Not a very nice-looking pier. It looked industrial/military, abandoned and dangerously tumbledown, with new caution tape surrounding old cave-ins on the pier's surface that were large enough to swallow cars. There were stern-looking signs in block letters, written in the Roman alphabet, but not in a language any of them could identify. Fragments of both Greek and Cyrillic could also be seen.

"I give up!" Alastair admitted.

"How about you, Willem?" Saskia asked.

"Former Yugoslavia? Macedonia?"

"Albania!" Saskia announced triumphantly and gave Willem a mock-stern look as if to say *What am I paying you for if you can't recognize Albania!?* She swiped through a couple of snapshots depicting a miserable port facility. "Right across the Adriatic from the heel of the boot of Italy."

"It looks like shit," Alastair said. "Not Cornelia's kind of place at all."

"Oh, but it is!" Saskia said. She'd come to a picture of a ruined stone building, very ancient, but vaguely recognizable as a church.

Willem had been speed-googling. "Albania only *has* two islands," he said. "Both of which used to be part of—"

But Saskia had beaten him to the punch line with a zoomed-in snapshot of the collapsed front of the church. Barely discernible, carved into a heavily timeworn stone lintel, was a winged lion. "The Venetian Empire!" she proclaimed. "Not since about 1800, of course. The Austrians gobbled it up, then lost it. Later it fell under Soviet control."

"But as we've seen, Cornelia's crowd have long memories," Alastair said drily.

"They seem quite good at maintaining these connections, down through the years," Saskia agreed.

"If this is the island I'm reading about," said Willem, scrolling on his tablet, "the Soviets built a chemical weapons plant there during the Cold War."

"That would explain so much," Alastair remarked. For, aside from the ruined church, all the other pictures were fully consistent with the decorative theme of "abandoned Warsaw Pact nerve gas complex and toxic waste dump on godforsaken island."

"One doesn't hear much out of Albania," Willem said.

"They've been active the last couple of decades, seeking foreign investment, trying to boot up a tech sector and all that," Alastair said. "Every so often they'll pop up in the City with a stock offering or a real estate scheme."

"Well, it would appear that Cornelia and her friends have risen to the bait," Saskia said. She was swiping slowly through a series of photos depicting a Land Rover journey up a switchbacked mountain road.

"That scans," Alastair said. "London and Wall Street are skittish about the Balkans because they don't understand the place. See it as unstable. With this unfathomable history. But if you're a Venetian aristocrat, it's . . . like Ireland is to England."

The road led to a summit where there was, at last, some new activity: construction trailers, a helipad, storage containers. All surrounding a flat area, in the middle of which was a drilling rig and a stockpile of drill rods.

"They're sinking an exploratory shaft," Alastair guessed. "The first step toward a bigger one."

Saskia looked at him. "Perhaps you could have a chat later with Willem about extending your contract."

"Oh," Alastair said, "it would kill me to walk away from this now."

Saskia flipped through the handout. "It would be illuminating to know how these maps and charts would all look if, in a year or two, a clone of Pina2bo were to go into operation off the coast of Albania." She looked up. "I believe that Cornelia has made up her mind to save her city from the sea. And heaven help anyone who gets in her way."

THE BLUE HERONS

There was a trope in the martial arts videos that was so shop-worn that even Laks, generally not one for fancy critical ter-minology, knew that it was a trope, and that it was called a trope. It would be the traditional move for a filmmaker to make at this juncture, were it the case that Laks was a fictional character in a low-budget martial arts film called, say, *Big Fish*. It was called a montage. Not a training montage, for Laks's training days were behind him. More of a "learning the ropes" sort of montage com-bined with a "meteoric rise to fame" one. The sort of montage that would conventionally end with Laks, head wrapped in a perfect Chand Tora Dumalla, climbing out of the back seat of a limousine in downtown Mumbai and cheerfully flinching from an onslaught of paparazzi and nubile fangirls.

In this particular case the montage would consist of quick cuts among a number of battle scenes up and down the Line of Actual Control, featuring various triumphs and setbacks. But mostly tri-umphs. Makers of martial arts videos did this so that they could cover a lot of story in a few minutes of screen time, and it worked. But in a way, what happened to the Fellowship next seemed even faster, more compressed in time, than that. Now obviously that wasn't the case; it was spread out over a few weeks. But there sim-ply was not time at any point to stop and collect one's wits and tally up the passage of time. Just mad dashing from one place to another. All those places were hot spots along the Line, where the services of Big Fish and his crew—which was rapidly growing— were deemed useful by people like Major Raju.

But if someone had come along for the ride and calmly watched it all happen and actually kept track, what they would have reported was that Big Fish ended up with a crew ("The School") consisting of: a dozen handpicked gatka practitioners in color-coordinated turbans, including Gopinder; a similar number of Gurkha rock-throwing specialists; and a ragtag irregular contingent of limited military effectiveness but mighty social media presence. Sam, Jay, and Ravi got shunted into that. Sam and Jay had become famous among British persons of South Asian ancestry. They had gotten some professional advice on how to wear turbans that would hide their scandalously non-observant buzz cuts. Since the School had started out with no particular color scheme, they took the path of least resistance and patterned their look after the red and yellow logo-wear used by Sam and Jay's football team in England. Ravi had his own following among non-Sikh Indians, which to put it mildly was a significant demographic.

Bella declared victory at some point and flew back to Argentina. Sue found an important role as the liaison between Big Fish's crew and the online community of K-Pop stans. Pippa gradually got nudged out of the way by Indian streamers chosen for them by the military. Laks tried to become indignant on her behalf. She insisted she didn't mind. Her career goals did not lie in grinding out propaganda. She had other objectives, difficult to articulate to anyone who did not live immersed in the film industry, having to do with portrayal of martial arts content in emerging three-dimensional formats, all under the heading of "performative war," a term it was pointless to google since she had coined it, and what few hits came back all pointed back to her. Apparently she had worked out an understanding with their minders that enabled her to tag along and gather the materials she needed provided she didn't get in the way. So Laks saw less of her, which was sad but probably good since he wanted to sleep with her in the most desperate way and that would have been a disaster. Somehow Laks's expired visa problem got ironed out and hints were dropped that the pathway to Indian citizenship was wide open.

Ilham faded from the picture with no explanation, but when Laks thought to ask about him—which, to be honest, took an embarrassingly long time—he was assured that the troubles of

Ilham and family were behind them, at least as far as immigration, food, and shelter were concerned. With a moment's reflection, of course, it was clear why Ilham—who still had family in Xinjiang—would not want to become world famous doing what Big Fish's School was doing.

The Chinese, of course, were not without resources of their own. So there were no more victories as easy as that over the Bonking Heads. Laks lost some fights against wushu stick fighters who knew what they were doing—and who, he realized, had spent time watching videos of Laks's earlier duels. "Opponent-specific training" was what Major Raju called that. Laks now had to do it too if he didn't want to fall off the leaderboard.

Meanwhile, the temperature was dropping, and even in these high arid places, snow was falling. The time would come quite soon when the Line of Actual Control would freeze in its current position until spring. Ski- and snowshoe-borne regulars might patrol, maneuver, and trade harsh language and snowballs, but almost all the volunteers would go home.

They were, in other words, building up to the season finale. And there weren't a lot of options as to where that would happen. When there were only a few pieces remaining on a chessboard, you could guess where the moves were going to be made.

It turned out to be a valley between two ridges that had been bare during the summer but during the last couple of weeks had become covered with snow to a depth of a meter. Farther up that valley, at about fifty-eight hundred meters of altitude, was the foot of a glacier whose meltwater created a stream that ran down the valley toward the salt lake of Pangong Tso. In former days, the glacier had extended quite a bit farther down. At its foot, after the 1962 cease-fire, the Indian Army had set up a base and constructed a few buildings, of which the only one that wasn't a total ruin was a barracks. This was a stone and mortar crackerbox consisting of two stories of soldiers' quarters above a ground floor with a mess hall and other common rooms. It had long since been abandoned by the receding glacier, which because of the valley's curve could not even be seen from its windows. The ridge to its west was almost always on the Indian side of the Line. From its top you could look west into territory that was, beyond all dispute, Indian. The ridge to its east was almost always on the Chinese side, and from there you could see the sun rising over China.

The barracks had been garrisoned by Indians until late in the current campaign season, when Chinese volunteers had broken into the ground floor and occupied it. The Indians who'd been using it as a base retreated up the stairs to the first story, then, a few days later, to the second story and the roof. Since then, after being resupplied by drones, they'd made some headway with a counteroffensive down a fire stairway, but at the moment held only a beachhead on the disputed first story, three-quarters of which was still Chinese-held. Barricades had been thrown up by both sides to fortify that line. The Line of Actual Control, in other words, had become a three-dimensional Surface of Actual Control, and you needed augmented-reality glasses to visualize its convolutions.

Which was not a mere figure of speech. The army had given Laks's crew access to such equipment. In virtual-reality mode, sitting far from the front, you could pull up a 3D map, Google Earth style, and pan and zoom up and down the length of the Line all day long, or until you were overcome by motion sickness. From a distance it looked fat and solid but as you zoomed in, it frayed to a loose-spun yarn. He remembered taking art classes in school, learning that instead of laying down a simple firm stroke you should make many fine scratches and gradually thicken the ones that were in the right place. That was how the Line looked when you zoomed in, each scratch being the record of where it had been for ten minutes three weeks ago.

When you put the device in augmented-reality mode it showed you nothing unless you were actually there, with line of sight to that fiber bundle. The day before Laks and the School were inserted, Major Raju drove him, in a snow machine, up to the top of the western ridge so that he could have a look down into the valley. The barracks, hundreds of meters below, looked like it had been trapped in glowing red cobwebs. Laks used the UI to filter out all but the last month's data. He was then able to watch in time lapse as the front crept down from the opposite ridgeline, then suddenly formed a fist-like salient that snaked down a tributary ravine and punched in the door of the barracks. For a few days this beachhead had been connected to the main Chinese position only by a frail stalk, but they'd broadened and fortified it while the Indian defenders had been distracted trying to maintain their toehold on the upper story.

The Indians weren't without tricks of their own. For a while they'd been cut off, since the Chinese salient completely surrounded the building. All resupply had been through drones. There'd been no way to send in or to evacuate personnel. But on the west or Indian side of the barracks, the valley wall was extremely steep: virtually a cliff rising to slightly above the height of the building before laying back to a more moderate slope that ran up to where Laks was looking down on it. During the last couple of weeks, the slot between the building and that cliff had become about half filled in with snow. Volunteers higher up the slope had encouraged more snow to avalanche down. In this way they had managed to fill it in entirely. The roof of the barracks, previously an island, was now connected to the slope just above and west of it by a snow bridge: a narrow tamped path that could be crossed by volunteers, one at a time, on makeshift snowshoes. To either side of that path the snow angled down like a rampart to the valley floor around the barracks.

The Chinese occupying the ground floor could, in theory, just go outdoors and walk right up that rampart to the path, but climbing it was nigh impossible when reinforced and well-fed Indian volunteers were raining down hard-packed snowballs the size of watermelons. The Chinese had made an effort to undermine it, but the volunteers above them on the ridge could fill in any new excavation with targeted avalanches faster than the Chinese could dig.

This was the point where the AR interface became more trouble than it was worth. Laks just shut it off and used the device as plain old see-through glacier glasses, the better to watch the arrival of Lan Lu.

Performative warfare (to adopt Pippa's terminology) followed a logic opposite to that of the twentieth century, when concealing troop movements had been all-important. So they knew exactly when Lan Lu was going to come down from the eastern ridge. They could watch it on the live streams from four different camera angles, with chyrons streaming across the bottom in layers showing the Vegas and Macao betting lines plus live comment feeds in four alphabets. For Lan Lu had been at the top of the leaderboard for three months.

The only reason *not* to just watch it that way from the warmth of a command tent kilometers away was so that they could grab some footage of Big Fish brooding down over the barracks as his soon-to-be nemesis made his triumphal entry to the ground floor at the head of his crew.

Laks didn't understand how Mandarin worked but it seemed like Lan Lu was both a singular and a plural noun depending on how you used it. Here, in its singular usage, it denoted one guy. It meant Blue Heron. Plural, it meant his whole crew of Blue Herons, who were called the Flock. They favored knee-length changshan jackets in dark blue slubbed silk, textured and yet shimmery, with protruding white cuffs, and gray trousers beneath. They were from Hong Kong. They practiced a style of wushu that had originated in Tibet but had been somehow exported to Kowloon late in the twentieth century and re-interpreted by wushu schools there. Much had been made of its Tibetan origins by Chinese propagandists who wanted to get people to believe it was an example of benign cultural integration. But this dude Lan Lu was a Cantonese speaker by upbringing, a Mandarin speaker when it suited him. And as far as Laks could tell there was no trace of Tibetan ancestry in any of the Flock. Their style relied on enveloping arm movements, said to be inspired by herons' wings, out of which came vicious pinpoint strikes like the ones that herons used to stun and impale small ground-dwelling creatures with their beaks. Whenever possible those strikes were aimed at nerve centers where they would inflict crippling pain out of proportion to their apparent power.

Laks could well understand how effective that system would be inside the barracks. He'd spent hours scouting the place in VR. The building was low-ceilinged and cluttered: not a good environment for whirling a long stick around. Lan Lu would have good odds of closing distance and getting into close quarters fighting range where he would have an advantage. Not that gatka fighters didn't know how to grapple. Kabaddi was half grappling. But by convention most of their practice took place in rule-bound competitions where the dangerous nerve center strikes were against the rules. So they didn't have that stuff programmed into muscle memory. And when the adrenaline kicked in your muscle memory was all you had to go on.

It took Laks all of about sixty seconds to come up with a plan of attack. It was simple and kind of obvious—but the more experience he got, and the more he perused old historical accounts of his forebears' tactics in the Punjab, the more certain he became that simple and obvious would defeat complicated and clever 90 percent of the time. "We'll play kabaddi," he said, "until we don't."

THE MARBLE MINE

All of Rufus's comings and goings were via New Marble Mine Road, which was passable even to ordinary cars once he had gone up and down the length of it and shoveled gravel into some big holes and removed a few rocks. These had tumbled down out of the high ground to either side. The road ran sometimes parallel to, sometimes right down the middle of, what was theoretically a watercourse. T.R. would have called it a stochastic river. In its upper reaches, within a mile of the mine itself, this was as dry and dead as any other part of the Chihuahuan Desert. Farther down, it was joined by a couple of other such arroyos in a flat pan that in any other part of the world might have been a pond, or at least a marsh. Here it was a stretch of low yellowed grass that apparently sunk roots deep enough to strike underground moisture. This was interspersed with cactus and other such plants. In a few deep crevices, actual standing water could be observed, especially as September gave way to October and the temperature dropped.

The only problem with this setup was that no vendor in the world would deliver packages to the minehead, and so almost every day he had to drive down the valley to High Noon to collect stuff he'd ordered online. One morning he was doing that, passing along right next to that low grassy patch, when two horses galloped across the road. It all happened fast. But he could have sworn that one of the horses was bloody.

He pulled up and got out to have a look around. Sure enough, there was blood on the grass next to the tracks that their unshod hooves had made in the dust. Unshod because, of course, the only horses you were going to see running around loose in a place like this were mustangs.

Then he heard an all too familiar noise: the squealing of a wild pig, not more than a hundred feet away.

His view was blocked by a swell in the ground, but when he vaulted up into the bed of his truck he was able to look over that and see another horse engaged in battle with a foe who was so low down that it could only be glimpsed through the grass and the thorny undergrowth. But Rufus knew what it was.

He jumped down into the cab and pulled the truck off the road and up onto that little rise. Then he took his rifle out from behind the seat, climbed up into the back of the truck again, and chambered a round. From this vantage point he could clearly see the wild boar, maneuvering around the mustang, trying to get one of its tusks into the horse's leg. The horse, of course, was having none of that and kept rearing up to strike down with front hooves or spinning round to kick out with rear. Both animals were mud-spattered. It could be guessed that they were disputing possession of a water hole. This pig had probably been wallowing down in one of those hidden wet places when the horses had come upon it hoping to get a drink.

They had been conducting these hostilities for a while. Both animals were tired. From time to time they would just stop and watch each other. During one of those intervals, Rufus put a .30-caliber slug through the boar's heart and dropped him like one of those stray boulders that sometimes peeled off the canyon wall. He might have expected the mustang to bolt at the sound of the gun. It startled, but it did not run. Rufus was able to get a good look at it through his scope and saw that it was a gelding. A very uncommon thing among wild horses, who generally were not big practitioners of surgical castration on the open range. Moreover, he was wearing a halter. Old, filthy, and tattered, but definitely a halter. And that was a shame because it could have got tangled on something and condemned this animal to a long slow death.

Rufus knew better than to try to approach it. Instead he got back in his truck and drove away. But to his list of errands he added a new item, which was that he made a detour to a part of the ranch where ordinary livestock operations were still underway and picked up some bales of hay. On his way back to the marble mine, he kicked one of these out of the truck and left it on the road just near where he had shot the wild boar. The horses were not in evidence, but when he came back the next day he found that they had demolished it. So he left another bale a few hundred yards farther up the road, trusting them to find it, which at least one of them did.

A week of this led to a moment when Rufus and the gelding came in view of each other, just a short distance down the road from the marble mine. Rufus avoided making eye contact, which only would have ruined everything, but instead turned his back and went quietly about his business, letting the animal understand that Rufus and his truck were the source of this incredible bounty of fodder.

Within forty-eight hours of that moment, horse and man were quietly and peaceably co-occupying the cool shady refuge before the opening of the mine, and Rufus was trying to figure out how he was going to supply this animal with water. He was going to need a bigger tank.

The horse seemed indifferent as to whether it would live the life of a wild mustang or hang around with Rufus. It was a pinto, mostly chestnut but spattered with white on the legs and belly. Mexicans, Indians, and horse fanciers had complicated names for different kinds of pintos, depending on the pattern of the spots, but Rufus had never made a study of it. A freeze brand—a row of white hieroglyphs on the left side of the horse's neck—marked him as a formerly wild horse that had at some point been rounded up and auctioned. A second brand on its shoulder marked it as property of one of the three older ranches that T.R. had, in the last few years, bought up and lumped together to form the Flying S. This animal must have got loose at some point during the merger and returned to its wild ways. The lack of shoes, and the condition of its hooves, suggested that it had escaped at least several months ago.

A good thing about horses, as opposed to some other domestic animals, was that they did not insist on being entertained. As long as they had food and water they would contentedly pass the time of day. So getting this animal put to rights was a side project that Rufus was able to prosecute in his spare time over a couple of weeks. He arranged for a farrier to come up and see to its hooves and get it shod, and for a vet to give it the recommended shots and pills and to care for some wounds it had presumably sustained during the conflict with the late boar. The ranch possessed a surfeit of saddles and other tack that was no longer being much used. This was made available to him when he let it be known that he had become the trustee of this particular animal. Online shopping caused a few other necessaries to show up at his locker down at High Noon. Once he had given the horse a day or two to get used to the look and the smell of the tack, he bridled and saddled him, whereupon he gave every indication of having been ridden in his past life.

Before mounting up for the first time, Rufus considered what the animal ought to be named. The Lone Ranger's horse had been Silver, but this creature was mostly brown. He considered "Copper." That, however, seemed like what a twelve-year-old girl would name her horse. Eventually he settled on Bildad, who in *Moby-Dick* was one of the three owners of the *Pequod*. In the Bible, he was one of the friends of Job, who came to him in the wilderness to lay a guilt trip on him.

T.R. had the habit, always surprising to Rufus, of shooting him a text message—usually swine- or drone-related—every couple of weeks. Most of these were just links or pictures. Rufus did not dare to suppose that this made him in any way special. He had sort of assembled the picture in his mind that he might be one of several hundred people in T.R.'s mental Rolodex who would occasionally be so favored, and that T.R. probably sent out dozens of such messages on every occasion when he got a snatch of time on the throne or whatever. Rufus was pretty sure that to send a whole lot of messages back the other way would get him blocked, or even fired. So he mostly kept his mouth shut. But a decent respect for another man's property did place him under an obligation to document Bildad, so he fired off a couple of pictures detailing the brands, as well as a few more intended to convey the general idea that the animal was safe and well cared for at the marble mine. T.R. seemed pleased by that out of all proportion to the actual monetary value of one stray horse. Rufus remembered their conversation about the importance of having good people on the property who could make decisions and manage things, and he reckoned that this was an example of that, and that, to the extent T.R. ever thought of him at all, it was now in a favorable light.

All pretty normal as Texas ranch management went, but with T.R. there was always some kind of extra, weird twist. One day in early October the peace and quiet of the marble mine were shattered by the strains of "The Eyes of Texas Are Upon You," which was the ringtone that Rufus had assigned to T.R., and only T.R. It was a video call and so Rufus propped his phone up against a stack of drone batteries on his worktable.

"I got a call from our Dutch friend," T.R. announced.

"Which one?"

"The jet pilot."

Rufus now had some cause to regret that he had turned on the video, because his heart started pounding and he was afraid that some consternation might be visible on his face. But if he was about to be fired for fornicating with the queen, there was really nothing he could do but take it like a man.

"How is she?"

"Fine. Sends her regards. Asked how you were doing."

"Oh, that's nice."

"I filled her in. She came up with an idea."

Just when he'd started to settle down, Rufus felt his face getting warm at this development. What possible ideas could Saskia be coming up with relating to Rufus? Did she want him back for more? Or did she hate him?

But it was nothing of the sort. "You ever see eagles up there?"

"You mean, like F-15s?"

"No, Red. Fucking eagles. The large birds."

"Plenty of buzzards." Rufus was visualizing a particularly energetic group of them who had lately been subsisting on the corpse of the boar that had attacked Bildad.

"I know that," T.R. said, somewhat exasperated. "It's *Texas*. There's gonna be buzzards. I'm not talking about those. I'm talking about eagles."

"I guess I've seen a few. More down toward the river."

"Well, a few years back, the Dutch had a program to train eagles to take out drones. They were worried about airspace security at Schiphol. Figured they could train eagles to pounce on any drones and take 'em down before they got sucked into a jet engine or whatever."

"Did it work?"

"No. Well, sort of. The eagles attacked the drones. But they were hard to control. I mean, they're eagles. Animal rights activists lost their minds, of course. But at the end of the day . . ."

"They just didn't need those darn eagles."

T.R. nodded. "There's other ways to take a drone down, as you probably know."

"Sure," Rufus said, "if you know it's there."

"Right, and at Schiphol fucking Airport you're gonna know, it's gonna stand out like a murder hornet on a pool table."

"Not so easy here," Rufus pointed out.

"Exactly, Red. Anyway, Her Majesty, with her interest in aviation, had a soft spot for that program and stayed in touch with some of the falconers who got let go when it was shitcanned."

"Falconers?"

"Folks who know how to wrangle these big birds. I guess 'Eaglers' would be a better term."

"Are there a lot of out-of-work Dutch falconers?"

"There's at least one," T.R. said, "but she's not out of work anymore, 'cause I just hired her."

While Rufus was absorbing that, T.R. was fielding an interruption from someone off camera, an aide or something who was in the car with him. "Okay, I stand corrected," he said. "She ain't Dutch. She's Icelandic."

"There ain't a lot of work for falconers in Iceland," Rufus said, thinking out loud, "so she worked on this Dutch project for a spell and then got laid off. But Saskia still has her on speed dial."

"Thordis, for that is her name, is in love with one Carmelita, a falconer in SoCal who has had her fill of hanging around garbage dumps."

"Why does Carmelita hang around garbage dumps?"

"That's where the work is. Crows go to dumps and pick over the discarded food, then drop chicken bones and whatnot on housing developments miles away. Carmelita gets paid, by homeowners associations and real estate developers, to use falcons to chase away the crows."

"Well, I can see how that would get old."

"I need you to go down to the airstrip tomorrow noon and pick up Thordis and Carmelita and Nimrod."

"Nimrod?" To Rufus this was a *Moby-Dick* kind of name, right up there with Bildad.

"An eagle. Don't worry, Nimrod travels in a box."

Nothing was ever simple and so Rufus ended up burning the whole next day on this. Thordis showed up first but Carmelita and Nimrod were delayed—something to do with logistics pertaining to Nimrod's box. Since the Flying S Ranch was nothing like a real airport, both of them were coming in on smaller planes that T.R.'s people had chartered. Rufus ended up cooling his heels in a prefab steel building next to the airstrip that had to all appearances been erected ten minutes ago. This looked like a warehouse from the outside but had all the amenities on the inside. There was a sort of lounge or waiting room with a view of the airstrip and the mountains beyond. Arranged around that were bathrooms, a couple of offices, and a conference room. When Rufus arrived, half a dozen men were seated around the table in there, having apparently just converged on the site in a couple of different planes that were now being refueled and fussed over outside. He couldn't hear what they were saying, not that it was any of his business. At the head of the conference table was a big screen running a video call with two talking heads on it. One was an efficient-looking woman probably in her forties. The other was Michiel, the ex-soccer player from Venice. Even though he couldn't hear a word of what was being said, Rufus understood the meeting. All the guys sitting around the table had come here on a mission. The overall boss was Michiel. Or to be truthful it was probably his aunt Cornelia, but she wasn't on the call. Michiel was hanging out in a nice room full of old stuff. The sun had gone down where he was and his handsome face was warmly illuminated by lamps. The efficient-looking woman was well pulled together but not glamorous. Her clothing and her bearing were formal. She had put more thought into her backdrop. So he could see that Michiel was basically calling the shots but had delegated the management to the woman. Michiel could be the informal nice guy who smiled and made witty comments, but the woman had to be all reserved and serious to prevent the whole thing from turning into a frat party.

After a little while the meeting broke up and the big screen went dark. The guys in the room stood up and began unplugging their gear and putting things back into luggage. One of them emerged towing a rollaway bag and went right outside and got on a plane. The others climbed into a big Flying S Ranch SUV and were taken off in the direction of Pina2bo. They all spoke English but not a one of them was a native English speaker. They must be from a mess of different European countries.

Based on the name, Rufus had been expecting Thordis to be built like an Olympic shot-putter, but he was wrong. She did have the expected level of blondness, and if anything was going a little overboard on sun protection. But she was maybe five feet five and built more like a badminton player. In birdlike fashion she constructed a nest of luggage and throw pillows at one end of a couch after she had exchanged pleasantries with Rufus. She did stuff on her phone for five minutes before pulling her enormous sun hat down low over her cheekbones and nodding off.

Inevitably then, Carmelita, who had the more delicate-sounding name, was a bit of a bruiser. She wore a tank top that exposed tattoos consisting predominantly of simple black rectangles covering large parts of her arms. She had long black hair in a braid. As a courtesy Rufus went out to her plane to see if he could help wrangle Nimrod's box, but it was plain at a glance that Carmelita could deal with it and didn't want him anywhere near her eagle. So he ended up towing her bag while she looked after the Nimrod containment system. "Box," while not wrong, hardly did it justice. A return trip to the plane's luggage hold was needed to fetch a large equipment case presumably containing other necessities of the falconer's trade. Rufus heaved that into the back of his truck while Thordis and Carmelita loudly and happily greeted each other. Both had kept Rufus at arm's length. He didn't take it personally.

When those two had come down a bit from the emotional high of seeing each other, and Rufus had got everything squared away in the back of his truck, they got into an interesting dance around the seating arrangement. The truck had a back row of seats accessible via small doors, both of which Rufus had left open in a manner that he hoped they would construe as inviting. Carmelita hopped right in and made herself at home, but Thordis—to the extent her facial expressions could be read under the reflective aviator sunglasses, spandex sun cowl, broad-brimmed hat, and half an inch of zinc-based sunscreen—deemed it maybe insensitive for the two guests to sit in back and be chauffeured. So she claimed that sitting in back might cause motion sickness and took shotgun instead. Rufus stayed impassive throughout. Making nice with these two was going to have a lot in common with how he had cultivated his relationship with Bildad. He just had to be cool and let them observe him. Which they did quite a bit of, during the drive. He could always tell when someone had googled him and pulled up the old newspaper stories.

On his way in to the airstrip this morning he had swung by the ranch office and picked up a fifth-wheel travel trailer that was supposed to be the lodgings of Thordis and Carmelita until better arrangements could be made. This jounced along behind them as the roads got worse and the mountains got closer. As a conversationalist, Rufus never got out of first gear until they came in view of the mine head and Bildad came strolling out to investigate. Thordis turned out to be a horse person. Apparently horses were a big deal in Iceland. So everything literally came to a stop as Bildad shoved his face into the back of the truck looking for hay, and jostled Nimrod's box. Carmelita urgently wanted out so that she could make sure Nimrod wasn't in a bad situation, but Thordis had to get out first because of how the seats and the doors worked. And Thordis had eyes only for Bildad. So after some delay the final leg of the trip was as follows: Thordis escorting her new best friend Bildad, followed at a distance by Carmelita carrying Nimrod on her arm—this involved a special glove—and finally Rufus in his truck idling along in low gear and towing the trailer toward a site he had taken the liberty of picking out that would keep it out of the midday sun while remaining far enough away from Rufus's trailer to give the ladies a feeling of privacy. Earlier those two had engaged in a minor public display of affection and then turned to look at Rufus to see whether he would spontaneously combust. He had given them the Bildad treatment. It seemed to have had the same reassuring effect. Which was all well and good, but

Rufus could have used a bit of reassurance himself as his formerly isolated hermit's retreat had suddenly acquired a horse, an eagle, and two ladies.

Just getting the trailer leveled and hooked up, and other such duties, consumed a fair bit of the afternoon. When the day began to cool off, he showed them how you could hike a couple of hundred yards back down the road and then double back on a path that ran steeply upward to the top of the peak that loomed above the mine's entrance. The maintenance crews who came out every so often to work on the radio tower or the solar array used ATVs for that leg of their journey. Thordis did it on Bildad, who turned out to be as sure-footed as might be expected of a horse who'd spent much of his life in the wild. Rufus and Carmelita trudged along behind, carrying the Nimrod containment device between them on a pole stuck through its top handle. When the top of the mountain came in view, Thordis rode on ahead, causing Rufus to feel a twinge of jealousy as to his formerly exclusive personal relationship with Bildad.

"How much does ol' Nimrod weigh?" Rufus asked, shifting the pole on his shoulder.

"Sixty-five hundred and eighty grams," came the answer from the other end of said pole.

Mere hours ago, this level of precision would have been startling to Rufus, but he had already seen enough of these falconry people to get the picture that they were a little different. He had to mentally convert six and a half kilograms to pounds, a skill he had developed in the army. It must be somewhere north of fourteen pounds.

Rufus shook his head. He might have whistled if his lips weren't dry. "Don't sound like much. But holding that on your arm for any length of time—" He risked looking straight at Carmelita. Deadpan, she flexed her bicep. As the tattoo rippled in the afternoon sun he saw traces of an older tattoo that had been covered up by the solid block of ink. Maybe in a few weeks, if she was still around, he'd ask her about that. For now he just tried to show due appreciation for Carmelita's upper-body development without seeming weird about it.

"You got to keep her close into your body to support her weight," she explained.

"Nimrod's a female?"

"Yeah. Females are, like, twice the size of males."

"Good to know."

"But then you get hit in the face a lot."

"Hit in the face?"

"When she moves her wings."

"I guess every job has its downside."

"What's the downside of your job, Rufus?"

"I'm waiting for that shoe to drop."

He had only been up to the summit a couple of times. Now he saw it through the fresh eyes of Thordis and Carmelita and he had to admit it was glorious. From here you could see much of the ranch, but the best view was south across the Rio Grande and into Mexico. The low sun had gone red orange. Everyone said Pina2bo would make for beautiful sunsets all around the world. He didn't know whether it was really having an effect yet. Whatever the cause, the angle of it was bringing out the shapes of the landforms bracketing the river. These stood out all the more crisply for being almost totally bare of vegetation.

"Yippee—ki-yi-yay!" was the exuberant verdict of Thordis. Seeing it through her eyes Rufus understood how it must look like a western. Not one of your low-budget spaghetti westerns but a big-budget wide-screen feature.

"Beats the dump" was Carmelita's more understated verdict as she got busy doing Nimrod stuff. Even a complete falconry ignoramus such as Rufus could guess that this was the best place in the world to be an eagle. Thordis dismounted to help out, and in short order they had Nimrod out of the box.

At first a hood covered Nimrod's eyes. But after conducting some pre-flight checks and unwrapping some raw meat—apparently some sort of incentive program—they took the hood off to expose Nimrod's eagle head, and her eagle eyes looked out to the south.

When T.R. had mentioned that an eagle was going to show up, Rufus's mind had immediately gone to the image of a bald eagle. But Nimrod was a golden eagle: all different shades of brown, edged with gold where the sunlight caught it just so. Her beak was edged with bright yellow, which Rufus interpreted as lips. Her eyes were yellow. The scaly dinosaur skin covering her feet was yellow. From her toes sprouted steel-gray talons. The toe and the talon combined were as long as one of Rufus's fingers.

Rufus convinced himself that the expression on Nimrod's eagle face was one of profound interest. But probably eagles always looked that way. She whacked Carmelita in the face as she spread her wings to take off, and then she was airborne, finding a thermal almost immediately above the sunbaked slope to the south.

"If you look thataway," Rufus said, making a blade of his hand and chopping it down along a certain azimuth, "you can see the parasails spiraling down and hitting the nets on the mesa." From this distance they were no bigger than dust motes in a sunbeam, but once you focused on them the eye was drawn to their neat spacing and orderly movement.

Thordis and Carmelita didn't respond. He glanced over and saw that they were having a private moment. So he turned his back on them. He'd noticed his phone buzzing a couple of times in the last few minutes, so he checked it.

> Shit's getting real in the North Sea!

This was from Alastair. It must be the middle of the night where he was. He had added a link, which took Rufus to some kind of scientific site. There was a map of the water between Britain and the west coast of Europe. Not a fancy map but a plain-Jane one that put him in mind of military documents. Numbered dots were scattered across it. When he scrolled down it was all just tables of numbers.

> What am I looking at?

Alastair responded with a five-digit number. This matched one of the labeled dots in the North Sea, between Scotland and Norway. Rufus zoomed in on that and gave it a tap. The result was a spreadsheet-like table of numbers. Left to his own devices for a while, on a larger screen, Rufus might have been able to make sense of it. Up here in bright sun on a screen the size of his hand was a different story. He panned around and stumbled upon a graph. The graph sort of meandered up and down for a while, but trending generally upward. Then at the very end it zoomed up to a high spike and then flatlined.

His phone buzzed again and a message from Alastair showed up at the top of the screen:

> That was a weather buoy until fifteen minutes ago
> What is it now?
> A projectile.

THE STORM

The storm was hitting in a few hours. Willem had put a coat of allegedly waterproof polish on his cowboy boots and gone in to The Hague to have breakfast with Idil Warsame. Apparently she'd read the weather forecast too and put on a very sensible pair of flat-soled boots. In spite of that she towered over him when she stood up to greet him; she must have been over six feet tall. She had classic East African features, reflecting a mix of sub-Saharan and Middle Eastern ancestries. She made a vivid contrast with her friend, a much shorter and stockier woman. Glimpsing them through the restaurant's window, already flecked with rain, Willem had assumed that the shorter person was from Africa. But when he got inside, and introductions were made, it became obvious that she was from Papua. Willem wasn't the first person to guess wrong. The reason Papua had been dubbed New Guinea in the first place was that, hundreds of years ago, a Spanish sea captain had mistaken the people who lived there for Africans.

Sister Catherine—for she was a Catholic nun—and Idil had grabbed a table in the back of the restaurant, next to an emergency exit, all likely pre-arranged by Idil's security team. These weren't obvious—they weren't slinging grenade launchers or anything—but Willem knew how to recognize them. They formed a gantlet spaced along the route that any assailant would have to take en route from the restaurant's entrance to the table where Idil and Sister Catherine were sipping their coffee.

Sister Catherine evidently belonged to one of those relatively modernized orders that didn't insist on wearing habits, though she was keeping her hair covered with a scarf. Now that Willem was across the table from her in better light he could see features that if he hadn't known better would have caused him to guess that she was Australian. The three of them together made quite the cosmopolitan table. In The Hague, this wasn't so out of the ordinary. People came here from all over because of the International Court of Justice and other global human rights initiatives. Most of them were here to represent populations that were being done wrong in one way or another, which was unquestionably the case with Papuans.

Willem looked at Idil and she looked at him and both of them simultaneously spoke the words "Beatrix says hello." So that broke the ice. To Idil Warsame, Willem, twice her age, would be an éminence grise of the Dutch establishment, a conservative parliamentarian turned royal retainer, and that could sometimes make the ice pretty thick.

Sister Catherine was most amused, and the look on her face spoke of great affection for Willem's first cousin twice removed. "You must be proud of her," said the nun, "such a firecracker!" Willem had trouble making sense of her English for just a moment until he got it that she was speaking with an Australian accent. Then it all snapped into place. "You'll have to be patient with my Dutch," she said, reaching across the table and touching Willem's forearm lightly. "Where I grew up, speaking it was discouraged."

Willem guessed her age at between forty and fifty. Papua's transfer from a Dutch protectorate to an Indonesian province would have been a done deal by the time she was born. So, yes, her schoolteachers might have been fluent in Dutch, but using the language wouldn't have been a great career move.

"We'll speak English," Idil announced in a tone making it clear this was not subject to debate. Willem had been warned to expect bluntness. "This is scheduled for one hour, and we're already ten minutes in; do you have a hard stop at the hour, Dr. Castelein?"

"I'm afraid I do. The weather."

"Time and tide wait for no man," Sister Catherine said.

Idil nodded and looked on the verge of delivering a statement but had to suppress frustration as they were interrupted by the waiter. While Willem ordered, she nodded at Sister Catherine, who began producing documents from a tote bag of impressive size. Willem guessed from its look that it had been produced by artisans in Papua.

"Look, there's no point dancing around," Idil said, as soon as the waiter was out of earshot. "It's obvious something is going on around T.R. Schmidt. Geoengineering."

"Where?" Willem asked. Not wanting to volunteer anything.

"Sneeuwberg. The highest mountain in Papua. Getting sulfur from there into the stratosphere."

Knocked me for a loop! was one of those down-home expressions that Willem had heard from the likes of the Boskeys during the sojourn in Texas. For a Somalian-Dutch woman to confidently announce that T.R. was pursuing additional geoengineering schemes on New Guinea's highest mountain knocked Willem for a loop. He somewhat prided himself on being ahead of the curve. An insider who knew such things before anyone else.

Idil must have read his stunned expression as *I can't believe you know about that!* instead of *Holy shit, first I've heard of it!* "I don't care," she said. "I'm not an environmentalist except insofar as it bears on those issues I *do* care about. Once we've gotten to the point where girls in developing countries are getting decent educations and being given control over their own bodies, then I'll concern myself with T.R. McHooligan's sulfur veil and its projected side effects. *Maybe.*"

"Some would say—" Willem began.

Idil ran him off the road. "That climate affects prosperity, and prosperity helps me achieve my goals. Of course. But climate's not getting better, is it? If some billionaire in Texas has a plan to make it less bad, fine."

"All right, well, glad we got that out of the way!" Willem said.

"Now, did your niece—"

"Cousin, technically."

"Did Beatrix talk to you about what she's been working on with my firm?"

For where there were courts, there were lawyers; and where there was an international court of human rights, there were law firms that specialized in that. Idil wasn't trained as a lawyer, but one such firm had set her up with a fellowship, endowed by a Bay Area tech zillionaire.

"No, she did not," Willem said. "But it's obvious. That branch of our family moved to Tuaba in the early days of the mine project and established a logistics business."

"Import of mining-related equipment from Australia, Singapore, Taiwan," Idil said, "as well as German equipment trans-shipped through Rotterdam."

"You've done your homework."

Sister Catherine was nodding sympathetically. "That is the way to survive, for people like the Kuoks. Become useful to a project that makes money for the powers that be."

Willem nodded. "Pre-war, it was oil installations in Java. Now it's the big mine in your homeland. The business has done well, but the political climate—well, I don't have to tell you about that."

Sister Catherine grimaced and nodded.

Willem continued, "Smart young people like Beatrix know that they have to get out before they get enmeshed in it."

"Or worse," Sister Catherine said. She was referring to the fact that people simply got murdered there, by Papuan freedom fighters, Indonesian secret police, or the latter pretending to be the former. "It speaks well of Beatrix that once she got out, and got a foothold in America, she's chosen to do some work on behalf of the people back home."

"I don't know much about the nature of that work," Willem admitted. "I know that the Papuans have been seeking independence for a long time. Which is complicated by the existence of the mine.

By the wealth that it represents. Which is not something that the powers that be in Indonesia are in any hurry to relinquish."

"Such things happen all the time in colonized countries that have resources, such as oil," Idil said. "What makes Papua unusual is that it's colonized by a country—Indonesia—that is itself a former colony. So your government—the former colonizer of Indonesia—has a special role that it could play."

"Here's where I issue the standard disclaimer that I work for the royal house—not the government," Willem said.

"And yet one reason you were selected for that role was your family connection back to the colonial past," Idil said. Calmly, without rancor.

"Fair enough," Willem said. "Is there some way, Sister Catherine, that I might be of any assistance in the work that you and my cousin are pursuing?"

"We seek independence," Sister Catherine said. "The Brazos RoDuSh mine has until now been a stumbling block. Like all mines, its fate is to become depleted over time. The less valuable it becomes, the lower the stumbling block. If what's next is that the site becomes a geoengineering complex—why, that looks to us like an opportunity."

Willem hadn't seen that coming. "How so? I'd have thought the opposite would be true. As you said, if the mine peters out, Indonesia covets it less. Becomes more willing to let Papua out of its clutches. But I'd think that if the site gets a new lease on life, all the old problems stay with you."

Sister Catherine was just looking at him. Not someone you'd want to play poker with. "It has to do with interests. *Cui bono?*"

"Who benefits?" Willem translated.

"Nation-states—some of which might be quite far removed from my homeland—that would benefit from injection of stratospheric aerosols from a high mountain near the equator will weigh in on our behalf. Even if, until now, they would not have been able to find Papua on a map."

Viewed from space, the twin gates of the Maeslantkering—the largest movable objects ever built—looked a bit like the pie-wedge-shaped wings that children scraped out in fresh snow when they were making angels. The curved rim of each pie wedge was the actual barrier meant to stand fast against the full force of a North Sea storm surge. Each was made to block one half of the width of the waterway joining Rotterdam to the sea. They came together in the middle, each swinging inward from a pivot on the embankment. The rest of the pie wedge—the triangle that spanned the 240-meter radius from the curved barrier to the pivot—consisted of massive steel tubes welded together to form a rigid trusswork. That structure transmitted the sea's force from the barrier to the ball and socket that might be thought of as the shoulder joint of the angel's wing. It went without saying that these were the largest ball-and-socket joints ever made. The balls were ten meters in diameter. They were cradled in sockets consisting mostly of reinforced concrete, set deeply into the ground and distributing the force into the surrounding earth through long concrete buttresses that splayed out like fingers and eventually ramped down below ground level to connect with massive subterranean footings.

Precisely curved trenches had been gouged into the banks to give the barrier arcs a place to abide during the long spans of time—on the order of decades—during which they were not actually needed. Like dry docks, these trenches lay below the level of the water, but most of the time they were kept empty, leaving the barrier arcs high and dry so that they could be inspected and maintained. The arcs themselves were hollow boxes, normally full of air. Once floated into position across the waterway, they could be flooded so that they would sink and form a seal against the floor of the channel.

The whole complex had been formally christened in 1997 by Saskia's grandmother and never actually needed until ten years later. After that, it had sat high, dry, and motionless—aside from regularly scheduled annual closures just to make sure it all still worked—for another sixteen years, when another surge had come along. Today, for the third time in its history, they were going to close it to protect the Netherlands from what was predicted to be the largest surge in the North Sea since the disaster of 1953. It was the first such closure in Saskia's reign.

Thanks to a program that had been set in motion by Willem in the days following her speech to the States General, Queen Frederika had spent much of the last three weeks touring the country in support of disaster preparedness. Now, trying to get Dutch people to prepare for disasters was a little like trying to get English people to watch football on the telly or Americans to buy guns. They were receptive to the message, to a degree that made the queen's efforts on this front completely superfluous. The very inaneness of it was just the sort of thing that caused anti-royals to roll their eyes and ask what was the point of maintaining such an institution if its work was to be that insipid. For all the good she was doing, Queen Frederika might as well have stayed home at the palace tweeting about muffin recipes. And yet, given the run of close calls and scares the household had experienced last month, this was actually just the ticket. Any royal-hater or royal-skeptic, any tabloid journalist who had become excited or suspicious by the whiff of mystery and possible scandal that had surrounded the queen around the time of her visit to Texas and the geoengineering kerfuffle on Budget Day, was now catatonic with boredom after twenty consecutive days of watching Her Majesty remind pensioners in Zeeland not to get trapped in their attics. She had gone to little towns along the Rhine to inspect their dikes. She had stood in the rain stomping the royal shovel with the royal gum boot. She had nodded thoughtfully as civil servants had pointed to maps of evacuation routes. She had laid wreaths on the graves of people who had drowned in 1953.

During the first half of that three-week span it had all bordered on self-parody. Even steadfast fans of the House of Orange had thought it was a bit much. The weather had been as non-threatening as it could be. But then it had turned decidedly autumnal. Not in a cozy way. Heavy rainfall inland had begun to raise the levels of the rivers. And long-range forecasts produced by computer models had raised concern about a low-pressure system forming in the North Atlantic, south of Iceland. This had intensified and begun to move toward the chute between Scotland and Norway. Curiosity had turned into excitement, then concern, then dread. Tides were going to be exceptionally high to begin with—simple bad luck, that. This thing was then going to push a monster storm surge ahead of it.

So they'd known for days that they were going to have to close the great gates of the Maeslantkering. Across the sea, the same precaution was being taken at the Thames Barrier below London. It was only a question of when the linked computer models that ran the thing would decide to pull the trigger. For along with all the other superlatives that characterized that system, it was also the world's largest robot.

They had a pretty good idea of when it would happen. And once it started, it took a while. Advance notice had gone out to mariners so that they would have time to move their vessels in or out of the gates before they swung shut. Saskia wanted to be there for at least part of it, as the capstone of her disaster preparedness jihad. So she went out a bit early and, to kill time, did an informal drive-by inspection of the nearby Maasvlakte.

This was an artificial peninsula that protruded, wartlike, from the nearby coast into the North Sea. Its purpose was to support an immense container port. Back in the age of sail, oceangoing ships had been able to glide all the way up to the ancient center of Rotterdam, some twenty-five kilometers inland. But as centuries had passed and ships had gotten bigger, they'd tended to drop anchor farther downstream. Accordingly the port had grown in that direction. The culmination of all that had been the creation of this

Maasvlakte, an anchorage that could be reached without entering the waterway at all. It was thus capable of servicing the very largest container ships in the world: absurdly enormous things, double the width of the biggest ship that could fit through the Panama Canal, that boggled Saskia's mind whenever she came out here to look at them. It was the place where the economy of China made a direct umbilical connection to Europe. The ships were two dozen containers wide and drew twenty meters of water when fully loaded. Some of them, fresh in from Asia, would unload part of their burden here just so that they would ride higher in the water, making it possible for them to move on to smaller and shallower European ports.

The Maasvlakte comprised several docks. One of them was named after Princess Frederika—a nakedly political move on someone's part, and yet it had given her a proprietary attitude about the place. There was an access road where you could go and park without getting in the way of port traffic, so that was where her three-car caravan went, just to see the sights and kill a little time before they got the go-ahead to drop in at the Maeslantkering, which was just a few kilometers upstream.

The Maeslantkering's status as the largest robot in the world seemed less exceptional when viewed from the Maasvlakte. The entirety of the Port of Rotterdam was a giant machine. Not that it didn't have plenty of greenery—you could hardly stop green things from flourishing here—but the soil in which it grew was just another component of the machine, graded and shaped and tamped just so to channel water or to support unbelievably heavy objects. The greenery had a purpose too: to keep important dirt from washing away. Decades ago one might have seen long strips of grass running parallel to the roads, railways, canals, and pipelines that serviced the docks. Those were still there, but they had all been turned into picket lines of wind turbines, all of which today were facing into the winds coming down out of the north as harbingers of the storm and spinning around as rapidly as their robot control systems deemed prudent. For space on the skyline they competed with looming queues of container cranes, parked oil rigs, and refinery stacks. These were arranged in layers that were interleaved at various distances as far as one could see, eventually blurring into a silvery mist.

The operations of the Princess Frederika Dock and its siblings around the Maasvlakte were as automated as technology and unions would allow. She could still remember cutting the ribbon on this thing as a teenager. One of the senior executives who'd been allowed to have lunch with her had reminisced about his former job deciding which container should be placed where on the cargo ships of his day: how to be sure that the load was balanced, and that it would remain balanced while the ship was being loaded or unloaded, while keeping in mind that the vessel might have to make several stops to discharge all its containers. He'd done it with index cards. The courtiers in attendance had tried to shut the poor man up, fearing that the princess would be bored, but she'd found it fascinating. Nowadays, of course, it was all done by software. When a big ship from China pulled into the Yangtze Canal—the deepest berth of all the Maasvlakte, the one closest to the sea—the over-reaching cranes that plucked the boxes from it and placed them on trucks or railway cars were robots that knew exactly what was in each container and where it needed to go. And the trucks themselves, shuttling containers to and fro, were for the most part driverless. Saskia, who had at one point in her young life been subjected to a battery of tests whose purpose was to find out whether her eccentric interests were a result of being on the autism spectrum, loved to just come here and watch the machine run, somewhat as a monarch of another era might have amused himself playing with his tin soldiers.

Things were a bit different today, though, because there was some concern that some areas of the Maasvlakte might get swamped by the storm surge, and so efforts were underway to move vulnerable stuff inland. And on the water, ships were making efforts to get out of town. In the middle of the Yangtze Canal loomed *Andromeda*, one of a fleet of Chinese container ships that vied for the honor of being the largest in the world. She'd apparently wound up her business ashore and was now being nudged away from the quay by tugboats. In old-school ports it might have required some hours before she could get underway, but here at Maasvlakte she already had a straight shot to open, deep water and needed only push down on the gas pedal, as it were. A couple of launches were shuttling back and forth between the shore and a pilot's door on her flank, presumably ferrying last-minute personnel and necessaries that had been left behind in the rush to get out ahead of the storm.

"I'm going to go survey the disposition of the enemy forces," Saskia announced and hiked off in the direction of what appeared to be a long low mound of gray sand running in a straight line along one edge of the port and separating it from what looked to be absolute nothingness on the other side. Any Dutch person would immediately recognize it as a dike, although most dikes were covered with grass. Other than a couple of lonely, opportunistic shore birds, this thing was as dead and colorless as the surface of the moon. Guessing her intent, the security team scrambled out of their cars and ran to catch up.

It started as a low flat beach of fine wet sand, then suddenly got steeper and coarser, with a vaguely scalloped shape that probably showed where a grab dredger had opened its clam shell bucket to dump huge gobs of muck. This was new work that hadn't yet settled to its natural angle of repose. Saskia helped that process along in a small way by wading and staggering up over knee-high mini-cliffs and touching off small avalanches. The levee was higher than it looked from a distance, which on a day like this was reassuring. Eventually she got to the point where she could see over the top, though. And what she could see—"The enemy forces"—was a whole lot of nothing. Visibility was cut off by mist at a distance of maybe a kilometer. The gray sea was churning and heaving, but there weren't a lot of breakers coming in against this steep artificial shore. Those that did attack it were flicked away by the dike's outer armor. For, soft as it was on its inner slope, the side facing the sea was another matter. The smallest and lightest objects that met the eye there were reinforced concrete cubes two and a half meters on a side. And, as had been explained to her at a level of detail that would have rendered most royals catatonic, this was only the uppermost layer of an engineered system that reached deep below the water.

But it wouldn't stop a rogue wave. One of those could come hurtling silently out of the mist and claw the queen off the dike at any time, as her security team well knew. Looking to her right she was pleased in a way to see that, if this were to happen, Amelia would share the same fate. Willem was on her left, performatively checking his watch. But when the royal photographer finally caught up and began snapping, he melted away. She hadn't actually come up here to have her picture taken, but she knew it was inevitable. And it would make for a fine picture.

If the Netherlands was a castle and the enemy was the sea, then this artificial island they were standing on was part of the bailey: the lightly fortified outer fringe, never meant to be held against a serious assault. It was now time for Queen Frederika to retreat inside the motte: the higher, more easily defended ground within. And along the way she was going to slam the gate behind her. Or rather she was going to stand in a suitably photogenic location and do absolutely nothing while half a million lines of C++ code slammed it for her. The drive to the Maeslantkering complex—or, to be precise, the half of it that was attached to the waterway's south bank—lasted only a few minutes. Still, when they got out of their cars there, Saskia had the feeling that the wind had picked up. A reminder that storms built slowly and predictably, except when they didn't.

The complex was surrounded by the same sorts of security

barriers and surveillance tech that in other countries might have been used to seal the perimeter of a nuclear submarine base. Not that it was a military target per se, but if some mad saboteur had gotten in there and vandalized a key part of the system, it would have been expensive to repair. If it had happened just before a big storm, and somehow prevented a gate from closing, the resulting damage would have been comparable to a nuclear strike.

Of course, they couldn't control the waterway itself, so their worst nightmare right now was a ship sinking in the channel right between the gates. Vessels large and small had been moving through in both directions during the hours since the notice had gone out. It was hard to miss the military and police deployment on land, sea, and air, keeping many eyes on every vessel that moved between the gates and making sure they kept moving. Tugboats were standing by to push or pull anything that got in the way.

Once they were through security they found themselves in a very un-Dutch world of things that were so preposterously enormous that even Texans might nudge their cowboy hats back on their heads and say, *holy shit, that's big*. There was a vast open triangular area whose sole purpose was to have nothing whatsoever on it: this was the zone across which the wing would sweep once it began moving. The trusses themselves were the size of seventy-story buildings that had toppled over onto the ground. The nerve center was a horseshoe-shaped building that rose above the level of any conceivable storm surge, commanding the waterway from a sweep of windows. Above that rose a reinforced-concrete tower topped by radars and antennas. A red box, small in comparison to everything else, housed the motor that would actually drive the barrier out into the channel. This, understandably, had come in for a lot of loving attention from maintenance crews during the last few days. As Saskia was whisked from her car toward the south bank's control center, she exchanged hand waves with a couple of crew members who glanced her way.

Looking up at the huge white vertical expanse of the barrier she had a moment of vertigo and put a hand on a railing just to steady herself. Then she realized that she was rock solid. It was the barrier itself that was moving. They'd already flooded its dry dock and set it afloat. The whole thing was bobbing ever so slightly, restrained by the 240-meter-long arms, but, thanks to those ball-and-socket joints, free to move up and down.

The control room proper was as small and spare as a ship's bridge. Everyone there was, of course, busy. But there was plenty of room along the panoramic sweep of windows where Saskia could see everything and yet not be in the way. Willem remained with her, and so did the photographer. The rest of her entourage stayed outside to watch from a green embankment, lashed by rain. But around here you were always lashed by rain. The photographer had already got pictures of the queen in her bedraggled and wind-swept incarnation up on the dike. Check. This was going to have a more formal vibe. Like christening a ship. Fenna had patched her up in the car. She hadn't gotten too ruined while quick-stepping from there to the building's entrance. Nothing she couldn't fix up in the women's toilet without professional assistance.

The actual closing of the gates was so smooth and quiet that she'd have missed it if she'd looked the other way. The only real clue it was happening was a mild rise in the chthonic thrumming of the motor in the red box. Stepping up to the window, she saw the barrier arc extruding into the channel. Looking across to the opposite bank, half a kilometer away, she saw its opposite number doing likewise. There was still that slow heaving as it responded to waves and currents in the channel, but its swing was as steady and relentless as the hand of a giant clock. The photographer danced around, trying to get the right angle, and finally clambered up on a table so that he could get both the queen and the front gate of her kingdom together in the frame. Slowly the gates severed the waterway. Off to the left, on the opposite shore, was the termi-nal at the Hook of Holland where the ferries went to and from England. That stretch, which was on the sea's doorstep, was still torn by whitecaps and shrouded by spray sliced off the waves by a scything wind. But to the right, upstream of the gates, the wild waves were subsiding. Big breakers seeking entrance to her country were slamming into the barrier arcs and sending up explosive gouts, but all those tons of steel soaked up the impacts as if they were gnats ticking into the windshield of Rufus's truck. She supposed that if you could go and rest a hand on the seven-hundred-ton steel balls in the shoulder joints you might feel a slight tickling in the tips of your fingers.

It would have been satisfying to hear a great boom and snap as the two gates touched in the middle, but that probably would have meant sloppy engineering. The low purr of the motor cycled down. The engineers whose job it was to make sure that those things worked could go home tonight and enjoy a beer. Other machinery was now engaged to open valves and flood the barrier arcs. The only way you could tell that was happening was that less and less of them showed above the churning surface. The long trusses, formerly parallel to the ground, tilted downward slightly. One had to use one's imagination a little to visualize the flat bottom of those arcs settling down along the full width, making contact with a channel bottom painstakingly sculpted and inspected to be as flat as a hockey rink. The seal wasn't perfectly watertight—nothing ever was—but it would hold for a day until the surge had passed.

The only way she knew it was done was by a sort of lightening in the atmosphere of the room, a change in the tone of the low conversation, a few laughs. She looked at Willem, hoping to share the moment with him, but he was fixated on his tablet.

A senior engineer approached, peeling off a headset and then self-consciously tucking his gray hair into place. The Netherlands *really* was just a constitutional monarchy. She had no real business here. She probably shouldn't have come here at all. If she'd been swept off the dike by a rogue wave, the same things would have happened at the same time. This man had no actual duty where she was concerned. But. He had to do it. "Your Majesty," he said, "I am pleased to report that the Maeslantkering is closed."

Willem had acquired an acute and finely calibrated sense for that moment when things suddenly got weird. Sometimes, of course, he could still be taken by surprise, as with the pigs on the runway in Waco. But more often than not this served him in the same way as the whiskers of a cat stalking through a maze in the dark. Today it had begun in the car during the brief drive back from the container port to the Maeslantkering. He had received a secure text from his contact in the security service:

> Meeting with him?

Then, a few moments later:

> Can't wait to hear the latest!

> Meeting with whom? Willem responded, already feeling badly far behind in the conversation.

> Winnebago

This was the code name that they had settled on for Bo.

> I've been killing time at Maasvlakte with Crash.

> You didn't cross paths with Winnebago?

> Are you trying to tell me he was there? At Maasvlakte?

> LOL I thought you knew he was there and had gone there to "meet him?

> No

> Well, he went there this morning.

> Maybe I'll touch base with him later when I get back.

> You won't. Winnebago has left the country.

> ???

> He took an Uber to Maasvlakte this morning and boarded a Chinese container ship on Yangtze Canal.

> Andromeda?

> Yes

> Saw the ship Willem responded. You couldn't not see something like that. He remembered the launches shuttling to and fro minutes before the *Andromeda* drove out into the North Sea, and now wondered if he might have been able to spy Bo aboard one of them, had he taken the trouble to peer with binoculars.

> Did not see Winnebago he added. Nor would have he expected to! This seemed an odd way for a man like Bo to travel. But what did he know? *Andromeda* could carry more than twenty thousand containers. Maybe Bo had his own personal shipping container kitted out like a penthouse. Hell, maybe he had fifty of them. Wouldn't have made much of a dent against twenty thousand.

> You're still at the Maeslantkering with Crash?

> Yes

> Let's catch up after the storm passes.

On the way back they got stuck in traffic. Saskia, sitting in the back seat of a car with Willem, idly flicking through messages on her tablet, suddenly asked, "What do you know about New Guinea?"

It gave him the start of his life. "What!?"

"You have family there, don't you?"

He frowned. "Is this about Idil Warsame?"

"She's from Somalia."

"I know, but . . ."

"Totally different place! I'm talking about *Papua*."

"I understand, but what causes you to bring up this topic today of all days?"

"Do you remember a few weeks ago when I showed you some selfies that Cornelia had sent me?"

"From that island in Albania? Yes."

"Well, the selfies have just kept on coming. It wasn't just a weekend cruise down the Adriatic. That yacht of hers can really haul ass. Thirty knots cruising speed, apparently. Faster if you don't mind a few bumps."

Saskia angled her tablet so that Willem could see it, and began flicking through a series of images, all apparently texted to her by Cornelia during the last three weeks. They told a little disjointed story.

The yacht passed through a waterway that was pretty obviously the Suez Canal. Cornelia went on a camel ride.

There were photos of spectacular landforms to either side of the Red Sea. Then a quick cut thousands of miles south and east: some low-lying coral reefs. Cornelia getting a tour from important-seeming locals. Lots of pointing and frowning.

"The Maldives," Saskia explained. "One of those countries that is going to end up completely underwater."

"Why are they squiring her around? It's not like she's a fucking ambassador."

"Anyone who shows up in a yacht like that and expresses interest in their plight becomes an ambassador," Saskia said. "Honestly, Willem, it's not as if any of the *real* ambassadors are giving these poor people the time of day."

"All right, fair enough."

Then another abrupt cut to Cornelia on an elephant in Sri Lanka. "She likes riding things," Willem commented. Saskia kicked him.

A photo of Cornelia at a Dutch war monument in Indonesia caused Willem to give out a little grunt of recognition. "You weren't kidding," he said. "She must be halfway around the world from Venice by this point."

"She's just getting started." The next selfie showed her having cocktails on the yacht's deck at sunset with Sylvester Lin and Eshma, the skyscrapers of Singapore in the background. In spite of himself Willem felt the little pang of emotion that comes from not being invited to someone else's party.

After some Indonesian island tourism the yacht anchored before a modern city of very modest scale, perhaps Waco-sized. "Don't bother guessing," Saskia said. "It's Darwin, Australia."

The next photo contained no buildings or signs of human activity at all for that matter. Just the alluvial fan of a river splitting a wall of jungle like a gray axe head.

"Aaand that would have to be New Guinea," Willem said. "I see where all this is going now."

"Then I won't keep you in suspense," Saskia said and began advancing more quickly. The next photo showed the yacht's helipad, because of course Cornelia's yacht would have one of those. A jet chopper was perched on it, painted in the corporate livery of Brazos RoDuSh.

The next few pictures had been shot out the chopper's window. Some snapshots of jungle far below. A small town carved out of said jungle. "Tuaba," Willem said. The fact that he would know this drew a curious look from Saskia. High mountains rising out of the jungle in the distance. And finally a huge hole in the ground, a spiraling roadway carved into its sloping walls, the size of it incomprehensible when you saw the motes spaced out along that road and understood that they were the largest trucks on Earth. "The famous mine," Saskia said. "Even I know that."

"*Your* famous mine."

"Touché."

The chopper came down on a pad staffed by Westerners slinging assault rifles. That plus the adjacent machine-gun nest left little to the imagination regarding the security climate prevailing around the mine.

The last selfie was just Cornelia and T.R. Schmidt, both in Flying S baseball caps, with New Guinea's tallest mountain as backdrop. T.R. was strapped with a shoulder holster, the weight of a big semi-automatic pistol under his left arm balanced by several loaded magazines under the other.

"The end," Saskia said.

"Yee haw!" Willem called out. "When was this photo sent?"

"Yesterday."

"Well, that explains a lot about my breakfast."

There was this delicious sense of having barred the door and battened down the hatches. After seeing to it that the queen was safely back at Huis ten Bosch, Willem got a lift back to Leiden in a government car. He Bluetoothed his phone to its sound system and, after apologizing to the driver, pulled up "Riding the Storm Out," a song by R.E.O. Speedwagon and a guilty pleasure from his misspent youth. He played it loud, once, and confirmed that it still rocked. Then he enjoyed spicy Indonesian takeout at home with Remigio in front of a YouTube feed simulating a crackling fire and went to bed mildly but pleasantly buzzed from a crisp New Zealand sauvignon blanc.

He was awakened at four in the morning by a call from his father in Louisiana making him aware that one-half of the Maeslantkering had caved in and was allowing the sea to flood Rotterdam and points inland. Hundreds of people were already missing. Most of them were probably dead. The storm hadn't even peaked.

Willem was dressed and on his way downstairs before it even occurred to him to wonder whether he and Remi were in danger. The natural and artificial waterways of this country were a maze. Could the floodwaters hook around through central Rotterdam, come north, and inundate Leiden?

Always an important question to ask oneself before surrendering altitude; and it came to him when he was halfway down the stairs. Remigio, who'd helped him pull his things together and get going, was standing at the top of the stairs in gym shorts and bathrobe, watching him quizzically.

"Could we get . . . flooded here?"

There turned out to be advantages in being espoused to a history professor. Remi shook his head. "Leiden predates the reclamation of the Haarlemmermeer."

"Of course."

"It was above sea level then. It's above sea level now . . . probably."

"Sea level," Willem said, making air quotes. He glanced down at his cowboy boots. After Texas he would never be able to use the term again with a straight face.

Remi sighed, taking his point. "Well, there is that. But if I had to pick a spot to wait this out, it'd be here or where you're going." Meaning The Hague. "Now, go. I'll stay above 'sea level.' Take care of yourself."

"Don't—"

"Get trapped in the attic. I know, I follow the queen's Twitter feed too."

Willem spent a few minutes comparing wait times on various ride share apps. All disastrous. Then he tried to sort out the train schedules, which had been thrown into disarray. Finally he just got on his bicycle and rode the few kilometers. He didn't even have to pedal. The wind pushed him there. He went straight to Noordeinde Palace because it was clearly going to be that kind of day. He changed into dry clothes and turned on all the TVs. The predominant image was of the north gate of the Maeslantkering, the barrier arc stove in, the truss crumpled, the whole thing peeled back, the North Sea rushing through the gap with such power that the south gate was bucking and shuddering in the backwash. He'd had time on the ride down to plot out in his head the shape of the waterways around Rotterdam and to form the opinion that, from there, the water was going to generally head south and inundate parts of Zeeland. Not that the flooding of Rotterdam wasn't a pretty big fucking disaster in and of itself.

In passing he saw a news flash from the BBC. The Thames Barrier had been circumvented by the storm surge and the water was rising in London. The drainage systems meant to handle storm runoff from north of the city had been overwhelmed and were backing up, flooding places inland. The Netherlands, he knew, would soon be facing a similar problem. They had no way to stop the great rivers that flowed in from fucking Germany. Those had to reach the sea eventually. One of their possible outlets was now flowing the wrong way. All the others had been temporarily dammed off to hold back the storm surge.

The question was—now that he'd reached his office, changed clothes, turned on the TVs, and got up to speed—what could Willem actually *do*? And the answer was nothing. During his former career he'd have had duties as a member of the States General on various committees. Now he was an aide to a theoretically powerless monarch. And *she'd* already done everything *she* could do by going about telling people to be ready for a disaster that was at this moment actually unfolding. There would be no repeat of her impromptu performance on the foam-drowned beach at Scheveningen. In a situation like this she had two jobs: to stay put, and to shut up, with the possible exception of maybe issuing a brief statement later in the day. Once the crisis had abated—tomorrow at the very earliest—they could arrange some photo ops and wreath layings.

So there was literally nothing for him to do. No reason for him to have gotten out of bed. He could watch TV from home.

> HOW COULD IT HAVE GIVEN WAY SO EASILY !? his father wanted to know.

Others would be asking the same question. Willem had a vague idea as to how, but he needed to confirm it.

Alastair had a rock on his desk. It had been there the whole time Willem had known him. Had it been quite a bit smaller, it might have been mistaken for a paperweight. It was an irregular oblong, smoothed by wave action, and totally unexceptional. Willem had asked him about it once and Alastair had explained that it had been retrieved from a lighthouse off the Oregon coast. The lighthouse keeper had heard a loud noise in the middle of the night and climbed the stairs to investigate. Halfway up was a window that had been smashed out by this rock. The window was a hundred feet above sea level. The only way the rock could have ended up there was by being entrained in a huge wave that had broken against the cliff on which the lighthouse stood. Alastair had somehow acquired the rock and kept it "as a memento mori" to focus the minds of shipping company executives who wanted to know (a) why insurance was so expensive and (b) why enormous ships sometimes ceased to exist without warning or explanation.

Alastair was looking as frazzled as one might expect. His extremely short hair required little maintenance but he hadn't shaved in a while and was just wearing an old T-shirt and a hoodie. "*You'll* be wanting to know why the Maeslantkering caved in" was how he started the conversation. His emphasis on the first word in that sentence, combined with a general air of distraction, suggested that Willem was just one in a long and ever-fluctuating queue of calls. "The fact that you called *me* hints that you suspect a rogue wave was the murder weapon."

"And what say you?" Willem asked.

"I say yes. Just by process of elimination."

"How so?"

"Those gates were engineered to take steady loads. Dead loads. The sea presses against the barrier with a force that gets larger as the storm surge gets higher. We call it a 'surge,' which sounds like something fast and violent, but it isn't. It's slow and predictable. Engineers can calculate the forces, work with the numbers. Oh, they add in a fudge factor to account for the odd wave. That is a stochastic figure that mostly stays within predictable limits. What hit the Maeslantkering a couple of hours ago was probably orders of magnitude outside the bounds of what those engineers planned for, what, forty years ago. And it was a live load, which just makes it all much worse from a structural engineering standpoint. The thing simply broke. There is not much else to say."

"And it's just bad luck," Willem said.

"That, sir, is my stock in trade. I am the bad luck man. Gandalf Stormcrow."

"Such a wave *could* have hit anywhere," Willem said, mentally organizing the press release. "Today it just happened to hit the Maeslantkering."

"It probably got funneled, intensified, by the entrance to the channel. We can analyze it later when there's more evidence. It might have diffracted around the Hook, bounced off the Maas-vlakte dike, picked up steam as the channel narrowed. You can't *predict* this sort of thing, sadly, but doing the postmortem is easy. Like you can't predict a car crash but it's easy to reconstruct it from skid marks."

"I'll let you get on with what must be a very busy day," Willem said, as he saw Alastair reaching for the red button that would terminate the call.

> Rogue wave, Papa. Impossible to predict. Impossible to plan for.

> WHERE IS THE BACKUP SYSTEM !?!?

> You know there isn't one. There can't be one.

> THESE DEFENSES ARE ANCIENT

Willem let the exchange lapse. Eventually his father would see that all the *other* such defenses were doing fine, despite being "ancient." Though a dike had been overtopped by waves in North Holland and would have to be repaired.

On the spur of the moment, he messaged T.R.

> How do you talk to people about randomness? Stochasticity?

> You don't. It's a fool's errand T.R. answered, as if he had just been sitting there waiting to hear from Willem.

> I guess that makes me a fool :(

> The Chinese had it right. The Mandate of Heaven and all that.

> So . . . wait for the stochastic outlier . . . then turn it into an opportunity?

> Worked for them!

Willem was getting ready to point out that it hadn't worked so well for the *outgoing* emperors. But as soon as T.R. had mentioned China, Willem had remembered Bo's weird, hasty departure from the country yesterday. Bo. Who had known, at least a week earlier than anyone in the Netherlands, that a big storm was coming. His scalp was tingling as nonexistent hairs attempted to stand up.

> I am sorry about your country's loss. Please give my best wishes to the queen T.R. added.

> Thx was all Willem could manage to thumb out.

THE BARRACKS

Another advantage of being supported by the Indian military was having access to Indian military intelligence. Sometimes this could mean having satellite imagery piped into augmented-reality glasses, but in other cases it was as old as the Bhagavad Gita: for example, talking to the caretaker about sneaky ways to get into the building.

For a couple of decades around the turn of the century, the barracks had been little used. During that time the army had hired a local guy, a Tibetan, to go up there every so often and look after the place. Major Raju had found that guy, and that guy had supplied the information that there was a coal hole. Most people nowadays would identify it as a manhole and would guess that it led down to a sewer or electrical vault. This thing had been set into the pavement right next to an otherwise featureless stone wall on the down-valley side of the barracks so that coal could be dumped from a truck down a chute into a sub-cellar that contained the boiler. The last of the coal had been burned twenty years ago, and the boiler long since devolved into a pile of rust. If the Chinese volunteers had any sources of heat at all, it must be from propane they'd brought with them.

One of the reasons Laks had gone up to the top of the ridge and peered down on the barracks through binoculars had been to look—without being too obvious about it—at this coal hole, which was easily visible. Even though temperatures rarely got above freezing, the warmth of the sun on that side of the building melted the snow and exposed the manhole cover.

The Chinese squatters had barricaded and fortified anything on the ground floor that looked like a door or window, but they'd done nothing at all about the coal hole. It was of smaller diameter than an ordinary municipal manhole. Laks could not have fit through it. But Gurkhas could.

They had to wait a day because of fresh snow. In the meantime, Raju provided Laks with the one new item he needed. This involved dispatching a jet helicopter to a shop in Kashmir, four hundred kilometers away, but was considered worth the expenditure of fuel.

That night the School's Gurkhas—who were normally rock throwers, but not today—came up the valley under cover of darkness. Following in their wake were the irregulars. The moon had come out after the snowstorm and was illuminating the western slope like a blue spotlight, so any attempt to come down from the ridge would have been obvious.

Indeed the School's stick-fighting contingent made use of that by mounting a fake attack (Major Raju, a walking thesaurus of military jargon, called it a "demonstration") shortly before the sun was due to rise over the opposite ridgeline. Laks stayed behind, prone on a sleeping bag just behind the ridge crest, watching his red-turbaned fighters descending through the fresh powder on snowshoes. They did that slowly, awkwardly, and obviously. But the fact that they were doing it in the hour before dawn, on the last campaigning day of the year (more snow was expected tomorrow, followed by more snow), made it *look* a hell of a lot like an attack to the Chinese sentries peering up at them through binoculars, as well as to various drones that soon took to the air.

Halfway down the stick fighters "got bogged down" and "encountered unexpected delays" due to "even deeper than expected snow," ruining their ostensible plan. Namely, to coordinate an attack with a breakout attempt by the beleaguered garrison on the top floor of the barracks. Those people went ahead and launched their attack anyway. This went absolutely nowhere, but in combination with the looming threat of Big Fish's School, apparently convinced Lan Lu that it was the real deal.

But who knew, really? Laks couldn't guess what was in Lan Lu's mind. All he knew was what he could see. And what he saw was the Gurkhas stealing through the shadows around the barracks—which seemed deeper and darker now, in partial daylight, than by the light of the moon—right up to the building's blank stone wall, where they were invisible to the occupants. In short order they had pulled up the iron lid of the coal hole and disappeared into it. Half a dozen of them, one after the other like fish on the same line. After which—a beautiful detail—the last of them pulled the manhole cover back into place above him.

There was nothing to see now for a minute and so Laks shifted focus to his stick fighters and verified that they had miraculously worked free of the unexpected difficulties.

Somewhere on the Internet there must be feeds from Chinese webcams on the ground floor of the barracks. These would no doubt make for entertaining viewing later. But the next event that Laks could actually see was his squad of irregulars, spearheaded by Sam and Jay, sprinting across the parking lot toward a side door. Which must mean that the Gurkhas had achieved their next objective, which was to climb up out of the boiler room and, by surprise if possible, violence if necessary, get to that door and open it.

So the raid—in the kabaddi sense of that term—was now on. The raiders had crossed the line into the enemy side and were tagging as many as they could before time expired. Which would probably be as soon as the Blue Herons got a grip on the situation and counterattacked in earnest.

The hardest part of the planning phase had been to get Sam and Jay to wrap their heads around the concept of tactical retreat. Apparently that just wasn't in the soccer hooligan DNA. Laks had been forced to reach centuries into the past and mention some of the battles in which Sikh cavalry had used the tactic with success. As soon as Sam and Jay had got it through their heads that they were permitted to go on fighting *after* the tactic had succeeded in drawing the enemy into the open, they grudgingly warmed to the idea.

So that was what happened next. In kabaddi terms, the raiders had done all the tagging they were ever going to do and now desperately had to get back to the safe side of the line. So out of the barracks door they spilled, some just sprinting in a reasonably convincing pantomime of blind panic, others fighting a rearguard action to keep the doorway clear.

People in combat obeyed instincts. The chase instinct was overwhelmingly powerful. In the School's wake came the Flock, spilling out into the open. The only member of the Blue Herons who wasn't in a retaliatory frenzy was Lan Lu himself, recognizable at a distance because his stick was a sort of cobalt blue with golden tips. Other members of the Flock had red or black ones according to seniority.

Laks stood up on the snowboard that Major Raju had procured for him and launched himself down the slope. His great stick, made of Kevlar laminate in a rocket factory outside of Delhi and maculated with corporate logos, made a fine balance pole. His turbaned gatka warriors, now most of the way to the bottom, had been warned over their earbuds. They looked up to see where he was coming down and cleared a gap in their line for him. They used their sticks to wave him toward it like the guys at the airport.

This was a pretty good board on pretty good powder—certainly an improvement on anything Laks had enjoyed at the crowded and waterlogged ski areas just outside of Vancouver. By agreement, Major Raju had procured a *used* board from a second-hand shop in Kashmir, and they'd scuffed it up a bit to make it look more ragtag, optics-wise.

Lan Lu certainly didn't see it coming. Or if he did he didn't understand how fast Laks was traveling. Not a winter sports aficionado, apparently. Anyway Laks was on him before he could get his guard up. Laks cut the Blue Heron's legs out from under him as he schussed by, then banked into a hard U-turn on the flat and came back around toward his fallen foe. He pulled up well short, though, to give himself a few moments to kick out of his hard plastic boots—not a good fit with light-footed gatka movements. As he was doing this he had a clear view past Lan Lu and back up the western slope, now in brilliant red sunlight—all the sunrises lately had been glorious—to check on the progress of the School. They were almost down, to the point where some members of the Flock were wheeling to meet them.

Toward Lan Lu he trudged in his stocking feet through knee-deep snow. The Blue Heron was up, dusting snow off his long changshan robe. Good. No broken legs. Keeping an eye on Laks, he looked around until he saw where his blue-and-gold stick had fallen, then picked that up. Looking past Laks he held up a hand to stop three Blue Herons who had been rushing to their master's defense. With his eyes he drew their attention to the barracks. Indian defenders from the upper stories were now emerging from it to close the jaws of the trap.

Then Lan Lu raised his stick and faced off against Laks and settled into the stately guard position that Laks had admired in so many YouTube videos.

Because of what happened afterward, Laks didn't get to watch Pippa's supercut of the fight until much, much later. But it was certainly his impression until close to the end that he was getting his ass handed to him. There was a reason Lan Lu had been at the top of the leaderboard for most of this year. Laks had been so focused on his opponent's close quarters techniques that he wasn't ready for the standoff fight that actually ensued. They never seemed to close to within two meters of each other. Lan Lu wasn't using stick technique at all. He was using spear technique. This turned out to work damned well. He had a way of making his stick flex around Lak's defenses and tag him in the ribs or the side of the head. Which was confusing and upsetting, because you don't expect to get hit in the side, or sometimes even in the back, by an opponent who is six feet away and in front of you.

But the weakness of all spear technique was what happened when you got close—too close for the spear's head to be of any use. Laks remembered Sam's first fight against the Bonking Head at Pangong Tso when he had just barreled in, absorbing damage until he was inside the other guy's preferred range. Laks finally managed to do that. He even put his big steel *kara* to use blocking, then deflecting a strike. Which brought him in range of the feared nerve center strikes of Lan Lu's kung fu; but unbeknownst to Lan Lu it brought Lan Lu in range of the short powerful strikes that Laks had grafted on to traditional gatka. Lan Lu got in one terrific shot behind the angle of Laks's jaw that nearly felled him and left the whole side of his face numb. But Laks fell toward Lan Lu, rather than away from him, which probably saved the day. For out of that collision Laks was able to emerge with a series of punches, using the last six inches of his stick as a force multiplier, that drove Lan Lu back shouting with pain and surprise and toppled him into the snow. He held up a hand. The fight was over. Big Fish had won. Money was changing hands in Vegas. Territory was about to change hands up here.

EINDHOVEN

I t had been a long time since Willem had read an official document produced on a typewriter. This one bore the date August 14, 1962. Its author was Freeman Dyson. Each page was stamped SECRET at top and bottom, but someone had gone through with a Sharpie and drawn a slash through each repetition of that word; apparently it had been declassified at some point in the last half century.

Not that it mattered in his case; he, and everyone else in this shipping container, had the clearances needed to read this document whether it was classified or not.

PROGRAM FOR A STUDY

Implications of New Weapons Systems for Strategic Policy and Disarmament

. . . followed by a quotation from William Wordsworth's *Sonnet on Mutability*, which was apparently the sort of literary touch you could get away with when you were Freeman Dyson and it was 1962. At a glance—which was all Willem had time for, as the presentation was getting underway—this was a survey of eight hypothetical new weapons systems that military planners in the United States had been worried about during the Kennedy administration. Some of them (supersonic low-altitude missiles, small portable ballistic missiles) still looked quite relevant. Which presumably explained why this chap from MI6 had gone to the trouble of reproducing the document and handing out copies. He'd flown over from London this morning and would fly back in a few hours. He was addressing a group of half a dozen Dutch colleagues in a SCIF—a Sensitive Compartmented Information Facility—near Eindhoven Airport. Inevitably, this particular SCIF was a portable unit built into a shipping container. This meant it was only eight feet wide, which made it a cramped environment for the invited guests. Most of them were military or intelligence. Willem wasn't, but he'd been invited anyway, for reasons that had not yet been made evident to him.

"You've probably heard of the Tsar Bomba," said the Brit, who was going by Simon.

"The biggest H-bomb ever detonated," said the minister of defense.

Simon nodded. "The Russians set it off about ten months before Mr. Dyson wrote this." He put his hand on the document. "The interesting takeaway was that despite its fifty-megaton yield, it didn't do as much damage as expected. Why? Because the earth is hard and the atmosphere is quite yielding—and only gets more so the higher up you go. So the explosion sort of ricocheted off the ground and went the only way it *could* go and basically punched a hole through the atmosphere and dissipated its power into the void. For those in the know, the lesson learned was that making bigger bombs was a waste of resources. But Freeman Dyson understood that large bombs could still have military effect provided you worked out a way to detonate them in a medium that would contain the blast and absorb its energy, rather than just venting it into outer space. Such a medium is water. The scenario he describes here, starting on about page 6, is that a very large hydrogen bomb—much bigger than the Tsar Bomba, even—is deposited on the floor of the ocean offshore from the coastal region to be attacked. This is easy to do covertly using a submarine or just kicking it off a ship. When the bomb is later detonated, all its energy is deposited into the surrounding water, creating an artificial tsunami that crests over the nearby coastline and, to borrow a homely phrase from the Yanks, breaks a lot of things and hurts a lot of people. And I do mean a *lot*, in Dyson's scenario. No one ever accused that man of not thinking big."

"Are you working up to tell us that we got nuked the other day?" asked one of the Dutch intelligence analysts, half serious.

"No. As you know, a nuclear explosion would have left isotopic evidence. It also would have done a lot more damage than just wrecking one half of the Maeslantkering."

"Then how is this old document relevant?"

"If you scan down to the bottom half of page 7 you'll see that Dyson says that the techniques for carrying out such an attack could be developed and rehearsed using H.E.—high explosive— charges in place of nukes." Simon adjusted his glasses and found the relevant quote: "'This part of the enterprise would not be expensive and would not require a high level of technological sophistication. Moreover, the installation and testing program could rather easily be camouflaged and kept secret.'"

Simon flipped the document over facedown, as if to emphasize that he was now going off Dyson's script. "So. Let's take nukes off the table altogether and talk about that 'part of the enterprise' to use his wording. He's envisioning a relatively small, cheap pilot program that consists, for example, of packing ANFO or TNT into a shipping container and shoving it off a ship at sea."

Since this meeting was being held *in* a shipping container, everyone looked around and tried to imagine every cubic centimeter of the space packed full of high explosive.

"Later," Simon continued, "you set it off and measure the result. What *is* the result? Well, the water above the explosion is going to bulge up. From there, waves are then going to spread outward. To give you a feel for magnitude, a standard shipping container full of TNT gives you rather more than a tenth of a kiloton of explosive yield. In round numbers, it would require a hundred of those to give you a Hiroshima-sized explosion. But even a single one, if the water isn't too deep, will produce a bulge and a system of waves."

"Spreading *outward* in all directions," Willem said, "if I'm following you correctly."

"You are, Dr. Castelein," Simon confirmed.

"Then it seems to me that the waves would spread out and dissipate."

"From a single such detonation, yes," said the visitor. "Now,

Mr. Dyson, or any other physicist who made it out of his sophomore year, would have known about constructive interference—the phenomenon where two wave crests, meeting at a given place and time, will sum to produce a much higher crest. That much is old hat in the world of mathematical physics. But what is different now, as compared to 1962, is that we have computers. Precision guidance systems. Split-second timing and communication technology. So. Our whole mentality around weapon design has changed. In Dyson's day, a Cold War military planner might have used a nuclear weapon to take out a whole city, just to destroy a single factory. Overkill, to be sure, but the best they could manage with unguided ballistic warheads. Today we would use a cruise missile that would strike a key component of that factory—say, a power transformer or a meeting of senior management—with a precision measured not in meters but centimeters. Much cleaner, much less collateral damage, much cheaper. Likewise, a modern approach to Dyson's 1962 scenario would be to get rid of the nukes straightaway and stick with those containers full of H.E. Drop those in precisely known locations not far from the target. Detonate them in a precisely timed sequence. The individual waves from any one detonation don't amount to much. By the way, that's a feature, not a bug. During a storm they aren't even detectable. They don't rise above the noise floor. But if you've set it all up right, there is one and only one location where all those waves sum together and create what seems to be a rogue wave, enormously bigger than all the others. If it just happens to cave in the Maeslantkering, why, the North Sea then rushes in and does your work for you."

Simon paused for a little while. Willem looked around the table. He could tell that some of his Dutch colleagues had known in advance what was going to be said, and others were surprised. Willem was one of the latter. It would take him a few minutes to absorb all this. But it *did* seem to answer the question of why he'd been invited. It must all have something to do with Bo, and his sudden departure from the Maasvlakte on the morning of the storm. Willem, in other words, hadn't been brought here to be briefed. He had been called as a witness.

"Are you suggesting that the flooding of Rotterdam and Zeeland was the result of a military attack by a foreign power!?" asked an incredulous army general. Clearly not one of those who had been briefed in advance. Therefore, just as surprised as Willem. And yet Willem had something of an unfair advantage. The series of weird encounters he'd had with Bo during the previous few weeks had inoculated him.

Simon said, "Yes. A similar attempt was, we think, made on the Thames Estuary, but it wasn't as effective because that is a more sheltered waterway. You can't come at it from as many angles." As Willem and everyone else knew, Simon was engaging in a bit of understatement here. There had been a lot of flooding in the Thames Estuary.

"Is there evidence? Other than this?" asked the general, slapping the Dyson report.

Simon carefully avoided making eye contact, in a way that suggested, to Willem's perhaps over-sensitive mind, that confidential sources and methods were involved. He would not speak of these. But he had not come unprepared for the question. "You would expect," he said, "to see seismographic evidence of those detonations. And we have seen it. It's quite clear. It tells us where we might go and search, were we so inclined, for debris—shattered containers or other residue left on the bottom of the sea. No doubt we shall. We'll coordinate any such efforts with the Royal Dutch Navy, it goes without saying. But we don't *need* to, really. The spikes on the seismograph tracings are as distinct as the sound of rifle shots in the forecourt of Buckingham Palace."

"So they—whoever they are—know that we know."

"I should say so, yes."

"What's the *motive*, though?" asked a woman from the Dutch counterintelligence service. "I mean, it's not as if they—whoever *they* are—can then follow up with an invasion of our country. It has no military value to anyone. It seems like a pure act of vandalism."

Her counterpart from Dutch foreign intelligence was sitting across the table from her. Janno. Willem had known him for decades. And it was clear that he'd been briefed on all this in advance. "We think it is a political gambit. An effort to sway the public conversation around climate change."

"But everyone already knows about climate change! Even the right wingers have changed their tune since"—she glanced toward Willem—"since the queen's speech. About geoengineering."

Since everyone was now looking—awkwardly, guiltily—at Willem, he felt it made sense to speak up. "The great question of our time is no longer whether climate change is happening but what to do about it. The right wing has recently snapped around to a hardline pro-geoengineering stance. Since then we're seeing hints that Shell and other oil companies are going to follow their lead. It has been made obvious to me personally during the last few weeks that China is providing covert support to those political actors in our country who advocate aggressive deployment of geoengineering schemes such as what is going on in West Texas. The disaster at the Maeslantkering can only strengthen their hand politically. I can't imagine what it's like right now to be Ruud Vlietstra."

"Since you mention the prime minister," said the defense minister, "I have some news, which none of you will have seen because we are in a SCIF and our phones don't work. As of—" She glanced up at the twenty-four-hour clock on the wall. "Literally ten minutes ago I am the *caretaker* defense minister. Ruud's out. The coalition has dissolved. He has notified the queen that a new government will need to be formed."

"Has Ruud been briefed on all this?" asked the woman from counterintelligence, rattling her copy of the Dyson paper. "Does he know he was—we were—set up?"

"Yes," said the now ex–defense minister. "But it doesn't matter. It doesn't help to know."

"So there will be a new government," Willem said. "Forming it might take months. The parties such as the Greens who are on the record as anti-geoengineering are likely to be shut out. Because the electorate will now be calling for strong measures. That means that Martijn van Dyck and his lot will probably be in. It's just arithmetic."

Heads turned toward Simon, who studiously ignored them. It was up to the Dutch people to work out among themselves what it all meant for them.

"Getting back to the question of motive," said Janno, "China—obviously this is all China—has spent a little bit of money and taken some modest risks and claimed the scalp of the Dutch government."

"Probably the British government as well," said Simon. "Things are headed in that direction."

Janno nodded. "The next governments of both those countries are likely to be pro-geoengineering to a degree that would have made them politically radioactive until a few days ago. In Texas, T.R. McHooligan has achieved a similar result, transforming the conversation around geoengineering by simply doing it. What does all this mean for China? It means that they can go on fueling their economy with coal and suppress its nastier side effects with geoengineering schemes of their own, while enjoying political cover from several countries in the West that might otherwise have raised a fuss. Good value for the money, if you ask me."

THE LINE OF ACTUAL CONTROL

The easiest way for the Chinese to retreat was up the valley toward the glacier, which is what they did. Following them, and pushing the Line of Actual Control in that direction, wasn't the smart move from an overall strategic perspective. The smart move was to ignore them and instead advance east up the slope of the ridge on the formerly Chinese side of the valley. The Line could thereby be fixed, at least for the winter's duration, in a more defensible spot. Besides which, stats-wise, it would add a larger number of hectares to India at China's expense. It was a way of running up the score. So as soon as they got things sorted at the barracks and made a quick count of who was injured and who was fit to keep going, they began to climb. Laks, who had borrowed snowshoes from one of the School who had suffered a broken cheekbone, led the advance. Spreading out to his left and right were his stick fighters, his rock throwers, his irregulars, a dozen survivors of the barracks siege, and various supporters and streamers. They were, at the moment, the living human embodiment of the Line. And the only thing that was holding back the Line's advance was snow, an uphill slope, and a lack of oxygen consequent to being at six thousand meters above sea level. But as Laks had discovered on that first exhausting climb up the Rohtang Pass, you just had to not stop. Just keep putting one foot ahead of the other. If you then had to pause and gasp in ten breaths, so be it.

He knew perfectly well that the Gurkhas could have scampered past him and beaten him to the top, but they politely refrained from doing so. Instead they spent their oxygen exchanging war stories from this morning and laughing. So Laks got there first, unless you counted the three video drones from competing Indian television networks hovering up there to record the planting of the flag.

Some ridges, some mountaintops, teased you with false summits. This was not one of them. It was a wind-sculpted snow cornice with an edge like a hatchet. One moment there was nothing in Lak's field of vision but fresh snow. The next he was looking a hundred kilometers into China.

Closer, of course, there was another valley much like the one behind him. Which was to say, new territory left open by another disappearing glacier. There was nothing down there.

No, wait a minute, there was a line of trucks, maybe four of them, invisible until now because they'd been buried in snow. Now, though, men were clambering over them, peeling back the tarps. The men were wearing those big fur-lined hats with the earflaps. Chinese winter military issue. Definitely regular army, not volunteers. For a moment Laks was afraid that the equipment on the backs of those trucks was going to be rocket launchers or something. That the cease-fire was finally going to be broken and that he would be the first casualty in a new shooting war. But the equipment didn't look like weaponry. It was just flat round panels mounted on pivots. Like solar panels? But they were not aimed at the sun.

They were aimed at him.

Crickets wasn't the right way to describe the sound. Crickets were quiet and peaceful and far away. Outside your body, anyway. This was inside his head. As if the cricket had hatched from an egg inside his skull and was sawing its serrated leg directly against his eardrum. He tried to wipe what he assumed were tears from his eyes, for his vision was blurred. But his eyes were dry. His view of China, the valley, and the trucks pivoted downward like a trapdoor as he toppled backward.

INFORMATEUR

The last power of any real significance that had been stripped away from the Dutch monarchy had been that of appointing the *informateur*. When a government had dissolved, someone needed to go around and have conversations with leaders in all the significant political parties and run the numbers and try to work out what the next ruling coalition might look like. When that picture began to come into focus, the *informateur*, as this person was called, would make a graceful exit and be replaced by a *formateur* who was usually the next prime minister.

The work of the *informateur* simply could not be done if all his meetings took place in the public eye, on the record. This gave it a smoke-filled room vibe that clashed with the overall style of Dutch politics. They couldn't do away with the role, because it really was essential to forming a new coalition. But they could at least take it out of the hands of the monarch. They'd done so by an act of the States General in 2012 and the then queen had, of course, accepted this further curtailment of her already minimal powers. It was still a bit of a sore point for those who wanted the monarchy to retain some power. But it satisfied those who looked askance at kings and queens, while bolstering the position of those on the other side who could now point to the monarch's utter lack of political power as a reason why keeping them around was harmless.

The upshot of it all was that during the day after the fall of Ruud Vlietstra's government Queen Frederika had no responsibilities whatsoever in that sphere and so was able to do what was considered proper for a monarch in the wake of a natural disaster, namely to visit shelters and ladle soup for people who, had this happened in a Third World country, would be called refugees. She was photographed shaking her head in dismay at the wreckage of the Maeslantkering, reading books to children sitting on the clean carpet of a high-and-dry shelter, nodding her head and looking extremely supportive as a coalition of charitable organizations kicked off a fund drive.

Her lack of any serious responsibility, combined with the fact that she didn't want to mess up any of the television shots, led her to shut her phone off during much of each day. Thus it was that while driving back from a visit to a breached dike in the eastern part of the country she turned her phone back on to discover the following series of messages from Lotte, delivered over a span of about half an hour:

> OMG ARE YOU OUT OF YOUR MIND

> ????

> I can't believe you did this

> crying

> Going to watch it now—finally downloaded. Don't know if I will ever speak to you again!

> ???

> WTF!?

> Don't remember any of this

> FUCKING WEIRD

> NEVER HAPPENED

> AM I GOING INSANE

> OK never mind all that mean stuff I said earlier

> WATCH IT AND CALL ME!

. . . followed by a link to a video.

Once Saskia had got through all of that, she saw a message from Willem:

> We need to talk about that video. 850,000 views and counting.

So far the most unsettling aspect of all this was that the normally cool and detail-obsessed Willem hadn't bothered to supply a link or even to give any specifics beyond just calling it "that video." He seemed to assume that Saskia would know what he was talking about.

Saskia hated doing this kind of thing in the car. She much preferred to just look out the window and enjoy the fact that she didn't have to do anything. But it seemed that duty was calling. So she pulled her tablet out of her bag and, fighting back a powerful sense of dread, brought up the video that Lotte had linked to.

It appeared to be handheld cell phone footage. It took only moments for Saskia to recognize the time and place: this was the dunes in back of Scheveningen beach on the morning of the foam disaster a few weeks ago. Probably just one of many such videos that had been shot and uploaded by random bystanders when they had recognized Saskia and Lotte. This one had been shot while Saskia had been shaking hands with members of victims' families who had gathered under the canopy to await news. It seemed that the streamer had been sort of weaving through the crowd, holding the phone up above his head, trying to keep the queen in frame, and not too far away, with varying levels of success. But at one point he managed to get a well-framed shot of Saskia looking almost directly at the camera, talking to someone who was not in the frame.

"One hates to be right about such a frightful tragedy," she said, "but sadly this is just the sort of thing I have been trying to warn the prime minister about, if only he would listen. I worry that the next such disaster will be ever so much worse."

Saskia had, of course, never uttered those words. She never *would* utter them. Though it was her face and her voice in the video, the diction was wrong. Like listening to Queen Elizabeth talking fifty years ago, running it through an English-to-Dutch translation algorithm.

Fake Frederika listened to some indistinct response from off camera and nodded.

"That is what I am saying. They—the current cabinet—are all

of that generation that believes the answers are to be found in riding bicycles to work and recycling newspapers. That's how out of touch they are. If they could see what I have seen while conducting my own research, they would understand that the climate crisis is a gushing wound. We are bleeding out. We need first to apply a tourniquet. Do we leave it on forever? Of course not. But it keeps the patient alive long enough to get him to hospital and stitch up the wound properly."

Fake Frederika listened again, then nodded. "Yes. Yes. Of course. I'm speaking of geoengineering. That is the tourniquet. It gives us time to put in place more long-term solutions such as carbon capture and emissions reductions. But anyone who doesn't think we need it right now is living in an ideological bubble."

Real Saskia ran the video back to the beginning and watched it again. Then a third time. Her phone was going crazy. She turned it off.

She'd read accounts of out-of-body experiences, where a patient who was at death's door, or pumped full of drugs, would seem to leave her own body and look down on herself from a corner of the room. This was like that. Including the part about feeling like she was high. Given that this was the single most scandalous thing that had occurred in the Dutch monarchy in many decades—a sitting queen meddling directly in electoral politics, basically calling for the downfall of the elected government—she ought to have been a lot more horrified than she was really feeling at this moment. Instead her basic impulse was to giggle at the fantastic absurdity of it all.

First things first. She texted Lotte.

> Your memory is correct, darling. I never said any of that as you know. I don't mind your being upset when you first heard about it. It is quite convincing.

> It is a deepfake Lotte answered.

Saskia had heard the term and knew what it was. But it had never occurred to her that anyone would go to the trouble of using such a technique on her, of all people. The president of the United States, maybe. The CEO of a big company. But her?

> Saw it she texted to Willem.

> Meet you at HTB? he responded.

> Yes. En route.

> Scrambling a video crew. We can have a video up within the hour. Doing some research on deepfakes. Writing a statement. Is Fenna with you?

> In the other car, right behind me.

> I'll coordinate with her.

> See you soon.

It wasn't often that the gates of Huis ten Bosch were surrounded by a scrum of photographers being held at bay by police. That was more of a Buckingham Palace kind of thing. But today was an exception. As they drove through it, Saskia just stared fixedly ahead. She didn't want to make any gesture, even any facial expression, that could be picked up and distorted by the media. But once she was through the gate and gliding across the private grounds of the palace, she wondered whether such precautions even mattered. It was all very 2010 to be thinking that way. They could create whatever they wanted in the way of fakery; it didn't matter what she actually did.

At least she didn't have to explain any of that to Willem. He knew the truth. He'd been there in that tent at Scheveningen. He was intermittently visible in the background of the deepfake video. He just walked into the palace by her side, Fenna bringing up the rear with a case slung over her shoulder. Without discussing it they turned in the direction of a certain room, lined with books and art and memorabilia, with windows looking out onto a secluded garden. It was the room they always used when they wanted to film a video message from the queen to the people. The film crew had it all down pat. They knew where to set up the lights, where to find the power outlets that wouldn't trip breakers, how to set the curtains and the diffusers and soft boxes just so to prevent awkward reflections and glare. Just down the hall was a bathroom where Fenna could ply her trade. Some outfits had been yeeted from the royal closets and laid out for inspection. But while Fenna was applying Face Two—the preferred Face for in-studio video shoots—they came to an agreement that the new video would look more legit if Saskia did it in the same outfit she'd been seen in earlier today during her appearance at the busted dike and just now while driving in through the gates. That settled, Saskia turned her attention to the script that Willem had written out for her and scanned it as best she could while turning her head this way and that in obedience to Fenna's commands.

In the end there wasn't that much to say, beyond the basics. Getting ready took longer than actually doing it. They'd moved the customary chair into its customary position and tweaked the lights to work with the overcast daylight coming in from the garden. Saskia sat in the customary demure pose, elevated her chin, and turned toward the teleprompter. Fenna beheld the royal visage in a monitor, then darted in to tuck a hair strand and snuff out a shiny bit with powder. Then Frederika Mathilde Louisa Saskia just read it straight out, one take.

"Earlier today, a video was released on the Internet that appeared to show me saying certain things about the cabinet and its positions on the geoengineering question. This video is a fake. A very sophisticated fake that was produced by digital manipulation of real footage shot on that sad day in Scheveningen and doctored by unknown persons apparently seeking to disrupt the normal functioning of our democracy. We do not at this time know who produced this forgery or what their motives might be. An investigation has been launched, but definite results may not be forthcoming for a long time, if ever. In the meantime, my message to you as queen is that my commitment to the basic principles of our democracy remains unshakable and that under no circumstances would I, or any other Dutch monarch, dream of interfering in domestic politics in the manner that is falsely depicted in the fake video.

"As anyone who follows Dutch politics will know, the government was dissolved yesterday and has become a caretaker cabinet. All this happened in a manner consistent with our constitutional norms and with no involvement or influence from me. Likewise, the process of forming a new government, which will unfold in coming weeks and months, shall be one in which I shall be a mere bystander. In keeping with our norms, I shall await the verdict of our duly elected political parties and respect the outcome of that process as has always been the practice in the Netherlands since the creation of our system of government in its modern form. In the meantime I would warn all Dutch citizens to beware of fake videos that appear to depict me, or any other prominent persons, making statements with political significance."

"Spot on" was Willem's verdict.

"I thought I tripped over some of the words halfway through."

"Just makes it seem more authentic."

"What's that supposed to mean?"

"Someone producing a deepfake would probably try to make it look perfect."

"Is that the sort of thing we must worry about now?"

Willem didn't respond. Probably because it was an idiotic question. Willem nodded to the streamer, who nodded back and popped a memory card out of the camera. "I'll clean it up, slap on the bumpers, and have it ready for review in half an hour," he said.

"Faster would be better," Willem answered with uncharacteristic snappishness.

"Putting out a garbage amateur video with bad sound and color isn't going to help given the nature of the problem we are trying to solve," pointed out the streamer on his way out of the room with the memory card between his knuckles.

Willem had no answer for that. But after the man had left he looked around at the crew, taking the lights down and pretending they hadn't heard. Then he looked at Saskia and gave a little toss of the head that meant *we need to talk in private.*

It took him about a quarter of an hour to lay out the basics of what he had learned yesterday in the SCIF at Eindhoven.

"Sorry to break this to you now," he said, "when there's this whole other crisis happening." He gestured back in the direction of where they had shot the video.

"Do you really think it's a whole other crisis?"

"No. Of course not."

"Because obviously all this is coordinated."

"Yes."

"The deepfake must have been produced some time ago. They—whoever made it—could have released it earlier. But instead they held it back until the day after the government had fallen apart on its own."

"I hadn't considered that," Willem said. "You're right."

"Why would they hold it back? Because if it had been released earlier, *before* the government had fallen, then the fall of the government would be blamed on *me*. It really would lead to a constitutional crisis in that case. Deservedly so."

Willem nodded.

"But," Saskia went on, "if it is released after the fall of the government is a fait accompli, then I can't really be accused of unconstitutional meddling . . ."

"Only of being blunt and outspoken. Saying out loud what ordinary sensible people are already thinking."

"The voice of the people," Saskia said. "Which I have never claimed to be. But it seems the role is being thrust upon me. Presumably by whoever sabotaged the Maeslantkering."

"That thing was the pride of the nation," Willem said. "A symbol of our engineering prowess. Its destruction a huge psychological shock. The kind of thing that makes people sit back and reconsider everything. Whoever did it is creating an opportunity to reshape the way our politics works for a generation. Setting you up. Not to take the fall. More the opposite."

"Well, I'm afraid whoever that is is just going to have to be disappointed," Saskia answered.

Someone knocked on the door. "It's ready," came Fenna's voice. "A triumph!"

"We're coming," Saskia called back. To Willem she said, as she was getting up, "First things first. Let's get this done and then we can continue this conversation."

A few rooms down the hall, the video crew had patched the streamer's laptop into a big flat-panel screen and cued up the edited video for their review. Like all the queen's official videos it opened with a "bumper" depicting the royal palace, with the arms of the House of Orange superimposed. Then it cross-faded to Queen Frederika sitting in that chair. And then she said the words she'd said. Then it cross-faded to the "outro."

Heads turned toward Saskia. In truth, she'd barely seen it. Her eyes had been open and aimed at the screen, but her mind had been all over the place. "It's fine," she said, "put it up."

That command was aimed at the royal webmaster. An antiquated job title—"social media coordinator" would have been more up-to-date—but it was common in royal courts to have outdated remnants of a bygone age. If Saskia could be guarded by men in bearskin hats riding horses, why, she could as well have a webmaster.

Accordingly, everyone looked at the woman who bore that title. She was oblivious.

She was staring at the screen of her tablet, completely aghast at some new horror. To be perfectly honest, that was the usual emotional state, and the customary facial expression, of anyone who worked in the social media industry. But even by those standards she looked shocked.

She finally became aware that all attention was focused on

her. She tried to say something but couldn't get it out. Instead she flicked her fingers over the surface of her tablet and spun it around so that everyone could see it.

It was playing a video. The same video they'd just finished watching, or so it seemed through the intro. When that cross-faded to show Queen Frederika sitting demurely in her special chair, however, she was wearing a different outfit. One she had, in fact, worn recently in front of cameras. But she had never sat in that chair and delivered a speech while wearing it.

Nor had she ever spoken the words that she now, on this video, appeared to speak.

"I come to you this afternoon with an apology and a promise."

"Where did you get this?" Willem demanded.

"It showed up on YouTube fifteen minutes ago!"

Everyone shushed them.

"Earlier today, a candid video was posted in which I was caught on film expressing certain views concerning the prime minister and the cabinet that should not have been said out loud by a reigning monarch. For that I apologize. Regardless of the frustration that I—along with all other Dutch citizens—may from time to time experience regarding our political process, it is not my place to utter such words in public. I did so thinking that I was merely expressing private sentiments to a small number of family members bereaved by the loss of loved ones in the disaster at Scheveningen. I was naive not to realize that my words might be captured and put up on the Internet where they have now become part of the public record. Again, for this I apologize.

"In retrospect, the disaster we experienced that day was but a foretaste of the much more devastating events of the last week— events that have among other sad outcomes led to the fall of the government. We must now look ahead to a period of at least several months during which a caretaker cabinet will look after the day-to-day running of the country while a new governing coalition is organized. It is the tradition during such periods that the caretaker government should avoid making major policy decisions or budgetary commitments. That is all well and good—in normal times. These times, however, are not normal. The nation is in the midst of a crisis that cannot be addressed *without* decisive action. I do not believe that we can afford to sit on our hands for several months during the endless negotiations that, in normal times, are needed to organize a new governing coalition. I therefore give you my promise that I will do everything that lies within my strictly limited powers as a constitutional monarch to speed that process along and goad the bickering parties into action. To that end I am putting forth the name of Willem Castelein to serve in the role of *informateur*. While I lack the statutory power to fill that office, nothing in the Grondwet or the law prevents me from stating my personal opinion as to who is best qualified to serve in that role. I hope that the leadership of the political parties will agree with me and name him to that position without delay, as a way of getting the process off to a faster than usual start. With that momentum established, I believe that Dr. Castelein will be able to shepherd a new and effective government into office in a matter of weeks, or even days—not months. Thank you and good evening."

Willem, aware that all eyes were upon him, took the risk of checking his phone. He had silenced it completely. But the sheer volume of messages was proof that they weren't just imagining this. It wasn't just a dream. Looking at the screen of the device was like staring into the chute of a slot machine that had just hit the jackpot.

"We have to release a statement—" Saskia was saying.

"To the effect that the totally convincing apology we just watched is actually a fake apology for the earlier totally convincing video that was also fake?" asked the streamer.

Maybe it was just his imagination, but Willem couldn't help feeling that some of the eyes now upon him were less than entirely friendly. He had felt a bit of this yesterday in the SCIF. To some Dutchmen he would always be an inscrutable combination of American and Chinese. Being gay didn't exactly help. His family links to China, his fluency in Mandarin, his recent interactions with Bo—which he had been at pains to put on the official record, to avoid the slightest hint of undue influence—all these could suddenly begin to look suspicious now that this second deepfake had been released.

His ID—the credential that got him through the gates of this palace, and many other secure facilities in the Netherlands as well, was hanging around his neck on a cloth lanyard that was riding up above his collar and touching his neck. It was suddenly feeling heavy. Before he'd even really had time to think about it he reached up and pulled it off and let it dangle from both outstretched hands in front of him. "Until this matter is resolved," he said, "to avoid even the appearance of any impropriety, I am placing myself on leave." He dropped the credential on the table and turned around. As he did so, his gaze swept across the queen's face. She looked stunned, stricken. Willem's impulse, born of habit, was to offer some advice. To coolly analyze the situation, make suggestions, execute a plan, smooth it all over. But there were situations that arose from time to time when the monarch actually did have to be the monarch. Alone. This was one of those. "Nice enough afternoon," he said. "Can I borrow a bicycle?"

EIGHT MONTHS LATER

There was an old joke about a man who is driving somewhere with an accordion in the back of his car. He parks the car outside a diner in a sketchy part of town and goes in for dinner. When he comes out he sees that the rear window of his car has been smashed out. He runs up to it and discovers that, while he wasn't looking, some miscreant has thrown a second accordion in there and made a clean getaway.

During Rufus's past life trying to operate a farm, he'd learned that this actually explained a lot about farm and ranch life. As soon as someone found out you had fifty acres, they'd remember a nephew with a dog that had outgrown his apartment, or nipped a child, and suggest that your farm would be the perfect place for it to live. Or they'd start talking about an old car that was taking up space in their garage that they'd been meaning to fix up one day and just needed to park somewhere for a spell—and a car wouldn't really take up that much space on fifty acres, would it?

This, more than anything else, explained the condition of a great many farms and ranches Rufus had seen in his day. You started with good and simple intentions, and a couple of decades later you were living in a slum/junkyard/menagerie. Unless you drew a hard line and risked getting a reputation as a difficult person.

But the marble mine was not Rufus's personal property and so he didn't have final say over such matters. When word got around among Flying S Ranch staff that he was looking after Bildad, and that he had set up horse-related infrastructure, such as a water tank and hay storage, before he knew it he had acquired another horse—a senior citizen named Goldie—and two mules, Trucker and Patch. It was explained, by ranch staff who towed these animals up the road in trailers, that livestock had to be redistributed around the property from time to time as various stables and other facilities were consolidated and rearranged. It was a strictly temporary measure.

Rufus knew perfectly well that this was a polite falsehood. But he said nothing, construing it as job security and as an opening to file requests for additional goods and services.

The presence of all these animals, and the scent of hay, attracted a mustang whom Rufus suspected of having been part of Bildad's herd back in the day. He named him Peleg, another *Moby-Dick* name. But everyone mispronounced it as Pegleg and took it to be a reference to the white sock on one of the animal's forelegs. Rufus soon grew weary of correcting people and of explaining that the character with the peg leg had been Ahab, so Pegleg it was. Thordis seduced him into the fold with hay and Rufus settled him down to the point where a large animal veterinarian was able to knock him out and cut off his balls, which had been causing trouble. After a short period of recovery Pegleg became a model citizen, and Rufus got him reconciled to bridle and saddle.

What was true of horses and mules was apparently true of eagles. The facilities that these birds required, the frequent deliveries of raw meat and exotic veterinary supplies, meant that if you were going to have one eagle you might as well have several. Which generally meant that you also had to welcome the falconers who came with them, since they tended to bond with individual humans.

Thordis apparently had her own personal text message hotline to T.R., a distinction she shared with Rufus and, apparently, about one thousand other people. And, like T.R., or anyone allowed to remain on that list for very long, she knew how to use it: infrequently and always with good news or interesting new developments that would brighten the great man's day or pique his interest when he scrolled past these little gems while sitting on the throne or waiting for a meeting to begin. The upshot was that, for reasons that were never quite explained to Rufus, a Mongolian woman named Tsolmon showed up with a golden eagle named Genghis who was half as big as she was. Three weeks later they were joined by Piet, a Dutchman who had worked on the original Schiphol Airport project. With him was Skippy, another golden eagle who was actually named after the airport.

All this coincided with a phase during which Rufus was asking himself what in God's name he was even doing here. He had long ago got the picture that T.R. was the living embodiment of what was now denoted ADHD. He went off on tangents, a small percentage of which made money. It was just the survival into modern times of old-time wildcatters running around Texas drilling wells and hoping to get lucky. Sooner or later these initiatives came under the heading of "special projects" in his bureaucracy and then continued to be funded in some irregular and hard-to-understand way until someone got around to pulling the plug—probably while T.R. was looking the other way. As long as Special Projects were suffered to remain in existence they could bang into each other in the dark and swap DNA. Setting Rufus up as the Drone Ranger had been one of those. The only thing that had come of it so far was some improvements to the marble mine and the rescue and rehabilitation of a stray horse with a market value of one dollar. It would be way overstating the case to claim that T.R. had any kind of coherent plan for bringing the falconers and the eagles up to the marble mine. But Thordis must be telling him *something* he enjoyed hearing. Rufus didn't know whether Tsolmon and Piet were being paid, or simply allowed to be on the property. Clearly it suited them. Tsolmon wasn't much of a talker but she obviously knew her way around horses. So that was a load off his mind. Piet, though probably in his forties, had the physique of a fifteen-year-old circus acrobat and was a fervid practitioner of the sport of rucking, which apparently was nothing more than running around with a heavy weight strapped to one's back. The general point was that neither of the new arrivals caused any trouble, and it cost almost nothing to keep them alive.

Rufus therefore came around to the view that his employment on the ranch was likely to be terminated at any moment without warning or explanation, but that while he was waiting for the axe to fall he might as well try to make himself useful to the falconers, who seemed to have momentum within what might optimistically be called the organization of T.R. This meant dropping the pretense that he could actually do anything useful, security-wise, with drones, over and above what Black Hat was already doing. Thenceforth he put all his drone-related know-how to work in the service of the Special Project that accounted for Skippy, Nimrod, and Genghis being here: the idea—pioneered years ago by Piet, developed further by Thordis, and still getting a bit of side-eye from Carmelita and Tsolmon—that trained eagles could be used to defend against hostile drones. The Schiphol project had been shitcanned partly because of protests from animal rights activists. Such people were, to put it mildly, neither common nor welcome on the Flying S, or any other West Texas, ranch.

First, though, Rufus had to settle some misgivings that had been rumbling in the back of his mind since the moment on top of the mountain when Nimrod's hood had been removed and he had realized that she was a golden, as opposed to a bald, eagle. At that instant this whole thing had suddenly turned into a family affair. For complicated reasons, he had to go back to Lawton and make sure he wasn't burning any bridges by taking part in a weaponized eagle program. So he took a couple of days off, got into his truck, and drove five hundred miles east-northeast to the place where he had been born, and, up to the age of eighteen, raised.

There was the usual amount of driving down streets that he had known since boyhood, and thereby having random memories triggered. Lawton and the immense army base of Fort Sill were wrapped around each other like two wrestlers on a mat. Much of the town's population were ex-, active, or future army. There were a few carefully delineated pockets of squalor, and the odd person who didn't mow his lawn, but those only emphasized the place's overall windswept tidiness.

It was a roomy place where all the development had long since gone over to modern commercial big-box strips. The only change since his childhood was that old signs had been ripped out and replaced with electronic ones on which managers could advertise the latest specials or job openings from the air-conditioned comfort of their offices. These provided a weird sort of digital peephole into their minds. A bakery was looking to hire a dependable baker. Two miles down the road, an auto parts store had a job opening for a dependable sales associate. Dependability was a major preoccupation of Lawton's managerial class. Rufus could see people walking, bicycling, or skateboarding up and down the same streets who, it could be inferred, had failed the dependability test.

Young Rufus might have assumed that this drought of dependability was a problem peculiar to Lawton, had he not joined the army and become aware of the fact that it was a worldwide phenomenon. If you did happen to be one of those rare people blessed or cursed—take your pick—with dependability, there were opportunities everywhere. The world's howling need for it would suck you into all kinds of situations that might look peachy if you had just fallen off the Lawton turnip truck but that, in the light of experience, probably needed to be vetted a little more carefully before saying yes. Which was part of why he was here. T.R. had checked the "dependable" box next to Rufus's name. Rufus now had better keep his wits about him.

Despite carrying a tribal ID card, he had always refrained from calling himself a Comanche. It seemed presumptuous, and it put him at risk of being called a Pretendian, which was absolutely not a label you ever wanted to have slapped on you. And yet that branch of his family had always been more welcoming and, for lack of a more devious way of saying it, loving, in an unconditional way, than any of the others, whenever he came around to visit. Possibly because he didn't come around that often.

He drove north out of town past the Comanche Reformed Church. This massive red-rock pile had always been there. It was where he had first heard names like Bildad and Peleg being read out from the pulpit. But recent developments in his life had made him aware that it had been founded by Dutch missionaries. So it was technically an offshoot of the Dutch Reformed Church, which in a roundabout way was the same church Saskia belonged to. He'd been to his share of christenings, weddings, and funerals in the place. But he had never been aware of its connection to the Netherlands, and certainly could never have imagined the whole Saskia thing, which as time went on seemed more and more like a dream or hallucination to him.

North of the military base the country became a little more rolling, with a good number of small trees casting shade on the ground but still letting enough light through that grass could grow and provide grazing for cattle and horses. The grid of streets was broken up by rivers, hills, and lakes. Roads rambled wherever the rambling was good. Strung along them like beads were the hundred-and-sixty-acre parcels known as allotments.

The allotment now controlled by his grandmother Mary was a bit smaller because part of it had been submerged in an artificial lake some decades ago, but on balance that wasn't such a bad thing because lakefront property was worth more. Like many of these things its ownership had, after a few generations, become splintered among a couple of dozen descendants of the original allotee. Making decisions had become difficult. Part of the property had been leased out as a sod farm. Some of the lower-lying ground near the water had become overgrown with juniper, cedar, and mesquite—all invasive species that back in the old days had been kept at bay by grazing bison. Rufus, fifteen years ago, had contributed to an effort whereby Mary and three of her other descendants had bought out most of the other co-owners. He'd also showed up with a chain saw on weekends to help clear away the unwanted brush along the lake. Now it was an RV park with seventy-five spaces. About half those were occupied by permanent residents, mostly military retirees with a weakness for fishing. The other half were available for short stays by transient vacationers. An L-shaped arrangement of mobile homes, spliced together with a pre-fab steel building, served both as front office and as a residence for Mary and some of her descendants—aunts, uncles, and cousins to Rufus. To get there, you had to drive along the edge of the former sod farm, which had now been fenced and turned over to three horses and a donkey. The horses were said to be descendants of some that had survived the depredations of the U.S. Army during the Red River War. Unable to defeat the Comanches on the battlefield, they had killed all the bison and drove herds of captured horses over cliffs, reducing the Indians to starvation and thus forcing them into captivity at Fort Sill.

"Weh! Weh!" was how they greeted Rufus, a word meaning "Come on inside!" It almost seemed as though they were expecting him, which made him wonder if he'd been spotted by some cousin while pumping gas in Lawton, and his arrival heralded on social media. Once he was through the door of the mobile home, all further conversation was in English. With one exception: his grandmother always addressed him as Eka, which was simply the Comanche word for Red. His hair had been red-tinged as a boy, and no visit was complete without her standing up on tiptoe and reaching up to tug at his locks, pretending to inspect for red roots.

It was a long reach. Like many of that tribe she was sturdy, but had not been of great stature even in her prime. Now she was pushing ninety. To find a genetic basis for the comparative tallness of Rufus, it was necessary to look elsewhere in the family tree. Perhaps to his great-great-grandfather Hopewell (though no one had ever measured him) but more likely to Bob Staley, his maternal grandfather, who had been some combination of white and Osage. And the Osage were as famous for their large stature as the Comanches were for the opposite; it was rumored that if the Osage branch of the family were traced back far enough it would include Heavy Runners, warriors who could chase down a Comanche pony in the middle of a fight, grab it by the tail, and bring it to the ground. For that reason Comanches, preparing to fight Osages, would bob or tie up their horses' tails.

Big Bob had been stationed in Korea with the U.S. Marines during and after the war there. He had married a younger Korean woman and brought her back to the States, eventually settling in the vicinity of Fort Sill where there were enough Koreans to prevent his bride from feeling completely isolated. Their oldest daughter had met, and briefly and unhappily married, Rufus's dad. That whole generation was a little bit of a sparse patch in the family tree, though. Rufus's mom had died young in a car crash and his dad, as the polite euphemism went, "was not in the picture"; a charming pathological gambler, he had faded away, when Rufus had been in his teens, as a steadily widening circle of family and acquaintances had called him on his bullshit. All of which helped to explain why Rufus had simply joined the army upon graduation from high school, and why he had completed his twenty years' service while still a young and healthy man.

On the Korean/Osage/white side—his mother's branch of the family—there had been a general turn toward extremely fervent Christianity and the production of a lot of cousins Rufus didn't know very well, since their incessant Jesus talk was so tiresome. By process of elimination, then, when he returned to this part of the country, the people he was seeing were his ninety-year-old grandmother, Mary, and the offspring of his two aunts on that side, who were enmeshed by many family and social ties in the KCA or Kiowa/Comanche/Apache network around Lawton.

An impromptu barbecue was fomented in the L-shaped compound as word got out that Rufus had slid into town. Various shirttail relations and friends began to pull up. Accustomed to solitude, Rufus had to suppress a fight-or-flight reaction as one person after another came up to interact with him socially. Most of these exchanges were either (1) rote friendly joshing about Rufus's unusual looks, stature, and way of life, frequently softened by the exclamation "kee!" meaning "not!" or "just kidding!" or (2) congratulating him in a more serious way about his destruction of Snout. This feat—minus the part of the story where a business jet did most of the work for him—had somehow made its way into the oral tradition. Everyone, of course, knew the first part of that story: what had happened to Adele. Word seemed to have got around that Snout was no more and that Rufus had something to do with that. People had filled in the missing details with a conjectural story line that made Rufus out to be pretty heroic. Explaining what had actually happened was, of course, completely out of the question, and so all Rufus could do was nod and accept their warm admiration.

It all delayed the real conversation that Rufus wanted to have, which was with Mary. Which meant also having it with his aunt Beth, who had become the chief Mary caretaker and living repository of Mary lore. But eventually when the barbecue broke up, everyone went home, and the younger kids were in bed, he found himself sitting around the remains of a campfire with Mary and Beth in the cool of the evening. And then he laid the whole thing out, as much as he could without violating his NDA.

"I don't want to burn any bridges with y'all or get mixed up in anything y'all would consider sacrilegious," Rufus said, where "y'all" here basically meant that portion of his surviving family who lived around Lawton and identified as Comanche. "But it looks like I'm getting involved in this project that involves eagles."

"Like the fighter planes?" Beth asked.

"No, ma'am. Birds. Some falconers—eagle tamers, basically—from different parts of the world, all come together to work on this thing I can't talk about in West Texas. But these eagles have been brought up around humans and trained to use their eagle superpowers in certain ways—"

"Bald eagles?" Mary demanded to know.

"No. Golden."

Mary nodded decisively. "Good."

Beth was nodding too. "Because fuck those things."

What was being referred to here was a long history of ambivalent feelings toward U.S. patriotic imagery, with bald eagles and the Stars and Stripes at the top of the list. Lots of Indians in this part of the country had served in the military and spent their careers saluting that flag, but they were all perfectly aware of the fact that effigies of bald eagles, and the red, white, and blue, were the last things that many of their ancestors had ever seen.

"That's my understanding," Rufus said hastily. "That when Comanches related to eagles it was always goldens. Balds were not part of the picture for us."

Mary nodded. Beth exchanged a few muttered words with her, including *pia huutsu*, which Rufus was pretty sure was the word for bald eagle, and *kwihnai*, which he knew for sure was the word for goldens. Then they looked at him expectantly.

"But that don't clear the picture up for me, ma'am," Rufus continued. "I get that y'all got no time for *pia huutsu* and that y'all have reverence for *kwihnai*. But that might just make the situation worse, if you see what I'm saying, if I am mixed up in a project where the *kwihnai* are being, for lack of a better term, used."

Beth totally got the picture and nodded. She discussed it with Mary for a minute or two in a rapid-fire mix of drawling Oklahoma English and Comanche.

"Our ancestors never did what these falconers do. Training them that way. We just captured them and held them captive," Mary said. "For eagle medicine—because, you know, for some people, their personal medicine was eagle medicine—and for feathers."

"Right! So do you think it's okay to—"

"You said these falconers came from all over the world," Beth said. "None of these people are Comanches, right?"

"Of course not."

"So we don't really have an opinion as to whether they should train golden eagles. It's a different group of people, different religion, none of our dang business."

"Yeah, but I'm involved and I don't want y'all to think I'm being disrespectful."

"What are these *kwihnai* being used for?" Mary asked. "What are they doing?"

"Catching rabbits?" Beth asked. "Isn't that what falconers usually do?"

"Fighting," Rufus said. "Fighting off invaders, I guess you could say."

"Oh, that's no problem then!" said his grandmother.

There had been some concern that spinning rotors might injure the birds' talons. Piet, like Tsolmon, wasn't much of a conversationalist, but it was easy to draw him out on this topic. He encouraged Rufus to reach out and grab Skippy's perch and compare the size of his hand to the eagle's foot. If you included the long curving talons, the bird's digits were as long as Rufus's fingers.

Not that Rufus would have relished shoving his hand into the rotors of a drone in flight. The blades of those things were extremely lightweight, but they spun quickly. They didn't pack enough of a punch to break a finger, but they could draw blood, and the impact hurt.

He now perceived an opportunity to be of service. Actually wrangling eagles was not a thing that he was ever going to learn. It was a whole world of fussy veterinary procedures, weird social man/bird interaction, and messing around with small dead raw animals that did not appeal to him and that he never would have become good at. Even if he were to somehow master all those skills, the fact was that the eagles they actually had at the Marble Mine had all bonded with specific human beings who were not Rufus.

But if the goal of this Special Project was to reboot the canceled Schiphol Airport Eagle vs. Drone project, then there were ways he could be of service. First of all by building practice drones, the sole purpose of which was to be ripped out of the air by eagles, using rotors with pivoting blades that would be less likely to damage the feet of an attacking eagle. These would make it possible for the falconers to train their eagles safely.

In actual practice, though, it wouldn't make sense to assume that the bad guys—whoever they might be—would be so considerate as to build eagle-friendly equipment. So the second part of Rufus's work was to construct eagle gauntlets: lightweight, hard-shelled gloves, like those on a suit of medieval armor, that could be slipped over the birds' feet and lower legs to take the impact from spinning drone rotors. Once those had brought the lightweight blades to a dead stop, the eagles' talons could close in around the body of the drone, the three front toes raking it back so that the hallux—the huge talon on the bird's "heel"—could close in, crushing and piercing the drone's hull just like the rib cage of a hapless bunny.

In the era before 3D printers, inventing eagle gauntlets would have been difficult, but now it was easy. Better yet, it gave him an excuse to purchase a fancier 3D printer that was capable of making stronger, lighter parts. Rufus was gradually getting clued in to the fact that dudes like T.R. actually liked it when you spent money, provided you did it within reasonable bounds. It proved that you were doing something.

In other words, he dropped, or at least set to one side, the pretense that he was actually patrolling the airspace of the Flying S Ranch with a personal fleet of drones and threw himself full-time into helping Thordis, Carmelita, Tsolmon, and Piet train their eagles. In military parlance, they were the Blue Team, preparing to defend the ranch against possible invaders, and he was the Red Team—a simulated opponent that the Blue Team could train against. And since all of them called him by his nickname of Red, it all seemed to fit. It gave him a story he could tell himself, as he sat down there in the cool recesses of the marble mine repairing drones torn apart by enraged birds of prey, as to why this all made sense. A story he could also relate to T.R., if T.R. ever asked. But he never did.

CYBERABAD

We think you are ready to walk," said Dr. Banerjee after they'd extracted him from the tank, removed the sphere from his head, disconnected the cables behind his ears, and given him a chance to shower and put some clothes on.

When he'd first regained consciousness, "clothes" had meant hospital gowns, but these days it seemed to be T-shirts, sweatpants, and a simple piece of cloth to cover his head. He never wore the same T-shirt twice. They just showed up. Most were blazoned with the names and logos of kabaddi teams, but there was also some hockey swag. He had only the vaguest sense of what kabaddi and hockey were, but their practitioners seemed quite generous with clothing.

As for the piece of cloth on his head: in the early going he'd been a little unclear on whether this was a medical thing—for they'd been doing a lot of things to his skull—or a form of attire. Some of the people who came to visit him—including most of the ones who claimed to be his friends and family—wore such coverings on their heads. Typically, they were a lot more elaborate than the thing he had. Large portions of his head had been shaved for medical reasons, but they'd left his hair long on top and in front. He could twist it into a sort of bun above his forehead and wrap that up in the cloth. Also, there was a metal band that he wore on his wrist.

Right now he was seated in a wheelchair in the living room of his suite, looking across a coffee table at Dr. Banerjee, a small woman in her forties. She was flanked by a couple of the usual crowd of—well, it was hard to tell who and what they were. Younger people who seemed smart and efficient and pleased.

"I've been walking for weeks," he said.

"I mean, without the rack," she clarified. She referred to a cube-shaped frame on wheels that until now had always surrounded him when he walked; it prevented him from injuring himself when he lost his balance. "Today's results were more than encouraging. Your proprioception has been improving steadily during the last few weeks, but recently it has just gone shooting off the charts. We have finally got those darned gyros dialed in. The neural interfaces are 'taking.' Combining those two advances, we can now say that your sense of balance is better than what we have measured in controlled experiments on Olympic gymnasts!"

"Well, screw it then," he said. In one motion he unbuckled the lap belt holding him into his chair and stood up. The backs of his legs impacted the chair and sent it rolling backward until it clattered against a wall. Dr. Banerjee was horrified. She needn't have been. He knew *exactly* where he was in space.

"No, too soon, Laks!" she exclaimed.

Laks. Yet another of his names.

"Please sit down! We wish to perform the trial under controlled circumstances!" Dr. Banerjee herself had jumped to her feet as if to physically restrain him—funny thought, since she weighed less than half of what Laks did. His lack of balance had not prevented him from working out on weight machines to gain back the muscle mass he'd lost during the months of lying unconscious.

Her colleagues, though, looked very pleased. They high-fived each other. One of them took a picture.

"Can you do this?" Laks asked. He lifted one foot off the floor so that he was balanced on one leg. Then he closed his eyes. "Count," he said.

One of them began: "One Mississippi, two Mississippi, three . . ."

When the count reached thirty, he opened his eyes. Rock solid. No flailing of arms or hopping around.

"I cannot," Dr. Banerjee admitted. "Few can."

During the half minute he'd been standing on one leg with eyes closed, that "Laks" thing had been sinking in. It jogged a memory—a recent one. He walked over to the floor-to-ceiling window of his suite. This was on something like the thirtieth floor of the building, so it had a fantastic view out over a sunlit cityscape consisting mostly of new office buildings ranging in height from five to fifty stories. Some were emblazoned with logos and funny words that he took to be the names of companies. The place was called Cyberabad. It was part of a much larger and older city called Hyderabad. These were all details he had picked up in fragments strewn among conversations he barely remembered, scattered across the last several weeks; but it was all coming into focus. It was beginning to "take," to borrow Dr. Banerjee's expression.

Dr. Banerjee inhaled sharply as Laks approached the window. She must be afraid that he was going to trip over his feet and smash through it. But he wouldn't. His sense of where he was could not have been more perfect. He even knew that he was gazing along an azimuth of about 325 degrees with respect to magnetic north.

Below, and across the street, was a building perhaps ten stories high. Its flat roof was fifty-seven meters below him. He wasn't sure how he knew that. The roof had a pea-gravel surface, sort of gray brown on the average. But someone had gone up there with white paint and rolled out the words "GET WELL SOON LAKS!" in letters several meters high. Strewn all around that was brownish vegetable matter flecked here and there with muted colors: flowers that had adorned the big white words but that had wilted and withered. Thousands of individual bouquets. Literally tons of old dead flowers.

His view of Cyberabad was cut off as the curtain was yanked across the window by one of Dr. Banerjee's flankers. "Sorry," he said. "The days of drones hovering outside your window are thankfully gone. But still, if anyone recognized you, social media would go ballistic. And we don't want expectations getting out of hand."

Laks stood there for a few moments absorbing that. This phrase "social media" was, on one level, new to his ears. Or the sensor pods screwed into the temporal bone ridges behind his ears that did what ears did, only better. And yet he could feel it lighting up big networks of connections in his head.

During the months he had lain flat on his back in the dark, trying not to be sick from vertigo, sometimes the sun would come out from behind clouds. Even through the blackout curtains next to his hospital bed, he could sense that it had done so. Not so much because of light leaking round the edges as because of the vague omnidirectional warmth radiating through the dark fabric. This was a little like that. On the dark side of the neurological curtain was Laks, trying to work out what "social media" denoted. On the other side was a large portion of his brain. And yet the curtain had a few moth-holes in it. Through those, he glimpsed clear images: a freckle-faced woman with a camera. The snowy top of a mountain. A Chinese man with a stick.

"Run it by me one more time," he said to the curtain-snapper. He knew he'd seen the guy before. He didn't wear scrubs or a lab coat. More a T-shirt and jeans kind of chap. Ponytail. Name tag "Kadar." Rhymed with "radar." Right now Kadar had an uncertain look on his face, which for him was unusual. He wasn't sure he understood Laks's question.

So Laks clarified: "Something happened to my brain."

The guy exhaled. As if to say *How many times are we going to have to go over this?* He broke eye contact. His gaze wandered over to a counter in one corner of the room where a microwave and a coffee maker had been provided for the use of Laks and the many people who came to his suite to have these weird conversations with him. Beneath the counter was a small fridge, and atop it were a fruit plate and a basket of snacks. A thought occurred to Kadar and he strode over to it.

Meanwhile Dr. Banerjee was saying, "You suffered an exposure to a pattern of energy that coupled in a deleterious manner to certain delicate structures inside of your noggin."

"Consider a spherical brain," said Kadar. He had plucked a single green grape from a bunch of them on the fruit plate. He now extracted a steak knife from the silverware drawer and used it to cut most, but not all, of the way through the grape. Laks drifted over to watch. Kadar opened the grape like a book. The uncut skin in the back held the two halves of it together like a hinge. "To most people, a piece of fruit not quite cut in half. To a radio engineer, a butterfly antenna."

"Antenna!?"

Kadar nodded solemnly and placed the grape in the microwave. He slammed the appliance's door shut and poised a finger over the "Beverage" button. "The last thing you saw before you lost consciousness on the top of that ridge was a Chinese weapons system that projects electromagnetic energy in a certain band. A little bit like this microwave oven." He hit the button while indicating with his other hand that Laks should observe. Laks bent over and peered through the perforated-metal screen behind the door glass to see the grape dimly visible trundling around on the glass turntable and presumably getting warmer. But suddenly there was a flash like a little lightning bolt and a sizzling noise. Kadar shut off the microwave, opened the door, and pulled out the two halves of the grape, which were no longer attached. "Hardly even warm," he said. He rotated the halves so that Laks could see the former place of attachment, now marked with tiny black smudges where the skin had explosively vaporized. "But in that one place, for a moment, it was as hot as the surface of the sun."

"How do you know that?"

"The color of the flash." Kadar held out the grape halves. Laks let them tumble into the palm of his hand. They were scarcely above body heat. "And that is the problem. The radiation from the Chinese weapon coupled *weakly* to most of your body but *strongly* to certain bits. Which got damaged. We're trying to get those bits to grow back—or provide substitutes where that isn't going to be possible."

Laks looked over at Dr. Banerjee, who seemed mortified. Presumably she felt that Kadar was being a bit blunt. But Laks didn't mind. "I'll keep the grape next to my bed as a reminder," he said. "So I don't have to keep asking you."

Kadar seemed slightly abashed. "I don't mean to suggest in any way that we are unwilling to answer any and all of your questions."

"In that case, I have one more."

"Shoot."

"Why go to all this trouble just for me?" Laks looked around. "I mean . . . this is a pretty nice hospital room, right?"

"*Very* nice," said Dr. Banerjee, with a depth of feeling suggesting that she had, in her day, seen some pretty fucked-up hospitals.

"It's because you are a hero of India," Kadar said, "but India is not quite finished with you yet."

THE BEAVER

From the river IJ—the water in the heart of Amsterdam—to the Lagoon of Venice was beyond the Beaver's range. So the former queen stopped off at Lake Como to refuel, to pee, to get a cup of coffee, and to drop off her co-pilot. She would fly the last leg solo. Partly that was for the visuals. Whenever there were two people in the cockpit, cynics assumed that Frederika Mathilde Louisa Saskia was just faking it.

But also she needed some alone time. She had abdicated the throne and seen Lotte become the new queen first thing in the morning. Since then she'd hardly had a moment to herself; and those moments had been interrupted by texts from Lotte asking her mother for advice and for reassurance.

She answered a couple of the more urgent questions while sipping her coffee beneath an awning by the water. Nobility and royalty had been coming to Lake Como since Roman times, often to lick their wounds after some kind of reversal in their fortunes. So its shores were strewn with spectacular old buildings with long, complicated, and not especially cheerful histories. Saskia could have found family connections to many of these, should she care to go rooting around in her ancestral tree. So having that cup of coffee, there in the dockside café of a luxury hotel that had once been the private villa of some great-great-uncle thrice removed, was a reminder that, if she so chose, she could while away the rest of her life in such a place. Just like many other defrocked, deposed, defunct, or disgraced persons of former importance down through the ages. To some that might be an irresistible siren's call, but it made Saskia's skin crawl. She couldn't finish that coffee fast enough. She had a sort of vision, sitting there enjoying the temperate breeze off the lake, that if the climate apocalypse happened, this place would be the last bastion to fall. And having now given up her throne in the pursuit of the climate wars, she didn't want to hole up in the last bastion. She wanted to go down fighting in the front lines.

So she stood up and tossed back the dregs of her coffee as soon as the lads down on the fuel dock were finished. She texted "OMW" to her contact in Venice, then shut off her phone. Under the lidless eyes of several paparazzi drones she marched down to the dock, climbed aboard her seaplane, and began to work her way down the pre-flight checklist. A few minutes later she was in the air, bound south down the Y-shaped mountain valley that clasped the lake. The plain of Lombardy then unfolded below her and she swung east toward the Adriatic, some two hundred and fifty kilometers away—an hour's flying time in this lumbering old pontoon plane. You could get faster, fancier ones, but this was a Canadian classic: a De Havilland Beaver. Her family had warm connections to Canada, going back to the war, and so this was the one she had picked out.

Once she had got the Beaver trimmed in level flight and headed in the right direction she spent ten minutes crying. Not that she was particularly sad. It was just that during important transitions you had to get this out of your system, and she hadn't performed that task yet. The Dutch didn't do formal coronations and so Lotte had become the new queen in a basically secular ceremony in Amsterdam's Nieuwe Kerk, which was a church only in name. No crown had been placed on her head. They didn't even *have* a crown. In attendance had been everyone who mattered in the Netherlands as well as a smattering of foreign royalty and international diplomats. Very convenient for Saskia who'd been able to exchange pleasantries with, and say goodbye to, many people in very little time. But when you had abdicated, you needed to get out of the country. To make a clean break and clear the stage for your successor. So after a quick change of clothes in the adjoining Royal Palace—as of ten minutes ago, her daughter's official

Amsterdam residence—Saskia had walked down to the IJ, jostling and dodging through pedestrian traffic like a private citizen, and climbed into the waiting plane and simply flown away.

Her Royal Highness Princess Frederika of the Netherlands, as she was now styled, reached the skies above Venice at the time of day movie people referred to as Golden Hour, when everything was softly lit by the warm colors of the western sky. In the life she'd just left behind, that would not have been an accident; it would all have been arranged by Willem and Fenna. Today it actually was an accident, though helped along somewhat by Pina2bo, which by this point had put enough sulfur into the stratosphere to make a noticeable difference in the sunsets of the Northern Hemisphere. The light of Golden Hour was famously forgiving to ladies of a certain age. Saskia liked to think she wasn't *quite* there yet, but Venice certainly was. And there could have been no better light in which to view La Serenissima.

Her plane was in its element chugging along at low altitude. She'd filed a flight plan that kept her out of the way of heavy commercial traffic at Marco Polo Airport, which was on the mainland to the north. She made a pass around the island city, shedding altitude, resisting the temptation to wave back at the onlookers watching her arrival from waterfront bridges, balconies, rivas, and piazzas. She banked the plane round into a light northwesterly breeze and brought it down gently into the soft waters of the Lagoon with the Giardini della Biennale on her right and the red spire of San Giorgio on her left. Water might have been a menace to the Venetians and the Dutch alike, but she loved to land planes on it. Waco had left her skittish about that critical instant when rubber met terra firma. But in a seaplane you had this long glide from flying to floating with no clear moment when one became the other.

The wind's direction made it easy for her to drive the plane right up to the quay at the park by the Piazza of San Marco. She only had to keep her peripheral vision engaged so that the propeller didn't chop up any excited boaters. When that simply became too stressful she killed the engine, shut everything down, unbuckled her safety harness, and climbed out onto the pontoon. From there she was able to toss a line into the cockpit of an approaching powerboat. Behind its wheel was Michiel, grinning beneath a pair of sunglasses that probably cost as much as Saskia's airplane. And worth every penny, if looks had value. His boat, naturally, was one of those handcrafted, all-mahogany runabouts. No fiberglass in this man's reality. The Venetians had been at great pains to set themselves apart from Italy, but they had no compunctions about Italian design when it made them look smashing.

With a little help from some friends in the boat, Michiel took Saskia's plane in tow and pulled her the last few meters in to the point where lines could be transferred to bollards along the edge of the quay. Suddenly divested of all responsibility, Saskia was able to just stand there on the pontoon, one hand braced on the wing strut, the other waving from time to time at people who had gathered in the park to greet her, to denounce her, or simply to watch. There was the usual variety of signs and banners. The Frederika who had awakened this morning in Amsterdam as Queen of the Netherlands had been tuned to pay careful attention to those. Saskia Orange could afford to shrug most of it off. And to be honest, the feeling was probably mutual. Venice had seen it all. Her arrival was not a big deal.

The park was separated from the docks by a stone balustrade. Along this someone had deployed a banner reading, in English: "Welcome Queen of Netherworld!"

Saskia well knew how to spot the differences between signs that really had been improvised on kitchen tables by amateurs, and ones carefully fashioned to seem that way. This was one of the latter. Nor did it escape her notice that when Michiel—who had vaulted up out of his beautiful runabout onto the quay—stepped forward to offer his hand as she stepped off the pontoon, it all happened with that banner in the background. So the image was all over the world before her foot touched what passed in Venice for dry land.

She had never before encountered that usage of the word "Netherworld," but she got it. Nederland—her kingdom until this morning—was a land that happened to be low. From a parochial Northern European standpoint it was *the* low country and so that was what people had always called it. From a global perspective, though, it was just one of many places where people lived close to sea level; and though, a hundred years ago, all such places would have seemed quite different—as different as Venice was from Houston or Zeeland from Bangladesh—when sea level began to rise, they all turned out to have much in common. A whole planet-spanning archipelago of threatened nether-places. Why not "Netherworld"? Whether it really needed to have a queen, though, was another question.

It was understood that she'd had a long day and so formalities at quayside were kept to a minimum: Saskia accepted a bouquet and an official greeting from the mayor as well as one from the leader of an entity called Vexital. After waving to the crowd and posing for a few photos she climbed into Michiel's sleek mahogany runabout and enjoyed a rousing dash across the Lagoon to a private island.

Dozens of tiny islands were strewn across the water around Venice, each with its own long history of use as a monastery, convent, prison, dump, cemetery, or fortification. Many were uninhabited and unused, a fact remarkable to Saskia, who would have expected that a charming private island only a few minutes' powerboat ride from the Grand Canal would be a hot property. The fact that they were all in danger of ceasing to exist had probably depressed the market. The one they were going to was less than a hundred meters wide. It was square except for an indentation on one side for a dock. Saskia had banked over this island a few minutes ago and got a good look out the side window of the plane. It was outlined on three of its sides by old buildings that had once served as the wings of a cloister. In medieval times those had risen directly from the water of the Lagoon, but sea level rise had forced the owners to expand the island's footprint slightly by dumping fill into the shallow water to build up a surrounding levee. Resulting environmental controversies had become a political flash point in a way that was suspiciously useful to Vexital: a local movement dedicated to the proposition that Venice ought to secede, not just from Europe ("Vexit") but from Italy ("Vexitalia").

Venice itself, at less than four miles long, would seem so small that it was superfluous to have a microcosm of it; but Santa Liberata, as this island was known, had been seen as just that. Cornelia, its owner, had appeared in a very well produced video sloshing barefoot down flooded corridors of its ancient cloisters, gazing sadly down through six inches of water at beautiful mosaics, and looking up at frescoes soon to be dissolved by rising seawater.

Anyway, Liberata was safe and sound for the moment behind those new levees, thrown up in defiance of the European Union's Infraction Procedure. The family of Cornelia had done a brilliant job of fixing the place up one bit at a time, bringing some rooms up to modern luxury-hotel standards while leaving others in exactly the right stage of dusty, weedy, comfortable decay. So upon her arrival Saskia was able to freshen up in a bathroom that sported sleek high-tech chrome-plated plumbing fixtures she couldn't even work out how to use; but then she was able to walk out onto a patio lit up by a red Pina2bo sunset and have a drink on thousand-year-old flagstones with Daia Kaur Chand.

"So, Your Royal Highness, what's it like to be an ex-queen?"

Wonderful was on Saskia's lips, but she held back. The last time she'd been in Daia's company was on the Flying S Ranch. Then Daia hadn't been working in her capacity as a journalist but tagging along with her husband, the lord mayor. This time, it was different. The conversation they were having now was off the record. But it was still a sort of dress rehearsal for the real interview they'd be conducting tomorrow with a full BBC production crew in attendance. So it would be wise for Saskia to get in the habit of being a little guarded. "It's nice to be relieved of some of those responsibilities," she allowed, "but of course Queen Charlotte—who has shouldered them in my place—is never far from my mind."

A wry look had spread across Daia's face as this carefully worded answer went on and on. If this was supposed to be informal off-the-record chitchat, it was already failing. "It's very different from the British monarchy, isn't it? I'll be certain to spell that out for our viewers."

"What, the tradition of abdication?"

"British monarchs—with one notable exception—never abdicate."

"But it's become the rule rather than the exception in the Netherlands, it's true."

"It's like retiring."

"Yes. And some retire earlier than others."

"Early enough to . . . pursue a second career, perhaps?"

"We'll see. It's a bit soon to be thinking about such things."

"Do you think you'd have stayed on if it hadn't been for all the controversies? The campaign of deepfakes? All the attention around geoengineering?"

"Oh, almost certainly. I was *raised* to do that job. I was good at it. People—even anti-monarchists—liked me. And it's a big burden to dump on Charlotte's shoulders at such a young age. But when you start becoming a distraction from the country's real business, it's time to leave. I just had to present Charlotte with the choice: we can all walk away, and put an end to the monarchy, or you can take over for me. She made her choice."

Saskia's phone had chimed several times in the last minute. It was Lotte. Saskia checked it, expecting some desperate plea for advice. But instead it was a selfie of her standing next to a ridiculously handsome prince from the Norwegian royal family. Smiling, she shared that with Daia, who laughed out loud at the beauty of the young man. "Somehow one suspects Queen Lotte will get along just fine."

There was that little pause that signifies a turn in the conversation. The two women sipped their drinks and took in the view across the flat water of the Lagoon to Venice, only a kilometer away.

"Your Royal Highness," Daia said, "as much as tomorrow is supposed to be a soft-focus puff piece, there is one question I can't not ask you. And that's just an ineluctable truth about who I am—who my people are."

Saskia nodded. She'd known this was coming. Daia was a Sikh. Her grandparents had come to England from the Punjab. She wasn't observant to the point of wearing a headscarf all the time. But any photo of a Chand family reunion would feature a lot of turbans. And she was said to be as fluent in Punjabi as she was in English. "Go on, by all means!" Saskia offered.

Daia nodded. "Here we are in the second week of July," she said. "The monsoon is late. So late that some in the Punjab are beginning to wonder whether it will come this year at all."

Saskia nodded. "What are the latest forecasts? I heard there was hope."

"The long-range forecast is not without promise. Thank God."

"Has it ever been this late before?"

"Of course. Some years it fails altogether. But that's not the point. The point is that people look at this"—Daia gestured toward the sunset, which was of rare beauty—"and they see that the rains are late in the Punjab . . ."

"And they can't not put two and two together."

They walked across the courtyard to join Michiel, Chiara, and Cornelia for a light, informal dinner in what had formerly been the convent's refectory. Also with them was Marco Orsini, the leader of the Vexital movement, sometimes called "the Doge" by the tabloid press. He was in his forties, conservatively attired, with an earnest, approachable manner that probably came in handy in his role of trying to promulgate what most would consider a daft idea. And Marco had brought with him his friend Pau, an activist from Barcelona—a city that, like Venice, was trying to get free of the country it had been lumped into.

The table looked a thousand years old; the molecular-cuisine tapas being carried in by the waitstaff had been prepared in a kitchen that looked like it had been refurbished by NASA. Art, mostly quite old, adorned those parts of the walls not covered by cracked and faded frescoes. Saskia could only imagine what this family's art collection must look like. She saw paintings she supposed were knockoffs of Titians or Tintorettos until she got it through her head that they were the real things.

The most prominent work on display was a Renaissance painting of Ceres in her winged chariot. The very goddess after whom cereals were named. She was flying over an idealized Tuscan landscape looking for her lost daughter Proserpina. Saskia knew the story perfectly well. The grief of Ceres over the loss of contact with her daughter—taken away to be the unwilling queen of the underworld—was the cause of seasons. Crops withered and died at the bidding of Ceres. But she was also the goddess of growth and fertility when she was in a more generous frame of mind. The choice of this painting to hang above this dinner table could not have been an accident, any more than the "Queen of Netherworld" banner.

"I wonder what the Romans would have made of that myth," Saskia reflected, "if they had understood the workings of the hemispheres and the fact that winter in the north was summer in the south? That you can't have one without the other?"

It was meant as a light conversational gambit, but Daia didn't take it that way. "Let's be clear about what you're getting at," she said. "Saving Venice from the sea might mean famine in the Punjab."

"That's actually *not* what I was getting at," Saskia said.

"No one wants famine in the Punjab, or anywhere else," Cornelia said. "It's not as simple a trade as that—fortunately for everyone."

"The Indian Academy of Sciences has published some climate simulations that suggest otherwise."

"In the scenario where Pina2bo is the *only* site of stratospheric sulfur injection in the whole world," Michiel said, "and it runs at maximum capacity year-round, maybe that is the case. That is why we are bringing Vadan online later this year. And it's why T.R. has begun work on Papua. Which adds a site in the Southern Hemisphere."

"How does that help us?"

"Historically, volcanic eruptions south of the equator are associated with stronger monsoons."

It turned out that Daia had never heard of Vadan. Saskia could hardly blame her. She'd never have known any of this had Cornelia not made her aware. So they took a minute to explain the basics: it was a rocky isle off the remote Albanian coast, formerly an outpost of the Venetian Empire, later a Soviet chemical munitions factory, and—as of about a year ago—the site of a project to build a clone of Pina2bo. From Venice, Vadan lay about eight hundred kilometers to the southeast. Along with other attendees, Saskia was scheduled to visit the place for a conference in a few days.

"You people are full of surprises," Daia mused. "Who knew that Albania was going to become a player?"

"North Macedonia?" Chiara guessed.

"You joke, but what's to prevent it? Why shouldn't North Macedonia build one, if Albania's doing it?"

"Because they don't need to. The effects spread out over a wide area," Michiel reminded her, "so North Macedonia gets a free ride. What's good for Albania is good for them, and everyone else downwind."

"In this hemisphere, prevailing winds are from the west," Daia pointed out. "Vadan's in the wrong direction from Venice, is it not?"

"Yes, if all we cared about was cooling the weather here," Michiel said. "Vadan won't do that. Instead it will cool down Turkey, Syria, and Iraq—places that are in danger of becoming uninhabitable because of rising temperatures."

"Just as Pina2bo has already made a measurable difference in Austin and Houston," Chiara put in.

"Well, that gives me a hint as to how you financed Vadan," Daia said.

This connection hadn't occurred to Saskia. She'd vaguely assumed that Vadan was all financed by mysterious Venetian oligarchs. But the look on the faces of Michiel and Chiara made it clear Daia had guessed correctly.

"The benefit to Venice is . . . indirect," Marco said. He'd been mostly quiet until now. Pau, his friend from Barcelona, hadn't said a word; he was content to enjoy the food and the wine and proximity to Chiara. It was clear that these two were an item.

"Oh, I *get* it. Sea level," Daia said. "So Venice's existential threat from the sea creates a natural alliance between you and overheated Persian Gulf states lying downwind of this island of Vadan, which is otherwise just a Soviet-era toxic waste dump that is useless to Albania but desirable to Venice in beginning to reassemble her Adriatic sphere of influence. Strange bedfellows!"

Cornelia said, "Strange bedfellows have been a constant throughout all history."

"It's just that climate change moves the beds around?" Saskia added.

"To cool off *this* part of the world, you'd have to build one upwind," Daia supposed. "In your neck of the woods, *mevrouw?*"

"T.R. had his eye on some coal mines in the southeastern Netherlands," Saskia said, "but the sonic booms could be heard across the border in Germany and it would have meant trouble with the neighbors. No, if people want to put sulfur into the stratosphere over Northern Europe, they'll have to build special aeroplanes."

"Back to the Punjab," Daia said. "The Breadbasket. Maybe I should start calling it that, just to make the stakes clear. *Where food comes from.* The climate simulations—"

"Were based on a different scenario. Pina2bo only," Cornelia said. "Not factoring in Vadan or Papua."

"And what do the simulations say when those *are* factored in?"

Cornelia, never a great one for diplomacy, broke eye contact in a way that showed impatience, even irritation. Michiel, in his role as smoother-over, glided in like a soccer player moving to intercept a pass. "That is a little like asking, 'What is the result of acupuncture?' There is no one answer."

"You lost me there."

"I used to have sinus headaches," Michiel said. "Nothing helped. Miserable. I went to see an acupuncturist. She put needles in my face, as you might expect. But also in my hands and feet! How can this possibly work!? How can a needle between my toes make my sinuses feel better?" He shrugged. "It all has to do with the flow of energy around the system."

"Which is never obvious," Marco added.

"But acupuncturists have that all mapped out, you're saying," Daia said. "We can trust them."

"In this case," Michiel continued, "maybe there are three points where we have the needles: Pina2bo, Vadan, Papua. Maybe more later. What does that mean for the Punjab? *There is no one answer.* It depends on how they are used. How they are tweaked."

"This is *why* we got involved with Vadan," Marco said. "Maybe we find out that if Pina2bo shuts down for two months in the winter and Papua runs heavy for six weeks in the spring, the monsoons in the Breadbasket come out perfect."

"But people starve in China," Daia said.

"China might have something to say about that," Cornelia said, in a tone of dry witticism.

Daia exchanged a look with Saskia, the import of which was *Do you understand what she's on about? I don't.*

"What do you mean, Cornelia?" Saskia asked.

"You could just as well point out that the United States could drop a bomb on Beijing, and hurt China! Why don't they? Because China doesn't like to get bombed and would retaliate."

"Also," Chiara put in, with a nervous glance at her aunt, "because it's just stupid to hurt people for no reason!"

"That too. Now, imagine if it took six months to transport the bomb from America to Beijing, and you had to do it in the open."

Daia nodded. "There can be no sneak attacks. No climate Pearl Harbors."

"The Alastairs and the Eshmas of the world know their business too well."

"But they are just voices crying in the wilderness," Saskia said, "if they're not backed up by some kind of muscle. China and India both have the big stick. What about, I don't know, Iceland? Myanmar? Chad?"

"Venice?" Marco added.

"Catalunya!" said Pau.

"All that boils down to," Cornelia said, "is that strong countries are strong and weak countries are weak. Which was true before." She picked up her phone and began shuffling through pictures. "You know, on the boat trip I took last year, we passed through the Suez Canal. The Bab el Mandeb. The Malacca Strait. All famous choke points to the navigation of the seas. People have been fighting wars over those places for hundreds of years. And when they are not fighting wars they are playing geopolitical chess games around who will control those 'acupuncture points.' This is the same. It's just that some places that most people have never heard of are going to become the Suez Canals of the future. And the great and small powers of the world will have to mark them out on their chessboards and maybe even prepare for conflict. But if you suppose any of that is new, you don't know history."

VADAN

hough he was not a licensed pilot, Michiel belonged to that class of people who spent a lot of time messing about in boats and planes and had some knowledge of how they worked. Saskia was old enough to remember when a man of that description might have been called a playboy. Among European royalty there was no lack of such. But no self-respecting man wanted to be called that anymore. Anyway, the Venetian didn't have a job per se, or any fixed slate of obligations relating to work or family. When it came time for Saskia to head for Vadan, Michiel asked if he might join her in the co-pilot's seat, and she said yes without hesitation. He was good company to be sure. And though she wouldn't have trusted him to take the Beaver off or land it, he could manage it in level flight when she needed the occasional break.

The journey lent itself to an easygoing, short-hop style of travel. They were essentially flying down the whole length of the Adriatic. They chose to follow its Italian, as opposed to its Balkan, coast. They could put the plane down almost anywhere, and it would usually turn out to be someplace charming. Michiel, who had roamed up and down this coast in pleasure craft his whole life, knew of good places to get coffee or a delicious meal while the Beaver was being refueled. They stopped once about halfway along in a little old Roman town, unspoiled by tourism and yet still well supplied with cafés and restaurants because of a local art scene. Then they flew a leg to near Brindisi, on the heel of Italy, at the narrowest part of the Adriatic. Here there was more modern hustle and bustle because of its maritime connections to Albania and Greece, but Michiel knew of a fantastic little waterfront bar, just colorful enough to feel like a real place, patronized by a hilarious mix of locals and old salts passing through. It was tucked in beside a fishermen's wharf across a cove from the fuel dock. The crew looking after the plane there, mostly Albanian immigrants, were in love with it and asked Michiel all sorts of questions. They were assuming that he, and not the woman by his side, was the owner and pilot. In other circumstances Saskia might have taken offense at that, but she was luxuriating in this brief spell of anonymity. None of these men had had a clue that she was Her Royal Highness Frederika Mathilde Louisa Saskia of the Netherlands. She was just the wife or girlfriend of this cool-looking Italian guy—who addressed her as Saskia. She didn't have to *do* anything. Didn't have to think twelve steps ahead or worry about how her every word and gesture would play on social media.

Once they were established in that waterfront bar with glasses of white wine and a plate of snails, Michiel squinted across the sun-sparkled water of the cove toward the fuel dock, then pulled his sunglasses down on his nose, looked over them at Saskia, and said, "Those men are fascinated by your Beaver. As am I."

Lotte had already made Saskia well aware of a fact that never would have occurred to her otherwise, namely that in English slang the word "beaver" meant a woman's genitals. The pun had since cropped up in conversation a few times. So Saskia was ready for the double meaning. Or at least she had to assume that Michiel was simultaneously making a perfectly aboveboard remark about aviation and hitting on her.

As with any double entendre, there was a need to proceed with caution, in case he actually *was* only talking of airplanes. But she doubted it. The plane was loud when it was in the air. Normal conversation was difficult. So they had spent much of the flight just looking and smiling at each other, and Michiel gave every indication of liking what he saw.

"You need to be aware," she said, "that it's old and complicated and takes a while to get up to speed. Not like the new models you're probably used to."

"Newer models have complicated features that are tiresome and high-maintenance in their own way," he pointed out.

"As long as you understand," she said, biting into a snail, "that the Beaver is mine, and it has other places to go."

After a short flight across the Adriatic, Vadan came into view. It lay fifteen kilometers off the mountainous coast of Albania's mainland and would have been a mountain in its own right if sea level was lower. There was still a good hour of daylight remaining and so Saskia made a low orbit around the island's summit so that she and Michiel could get a look at how the work was progressing. A lot had happened since the last photos Cornelia had sent her, back in the autumn. The road that zigzagged to the summit had been paved. Additional construction trailers had been hauled up and arranged around the head frame. A considerable heap of spoil gave a sense of the depth of the shaft. From having been to Pina2bo, Saskia knew what else to look for: a pile of sulfur, plumbing for natural gas, and a separate complex of new buildings, a couple of kilometers down the road, where people could live and work with at least some separation from the sonic booms.

The island only had one decent anchorage, in a rocky cove on its northern end. Even if they'd lacked a chart, they'd have been able to find it just by flying along the road—*the* road, for there were no others on this island—until it met the water. Running parallel to it was new-looking infrastructure, most notably a gas pipeline. All of it terminated at the dock where Venetian merchants had called a thousand years ago, sailing to and from Constantinople, and which more recently the Soviets had beefed up into a military compound. Those days, of course, were long past, and so what was left of that infrastructure was as shabby and forlorn as might be expected. But within the last year the pier had been upgraded to modern standards, and other improvements were shouldering the rubble of the Warsaw Pact off to the margins. One day soon, the ships calling here would be bulk carriers bringing sulfur and natural gas to feed the gun.

Today, though, the only vessels of any consequence were pleasure craft. Two of them. Tied up on opposite sides of the pier. They couldn't have been much more different. The larger—*much* larger—of the two was one of those yachts so huge it might be mistaken for a cruise liner if not for its rakish and cool-looking design. It had *two* helipads, both occupied at the moment, and a berth out of which a smaller, more nimble superyacht could be deployed.

The yacht on the opposite side of the pier might have looked big in some anchorages, but not here. It was perhaps half the length of the other. Nearly as tall, though, because of two sails projecting from amidships. Really not so much sails as wings that were pointed straight up.

Saskia swung the plane round past the mouth of the cove, shedding altitude, then banked back and brought it in for a landing. It came nearly to a stop several hundred meters abaft of the larger yacht. The name *Crescent* was emblazoned across her stern in both Roman and Arabic script. As Saskia piloted the Beaver toward the end of the pier, the stern of the sail-powered vessel came into view; she was christened *Bøkesuden*. Staff were on hand to help make the plane fast and handle luggage and so on, but some crew from the yachts had also come down to greet them. The ones from *Crescent* were Arabs and Turks. Those from *Bøkesuden* were Norwegians. Two ethnic groups that had little in common, save that they got all their money from oil.

And the similarities ended there. The differences were conspicuous in the way each group felt about the protocol around welcoming a royal visitor. Both ships' captains had come down to greet her. The Norwegian captain, a woman in her forties, treated her in a respectful but basically matter-of-fact way a Dutch person would. Saskia got a clue as to why as they walked down the pier and she saw the coat of arms of the Norwegian royal house blazoned on the stern of *Bøkesuden*. This thing was actually a royal yacht. She'd heard about it. It was completely green, wind- and solar-powered from stem to stern, a floating showcase both for the latest climate-conscious technology and for traditional Norwegian shipbuilding know-how. But the royal ensign was not flying from it today, so apparently the king was not aboard.

The captain of *Crescent* was English and treated Princess Frederika with the deference he might have shown to the reigning monarch of his native land. Below him, in the yacht's considerable org chart, tended to be Turks near the top giving way to Filipinos and Bangladeshis filling out the ranks of deckhands, housekeeping staff, and food service.

Saskia wasn't a yacht person. But she knew people who were, and had got the picture, through them, that when boats like this exceeded a certain size, the expectation was that they would basically be staffed and operated as resorts. If you were going to provide toys—parasails, Jet Skis, scuba gear, fishing tackle, and all the rest—you had to provide staff who knew how to keep all that stuff running and who could show the guests a good time while making sure no one got killed. Those staff all needed places to sleep and to eat, separate from guest cabins of course. Throw in a full-time security detail and the yacht had to be that enormous just to carry out its basic functions.

Crescent was one of those. The owner was a Saudi prince. Which wasn't saying much; there were many. As far as she could tell, this guy—Fahd bin Talal—wasn't the type who cut journalists up with bone saws. Dressed in a long white dishdasha and red-and-white headscarf, accessorized with gilt-edged sunglasses, he greeted Saskia at the gangway, flanked by at least a dozen uniformed crew members, and handed her a bouquet before escorting her aboard—where a woman was waiting just so that Saskia could hand the bouquet off to her and not have to lug it around. After a brief walkaround she was escorted to the royal suite, or at least *a* royal suite, and introduced to a phalanx of butlers, stewards, housekeepers, and so on who would see to her every need.

None of which was exactly unheard of, when you were a queen; but Dutch royals steered clear of it. She knew she'd have felt much more at home on the Norwegian eco-yacht.

She'd lost track of Michiel during all this. No formal activities were slated for this evening. She spent a few minutes freshening up and changing clothes, then ventured out, bracing herself for more aggressive hospitality. Michiel had sent her a selfie as a clue as to where he might be tracked down. The sun was dropping below the horizon when she found him sitting in one of the yacht's bars, an open-air, tiki-themed establishment beside the swimming pool. Why you'd have a swimming pool on a boat that floated in the water wasn't clear to her. Maybe so that you could have a poolside bar. Anyway, Michiel—who'd been assigned to a slightly less palatial stateroom—was sitting there in a Hawaiian shirt and white slacks enjoying a cocktail with a shirtless and even more good-looking man who bore an uncanny resemblance to—

He stood up when he saw her coming. "Ma'am," he said. Then, worried—hilariously—that she wouldn't recognize him, he added, "I'm—"

"Jules. The Family Jules. Such a pleasure to see you again."

He seemed chuffed to be recognized. Michiel was just grinning, enjoying the moment.

"In case you're wondering," Jules offered, "I was looking for work on this side of the ol' pond, so I could—"

"So you could be within striking distance of Fenna!"

He nodded and grinned. "Oil rig work and such is hard to break into because of unions and certs, but—"

"There was an opening on a yacht, for a personable young man who could teach guests how to scuba dive."

"Exactly, ma'am."

"Well! That explains—"

"Why Fenna's coming to help you get ready for the big party tomorrow evenin'!" Jules said, now smiling broadly.

"She seemed incredibly eager to do so. I fancied she was doing me a favor."

"I'm real glad it worked out!"

"Not as glad as you're going to be, I'm quite sure."

If it was possible for a man as deeply and perfectly tanned as Jules to blush, he did so.

Something about the knowledge that Fenna and Jules were tomorrow going to be fucking each other's brains out in the manner that had been so conspicuous in Texas made it seem not merely okay but almost a matter of some urgency that Saskia and Michiel get to it first. After Jules politely excused himself and left them alone together, they had dinner brought out and they dined poolside, al fresco, in a setting as romantic as it was possible for a decommissioned Cold War Soviet nerve gas depot to be. Then they went back to Saskia's suite and got the Beaver up to cruising altitude. The next morning they had another go. After a little doze, Michiel got out of bed and began taking a shower. Saskia put on one of the provided bathrobes, ordered coffee, and was sitting there in a condition of pleasant post-coital disarray when a knock came at the door.

"Come in!" she called, and it opened to reveal a waiter carrying a silver tray. And, right behind him, a young man. Blond, bearded, oddly familiar-looking, clearly not a servant. The look on both men's faces suggested it was an awkward coincidence. The blond man politely held the door open for the waiter, but then averted his gaze from Saskia, backed out into the corridor, and allowed it to swing closed.

Saskia only had to turn her head and look out the window across the pier. *Bøkesuden* was still tied up there. But this morning it was flying a new flag, bearing a royal coat of arms. Not the purple-mantled one used exclusively by the king but the red-mantled version used by the crown prince.

She strode past the bewildered waiter and peered through the peephole in the door. Prince Bjorn of Norway was still standing there, looking indecisive. When she hauled the door open, though, he looked astonished and unnerved. It didn't help that her robe almost fell open when the door snagged it. She caught it with her free hand just in the nick of time and retied it while the prince gamely tried to keep his eyes on her face. He was wearing a navy blue blazer and a well-tailored dress shirt over khakis. Looked as though he'd have been more comfortable, though, skiing through the mountains.

"Prince Bjorn!" she exclaimed.

"Your Royal Highness. When we last met—"

"My husband's funeral. You were just a boy. How you've grown! Are you here to talk to me about my daughter?"

"Well, yes."

"Come in."

They sat down across the coffee table from each other. The waiter poured coffee for both of them. Saskia took advantage of the delay by pulling up a certain selfie on her phone. She showed it to Bjorn: Lotte in the gown she'd worn to the ball on the day she'd become Queen of the Netherlands, making a comically exaggerated wink as she posed next to Bjorn, who here was looking even more uncomfortable in black tie. Bjorn blushed as deeply as Jules had yesterday, but he was a lot more careful about using sunscreen—something of a professional obligation when you were the crown prince of a country full of outdoorsy melanin-deprived people—and so it really showed.

"Well then, I'll get right to the point," he said, as soon as the door had closed behind the waiter.

"Oh my god, is she pregnant?"

Bjorn barked out a nervous laugh. "Certainly not! My god. We haven't even *done* anything."

"I'm just joking. If she were pregnant, you couldn't possibly know yet."

"The point is, she's seventeen."

"I was aware of it."

"I'm twenty-two." He shrugged. "It might seem a small difference to—to—"

"To someone as old as me? Go ahead, it's okay."

"But I just wanted to say—because there have already been false reports on the Internet—"

"Someone on the Internet is wrong? I don't believe it!"

"Nothing has happened. And nothing will, until she is of a proper age. But—" Here Bjorn got stuck again.

"But you would like it to happen."

"I believe there is potential there. Yes."

"Potential. A dry and somewhat technical-sounding way to say it. You're an engineering student?"

"Not anymore. Got my degree."

"Congratulations!"

"I'm going to work on carbon capture."

"Well, you seem like a wonderful young man. Serious and self-disciplined. Respectful in the way you treat women. I wouldn't want anyone in my family to end up with some playboy."

From the look on Bjorn's face it seemed that this term was unfamiliar to him. Once again, she had dated herself. "I think now they are called fuckboys or something."

The bathroom door opened and Michiel strode out, staring down at the screen of his phone. His bathrobe was wide open, sash dragging on the floor, flat stomach glistening, his erect penis sticking out like the bowsprit of the royal yacht. "Something came up while I was in the shower!" he announced, snapping a photograph. Then he looked up.

"His Royal Highness Prince Bjorn of Norway," Saskia announced, but before Bjorn could scramble to his feet Michiel had retreated into the bedroom.

"Like that," Saskia said coolly. "Don't be like him and we'll get along fine, you and I."

It occurred to Saskia that if she moved fast she might be able to reach Michiel before it was too late. "See you at the opening session, Bjorn, in—what—an hour and a half?"

"Thirty minutes, in fact," Bjorn said apologetically, getting to his feet. His eyes darted to the bedroom door. "But, you're a queen, you know."

"More of a Dowager at this point."

"Anyway, you can show up whenever you like, of course."

"I'll be there in forty-five," Saskia said. "Tell them I'm powdering my nose."

Crescent had many fine qualities, but at the end of the day it was a pleasure barge and its largest single room was a disco. That was the backup location for the conference, if the weather turned bad. But it was fine and so they met under a canopy that the event planners had pitched a short walk up the road from the pier, amid the ruins of the old fortified town that the Venetians had built there a thousand years ago. The remains of a church could be seen, with a pitted and broken frieze of the winged lion that was the emblem of that city and its long-forgotten empire. Across the way from that was a loudspeaker thrust into the air on a pole from which the Muslim call to prayer was broadcast five times a day. The construction of the big gun had drawn a couple of hundred Albanian workers to the island, and this was a largely Muslim country, so they were making do with this simple workaround while a proper mosque was being constructed nearby.

An Audi was waiting for Princess Frederika on the pier, but it hardly seemed worth the trouble of climbing into it, so she walked up to the site in time for the tail end of the pre-meeting coffee-and-pastries mixer. Michiel would follow later; he had some things to catch up on with Cornelia, who was inbound from Brindisi. The day was sunny and looked as though it might turn warm, but a cool breeze was coming up from the Adriatic and the event planners had stockpiled electric fans that they could deploy if they noticed guests fanning themselves with their programs. But with the exception of the Norwegians and a City of London contingent— which included Alastair—most of the people here came from hot places. A lot of Arabs. Some Turks. Texans and Louisianans. Contingents from Bangladesh, West Bengal, Maldives, Laccadives, the Marshall Islands. Indonesians displaced by the flooding of Jakarta, Australians from a part of their country that a few months ago had been the hottest place in the world for two straight weeks. If any audience could put up with a balmy afternoon, it was this one.

The name of the conference was Netherworld. It had a logo, inevitably, and swag with the logo on it. The image was a stylized map of the world showing only what T.R. would have described as stochastic land: everything within a couple of meters of sea level. Deep water, and the interiors of continents, were blank. So it was a lacy archipelago strung about the globe, fat in places like the Netherlands, razor thin in places like Norway or America's West Coast where the land erupted steeply from the water.

It was always a pleasure working with a fellow professional. Prince Bjorn had the royal thing down pat. He understood as well as Saskia that his job at an event like this one was to say a few words—just enough to sprinkle the royal fairy dust over the proceedings—and then sit down and shut up, smiling and nodding and applauding on cue. So he said his words, and Princess Frederika, newly abdicated but always a royal, said hers, and they sat down next to each other in the front row and did their jobs. Prince Fahd bin Talal, on the other hand, was from a place where royals still had some real authority, and so he took a more active role.

A series of panel discussions and solo talks had been artfully programmed to give equal time to the likes of the Marshall Islands. But the money was Norwegian and Saudi. Bjorn was here as figurehead, but the real power was a trio representing three-eighths of the executive board of the Oil Fund. That wasn't its official name, but it was what people called it, because that's what it was: a sovereign wealth fund into which Norway had dumped the profits of its North Sea oil production over the last fifty or so years. Last Saskia had bothered to check, it was well over a trillion dollars—the largest such fund in the world. And she should know; the oil from those rigs came ashore at Rotterdam.

So the Oil Fund contingent was two men and a woman, all in their fifties or sixties, dressed in business casual as per the invitation, in no way famous or recognizable. They could have been lecturers at a Scandinavian university or docents at a museum. But they controlled a trillion dollars that had been earned by injecting carbon dioxide into the atmosphere. No accident that Prince Bjorn's engineering talents were going to be dedicated to carbon capture technology; this was very much a case of a royal leading by example.

The Saudis had made a lot more from petroleum than the Norwegians, but spread the money out among funds and companies and individuals in a way that was more difficult for Westerners to keep track of. But it wasn't unreasonable to guess that their host could tap into an amount comparable to what the Norwegians were looking after. And he probably had greater freedom to spend it.

Prince Fahd did have some skill at public speaking. Not for nothing had he earned degrees at Oxford and at Yale. "Some of us live in places that are too low," he said, with a gesture of respect to Saskia, and a nod to the Marshall Islanders, "but I live in a place that is too hot. Perhaps we can work together. Those of us who have reaped great rewards making the situation worse"—this with a glance at the Norwegians—"are sensible that we might have a role to play in setting things right. One who could not be here today has amazed the world by taking aggressive action to shield our world from an angry sun. Later we'll go up to the top of the mountain to see another such facility launch its first projectile into the Albanian stratosphere. As the veil spreads downwind it will, I hope, provide a measure of relief to our brothers and sisters in Turkey, Syria, and Iraq. Other such projects are being contemplated in places farther to the south, where we hope they will benefit my home country as well as helping to combat rising sea levels all over Netherworld." This the first, albeit oblique, public acknowledgment of something Saskia had got wind of from the Venetians, namely that the Saudis had been busy with a little project of their own.

"Many are the voices who will say—who have already said, quite vocally—that this is at best nothing more than a stopgap solution. I'm sure our friends from the Maldives, the Laccadives, and the Marshall Islands would take a different view! But of course the detractors have a point. It is absolutely the case that we cannot long survive on a program that consists exclusively of bouncing back the sun's radiation using a thin veil of gas. We must take advantage of the brief respite that such interventions give us to *remove carbon from our atmosphere*." This the big lectern-thumping applause line. "And we must do it," he continued, raising his voice over the clapping, "on a scale that matches—no, even exceeds—the scope of the coal and petroleum industries' global operations during the last hundred and fifty years. They had a century and a half to put carbon into the atmosphere; we have only decades to take it back out. It will be expensive. But we have money. Abraham Lincoln, in his second inaugural address, said, 'Yet, if God wills that the Civil War continue until all the wealth piled by the bondsman's two hundred and fifty years of unrequited toil shall be sunk and until every drop of blood drawn with the lash shall be paid by another drawn with the sword . . . so still it must be said that the judgments of the Lord are true and righteous altogether.' If, at the end of all this, the pensioners of oil-rich countries are once again only being supported by the proceeds of modern clean industries, then we will truly know that the money has been well looked after."

Strong words. Saskia smiled, nodded, and applauded at all the right moments. She really couldn't tell whether Fahd bin Talal was full of shit. He might sincerely believe every word he said, and he might not. If he was sincere, he might be completely delusional. It could be that tomorrow he'd fly back to Riyadh and never be seen or heard from again. But a big part of her job had always been signaling agreement with people who were some combination of delusional or disingenuous, so, for the moment, it didn't matter to her. He was proposing to spend a lot of money to fix the atmosphere. How could she find fault with that?

It was a sufficiently effective keynote speech to make the remainder of the conference seem almost superfluous. Prince Bjorn moderated a panel of experts discussing the pros and cons of various carbon capture schemes. A questioner from the City of London poured cold water over it by pointing out there was no way to pay for any of this. They watched an expensively produced presentation about a proposal to carpet a large part of the Sahara with photovoltaic panels. Another speaker talked about the notion that everything T.R. was doing could one day be replaced by a cloud of giant mirrors between the earth and the sun.

The afternoon was going to be breakout sessions on a range of topics. But first there was a long lunch break. Everyone piled aboard buses that took them to the top of the mountain. There they sat beneath another canopy and ate box lunches and sipped bottled water as the Albanian minister of infrastructure and energy said a few words and then slammed the palm of her hand down on a big red button mounted in a mocked-up control panel. The muzzle flashed, the shell flew, and the sonic boom—despite the fact that they had been warned and had all put in their free earplugs—scared the hell out of everyone. Everyone, that is, except for those who'd heard it before in West Texas: Saskia, Alastair, Michiel, and Cornelia—who'd made an uncharacteristically low-key entrance at some point during the morning session. Naturally this made Saskia think of those who couldn't be here today. Fenna was apparently on her way in from the airport in Tirana and might have heard the boom. But Willem was enjoying a prolonged vacation in the South of France, and Amelia was pursuing a new career with a private security firm based out of London. Saskia took out her phone and texted Willem.

> They just fired it. Wish you were here!

> Glad I'm not :)

Willem followed up with a picture of Remi lounging next to a pool raising a drink.

A socially awkward situation came up later in the day, when the prince—the Saudi, not the Norwegian—attempted to give Princess Frederika a jet airplane.

He had the good sense to be somewhat discreet in how he went about it. After the conclusion of the afternoon program, but before the cocktail hour that would precede the big dinner party, he asked Saskia if she wouldn't mind accompanying him down to the island's airstrip to have a look at something she might find interesting. "Airstrip" maybe was the wrong word for a four-thousand-meter runway that the Soviets had dynamited out of the island's southern plateau to accommodate heavy military transports. But there was no point quibbling over it. She had to send a message to Fenna, who was poised in the royal suite on the yacht, just waiting to get her hands on Saskia's hair and face, letting her know that there would be this slight delay. Then it was off to the "airstrip" in a short motorcade consisting of three Bentleys: one for the gents, one for the lady, and one for the short-haired men with guns and earpieces. A few business jets were parked at the end of the runway, as well as a couple of 737s that had been chartered to bring various contingents in to the conference. Only one airplane, however, was adorned with a giant bow. Just like the ones that appeared on new SUVs in Super Bowl television ads. This bow happened to be bright green, which could have been taken as a symbol of Islam or of the global environmental movement. The plane was of an unusual configuration and it had weird-looking engines. Its stair had been deployed to the tarmac. At its base a uniformed pilot and a man in a business suit were waiting for them. They were trying to act all casual about it.

Saskia was glad to be alone in the ladies' Bentley so that she could react with some amount of privacy. When you were a queen, people gave you things. Sometimes weird—very weird—things. Sometimes things that were inappropriate, in the sense of raising questions about conflict of interest and undue influence. She'd thought she'd put all that behind her by abdicating the throne. Apparently not, though. Apparently it only got worse from here, since she was no longer subject to the same level of scrutiny. So she laughed, groaned, put her face in her hands, and writhed in almost physical discomfort for a few moments before pulling herself together and putting on her fake, queenly smile just in time for the chauffeur to circumnavigate the Bentley and open the door.

One thing she absolutely *couldn't* do was beg off. Frederika Mathilde Louisa Saskia had to play the role. Had to take the tour. Had to sit in the pilot's seat and look fascinated as it was all explained to her by Ervin—the pilot—and Clyde, the guy in the suit. Both Americans. Clyde had founded the company that made this thing: a bizjet that was fueled by hydrogen, running it through fuel cells to power electric motors. The prince had invested in it. And now they wanted to give her the plane.

"Because of Waco," she said to Alastair, a few hours later, "part of me just wants to say 'fuck yes, I'll take that plane.'"

Alastair, in black tie—for this was that kind of party—just gazed into his after-dinner whiskey and tried not to look any more amused than he already did. He'd already made the obligatory point that no one ever tried to give *him* jet airplanes. It would have been simply boring and stupid of him to have kept pounding away at that topic.

"Like karma. *Good* karma, I mean to say," he said.

"Absolutely. I crashed that plane to be sure."

Alastair raised an eyebrow. "Some would blame the pigs."

"Or the alligator that chased the pigs. Or the refugees who chased the alligator. Or the fire ants that burned out the relays in their air conditioners. You can go on spreading the blame as far as you like. But I was flying the plane. The buck stops at the pilot's chair."

"Formally, it was your responsibility," Alastair agreed. "And yet at some level you feel that the universe owes you a free jet airplane."

"I'd never come out and say it like that. But yes."

"Do you know how to fly it?"

"Absolutely not! Since the crash the only thing I've flown is the Beaver. Clyde would have to loan me Ervin until I could get certified."

"So they're throwing in a pilot. Probably just a round-off error at this point." A thought occurred to Alastair. "Where does one gas it up? Can you buy hydrogen at airports?"

"I have no idea. Maybe the crown prince of Norway would know!"

Prince Bjorn had been edging closer, waiting for an opening. "Your Royal Highness," he began, "I have been admiring you from the other end of the table all evening. You are magnificent."

So Bjorn—unlike Alastair, who hadn't said a word about her hair and gown—knew how it was done. Saskia accepted the compliment with a wink. "It's amazing, I just sit there checking my Twitter and it's all handled for me by people who actually know what they're doing."

She went on to introduce Alastair as a close adviser. Which was no longer technically the case; but whatever. The point was to signal to Bjorn that he could speak as though among friends, should he so choose. "I heard," he said, "about your new plane."

"It's not mine until I accept the gift," she cautioned him.

"Well, should you decide you are in an accepting mood," he said, "on behalf of my father, I am offering you the unlimited use of the royal yacht *Bøkesuden.*"

"Really?"

"Really. The hydrogen-fueled jet can, of course, take you to many places much more quickly . . ."

Saskia held out one hand, palm down, and bobbled it from side to side. "I can't *leave*, though, until a truck full of hydrogen shows up. Could take a while!"

"My point exactly. For some missions, a boat is really what you need."

Saskia raised her eyebrows. "So it's *missions* I'm to be going on now, is it?"

"Perhaps the wrong choice of words. We talked about this before. I am too much the engineer sometimes."

"You're forgiven, Bjorn, since you're trying to give me a yacht."

"*The use of* a yacht," he corrected her.

"What if His Majesty the King of Norway has a mind to go boating? While I'm on his yacht, on a *mission*?"

"It's Norway. We'll make another."

She went to bed thinking that it was all perfectly ridiculous—just a case of some well-meaning friends with too much money, taking this "Queen of Netherworld" gag too seriously, and acting on impulse. Tomorrow, the second and last day of the conference, she would find a way to take these guys aside one at a time and let them down easy.

Saskia woke up in the opposite frame of mind. Looking down at the snoring Michiel, she realized it was *him* she was going to have to let down easy. The other guys she had to begin taking seriously.

What had changed was a series of messages and news reports that had come in while she was sleeping. It seemed that a lot was going on in both New Guinea and West Texas. India was making noises about "climate peacekeeping" and denouncing the firing of the gun in Albania yesterday—in a way hinting that it justified their taking unilateral action. China was talking in an equally menacing way about the instability in Papua. Indonesia, they were saying, might claim the western half of New Guinea for their own, but that was really just a holdover from the days of Dutch colonialism—a discredited way of thinking. The United States—which used to intervene in such situations—was a basket case and global laughingstock; the United Nations couldn't act fast

enough; something had to be done to protect the defenseless Papuans and incidentally safeguard the world's copper supply. Jumping out from all these news feeds were words like "Sneeuwberg"
and "RoDuSh"—constant jabbing reminders of the connections
back to the Netherlands.

Yesterday, during all the talk about carbon in the atmosphere,
Norway had been taking a bullet that might otherwise have been
aimed at the Netherlands. Royal Dutch Shell had been one of the
world's great petro-powers and had amassed great wealth during
the twentieth century. It was only in the last five decades that Norway had turned into a petro-state and eclipsed the Dutch—who at
the same time had been retreating from their colonial empire. The
workings of the stock market had spread the ownership of Shell
and its profits and its liabilities among shareholders all over the
world. Saskia's country had been happy to quietly park Norwegian
crude in vast tank farms at Rotterdam, to refine it, and to pipe it
up the Rhine.

It was all what Alastair described as "cruft," meaning complicated and messy holdovers from obsolete code and discontinued
operating systems. This was cruft of a geopolitical sort. But cruft
was a real thing, it had consequences, and it had to be managed.
It seemed that the world was asking Saskia to play some part in its
management.

THE LINE

There was a catch, sort of. When in life, though, was there ever *not* a catch? During the after-dinner chitchat, Prince Fahd had strolled over for a bit of airplane talk. In an apologetic and self-deprecating tone—as if he had embarrassed himself by giving Princess Frederika the wrong type of jet airplane—he mentioned that its range was nothing like what a modern bizjet was capable of. Gone were the days of nonstop flights from Schiphol to Sydney. No, getting around in that thing was going to be more akin to traveling in the Beaver: shorter hops, more frequent stops. And, further compounding his shame, the stops couldn't be just anywhere: obviously you had to put the thing down at a location where hydrogen was available. Of course, very few airports had that on tap. But in many of your more technologically advanced countries it was possible to have a truck deliver the stuff to the tarmac and pump it directly into the plane. It just required a bit more advance planning, which the prince's staff would be glad to assist with until Princess Frederika and her people got up to speed.

Saskia had to suppress an impulse to confess that she no longer *had* "people" in that sense of the term. She was meaning to get some sooner or later. She could support a modest staff. But, for now, she was still enjoying the simplicity and freedom of not being anyone's boss.

"If you are interested in taking the thing on a little shakedown cruise," Fahd bin Talal went on, "I would draw Your Royal Highness's attention to the Line. It is just within range from here, and as part of the kingdom's commitment to decarbonization, we have, as a matter of course, equipped the airport with state-of-the-art facilities for the storage and delivery of hydrogen. It is easily the most hydrogen-friendly air terminal in the world today."

Saskia had heard of this Line place. It was a completely new city, a hundred miles long and only a few blocks wide, that the Saudis were constructing on mostly unoccupied land. Its western end was on the Gulf of Aqaba at the head of the Red Sea, its eastern reached deep into the desert. They'd started the project years ago with high aspirations and a great deal of fanfare, but it had stalled out after the Khashoggi assassination, which had led many international corporate partners to back away from it.

The prince's description made sense, though. When you were building a completely new airport from scratch, drawing on an infinite fund of petro-dollars, why not plumb it for hydrogen? Why not pave the runways in gold?

She wondered if she was being set up here for a photo op. And to his credit, Fahd scented her misgivings. "This would not, in any way, be a public visit," he hastened to add. "On the contrary. Publicity would be counterproductive. Fortunately, we control the airspace."

On that promise, Princess Frederika allowed as how she might consider a spontaneous shakedown cruise to the Line the next day, provided she could then fly back and be reunited with her good old Beaver. The prince took this as an unconditional yes and nodded. "Everything will be made ready," he announced. "Departure will of course be at your convenience, but might I be so forward as to propose wheels up by nine in the morning?"

He was a hard man to say no to. He knew what he wanted, he was used to getting it, and his politeness was as a veil of finest silk draped over a brick. Thus did Saskia find herself suddenly obliged not only to accept the gift of the airplane but to sit in the co-pilot's seat the next morning as Ervin flew it to the Line.

On the contrary. Publicity would be counterproductive.

Saskia ought to have been paying attention to the advanced controls and unusual features of the hydrogen-powered plane. Ervin was keen to show her these, on the assumption that one day she'd be piloting it herself. And she did manage to show a polite level of interest, but only by dint of a lifetime's royal experience pretending to pay attention to things for the sake of other people's feelings. She got the sense that Ervin was frustrated, or at least a bit nonplussed, by her tendency to drift off into long silences as she pondered the prince's words.

Fahd wanted to show her something connected with the Line, something that must be climate-related but that was meant to be kept under wraps.

And there had been that stinger at the end: *"we* control the airspace," with the emphasis on "we." Kind of an obvious statement. Of course Saudi Arabia controlled Saudi Arabian airspace. Why bother even pointing it out?

Because he was emphasizing a contrast between the Saudis, and someone else who *didn't* control the airspace. Probably T.R. Who had designed his whole system to punch bullets straight up through airspace he didn't legally control. If you wanted to do what T.R. was doing, and you didn't have to worry about the FAA shutting you down, what would you come up with in place of giant guns?

From the plane's cruising altitude over the barren mountains of the Sinai, it was just barely possible to make out the two splayed prongs of the Red Sea curving along the horizon to right and left. The one to their right was the Gulf of Suez, visibly congested with shipping even from this distance, the air above it stained with their sooty exhaust. A good many of those huge container ships were, she knew, bound to or from Maasvlakte, the only port capable of accommodating them. The one to the left was the Gulf of Aqaba, running up the Sinai's eastern shore, separating Egypt from Saudi Arabia along much of its length. It was less busy because it was a dead end. The Israelis and the Jordanians had footholds at its northern terminus and used it as a shipping outlet to the Red Sea and points east.

Just south of there, the Line was anchored to the eastern shore of the Gulf of Aqaba on Saudi territory. From the waterfront it cut straight across the desert for more than a hundred miles. From the looks of it, the spine of the city—a pair of tunnels that ran its whole length, whisking people and cargo from one end to the other in high-speed maglev trains—was largely complete. Along most of its length it was just a faint scar on the desert where they'd backfilled lifeless and bone-dry earth over the completed tunnels. The beginnings of train stations and settlements were tidily spaced along its length. The far eastern end of it, 170 kilometers away on the other side of some mountains, she only glimpsed. But in that glimpse she saw neat phalanxes of black rectangles marching across the desert: photovoltaic panels taking advantage of the kingdom's virtually infinite supply of sun-battered land. Much easier to see, since the airport lay near the Line's western end, were the port facilities. There were two Chinese ships unloading and another waiting its turn out in the gulf, spewing a plume of soot into the languid, sunny air. In contrast to the ships at Rotterdam, which were a colorful, random mosaic of differently logotyped containers, these were virtually monochromatic. All the containers, with a few exceptions, were yellow, with a green logo. They were all, she could guess, carrying photovoltaic panels or related equipment from the same supplier, and they were all destined for the blank space on the map at the opposite end of the Line.

The plane landed itself adroitly. The weird ducted engines could vector their thrust, and so it didn't need a lot of runway, especially when the hydrogen tanks were nearly drained. Formalities on the ground were nonexistent. That was only in part because she was a royal being greeted on the tarmac by a prince. The Line was supposed to have some kind of transnational status, free of the visa requirements and so on that made travel to the rest of Saudi Arabia burdensome.

The prince got the princess into an ice-cold Bentley as soon as he could, then surprised her by climbing in opposite her. Apparently they were going to dispense with the pretense he had observed on Vadan of having men and women travel in separate vehicles. Or maybe he was just running low on Bentleys. Their apparent destination was not far away: a colossal but nondescript hangar on the other side of the airport's web of runways.

"Did you see the container ships?" Fahd asked, as they dodged around an incoming hydrogen tanker and set a course along the edge of a taxiway.

"Yes, clearly the Chinese have taken an interest!" In other company, she might have added *while Western companies were sleeping on it* but thought it better not to.

Fahd made a faint grimace and tossed one hand as if shooing something away. "We are buying what they are selling, no more," he said. "Chinese aid comes at a high price—a price we don't need to pay."

"How much of the Empty Quarter are you planning to pave with photovoltaics?"

He leaned forward, elbows on knees. "We have grown rather attached to the practice of selling energy for piles and piles of money, and we intend to continue it long after we have run out of oil. To be blunt, we will install enough photovoltaics to alter the climate."

She nodded. "Those panels are going to keep a hell of a lot of CO_2 out of the atmosphere!"

"Yes, but that's not what I meant."

"Oh?"

"The desert has high albedo for the most part—sunlight bounces back from the light-colored soil and returns to outer space where it cannot warm the planet. Solar panels, on the other hand, are dark. The whole point of them is to absorb, not reflect, sunlight. They get hot. Hotter than the light sand that they are covering. Convection grows more powerful as hotter air rises with greater force. This changes the weather directly."

"Have you modeled it?"

"No, but those guys have." Fahd gestured toward a row of unmarked mobile office trailers huddling in a narrow strip of shade along the north wall of the huge hangar. What few windows they had were covered with mirrored film. Rooftop air conditioners shot plumes of heat into the air.

"Who are 'those guys'?"

"Israelis."

And so what she was expecting—completely illogically—was that the hangar would turn out to be full of racks stuffed with computers, all chugging away on climate simulations.

But no. The Israelis didn't need to do that here. The hangar turned out to be occupied by a single enormous airplane. A type she had never seen before. It was complete, just in the sense that two wings and a tail were attached to its fuselage, but it was imprisoned in a web of scaffolding. Workers in hard hats and high-vis vests were busy here and there. Not a *lot* of workers and not *super* busy. This was not some mid-twentieth-century assembly-line operation. It felt more like one of those facilities where space rockets were meticulously pieced together.

And yet the overall lines of the giant airplane were not at all rakish or science fiction. It looked like a child's model, scaled up. The wings, which were extraordinarily long, stuck straight out from the sides. Nothing was swept back, nothing optimized for amazing speed or maneuverability. It really looked like a sailplane—a glider. But it had engines.

A hard-hatted man with an East African look about him was waiting behind the wheel of a golf cart. Saskia was a bit sick of being whisked around from place to place in vehicles controlled by others. She was a pilot for a reason. In the Netherlands, in front of cameras, she'd have made a point of walking. But . . . when in Rome. After donning the inevitable pair of safety glasses, she and Fahd were treated to a slow pass down one side of the plane and up the other.

"If you were anyone else, I would give you a laborious explanation of what this is," said Fahd, as the golf cart swung wide around the slender, exquisitely sculpted tip of one wing. "But since it's *you* . . ."

"It's modeled after a U-2 spy plane," Saskia said. "Those, in turn, were modeled after gliders. It is designed to operate at extremely high altitudes—seventy or eighty thousand feet. The thin air makes it tricky to design and even trickier to fly. It's probably not even stable unless there are computers in the control loop."

"Very good," said Fahd. "And the cargo?"

"The fuselage will be full of tanks, with baffles to control sloshing and weight distribution. The tanks will be full of sulfur dioxide when it takes off, empty when it lands. Because the whole purpose of it is to inject SO_2 directly into the stratosphere."

"Clearly my presence here as tour guide is superfluous!" said the prince, allowing his usual mask of stony dignity to be cracked open with a grin.

The compliment was appreciated, but she knew flattery when she heard it. People had been talking about making a plane like this for decades. She'd seen CGI renderings. Not of this exact plane, of course, but of ones very like it, in PowerPoints and videos envisioning how solar geoengineering might change the climate for better or worse. Depending on how you felt about the idea, you could soundtrack the animation with scary war drums or with soaring anthemic strains and make it seem like the end of the world or the dawn of a new era. In any case, she'd have to have been pretty ill-informed not to know this for exactly what it was.

"You had the airframe designed by . . . someone who knows what they're doing," she continued. "Composite wings made by people who do wind turbine blades. I recognize the engines—but you've had them modified for high altitude. The airframe is built, but that's the easy part. Now the fancy systems are being integrated into it by contractors from around the world." The coveralls worn by various teams were blazoned with corporate logos, most of which she'd seen before. But it was all pretty understated and you had to get up close to make them out. Americans, Germans, Israelis, Japanese were working on different subsystems, many using AR goggles to gesture at figments in the air.

"With all due respect to Dr. Schmidt," Fahd said, "who really has accomplished something quite remarkable, we think that this is the future of solar geoengineering. The second wave, if you will. The first wave is a stopgap measure. Hurling enough SO_2 into the stratosphere to begin making a difference. All well and good; when a house is on fire, you throw water on it. The second wave will be about tuning the distribution of the veil so as to achieve the results . . ."

Saskia looked him in the eye. She got the idea he was about to conclude the sentence with "we want" but after the briefest of hesitations he said "that are most beneficial."

Their loop around the plane ended at a cafeteria that had been set up in the corner of the hangar. Several rows of folding tables, a buffet line staffed by what she guessed were Filipino and Bangladeshi food service workers, the very latest in coffee-making robotics. "You must be famished," Prince Fahd said, extending a hand to give her unnecessary help in alighting from the golf cart. She had to admit that a cup of coffee sounded good. Maybe a pastry. Lunchtime was over. So only a few workers were here, taking solo breaks or holding impromptu meetings. Saskia peeked over the shoulder of a man with close-cropped, sandy hair and a deeply tanned neck as he fluidly worked his way through the user interface of a coffee machine. By the time he had finished, she had an idea what to do, and without too much floundering was able to get away with a decent enough macchiato. She turned around and scanned the tables until she picked out Prince Fahd, who had chosen a seat conveniently far away from any other diners. He was scrolling messages on his phone. She sat down across from him and began to enjoy her coffee and her Danish. "A thousand apologies," he mumbled, "something has come up, you know how it is."

"On the contrary, this lets me enjoy my snack!"

She had been enjoying it for no more than thirty seconds when Fahd's phone signaled an incoming call. "So sorry, I must take this," he said, and stood up. He walked away, beginning the conversation in English but then switching to Arabic. Saskia gazed through the vacancy he'd left in his wake and saw that the sandy-haired man had taken a seat at the next table, facing her squarely. And his green eyes were looking at her squarely, with no trace of the atavistic deference that some people still afforded to royals.

"Your friend T.R. is quite a character," he said. He spoke in a somewhat lilting, bemused accent that might have been Eastern European. But she'd seen enough circumstantial evidence to know that this guy was Israeli.

"Friend might be too strong a word? He *does* have some likable qualities."

"Well, a person in whose company you have been seen from time to time, let's say."

"Only by people with truly exceptional powers of observation. But do go on."

"He might be wrong, he might be crazy, but you have to admire his focus." The Israeli emphasized that word. He liked focus. "Very important. Very good! But sometimes when you're focused, you get tunnel vision. You don't see the bigger picture."

"What do you mean by that?"

"You know, things that come at you from the side."

"I haven't seen him in a while but I'll be sure to pass that on."

"He wasn't at Vadan."

"No."

"You'd think he would have been there. To see his big gun go off."

"It surprised me a little. But apparently he's quite busy in some different part of the world."

The Israeli snorted. "Different is for sure the right word. He has an eye for strange places, that one." He took a sip of his coffee. "Look. I just wanted to say you might want to have a talk with your friend. Tell him to raise his head up out of that hole in the ground and look around. To be a little more aware."

"Can you be more specific?"

"Sources and methods," he said. Intelligence-speak for *I can't tell you what I know because by doing so I might inadvertently reveal how I came to know it.* "Maybe look to the north."

"How far north? Oklahoma? Canada?"

"You don't know where he is," the Israeli realized. "He's in New Guinea."

Saskia was taken aback. It wasn't so much that she was surprised by the news. Rather it was a sense of inevitability. Brazos RoDuSh, the selfies from Cornelia, Willem's contacts with the Papuan nationalists . . .

"I suppose I ought to have seen it coming."

"You're a shareholder! You have to keep an eye on your investments!" he said, in an amused, world-weary tone. "Look. We like the guy. We like what he's doing. It helps us"—he flicked his green eyes toward the plane—"do what we're doing. But we have reason to believe that the time has come when he should just keep his wits about him a little more."

"And I am somehow the person who needs to deliver this message."

"Texans!" The man threw up his hands. "Like some other ethnic groups I could mention, they seem to place great stock in personal relationships. He respects you. That's all I'm saying."

Saskia nodded. "What's in this for you guys?"

"You ever wonder why people in the Bible are always fighting over our tiny scrap of land? Why the Romans even bothered with it? Israel used to be sweet real estate. The land of milk and honey. Now it's kind of a shithole, climate-wise."

"So it's all about bringing back the milk and honey."

"Sure."

"Nothing more than that."

"You thought otherwise?"

"Maybe I'm just of an overly cynical nature," Saskia said, "but it occurs to me that you and the Saudis might be working together to completely fuck Iran."

The man shrugged. "Personally, nothing would give me greater pleasure. But the models are complicated."

"The Arabian Peninsula, all by itself, is vast. If you add Israel and Jordan to the north, it spans a huge range of latitude. If you fly those planes south . . . well, I don't think Somalia has the technology to shoot planes out of the stratosphere. You could fly to the equator and beyond. You could dispatch those planes anywhere you like across that range. Put the SO_2 exactly where you want it. Do acupuncture on the region's climate."

The Israeli took another sip and stood up, sighing as if he regretted leaving this fascinating conversation and abandoning his nearly full cup of coffee. "I like the acupuncture analogy. I might steal that."

"It wasn't mine."

"Thanks for your time, Your Royal Highness."

Saskia waited for him to clear out, then scanned the area until she caught a glimpse of Fahd bin Talal. He was still talking, or pretending to, on his phone, keeping a sidelong eye on her.

She texted Willem.

> The day has arrived. A year or two sooner than I thought.

Meaning, as he'd understand, the day when her "retirement" would end, and she'd need him for something.

> Ha! Even sooner than I predicted. What do you want?

TUABA

Willem could have afforded a suite at any of the modern hotels that had been thrown up within striking distance of Tuaba's one-runway airport during the last few decades. Instead he would be sleeping on a futon in a back room of Uncle Ed's compound.

On an aerial view—even one so far zoomed out that it took in the entirety of Australia, Indonesia, and Southeast Asia—you could easily pick this place out by looking for the gray scar on New Guinea's southern flank. This was the alluvial spew of the river that flowed down to the Arafura Sea from glaciers along the island's spine: the highest mountain between the Himalayas and the Andes. Unlike all the other rivers draining that slope— and there were a lot of them, given that the glaciers were melting, and rainfall could exceed ten meters per year—the one that ran through Tuaba was gray because the sediments coming down from the copper mine hadn't weathered naturally and hadn't had time to oxidize.

Uncle Ed wasn't named Ed and wasn't Willem's uncle. He'd come to this place in the 1970s and established what was imaginatively called a logistics depot for bulldozer parts. Later he had branched out into helicopter maintenance, pipeline supply, and drilling rigs. He had started by simply using a bulldozer to scrape all life off a patch of jungle near the banks of the river, then sold the bulldozer to Brazos RoDuSh. The boomtown of Tuaba had taken shape around him, prompting him to upgrade his security perimeter from time to time. In the early going this had consisted of an earthen embankment topped by barbed wire, but nowadays the compound was outlined by rusty old shipping containers stacked two high, with long snarls of razor ribbon strung along their tops. Within those steel walls, trucks and heavy equipment trundled back and forth across a gravel lot that at any given time was 50 percent gray puddles. When a given puddle became deep enough to impede commerce, Uncle Ed would emerge from the building—not quite a house, not quite an office—in the corner of the lot nearest the street, fire up one of the clapped-out, rust-encrusted bulldozers lined up nearby, and sally forth, dragging in his wake long skeins of strangler vines that had been using the machine as a trellis, and scrape some muck off a high place and shove it into the offending depression. Then he would park the dozer and go back inside and resume his primary occupations of watching basketball on TV while conducting a range of disputes with random people all over the world on social media. Every so often he would see a familiar face looming in a security camera feed and press a button that would buzz them through a door into the compound. As often as not these were old friends who had come to play badminton on a rectangle of Astroturf that Ed had imported in 1982 by making arrangements for it to be wrapped around a replacement driveshaft for the largest truck in the world, which was being barged up the river from the Arafura Sea. Badminton apparently kept him immune from the ill effects of smoking.

It would be conventional to assume that Tuaba had been expropriated from indigenous people, but as far as anyone could tell, no one had ever lived here until the likes of Uncle Ed had showed up. Farther south, along the edge of the sea, people had long roamed among the inlets and swamps in dugout canoes, living off fish, prawns, birds, and sago palm while trying to stay one step ahead of malaria. Farther north, small populations had lived in the mountains, above the swamps but below the tree line, eating sweet potatoes, wild pigs, and small marsupials, suffering from yaws, anemia, and the depredations of their fellow man. But the belt of land in between was the worst of both worlds, and simply not worth living in. Unless, that is, you were a company from Texas who wanted to construct the world's largest open pit copper mine on top of the island's highest mountain.

Tuaba was the highest point on the river reachable by barges from the sea. It was only meters above sea level. There, cargo had to be offloaded and transported by road the remaining hundred clicks to the site. A key detail being that this entailed an altitude gain of some four thousand meters. Since said road had not existed at the beginning, the first cargoes, back in the early days, had been mostly road-building equipment. The lineup—some would call it a junkyard—of ancient, rusty hulks in Uncle Ed's lot constituted a sort of archaeological record of that endeavor. Albeit a selective one, for many bulldozers had simply disappeared into swamps.

Nowadays, 150,000 people lived in the city, which occupied a couple of miles of the river's western bank and stretched about a mile into the former jungle. Surrounding that were suburbs that didn't feel quite so much like a hastily thrown-together boomtown. Many of Ed's badminton buddies had relocated to such neighborhoods, but Ed was quite happy where he was; he seemed to believe that if he set foot off the compound for more than a few hours it would succumb to some combination of jungle rot and rampant hooliganism. Nowadays the business was run by younger members of the clan, many of whom operated out of branch offices in Singapore, Taiwan, and the northern Australian city of Darwin. These people went for months, even years at a time without setting foot on the island of New Guinea.

The business was simple enough: they caused certain very specific objects to show up when and where they were needed, incredibly reliably. The mine operation as a whole consumed tens of thousands of gallons of diesel fuel per hour. The engines that did the consuming were distributed across a wide range of equipment both stationary and mobile. Almost none of it was run-of-the-mill. Run-of-the-mill equipment couldn't operate at four thousand meters of altitude on some of the world's worst terrain. It was all weird special equipment. Helicopters had to be fitted with special blades to get purchase on the thin air. A burned-out bearing or snapped driveshaft could burn astronomically more money in downtime than what it cost to replace it. Uncle Ed's company was far from the only one serving that market, but they were holding their own against the competition—enough that members of the younger generations, like Beatrix, could get expensive educations and passports to First World countries.

Most of the business was transacted over the Internet. But they had to have a physical depot here. So Uncle Ed pinned down both tails of the bell curve. He was the founder and CEO. But he was also the guy filling in chuckholes. Everything in between those two extremes he delegated to the juniors. He could have moved, of course, and lived out the rest of his life in a part of the world characterized by greater political stability. But having seen shit you wouldn't believe in Indonesia, he had arrived at the conclusion that political stability *anywhere* was an illusion that only a simpleton would believe in. That (invoking, here, a version of the anthropic principle) such simpletons only believed they were right when and if they just happened to live in places that were temporarily stable. And that it was better to live somewhere obviously dangerous, because it kept you on your toes. Willem had thought all this daft until Trump and QAnon.

So the first humans to live here had been Texans. They'd brought Dutch and Australian expats in their wake. Not long after, people like Ed had begun to show up. Ed was an Indonesian citizen on paper, but culturally was overseas Chinese, conducting business in English, speaking Fuzhounese otherwise and Mandarin when he had to. In Irian Jaya (as Western New Guinea was called in those days) he did for Brazos RoDuSh what, before the war, his forebears had done for Royal Dutch Shell in Java.

The mine had attracted Indonesians—almost all Muslims, of a different race and culture than the indigenous Papuans. So the second layer of settlement had seen Indonesian neighborhoods, mosques, schools, playing fields, and shopping centers growing up around the airport, the hotels, the bars, and the office buildings that the white expats had thrown up just as table stakes. Efforts to train and hire native Papuans, and allow them to share in some of the wealth, had got underway. They'd migrated to the area in numbers. As part of their overall deal with the Indonesian government, Brazos RoDuSh had provided schools, modern housing, clinics, and helicopter rides. Their numbers had grown because of natural population increase over the fifty years that all this had been here, combined with the in-migration of people from surrounding areas drawn by the availability of all these goods and services.

According to an informal pact dating back to colonial times, the half of New Guinea north of the mountains was the turf of Protestant missionaries and the south was Catholic. This explained the existence, in Tuaba, of a new Catholic cathedral and an associated complex of religious schools, convent, hospital, and so on. White European Catholics could, of course, go to church there; but it had all been built mostly to serve a flock of Papuans who had been converted by missionary activity that was still going on. Thus Sister Catherine, the Papuan nun Willem had broken bread with in The Hague on the morning of the great storm, which now seemed a hundred years and a hundred light-years away.

Sound arguments could be, and often were, constructed as to why all these different groups should not get along. To nationalist Indonesians, the white mining companies were colonizers pure and simple, only allowed to be here because the people who had been in charge of Indonesia in the 1970s had realized that if they were ever going to attract development capital they were going to have to make things good for the likes of Brazos RoDuSh. That company's efforts to train Indonesian engineers and managers— effectively nationalizing the operation one head count at a time— were, from a certain point of view, particularly sneaky forms of cultural imperialism.

To the Papuans, it was the Indonesians who were the foreign colonizers, moving to places like Tuaba in their tens and hundreds of thousands and putting up mosques and such. The Christian whites were no better in principle, but they had ties to media outlets, human rights organizations, and the United Nations, which might be of some help in enabling the Papuans to get their country back. For its being part of Indonesia made no sense on any level. Most activists were in the orderly, systematic mold of Beatrix and Sister Catherine. But there were enough angry young men up in the hills with guns, machetes, and dynamite to justify the presence in Tuaba of Indonesian black ops security forces. Obvious targets had been hardened—as anyone who tried to sneak into Uncle Ed's compound would soon discover—and so when violence happened it tended to be on weak links in the security chain: people getting shot by assailants on motor scooters while out running errands. Slurry pipelines dynamited in inaccessible swamps. Truck engines sabotaged. Adding to the overall feeling of paranoia and dread was the perception—right or wrong, it didn't matter—that some of those outrages had actually been committed by Indonesian security cops *pretending* to be Papuan nationalists, to justify their presence here and boost their budget. Living in a separate bubble from all that were the expats in their gated communities with their private security forces drawn from a pool of mostly Western ex-military.

"What the hell are you doing here?" asked Uncle Ed, after giving Willem a decent interval to unpack and get settled.

"Getting drunk," Willem said, which was not wrong. He had found his way out to a sort of screened-in patio adjacent to the badminton court and uncorked a bottle of duty-free whiskey he had scored while changing planes in Jakarta. Not at the old airport, which was usually underwater, but at the new one they had just built on higher ground. Ed was finishing up a sweaty doubles match with some of the usual crew of Chinese gaffers. This was the coldest part of the year. It was a little above room temperature, but extremely humid. Willem was almost comfortable in a dress shirt with the sleeves rolled up. No rain was spattering the tin roof at the moment, but it had been recently and it would be soon.

"I thought you were going to be the prime minister of the Netherlands or something!"

"For a brief moment, it looked like it was on the table, but . . ." Willem sipped his whiskey and tried to remember that brief moment. For all its apparent stability, Dutch politics could be convoluted. It had been in—what—December? No, after the holidays. He shook his head. "I don't want to talk about all that stuff."

"Instead you are retired. And you come . . . here!?" Ed looked around. "Don't get me wrong, you are most welcome. Would you like some tea, or are you going to stick with whiskey?"

"Whiskey is fine, thank you."

"Then I will smoke." Ed knocked an unfiltered cigarette from a pack—some Chinese brand—and bit slightly into the middle, creating a tear in the paper. He put the cigarette in his mouth crosswise and lit both of the ends, a glowing coal projecting to either side as he inhaled through the central hole. In Papua it was not an unusual practice, but for new arrival Willem it took a little getting used to. "You said another person is coming? A woman?" Ed asked. He knew that Willem was gay and so there was an implicit question.

"Amelia Leeflang. Ex-military. She used to be on the queen's security detail."

"And now she is on yours?"

"I was told it might be a good idea." Willem glanced out over Ed's compound. At least two men could be seen strolling around in a sort of Brownian-motion style, picking out irregular paths to avoid puddles. Each had a pump shotgun slung over his shoulder. They looked Papuan. From the taller coastal tribes, Willem guessed. "Amelia has left the government payroll and is working for private clients now."

"You mean she was fired?"

"The Netherlands holds its politicians to a very high standard. The royals as well. And the staff who surround those people."

"Such as you."

"Sometimes it is clear which way the wind is blowing. You don't have to get fired to see that there might be other opportunities. Amelia joined a private firm."

"Mercenaries?"

"If you will. I requested her by name."

"Will she be staying here?"

"Is that a possibility?"

"I can have a trailer dropped over there." Ed indicated an unfrequented corner of the lot. "She'll need to talk to locals who know how things work here. I can get you in touch."

"Papuans?"

Ed looked at him incredulously. "Australians."

Willem took a sip of whiskey. Ed took a drag on his double-barreled cigarette. Exhaling, he said, "You're not actually retired, are you?"

"In a sense, if you love your work, you're never truly retired."

"Are you going to make trouble for me? For the family business?"

"I've seen the numbers on the mine." Willem nodded vaguely in the direction he thought most likely to be north. The mountains as usual were completely invisible behind a blank white sky. "Eventually the ore will run out—or become so difficult to extract that it can no longer compete on the world market."

"Decades from now," Ed said dismissively.

"You've *been* here for decades. It's not that long. What happens to the family business then?"

Uncle Ed didn't have a ready answer.

"Do you move to some other part of the world? Or stay here?"

"Why would we stay in this hellhole?" Ed asked. As if on cue, a gunshot sounded in the distance, then two more. The men with the shotguns did not seem to find this remarkable.

"Maybe something new happens."

"Where?"

"Up there." Willem nodded to the north again.

"What could possibly happen up there besides the copper mine?"

Willem got up, took a few steps across the patio, and stepped down to the gravel lot. He bent over and scooped up a handful of gray muck from the edge of a puddle. He held it up to the skeptical, bordering on worried, inspection of Uncle Ed. "Do you know what this is?"

"The shit that washes down from the mine. Tailings that don't have enough copper to be worth refining."

"Do you know what else it contains besides copper?"

"Gold. A tiny amount."

"What else?"

"I don't know, I'm not a geologist."

"Sulfur."

Ed snorted. "There are easier places to get sulfur, even I know that."

"None that are so close to the stratosphere."

COOLATTIN, BRITISH COLUMBIA

"his time, Uncle, I'm headed *down*stream. Just following the flow of the river," Laks said, "like a fry becoming a smolt."

Uncle Dharmender crossed his arms across his belly and regarded Laks in a way that might best be described as alert. "Is that some kind of fish terminology? You forget I am not a fish guy." He held up both hands as if to say *look about you, boy!* and then re-crossed his arms.

Laks didn't need to look about himself. Now that he had got most of his long-term memory back he knew exactly where he was: a small town in British Columbia, on the banks of the Columbia River about twenty miles north of the Canada-U.S. border. When Laks had been a boy, Uncle Dharmender's holdings here had been limited to a mere gas station, but a few years ago he had, during a COVID-related tourism slump, purchased the adjacent, down-at-heels resort and begun fixing it up one unit at a time.

"Resort" was a grand term. It was a rustic affair comprising a dozen small cabins scattered through woods surrounding a larger building that served as reception, kitchen, laundry, and banquet hall. In the latter facility, Aunt Gurmeet—the wife of Dharmender—and various cousins and family friends had accorded Laks a hero's welcome this evening with a reception, a lavish meal, and a party hosted by a Punjabi MC/DJ team out of Vancouver.

When the guests had taken their leave, Dharmender and Laks had been deemed surplus to requirements and been shooed into the conference room. This was a B.C. classic with a stuffed bighorn ram's head on the wall and curtains in a vintage North Woods print featuring ducks, moose, and men in plaid shirts paddling canoes.

To show respect for the occasion both men had put some effort into their turbans. It was a matter of perspective, really, what should be considered exotic in such a juxtaposition: the decor, or the occupants? Dharmender seemed very much at home. If that bighorn sheep were still alive, his dark, slit-like nostrils, spreading like wings from the center of his lip, would be filled with the aroma of Punjabi cuisine, as well as some rare perfumes that some of the guests had put on during this occasion—somewhat out of the ordinary, here—to get all dressed up.

Not that Laks could smell any of it. His nose was as dead as that ram's. The place did, however, smell *safe* to him, thanks to certain upgrades that had recently been implanted in his skull.

Above the opposite end of the conference table was a king salmon mounted to a varnished plank. A brass plaque, dark with age, provided statistics on its weight and the circumstances of its demise. Dharmender gave it the side-eye, as if hoping it might supply a clue that would help him solve Laks's gnomic utterance about fry and smolt. But the dead glass eye of the stuffed fish stared back at him, pitiless and baleful.

"What the hell are you trying to say, Laks?"

"If you could give me a lift down to Trail, or even a little farther, tomorrow morning before sunrise—"

"We are practically at the North Pole here," said Uncle Dharmender, with hyperbole that Laks decided to overlook. Actually, as Laks could tell without looking at a map, they were at a latitude of 49.3196 degrees North, so, more like halfway between the equator and the said pole.

"It is the middle of summer, the sun rises at three in the morning!" Dharmender went on. Also an exaggeration; the correct figure was 5:09. "We should have gone to bed five hours ago if that was your intention!"

"Sorry to spring it on you like this."

"You weren't kidding. You literally are going to go down the river." He was referring to the Columbia. "Into the United States." Which was where the Columbia flowed.

"I have a wet suit," Laks volunteered, in case Dharmender was getting ready to give him a hard time about hypothermia.

"Why don't you just cross on the land like a normal person? I mean, the United States is a mess, sure. But it's not like going to North Korea."

"I'm not at liberty to say, but—"

"You're on some kind of secret mission?"

Apparently Laks's face was quite easy to read.

Uncle Dharmender raised his voice. "Gurmeet!" His wife, two rooms away, could not hear him in the clatter and chatter of the kitchen. "Gurmeet! *Gurmeet!* Our nephew is going on a secret mission!"

The kitchen suddenly became a lot quieter. Gurmeet bustled into the room, drying her hands on a simple cotton apron she had tied on over a spectacular getup that made her look, in small-town Canadian eyes, like the wife of the Romulan ambassador. In her wake were several younger women, as well as Gurmeet's mother. They were all dressed to party.

"For the Indian government?" she asked.

"Who else would he be doing it for?!"

"You'll need food!"

"He's sneaking into the U.S. They have food."

"It is carrion."

"He's probably carrying a ton of cash money, he can buy proper food." Dharmender looked at him. "They gave you money, yes? American cash? Bitcoin?"

"Yes, Uncle." But Laks now became distracted by the sight of Tavleen—one of the younger women—whipping out her phone and getting busy with both thumbs.

"Tavleen!" Laks shouted. "Are you *Facebooking* this?"

Far from seeming in any way mortified, Tavleen glared back at him as if to say that the answer was so ridiculously obvious as to be not worth giving. "Your *last* secret mission was the biggest thing on the Internet! I'm just giving you a signal boost!"

"This *actually is secret*," Laks protested.

Dharmender explained, "If you put it on social media, he will be arrested for swimming across the border and put in real handcuffs."

"Then why are you telling us?" Gurmeet demanded.

Dharmender checked his wristwatch, a momentous bauble that he kept with him at all times in case everything went sideways and he had to trade it for a jet airplane. "Because at this point we are going to be up all night, and you'll notice."

SNEEUWBERG

T.R.'s logistics people had warned Willem that he might need oxygen just to remain upright and conscious at the mine. This information had reached him in the form of a link copy/pasted to the tail end of the calendar invite. They hadn't bothered to warn Amelia, so maybe it was an age-related thing. But they had hastened to assure him that oxygen tanks on wheels would be available at the helipad and he shouldn't hesitate to just grab one on his way past.

With that as prelude, the chopper ride from Tuaba did not disappoint. In mere seconds they'd left the town behind them and were flying over jungle that was as dense as any Willem had ever seen. The chopper's main task was not to cover ground—they were only going a hundred kilometers—but to gain altitude, which it did by ramping up steadily along the whole duration of the flight. So at first the jungle plummeted far below and became veiled in clouds. A single gossamer strand of road was laced through it, often hidden beneath the canopy but sometimes breaking into view when it ran across a swamp on a causeway or skirted the river.

Looking out the front they could see the mountains rising up in their path to the north. Over the next half hour the land shouldered up out of a sea of low clouds. By that point the works of Brazos RoDuSh had ramified away from the road to cover large patches of the landscape: settlements where workers could live, close to the mine as distances were measured on a map, but still thousands of meters below it in altitude. Spurs reached out to depots and industrial works the nature of which Willem didn't understand. But he knew that the gist of it was to crush the ore into powder and concentrate it using some water-based process and send the resulting slurry down a pipeline that ran through the jungle, parallel to the road, all the way to the coast, where it could be poured into huge ships bound for places where the red metal was smelted. His Green instincts, drilled into him by a life spent in a modern Western social democracy, told him to be outraged by what the miners had done to this part of the planet. But he knew that every wind turbine feeding green electricity into the Netherlands' grid had copper windings in its generator and copper cables connecting it to the system. And that the copper had come from here.

Never in his life had Willem seen such rugged terrain. Range after range of vertiginous mountains, each much higher than the last, passed below them and then plunged into valleys of Grand Canyon–like depth. And yet the mine proper was still far above all that, connected to its outlying works by tramways and pipelines that ran nearly vertically.

Finally, after the sky above had grown a very dark shade of blue, as if they were halfway to orbit, he saw a place where the top of a steep mountain had simply been sheared off. Above one side of it rose tiered ramps connecting it to a higher plateau beyond, for use by the special high-altitude trucks and excavators that were Uncle Ed's stock in trade. Atop all that was a plateau almost at a level with New Guinea's highest peak, which lay just a few kilometers farther inland. As they came in for a landing, Willem glimpsed a whole additional mining complex beyond: a pit that could have swallowed central Amsterdam, a ramp spiraling down to its bottom, trucks he knew to be the size of seven-story office buildings scuttling up and down looking no bigger than lice.

Amidst all that hugeness, he had to re-calibrate his eye just to see what he had come all this way to look at. In the desert of West Texas the Biggest Gun in the World had looked big just because it was the only sign of human activity, other than barbed-wire fences, for miles. Here, though, the head frame of the gun could have been overlooked as just another mysterious bit of mine infrastructure. Likewise, the sulfur heap was dwarfed by mountainous piles of mine spoil. It stood out only because it was yellow.

As advertised, little oxygen tanks on carts were lined up for the taking to one side of the helipad. There was also a rack with ski jackets, so that people who'd just flown up from the equatorial jungle didn't have to bring warm clothes with them. But T.R. was standing right by the helipad next to a Tesla SUV (didn't burn gasoline; didn't need air) with its gull wing doors open. So Willem just quick-walked over and climbed into that, then leaned back and waited for his heart and lungs to scavenge enough oxygen to return his body to some kind of equilibrium. The seat was warm and so was the air once T.R. had got in and closed the doors. If there had been a chauffeur, Willem would have sat in the back with T.R. and Amelia would have rode shotgun. As it was she rode in the back so that T.R. and Willem could occupy the two front seats.

"You do have a taste for weird, difficult parts of the world," Willem gasped, when the oxygen panic had subsided.

T.R. considered it carefully. "A thing you learn real fast, when you are in the oil business"—he pronounced it "ol bidness" and Willem honestly didn't know if it was wry Texan self-parody, or actually how he talked—"or mining, is that almost every part of the world is weird and difficult. We don't see those parts because we prefer to build our habitations in more hospitable areas. Which are rare. We come to think of Connecticut, Florida, France, and all that as how the world is. Places like this being aberrations. Thing is, geology don't care about our convenience and so it puts the oil and the minerals in locations that are truly random. You put on a blindfold, Dr. Castelein—"

"Willem. Please."

"You throw darts at random into a spinning globe, the odds of hitting Connecticut are small. The odds of hitting what you call a weird, difficult part of the world are high."

"Fair enough."

"But I'll give you this much: this is the worst place of all, with the possible exception of Antarctica. The first map of New Guinea was drawn up just a little over a century ago. It killed seventy-nine out of eight hundred men who worked on it."

"Drawing the map!?"

"Drawing the map. The first European expedition to these parts involved four hundred men and took over a year. Only fifteen of those four hundred stuck it out—and they didn't even come close to reaching where we are now! When some crazy Dutch mountaineers finally made it up here in the 1930s they described it as a mountain of ore on the moon. This here"—T.R. made a "look about you" gesture—"was then the highest point on Earth between the Himalayas and the Andes. Because it was buried fifty meters deep under a glacier. Hence, the Dutch name of the place. Sneeuwberg. Snow Mountain. Since then the glacier has melted and the mountain has been leveled. No snow, no mountain. So now *that*"—he pointed to the brown rock crag that loomed over all this, so close they could, with oxygen tanks, simply hike over to it—"is the highest."

"Five thousand meters, give or take," Willem said.

"That is correct."

T.R. during this had been piloting the car over a terrible road at little more than a walking pace. They had put the helipad behind them and passed through a security gate staffed by Caucasian men armed with submachine guns. There was a sort of buffer zone consisting of strewn cargo pallets and parked equipment. Here and there, Papuan men in hard hats and high-visibility vests were working on engines or driving forklifts. Then they passed through another belt of armed security and came alongside a row of office trailers. "Fiefdoms of different subs," T.R. explained. "Brazos RoDuSh is a mining company. Period. Don't wanna run medical clinics, commissaries, housing, anything that ain't mining per se. So, subcontractors. You might remember this one."

He had pulled up in front of a trailer that was unsigned and unmarked, other than a blank sheet of white printer paper taped to the door. "Welcome to the Papua offices of White Label Industries! Breathe deep and don't go into oxygen debt as you ascend the four steps to the door!"

The interior was true to White Label form. The ends of the trailer featured a couple of smaller offices and a toilet, but most of it was a conference room. The walls were sheathed in cheap fake wood paneling with whiteboards drywall-screwed into place. A watercooler and a coffee maker sat in the corner on a makeshift table consisting of the cardboard boxes they had arrived in. The flimsiest, cheapest obtainable folding plastic chairs surrounded a couple of plastic folding tables jammed together. "Sometimes the glamour of it all is just a bit much," T.R. gasped as he collapsed into one of those chairs and nearly buckled it. Next to it was an oxygen tank. He cranked its knob and took a few deep breaths as Willem tottered back to the toilet.

"Have you considered simply piping oxygen into rooms like this one?" Willem asked when he came back.

"First question I asked," T.R. said. "Turns out it's dangerous. You add too much oxygen, and stuff burns you didn't know was capable of burning."

Willem nodded and sat down. Amelia, who had better cardio, prowled up and down the length of the trailer looking out the windows. These had all been covered on the inside with steel mesh, affixed with drywall screws and washers. She gave one a rattle. "For grenades?" she asked.

"Correct. Wouldn't stop a burglar. Protects upper management from casual fragging. Sandbags on the roof—before you ask." T.R. turned his attention to Willem and winked at him to indicate that he approved of Amelia. "Welcome to the Southern Hemisphere branch!"

"Just barely."

T.R. considered it. "You refer to the fact that we are only a couple hundred clicks south of the equator. It's enough, though! The circulation patterns of north and south are surprisingly well separated. And the special circumstances here make it possible for us to reach farther south yet—we pulled off a few tricks that were not an option in our little old pilot project down Texas way."

"Pilot project!" Willem said under his breath, shaking his head in disbelief.

T.R. had been fussing with the AV system while they chatted, and now pulled up an image on a 3D holographic projector that was mounted to the ceiling: the one concession in this place to fancy high-end office equipment. As if reading Willem's mind, T.R. said, "Cost more than everything else combined. But we gotta put on some kind of show for folks like you who go to the trouble of coming all the way out to this godforsaken shithole!" Left unspoken was the question *What the hell are you doing here?* but Willem was pretty sure they'd get around to it after T.R. was finished putting on this big show of hospitality.

Hovering in the middle of the conference room was now a semi-transparent model of the entire mine complex. This slowly zoomed in on an area not far from the trailer where they were having this conversation. Hard as it was to make sense of the vast complex when viewed from a chopper, this rendering made it all even more confusing as it revealed all the underground works that had been cut into the mountain during the half century that Brazos RoDuSh had been working here. Not for the first time, Willem was awed, staggered, and even a little humiliated by the sheer scale at which the oil and mining industries operated—year in, year out, in a way that was basically invisible to the people on the other side of the world who benefited from what they were doing, and who funded these works, every time they checked their Twitter.

To help make sense of it T.R. did something that grayed out most of the complex while highlighting a narrow shaft that angled down into the rock from the head frame Willem had noticed as they drove in. "Looks small compared to all this other shit," T.R. said, "but it ain't. Here's the Pina2bo shaft for comparison." He somehow caused a red tube to materialize on the map, beginning at the same site. It went vertically downward and it only went half as deep. "Point is, conditions prevailing here—availability of equipment, competence of the rock, et cetera—make it possible to bore at an *angle* and to bore deeper and wider. More barrels. Higher muzzle velocity."

He made the red overlay fade out to provide a clearer look at the angled shaft they'd apparently finished here. "Projectiles coming out of that gun are going faster. They are starting halfway to the stratosphere already, so they don't lose as much energy fighting their way through the lower atmosphere. And they are angled *southward*, away from the equator, with an over-the-ground velocity component of almost two thousand miles an hour."

He cut to a different view, zoomed way out, showing a trajectory that started at the top of New Guinea and arced toward the Arafura Sea. The boundary of the stratosphere was helpfully delineated. The shell soared well above that, passed through apogee, and began to arc downward again as it approached the southern coast of the island. Its trail then straightened, leveled off, and became a thickening plume of yellow gas drawn southward across the airspace between New Guinea and Australia. "The burn phase," T.R. explained. Having been through all this at Pina2bo Willem understood that this was the part of the shell's flight when the molten sulfur was burned to make thrust, extending the duration of the flight.

Once it had consumed all the sulfur, the shell's trajectory became a long straight glide that angled down until it hit the sea between New Guinea and the northern capes of Australia. A zoom-in showed a flotilla of barges and ships with nets like the ones on the mesa above the Rio Grande on the Flying S Ranch. Willem knew enough about the West Texas operation to guess that the shells and parasails would be refurbished and ferried back to Tuaba, whence they could be trucked back up to Sneeuwberg.

A further zoom-out provided a view of the whole Earth, but from a perspective you normally didn't see: the South Pole was up.

Willem had recovered his wind to the point that he felt it was safe to stand. This enabled him to look down on the whole Southern Hemisphere. The trails of sulfur dioxide—shown here as bright yellow smoke, for visibility—began as faint curved scratches over the Arafura Sea. But prevailing winds blurred them together into a blob and then stretched the blob westward. Over Western Australia it was dense, but it feathered out over the Indian Ocean until it had become a diaphanous veil.

"Pina2bo? Vadan?" Willem said.

"Glad you asked." T.R. made a scooping gesture that caused the globe to spin about until it was north up. Smaller blobs could now be seen originating from West Texas and the Adriatic, spreading and fading as the Northern Hemisphere's prevailing winds carried them eastward.

Willem regarded it for a minute, walking slowly around the table to view it from different angles. "I'm looking at this," he said, "and I'm seeing causes but not effects. The plumes of sulfur dioxide fade and dissipate. They just look like localized sources of pollution, diluted by the immensity of the atmosphere. But you and I know that the effects will make themselves known all over the globe."

T.R. nodded. "You're correct that this particular visualization does not attempt to show that. I could pull up others that do."

"And those would show—?"

"Good things for your country. For Houston, Venice, Jakarta, Bangladesh."

"And bad things for—?"

The trailer resonated with a deep boom, felt rather than heard. All the flimsy bits, of which there were many, rattled and buzzed. Amelia pivoted toward a window, more curious than alarmed. "ANFO," T.R. said. "We use tons of it. You get used to it." He turned back to Willem. "It's a smartass, gotcha question, as I think a man of your sophistication knows, Dr. Castelein. 'Bad things' can mean a drought, a flood, a heat wave, a cold snap. Bad things tend to be localized in time and space. Harder to predict.

But we *can* predict them to some extent. And the more sites we have operational, the more knobs and levers we have on the dashboard, so to speak. So instead of just blundering around we are managing the situation to maximize the good and minimize the bad."

"And who is 'we' in this case?"

"Whoever controls the knobs and levers, obviously."

"How long do you expect you'll be allowed to control them? What if someone else decides they want the knobs and levers for their own?"

T.R.'s phone had buzzed, and he had put on reading glasses. He looked at Willem over the lenses. "My granddad built a mine in Cuba. Castro took it away from him. Does that mean he shouldn't have built it?"

While Willem pondered this not uninteresting philosophical conundrum, T.R.'s phone buzzed a couple more times. The man was making a Herculean effort not to look at it, but the effort was taking a toll on his patience. "Look, this is a whole very interesting question unto itself, which I would love to discuss at the bar at the Sam Houston Hotel down in Tuaba or just about anywhere that has more oxygen. But maybe you overrate the value of discussing things. There is a reason why I don't hire a lot of Ph.D.s. I *have* a Ph.D., Dr. Castelein. I seen how the sausage is made. And the problem with Ph.D.-havers is overthinking. Y'all live in this alternate universe where everything has to be made perfect sense of before y'all can do anything. Is that why you came here? To help me make perfect sense of everything?"

"Are you sure you're getting enough oxygen?"

"Your bluntness does lead me to ask a blunt question of my own, if you would not take it amiss: What the *fuck* are you doing here, Willem? Don't get me wrong, visitors are always welcome. We will show you nothing but hospitality. But out of all the places in the world you could be, why here?" His phone buzzed again.

"I've been sent to talk some sense into you."

"Many are those who have tried," T.R. said absentmindedly while finally succumbing to the siren song of his phone.

"Also, I thought I could make myself useful."

"In what capacity?"

"Politics," Willem said, "which you suck at." He glanced over at Amelia, then did a double take. A gun had appeared in her hands. She dropped the cheap plastic venetian blind over the window, then tweaked the angle so she could see out without presenting an obvious silhouette.

Another boom rattled the trailer. As its echoes rolled back and forth among the surrounding mountains, individual gunshots, then fully automatic fire, started up.

"Coincidence, Willem?" T.R. said, getting to his feet.

"Of course not," Willem said. "Saskia suggested I come here for a reason."

"Know how to shoot a gun?" T.R. asked, in a fairly light conversational tone, as he brushed past Willem and trudged down a narrow passage to the office closest to the trailer's front door. There, he hauled open a vertical gun safe and pulled out a long weapon with a fat barrel. Willem guessed it to be a semi-automatic shotgun.

"I could maybe be trusted with that Glock," he said.

"Be my guest," T.R. said, pulling it from a felt-lined slot and holding it out, pointed at the floor. Willem accepted it. He was no gunslinger but he'd had enough basic security training that he knew what and what not to do with this style of weapon.

T.R. remarked, "The odds you'll have to use it are minimal. My security detail is right outside. They will get us to the chopper. Please do us all the courtesy of pointing it at the ground or the sky when not trying to murder someone."

"Happy to," Willem said.

"Very much obliged," T.R. returned, stepping past him to the door. He turned his back to the wall, dropped to one knee, reached across the door, unlocked it, and hauled it open. Several holes appeared in the opposite wall of the passageway; apparently someone out there had fired a burst when they saw the door move. This touched off an answering fusillade from right in front of the trailer: T.R.'s security detail, apparently filling the air with lead to discourage any more such unpleasantness. A man in a plate carrier pounded up the steps carrying what looked like the heaviest blanket in the world and wrapped it around T.R., then essentially picked him up and threw him down the stairs. You could get bulletproof blankets? It was a new concept to Willem but he saw the good sense in it, in a world full of bullets.

Amelia followed those guys out, perched on the top of the stairs to look around just for the amount of time it would take someone to pull a trigger and send a bullet her way, then nodded back at Willem and dove down the steps. Willem ran out the door, tripped down the last couple of steps and sprawled facedown on cold wet ground. A moment later he felt Amelia's weight on top of him. Everything was insanely loud. He was more worried about his hearing than his life. His breathing and pulse had shot up to what seemed like inevitably fatal levels. But all that heart/lung action didn't seem to help, made no change in the world. He finally just allowed himself to go limp and be manhandled by much bigger, stronger people. The next time he was fully cognizant of his surroundings he was in the back of an SUV under a pile of plate carriers that sprang into the air and crashed down on him whenever the thing went over a chuckhole. Someone was operating a jackhammer. Here!? Now!? No, it was a fifty-caliber machine gun. "Choppers are all in the air," said an Australian, "S.O.P. or else they'd be sitting ducks."

"I understand," T.R. said.

"We'll have to time it."

Apparently they timed it. Willem didn't know. He'd slumped down until he was on the floor of the SUV. All he could see out the windows was the blue-black stratosphere, as yet unmarked by streaks of SO_2 but occasionally diced by the rotor of a helicopter. There was another helter-skelter transfer. Not at the official helipad—which frankly was nothing to write home about—but some alternate site. And then they were in the air. Were people shooting at them from the ground? One had to assume so. But you couldn't see the bullets, so they'd have no way of knowing unless they got hit. To make that less probable the pilot was operating the chopper in a way that involved all the passengers getting slammed to one side of the cabin or other every couple of seconds. They hadn't had time to buckle their safety belts; the chopper hadn't even really landed, getting into it had been like diving through the window of a moving car. Willem ended up supine on the floor, gasping like a landed fish, vision desaturating until Amelia's hand grew vast in his field of view, reaching toward his face with a hissing oxygen mask.

TRAIL

Who have you been talking to?" Dharmender asked him a few hours later as they were pulling out of the gas station under cover of darkness. Laks was naked in the back seat of Dharmender's Subaru, the better to writhe into his black wet suit. His black waterproof pack was strapped into the passenger seat. On the floor in front of that was a not-so-waterproof care package that had been assembled during the last few hours by Gurmeet and others, containing sufficient provisions for Laks to crawl to Texas on hands and knees. Dharmender had already solved a potentially awkward problem for Laks by indicating, discreetly, that all of it would end up being eaten by bears at a nearby campground.

"What do you mean?" This was one of those conversations that was going to happen through eye contact in the rearview mirror.

"You flew straight to YVR from Hyderabad. But you only spent a couple of days in Vancouver before you came here."

"That's true, yes."

"Do your parents know?"

"No."

"So you did not talk to them about what you are doing."

"I was told not to. They think I am going to relax in one of your little cabins and do a lot of fishing."

"So all your conversations with friends and family, until now, took place in Hyderabad."

"Cyberabad."

"Whatever. Did you feel that your friends and family were speaking freely there? As freely as you and I are speaking now?"

"I don't know. For much of that time, you know, I was not quite myself. It was only in the last few weeks that—"

"Did you ever see people doing this?" Uncle Dharmender glanced theatrically up at the Subaru's dome light.

"I don't understand."

"It is a gesture people make, meaning, *this room is bugged, we are being listened to, I am not really speaking my mind.*"

"Perhaps. I don't remember."

"What about the people who recruited you for this mission? Who briefed you?"

"People I got to know during the fighting along the Line of Actual Control." He referred here to Major Raju, who had "befriended" him during his Himalayan exploits and who had stayed in touch with Laks during his convalescence.

"Indian Army."

"Yes."

"Not people like us."

"No."

"What did these people say to you that made you want this?"

"Want what?"

"To be in the back of your uncle's car getting into a wet suit so that you can sneak into a foreign country."

"Our country is in danger."

"India? Or the Punjab?"

"Same difference. If there is drought in the Breadbasket, all of India suffers."

"And was this their claim? That there is drought in the Breadbasket?"

"The monsoon was late."

"Late, yes. But it came. It did come, Laks."

"Next year it may be later still."

"That's always true. To be Punjabi is to live in continual anxiety about next year's monsoon."

"But now people are messing with the weather."

"You're talking of this thing in Texas. That's what they told you, isn't it?"

"They showed me pictures. Explained the science."

"I'm sure they did."

They passed through a roundabout on the southern fringe of town, where three roads came together. "This is not the fastest way," Laks said.

"What!?"

"You should have taken the first exit. Not the second." He considered it. "This will get us there, though. It's only 1.23 kilometers farther."

"How would you know these things? That intersection was just built last year."

"I can just feel where I am. Where I need to go. Like a sixth sense. I was leaning into the turn—but it never came."

"Perhaps your uncle doesn't want to take you down that first road because it is notoriously rough and winding, and your uncle wants to make it easier for you to get that crazy thing on."

"Thank you, Uncle. I'm sorry I questioned your navigation."

"Also, perhaps getting there absolutely the fastest is not most important thing in world."

"Why not?"

"Perhaps I can talk a little sense into you. This is apparently the first real conversation you have engaged in since your brain got scrambled at the Line of Actual Control."

"All right, well, let's make the most of it then," Laks said, a little absentmindedly. Getting all the bits of the wet suit on really was amazingly difficult. He wondered if the staff of the Indian consulate in Vancouver—who had provided him with all this stuff—had been given his correct measurements. Like many big men, Laks didn't think of himself as big. He was just normal sized. Trying to get into a wet suit in the back seat of a Subaru gave him a different perspective.

Unspoken here—because it would have been awkward—was something about the family dynamic. Laks's father was not very outgoing, his mother somewhat naive. Dharmender had guessed, correctly, that Laks's reception at home in Richmond had been affectionate, but completely devoid of any meaningful conversation.

Dharmender was talking in bursts as he negotiated unfamiliar roads. This stretch of B.C., along the river south to the border, was not the B.C. of tourism brochures. It was the real B.C. of small blue-collar communities built around resource extraction: here, mostly mines and gravel pits, using the river as a convenient means of moving extremely heavy things. Scenic riverfront drives were in short supply. Where the bank neared the road, it was as likely to be occupied by barge docks as by campgrounds.

"During your fifteen minutes of fame last year," Dharmender said, "we were all proud, for sure. But there was some concern that we have seen this movie before and it is not always one that has a happy ending for the man in the turban."

"What kinds of movies have you been watching!?"

"Let's put it this way. You were planning to join the Canadian Army, right?"

"Yes."

"That would be a fine thing to do. Don't get me wrong. But I will just point out"—and here Dharmender held up one index finger and made eye contact in the rearview—"that it is just what people want of us. They want us to follow orders and put ourselves in harm's way. On their behalf. 'Oh look, those weirdos turn out to be useful to have around.' We are useful, in other words, for going to the front lines and getting killed. So they are happy to overlook the turbans and so on."

"That's putting it pretty harshly, Uncle! *Someone* has to be in the military, if we are going to have a military."

"I overstate to make a point." Dharmender slowed the car. For the nav system was depicting a turnoff that was by no means in actual evidence. One of those roads that only the computer thinks is real. It allegedly ran for a few hundred meters to a dead end near the bank of the river, which was now depicted as a slab of blue occupying half the screen.

"It's here," Laks said. "Turn the wheel . . . now!" His uncle was not inclined to do so; but suddenly it was just there, a pair of ruts in tall grass leading away into scrubby trees. They were on the dry side of the province and tall trees were rare, but here deep roots could draw off enough river water to carpet the stony landscape with stunted pines. A few moments' drive took them to a turn-around where empty beer cans gleamed in the black scars of old campfires.

"This is it," Laks said.

"You sure?"

Laks opened the passenger door and swung the pack onto his shoulder. "It's hard to explain, but I can *literally* feel it in my bones."

Also, it smelled safe here; but Laks didn't want to launch into a whole sub-conversation about how the researchers, or whatever they were, at Cyberabad had re-wired his useless olfactory system.

"Like a fry or a smelt or whatever it was you were going on about," Dharmender said, peering at him with a little more intensity than Laks was really comfortable with.

"Smolt."

"You just *know* it's time to head downstream."

"It's my . . . I don't know what to call it. Destiny." Laks looked down. Beneath his feet the ground was basically level, with little rocks and sticks perceptible through the neoprene soles of his wet suit booties. But his inner ear was auguring an irresistible down-hill slope toward the water.

"Did you hear a word I said? About how people take advantage of us sometimes? About how *convenient* we are to them?"

"Every word, yes," Laks said. "I'll think about it." He looked guiltily at the lavish care package, soon to be bear food in the pro-vincial park up the road. "Tell Aunt Gurmeet it was delicious." Not technically a lie.

Something gleamed under the dome light: the steel band Laks

wore on his right wrist. He'd taken it off when struggling with the wet suit. It must have fallen onto the floor. "Don't forget this," Dharmender said, holding it out. Even Laks, in his distracted state, got the double meaning. He took the *kara* from his uncle's hand, kissed it, turned his back, and began jogging toward the black waters of the river. It felt like running downhill. He slipped the *kara* on.

ST. PATRICK'S

Well, that escalated quickly!" T.R. said.

Some combination of pure oxygen from the mask and a precipitous drop in altitude had revived Willem to the point where he was able to be annoyed by the joke. It was a callout to an old Internet meme. He decided to let it go. "Yes," he said, "but it kind of seems like you were expecting it."

"We were *prepared* for it."

Amelia wasn't having it. "You have multiple fifty-cal emplacements with interlocking fields of fire. The whole mountaintop is diced up into compartments with anti-personnel and anti-vehicle barriers. Choppers keep their engines running so they can get out fast if mortar rounds come in. It is a straight-up combat zone."

"Well, it is *today*," T.R. allowed. "Most days it ain't. It's probably over and done with already. These are pinprick raids. They happen once a year, tops."

"Papuan nationalists?"

"Or Indonesian black ops angling for a budget hike," T.R. said. "Impossible to tell, since they do exactly the same shit. What they have in common is that they don't actually want to destroy the cash cow."

"The mine?"

"The mine." A thought occurred to T.R. "Hey, you still have that Glock?"

"No."

Amelia held it out, action locked open, magazine removed. "I took the liberty. You want it?"

"No," T.R. said, "I just don't like loose ends."

Amelia shrugged, then slid the weapon across the floor to Willem. The magazine followed a moment later. Willem decided to keep them separate for now. He normally carried a shoulder bag, which his father derisively called a man-purse and Remi just called a purse. This was now somewhere on top of Sneeuwberg. So he put the pistol into his belt at the small of his back and slipped the magazine into his pocket.

T.R. had been summoned forward by the pilot, who had put the chopper into a banking turn. Then he leveled it out and angled it back a hair until they were basically hovering, perhaps a thousand meters above the jungle. They were about halfway from Sneeuwberg to Tuaba. The land beneath them had shed most of its altitude and flattened out somewhat. From the jungle below they could see a pall of smoke swirling around a clearing near the highway. "Aw, shit, that's the pump station," T.R. said. "Those fucking assholes."

On a closer look the clearing was a puddle of gray liquid, like wet cement, spreading out into the surrounding jungle. "System should shut off automatically before the spill gets too much worse," T.R. said. He came back into the cabin, checking his phone. "Aaand the fucking cell towers are down." He called back to the pilot. "Get on the horn back to Sneeuwberg and make sure they are aware the slurry pipeline has been breached."

"Roger that," came the answer. T.R. slammed down into his seat as the chopper tilted forward to resume its flight back to Tuaba. "Fucking assholes," T.R. said. "They do this every few years. Blow up the pipeline. They know it's how copper leaves the island. But it's also the only reason money comes in. Very self-destructive. It is an escalation to be sure."

"So, just to calibrate," Willem said, "shooting up Sneeuwberg and detonating some ANFO is a common occurrence but blowing a hole in the pipeline is a big deal."

"Correct. Forces us to shut a whole lot of things down, higher up. The mine is like an engineered avalanche, running on gravity, material in motion on a scale you can't believe until you see it. Momentum that is inconceivable. To stop it is like diving in front of a freight train." T.R. checked his phone again but the look on his face said he wasn't getting any bars. Finally he slapped it down, put his chin in his hand, and looked out the window. They were almost there. Looking out, Willem could see the outskirts of a town passing below them. And there was only one town.

"We're gonna land on top of the Sam," T.R. explained, suddenly remembering his duties as gracious host. He meant the Sam Houston, which was one of the Western-style hotels that had been put up in Tuaba as a base of operations for visiting engineers, business executives, and the like. "From the helipad there, we can get you down to a room where you can hang out while we arrange a convoy to take you to Ed's compound. Or anywhere else you prefer." Beyond him, through the chopper's side window, Willem caught sight of the airport's control tower in the middle distance. The Sam Houston was in the belt of Western-style hotels and amenities near the airport, so they must be close.

But instead of banking toward the Sam, the pilot swung the other way and put the chopper into a climb. The world rotated slowly around them, and in a few moments the Sam Houston Hotel complex came into view out the window on Willem's side. It looked like any other generic modern hotel, rising a dozen-and-a-half stories above a parking lot ringed by palm and banana trees.

But the grounds were a lake of flashing cop lights. Hundreds of people were milling around, but almost all of them had been banished beyond a radius of a few hundred meters from the structure. Inside that radius were just a few cops and some stragglers—hotel employees, it looked like—being hustled away from the building.

"The Sam is evacuated," the pilot reported. "Suspicious vehicle."

"What's so suspicious about it?"

"It crashed into the lobby and the driver ran away."

"We okay on fuel?"

"Fine, sir."

"Where would you like to go?" T.R. asked Willem. "There's enough room in Ed's compound we could set this thing down right in the middle."

Willem liked that idea. Amelia didn't: "With respect, landing a Brazos RoDuSh chopper *anywhere* marks the location as a target. We won't be doing Uncle Ed any favors—"

"Painting a bull's-eye on his property. Understood," T.R. said.

"Saint Patrick's has a helipad," the pilot pointed out.

"That's it," T.R. said. "Go there."

"The hospital," Willem explained, in case Amelia didn't catch the reference. Though the hospital was just the biggest part of a complex that included a school, convent, and church.

"A chopper landing there is just gonna look like a medevac flight," T.R. said, "bringing casualties down from the mine. If it's really Papuans behind this—well, they know the R.C.s are on their side."

"R.C.s?" Amelia asked.

"Roman Catholics. If it's the Indonesians *pretending* to be Papuans, they gotta do what the Papuans would do—leave the R.C.s alone."

Some part of Willem's brain was registering an objection to this gambit on ethical grounds. They were not, in fact, casualties in need of medical care. But he was not in control of this helicopter. And in any case it took a little while for such high-flown considerations to form up in one's brain; Tuaba was tiny; and jet helicopters were fast.

So fast, as a matter of fact, and so convenient that some less noble part of Willem's brain was beginning to question the wisdom of disembarking from this one. Might this thing have enough fuel to reach the coast? Or even Australia? Could they just get the fuck out of here?

Anyway the decision was made for him as the Sam Houston Hotel, still clearly visible perhaps a kilometer away, exploded. It happened as the chopper was settling in for a landing on the flat roof of the tallest building in the St. Patrick's compound, a modern ten-story structure. Because of the prevailing atmospheric conditions—humid, just above dew point—the explosion manifested as a bolt of yellow light almost immediately snuffed out by a sphere of white vapor expanding outward from the blast at the speed of sound. It took all of about three seconds for this thing to strike the helicopter: long enough that everyone knew that it was coming, and knew that they were going to get hit, but too quickly for the pilot to do anything about it. And what *could* he have done, really? The chopper—which was aimed almost directly toward the Sam Houston—rocked backward, nose pitching sharply up as if it had just taken an uppercut from King Kong. It skidded back across the helipad until it was stopped by a parapet running along the edge of the building's roof. It all happened more slowly and with less overt violence than you might think. Or maybe Willem's brain just couldn't run fast enough to process the violence in real time. The chopper settled back down on its landing gear as the pilot killed the engine. But it was obvious just from the sounds that this thing was not going to take off again anytime soon. And that was confirmed when they got out—which they did very, very hastily—and had a look. The tail rotor had been gnawed down to fibrous stumps and the tail itself was bent upward.

As eye-catching spectacles went, it was hard to choose between a wrecked helicopter close by, and a mushroom cloud of copper-red ammonium nitrate smoke rising above the collapsing remains of a luxury hotel in the distance. And yet only a few minutes later Willem found himself staring at something else. Drawn by the sounds of the hotel being blown up and the helicopter crashing, hospital staff began emerging in numbers from the little hut in the corner of the roof that marked the upper end of the stairwell. More pulsed forth from an elevator near the helipad. They looked much the same as nurses, doctors, x-ray techs, and so on anywhere else: color-coded scrubs, stethoscopes, name tags. Of course there were regional differences: lots of ethnic Papuans, lots of women wearing the headgear that marked them as Catholic nuns. As minutes went by, they were joined by some others who did not appear to be medical professionals. Patients, perhaps, who were well enough to be ambulatory, or people who had come to visit patients. The one who stood out, for Willem, was a grizzled Papuan gent who was naked except for a penis gourd. Willem had read about these, but always assumed they would be smaller. More penis-sized. This one was much, much longer than any human penis Willem had ever seen, and in his younger days he had seen a few. Its wide end—just wide enough to accommodate a penis—was lashed to the man's groin. From there it curved upward along his belly, restrained by a cord around his waist, and then twisted about in free space to end in a sharp point somewhere out in front of his sternum. Willem wondered if it was rude to stare; or if you went about in that getup, would you find it more insulting *not* to be stared at?

They shoved the helicopter off the roof. More choppers—legit medevac choppers—were coming in. They couldn't land while T.R.'s helicopter was in the way. It was not capable of taking off. So a contingent of the hospital's security staff was detailed to cordon off a generous stretch of lawn below. Once they gave the all clear, a couple of dozen of those on the roof converged on the chopper and rotated it until its glass snout was protruding over the edge of the parapet. Then they used its long tail as a lever arm to pitch it forward. This quickly elevated beyond reach and so people rushed to get their shoulders under the landing gear and push on that. Willem found himself between Amelia and the man with the penis gourd. Whatever strengths and weaknesses this guy might have had as far as his grasp on technology and the ways of the modern world were concerned, he understood the helicopter-tipping procedure as well as anyone here, and even used hand gestures to make polite suggestions as to how others might position their hands and use their muscles to best advantage. Eventually the crowd settled into a rhythmic heave-ho procedure, and finally shifted it past its tipping point. It lifted free of their outstretched hands and somersaulted over the edge in perfect silence. The man with the penis gourd watched it fall and smash into the ground with only modest curiosity. It simply wasn't as big a deal to him as it was to those of a more modern mindset. Having made friendly eye contact with Willem earlier, he now made gestures the import of which was *Hey buddy, got a smoke?* and Willem had to pat himself down and show empty hands. "Does anyone have a cigarette for this man?" Willem asked. In short order one was conjured from a janitor's pocket. The man, after expressing due gratitude, snapped it in half and smoked it double-ended as he watched the first medevac chopper come in for a landing.

T.R. led them toward the stairwell. As they walked past the elevators that serviced the helipad, Willem did a double take. A sign above the doors proclaimed T.R. AND VICTORIA SCHMIDT MEDICAL PAVILION, with the same—or so he assumed—repeated in Indonesian and one of the eight hundred some local languages of New Guinea.

"Where are we going? Just curious," Willem asked, after T.R. had led them down eight flights of modern, reinforced-concrete stairs and then into a much older wing of the hospital—walls lined with glazed cement blocks, linoleum floors, wooden doors, the smell of disinfectant. Like a certain number of post-war institutional buildings in the Netherlands.

"L & D."

"Which stands for?"

"Labor and Delivery," T.R. said.

An odd choice, but logical in a way? The trauma center, surgery, x-ray, ICU—all probably swamped, or about to be. Labor and Delivery, no more so than on any other day.

It was an endless maze like all other hospitals, but eventually they found L & D. It did not seem particularly busy. Behind one closed door a woman in labor was crying out in pain. Clusters of family members sat in hallways. Nuns bustled around and glared at them. But T.R.'s was a face they soon recognized. No wonder, since portraits of him and Victoria were prominently featured in the eponymous Medical Pavilion. So they went unchallenged as T.R. led Willem, Amelia, and one of his security guys down a long corridor and then through a wooden door into a hospital room. No one was using it. No one had used it for a while. It looked next in line to be gutted and modernized. It was half full of stacked boxes of medical supplies.

"Thanks for bearing with me," T.R. said. "I just had to stop by and see this, long as I was in the vicinity."

"Why? What's it to you?" Willem asked.

"I was born in this room," T.R. said.

Before long an important-seeming man—a Filipino in a clerical collar—tracked them down and escorted them to an office suite elsewhere in the complex, where they camped out for a bit while T.R. tried to sort out his next move. To judge from listening to his half of various conversations, he would not be averse to simply leaving the country. But there was some kind of shutdown affecting Tuaba's airport and so his jet was grounded. His people were organizing an armed convoy of SUVs that would take him to a residential compound on the edge of town, easier to defend than a luxury hotel. Willem and Amelia could tag along, or—

The "or" was abruptly resolved by the advent of Sister Catherine, whom Willem had last seen at breakfast in The Hague, last October. She denounced T.R.'s plan as nonsensical, though T.R. didn't hear any of that because he was on the phone the whole time she was in the room. "We could offer you sanctuary here," she said. "But to be frank you would be taking up space needed by others."

This sounded like an opening for Willem to declare he wouldn't dream of doing so, and so he opened his mouth. But Sister Catherine ran him off the road. "I can provide easy and safe conveyance to your uncle Ed's if that is where you would prefer to wait this out."

Her phrasing could not help but raise a question in Willem's mind as to what "this" was and how long "this" was projected to last. Part of him wanted to stick with Western-style accommodation near the airport. But a lot of people who'd been staying at the Sam Houston had probably felt safer there, until they'd been hustled out of the building by cops and watched it blow up.

So he accepted Sister Catherine's offer. Five minutes later he and Amelia were lying down in the aisle of a yellow school bus as Sister Catherine fired it up and pulled it out of the school grounds and onto the streets of Tuaba. Her proficiency with the vehicle's manual transmission, the adroitness with which she gunned it through traffic, her hair-trigger approach to application of the horn, all made Willem wonder what other skill sets this nun had acquired during her (he estimated) three decades as a bride of Christ.

"You saw the gun?" she asked him, in Dutch. "Up on Sneeuwberg?"

"A very quick glimpse," Willem said. "Then there was some sort of attack and we had to evacuate."

"Still, it's good that you saw it," Sister Catherine remarked. "Not just the gun. The whole mine. So you know what we are dealing with. The scale of it."

Noteworthy to Willem was the nun's utter lack of curiosity about the attack. He raised his head from the floor of the bus and exchanged a look with Amelia.

He asked, "Do you think that the attack was related to the new gun project or—"

"No!" she said, with a brusqueness that gave Willem a glimpse of what it would feel like to be a dull pupil in her classroom. "No one here cares about any of that."

"Climate change, geoengineering . . ."

"No one cares. Except foreign countries. And it is those who decide our fate."

"Whether you will remain part of Indonesia or—"

"We are 'part of Indonesia' in the same sense that Indonesia used to be 'part of the Dutch Empire,'" she said, and, in the scariest thing Willem had seen all day, turned around to look back and down at him while removing both hands from the steering wheel to form air quotes.

"Please overlook my poor choice of words," Willem said, suppressing the rest of the sentence *and keep your eyes on the fucking road*.

"Go and sin no more," she cracked, swinging the bus decisively onto a side street. Judging from the frequency with which Willem's skull was slamming into the floor, this one was not as well paved. They were plunging into puddles that began, but never quite seemed to end. Canopies of trees were looming above the windows. The verdant scene was interrupted by the hard corner of a rusty shipping container. Standing atop it, well back of a coiling fumarole of razor wire, was a young man in a backwards baseball cap and mirror shades, cradling an AK-47 and smoking a cigarette. Others like him came into view as the bus slowed and then stopped. Sister Catherine put it in neutral and stomped the parking brake with a vehemence she might have used to crush a scorpion threatening a pupil. "School's out," she said.

"Home sweet home," Willem said, and stood up. "Thanks for the lift, Sister Catherine."

"I'll be in touch," she said, "as this plays out." Again, this clear sense that there was a specific "this" and that she knew what it was. To Amelia she said, "There's probably no safer place for you to be. It's where we used to take Beatrix and the others when there was trouble." Amelia didn't know who Beatrix was, but she smiled and nodded politely.

Willem had been anticipating a potentially awkward delay out in front of the gate, during which he would gesticulate in front of Uncle Ed's security camera in an effort to get buzzed in. But their arrival happened to coincide with the departure of several badminton buddies, whose taxi was waiting for them on the street. Clearly these men were not about to let a small insurrection alter their plans for the day. The last of them recognized Willem and simply held the door open for him by sticking one leg out. He made the most of the slight delay by lighting a cigarette. "See you tomorrow," he said to Willem in Fuzhounese, as Willem walked past him.

THE COLUMBIA RIVER

aks's sixth sense—or maybe his seventh or eighth, he'd lost count—told him when it was time to dog-paddle to the left bank of the Columbia and clamber up onto the rocky shore. The sun had broken the horizon as he had snorkeled along beneath the dark surface of the river, but the place where he crawled up onto the land was still deep in the shade of the precipitous eastern bank. On the opposite shore there was practically nothing visible in the way of human habitation—just the same sort of pine scrub where his uncle had dropped him off north of the border. Laks peeled out of the wet suit and changed into the outfit that had been stashed at the top of his waterproof pack: T-shirt, jeans, sneakers, and a bandanna that he could use for the time being as a keski. He weighed the wet suit down under rocks beneath the water. The pack itself looked scarcely less ominously tactical, but it contained a rolled-up duffel bag into which he transferred the other stuff they'd given him: a change of clothes, some American snack food, a water bottle.

It was very quiet here, as there was next to no traffic on the roads and only a faint lapping of water along the bank. Laks's ears—which were better now than they had been before he'd been fixed up in Cyberabad—picked up a faint whir. He swiveled his head to and fro until he picked out its source: a little drone hovering just above the river's surface about a hundred meters away. It smelled safe. He paid it no further mind. There had been no drones shadowing him in Canada, but apparently the United States was a different story. It was, as all the world knew, a completely insane and out-of-hand country, unable to control itself. Men like the Texan could get away with anything; but by the same token, so could Indian military intelligence.

A two-lane highway ran along the top of the bank. He followed it south along a sweeping curve and came in view of an old bridge where the river was crossed by another such road. Around their intersection, half a mile farther along, was a small town built on a generous stretch of flat territory. The shoulder of the road broadened and flowed without any clear dividing line into the gravel parking lots of a few roadside bars, diners, and convenience stores. Laks's ride was idling in one of those. It was a semi-trailer rig carrying a forty-foot shipping container. They hadn't told Laks anything he didn't actually need to know, but it was easy enough to guess that the container had arrived recently at Tacoma or Seattle and been collected by this driver. Laks walked right past it without looking very closely. But there was nothing to see. It looked like a million other trucks.

Half a minute later he heard it revving up, now a couple of blocks behind him. It pulled out onto the road, which doubled as the town's main street. Laks turned around and stuck out his thumb. The truck slowed.

It could be inferred that the driver—who looked Indian—had been instructed to talk to him as little as possible. When asked his name, he simply glanced up at the dome light and then looked pityingly back at Laks. Thanks to Uncle Dharmender, the meaning was clear. "You can sleep back there" was the extent of his conversation. Oh, and he held up a certain kind of widemouthed plastic container that Laks well recognized. During the months he'd spent bedbound from vertigo, he had made frequent use of them. "For urination, please!"

Running athwart the semi-tractor behind the seats was a foam mattress. Tucked into clever built-in cabinets around that were a tiny fridge, a microwave, and some other conveniences. An overhead rail supported a blackout curtain that could divide the cabin in two. It looked tempting to Laks. On the other hand, it was a beautiful morning in eastern Washington. So he sat there and gazed out the windshield for an hour or so as the driver silently, patiently, and at no point exceeding the posted speed limit, maneuvered the rig along a country road that wound through rocky, rolling ranch territory, going brown in the heat of summer, framed by hills carpeted with dark evergreens. It was evident from the sun and from road signs that they were headed generally south, toward Spokane. They passed through a couple of small towns and a reservation for the other kind of Indians. In due time they verged on the outer fringes of the city, with the same lineup of big-box stores and fast-food places as everywhere else, and sleepiness overtook Laks. He took off his shoes, crawled into the back, and pulled the curtain.

He was awakened by the unaccustomed stillness of the truck. Its engine was still idling but it had ceased moving. He pulled the curtain back and was surprised to see that dusk had fallen. He must have slept for something like ten hours. They were just off an interstate highway, in the vast parking lot of some kind of commercial truck stop. The highway ran north-south and was bracketed between ranges of rugged hills. The last light of a gaudy sunset was silhouetting the ones to the west and reddening the scrub-covered slopes of those to the east. The truck driver was nowhere to be seen.

When Laks leaned forward to look around, he was able to get a better view of the plaza's main building, a flat-roofed, mostly windowless corrugated-steel slab. This was surrounded by a branching system of walkways protected by roofs on high steel stilts and feeding out to a vast array of gas pumps and electric vehicle charging stations. At least a hundred of them, with special affordances in some areas for trucks, RVs, and other rigs that needed a lot of room to turn around. Signage on the main building announced that restaurants and other amenities were to be found there. The driver must have gone in for a well-deserved meal.

Laks was glad of the truck driver's absence; this was the first moment he'd had to himself in a long time, unless you counted snorkeling down the river, which had not exactly been relaxing. He peed in the urinal and screwed the lid on carefully. But this somehow caused his bowels to start moving and he realized he was going to have to go inside that huge building and find a proper toilet.

He opened up his bag and found basic toiletries, including a small wooden comb. Traditionally this would have been tucked into his hair, but the circumstances of the wet suit and so on had not allowed it. He used this to comb out the hair that was still long and to remove strands that had naturally broken or fallen out. Behind his ears the areas that had been shaved by the medics were still growing back in, but the hair was still short enough that scars and ports could be seen in his scalp. He'd have wanted to cover that up even if it had not been part of his identity to wear a turban.

In the bottom of his duffel was a bolt of black fabric neatly folded. After he had put his hair up into a knot and covered that and the little comb with his bandanna, he unfolded the black fabric and tied one end of it to the rim of the steering wheel with a slipknot. This enabled him to stretch it back across the cab into the sleeping area. That in turn made it possible to get it pleated lengthwise in the correct way, making sure that its raw edges were neatly folded inward. Which was half the battle. That done, he untied it from the steering wheel and clamped the end between his teeth temporarily while he began to wind it around his head. A few minutes' wrapping and tucking later, he had a reasonably presentable turban that covered the scars and so on left over from the surgery. It passed high across his forehead, allowing a neat triangle of the bandanna under-turban to show—a touch he hoped would be noticed and appreciated by the locals. For he had no idea where he was, other than the western United States. Cowboy country for sure.

He was able to do the first part of this operation by feel, sitting cross-legged on the mattress, but some of the details at the end required a mirror. So he moved up to the passenger seat, flipped the sun visor down, and discovered a small vanity mirror on the back of that. It was flanked by a couple of lights, which he turned on, since it was now close to full dark outside. In another minute or two he was able to finish the wrap and get everything neatly and securely tucked away.

It was only after Laks turned the light back off that he got a good look outside the windshield and saw two people standing in front of him, staring up at him from perhaps ten meters away. He had, during the last minute or so, begun to notice a distinctly foul odor. Since his sense of smell was next to useless, he'd assumed it was but a faint whiff of some incredibly disagreeable stench blowing over the truck stop from a nearby hog lot or chemical factory. Perhaps a tanker full of toxic waste had jackknifed. But he now understood that nothing of the sort was true and that the stink in his nostrils was perceptible only to him. It wasn't real. It was a signal from the early-warning system that had been wired into his skull in Cyberabad. It was trying to let him know that there was something dangerous about his situation. It had started perhaps one minute ago and gotten rapidly worse until the moment he had switched off the light and seen those two people watching him. A man and a woman, both in their late forties or early fifties, white, fat, informally dressed as you'd expect in a truck stop parking lot in the intermountain West. Absolutely normal and unremarkable, in other words, for this time and place.

It was, of course, *he*—Laks—who was the weirdo. He could guess that this couple had been on their way to or from the truck stop when they'd happened to pass directly in front of him. Their gaze had been drawn by the light. They'd stopped to watch him putting the finishing touches on his turban. A procedure neither of them had ever seen in their lives.

Laks reached for the door handle. He had a notion to climb out of the vehicle, greet these people, introduce himself, and politely explain what they'd just seen. But before he could act on it they moved away suddenly, quick-stepping toward the truck stop. The man gripped the upper arm of the woman, who was a little less nimble than he was. A hip replacement was in her future. His lips were moving. She turned her head and threw a look back in Laks's direction as they hustled away. It was not a good look. But the foul smell was abating. The system—whatever it was, however it worked—was letting him know that the threat was subsiding.

Still, he didn't want to alarm these poor people any more than he apparently had already, so he waited until they had gone inside the main building before opening the truck's door and climbing down to the pavement.

And then he stopped for a few moments and gazed almost vertically upward at a bright prodigy blotting out much of the sky.

Visible nearby, out the truck's side windows, had been a pair of stout pillars: steel tubes, anchored to concrete plinths by nuts the size of his head, erupting vertically until they passed above his field of view. Now that he was outside, though, he could follow them up and see what they supported: a sign that, laid flat, would have covered half of a football field. It was thrust high into the air so that it could be recognized by travelers from miles away. It was a cartoon rendering of a smiling and winking man with a white cowboy hat pushed jauntily back on his head. He wore a checked shirt. One hand was extended invitingly toward the truck stop. The other hand was thumb-hooked into a wide orange belt with a buckle shaped like Texas. Below that, the sign consisted of huge glowing letters: T.R. MICK'S.

Some kind of chain operation, evidently.

When Laks had had his fill of that and enjoyed the starry sweep of the big western sky, he lowered his gaze and began walking in toward the central building. A moving walkway was available. Normally he'd have walked, just to stretch his legs, but his inner ear was acting up suddenly, as if trying to pull him back to the truck. So he stepped aboard and grabbed the handrail. In the distance behind him, barely perceptible under the whoosh of tires on the interstate, he could hear the comforting whir of drones shadowing him in the dark.

UNCLE ED'S

nteresting developments up at the mine!"

This exclamation, in English, came from a man of a certain age sitting in a folding chair by the side of Uncle Ed's badminton court, apparently taking a breather between sets.

Almost twenty-four hours had passed since Sister Catherine had dropped off Willem and Amelia. Sometimes, when a lot happened at once, time got compressed, or something, and then it had to relax to bring the universe back into balance. Willem had passed the remainder of yesterday doing nothing in particular, then failed to get to sleep until well past midnight, then slept until almost noon. Now he was stumbling around feeling like he'd missed the whole day, and these eager beaver geriatric badminton players just accentuated that. He blinked and looked at the guy who had just spoken to him. White sneakers, white socks, lime-green gym shorts, a loose sleeveless T-shirt providing an all too graphic view of a physique that, if it had ever seen better days, had not seen them in a long time. A floppy cloth hat to keep the sun off his head, big sunglasses. He was guzzling tea from a stainless-steel thermos. He sat apart from the other gaffers. An out of town visitor, perhaps, an invited guest but not one of the regulars.

Willem felt blood rushing into his face as he realized that this man was Bo.

"Holy shit," he said. "You *do* get around."

"No more than *you* do," Bo pointed out.

Willem could not gainsay Bo's logic. "Hang on, I have to piss and so on."

"Don't let me stop you. There's still some time."

Willem did not get the sense that Bo meant "some time before the next badminton match."

He went back to his room and spent a few minutes doing the usual things in the toilet. When he could, he glanced at the screen of his phone. More violence had happened locally. The Sneeuwberg mine had gone to full shutdown. He decided to simply ignore most of his email and message traffic—he'd already marked himself "safe" on all the platforms that mattered, and he'd checked in with Remi. He peered out the window to the trailer where Amelia was lodging and saw her moving around in there.

"India is getting feisty!" Bo declared, when Willem came back out and snapped out a folding chair next to him.

"Just saber rattling?" Willem asked. "Or is it the real deal?"

"Now you are asking me to read the minds of our good friends south of the great mountains," Bo admonished him. "Never easy. But they have dropped a hint."

"Which is?"

"A new phrase they have just begun using in their public pronouncements. 'Climate Peacekeeping.'"

Willem rolled it around in his head. Interesting. "And what do you think of this phrase, Bo?"

"Oh, I quite like it. Covers a lot of political territory."

"Too much, in my mind," Willem said. "It could be used to justify almost anything. But then, I live in a democracy."

Bo raised his eyebrows as if an amazing new thought had just come to him. "Perhaps the Netherlands should adopt this phrase! You who have suffered such depredations from rising sea level." He took a sip of tea. "Or Netherworld or whatever you're calling it."

"Thanks. Would that help give you political cover for whatever you're doing here?"

"It wouldn't hurt."

"Be that as it may, I cannot help you, for I am freshly retired."

"So I see!" Bo gestured all around. "And such a fine place you have picked for it. State-of-the-art security . . . unmatched culture and recreation . . . and only eight thousand miles away from your husband."

"I needed to get away for a bit. It was suggested I come here for a visit to clear my head."

"Suggested by your ex-boss?"

Willem declined to rise to the bait.

"How's your head? Clear now?"

"I got to help push a helicopter off a hospital."

"Saw that. Amazing visual. Helpful."

"Helpful how?"

"Though China has its well-known differences with India, there are some things we can agree on. One of those is the desirability of peace."

"*Really!?*" Willem exclaimed.

Bo nodded.

"China is coming out in favor of *world peace*."

"It is our constant preoccupation," Bo affirmed.

"So are you going into the climate peacekeeping game as well?"

"A more holistic approach is better. Climate is just part of it. When we see hotels exploding and helicopters being thrown off hospitals by excited mobs of doctors and men with penis gourds, in an area that bestrides our copper lifeline, it forces us to ask tough questions about whether our Indonesian friends really have the situation in hand."

"Holy shit."

"Distressing reports have reached us from the likes of Sister Catherine and your cousin Beatrix concerning the conduct of the foreigners who occupy this land."

"Indonesians. Who don't consider themselves foreigners, by the way. Because this is part of Indonesia."

"Yes," Bo said, waving away Willem's annoying cavils. "Now the situation seems quite out of hand. Copper prices have spiked, threatening our economic interests. There is also concern that shipments of coal and iron ore from Australia may be threatened. In the old days we might have looked to the United States or Great Britain to intervene. But those days are behind us, I think you'll agree."

"All quite above my pay grade, I'm sorry to say."

"Oh, I don't know. The former Queen of the Netherlands, Dr. Schmidt, Sister Catherine, all seem to think you are a valuable person to have around."

"She's going to end up running the place, isn't she?"

"Sister Catherine?"

"Yes."

"You have someone else in mind? Someone better qualified? More deserving of trust?"

"No, but I just got here."

"Maybe your uncle Ed?"

"Too Chinese. Has to be Papuan."

Bo nodded. "My thinking as well. The nun it is."

"When are you guys going to . . . do . . . whatever it is you're going to do?"

Bo rolled his eyes. "Oh, the powers that be wouldn't dream of entrusting *me* with such sensitive information."

"Of course not. But you're not here in any professional capacity. I mean, look at you."

Bo looked at himself and adopted a mildly put-upon air. He plucked at the limp tank top. "You don't like it?"

"In your capacity as visiting tourist, shooting the breeze by the side of the badminton court, what would you speculate?"

"I'm not one of those old Chinese men who is always trotting out quotations from Sun Tzu's *Art of War*," Bo said. "Tried to read it once. That guy is, what do you call it in the West? Captain Obvious."

"Good, because I was hoping for something more directly applicable to Tuaba, *today*."

"In my reading of military history, I'm always coming across references to the night before battle. It's a trope. I've never once read about people having lunch before battle. No one wants to launch anything in the afternoon. It's a foregone conclusion you'll run out of daylight. Just an observation."

"All right." Willem checked his phone to see if he had connectivity. He did, thanks to Uncle Ed's satellite uplink. It was 1:30 in the afternoon. Tuaba, Western Europe, and West Texas were evenly spaced around the globe, eight hours apart. In Texas the sun had probably gone down at least an hour ago. Where Saskia was, in the Adriatic, it would be shortly before dawn.

He sent T.R. a text.

> Let's talk about being overrun by China. Also about India's climate peacekeeping initiative.

> What do you know?

> More than you. Shall we meet where it all started?

> Can it wait until dinner?

> Up to you, you're the one with the jet.

> Rijsttafel?

> Sounds delicious

> C U there.

Willem replied with a thumbs-up emoji and pocketed his phone. "I have no idea what the fuck I'm supposed to do," he said.

"Well, don't look at me," Bo answered. "Oh, I'd love to make myself useful somehow, don't get me wrong. But you and your friend Frederika are doing something that has never been done before. Quite beyond my powers of imagination."

"And what is it you imagine we are doing?" Willem was trying not to giggle. He'd spent yesterday being flung around like a rag doll in a chopper, various SUVs, and a school bus. The idea that he was "doing something" in any kind of systematic way was pure comedy.

"Booting up a new country. Netherworld. Cool name."

"Thanks. But the name wasn't my idea. Some Venetians came up with that."

"They are always at the forefront in matters of taste and creativity."

"And it's not a country. You know this."

"It could be a political force, though. More powerful than many so-called countries."

"Yes, the Marshall Islands, the Maldives . . ."

"I was thinking the United States. A clown show."

"We're agreed on that."

"And yet the chaos of America gives people like T.R. the leeway to do things like Pina2bo that simply wouldn't be tolerated anywhere else."

"It's an asset, you're saying. The sheer incompetence of the United States."

"People have come to rely on it."

"It's true."

"The crazy place where people can do crazy things!" Bo exclaimed. "But then countries like India feel as though some intervention is needed. In *my* opinion, they are going too far."

Willem threw up his hands. "Well, since I don't know what they're doing—"

"Trust me, they are going too far. But it will play well in their media. And they know they'll get away with it. America will be very angry for forty-eight hours and then get bored and get angry about something new. A movie star will kick his dog or a quarterback will park his Lambo in a handicapped space."

"Sounds like T.R. is screwed then."

Bo shrugged. "Perhaps a *real* country could be persuaded to step in and restore calm."

SQUEEGEE NINJA

At nine A.M. Texas time every Monday and every Friday morning, Black Hat Practical Operations held a virtual stand-up meeting. They had started inviting Rufus to these shortly after he had set up operations at Marble Mine. It all happened over augmented-reality headsets. They had delivered one such device to him. You could use the thing anywhere and see the same stuff, but the overall effect was more convincing if you did it in a big dark empty space. By virtue of living in an abandoned mine, Rufus had access to one. So every Monday and every Friday just before nine A.M. he would go to a big empty space down in the mine and put the thing on his head. As the meeting started, people would begin to appear, standing in a circle around the room. Head count was never less than a dozen, sometimes as much as two dozen. Most of the participants seemed to be in charge of teams. Rufus, of course, was not in charge of anyone. He was on the invite list, as he well understood, because otherwise he'd be totally isolated. He'd have no idea what was going on and no one would know who he was. This could lead to confusion and friendly-fire fuckups. So he always showed up for the meetings. But he never spoke unless spoken to, which was never.

The majority of the avatars in the biweekly stand-up talked like Americans and had low latency, meaning that they exchanged words and gestures in something close to real time. Some attendees had high latency, which as Rufus could guess meant that they were far enough away for the speed of light to become a limiting factor; no matter how adroitly networks routed those packets, they could only travel down the fiber-optic cables or bounce off the satellites so fast. Frequently the high-latency avatars spoke with non-American accents. He recognized some as British, Australian, or South African. Others he didn't recognize at all.

And some moved around. T.R. was one of those. Sometimes his latency was high, sometimes low. Rufus had noticed a few things and put two and two together. Sometimes when T.R. was in high-latency mode—suggesting he was on the other side of the world—he breathed heavily and rapidly, as if short of breath. Rufus hadn't understood this, and in fact he'd actually begun to worry about T.R.'s cardiovascular, until he had taken to noticing the word "Snowbird" coming up in conversation. Then he'd realized it was actually "Snowberg." Then he'd heard one of the South Africans—an Afrikaner—say the name of it with different vowel sounds: "Snayoobergh." Rufus had figured out it was a Dutch word, "Sneeuwberg," and that it was a place on the island of New Guinea. The Dutch had named it "Snow Mountain" back in the days when it actually did have snow on it. Nowadays it did not. That was partly because of global warming and partly because Brazos RoDuSh had converted it into a hole in the ground. Anyway, the elevation was quite high—something like fifteen thousand feet, depending on which part of the mine complex you were at—and so T.R.'s noticeable shortness of breath did not reflect any underlying deficiencies on the cardio front. There just wasn't that much oxygen where he was.

So, though they didn't talk about it directly—Black Hat had pretty good comms discipline, everything "need to know"—Rufus had pretty easily been able to piece together the picture that another big gun was in the works at Sneeuwberg. As well as a third complex at some place called Vadan, in southern Europe. With yet more sites apparently being evaluated.

Which was all very interesting but, from a Black Hat standpoint, a potentially dangerous distraction from the task at hand, which was to secure the Flying S Ranch. Anything not directly related to this property was above Rufus's pay grade. He knew the military mind well enough to know that for him to express even mild curiosity about Sneeuwberg or Vadan would get him in trouble; and to do it a second time would get him fired. And along with that came a certain feeling of being out of the loop. Flying S was a done deal. The Pina2bo gun had been operating with only occasional episodes of downtime for almost a year. The initial pushback against what T.R. was doing here had more recently been muted by countervailing arguments around the idea of termination shock: the fear that if the gun stopped, it would lead to a backlash in the world's climate system. The cool kids in T.R.'s organization were now popping up with high latency in Vadan and Sneeuwberg. The medics at High Noon had started urging Rufus to get all kinds of vaccinations for diseases whose names he hadn't heard since the army had shipped him off to fucked-up parts of the world.

It wouldn't be quite fair to the staff left behind at Flying S to say they were complacent. But it was definitely the case that they were no longer in the spotlight. Flying S–related topics were now deep in the agenda and tended to be dispensed with by Colonel Tatum reporting that there was nothing to report.

The next, and always the last, agenda item was called Trigger Warning. It always consisted of a video, typically from YouTube. Sometimes T.R. picked it out himself, other times it was a suggestion from one of the team. Most of the Trigger Warning videos had at least some connection to the over-arching theme of practical applications of violence, which was, after all, the profession, or at least the constant preoccupation, of everyone present. A typical example might be a cop getting stabbed by a distraught housewife while his attention was fixed on the husband, or a fistfight in front of a liquor store with some unexpected twist. In general, to be considered for the honor of appearing on the Trigger Warning segment, a video needed to have some *Whoa, I did not see that coming!* element that would leave the team members entertained and yet questioning their assumptions—and, as such, more on their toes and less likely to end up being featured in such a video.

One Monday morning, the Trigger Warning video featured a man known to the Internet as Squeegee Ninja. Very low-quality cell phone video of this guy had been circulating during the last twenty-four hours, but it kept getting taken down as the people who'd posted it figured out that they were incriminating themselves. T.R., though, had exclusive access to much better footage, all from security cameras controlled by his organization. Because the whole thing had gone down at a T.R. Mick's.

The quality of these videos made Rufus feel old. When he heard someone speak of security camera footage—from a gas station, no less—he still thought of old-school black-and-white imagery with terrible resolution. Of course, it wasn't like that anymore. This footage was Hollywood movie grade. Even the sound quality could be pretty good.

Another drawback of classic security camera footage was that nothing was ever framed correctly. The camera was never pointed in exactly the right direction. The bozos and miscreants and flailing, hapless victims who tended to star in these little dramas always went out of frame at the worst possible moment. But of course that too was a thing of the past. The cameras now used AI to pan and tilt and zoom, centering whatever the AI considered most interesting—most legally actionable, anyway—and in one of your better planned-out systems, practically all parts of the facility could be covered from multiple camera angles. So really it was all about choices—about editing. Someone in T.R.'s chain of command had apparently handed off all the Squeegee Ninja–related footage to a gifted film editor who had cut it all together into a five-minute sequence that was as watchable as any Hong Kong action flick. In real time it hadn't lasted that long, but the editor had chosen to use a lot of freeze-frame, slo-mo, and multi-camera instant replay during especially watchable parts of the action. It was safe to say, based on the reactions of the virtual audience gathered around Rufus in the depths of the marble mine, that no one had any objections to taking the additional couple of minutes out of their day to watch the extended director's cut. Even T.R. allowed as how those members of the team who were in time zones where it was after five P.M. should feel free to crack open a beer. Today, T.R. was high latency (he was on the other side of the world) but seemed to have plenty of oxygen (low altitude).

Like any well-structured narrative the story began with some setup: it was just a normal, pleasant summer evening at this random T.R. Mick's Mobility Center somewhere in the western United States. A middle-aged couple came in, looking concerned but not yet what you would call agitated, and requested to speak to the manager. They made that request of an employee running a cash register near an entrance. It took a minute for the manager to show up. During that time, the couple chatted with some of the other customers in the queue. It was hard to make out exactly what they were saying, but there were a lot of apprehensive glances in the direction of the parking lot. Eventually a manager—wearing a white cowboy hat as badge of rank—did show up. The couple— now surrounded by several other customers who had been drawn into the story—began to point out into the parking lot and to explain something. But as luck would have it they were barely able to get started when the door opened and a man walked in. He was a big fella with an athletic build, like a tight end or a power forward. For the most part he was dressed in completely forgettable clothing: jeans, sneakers, unmarked T-shirt. But he was wearing a turban. A standard-issue N-95 mask completed the ensemble. Around the fringes of the mask a healthy black beard could be seen. He was brown skinned, not a white guy but probably not African American. Not far off from Rufus in skin color.

Whenever you watched a movie, and new characters began to appear on the screen, you had to pick sides. To decide who to root for. From the word go, Rufus was on the side of the guy in the turban. How many times in his life had he been that guy? And the conspiring, finger-pointing white people he couldn't have hated more.

Here the video had to be paused because a discussion had broken out among various Black Hat operatives. "Dude is Arab!" some-one objected.

"So?"

"It's kind of racist to call him Squeegee Ninja."

"Why?"

"Ninja is a Chinese thing."

"Japanese," someone corrected him.

"Okay, whatever, but the point is, not Arab."

"He's not Arab," said another voice. "Dude is Indian."

"I never heard of any Native American tribe wearing turbans."

"I mean, from India."

"Oh."

"He's not Indian. He's Sikh," said yet another voice.

"Sikhs are Indian!"

"No, they are from Pakistan."

"Arabs then."

"No, Pakistanis are not Arabs!"

The pace of the discourse had slowed down as mad typing on multiple keyboards was taking over the audio feed. "According to Wiki—"

"I'm gonna restart the video now," T.R. announced. "Y'all can take this offline."

The guy in the turban was clearly oblivious to the little drama playing out at the cash register. Even if he'd been paying attention there'd have been nothing to see, because as soon as he came in, all those people clammed up and made a big show of not star-ing at him. He looked around to get his bearings, then lurched in the direction of the bathrooms. "Lurched" being the operative word here because something about his gait was off. Like invisible hands were trying to pull him back out toward the parking lot and he was tearing loose from them. Once he'd got well into the building he seemed to recover his equilibrium, and then made a beeline for those world-famous surgically clean T.R. Mick's toilets.

It transpired that he needed to go number 2, and so there was now an interlude during which the cash register caucus resumed its deliberations and acquired new members. A couple of these were open carrying, and as the conversation went on and began to include words like "Arab," "terrorist," and "bomb," these reached around to pat their weapons. One drew his pistol from its holster and pulled the slide back to inspect the chamber.

A different nonwhite, non-Black man entered the frame from the other direction carrying a foil-wrapped burrito and exited to the parking lot. He seemed oblivious to all this drama and was scarcely noted by its participants. Rufus might not have noticed him at all had T.R. not paused the video and remarked, "We think that is the driver."

Eventually Turban Man finished his business in the toilet and headed straight for the exit. His utter lack of interest in any of the food, beverage, or leisure time modalities on display in the T.R. Mick's was construed in the darkest possible way by those observing him. A contingent hastened to the bathroom to look for (guessing) bricks of plastic explosive stuck beneath toilets. In this they were disappointed; but by that time the man in the turban had already checked in for his appointment with destiny and the truck stop was on fire.

For three members of the self-appointed posse had followed him outside. Camera angles flickered around for a spell. The principals were all on the move through a relatively camera-impoverished part of the property and the editor had had to make do and fill in with some less than ideal cuts. But as luck would have it there were a couple of strong angles on the place where the posse caught up with its prey: a vacant gas pump, 37G, about a hundred feet away from the building.

One interesting detail that caught Rufus's eye here was that the guy was no longer unsteady on his feet. More the opposite. While Rufus was just a mediocre athlete himself, he'd played football with a couple of guys who had gone on to the NFL. He'd always known there was something different about them, just based on the way they carried themselves, the way they moved. The guy in the turban was one of those. By the time he reached Pump 37G, the posse had been hassling him for a little while, questions hardening into threats and commands. He was ignoring them, pretending not to hear. But he was keeping his hands in view and well away from his sides, which was smart of him.

Finally one of the posse lost his temper and drew his sidearm, which happened to be a revolver. One of those ridiculously large-caliber revolvers that a certain kind of gun nut had a hard-on for. He put his thumb on the hammer and drew it back, cocking the weapon, which for the time being was still aimed at the ground. The click of the gun's action wasn't audible on the soundtrack. But apparently the guy with the turban heard it, for in one smooth motion he lunged sideways and grabbed the handle of a squeegee, provided for the convenience of T.R. Mick's customers who wished to scour their windshields clear of dead insects using T.R.'s patented Bug-Solv formula. The squeegee was soaking head down in a bucket of same. The man in the turban pulled it out, executed a full pirouette, and whipped it around, causing Bug-Solv to spray from its end in a scythe-like arc that, under the powerful motion-activated lights of Pump 37G, shone like Star Wars light saber shit. It perfectly sliced across the middle of Revolver Man's face, delivering a load of slightly used Bug-Solv directly into his eye sockets. The man toppled back. Rufus noted with approval that he maintained control of the weapon, though. The Bug-Solv also spattered one of the other men, who reflexively cringed away from it; Squeegee Ninja took advantage of this to step close to him, hook his arm with the T-shaped head of the squeegee, and get him in a sort of complex joint lock that made it possible for him to pull the man's pistol from his belt holster and toss it lightly up onto the moving walkway. This, of course, carried it away.

"Picked up by a ten-year-old Boy Scout at the front door and handed in to a cashier," T.R. said.

The third posse member, correctly eschewing the use of firearms in such a fraught close-range melee, jumped on Squeegee Ninja's back, obliging the latter to disentangle his weapon from number 2's arm. He punched its handle back several times in reverse pool cue style, delivering powerful, rib-snapping, spleen-rupturing jabs to the assailant's midsection, then shrugging free as number 3 collapsed back onto the pavement.

"Choppered to the nearest tertiary trauma center, critical but stable," T.R. said.

Number 2 had been patting himself down like a man who has lost his car keys; he had no idea what had become of his gun. He took a wild swing at Squeegee Ninja, who dodged it. Then another. The third punch was never delivered; the guy drew his fist back but the move was so obviously telegraphed that Squeegee Ninja had time simply to plant the head of his weapon across the guy's bicep, just above the elbow, freezing his arm. And leaving his face wide open for a double-handed butt-stroke with the squeegee's opposite end. He fell on his back with a finality that elicited a round of light applause and some "woo!" from the enraptured Black Hat staff in their virtual meeting.

The guy with the Bug-Solv in his eyes had got to his knees. To his credit he was still observing correct trigger discipline; his cocked revolver was pointed straight up and his finger was laid alongside the cylinder. He had his face buried in the crook of his other arm. He lifted his head. If it made sense to describe a motion of the eyelids as violent, then he was blinking violently. He was trying to see something. His gun began to descend in the general direction of the blur he had identified as Squeegee Ninja. Who was looking the other way; but he pivoted as if he had eyes in the back of his head. With a curious little hop and skip, like a seventy-pound girl playing hopscotch, the big man took to the air, light as a tumbleweed, and lashed out with the squeegee in a two-handed home run swing that connected with the revolver and knocked it clean out of the man's hand. It flew out of the frame. Had this been a real Hollywood movie, its trajectory from that moment on might have been lovingly captured in slo-mo from all sorts of camera angles as it spun through the air. Matters being what they were, however, everyone just had to put two and two together and use their imaginations a little bit to infer that it had taken a bad bounce, which had caused it to discharge: an inference made more than obvious by the detonation of the liquid propane truck a hundred yards downrange, currently refilling a large reservoir placed there for the convenience of T.R. Mick's RV-driving customers. Which exploded too.

"No casualties, believe it or not," T.R. said. "The driver of the propane truck was watching all this shit go down and had already taken cover."

"He got away?" someone asked.

This elicited a guffaw from T.R. "He ain't a *criminal*. He din't do one single thing *illegal*. We don't say of such a man, 'he got away.' We say, he took his leave."

"In Burrito Guy's truck?"

"A semi, yes. Burrito Guy pulled out when the LP tank exploded and drove to a safe spot on the far edge of the parking lot. Squeegee Ninja *took his leave* from the well-regulated militia at Pump 37G and went looking for the truck—eventually found it—and climbed in. Off they went."

"Did you get a license plate?"

"I suppose we *could*," T.R. said, "and maybe we *will* if there's a criminal investigation, and some local yokel D.A. sends us a subpoena. But I hope they just let sleeping dogs lie. The poor man was attacked. He defended himself. No one died. We have insurance. And when you have spent as much as I have, cumulatively, on insurance, nothing brings greater satisfaction than to lay a horrific claim on your insurer. The end."

During this discussion the video had remained up, hanging in space, projected on a virtual screen—a rectangle hovering about ten feet in front of Rufus. It was frozen on the last frame, which was just a wall of billowing orange fire.

Now, of the score or so of persons attending this meeting, Rufus probably had the best view of it. The others—scattered around the world in hotel suites, conference rooms, departure lounges, or spare bedrooms—were in environments that were, by and large, more brightly lit and more cluttered. The same pixels were being displayed in their glasses as Rufus's. But only Rufus had the advantage of being able to view those pixels in a dark place against a featureless matte backdrop. He noticed something. And for the first time in three months, he spoke during a meeting.

"Those your drones, T.R.?"

Silence for a few moments as people tried to identify the speaker. "That you, Red?" T.R. asked.

"Yes, sir. I was asking about the drones. Are those T.R. Mick's equipment? Just hovering around the mobility center for security or whatever? Or someone else's?"

"I'm not aware of any—" T.R. paused now for several seconds. "Well, ho-lee shit."

"Just above and to the right of that Tesla," someone confirmed.

T.R., or someone who had control of the video interface, zoomed and panned. The wall of fire occupied basically the whole frame of the video. Any object between it and the camera showed up as a crisp silhouette. This included objects that had been invisible until they had been backlit by the conflagration. The thing Rufus had noticed was a small quad-copter drone, hovering ten or twelve feet above the ground.

"There's a second one off to the left, near the edge of the picture," Rufus said.

The view panned leftward, seeming to move at great speed because it was so zoomed in. With a bit of hunting around, a second drone, just like the first one, became visible. It was harder to see because of how it was lit, but it was definitely there.

"Triangulating on Squeegee Ninja," Rufus said. "Leastways that's how it looks to me."

"You think maybe the well-regulated militia got drones in the air to track the 'Ay-rab terrorist'?" T.R. asked.

"I guess that's . . . possible?" Rufus allowed. "If someone was real quick on his feet."

There was a silence as everyone thought it through. During the time Squeegee Ninja was taking his dump, might some member of the cash register posse have run out to the parking lot and got a couple of drones in the air? Rufus could sense everyone swinging round to the opinion that this seemed unlikely.

"Or maybe," T.R. speculated, "some hobbyist just happened to be playing with two identical drones out in the parking lot when all this happened?"

"Two that we know of, sir," Rufus corrected him.

"Ha! You think there's more we can't see, Red?"

"The more the merrier."

"Well! I only showed y'all this video as a little bit of light entertainment to wrap up the meeting and send y'all on your way with a bang and a chuckle," T.R. said. "Thanks to Eagle Eyes here, seems we got a mystery on our hands."

"Can we take it offline?" asked Tatum. "This is a T.R. Mick's thing. It's not related to any of our operations, is it?"

Rufus was thumbing a message to T.R.:

> If you get me access to the videos I will investigate.

> You got it T.R. texted back, even as he was saying out loud, "Hell no, it's a thousand miles away from Flying S. You're right, Tatum. This meeting is concluded."

RIJSTTAFEL

ndia's pissed off."

This obviously wasn't news to T.R., but it was enough to pull him away from his phone for a minute. He had just concluded some kind of virtual meeting in the conference room on the top floor of the T.R. and Victoria Schmidt Medical Pavilion. Willem and Amelia had been loitering in the reception area along with something like a dozen members of an Indonesian family who had come here to serve them dinner. Now they had all flooded through. Willem and T.R. retreated to a corner while the conference table was set and the dishes arranged.

"What are they pissed off about now?" T.R. asked.

"The monsoon."

T.R. cackled. "The monsoon that's in full swing right this minute?" He pulled his phone back out. "Hang on, let me check the weather in Amritsar. Oh, look!" He held it up so that Willem could see a pictorial weather forecast. "Right now it's raining cats and dogs in Amritsar." He put his phone back in his pocket. "So what's India got to be pissed off about?"

"Perhaps," Willem said, "they regret you did not consult with them before building a giant machine that fucks with the weather."

It was almost midnight. The view from this corner was as good as it got, in Tuaba. The nighttime cityscape was spread out before them, and they could see part of the airport's single runway. The most prominent thing on the skyline was the half-collapsed ruin of the Sam Houston Hotel, lit up by work lights that had been trucked down from the mine. All the fires had long since been put out, but recovery and demolition work were putting enough dust into the air that the ruin appeared to be wreathed in smoke.

The signal to eat was given. Most of the restaurant clan cleared out, though the matriarch stayed for a minute while Willem switched into her language to express his gratitude for their staying up so late, and to remark on the astonishing beauty of the dishes' presentation.

When she had finally taken her leave, beaming, Willem turned to see T.R. appraising him.

"That's what you do, ain't it?" T.R. said.

"What? Talk to people and make them feel seen and appreciated? That's part of it." He sat down and reached for his napkin. "I can also be a cold-blooded son of a bitch."

"And under what circumstances, pray tell, would you allow that side of your personality to come out?"

"When it was necessary to achieve the goals of the state."

"Would that be . . . *Netherworld?*"

Willem laughed. "Seems everyone has heard of it."

"Is that why you're here? To bring Papua into Saskia's orbit?"

"It's fascinating," Willem said, "that people have such inflated notions about Netherworld, which a few days ago was just a word painted on a bedsheet in Venice."

"It's fascinating to *me* that you're so clueless about marketing. If I saw a hashtag go viral that fast, I'd have a hundred people on it the next day."

"For all I know, Cornelia has done just that. It's all her doing."

"Mm!" T.R. exclaimed. "We Texans brag about our tolerance for spicy food but our stuff is child's play compared to Indonesian! This is fiery!"

Willem let the remark pass without comment. T.R. had been born here. The hotness of Indonesian food could not actually have come as a surprise to him.

"Look, man," Willem said, after they had spent a few moments enjoying the meal, "you have to have known from the beginning of all this that the great powers of the world weren't just going to sit by and watch while you implemented a scheme on your ranch that was bound to alter the climate everywhere."

"I would remind you," T.R. said, "that I convened a group of people last year, including you and Saskia, to start the conversation."

Willem was irritated by T.R.'s offhand use of the familiar name "Saskia," but decided to let it go. She *had* encouraged people to call her that during their sojourn in Texas. "Start it, yes. But you chose small countries. Microstates. Venice, for god's sake."

"Gotta start somewhere. I invite China and India to such a meeting, what do you think's going to happen?"

"Nothing," Willem admitted. "They'd find ways to stop it."

"My point exactly."

"And now you've gone and done it . . . and they are stopping it by other means."

"Is that what you think is happening? To me it looks like they are demanding a seat at the table. Now that I gone and *done* something. They're *happy* someone did it."

"They've a funny way of showing it."

T.R. scoffed and waved him off. "It's just full-contact football," he explained, in a helpful tone. "Like when the linebacker comes through and lays a good lick on the quarterback. A sign of respect. Game on!"

Willem was only beginning to organize, in his mind, some of his objections to this metaphor, when there was a light knock at the door. Then it opened a bit and Sister Catherine stuck her head in. She had a shy-schoolgirl look about her very different from the bus driver avatar in which she had manifested yesterday. Both men threw their napkins down and stood up. Willem was closer to the door; he got to it first and held it open for her as she bustled into the room. Looking over the top of her habit—not difficult, for she was of not very great stature—he saw the anteroom, and the corridor leading to it, now populated by at least a dozen Papuan men slinging weapons ranging from AK-47s down to the machete-like choppers known as parangs. Engulfed in them was Amelia, looking at him wryly. Willem gave what he hoped was a polite nod to the one who looked oldest and best equipped, then gently closed the door. T.R. was greeting Sister Catherine, even trying out a few words in one of the local languages.

She took a seat at the table and partook of the meal. The conversation that followed was polite, awkward, and peculiarly dull in the way that important conversations sometimes had to be. Everyone here must know that something was up. But they couldn't yet talk about it directly. Ultimately it was about copper and gold mines—not really of interest to Willem. As Sister Catherine had made crystal clear yesterday, these people would worry about climate change later.

"It is my recommendation," Sister Catherine said, when they'd got through the polite stuff, "that you get out of here."

"What do we know about conditions at the airport?" Willem asked. He directed the question at T.R., supposing that T.R. might actually know something. But—a bit disconcertingly—T.R. just looked across the table at Sister Catherine. She made a gesture indicative of her mouth being full, so T.R. looked back at Willem. "Need a lift?"

"Now that you mention it, if you could find room for me and Amelia . . ."

"Certainly. As long as you don't mind going to Texas."

"We'll find a way to make the most of it."

> Going to Texas apparently Willem texted Princess Frederika.

Sister Catherine washed down her food with a swallow of beer and said, "Now would be a bad time. Indications are that the airport will be up and running by mid-morning. You might need special clearance to take off, but . . . arrangements can be made."

T.R. nodded. "For the benefit of my people who are trying to wrangle the logistics of it all, who do we need to talk to about that?"

"You need to talk to me."

Willem's phone vibrated and he glanced down to see a cowboy hat emoji.

> C U there.

The meal didn't reach a firm conclusion but sort of devolved into what showed every sign of becoming a slumber party. Sister Catherine basically lived here, albeit in another part of the complex. The compound where T.R. had been staying was across the river, not convenient to the airport, and so if they really were looking at a departure in less than twelve hours there was no point in his risking the drive back just so he could then risk a separate trip to the runway a few hours later. For the night had become lively with sporadic exchanges of gunfire and occasional deep booms audible through the conference room's windows. More than once, Willem looked at those askance, wondering if they might at any point turn into a horizontal storm of glinting cubes propelled into the building on a shock wave. But Sister Catherine seemed to think it was in God's hands. So it turned into a game of chicken, which Willem was not about to lose to a five-foot-tall nun.

For their parts, Willem and Amelia had shunted into that mode of carrying all their luggage with them at all times. With equal ease they could hole up here, go to the airport, or try to get back to Uncle Ed's in one piece.

Someone finally just propped the conference room doors open. Various aides to T.R. and Sister Catherine began to dart in and out without ceremony. Senior ones claimed table space and unfolded laptops. Amelia found a comfy chair in a corner and dozed.

It was still dark, but only a little before dawn, when it came to Willem's attention that he was surrounded by heavily armed Chinese men who had not been there a few moments earlier. He had gone up to the roof to get some air. It was as cool as it ever got in Tuaba. Not what you'd call peaceful though. The gunfire and the booms had abated somewhat, but their aftermath kept rolling up to the emergency department on the ground floor. In a pool of light down there, bloody people were being dragged out of cars, triaged in the parking lot, laid out dead or dying in the grass if it was too late, hooked to IVs if not critical, hustled inside if they were somewhere in between. These were decidedly *not* the kinds of patients apt to be brought in on helicopters and so the roof was pretty quiet: just a few employees up here on cigarette breaks and a couple of guys with rifles.

Which just made it all the more startling to be suddenly in the company of young Chinese men. Had he gone to sleep on his feet and slumbered through something? There had been an outbreak of raucous hissing noises in the last minute or so, which he'd guessed might be steam venting from a boiler.

A flat silvery-gray object—a Frisbee-shaped disk the size of a compact car, but apparently not as heavy—clattered down onto the roof in a burst of dust and pea gravel. A second one landed right on top of it, neatly stacking.

He heard another of those intense hissing sounds and realized it was right out in front of him, above the hospital courtyard where they'd dumped the chopper yesterday. Enough light was radiating outward from the windows of the building to make the source clearly visible: another of those silvery disks. When he caught sight of it, the thing was still falling. For it had simply dropped out of the sky. Plumes of white fog were screaming out of nozzles spaced around its perimeter—just like rocket exhaust, but cold, with no fire.

And people were falling from it. Four people.

Not exactly falling, though. They were being dropped on thin cables. At first glance it looked like a quadruple suicide. But the disk stopped falling almost violently under the influence of those cold thrusters. It slowed to a momentary halt and then sprang back up. The four humans—who, just a moment ago, had been plunging toward the ground at what looked like fatal velocity—fell slower and slower the closer they got to terra firma. Those cables were being paid out in a programmed way, killing their velocity. It all unfolded in maybe two seconds of elapsed time from the moment the thing had begun hissing to the point where those men were safely on the ground. The object that had dropped them, having just shed probably five hundred kilograms of human baggage, sprang into the air just as those thrusters petered out.

At that point Willem's attention was captured by another hiss, this one above the helipad. He couldn't see the source, but the helipad was well lit and so a second later he saw four men plummeting toward it—again, at a speed that seemed sure to prove fatal. But again they were being slowed down the whole way. The cables released when they were mere centimeters above the pad, and then they were just standing there. It was a squad consisting of three men with rifles and one carrying a larger automatic weapon. In unison they reached up to their faces and pulled off what looked like oxygen masks.

He'd seen similar mechanisms depicted on NASA animations when they landed rovers on Mars. Sky Cranes. Once they had let their payloads down to the Martian surface they usually just flew away and crashed somewhere. But these things apparently had enough smarts and enough battery power to manage a controlled landing nearby. And, when possible, they politely stacked themselves.

Most of the groups being landed were squads like the one that had just touched down on the helipad. Others looked like snipers or comms specialists. None of them showed much interest in Willem, so he wandered over to examine a sky crane that had landed nearby a few moments ago. It had a spherical bulge in the middle, like a classic depiction of a flying saucer. Probably the vessel where the compressed gas was stored under some heinous pressure.

He couldn't understand why these things were basically white—which didn't seem very stealthy—until he got close. Then he saw that the whole thing was jacketed in a thick layer of frost. Humidity had condensed out of Tuaba's air and frozen on contact. It must have been dropped from the stratosphere—from an airplane flying so high it couldn't be seen. It had fallen for miles through air at nearly cryogenic temperatures and become ice cold. That explained the oxygen masks that these guys all wore.

Those hisses seemed to be coming from all over the place. They died down, but then they started up again. Waves of planes, flying dark, invisible in the stratosphere, deploying these things by the rack.

A man less tired, more on the ball than Willem would have counted the hisses and multiplied by four to estimate the total number of troops the Chinese had dropped. But it was too late, he had long since lost track. There were at least a hundred just on the grounds of St. Patrick's. Presumably more at other key points—the bridges, the airport, the barge port on the river. And now, as the sky grew brighter, he began seeing parachutes as well: big triple chutes dropping cargo pallets at the airport and on the floodplain, and paragliders carrying individual men, spiraling down into areas that the skyhook guys had already secured.

A chopper came in. It descended vertically from a great height, maybe to avoid small-arms fire. If so, an unnecessary precaution, for the city had grown quiet, except for a few localized bursts of intense fighting. Willem was expecting this thing to have Chinese military markings. But it was a Brazos RoDuSh helicopter, probably just flown down from the mine.

T.R. emerged from the elevator. In tow were a couple of his senior staff and Amelia. She was pulling her wheeled bag with one hand and Willem's with the other. Willem strode over to join them. T.R. saw him coming. "We got word," T.R. explained. "Wheels up in fifteen. After that the airport's gonna get real busy."

Once they were all in that helicopter, it took all of sixty seconds to reach the airport. They set down near a business jet parked at the south end of the runway, lights on, engines running, pilots and flight attendant waiting for them at the foot of the fold-down stairs.

There was a minute's delay while the bags were taken by the pilot, one at a time, and stowed in the jet's luggage compartment. Willem had positioned himself at the end of the short queue of passengers so that he could snap a selfie to send to Remi. For Remi would be getting ready for bed in Leiden, worrying about the latest reports from Tuaba, and he'd sleep better if he had a picture of his husband about to board a plane that would take him to a more stable part of the world. Or to Texas at any rate.

He saw an opportunity to frame the shot more perfectly by walking a short distance away from the plane and positioning himself with the plane behind him and a spectacular Pina2bo dawn behind that.

"May I?" someone offered. One of the Chinese guys who was hanging around. A senior military officer who had broken away from his claque of aides, just to come help Willem with his selfie.

"Thank you," Willem said, handing him the phone.

"Is this for Remigio?" Bo asked, maneuvering around and trying to figure out how the zoom feature worked.

"The uniform suits you," Willem said. "Much better than the tank top."

"I had it tailored in Hong Kong," Bo explained. "The standard issue are rubbish." He was tapping the shutter button over and over. "Off to Texas?"

"No," Willem decided.

"No!?"

"I'm going to stay. Keep an eye on you guys."

He realized Amelia had come over to collect him. She'd heard.

"It has been great working with you," Willem said and held out his hand.

Recovering her poise quickly, Amelia reached out and shook it. "Back to Uncle Ed's for you?"

"Too gritty for a prolonged stay. I can't see Remigio coming to visit me there. No, I'm going to check into one of the hotels Bo hasn't blown up yet."

"Terrorists did that," Bo demurred. "Believe me, the Sam Houston was no great loss. Black mold and bedbugs everywhere. I recommend the Mandarin."

"T.R. likes you," Willem said to Amelia. "Maybe he'll offer you a gig."

Amelia's face reflected skepticism. "Ehh, I'll bet there's openings in Netherworld." She was turning to leave.

"Defense minister. I'll put in a word for you."

She looked back over her shoulder. "You going to visit?"

"This place is going to need a foreign policy now that it has been . . . liberated." Willem nodded into the southern sky above the end of the runway. Lined up on approach, still miles out, were the lights of an approaching airplane. Behind that, another. Behind that, yet another. Like a train in the sky.

"We have to leave *now!*" shouted T.R.'s pilot through cupped hands. Amelia took off at a run. They didn't bother stowing her bag, she just heaved it up above her head and pounded up the stairs. The cabin door closed right behind her. The jet was already rolling. It made a turn to get lined up on the runway. Framed in one of its big oval windows was the head of T.R. Schmidt. He tossed Willem a salute as the jet's engines whined up to a shriek and it sprang forward.

It had barely got its landing gear retracted when the first of the heavy Chinese military transports touched down in its wake.

"Well," Willem said to Bo, "I'm sure you have a lot to do."

"On the contrary, my work here is essentially finished," Bo said, "but I would imagine you are about to become quite busy."

PERFORMATIVE WAR

I t took about a day for T.R.'s people to set Rufus up with the access he needed, and another day for him to find his way around the various directories where the surveillance videos were archived, and to make sense of what he found there.

Rufus was able to rule out the theory that those drones had been put in the air by members of what T.R. referred to as the well-regulated militia. Or the even more far-fetched notion that it had just been some random hobbyist in the right place at the right time. The drones had been launched from a small RV, a converted Sprinter van, which had pulled into the Mobility Center a few minutes ahead of Burrito Guy's truck. During their brief stay, the occupants—two black-haired men in baseball caps and dark glasses—had refueled their RV but shown a marked lack of interest in using the toilets or getting food. One had looked after the refueling while the other had opened the vehicle's side door and got three identical drones in the air. They'd done this at an outlying gas pump, far away from any other vehicles. They'd parked in such a way that the only things on that side of the van were a barbed-wire fence and a hundred miles of open range. So no other customers would have seen them launch the drones. The dark glasses they wore (at night) must have contained AR gear. Darkness made it impossible to know where those drones had gone between the time they were launched and the moment that two of them had been silhouetted against the flames.

After the tanker exploded, Squeegee Ninja ran down the line of gas pumps to the parking lot beyond, obviously headed for the location where Burrito Guy's semi rig had been parked. It was no longer there because Burrito Guy—who had got back to the rig without incident a couple of minutes earlier—had put it in gear right after the explosion and pulled out to a greater distance from Ground Zero. The bafflement of Squeegee Ninja was clear from his body language—one could almost see a huge exclamation point and question mark hovering in space above him—but then he turned his head in the direction of the truck and homed in on it. Fifteen seconds' sprint across the parking lot took him to the passenger door of the rig, which was already rolling forward as he scampered up into it. Within moments they had passed beyond the purview of T.R. Micks's security cameras. From one angle, though, it was just barely possible to see the rig's turn signal flashing out on the main road as it approached the on-ramps to Interstate 15. The truck was headed south.

At the same time, the drones were headed back to the little RV. Three had gone out. Two came back. The consternation of the RV's occupants was obvious. Where was the third drone? Equipment was fiddled with. Heads were shaken. Fucking *binoculars* were produced and used to scan the disaster scene. Again though, body language was eloquent as these two guys concluded, *Fuck it, that thing is toast, let's get out of here!* Which they did, signaling the same southbound turn as the semi had done a few minutes earlier.

> There will be a drone that was left behind at the site. Maybe destroyed. But maybe someone there has found it.

> Will inquire

Rufus turned his attention now to the strange case of this turban-wearing badass who roamed the western U.S. in an anonymous semi rig shadowed by high-tech drone geeks in a small but expensive RV (those Sprinter conversions didn't come cheap, and this one looked new).

It was but a few moments' work to turn up many examples from all over the Western world of turbaned Sikhs being mistaken for Muslims and persecuted as such by people who took a dim view of the religion of Islam. So this was just another case of that.

Noting his sudden interest in the Sikh religion, YouTube help-fully revamped his feed, expunging videos about wild horses, feral swine, drones, eagles, the Dutch royal family, and climate change, and replacing them with a slate of content featuring various aspects of that religion and culture. Scanning through those, Rufus's gaze snagged on a clip showing a dude in a turban brandishing a sword and standing in the middle of a ring of spectators, giving some kind of martial arts demo. Or maybe a dance performance? His hopping and twirling movements seemed far removed from any fighting style that Rufus had ever seen. But he *had* seen a similar move performed recently, at Pump 37G, when Squeegee Ninja had inexplicably sensed that Revolver Man—*who was behind him*— was fixing to shoot him in the back.

This—once he'd confirmed it by split-screening the YouTube guy and Squeegee Ninja—sent Rufus down two parallel tracks. One, which was fairly trivial, was familiarizing himself with the martial art in question. It was called gatka and it made a lot of use of sticks—which explained why the subject of this inquiry was so handy with a squeegee. The other, which was more of a brainteaser, related to the drone operators in the RV and the nature of their relationship to Squeegee Ninja.

> Found it. You will have it later today

> Thanks

Rufus replied, pausing briefly to wonder how that delivery was going to be accomplished. Was T.R. going to charter a jet? A jet helicopter? Both? Probably.

His initial, obvious assumption had been that the guys in the RV were in some sense adversaries of Squeegee Ninja and Burrito Guy. Because they were all kinds of sneaky and sinister. The fly in that ointment was obvious, once Rufus gave it a moment's thought: the RV had pulled in *ahead of* the semi. It must have been miles ahead of that rig on the interstate. If they were covertly tailing the rig, they would have to, well, *tail* it. Not drive way ahead.

So maybe they were all members of the same team, split across two (or more?) different vehicles. This would help explain certain other oddities that Rufus had noticed about the actions of Squeegee Ninja. There were a couple of moments when he had exhibited situational awareness that was pretty fucking exceptional. Rufus had frame-by-framed the interval between Revolver Man cocking the hammer of his weapon and Squeegee Ninja making his move for the Bug-Solv bucket. It was—well, either a mere coincidence or superhuman. And shortly thereafter he'd made his eyes-in-the-back-of-his-head move.

Rufus was not a religious or woo-woo sort of guy; Snout had put paid to all that. He didn't believe in ESP or any other literally superhuman shit. But if you were somehow patched in to a mesh network of drones—if you could somehow sense what they sensed—that could give you such an edge. And if the drones were hovering invisibly in the dark, observers wouldn't have any rational way of explaining it.

Suddenly he couldn't wait for that third drone to be delivered.

In the meantime, he just had to pursue other leads as best he could.

He knew nothing about this martial art of gatka, had never heard of it until this morning. Were there gatka champions? Did they even compete? Did they participate in ultimate fighting tournaments like the Muay Thai and the Brazilian jiu-jitsu guys? The answer generally seemed to be no, it was more of a niche thing in the Punjab (a name that triggered some vague associations in his head; but he decided to let that sleeping dog lie for now).

Sometimes the dumb, simple approach was best. He googled "who is the greatest gatka fighter?" and the answer came back: Big Fish. There wasn't even any controversy. No welter of anonymous Internet fucktards arguing about it in chat rooms.

Just like that, his YouTube slate was once again wiped clean and filled up with a simply unbelievable number of videos featuring Indians and Chinese fighting with rocks and sticks at the Line of Actual Control—a thing of seemingly immense importance that

Rufus, in his whole life, had never even heard of. But he had somewhat grown accustomed to there being such things and to the Internet suddenly revealing them to him and so he got over it pretty quickly. Keeping his head down and plodding relentlessly was his way. So there was a period of a few hours, coinciding with the hottest part of the afternoon, when he just took all that in. Just sat down in the coolest part of the marble mine and let the YouTube wash over him. Learned about the history of the LAC and its geography too: the Yak's Leg, Sikkim, the Kunchang salient, and other hot spots. Followed the stories of different Chinese and Indian crews: where they hailed from, their uniforms and other branding, what styles of kung fu or other martial arts they favored, their won/lost records, their positions on leaderboards, their Vegas and Macao odds, what kinds of people belonged to their fan bases.

It was a lot to take in and he found himself getting a little stupid-headed. So he took a nap, or what his compadres south of the Rio Grande would call a siesta. When he woke up, a mere forty-five minutes later, he found that his brain had sorted things out for him and it was all in better view now. He was seeing the forest instead of the trees, as the saying went. Why had he gone down this particular Internet rathole? Because it seemed like Squeegee Ninja was a gatka man, and so he wanted to learn more about gatka. About who was best at it. And the Internet said that the answer was Big Fish. According to various adulatory fan sites—none of which seemed to have been updated recently—he had burst from obscurity last year to become the leader of the most badass crew on the Indian side of the LAC and recovered many square kilometers of territory that had been stolen by China. But then he had fallen in battle under circumstances that were poorly understood. A stroke or exposure to invisible death rays from a Chinese superweapon were the two leading hypotheses. Long exposure to the ways of the Internet led Rufus to favor the stroke theory. Anyway, Big Fish had disappeared from the front and been helicoptered to a first-rate medical center elsewhere in India and then fallen out of the spotlight just as rapidly as he had ascended to fame. A more recent news item from a tabloidesque Indian site suggested that he had gone back home to Canada to continue his convalescence. He was depicted in a wheelchair, struggling to perform a simple thumbs-up gesture. Which was a shame, both as such (national hero cruelly cut down in his moment of triumph) and for Rufus's own selfish purposes. His research program, if you could call it that, had become centered on Big Fish. Not only because he was a close physical match for Squeegee Ninja, but also because he was so well documented. Practically every waking moment of his rise from hitchhiking vagabond to epic hero had been chronicled in videos, initially by a New Zealander named Philippa Long, and subsequently, in a more blatantly propagandistic style, by Indian filmmakers who seemed to have more resources to play with. Like symphony orchestras to juice up the sound track.

To Rufus, the more low-key style of Philippa Long conveyed greater credibility, so he learned about her a little bit. She seemed to keep up with her social media feeds pretty regularly. She had moved to Los Angeles in the last few months and was working on an indie film project there. Rufus created an account under the moniker RedASDFJKL and dropped her a line just for the hell of it.

Then he clicked back over to one of the other video sites he'd been using and was a little startled to discover some truly awful cell phone footage of what appeared to be a party in a disco. Not one of your fancy high-end discos but a down-at-heels ballroom outfitted with a few strobe lights and strings of blinky lights strung over the antlers of a stuffed and mounted moose head. The music was what he had, in the last few hours, learned to identify as bhangra: tunes that could compete with the very best that the Western world had to offer in the way of high-energy danceability but that were firmly grounded in the traditions of the Punjab.

But the Internet had at least as many high-quality bhangra videos as it did ones from the Line of Actual Control, so why was this terrible piece of cell phone video at the top of his feed? Some glitch in the algorithm? Some malware on his computer? He clicked the "Why am I seeing this?" button and was earnestly informed that it featured a friend of his. Reviewing the video frame by frame, he saw no friend of his. Centered in the picture was a lovely young woman of South Asian ancestry, dressed to the nines and dancing. No friend of Rufus, sadly. He was about to shrug it off as some arcane malware phishing attack when, in the final few frames, in the background of the picture, off to the right, a big man became visible. He was dancing in a style that recalled those gatka moves that had started Rufus down this path earlier today.

He was all ready to dismiss this as a series of coincidences. Three vaguely similar men. Big Fish: an invalid being rolled around in a wheelchair. The dancing man in this video, which according to metadata had been shot in a small town in southern British Columbia about twenty-four hours before the incident in the T.R. Mick's. And last but not least, Squeegee Ninja.

Now, though, Rufus came up with a wild surmise, which was that they were all the same person. It was all possible if you were willing to accept the hypothesis that Big Fish's invalid status was just a cover story. In other words, maybe the algorithm had actually nailed it: seen something no human could have.

Philippa Long had responded to his earlier message with an emoji. On an impulse, Rufus direct-messaged her the video from the bhangra party and asked her whether the man in the background might be Big Fish.

Ten minutes later he was on a video call with her. He was just a grainy cloud of pixels in the darkness of the marble mine, so he carried his laptop outside as they worked their way through the inevitable opening rounds of troubleshooting the video and audio.

Based on her name, which sounded fancy to Rufus, and on her profession as globe-trotting indie filmmaker, and also on a profile photo associated with her social media presence, which showed evidence of intervention by hair and makeup professionals, he had been expecting someone more glamorous and intimidating.

But she was very girl-next-door, like she'd just stepped away from milking a goat. Almost unsettlingly open and approachable, but with a cool confidence about her that kept things at arm's length.

It was still pretty warm in the box canyon before the mine's entrance, mostly because of stored solar heat now being dumped into the void by the stone walls. But the air itself had cooled down quite a bit and would keep doing so until he'd be obliged to put on a jacket. Thanks to Pina2bo there was still enough light in the western sky to cast warm gentle illumination over everything. Rufus set his laptop on one of two plastic tables they'd set up in the little compound of trailers and equipment. Behind him, Pippa—which was the name Philippa Long went by—would be able to see a couple of trailers, a campfire straddled by an iron tripod, random sun-bleached lawn furniture, Bildad wandering around in a futile search for grass, and the odd falconer. No eagles were in evidence just now, but the point was that Pippa was seeing a whole different picture than just Rufus sitting alone in a dark abandoned mine. A somewhat misleading picture to be fair, since Rufus, in truth, was a dark abandoned mine kind of guy, but anyway a picture that might lead Pippa toward a cautiously favorable opinion of Rufus. As opposed to just terminating the call and blocking him. He cracked open a beer.

"I read classics at uni," Pippa said, "and got interested in the performative aspect of war. I'm talking specifically about the *Iliad*."

Rufus couldn't make heads or tails of "I read classics at uni" but he could guess the meaning of "performative." The *Iliad* he had listened to during his perambulations around Texas. "Like Achilles dragging Hector around the walls of Troy?" he guessed. "Putting on a li'l show. For the psy-ops impact. But zero tactical value."

"Exactly. I won't bore you with all the other examples that could be cited, down through the ages."

"I got you," Rufus assured her. "Comanches did that shit all the time. White men couldn't understand it."

"You're a Comanche?"

"Sort of." Because Pippa seemed so interested in this, Rufus did something he did only rarely: pulled out his wallet, extracted his Comanche Nation ID card, and held it up to the camera.

"I've been studying their . . . practices," Pippa said.

He knew what she meant. "Pretty gruesome stuff."

"Undeniably. But the latest research says that they were masters of performative war. They knew how their actions played in the newspapers. All that gruesomeness was *designed* to make them famous. To scare the shit out of people."

"It worked," Rufus said.

"Absolutely. It had a tactical effect. Kept Comancheria free of white settlers for decades. But it all came at the end of an era."

Rufus nodded. "The era of Indians living free," he said.

"Well, that too, of course. But I was actually referring to a worldwide transition. Beyond a certain point—which happened at different times in different parts of the world—hard tactical outcomes were all that mattered."

"Performative war didn't work anymore," Rufus translated. He was thinking of the heaps of dead bison on the plains, the Indians starved into submission.

Pippa nodded. "Like, it would not have made tactical sense to chain Paulus behind a T-34 and drag him around Stalingrad. It wouldn't have moved the line of battle one inch. It would have been seen as savagery."

"Savagery. Important word in these parts."

"That's one way people were defined as savages: by their willingness to let that kind of performative display affect the outcome of battle *for real*."

Rufus nodded. He was thinking of the Little Robe Creek fight in which the Comanches had been routed by a small force of Texas Rangers after their chief, Iron Jacket, had been brought down by a sniper. The Comanches had then tried to talk the Rangers into settling the battle by single combat between champions, as in the days of chivalry. Hadn't worked.

"Now, that all changes with Hiroshima and Nagasaki, which were basically performances. Deadly for real, obviously—but the point was the spectacle of it, and its psychological impact."

"After that we're *all* savages."

"Yeah, and it leads to things like 9/11. Which again is horrible— but with a lower body count."

"Until we invaded Afghanistan and Iraq!" Rufus pointed out.

"Using Shock and Awe," Pippa countered. "Anyway, we could talk about it all night, but that's how I got interested in what was going on at the Line of Actual Control and met Laks."

"Locks?"

"Big Fish. His friends and family call him Laks."

"Is that him in the video I sent you? Dancing at the party?"

"Absolutely."

Rufus had been expecting a more guarded response, so Pippa's certainty knocked him off balance.

"So he's recovered."

"Yeah, and people who knew him were aware of it. The story of him being incapacitated was put out on the media by someone. I've no idea why."

"Someone who wanted folks to believe that Big Fish was still out of commission," Rufus said. "Still a non-combatant."

"Well," Pippa said, guardedly, "he's *definitely* a non-combatant. He's partying in Canada. No longer beating up kung fu masters in the Himalayas."

"I think he's in the States now," Rufus said.

"Same difference. Still a non-combatant."

"I wouldn't be so sure," Rufus said, wondering if he'd get in trouble if he sent Pippa the video from the T.R. Mick's. "Try googling Squeegee Ninja," he suggested. "All the videos might have been taken down, though."

But it very soon became obvious from Pippa's gestures and the movements of her eyes that she had found something. "Holy fuck," she said. It was all she needed to say. "Let me Google Map this place, my American geography is rubbish." She did so. "Where do you suppose he's headed?"

"If you draw a line from the Canadian bhangra bash through that T.R. Mick's, it points to me," Rufus said.

"You're in Texas."

"How'd you guess?" Rufus answered, half serious.

"The beer. And you mentioned savagery."

Rufus looked at his beer. Shiner Bock.

"West Texas, to judge from your imaginary line on the map." A thought occurred to her. "Say, are you anywhere near that huge—"

The rest of her question was drowned out by a sonic boom. Rufus just nodded.

Pippa sat back in her chair and pondered for a spell. Rufus let her do it. The beer was enjoyable. The temperature in the canyon was now perfect. He was in no particular hurry. He checked his phone, which had buzzed a couple of minutes ago.

> Incoming!

He could hear a drone coming up the valley, following the road. He could tell from the tone of its rotors that it was a big boy—the kind they used to deliver sacks of groceries. Rufus got to his feet, cupped his hands around his mouth, and hollered up to the peak that loomed over the mine entrance. "Drone coming!" he shouted. "We got any birds in the air?" Eagles—especially when they were wearing 3D printed gauntlets—could take down smaller surveillance drones with impunity, but the rotors on cargo carriers were beefy enough to cause injury. Carmelita hollered down with the information that all birds were safely in their boxes.

The big drone banked into view, slowed momentarily, then came right for him. Someone back at High Noon was piloting it off a video feed. As it came closer he gestured toward the other table, a few feet behind him. The drone settled there, released a cardboard box that had been grappled to its belly, then whooshed straight up until it was clear of the canyon walls and headed back north. Rufus pulled a knife from his pocket, unfolded it, and slit the tape.

Inside, under a layer of wadded-up paper, was a drone, bigger than his hand but smaller than a dinner plate, looking a little the worse for wear. Had it been one of his, he'd have rated it as just barely worth fixing. It had been slammed against something hard and lost a rotor. The motor's axle was bent and the chassis had taken some structural damage.

He carried it back over to his laptop and sat back down. Pippa was evidently using other windows on her screen to look stuff up, but she was still on the call.

"What do you know about the Punjab? The monsoons?" Pippa asked. "I don't want to tell you stuff you already know."

The mention of monsoons put it all together for Rufus. He still talked to Alastair from time to time. That topic had come up once or twice earlier in the summer, when people had been afraid the rains would never begin.

"There is concern," Rufus said, "in the minds of some folks, that Pina2bo here is going to mess up the monsoons and create a big problem for farmers who depend on that rain."

Pippa nodded. "To tell you the truth, it's probably a bigger deal than all that drama around the Line of Actual Control. If I'm an Indian military planner, a few hectares of gravel and ice at six thousand meters above sea level is symbolically important, sure, but famine in the Breadbasket is where I really need to focus."

"So what am I going to do?" Rufus mused. "If I am that military planner, I mean. Send troop ships up the Rio Grande and make an amphibious landing at the Flying S Ranch?"

He thought better when his hands were busy. He found that he had deployed a little screwdriver from the multitool he kept on his belt and was removing the screws that held the drone's outer shell to its chassis. "Send long-range bombers halfway around the world? Does India even have those?"

"They are more about rockets, I think," Pippa said. She was multitasking too. "Nine hundred miles."

"Eh?"

"I'm nine hundred miles away from you. Depending on which part of that huge ranch you are on."

"The old marble mine."

"Got it. What's that, a day's drive?"

"A very long day," Rufus said. "Depends on how you drive."

"Conservatively, as befits a guest in your country," Pippa said, "but I have friends."

Rufus had got the drone opened up and was checking out its guts. He already knew that it was of no make or model he had ever seen before. There was not a speck of branding on the thing. Not mass produced. 3D printed from carbon fiber composite—an expensive process. Too polished, though, to be what you'd call a prototype. Some of the parts, like batteries and motors, were off-the-shelf—stuff you could source over the Internet anywhere in the world. Made sense. Even the kind of esoteric R & D program that had 3D carbon fiber printers wouldn't bother manufacturing its own batteries from scratch. Same went for ribbon cables, connectors, fasteners, and a lot of other bits. Circuit boards were what mattered. Those, and the propellers. The propellers were machined out of some light metal and anodized black. He could tell by the shape of them they'd been optimized to a fare-thee-well. They reminded him of the rotor blades on the most advanced stealth choppers he'd seen in the service, the ones used by JSOC squads for insertions into crazy places. But why go to all that trouble to optimize the rotors on a quad-copter drone? To eke out a little more range? To make them quieter? Or just to flex?

Most circuit boards had markings silkscreened onto them: a part number, a company logo, labels for the I/O connectors. Not these. Just chips. And even the chips were unmarked. Who the fuck made their own chips? More to the point, why bother?

Ribbon cables ran from the edges of the board to various sub-systems. But there was also a pair of plain old wires, red and black, that ran to a plain old switch mounted on the outside of the chassis. He flicked it on and was rewarded with a green LED coming on. Normally it would be hidden beneath the black carapace. For this thing had been made to run dark.

Pippa meanwhile had gone into another round of clicking on things. "Look, India's not going to mount a twentieth-century-style military operation against West Texas. No matter how bad it gets."

"Let me guess," Rufus said. "They've been getting shit done in the Himalayas without firing a single bullet by using the new tactics of, what did you call it—"

"Performative war, Red." In the Kiwi accent it came out as "Rid."

"Pina2bo's more of a threat—which means, more of a target—than a bunch of kung fu fighters freezing their asses on the top of the world," Rufus said. "But old-school war ain't an option. So what they gonna do? Performative war. And who's the best they got?"

"Big Fish," Pippa said. "I'll see you in a day, Rid."

Rufus was getting ready to explain to Pippa why this was not a good idea when he was distracted by joyous, excited whooping from the top of the peak. Thordis and Carmelita were up there, taking the evening air. "Shooting star!" were the only words he could make out. He looked up at them and saw them pointing excitedly into the northern sky. He turned his head that way and saw a line of brilliant white being drawn across the navy blue heaven. It did indeed look like a meteorite. But after a certain point it seemed to stop moving. It just kept getting brighter.

Rufus hadn't played that much baseball, but he'd caught enough fly balls during his day to know that if you are staring at the ball, and it doesn't seem to be moving, you're in the right place to catch it.

"Don't look at it!" he shouted. *"Don't look at it!"*

"Don't look at what?" Pippa was saying. "What's going on, Rid?" But he was moving away from his laptop. He'd turned his back on it, and on the shooting star, and was looking up at Thordis and Carmelita, trying to get their attention.

He needn't have bothered. The shooting star had grown so bright and so close that it was illuminating the whole north-facing side of the peak, casting stark shadows. No one *could* look at it. Thordis and Carmelita had both turned their backs to it.

Then there was a momentary flash that was even brighter, and then darkness.

Absolute darkness. The screen of Rufus's laptop had gone black. The lights in the windows of the trailers had gone out. The generators had stopped running. He pulled his phone out of his pocket and tried to turn on its flashlight app. It was bricked. In his other pocket he had a little LED flashlight. It didn't work either.

His eyes had adjusted to the darkness, though, and now they picked up one mote of green light. He stepped toward it. It was on the table next to his dead laptop.

It was the power LED on the drone's main circuit board. That was still working just fine, apparently.

FLYING S

As first world problems went, it was hard to top this one: being limited to relatively short-hop flights because of the unusual fuel required by the brand-new, state-of-the-art private jet that had been given to you as a personal gift. And yet by the time the airstrip at the Flying S Ranch finally rolled into view over the jagged horizon of West Texas, Saskia did feel she had some legitimate grounds for complaint. She and her new best friend Ervin, an ex–U.S. Air Force pilot from Baldwin Hills, California, had flown from the Line back to Vadan, where a hydrogen tanker still awaited them, and thence to Schiphol for an overnight stop and a quick check-in with the new Queen of the Netherlands. Fenna and Jules had hitched a ride from Vadan to Schiphol and then talked their way aboard for the remainder of the journey, cramming into the two passenger seats in the back of the jet's tiny cabin as they tacked back and forth across the great circle route. From Schiphol they had flown to Aberdeen, then Reykjavik, then someplace called Nuuk in Greenland, where they'd been stuck for a day awaiting hydrogen. Then Gander, Newfoundland. Then Ottawa, Chicago, Denver, and finally the Flying S Ranch. They were low on fuel by the time they landed, but they'd solve that problem later. Or to be precise, Jules would. Managing hydrogen deliveries over a sketchy voice connection had turned out to be this young man's unheralded superpower. There was, Saskia supposed, a kind of logic to it: divers had to know all about compressed and liquefied gases or else they would die. Hydrogen was only a small stretch once you knew everything about compressed air, oxygen, helium, and other staples of the diver's trade. But a professional background in that area was only part of his qualifications. More valuable, as far as she could determine from overhearing his half of conversations with ground personnel, was his manner of talking.

The reputation of America and Americans might be in tatters in elite cultural and diplomatic circles, but on the nuts-and-bolts level of the petroleum and mining industries, they still seemed to get a lot done in the world. The easygoing southern drawl, stiffened with traces of calm cool military discipline and implied know-how ("Yes, sir!" "No, ma'am." "Copy that!") seemed to open doors, or at least prevent random strangers worldwide from immediately slamming down the phone when Jules cold-called them out of nowhere with his outlandish requests.

Not that anyone actually slammed down the phone nowadays. Those things were delicate and expensive. But the point remained that Jules was good at this, to the point where Saskia wondered, during endless hours of flying across the North Atlantic and the Canadian Shield, what would happen if she were to task Jules with sourcing a plutonium bomb core. She was a little afraid that after a few hours of polite, laconic phone work, he might succeed.

"No, sweetheart, I can't have you doing this! You are no longer my employee but a beloved friend."

"A beloved friend who knows what you need," Fenna said. "Shut up and look at the ceiling!"

Saskia obeyed, and saw corrugated steel, obstructed from time to time by the briskly moving hand of Fenna, who was up to something involving the increasingly complicated zone between the ex-queen's lower eyelid and her cheekbone. "It's not like I have anything else to do here!"

They were in the tiny settlement called Bunkhouse, in a shipping container that had been converted to a barracks and then buried in sandbags to muffle the sonic booms. Still, one could feel the thuds every few minutes, transmitted through the ground.

"We'll figure out a way to get you and Jules to New Orleans," Saskia assured her.

"Don't worry about it. Jules wants to visit the gun. See how it works."

"Then his best bet would be to just come with me now. I could ask T.R. to arrange a tour tomorrow, but he's a little distracted."

"Not as distracted as he's about to be," Fenna predicted, with a degree of confidence that Saskia had not felt about anything in decades. "You are going to look fantastic while he will be ruined from the endless flight from China or whatever."

"Papua, dear." Though if things kept going the way they had been, it would soon enough be Chinese.

"Whatever. Point is still the same."

Not for the first time, Saskia wished that Fenna's conception of reality—according to which people with the best styling inevitably prevailed—actually made sense. But it didn't hurt to pretend that it did.

"Would you care to join us?" Saskia asked.

Fenna wrinkled her nose in some combination of disbelief and horror. "Visiting the gun?!"

"Yes."

"I've seen it before. And again at Vadan. Loud bullet-shooting things are not my area of interest!" She threw a wry look at Jules. He had the military man's ability to sleep anywhere, anytime, and was taking advantage of it in the corner, sprawled out on a pile of luggage. "He'll be thrilled though. As for me, I have a date with Amelia! We are going to get beers and burritos from the vending machines."

"Sounds like a good time. Raise a glass for me."

"Can is more like it. Do they have a golf cart or something to take you to the gun?"

"No, Jules and I are going to walk."

"Walk!?"

"Yes. I haven't walked more than a few strides in days and days, as you know."

"You should have told me, the wind will—"

"There is very little wind, I checked. It will be windy tomorrow. But not now."

"Maybe you should ride a horse! That would be so cool to see."

"They don't take them near the gun. It would be cruel. And anyway the last thing they need is horse shit all over."

"It can't be that pleasant for you either."

"Every evening, during the shift change, the gun goes silent for an hour. It's a chance for the system to do some kind of maintenance and recalibration or some such. The engineers inspect things. I don't know all the details. Anyway, T.R. is going to be there for that and he said it was all right for me to 'tag along,' whatever that means." Saskia checked her watch. "I need to get going. Jules! Let's go!"

The young man could wake up as quickly as he could fall asleep. "Yes, ma'am," he said, rolling up to his feet.

"Aren't there snakes?"

"Yes, but there is also a paved road that we can walk on, where snakes will have no place to hide. Besides—look!" She stuck out one leg to draw attention to the fact that she was wearing cowboy boots. Scored half an hour ago from Bunkhouse's self-serve swag kiosk. "I'd like to see the rattlesnake that could punch its fangs through these!"

"I wouldn't."

By the time those cowboy boots were striding down said paved road, the sun had set behind the mountains separating Pina2bo from the Rio Grande. Conditions would have been downright pleasant if not for the flash and boom of the gun. Through some peculiarity of how the sound waves propagated, standing near the gun itself—directly in the shell's wake—wasn't as bad as being off to the side.

Once or twice as she and Jules strolled along, Saskia turned back and let her gaze follow the serrated ridge of the mountains north and west, until it melted into the dark purple sky.

"What's to see up there, ma'am?" Jules asked.

"Do you remember Rufus? Red?"

"Oh, of course."

"Well, somewhere back thataway, unless I've got my directions mixed up, is a mountain made of marble. Tunneled into it is an old mine where he's been living."

She'd got occasional reports and a few pictures from Thordis and Piet. As far as she could make out, Rufus was gainfully employed there doing work he found interesting, which in a way was a big part of being happy. She wondered if he *was* happy, though, and if he thought of her from time to time.

She noticed that she was casting a shadow on the pavement ahead of her. This made no sense. The sun was down. The moon was off to her left, low above the mountainous spur that framed the other side of the valley. In other words, it was in the wrong place, and in any case not bright enough, to cast her shadow there. Someone must be shining a light on them from behind. But she hadn't heard anyone approaching. A drone, perhaps? Maybe some nervous Black Hat had decided to shadow them and make sure they didn't wander off into the desert to be eaten by pigs. Somewhat annoyed, she stopped walking and turned around. Jules was already doing likewise. The source of the light was blindingly obvious in a quite literal sense—she couldn't look right at it. It was moving across the sky, shortening her shadow. Who flew drones with such powerful lights on them?

Because her gaze was averted, she noticed that the entire valley was lit up by this thing. It wasn't just a narrow spotlight focused on her and Jules, but a floodlight somehow illuminating the mountain walls on both sides as well as the steel frameworks enclosing the gun barrels, the pipes and conduits converging on it, the big yellow sulfur pile nearby.

It really did blind her for an instant, and then all went dark. She was afraid her eyes had been damaged. But over the next minute or so, they adjusted to a world lit only by the moon and by the light lingering in the western sky. Most of the lights in the complex ahead of her had gone out. She turned around and saw that Bunkhouse was completely dark. She took out her phone, thinking to use its flashlight feature. It was dead.

"I'll be darned" was all Jules could say. "Meteor?"

"It looked like one of those meteors that burns up before it hits the ground," Saskia said, "but that wouldn't explain why the power's out. Why my phone is dead."

Jules checked his phone and found the same.

Without further discussion, they lengthened their stride toward the big gun. No longer the Biggest Gun in the World, but still pretty big. T.R. was there. He'd know what was going on. Anyway it was the only thing she could see that still had power. Many of the outlying structures—the low steel building where robots filled and prepped the shells, the cooling tower, the natural gas cracking facility where they made the hydrogen—had gone dark. But the gun itself seemed to have at least some systems up and running. The tips of its six barrels and the muffler-like housings that surrounded them were illuminated from below by light shining up the main bore of the big shaft. The steel framework surrounding all that was speckled with lights focused on stairways, catwalks, and hatches. As Jules and Saskia drew closer she could hear the low hum of machinery: pumps moving cold water down to the combustion chamber two hundred meters below and drawing hot water back up, routing it to the cooling tower, which, though darkened, was still burbling and steaming. The higher-pitched whoosh of fans suggested that essential ventilation was still going on. Valves snicked and clunked, gases hissed in pipes, transformers droned. As they got closer yet, Saskia heard voices, mostly male, mostly Texan. Agitated, alert, but controlled.

She had no idea what had happened. She'd never heard of a meteor blacking out electronics. This had to have been some sort of attack making use of an electromagnetic pulse device—a thing she'd heard mentioned in military and intelligence briefings. It had killed all the electronics in the valley except, apparently, for some systems buried deep underground. The stuff that absolutely had to keep working no matter what. They must have generators down at the bottom of the shaft, shielded by two hundred meters of rock, burning natural gas fed down in pipes and sending back electrical power to key systems topside.

So Pina2bo had been attacked—or maybe was only starting to come under attack. But it was an unusual type of attack and so the security and operations people around the gun were only beginning to realize it. Firearms probably still worked just fine. Saskia didn't want to stumble into the crosshairs of some jittery Black Hat, so she began making noise as she drew closer. Personnel who'd emerged from darkened buildings around the complex were gravitating to the only area that still had light, which was the gun. Saskia began to make noise as soon as she was within earshot. "Hello! Hello!" Not very original, but hopefully nonthreatening. "It's me, Saskia! And my friend Jules!"

"Saskia who?" came a man's voice back.

"Frederika Mathilde Louisa Saskia of the Netherlands," she returned.

"Welcome back, Your Majesty." That was T.R. talking. She saw him detach from a cluster of men and begin walking toward her.

"Your Royal Highness," she corrected him.

"Oh, yeah. Forgot. Sorry, long couple of days."

"So I heard."

A couple of Black Hats had strode forth to flank T.R. They had broken out the assault rifles and were carrying them with muzzles pointed at the ground. Looking at their tactical pants and vests and gear harnesses, all bedecked with lights and optics and comms gear, Saskia was struck by how little of it was actually going to be functional in the aftermath of the EMP. They could peer over iron sights into the dark and shoot bullets at what little they could see, but that was about it. They could walk around under their own power but any modern vehicle, dependent on hundreds of microchips, would be useless. Horses and bicycles would work, but she didn't see any.

T.R. stopped a few paces short of her. So this was the moment Fenna had envisioned with such relish: Saskia still more or less impeccable, T.R. a ruin. But it didn't have quite the same impact. Saskia was directly illuminated by the lights in the gun complex, which she was facing. T.R. was backlit: just a stocky, vaguely cowboy-shaped shadow outlined in a fringe of dusty light. "Who would have imagined," T.R. said wearily, "that one who has so recently passed a night in Nuuk could pull together such effortless elegance."

"Your wife has trained you well!"

"Still it's true."

"I had help."

"How is the lovely Fenna?"

"Scared and in the dark, I would guess," Saskia said, with a glance toward Jules. He had politely stepped to one side and approached a cluster of men—not Black Hats, so probably White Label engineers—who were standing around discussing what had happened.

"We are scared and all lit up, as you can see," T.R. said. "Please join us."

"Do you know what we are being scared of? What is going on?"

"Did you see that goddamn thing fall out of the sky?"

"Yes."

"I'll not insult your intelligence by saying what it was."

"I thought EMPs were a kind of nuclear weapon, though?"

T.R. looked back toward his security guys. "I am informed that you can make a small one that ain't a nuke. Derives its energy from the heat of reentry, which is considerable. Generates the pulse through a thermochemical reaction. Affects a correspondingly smaller footprint on the ground. Surgical. Just the thing for whatever our adversaries have in mind. Whatever that is."

He turned sideways to listen to a few tense words from a grizzled Black Hat who had strode up behind him. In profile Saskia could see him nodding.

"My fellas," T.R. said, turning back to face her, "are expressing keen impatience with the easygoing and protracted pace of this conversation. The words 'sitting duck' have been used. They would like me—and you, goes without saying—indoors and belowground."

"I'm happy to do whatever they consider best." Saskia began closing the distance between them.

"If it weren't for that damn EMP we would have our pick of hidey-holes. Things being what they are, there is only one reasonable choice. The elevator still has power. It can take us down to places you have seen before, where nothing short of a nuke would trouble us. And let's face it, if they just wanted to nuke us, they'd have done it. The power is on down there and will remain so. It's a no-brainer."

"Lead and I shall follow," Saskia said.

THE PECAN ORCHARD

Laks's driver, though not much of a conversationalist, had been the living embodiment of professional competence until around dusk, when he swung the wheel hard left, crossed the road's oncoming lane, smashed through a barbed-wire fence, and let the rig's momentum carry it some distance into a pecan orchard. There it rested for only a few moments before all its electronics went dead and the engine stopped running: an event that seemed to coincide with a blinding flash of light in the sky off to the right.

This road ran through country that, for sparseness of population, rivaled the Himalayas. The pecan trees now surrounding them were the only vegetation they'd seen all day more than about the height of a man's knee. So it seemed like they'd crashed with some degree of privacy. The pecan trees were planted in a grid. The driver had aimed down a lane between rows. Their foliage was thick; someone must have put a lot of money into irrigation. When Laks opened the door and climbed out, he saw no lights except for the stars. The only witnesses to the crash of the truck would have been the men they had passed about three seconds before the driver had swerved. They'd been standing next to a van parked on the shoulder of the road. A very old van, like something from the 1960s. One of the men had, in retrospect, been using a flashlight to cue the driver.

Now that van was approaching, following the rut left in the truck's wake. Its lights were off and so it was sort of feeling its way along at little more than a walking pace. Too slow, apparently, for the taste of one man sitting in the back. He slid the side door open and alighted, then jogged ahead. Ignoring Laks, who had walked back down the length of the rig to investigate, he made a beeline for the back of the shipping container, clambered up onto the rear bumper, and got busy with a keychain. After a few moments Laks heard the heavy clunk of the massive latch bolts moving and hinges moaning as the doors were swung open.

By now the van had parked about ten meters behind. Its driver turned on the parking lights just long enough for the guy with the keys to step up and punch some numbers on a keypad inside the door. This caused a lot of red LEDs to come on. Once the van's lamps were extinguished, Laks could see up into a volume forty feet long, eight feet wide, and eight feet high, with just enough of that red glow to let people get a sense of where things were— like the combat lighting on the bridge of a warship. Silhouetted were long racks mounted to the ceiling and to the walls, running the full length of the container. Queued up on those were hundreds of skeletal black shapes that he recognized as drones. They were of more than one size and shape. Some were barely larger than the palm of his hand, others as large as a bicycle. It was difficult to sort it out visually because, as he gradually figured out, there were drones mounted on other drones—mother ships carrying several smaller children. The closest analogy from nature would be a cave in which a large number of bats were sleeping all crammed together, wings folded around them. The wings here were rectangular, creased, and folded like fans: deployable panels of photovoltaic cells.

The van rocked on its suspension as the guy who'd been riding shotgun vaulted up onto its roof. He got down on one knee and unslung a rifle from his shoulder. He laid this gently on the roof, then got into a prone position, his face and the barrel of the weapon both aimed back the way they had come. Not that there was anything approaching from the road; but apparently he intended to keep it that way.

The driver of the semi—Laks's companion of the last few days— got out of the truck's cab and climbed down to the ground. He had a duffel bag slung over his shoulder. He walked back, favoring Laks with a quick nod, and climbed into the rear seat of the van.

The guy with the keychain had extracted a laptop from a compartment just inside the container's door. He let himself down to the ground, then opened it up and used a fingerprint scanner to log on as he was carrying it back toward the van. He got into the passenger seat. The screen illuminated his face: Indian, neatly groomed, lean, mustache. He was gazing alertly out the windshield.

Laks startled as several rotors whirred up to speed. Half a dozen drones—the ones closest to the container doors—took to the air and hummed off into the night.

Revealed behind them was the largest single object in the container. This one was mounted on floor rails and sort of set back into a pocket of space surrounded entirely by the smaller devices.

The driver of the van, and another man who'd been riding in its back, stepped up on the truck's rear bumper, reached in, and (to judge from sounds) undid some latches. Then they slid the big thing back until it was perched on the container's threshold. Not a word had been spoken yet but Laks got the gist of what they were trying to do. He helped them lift the thing up, pull it free of the container, and set it down in the stretch of open ground behind the semi and in front of the van. It was awkward but not that heavy. Laks couldn't make sense of it until the men began swinging parts of it around, unfolding it like a pocketknife. He then understood that the first end of it to emerge from the container had been a sort of hub, and the rest consisted of spokes that had been folded back for storage and shipment. When those were all rotated and snapped into position, the thing was revealed to be a six-rotor drone several meters across. Its central hub appeared to have ample space for batteries and other gear, but the largest part of it was a human-sized vacancy equipped with a seat and a safety harness. Resting on the seat was a beach-ball-sized mass of bubble wrap, strapped down with tape. Once this was unwrapped it proved to be a pair of goggles of a size to cover the whole upper half of his face. One of the guys handed this to Laks and looked at him expectantly. Maybe even a little bit impatiently. Laks, now beginning to struggle with his emotional state, but not wanting to ruin what showed every indication of being an extraordinarily expensive set of plans and preparations, tried to put it on, but had a bit of trouble getting the head strap to fit over his turban.

The other men were all Indians, but none was a Sikh. They were all boring holes through his skull with their eyes. Body language suggested that they were terrifically impatient for him to climb aboard the big drone. The guy with the laptop was just running the palm of his hand up and down over his face, as if windshield-wiping sweat. Challenging as it was for those guys, however, this turban-related delay gave Laks some time to review the events of the last few minutes and to ponder what might await him.

He could refuse. He could claim *I didn't sign up for . . . whatever is about to happen.* But by the letter of the law, he actually had. He had, shortly before checking out of the hospital, or whatever it was, in Cyberabad, taken an oath and volunteered for a mission whose exact details were undisclosed. Which was almost always the case in the military, right? Soldiers didn't know where they were going, what they'd be asked to do. Even the officers probably didn't know until circumstances unfolded. Still, he had—very naively, as he now saw—kind of assumed it would be more like the fighting at the LAC. More of him deciding where he wanted to go and what he wanted to do next, and less of blindly following unexplained orders.

None of which changed anything about the actual situation. But it gave him a few moments for his mind to catch up. He let the goggles dangle around his neck for now. He finally complied with the furious gesticulations of the men waving him toward the big drone. He sat in the cockpit and immediately felt a rising hum as the rotors began to spin up. While being flown around the Himalayas and the Karakorams in military choppers he'd learned how to buckle a five-point safety harness, so he did that as the drone was lifting off in a cloud of dust. The drone leaned forward. Air began to stream over his face as it picked up speed. He pulled the visor up to protect his eyes from wind blast. Once he'd blinked the tears from his eyes he saw the edge of the pecan orchard disappearing beneath him as he crossed the road. Beyond the barbed-wire fence on the road's other side, a wild desert landscape stretched to the horizon, lit by a full moon. Some kilometers ahead was a range of mountains. The drone banked left to circumvent them on their moonlit southern flank, which ramped down a long rocky slope for a while and then fell off into the valley of a river.

This wildly beautiful vista was then blotted out by the splash page of a PowerPoint deck.

MISSION BRIEFING
PHASE 1
NET SYSTEM DEMOLITION
U.S. BANK OF RIO GRANDE RIVER

In the upper-right corner were two time readouts, updating once per second. One was labeled MISSION ELAPSED TIME and seemed to show how long it had been since Laks had lifted off from the pecan orchard. The other was TIME TO INSERTION and was counting downward from about fifteen minutes.

He'd assumed NET SYSTEM DEMOLITION was something to do with a computer network. But the next couple of slides showed pictures of literal, physical nets stretched between steel poles that stuck out of the ground on a plateau above a river. Presumably the same river the drone was carrying him toward right now: the Rio Grande. It was explained that his task was to topple the steel poles. He would be using a machine called a plasma cutter, which would be supplied. There followed ten minutes of instruction on how to operate a plasma cutter, which was all old hat as far as Laks was concerned, since he had used to do it for a living: you clamped a ground cable to the object you wanted to destroy, opened a valve on a gas tank, turned the machine on, and pulled a trigger. The goggles would prevent him from going blind as he sliced through the steel poles. Good advice was supplied on where to stand to avoid being crushed when these fell over.

Almost as a footnote, a mere afterthought, there was information on "hostiles." The whole site was studded with surveillance cameras, which would not be operational, and motion-activated lights, which would not be operational. These were reinforced by camera drones. Those would not be operational. All were connected over a private, secure network, which would not be operational, to a command center some miles to the north. Security personnel at the actual net site usually got around on four-wheeled ATVs, which would not be operational, and communicated over encrypted radio headsets, which would not be operational. All, because, as Laks understood, what had happened to the electronics in the semi had also happened to all the other electronic devices in this whole area. It all had to do with that flash of light in the sky. It was some kind of special bomb that fried electronics but didn't do a lot of other damage—at least, not when you set it off miles above a godforsaken desert. Even mechanical systems like the engines of trucks and ATVs had electronics in the loop, and so those were all dead.

Of note was the obvious fact that all the gear that had been in the shipping container still worked perfectly. Perhaps the container was shielded from the effects of the detonation? But the stuff they'd planted in Laks's head to help fix his brain seemed to be working normally too, so maybe they had ways of making chips that were invulnerable to that kind of attack.

And the van they'd been driving. Vintage, almost antique. From the 1960s, probably—before the automakers had put chips in everything. They'd gone to the trouble of sourcing a getaway vehicle that would keep running even after every other car, truck, and ATV in the vicinity was bricked.

Security personnel themselves were presumably feeling just fine, unless they had pacemakers. And their guns, unless they were very special and weird, would presumably shoot bullets just as well as usual. This was a detail that Laks only began to ponder toward the very end of the flight, when the mesa above the Rio Grande was rushing up toward him and the stretched nets—gleaming in the moonlight like pools of fog—were filling most of his visual field. For a moment he feared that one or more of the drone's six propellers would snag in a net and culminate in a Cuisinart-tangle-blood storm. But whoever, or whatever, was piloting this thing tilted it back hard at the last minute to kill its velocity and then brought it down softly on the ground, only a few steps away from a concrete plinth from which erupted a thick steel tube. TIME TO INSERTION had counted down to zero.

Laks unfastened the safety harness while waiting for the propellers to stop moving. When it seemed safe to do so—"Safe" being a relative term here, of course—he climbed out. No one was nearby. No lights were operational. It seemed a tidy, orderly facility. About a hundred meters away was an ATV that had just been abandoned where it had died. There was a system of dirt roads that looped around all these big nets and connected them to a cluster of office trailers and shipping containers that seemed to be the nerve center. That was a few hundred meters away.

It wasn't entirely clear what he was supposed to do now. He'd been told that a plasma cutter would be supplied. He did not see any lying around.

The brink of the mesa was not far away and so he ambled over to it and had a look down toward the river, which was maybe a hundred meters below. Some patches gleamed and rippled in the moonlight. Others were stamped with the sharp-edged silhouettes of scrubby vegetation growing on its banks and bars. He could hear the purr of a small engine down there, its tone rising and falling as it revved up and down. His revamped ears were pretty good at direction-finding. He swung his head back and forth until he was able to identify the source: just a gray mote angling up the slope below him, cutting its own switchback up the flank of the mesa in a rooster tail of churned-up dust. So at least one vehicle—it sounded, and moved, like an ATV—had survived the flash. And, allowing for switchbacks, it seemed to be headed in his direction.

"Freeze!" someone shouted. "Hands where I can see 'em, Abdul!"

Laks wasn't surprised. During the last minute or so he had begun to smell danger, and its odor was now very strong. He extended his hands out away from his sides and turned around slowly to see a man in a sort of military getup, standing about five meters away and aiming a shotgun at him. Approaching from the direction of the compound, he'd crept up on Laks while Laks had been enjoying the vista.

Before either of them could take any further action, a light came on above, creating a pool of illumination around this man. A second and a third light appeared, catching him in an equilateral cross fire with the intensity of the midday sun. Three drones, making practically no sound, that had been stalking this guy through the night.

A fourth drone descended into the pool of light until it had interposed itself between the barrel of the shotgun and Laks. This one had a short tube projecting from an apparatus in its belly. The tube was on gimbals that enabled it to pivot this way and that, and to angle up and down. Initially the tube was aimed right at the man, but once it had got his attention it angled downward. A bolt of fire spat from it and dust erupted from the ground just to one side of the man's boots. The drone jerked back from recoil as a loud bang reached Laks's ear. A spent shell casing twinkled as it bounced in the dirt.

"You are surrounded," said a woman's voice from the drone. Perfect English with a light Indian accent. Laks thought it might be the same lady who did the recorded announcements at Indira Gandhi International Airport. With the same tone of mild regret that she might have used to inform passengers that their departure gate had been changed, she instructed this man to disarm himself and then march in the direction helpfully pointed out by "the arrow."

Which raised the same question in Laks's mind that it probably did in that of this security guard: *What the fuck was the arrow?* But no sooner had Laks begun to furrow his brow in puzzlement than an arrow appeared on the ground, drawn out by a scanning laser. There was enough dust in the air that Laks could see the laser beam and back-trace it up to its source: yet another drone hovering perhaps twenty meters above them. The arrow, painted on the dirt in brilliant emerald green, began right in front of the security guard's boots and executed an immediate U-turn, pointing back in the direction of the main compound.

The guard had now recovered his wits to the point where he had put a plan together in his head. Not a great plan, but a plan. He took a couple of steps forward as if following the arrow, but then suddenly pivoted, dropping to one knee, and fired his shotgun at the closest drone—the one with the built-in gun. This shuddered back from the blast and skittered across the ground leaving a trail of shattered parts in its wake.

Immediately the green arrow disappeared. Or rather the cone of grainy green laser light shrank and collapsed inward until it was just scanning back and forth across the man's eye sockets. "Fuck!" he shouted and bent his face downward. The back of his head was now just an incandescent blob of green laser light. Another gun drone hummed in from a different angle and fired a second round. The shotgun jerked and spun out of the man's hands and came to rest on the ground out of his reach.

Holstered on the man's hip was another gun—a semi-automatic pistol. Laks wondered if the drone would try to shoot that as well. But it seemed that such measures were not even necessary. The man raised his hands and laced his fingers together on the top of his head. The blinding blob of green light spread out and reconstituted itself as the arrow telling him where to go. He began to follow it; and it changed its shape in response to his movements and preceded him across the mesa as he walked back toward the compound.

"Abdul's an Arab name!" Laks shouted after the man. But the man either didn't hear, or chose to ignore it. En route his arrow met, and merged with, that of a colleague who was being marched along by a different squadron of drones.

The smell of danger abated in Laks's nostrils, or, to be precise, whatever equipment the medics had inserted between his nostrils and his brain. It was replaced by the scent of smoke. He turned around. The ATV he'd noticed earlier had gained the top of the mesa and parked. Two men were getting out of it. One was smoking a pipe: the source of the smoke. The other, who had been driving, heaved a backpack out of the cargo storage area behind the seats, got one arm through a shoulder strap, and began to lug it along in Major Raju's wake. For the pipe-smoking man was he.

"Sergeant Singh!" Raju hailed him. For as of a few weeks ago this was Laks's correct designation within the Indian military. Purely a formality, he'd been assured—a requirement of paperwork and documentation that would only ever become relevant under certain highly improbable circumstances. "A salute is traditional," Major Raju reminded him.

Laks had seen characters saluting in video games and tried to imitate them as best he could remember. "You see," Major Raju said, returning the salute, "if we're seen observing these niceties, it's easier for you to claim you were only following orders."

"Wouldn't that shift responsibility to you?" Laks asked. Then, noting an expectant look on Major Raju's face, he added ". . . sir."

"I'll be on the other side of the river," Major Raju said. "Shame, really. One feels that a leader should . . . well . . . lead. Command his men from the front. Not be shouting at them from the rear. Alas, I have clear directions to the contrary, from officers of even higher rank, even farther from the action." He put his pipe in his teeth and spent a few moments taking in the scene. "Oh, see there!" he mumbled. "One's just coming in now." He pulled the pipe from his teeth and used its stem to point up into the air.

A ghostly shape, like an albino bat the size of a 737, was gliding in from the other side of the river. A gracefully curved airfoil with shroud lines converging down to a bullet-shaped burden. It passed over one of the nets in perfect silence and dropped the bullet, which plummeted into the net. The airfoil crumpled and drifted into the night on a light breeze.

"A safe re-entry from a brief sojourn to the stratosphere," Major Raju said. "You know what it was doing up there, Sergeant Singh?"

A second ATV had crested the lip of the mesa and pulled to a stop next to the first one. Two men had climbed out of it. They did not carry guns or any other sort of equipment, save for cameras mounted to the fronts of their helmets. During Laks's exploits in the Himalayas, he'd gotten used to people like this following him around. They had elbowed Pippa out of the picture very early, which he still regretted. They had a curious style of moving around and looking at things that, as he now understood, was all about trying to find the best angle. And looking directly at them was to be discouraged. So he looked at Major Raju. Who had positioned himself with his back to the moon so that its light would fall on Laks's face as they conversed.

If you could call this a conversation. Laks began to answer the question. "They were . . ."

"*What* were?" Major Raju broke in, like a schoolteacher trying to be of assistance to a slightly dull pupil.

"The shells landing in these nets," Laks said, waving an arm toward them, "have just come back from spewing toxic chemicals into the stratosphere. It's a layer of the atmosphere that knows no national boundaries—shared by all the peoples of the world. If you want to know why the monsoon was late this year, my brothers and sisters, look no further."

"Well said. Now let's do something about it, shall we?"

The guy with the backpack had just been standing there stolidly during all this. At a signal from Major Raju he stepped forward, swinging the pack down from his shoulder in a way that indicated he meant for Laks to take it. As Laks got a better look at this object he found it strangely familiar-looking: it was the rig he'd spent the last ten minutes learning how to operate via the PowerPoint deck. It comprised a tank of compressed air, batteries, and some electrical gear that fed a handheld pistol-grip business end on the end of a thick umbilical.

Laks turned his back and let the guy hold the rig up for him while he shrugged it on. The nearest net stanchion was only a few paces away. He hiked over to it, adjusting the shoulder straps. The valve knob on the air tank was sticking out next to his left ear. He reached across with his right hand and cranked it open, hearing the gas hiss into the system's plumbing. The power switch was conveniently located down by one hip. Status lights came on. He double-checked the position of his visor, walked up to the plinth, and connected a beefy spring-loaded ground clip to a metal flange, worrying it back and forth so its serrated jaws would gnaw through the paint and make good electrical contact. He stood in what the PowerPoint deck had assured him was a safe location, put the nozzle to the steel, and pulled the trigger. A purplish-blue plasma arc jumped between the nozzle and the pillar. Hotter by a long shot than the surface of the sun, it would have turned his retinas into gravy had his visor not auto-darkened. In the night above the Rio Grande, with all other technology dead, it must have been more than a bit obvious. They could probably see it, not just in Mexico, but in Guatemala. At first he moved the arc too slowly. Then he noticed he was just widening a chasm in steel that had already been obliterated, and began to move it faster. Beyond a certain point, the slot he was cutting began to widen of its own accord as the tension on the net at the top of the pole began to pull it inward. Then he just had to make a quick slice around the other side and watch the thing topple. Still attached to the foundation by a flap of metal he had not got around to cutting through, the pole fell into the middle of the net and bounced gently up and down.

He stepped back and raised his visor. The cut edges of the steel were still glowing red.

In addition to pipe smoke, Major Raju reeked of satisfaction. "That contraption is as amazing as they say!" he remarked. "Imagine what one could do with a suspension bridge. Or a skyscraper. Or—well—*anything* that conducts electricity and is big and important!" He puffed on his pipe for a moment, staring up into the moonlit sky as visions of collapsing bridges danced in his head. "You could mount one on a drone," he mused. Then, as if arguing with himself: "But that would leave out the human angle." This snapped him out of his reverie. "Sergeant Singh! Big Fish! What did you just do?"

"We have just—"

"You. *You.*"

"I have just struck the first blow in the defense of our Breadbasket against the toxic and aggressive actions of those who would seek to, uh, change the climate in a way that is, uh, deeply toxic and racist."

"Cut everything after 'Breadbasket,'" Major Raju muttered to one of the cameramen. "You have work to do, Sergeant Singh! Very good work! Best get on with it!"

"Yes, sir!" Laks started making tracks for the next net stanchion. As he did, he could hear the major giving an order to the subordinate who'd given him the backpack: "If I'm not mistaken, we have some additional *materiel* that needs to be transferred into Sergeant Singh's flying chariot for use during Phase 2."

PINA2BO

The touch screen that was supposed to serve as the elevator's UI was dead like everything else that had been reached by the electromagnetic pulse. But the system still had power from below. Someone had to rip the control panel off the wall and then figure out how to hot-wire it. This was far from being the most difficult technical challenge tackled by White Label Industries engineers during their years-long quest to alter world climate, but it still took some doing. For example, it was decided that they needed someone to climb the ladder all the way down to the bottom of the shaft to flip a switch and poke at some wires. Jules volunteered and scampered down the shaft. Several minutes later his voice could be heard echoing up from below. He began to follow instructions hollered down to him by Conor, the engineer who'd taken the initiative with the crowbar and was now standing in the elevator, hands in pockets, evaluating a tangle of wiring harnesses and connectors.

During that procedure T.R. and Saskia—whose only role, here, was to be protected by all the other people—had nothing to do but pace around and drink water. It had been years since she'd been completely disconnected from all electronics, and she found herself wishing she'd brought one of the many unread books piled up on end tables and nightstands in various residences.

About forty-five minutes after the EMP they saw lights gliding through the air down around Bunkhouse. It was obvious from the way they moved that they were drones and that they were swarming in a coordinated fashion. Saskia's first assumption was that the Black Hat people around High Noon had deployed a fleet of these things that had somehow survived the EMP and were setting up an air patrol over Pina2bo. The first wave of them only came up as far as Bunkhouse. A second wave, however, soon began to advance toward the gun complex.

Gunfire sounded from Bunkhouse. The boss of the Black Hats, one Tatum, ordered his men to begin dispersing into positions where they could find cover. Saskia and T.R. he herded into the elevator. "Close this door," he said to Conor, the engineer who had been messing with the wires, "and get them to the bottom. Even if it means y'all gotta climb down the ladder."

Closing the door was a thing that Conor had figured out how to do pretty early, and so that was the last they saw of Tatum or of anyone or anything else on the surface. Saskia and T.R. were now sealed up inside a rather small box with this Conor. He was a short, stocky white guy, probably in his mid-thirties, who had given up trying to cope with the complexities of male pattern baldness and just gone over to stubble. His burly physique took up more than its share of space in the elevator but Saskia would not begrudge him that if he could get the thing to move.

"I was trying to figure out how to do this the nice way," he remarked. "The terrible way is easy." He evaluated his fellow passengers, seeming to assess their overall health and state of mind, in a way that suggested he really wasn't kidding.

"What's the terrible way?" T.R. asked.

"Just turning the motor on and off."

"That doesn't sound so bad."

"You might want to sit down on the floor. No, on second thought, let's keep your tailbones out of it. More of a squatting posture might be good." Conor demonstrated by backing into a corner of the elevator within reach of the gutted control panel, then sliding down until he was sitting on his haunches.

Saskia was with T.R. in thinking it didn't sound so bad, until the first time Conor touched two wires together and the motor came on. Then the bottom seemed to fall out of the lift and they dropped what seemed like a hundred meters in a fraction of a second. Then they stopped so hard she thought they must have smashed into something. To her embarrassment she let out a scream.

T.R. broke the silence that followed by saying, "Gotcha."

"Yes, sir."

"It's like popping the clutch in a truck. Full power all at once."

"Good analogy, sir."

"How far did we drop?"

"I have no idea." Conor, displaying admirably good knees and leg muscles, stood straight up and looked through the mesh wall of the lift, through which it was possible to see the shell hoist and much more routed-systems clutter choking the mine shaft. This was dimly, unevenly lit by emergency lights. He craned his neck and put his face close to the mesh so that he could peer upward. "Not that far," he said.

But this could have been guessed anyway from the sound of gunfire echoing down the shaft. It sounded close. Saskia's impression that they had dropped a hundred meters was totally wrong. Ten was more like it.

The gunfire wasn't heavy. This was not a full-blown firefight. This was selective and it seemed to come from several directions.

"Shotguns," T.R. pronounced them. "Our boys trying to take out drones." He listened a little more. "That there was a pistol round." He looked down at the others. "Much as it shames me to run from a fight, I do believe we should descend farther. You okay, Saskia?"

"Perfectly fine, thank you."

"So why don't let's get comfy and you pop the clutch again and—"

"Sir?"

Conor had slid back down into his squat and was poised to touch two stripped wires together, which Saskia knew would lead to another drop. But he was looking at T.R. who had held up a hand to signal *wait just a sec*. T.R. had turned his face upward and opened his mouth. He was listening. So they all listened. Gunshots were still popping off here and there. But something very weird could now also be heard. It was a woman's voice, electronically amplified, speaking calmly: "Place your weapons on the ground and lace your fingers together on top of your head. Proceed in the direction indicated by the green arrow." Though they had to listen for a while to completely decipher it, the same announcement seemed to be emanating from multiple drones in different places at different times.

"Sounds like a fucking airport," T.R. remarked. His eyes rotated down toward Saskia. "Would you call that an Indian accent? As in, from India?"

They all listened to a few more repetitions of the message.

"Definitely," Saskia said.

"I concur, Your Royal Highness." He looked at Conor. "Hit it."

Conor had to "hit it" at least a dozen times before they got to the bottom. Toward the end he was just tapping the wires together for the briefest instant possible, producing a series of jolts that dropped them only a meter at a time. But he didn't have to explain that this was preferable to slamming full-tilt into the bottom of the mine shaft. When they got to within about a meter of the Level Zero lift stop, all aboard wordlessly agreed that this was close enough, and that clambering down the rest of the way was preferable to the sickening lurch-drop-jolt of "popping the clutch."

Conor did the thing that caused the door to open. They looked out into the side chamber at Level Zero, which Saskia had last seen the better part of a year ago, on the day the gun had first been fired. It looked the same, just a bit more lived-in. Conor climbed down to the floor and helped T.R. out. Both men then made a show of trying to help Saskia until she pointed out that they were merely getting in her way. Waiting for them was Jules.

Though partly obstructed by all manner of plumbing and mechanical equipment, the whole length of the shaft from here up to the surface was basically open. Air and light could filter up and down it, and sounds echoed down from above. At this distance they would no longer hear the Indian lady delivering her calm but firm instructions. Gunfire was audible, though. As before, that was sporadic. The shots seemed to come fewer and farther between as time went on.

"What's going on up there?" Jules finally asked.

Saskia realized he hadn't seen the drones or heard the voice. "It sounded to me," she explained, "as if drones were being used to somehow round people up and march them off."

"Off to where?" Jules asked. It was, come to think of it, a perfectly obvious and sensible question.

Saskia threw up her hands. "Not here."

Jules was stricken, obviously thinking that he should have stayed behind with Fenna. "What's wrong with here?"

"This may become a question of some relevance to us," T.R. remarked.

The image stabilization system in his fancy binoculars was on the fritz. To get a steady view of what was happening down on the mesa, Rufus had to go full Stone Age, holding them down on an outcropping of rock near the summit of the peak. The distance was so great that the binoculars weren't a huge improvement on the naked eye. Every few minutes a purplish star would ignite at the base of a net stanchion and burn for a couple of minutes. Then that pole would fall inward. One by one the nets were hitting the ground.

Pina2bo had stopped firing shells around the time of the flash—which as near as he could tell had detonated in the sky right above it. But there would still be dozens of shells in the air, spiraling down out of the stratosphere beneath their parasails. Under normal circumstances, they'd be talking to systems on the ground that would tell them which net to aim for. Rufus didn't know what happened in the case when a shell couldn't phone home. It was maybe kind of an interesting question but not the thing to be focusing on right now.

Pools of light were gliding around the mesa in an orderly way, sometimes preceded by—unless his eyes deceived him—huge glowing green arrows. He could not make out what it was they were illuminating, but a reasonable guess would be people. They converged on one location in the facility's parking lot: a ring of green laser light surrounding a lit-up circle. People were being herded and penned, he guessed.

Up here at the marble mine they didn't have lights at all, other than a few candles. All their flashlights were LED-based. Instead of simple on-off switches, they had buttons you could press multiple times to get different brightness levels or check the batteries or what have you. There must be a little microprocessor inside the unit counting the button presses and deciding what action to take. Those were fried. So the lights didn't work. Fortunately the moon was full. It was what they used to call a Comanche moon on the Texas frontier, for the warriors of that people had taken advantage of its light to mount nocturnal raids. Rufus was thereby able to hike down from the peak and find his way back to the campfire without turning an ankle. He'd had an idea that he could hot-wire some flashlights by opening them up and soldering wires directly between the battery terminals and the LEDs.

Or, of course, they could all just go to bed and wait for the sun to come up. But after that it would soon become so hot that they would have to lie low until it went down again. The ability to move around and get things done during the hours of darkness was going to be important.

Besides, he had nothing else to do.

His trailer had some twelve-volt circuits that ran off battery power, and these still worked. So he was able to go in and grab his soldering iron. But it required 120 volts AC. Normally this would be supplied by the generator. But the generators were all dead because they were controlled by systems that had microchips in them. For that matter, so did the soldering iron; it had a built-in thermocouple and some logic that varied the power to keep it at a set temperature, turned it off when not in use, and so on.

So Rufus's first project was to hot-wire his own soldering iron by holding its tip into the glowing coals of the campfire until it was hot enough. He was able to bypass its power supply and hook it directly to a car battery. This gave him the ability to hot-wire flashlights. This in turn gave him a well-illuminated workspace on one of the plastic tables.

He did not, of course, fully know what was going on, other than that the ranch was under some sort of attack. His conversation with Pippa pointed to some kind of performative war project starring Big Fish. Such a thing could not possibly have worked if it was Big Fish single-handedly taking on Black Hat. But Black Hat without electronic devices was just a few guys running around in the dark with guns, strewn across a vast stretch of desert. Desert where it was nearly impossible to move because of climate and terrain. They'd have no way to communicate save mirror flashes and smoke signals.

In the land of the blind, the one-eyed man was king. Big Fish must be down on that mesa, performatively bringing the nets down. Why attack the nets? Because they were a great big obvious symbol and it would look good. Maybe they could get some video of spent shells crashing ignominiously into the ground.

Pina2bo, on the other hand, was all underground. Nonetheless, he'd have to go there eventually. He'd have to do it soon, before reinforcements could be sent in. Personnel there were probably being rounded up and herded and kettled just like the ones down on the mesa. The next move—the big payoff—would probably happen tomorrow, in daylight where it would look better on the videos.

To do anything about it, Rufus would have to cover ten miles of rough ground. He was going to be out in the open. He was going to need his earthsuit.

The earthsuit was a whole basket of technologies, some of

which belonged to the realm of materials science, such as fabric, or of mechanical engineering, such as pumps and fans. But the key thing for his survival tomorrow was going to be the refrigeration system.

The fancy suits issued to Black Hat personnel did not show up on the loading dock as suits, but as rolling footlockers crammed with modular parts, so the user could configure them for different conditions. The module that was responsible for the user's not perishing of heat stroke was branded as the Me-Frigerator. More than one type of Me-Frigerator was in the kit. One of them was optimized for conditions where direct intense sunlight was the primary threat. Which was decidedly the case in the Chihuahuan Desert on an August afternoon. It was built around a technology that had been invented and patented a hundred years ago by none other than Albert Einstein, teaming up with a future A-bomb physicist named Leo Szilard. It didn't have moving parts, other than some valves. It was just a particular configuration of plumbing containing certain fluids. One part of it just happened to get cold when another part of it was exposed to heat. You didn't need a motor to drive a compressor or any of that. It just worked, provided you could open the valves and make one part of it hot. And that last was pretty easy in the desert sun, especially when there were new blacker-than-black light-absorbing materials and certain other innovations that Einstein hadn't known about. During the first century of its existence, Einstein's invention had not seen very much practical use because it was less efficient than other ways of making things cold. But more recently, researchers had been spiffing it up with an eye to using it in developing countries where heat, in the form of sun and fire, was easier to get than reliable electricity. The manufacturers of the fancy earthsuits favored by Black Hat had piggybacked off such innovations to make these Me-Frigerator systems. Rufus dug into one of them as soon as he had good light and a functional soldering iron.

That implement—the soldering iron—was an example of the

same kind of problem he was facing with this Me-Frigerator. The part of the soldering iron that really mattered was just a dumb coil of wire that got hot when electrical current ran through it. Everything else was electronic brains that added features. When the brain got fried, it just had to be bypassed. The added features went away, leaving a soldering iron that was a throwback compared to the one with the brain. But it did most of what the brainy version could—especially if the person wielding it had some brains of his own.

Likewise, the maze of plumbing and sealed containers of special fluids in the Me-Frigerator were simple enough that they would do their basic job without a brain. That had to be the case, because ol' Albert had patented the thing before thinking machines existed. The trick was to work a bypass, just as Rufus had with the soldering iron. He might have to turn it on and off by hand. But since he was a pretty acute judge of when he was and wasn't hot, that should be easy.

"What the hell are you doing? Everyone wants to know." This was Carmelita, whose role in this strange little community was to be the Rufus whisperer. Thordis talked to horses. Everyone except Rufus talked to eagles. Rufus talked to drones. Carmelita talked to Rufus. She had acquired the skill early in their relationship, when they hadn't liked each other. As such it had been easy for her to speak to him bluntly. Now they'd come to like each other fine. The habit had stuck, though.

"Before you settle in to bothering me could you throw a couple more logs on the fire?" Rufus asked, without looking up. "Gonna need a heat source to see if this thing works." Carmelita did so, then sat down across from him. "Seriously, Red. What the fuck?"

"We are at war," Rufus said. "Gonna ride to the sound of the guns. Leaving before daybreak, I reckon."

"The guns aren't making any sound!" Carmelita objected.

Rufus sighed. "It is a Civil War joke. Not so funny apparently. It means I need to go to where the action is gonna be. Pina2bo."

"And you think you're gonna get that suit working."

"Gonna try."

"Then what, Red?"

"Head out before sunrise, like I said." He heard footsteps and looked up to see Thordis approaching. Trailing behind her were Piet and then Tsolmon.

"On Bildad?" Carmelita asked.

"Pegleg. I'm too big for poor ol' Bildad. Pegleg's more my size." Also, though Rufus was embarrassed to admit it, he'd held an irrational grudge against Bildad ever since the gelding had made his preference for Thordis clear.

"Pegleg does not have a Me-Frigerator."

"By the time the sun is high enough to be a problem for Pegleg, we'll have reached a waller I noticed, a couple of miles from the big gun."

"Waller?"

"Low spot in the ground where there's some water. Pegleg can rest easy there until the cool of the evening. Then he'll find his way back."

"While you cover those last couple of miles on foot."

"Yep."

"Here, let me hold that for you." Carmelita picked up a flashlight that Rufus had balanced on a rock and angled it into the control unit of the earthsuit to give him a better view. He had a big magnifying glass that he used to work on tiny components and was putting it to good use now.

"What are you going to do about the drones, Red?" That was Thordis talking. She and the others had now formed a little circle around the table. Piet came up behind him, stood a little too close, and peered over his shoulder. He was meticulous, on the spectrum, one of those guys who'd figured out by trial and error that he got along better with critters than with people. "Guess you might as well take notes, Piet," Rufus suggested. "Maybe we can come out of this with a procedure. Or at least a list of what *not* to do."

Piet didn't say anything, but Rufus could hear the click of a ballpoint pen and the rustle of pages in the little graph paper notebook he always carried in a certain pocket.

"You didn't answer Thordis's question," Carmelita pointed out.

"We've been up there watching," Thordis said. "Whoever those people are—"

"India," Rufus put in.

"They must have hundreds of drones. And I don't know how many people."

"Very few, would be my guess," Rufus said.

"Anyway, the drones have guns on them. And who knows what else."

"I figured the same, Thordis."

"There's no cover out in that desert. The drones will see you coming a mile away."

"Well, I can and will go alone," Rufus said. "Someone got to be Hector in this *Iliad*."

"Hector?"

"The opposition. Someone gotta play defense. Staff at Pina2bo gonna be neutralized, rounded up, just like those ones down on the mesa. But they probably don't know about me, coming down the back way from the old marble mine. That won't be in their plan."

"You'll go alone *if you have to*. Is that what you're saying, Red?" Carmelita asked. "And those drones will fuck you up. But if we've got your back—"

"How do the eagles fare in the heat of the day?" Rufus asked.

"They ride the air to where it is cold," Tsolmon said. Her first and quite likely her final contribution to this conversation.

"Thing is," Rufus said, "whatever these guys are gonna do, they got to get it done quick. Electronics might be on the fritz *here at the ranch*. Giving them the upper hand. But—"

"There must be some safe radius outside of which everything will still be working," Piet said.

"Yeah. And so the cavalry will be on its way tomorrow. Bad

guys know this. Maybe they can use hostages to delay the inevitable. But they gotta do something tomorrow, something big to justify all this. I do mean to be there. You want to bring the eagles and join the party, be my guest. We got all night to get the meefs fixed," he concluded, using the inevitable slang term for "Me-Frigerator."

He got to his feet and lifted the meef from the table. During the last few minutes he'd identified what he believed to be its on/off switch: a pair of valves, electromechanically actuated, that controlled the circulation of fluids through the plumbing circuits. He had teased the wires free and hooked them up to new leads in a simple circuit consisting of a battery, a switch, and a resistor. When he flicked the switch he could hear the valves moving. He was pretty sure he had just turned the unit on. There was an easy way to find out. He carried it over to the campfire, which had developed a nice bed of coals. He turned the unit's hot plate—just a flat expanse of bottomless black—toward it, using his hand to verify that it was getting warm. A watched pot never boils, so he waited for a minute. "Y'all are the custodians of those beautiful birds," he said. "Y'all can decide."

"The drones they're using might be big ones," Thordis pointed out.

"Go for the little ones first," Carmelita suggested. "The video drones. Peck out their eyes."

Thordis didn't seem mollified. "The real question is, why are we doing it? Why go to war for T.R.?"

"We're going to war for Red," Tsolmon answered.

"Why are you doing it then, Red?"

"You mean, other than the fact that T.R. has been paying me to look after his property?" Rufus asked, looking Thordis in the eye. But he already knew that an argument of that type wasn't going to cut much ice with her. How impossibly old and out of date he was, making decisions based on some frontier notion of honor. And she was right, in a way. All their vehicles and comms were down.

They could all just stay put right here and wait for the cavalry and T.R. wouldn't think less of them.

Rufus was debating whether he should just come out and tell them the real reason: Saskia was down at Pina2bo. He'd heard the news over the Black Hat comms network before everything had gone down yesterday afternoon. She was probably being menaced by those drones. And a certain atavistic logic dictated that he must, therefore, ride to her rescue. But he wasn't sure how that was going to play with this crowd.

"Why take those kinds of risks," Thordis said, "to protect this crazy plan to mess with the climate?"

Rufus considered it. "It's already been messed with," he said. "It's like, we've been in a car with a brick on the gas pedal and no one at the wheel, careening down the road, running over people and crashing into things. We're still in the car. We can't get out of the car. But someone could at least grab the wheel. T.R. ain't the perfect man to grab it, but I don't think his whole plan is just to fuck up the Punjab and starve India. He's trying to get a global system up and running. Criticize it if you want. But I don't mind helping when an opportunity presents itself."

He reached into the meef. His hand encountered something that had, over the last couple of minutes, grown very cold. But his eyes were fixed on the campfire: dry mesquite popping and crackling. "That's my fancy explanation," he said. "But the real answer is in the words of the Bible. Man is born to trouble as the sparks fly upward. I been holed up in this place long enough."

By the time Laks climbed back into his six-rotor flying chariot, it had become a five-rotor flying chariot.

Major Raju had long since taken his leave and gone back across the river into Mexico. For at least an hour, it was just Laks walking around the site chopping down net stanchions, trailed by the videographers. From the way those guys went about their work, and the nature of some comments he overheard in Hindi, they were not livestreaming. They were going to edit this footage and release a cut later. Which made total sense, considering. Since he had come back to his senses and got most of his memories back, Laks had familiarized himself with the amazingly vast corpus of Big Fish–related content that had gone up on the Internet during his rise to fame and sudden fall from glory. It made much of his supposedly humble blue-collar origins as a fisherman and a welder. At one point his handlers had even gone to the trouble of renting out a welding shop for a day and shooting footage of him grinding metal and operating a cutting torch: two operations beloved of filmmakers because they generated lots of sparks. The images of him cutting down stanchions on the mesa would fit perfectly with that story.

Anyway, it all went pretty much according to plan (or so Laks assumed; it wasn't like anyone had talked to him about what the plan actually was) except for an element of randomness introduced by those spent shells gliding down out of the sky every seven and a half minutes. These were the very definition of an accident waiting to happen. Laks didn't know how they worked, but it was easy enough to see that they were supposed to home in on the nets. And maybe they had enough built-in smarts to find their way back to this general vicinity on their own, and perhaps line up a final glide path aimed roughly toward the mesa. But maybe there was some kind of robotic air traffic control system that was supposed to take over at that point and guide them in on final approach. If so, it was on the blink. Sometimes the shells happened to hit the nets, like the first one that he and Major Raju had watched, but sometimes they didn't. And even when they were on target, they were dropping into nets that Laks was here to cut down.

Half an hour into the operation, he stood and watched as a shell plummeted directly onto hard ground that was covered with a completely flattened net. The thing belly-flopped in a cloud of rocks and dust and tumbled end over end for something like a hundred meters before coming to rest in a big tangle of shroud lines and silky fabric. For the mechanisms that were supposed to disengage the shells from the parasails were sometimes failing and so the tumbling shell was getting wrapped in its shroud lines as it careered across the mesa.

It made for great video but the potential hazard was obvious and so for the remainder of the mission the videographers were torn between fascination and terror as they waited for these ghostly visitations to glide out of the sky along slightly random vectors and crash somewhere nearby. Laks requested that they please inform him if any were headed directly for him, then adjusted his visor and went about his work.

Because he did not hear any such warnings from them, he was surprised but not especially worried when they suddenly began to cry out in dismay. He was in the middle of cutting down a stanchion. He could hear the distant sound effects he'd learned to associate with a shell crash-landing. It was far away and it wasn't getting closer. So he ignored it until he was finished dropping this pole. It took longer than usual—he had the sense that the plasma cutter's batteries were dying, and there was no question that the air tank was nearly empty.

He switched off the machine, pulled his visor down onto his chest, and looked around to see what all the fuss was about. He had been abandoned by his videographers, who were trotting across the mesa's treacherous surface as best they could in the dim moonlight, headed back toward where the drone was parked. Laks ditched the backpack and followed them.

The drone had not taken a direct hit, at least. It was somewhat difficult to reconstruct what had happened because the drone's six arms and eighteen rotor blades had become all involved with the shroud lines of the shell that had caused the problem. Consequently shell and drone had been dragged and tumbled, with multiple small impacts, a visual record of which was inscribed across a dozen meters of ground. Laks had a folding knife, which was fortunate since otherwise they'd have been untangling the mess until the sun was up. As it was, it took a quarter of an hour to cut it free to the point where they could assess damage.

One of the six arms was damaged beyond repair. It was a hollow tube of carbon fiber composite that buckled and creased but didn't completely give way. About halfway along it just lost all structural integrity and dangled askew.

One of the other arms had a damaged propeller, but this seemed like it would probably still work. The videographers had found a new role for themselves, sending pictures of the damage back to experts in India.

The central hub, comprising the cockpit and some storage compartments, looked worse than it was. At first Laks was afraid to inspect it, because at a glance it looked disastrous. But when he did take a close look he understood that while most of it was quite sturdy, the hatches that closed over the storage bins were as flimsy as they could be. Those had taken quite a beating. One was just dangling by a few strands of carbon fiber. But this damage was basically cosmetic. The only possible consequence was that stuff might fall out during flight.

Inevitably, the tool chest in the remaining ATV contained a roll of duct tape. One of the videographers brought this back at a run, holding it out in front of him like Gollum with the One Ring. Laks—carefully filmed at every step—used it to patch up the damaged hatches. Along the way he got a look at their contents, which until now had been unknown to him. The biggest compartment with the most seriously damaged hatch contained what was obviously an earthsuit in a desert camo pattern. Others contained food and water. One contained a briefcase that was shockingly heavy. A sharp voice in his earbuds told him not to mess with that, but to make sure it was well secured.

The drone booted up with an array of warning lights and system errors that made it look like a portable disco. Following instructions from India, Laks used a folding camp saw from the tool box to amputate the damaged arm. Then he taped off the cut ends of the wires that dangled from its stump. The drone, he was assured, was perfectly capable of flying with one rotor out. The damaged rotor on the other arm was a concern, but a brief flight test indicated it could still move enough air to get the drone off the ground. A few more minutes were then devoted to silencing alarms, clearing error messages, and overriding safety interlocks just to get the operating system calmed down to the point where it was willing to consider taking Laks on the next leg of the mission.

And then he was in the air, headed deeper into Texas. He hadn't finished taking the last two nets down, but no one seemed to care about those. The good video had been shot, he guessed, and uploaded to a server in India. The cameramen were headed back down Mexico way. The overall tone of the last hour's discourse had been that he was well behind schedule and it was a now-or-never kind of situation.

During Laks's convalescence, after he'd come out of the coma but before they'd restored his sense of balance, they had pushed him around Cyberabad in a wheelchair. And needless to say, not being able to walk had been miserable for him. But added to it had been this other, less obvious source of annoyance, which was that he had no control over where he was going. The person pushing the wheelchair decided that. But at least in those days he'd been able to talk to that person. To ask where he was being taken, to make requests.

This felt like that. He was not actually flying the drone. He couldn't have flown it if he'd tried, because it had no controls. As soon as he climbed in, some pilot who might be on the other side of the world—in a military compound outside of Delhi, say—made the thing take off and go wherever they wanted him next. But he couldn't talk to that person the way he could to a wheelchair pusher.

So it was actually with some sense of relief that he watched the drone run out of juice during the flight north and make what was obviously an unscheduled emergency landing in the mountains around one o'clock in the morning.

At least the drone had what Uncle Dharmender referred to as idiot lights. That's what they were called on the dashboard of a car. They told the driver when to check the oil or whatever. As such, they were a pillar of the family's business; a large portion of the clan's overall cash flow was traceable to motorists noticing idiot lights.

On this thing, they were idiot icons scattered around on a screen. But they served the same purpose. The most important of which was to prevent the occupant/pilot from being high aloft at the moment the batteries died. They had been yellow when Laks took off from the mesa, they turned orange shortly afterward, and they turned red as the drone was gaining altitude in an attempt to get over the summit of a mountain ridge. No one was bothering to tell Laks anything, but it could be inferred that said ridge stood between him and wherever it was they wanted him to be. Somewhere in the bowels of India's military-industrial complex, people were probably getting demoted, fired, maybe even arrested right now for having failed to predict the mishap with the shell, for having miscalculated the battery charge necessary to get him over those mountains.

Anyway, the drone broke off from its laser-straight trajectory and came under what showed every sign of being manual control. After hunting and seeking around the mountainside for a few moments it settled down on an angled patch of gray scree. The red idiot light had taken to flashing on and off and counting down the seconds. It landed with six seconds of flight time remaining. Some small reserve of juice was then spent unfolding an array of photovoltaic cells. When the sun came up, this thing would begin to recharge.

It must be a huge fail for the planners of this mission but it was fine for Laks. He unbuckled himself, climbed free of the Sky Wheelchair, and strolled up-slope to a ridgeline clearly visible in moonlight a few hundred meters away. Like so many other ridgelines this did not afford him a clear vista once he had reached it, just a view to some more possible vantage points farther away. But he did get a sense that if he kept going in that direction the ground would soon break downhill and take him into lower terrain beyond. That would probably be the valley that contained the Pina2bo gun and its support complex.

As he was hiking back down to the drone, a new PowerPoint flashed up in the visor, blocking his view of the treacherous rocks ahead and nearly causing him to sprain an ankle. Laks ripped the visor off over his turban, stood still for a few moments to recover his night vision, and kept going. He'd seen just enough to read the deck's title page:

MISSION BRIEFING
PHASE 2 (REVISED)
PERMANENT DECOMMISSIONING OF PINA2BO CLIMATE
WEAPON
FLYING S RANCH, TEXAS

The moon was casting long shadows that made finding his way a bit tricky. For a few moments it crossed his mind that he might actually have gotten lost! But soon he came in view of a red light: one of the idiot icons on the drone's screen. A troubling connection had been made in his head now between idiot lights; Uncle Dharmender, who had taught him that term, and who had implied, during their last conversation, that Laks was being kind of an idiot; and Laks himself, now using an idiot light as a guide star to find his way through the night.

Piet was a rucker, meaning a practitioner of a sport that consisted of putting on a backpack loaded with weights and then covering ground on foot in open country. When he'd first explained this shortly after his arrival in West Texas, Rufus had suspected the Dutchman was pulling his leg. It sounded to him like army boot camp stuff. As if peeling potatoes or scrubbing toilets had been made into an extreme sport. Why would a forty-year-old man like Piet do this voluntarily? Why would he consider it fun? But he had to admit it went well with Piet's personality type. And it explained why the man had said yes to this gig out in the middle of nowhere. During the winter months, when daytime conditions here could be downright pleasant, he'd even talked Thordis and later Tsolmon into going on some of these jaunts with him. They'd always come back looking pleased with themselves. So maybe it was an easier way for a guy like Piet to relate to other humans than, say, going to a party and dancing. His rucking regimen had tapered off a bit during the summer months; he'd shifted to early mornings and it looked like his body fat percentage had skyrocketed from maybe 1 percent to 1.5 percent. But he was totally game for what had to happen next.

Piet's ruck on tonight's trek consisted of an earthsuit and a few liters of water. He departed after a briefing with the other falconers about the idiosyncrasies of Skippy. Skippy was chilling out in her box unaware of these goings-on, but when she awoke she'd find herself being handled by humans to whom she was not as accustomed as she was to Piet. Overhearing this conversation Rufus could tell it was mostly about Piet working through his misgivings and perhaps grief wasn't too strong of a word re being separated from Skippy for a few hours. Duly reassured by the other falconers, he chugged a liter of water, shouldered his pack, and jogged off down the road. Rufus had equipped him with a revolver, not for humans but for feral swine. As soon as he broke free from the confines of the canyon's nearly vertical walls, about a mile down the road, he would cut up into the lower slopes of the arc of mountains that embraced Pina2bo and traverse that until he came in view of the gun complex, probably around sunrise. He would scout things out, try to get a sense of what was happening, and try to link up with the others—in person if that was possible, using mirror flashes otherwise.

Hot-wiring the earthsuits went fast once Rufus worked out the procedure. He had the notion he'd make everything ready during the wee hours, then catch a couple of hours of shut-eye, setting his alarm for a four A.M. departure. Then he realized he had no way of setting an alarm. All his timepieces were electronic. He had never owned a mechanical clock or watch in his life. If he had a star chart, he'd be able to estimate the time from the elevations of astronomical bodies, but you couldn't do that while you were asleep. And the only way he knew to obtain a star chart was to download it from the Internet.

So he just stayed awake. Which, to be honest, he probably would have done anyway. The more he thought this thing through, the more obvious it was that Big Fish was going to have to do whatever he was going to do sooner rather than later. Might have done it already. Because it just wasn't going to take that long for some kind of reaction from Black Hat, or from the cops. And when it came to that, the only way for India to hold them at bay was going to involve hostages. Such as Saskia.

"We should just leave," he announced. "As soon as we're ready." He stood up from his soldering table, having finished with the last of the earthsuits. His eyes were still adjusting to the dark. With great care he walked, planting one foot at a time, toward the place a hundred feet away where Thordis, Carmelita, and Tsolmon had been working with Bildad, Pegleg, and the mules Trucker and Patch. And what he saw there was testimony to the power of something that Rufus had never really got the hang of: working in a coordinated fashion with other human beings. In his personal experience, this had always been pure foolishness, because you had to get them to do what you wanted them to do.

And getting other people to do what you wanted them to do had, for Rufus, always been a sort of black art. Not worth the trouble of learning. In the army, they had people for that. Whole echelons of people.

But these three women might as well have been of a different species. Working quietly and assiduously while he'd been busy with his soldering iron, they had simply got it all done. The boxes containing Nimrod, Skippy, and Genghis were perched on the horses' and mules' croups. Looked like a bumpy ride to Rufus, but what did he know about eagles and their ways? If home for you was a tangle of sticks in the top of a tree on the edge of a cliff in the mountains, why, maybe riding on a mule's ass was a Sealy Posturepedic.

And they'd packed all the other stuff too, looked like. Rufus was about to ask them if they had plenty of water but thought better of it since it would border on insulting.

Carmelita came out to meet him as he approached. "We decided we have to do it," she announced.

"Why?" Rufus responded. "If I may ask."

"For the profession."

"The profession of falconry?"

"Yeah. If an opportunity to do something was presented to us like this and we just said 'Naah'—"

"How could you look other falconers in the eye after that?"

"Yeah."

"Anyone have any idea what time it is?"

"One fifty-six," said Carmelita, checking a mechanical watch on her wrist.

"Let's saddle up."

"*We're* ready. Are you?" Carmelita looked him up and down. "I was expecting you to be more strapped."

Rufus had heard the term in old rap music. "You are referring to guns," he said.

"Yeah. You don't have any."

"I'll go and see to that now," he said. "Shouldn't take long. Y'all drink some water."

PERMANENT DECOMMISSIONING OF PINA2BO CLIMATE WEAPON

Laks did not have the ability to page back to the first slide of the PowerPoint. These things only played in one direction. They were monitoring the movements of his eyeballs or something; they could sense when he was finished reading a slide. Then they'd turn the page and electronically shred the previous one. Still, he could remember seeing those words during the few moments before he pulled the visor off his head. What did they actually mean?

He had to wait a little while to find out. When he got back to the downed drone, he was instructed to eat food, drink water, and get some shut-eye if possible. Somewhat amazingly under the circumstances, he actually was able to get to sleep for a bit. He wondered if they'd wired a switch into his head that would knock him out from the other side of the world and wake him up again when his services were needed.

It seemed that during this little breather the powers that be had been figuring out whether it was faster to wait for the sun to come up and recharge the drone, thus enabling him to fly straight to "the objective," or for him to simply walk. Laks could have told them that walking would be faster, but he sensed a large bureaucracy at work. Anyway, they got back to him at around three in the morning with a revised mission briefing that was all about walking. Stashed in one of the drone's luggage compartments were a few sticks of black plastic and bits of black webbing that, as it turned out, could be snapped together into a sturdy backpack frame that weighed essentially nothing. Immediately, though, it began to weigh rather a lot as the first thing he was told to load onto it was the shockingly heavy briefcase he'd been told not to touch a few hours earlier. Getting that firmly attached consumed most of the available straps, bungee cords, and duct tape. With what remained he loaded on a few key earthsuit parts and several bags of water. Then he heaved the thing up onto his back, adjusted the straps, and started walking.

A few minutes later he was at the ridgeline he'd checked out earlier. He paused there to make a few adjustments. Something caught his eye. He swung his head around and looked back toward the big drone. It was engulfed in flames.

He turned his back on it and continued walking across the crest of the mountains. The night was silent except for the faint whirr of drones, shadowing him all around in some kind of intricate formation he could feel but not see.

The next sound Laks heard, other than his own footfalls, and the little avalanches they sometimes touched off as he descended toward the valley, was a human voice. A cheerful one. Surprisingly close by.

"Splendid morning for a ruck, isn't it?"

Until that moment he had been in a reverie. At its beginning, it had been dark and he had been striding across level, bare ground at the top of the ridge. Now the sun was not exactly up, but the sky was bright enough that it might as well have been. He was picking his way down steep and extraordinarily treacherous terrain covered with viciously spiny vegetation, headed for the Pina2bo "climate weapon," which was in plain sight a couple of miles ahead of him. To the extent his mind was up and running at all, it was entirely focused on deciding where to plant his feet so that he could absorb the massive burden of the weight on his back without turning an ankle, blowing up a knee, toppling forward, or impaling himself on a plant. He kept thinking he was almost to the bottom and that the going would soon get easier. It did not.

So the last thing he'd been expecting was to bump into another pedestrian at random. What were the odds? Slim enough for it to seem suspicious. And why had all those fucking drones not noticed this guy and given him some warning?

Out of batteries, probably. They hadn't planned on Laks walking through the hours of darkness. Pretty soon, though, they'd all be able to recharge, and then they'd catch up with him.

The stranger was tall and lean, with thinning blond hair and a creased face. He seemed to understand that some explanation might be warranted for his startling appearance directly in Laks's path. "I saw you up there half an hour ago," he said, "silhouetted against the skyline, and it looked like the way down was tricky, so I decided to take a little break and just make sure you got down all right." He spoke with a crisp accent Laks couldn't quite place.

"Thanks." Laks had been thinking of taking a little break anyway, so he unbuckled the pack's waist belt and swung it down onto the ground. Then he stood up straight, rolled his shoulders back, and stretched.

"Communications are down, you know, and so if someone has an emergency, we all have to rely on each other."

Something about this guy's nervous insistence on explaining himself was setting off alarm bells in Laks's head. "That's very considerate of you," he said.

But he was interrupted by the voice of the lady from the airport. "Halt! Move your hands away from your sides and keep them in plain view. Refrain from sudden movements, as a defensive response may be initiated under algorithmic control. Serious injuries may result."

Both men looked around to see several drones silhouetted against the sky, which, because of stratospheric sulfur that had been hurled into it by that big gun right over there, was bright. Anyway, the drones were obvious now. They must have been hanging back, lurking, conserving power. But now they were out in force. Expending their reserves.

"Goodness! This is unexpected!" said the man, not very convincingly. He was complying exactly with the instructions, with the gratifying side effect that the announcement was not repeated. He squinted at one of the nearby drones. "Does that thing have a *gun* on it!?"

"Yes."

"How very Texas."

"They are not from around here, actually," Laks said. "I don't think it's going to shoot you if you follow the arrow."

"Arrow?"

Laks looked around. The man followed his gaze. The laser arrow was harder to see in the daytime, but it was there. He shrugged. "Just do what it says. I think you'll end up with the other . . ." Hostages? Detainees? Prisoners? ". . . people."

The flash caught Rufus's eye about an hour after the sun rose above Pina2bo. He was alone, riding Pegleg across flat open terrain along the base of the ridge. He was still in the shadow of the mountains, but the complex was awash in the amber light of early morning. Closer to him, about a mile away, was Bunkhouse. Farther in the distance was the gun complex, mostly concealed under stretched camo netting, but easily seen because of the head frame and the exposed muzzles of the six barrels with their bulky flash suppressors. The flash that had caught his eye, though, had not come from the big guns. It originated from open territory between the base of the ridge and the Bunkhouse.

His first thought was that there'd been an explosion. An old instinct left over from working in places where IEDs were a problem made him tense up, awaiting the crack of the shock wave. But then he understood that someone out there was signaling him with a mirror. And he had a pretty good idea of who that would be.

The others had been shadowing him along a parallel course, higher up the slope. They were on rougher terrain and trying to be less obvious than Rufus, so they made slower progress. Rufus dismounted, giving them a chance to catch up, and took his rifle from the soft fabric case he'd strapped alongside the saddle. This was not the Kalashnikov but the long bolt-action number with the scope, the one he'd built for drilling big boars from long range.

Another flash caught his eye. Turning around and looking up, he could see a hot spot of bluish light scribbling all over the mountainside as Piet wiggled the mirror around. He must know it was hopeless to hit Rufus, or any other fixed target, with anything more than the odd lucky flash. There'd be no Morse code transmissions on this channel. But a lucky flash carried a lot of information. Rufus found a patch of ground where he could lie flat on his belly without collecting hundreds of barbed spines in his flesh. He stacked a rock on another rock and used that to steady the barrel of his rifle, then pulled the dust covers off the ends of the scope. He peered through it, sweeping it this way and that across the area where he thought he had seen the flash. This took several minutes. But finally he saw a human figure walking alone across the alluvial flat, headed down off the mountain. As best as he could tell at this range, he was not headed toward the gun, but rather toward Bunkhouse. Which fit with Rufus's general picture of how this was going to go: personnel herded into a pen, and forced to remain there, by drones. At this range he could not see drones in the objective lens of the scope, but he knew they must be shadowing Piet. Piet must have slipped the mirror out of his pocket and used it while he was taking a piss break or something.

Rufus wished he had a way to communicate with Thordis, Carmelita, and Tsolmon up above him, but he didn't. They too might have been hit by the strafing beam of light from the mirror. They might have seen Rufus peering through his scope. In case they'd missed all that, he stood up, tapped the telescopic sight, and then used two fingers to pantomime looking down the valley. They had the binoculars with them. If they saw and understood the gesture, they might use those to see what he'd seen.

The sun had hove up over the ridge during all this and felt

warm and welcome on his skin for about ten seconds before turning unpleasantly hot. As long as he was stopped anyway, Rufus opened up the saddlebag where he had stashed his earthsuit and changed into its under-layer, which as far as he could tell was a glorified spandex bodysuit. It was khaki, so it wouldn't stand out too bad in the desert, but it would be going too far to call it camouflage. He put on a white broad-brimmed hat to protect his head and then got "strapped," to use Carmelita's terminology: a semi-automatic pistol on his hip and a pump shotgun slung over his shoulder on a strap pendulous and gleaming with extra shells. He had the idea that such a weapon might be capable of taking down drones. If it worked on clay pigeons . . .

Fussing with these things was one of those deals where the longer it took, the longer it took. Between that and the slowness with which the three falconers were obliged to travel, Rufus began to feel that they were terribly behind schedule and that they had wasted the cool part of the day. He couldn't believe, in retrospect, that he had contemplated grabbing a couple of hours' sleep last night.

Finally he climbed back up into the saddle and began to ride Pegleg toward the Biggest Gun in the World.

By the time he was, at long last, able to lengthen his stride down into the flat between him and the big gun, Laks was in a quite ambivalent frame of mind about the whole drone thing. On the one hand, this whole operation would have been unthinkable without them. On the other hand, batteries. The big drone had been forced to land well short of its objective because it was low on batteries, and this had led to knock-on effects as the smaller drones escorting him had run low on juice in the dark. Several of the ones that still worked had then been spent on the weird blond hiker, leaving Laks bereft of air cover. So he'd been ordered to sit on his ass for a while as a couple of mothership drones spread their photovoltaic wings in the sun and recharged their broods.

On the other, other hand, he'd made an honest effort to read some military history, since it seemed he was bound for a military career, and found it to be a whole lot of repetitive accounts of armies running out of things. Usually energy. Whether that meant food for troops, grass for horses, or fuel for trucks. Electrons for batteries was just the modern equivalent of that. Hitler's invasion of Russia had stalled in the dead of winter, in a place from which the Germans could actually *see* Moscow. Now, in the dead of the Texas summer, India's invasion of the Flying S Ranch was stalled at a place where Laks could see the huge flash suppressors on the gun's six barrels, protruding from a lake of camouflage netting. Choppers and planes were beginning to cross high overhead as word apparently got out that something bad was happening here.

To the extent Laks understood the plan, anyone who looked down from those planes and choppers would see a congregation of ranch personnel all together in the residential part of the valley, and it would be understood that—for their own protection, of course—they were being temporarily detained there while the Indian military conducted a "climate peacekeeping" mission— the smallest and deftest of surgical strikes—at the gun complex. Which was Laks's job. In his mind's eye he reviewed the instructions from the most recent PowerPoint. He was to hike to the "head frame," which was easy to find; he could see that already. At ground level there would be a door to a lift. The lift ran down a deep shaft into the ground, where the guts of the gun were protected beneath hundreds of meters of rock. His job was to get the heavy briefcase down to the bottom of that shaft. If the lift was operating, he could just walk into it and hit the "down" button. However, this was deemed the unlikeliest of scenarios. The shaft, according to their intelligence, was a chimney, open at the top. It was cluttered with equipment, but not so cluttered he couldn't simply drop the briefcase down it and let gravity handle the rest.

That done, he was supposed to just travel upwind as fast as he could manage.

Laks would have to have been an exceptionally dense and slow-witted fellow not to have asked himself the obvious question: *Am I carrying a nuclear weapon on my back?* He wasn't sure how small you could actually make such things. He'd heard of backpack nukes and suitcase nukes. This thing was smaller yet. A briefcase. And it felt like most of it consisted of lead. Not much spare room on the inside, then.

His mind circled around it, considering various possibilities, as he just sat there on the ground waiting for batteries to charge. It was a beautiful place, in its way. Pretty quiet, since not much was alive. Lizards began to come out and dart around. Far away on an opposite slope he could see a brown dog. No, of course that would be a coyote. There were a few birds hopping and flitting about. A screech high overhead drew his gaze up into the sky. An eagle, or at least, some kind of big raptor, soaring on a thermal high above the flats beyond Bunkhouse. Laks leaned back and propped himself up on his elbows, to enjoy a better view. The eagle banked round once, twice, then folded its wings and went into a power dive. Before it reached its prey it disappeared from view behind a rise. Must be a bad morning for some poor gopher or whatever it was eagles feasted on in these parts.

It was only a few minutes later that the peace of the morning was disturbed by a familiar humming sound as an echelon of drones passed over him: small camera drones first, at higher altitude, followed by the bigger ones that had guns and lasers and such. They conducted a crisscross grid search over the area that Laks would pass through next, if he simply stood up and walked in a straight line toward the gun complex. It all seemed a bit silly until he heard Airport Lady's voice issuing a now familiar set of commands. A few hundred meters away—a place he'd have walked through only minutes from now—a man had just climbed to his feet. He looked like a rag doll. He was wearing one of those camouflage suits—Laks couldn't remember the name—that was a mess of fabric strips, flopping loose all round, to blur a man's outline and make him nearly undetectable by the human eye. He was holding his hands out to his sides, making him look even more like a scarecrow.

That guy had just been *waiting* for Laks. Hunting him like an animal. Laks would have walked right past him. Laks was still just gaping at the man, being amazed by this fact, when the man did exactly what you weren't supposed to: made a sudden move. Laks saw a pistol in his hand, silhouetted against the bright sun shining on the valley floor in the distance. He jerked this way and that, as if doing some kind of weird dance. As he was collapsing to the ground the reports of three gunshots reached Laks's ears.

During the hours after Saskia took refuge with T.R., Conor, and Jules at Level Zero, gunshots continued to echo down the shaft from time to time, but less and less frequently. And it seemed to Saskia that they were becoming more distant, though this was difficult to judge. One thing that certainly did *not* happen was any communication of any sort from above. The picture she conjured up in her head was that the drone swarm had basically succeeded in forcing the people on the surface to disarm themselves and march away and was now sweeping the area around the gun to ferret out any die-hard Black Hats who had concealed themselves. Every so often, they found one.

Meanwhile they took stock of what was down here. Plenty of water. A cache of snacks. A toilet of the type seen on RVs and boats. Few weapons. Though it appeared weapons were pretty useless against the drone swarm topside, and so T.R.'s sidearm, a semi-automatic pistol with two spare magazines, would be more than enough, assuming it had any value at all. Levels Zero and Minus One, since they served as a sort of control room, were furnished with rolling office chairs, a couple of tables, whiteboards, and flat-panel screens. But everything was run off laptops now, so there was little in the way of control panels as such. Life safety equipment was ubiquitous and clearly marked. This mostly took the form of full-face respirators with compressed air tanks, to be donned in the event the complex had to be flooded with argon as a last-ditch anti-explosion tactic.

Below Minus One, there wasn't much to see until you got to the bottom. Those levels were really just there to provide access during inspections and maintenance. Boxes of tools and other gear were stacked here and there. Some of it looked to be left over from the early phases of the project. In one of them Jules found a cache of climbing gear: long, neatly coiled ropes of the kind used by mountaineers, a couple of climbing harnesses, and a device called a descender that could be used to ratchet one's way up a rope or, on a different setting, to slide smoothly down it. He took the initiative to sling this stuff over his back and climb the ladder partway up the shaft above Level Zero in the hopes he might be able to see or hear something. He anchored a rope up there so that he could use the descender to come back down rapidly if he had to. But after going to all that effort he came back down with nothing to report. It was quiet up there and he daren't climb too high lest he be detected.

Jules and the others just wanted to feel that they were doing something. There was, however, nothing *to* do except wait for the situation to be resolved. Painful for them, but business as usual for Saskia, who'd made a living standing around in situations like the foam disaster at Scheveningen waiting for others to do their jobs.

This would have to get resolved soon. The attackers had bought themselves some time by knocking out all electronic devices within a certain range, and it sounded like they had parlayed that into some leverage by rounding up hostages. But this couldn't possibly last more than a few hours, or at most a day. The cavalry must be inbound; it was just that they had to travel a long way. So all they could do was wait.

Accordingly she climbed down to Minus Five, made herself as comfortable as she could, and went to sleep.

As a young man Rufus had disappointed some of his white army friends who had wanted him to be a whole lot more authentic, according to their version of what that was. But this had been back in the days before Rufus had developed his theory—the theory he'd explained on the train to Saskia—that Comancheness was a viral thing that could hop from brain to brain, regardless of skin color, and that—using the early Texas Rangers as a vector of infection—it had completely taken over America a long time ago. Old-school Christian values and straight-out racism had held it at bay through the world wars and the fifties, but then the barriers had fallen one by one and before you knew it there was a white guy in red-white-and-blue war paint sacking the U.S. Capitol in what the media described as some kind of Viking getup but Rufus knew perfectly well was a Plains Indian–style bison headdress. And just like Comanches with their raids, those people didn't stick around and try to plant their yellow rattlesnake flags on the Capitol dome. They just wandered off, having counted coup on democracy and taken a few cop scalps, and melted back into their nomadic trailer park encampments. Point being, Rufus hadn't worked all that out in his head back when he'd been a buck private; he had not had the mental equipment to explain to his white brothers in arms that the Comanches had won the long war. The war between men's ears.

Which went some way toward explaining why at this moment they, the Americans, were getting their asses handed to them by a meticulously planned invasion originating on the other side of the world. Because that seemed to be the timeless doom of fierce independent-minded tribespeople. The world just didn't fucking like them. And if you were too disorderly for too long, and it started to cause problems for people, then order was going to be imposed. White people had done it to Indians by slaughtering all the bison. Indians from India were doing it to Americans now by wiping out their electronic devices.

All this passed through his head as he was riding up the valley trying to make sense of what was going on with the eagles. Back in the day, his Indian ancestors hadn't had walkie-talkies or GPS or drones. They'd been forced to figure things out by watching the world around them, which was mostly a natural world. They'd had to make surmises about what was going on. Like the guys up in the crow's nests on the *Pequod*, interpreting far-off whale spouts, sensing the direction of the wind and the waves.

He was a far cry from any of those dudes but some things were clear even to a guy like him: the falconers up on the ridge had released Skippy. Maybe they'd seen Piet through the binoculars or maybe it was just a lucky hunch. Then they'd let Nimrod out too. Skippy had taken to the air and recognized Piet. Which seemed damned near impossible at such a distance. But if Rufus had picked up one thing about eagles it was that "eagle eye" actually meant something, their powers of vision were simply unreal. So of course Skippy had picked out the lone human figure walking toward the Bunkhouse, which Rufus had needed a telescope to see. And if she didn't recognize Piet instantly, she did so pretty damn soon. She flew toward Piet. She saw drones flying around Piet. And apparently *fucked them up* though it was difficult for Rufus to make out details. Nimrod came along a minute later and went after some other targets—extra drones, maybe, that were trying to reinforce the first batch?

Piet then changed course and began moving in the direction from which he knew Rufus and the others would be approaching. When the drones had been escorting him, he had been moving as slowly as he could get away with. But now he came on fast. He'd found a dirt road along the valley floor, a terrible road by any standard, but for him a racetrack compared to what he'd been picking his way across for the last few hours. Rufus could track his progress by watching Skippy, who was running combat air patrol above him. Nimrod was headed back toward her girl Carmelita, somewhere up above the road.

"I talked to him!" Piet shouted when he guessed he was in range.

"Big Fish?"

Piet nodded. He talked in bursts, hands on knees, breathing

fast but controlled. "Unless there is more than one turban-wearing Hercules in these mountains."

"Headed for . . . ?"

"The gun."

"Sure."

"Red. Listen."

"Okay. I'm listening."

"I have to tell you something."

"Shoot."

"He's carrying something on his back. Strapped to a frame. Quite heavy."

"How do you know?"

"The way it moved. When he swung it down off his back."

"Okay. Any markings or . . ."

Piet shook his head. "Of course not. Red, I think it's bad. Very bad."

Rufus exhaled and gazed off into the distance. There were more questions he could have asked. But there was no need. He just knew without hesitation, without doubt, that Piet was right. Because that one detail made everything else about this make sense. How else were they expecting to put the gun out of commission? They couldn't bomb it from the air. It was all underground. They had to physically insert some kind of team to get down to the bottom of the shaft and damage the fancy shit. But that would be open war. But if they could just send in one guy . . .

"Well then!" Rufus exclaimed. "I am gonna just ride down there and put a stop to this. I suggest you go up and find the others and tell them what you told me and get you gone. Get the mountains between you and Pina2bo, head upwind, keep moving. Upwind being the important part."

Piet shook his head. "It's too late," he said. "Big Fish must be there already."

Pegleg startled as a trickle of rocks and sand came down a

nearby slope. It was a tiny avalanche touched off from somewhere above. Rufus looked up to see the rest of their party descending. Thordis, Carmelita, and Tsolmon were all dismounted, loosely holding the reins of Bildad, Trucker, and Patch, who were sure-footedly picking their way down through the stones and the cactus. They'd be here in a few minutes and then they'd be looking at a pretty direct gallop along the road in one direction or another. Into the fight, or away from it.

"I got no time to debate the matter," Rufus said. "Y'all decide amongst yourselves which way y'all want to go. Pick you a direction. Ride fast, either way. I got no choice."

The look on Piet's face said that he had no idea what Rufus was talking about. Rufus had never sat down with him and explained matters. Never told the story about Snout and Adele. About how his big Ahab moment had been spoiled by Saskia's airplane coming out of the sky and doing most of the job for him. And how that had somehow gotten him into this. He was feeling now like time had stopped when that jet airplane had hit Snout on the runway. Like hitting the pause button on a video. He'd enjoyed the night he'd spent with Saskia, the sojourn at the marble mine. But now the video was running full speed again. Rufus drew gently on the rein that aimed him toward the Biggest Gun in the World and got Pegleg moving down the road at a walk. But before he'd covered too much distance he turned around in the saddle and said, "I ain't gonna lie. Thordis and Piet, I know you have a special relationship with Saskia."

"Are you referring to Princess Frederika!? The former Queen of the Netherlands!?" Piet exclaimed. It was just like that guy to get hung up on the protocol.

"Yeah. She's down there. Might need our help."

Thordis and Piet turned their heads and stared at each other.

"Well, fuck!" Thordis said and mounted up on Bildad.

Rufus turned to face the enemy and let Pegleg know it was time to cut loose.

It seemed that she was waking up every five minutes, which gave Saskia the idea that very little time was passing. But when she came awake for good, and threw off the emergency blanket she'd been using to keep the light from her eyes, and gazed up through the multiple layers of gridded catwalks above her, she saw more light—a lot more—filtering down the mine shaft. So convinced was she that it was still the middle of the night that she imagined, at first, that they were being attacked or rescued. But when she ascended the ladder to Level Zero and looked at the wall clock, she saw that it was morning. The light coming down the shaft was that of the sun.

Conor and Jules had bunked down on opposite sides of Level Zero. Jules was curled up under a table, Conor had simply leaned back in an office chair and propped his feet up on a desk. On her way up the ladder, she'd passed a human-sized bundle of blankets on Minus One that must have been T.R. They all woke up over the course of about fifteen minutes and took turns using the toilet. They then had what in other circumstances would be called a stand-up meeting, drinking bottles of water and eating energy bars and wishing someone had bothered to install a coffee maker. Above, it seemed perfectly quiet. They decided it would make sense for Jules to ascend nearer to the surface. If he had to come back down in a hurry, he could slide down the ropes. He'd found three of them, each 60 meters long. From Level Zero to the surface was 215 meters. The ropes would cover 180 meters of that, leaving a gap of 35. The idea then was for Jules to climb about 95 meters up from Level Zero, anchor a rope there, and let it dangle. Then he'd climb up another 60 meters and anchor a second rope, hanging to the level where he'd anchored the first. Beyond that, another 60-meter ascent would bring him near the surface, where he could anchor the top rope. He'd keep his harness clipped to that and do some reconnoitering. At the first sign of trouble he could trust his fate to the rope and drop 60 meters below the ground in a few seconds. By transferring to the other ropes he could then get down to a point 35 meters above Level Zero almost as quickly. By that point, hopefully, he'd have enough of a head start on anyone or anything pursuing him that he'd be able to scamper down the ladder before it caught up with him.

Which raised the question: What then? If bad guys with guns were chasing him, then there wasn't much they could do. But there didn't seem to be any of those. Only drones. Where might they take shelter from a drone attack?

The answer was obvious: the steel cylinder that occupied the entire five-meter diameter of the shaft below Level Zero, all the way down to Minus Six. There were two access hatches, massive as bank vault doors, cut into the side of it. Saskia had stepped through both of them during her tour last September.

The one at the very bottom, Minus Six, provided access to the part of the cylinder below the piston, known as the combustion chamber, where a natural gas/air mix was ignited to drive the piston upward on a column of fire. The hatch at Minus Four was above the piston, at least when the gun wasn't operating. It provided access to the so-called pump chamber, normally full of hydrogen, that got pressurized by the piston when it shot upward.

During normal operation, both combustion and pump chambers were hell on earth. But the gun hadn't fired for almost twelve hours. Cooling water had been circulating that whole time through a jacket surrounding both chambers. They were now down to ambient temperature. They had been purged with plain old atmospheric air to remove all traces of anything flammable or toxic.

They could, in other words, simply open those hatches and step into the combustion chamber or the pump chamber and just hang out there in comfort and safety. If they stayed for too long the air would get stale, but they could always simply open a hatch and let in fresh air. And as a backup plan they had a supply of respirators, each with an air tank.

So after a lot of discussion and talking through of scenarios, they agreed that Jules would go up for a look-see. But as a precaution T.R. and Saskia would station themselves at Minus Six, next to the open hatch. They had pre-stocked the combustion chamber with water, snacks, lights, respirators, and a bucket to pee in. Above, on Minus Four, similar preparations had been made in the pump chamber. Conor would hang out up there. When Jules went topside, he'd be carrying a plastic water bottle. If he saw anything bad, he'd simply drop it down the shaft. A few seconds later it would slam into something near Level Zero and burst open, a signal they could not fail to notice. T.R. and Saskia would immediately take refuge in the combustion chamber. Conor would wait a bit to give Jules a chance to come down the rope, whereupon they'd seal themselves up in the pump chamber.

So after seemingly hours of dithering and preparation, that is how they set it all up.

And after all that it seemed almost anticlimactic when, ten or so minutes after Jules had begun his ascent, the water bottle hurtled down and exploded.

The road got better, but still not good, as it drew closer to Bunkhouse. That place seemed sure to be one big humming swarm of drones and so Rufus gave it a wide berth and then swung round to angle across the open stretch that separated it from the gun complex. This was the area where the Flying S Ranch Model Rocketry Club had held its launch months ago, just before T.R.'s big gun had gone into action for the first time. Since then much of the open ground had filled up with shipping containers, heavy equipment, and cargo pallets. These had been arranged in a grid of lanes wide enough that trucks and forklifts could maneuver among them. Nets had been stretched over some of the area to catch sabots and to cast shade. The area immediately next to Bunkhouse, where they had set up the bleachers and launched the little rockets last year, had been kept as open space. This was a considerate gesture for those hobbyists but a problem for Rufus. He'd been thinking about those drones and how to get from where he was now to the gun complex without getting surrounded by those things and picked off. And it was clear to him based on his own experience flying drones that they were going to be at a disadvantage in the cluttered environment of the depot. But to reach that he had to cross this few hundred meters of open ground where they could come at him from all directions. There was nothing for it but to take it at a dead gallop, so he pointed Pegleg's head at the closest corner of the depot and spurred him on.

He might have just imagined it, but he thought he heard whooping and cheering from Bunkhouse. Which was real nice and everything, but if the hostages penned there could see him, so could the drones. He unslung the shotgun from his shoulder, thumbed the safety off, and pumped the forearm to chamber a round. Didn't need it just yet, so he yanked a shell from the strap and shoved it into the magazine to replace the one he'd just chambered. These shells were birdshot, like you'd use for going after pheasant or small game. He'd fitted the weapon with a choke to improve its range. He heard the screech of an eagle above and off to his right and turned his head back to see Genghis pounce on a drone and smash it to the ground. The birds all looked the same to him, but he could tell them apart by their gauntlets, which he'd printed up using different colors of plastic.

Some more eagle-related action happened on his left but on the galloping horse he couldn't track everything. He had to focus on what he could deal with himself and leave the eagles to their work. If there were drones behind him, there might be drones ahead of him. He raised the shotgun and sighted along the top of its barrel. No point seeing anything he couldn't shoot. The damned things were so small. A whirring mote swam into his vision and he pulled the trigger, pumped the forearm to load another shell, swung the barrel toward another veering, humming phantom, fired again. A shell casing tumbled from the target, gleaming in the sun, as his blast struck it and turned it into a cloud of carbon fiber. The thing had taken a shot at him! He pumped and swung the barrel the other way and almost committed a friendly-fire mistake: it was Nimrod grabbing another gun drone in one of her talons.

He was halfway to the nearest shipping containers. Saw no bogeys around him. Seemed like they came in waves. He loaded shells to replace the ones he'd fired.

A problem with the eagles had been getting them to drop drones they'd struck—that wasn't their instinct. Skippy, who'd been part of the Schiphol Airport program, was better than the others, but Genghis and Nimrod were working on it.

Another wave of gun drones—Rufus guessed three of them—dropped into place around him when he was still fifty yards shy of the depot. Half a football field. One was just dead in his sights. He blew it out of the air, pumped. Sounds behind him and on his left made him think that Skippy was tending to a drone on that side. He turned to his right, saw a drone gliding along behind, bringing its gun around to bear on him. It put him in mind of an eagle diving on prey: wings and such all over the place, but gaze steady on the target. The angle was awkward. He had to take his left hand off the gun's forearm, aim behind him with his right, and fire one-handed. The recoil snapped the barrel up and almost whipped the gun out of his hand. A shell casing spun out of the drone's belly as it fired back. He threw his left hand across his torso, pumped the shotgun, fired again, apparently missed, saw another shell casing eject from it. An eagle punched it out of the air just as his view of it was being blocked by the corner of a shipping container. Pegleg let out a sound that came unsettlingly close to a human scream and pulled up short beneath the shade of a camo net. His gait was all awry and he looked to be going down. Rufus pulled his right boot from the stirrup, swung his leg back over Pegleg's croup, and spun away as the horse settled to his knees. Rufus's left boot was still in the stirrup as he slammed full-length into the ground, but this was groomed earth, no rocks or cacti. Landing on it didn't feel good but it didn't cause any damage that couldn't wait until later.

Fortunately Pegleg didn't roll onto his left side, which would have pinned Rufus's leg. He seemed content to just stay on his belly. Rufus yanked his foot out of the stirrup, raised the shotgun, and looked back the way he'd come. A trail of downed drones and furious eagles was spread across the track Pegleg had taken, but there were no drones aiming guns at him now. He reloaded the shotgun's magazine before doing anything else, then stood up, bent over Pegleg, and drew the rifle from the padded case alongside his saddle. Blood was running down Pegleg's right flank from an entry wound to the right of his tail. Deep into the muscle. Enough to bring the animal down but probably not enough to kill him. Rufus felt that some kind words, some expression of gratitude, was now in order, but there was no time to lose, so he just stroked the horse's nose as he took his leave and told him what a fine fella he was.

Then he ran down to the far end of the shipping container and ducked around a corner. He could hear a drone overhead, above the net, but it probably couldn't see him. He aimed straight up through the net and blasted it, then pivoted and ran for a gap between two more containers.

A freight train was parked on the railway that ran along one side of the depot and continued directly to the gun complex. It consisted entirely of hopper cars loaded with sulfur. At the opposite end of the train from where Rufus was, a pile of sulfur—a smaller version of the one on the Houston waterfront—sat on the ground like a huge yellow traffic pylon. Near it, he knew, was a shallow pit under the railway where the hopper cars, one by one, discharged their loads. Empties then coasted under gravity power onto a siding where they could be reassembled into trains that would deadhead back to Houston.

From that pit under the tracks, an angled conveyor carried sulfur up from the pit to the apex of the pile; and from the far side of the pile, other conveyors took the stuff into a building where it was melted and poured into shells. Anyway, the pile was a conspicuous landmark that Rufus could aim for. From there it was a couple of hundred yards to the head frame.

Rufus had the idea that by running alongside the parked freight train he'd be able to cover some more ground while enjoying at least partial cover. In the open, the drones could come at him from all sides. If he was next to a hopper car, that gave him cover on one side. Better than none at all.

Movement through the depot was a mixed blessing as the nets made trouble for the drones but also kept the eagles out of the action. He just had to keep moving and not let the drones zero in on him. Whenever he ventured into an open space there was a few moments' grace period before a drone was able to swing around and aim its gun at him, and he could take advantage of that by moving to cover, or just blasting it. The shotgun had been the right choice. But he had to be conservative with ammunition and so finding cover was better. Moving in a somewhat random path—partly out of necessity, partly by design—he was able to approach the railway siding within a few minutes, spending half a dozen shells in the process and twice getting shot at without result. If the drones were being aimed by humans, the latency of their network connection had to be a factor. As long as he kept moving he could use that to his advantage. Standing still and staring a drone down, *High Noon* style, was not his move.

When he reached the strip of open ground along the railway siding, he found that all three eagles had taken down drones that had apparently been lying in wait for him there. Rufus ran across it, thumbing shells into his magazine, and crouched to duck under the closest hopper car just as a round pinged off a steel wheel. On one knee he pivoted toward the sound of the shot and punched the offending drone out of the air with a shotgun blast, then got up to the other side of the train and ran along it for a car length before ducking under to avoid a drone and coming out the other side. He ran another half car length and then ducked and rolled across the tracks again. Any drone chasing him down the left side of the train would be out of luck when he dodged over to the right, and vice versa. After a few repetitions of that, one of them got the idea and tried to follow him by crossing over the top of a hopper car just as he was diving under it. Which might have actually worked—except that the downwash of its rotors kicked up a cloud of loose powdered sulfur as it skimmed over the top. Rufus rolled over on his back and looked straight up to see the thing hovering, blind in a sunlit yellow cloud. He shot it out of the air, kept rolling, pulled a shell from the strap, reloaded. Down to half a dozen shells now. An eagle came out of nowhere twenty feet ahead of him and crunched its talons into a drone he hadn't even seen.

He was measuring his progress in hopper cars. Three more to go before he reached the pile. Two more. He'd been running on adrenaline since he started his gallop. His ticker was going like crazy and tiredness was beginning to take hold of him. Diving and rolling across railroad tracks was brutally unpleasant even for a man half his age. He knew he was covered with bruises and abrasions. He could sense himself beginning to flinch from the impact of shoulder on gravel, beginning to slow down.

A human figure caught his eye, crossing the open ground between the depot and the head frame. Carrying a heavy pack and dragging one leg. But still making better time than Rufus with all this foolishness about the drones. This man kept turning his head to look toward the sounds of the gunshots. He was a couple of hundred yards away. Hard to see details, but obviously Big Fish. Piet was wrong; Rufus wasn't too late; Big Fish had been delayed, hadn't reached the objective yet.

Rufus lost sight of him, though, during a nearly fatal clusterfuck that took shape at the head of the train—the last hopper car, poised over the unloading pit. Multiple drones were waiting for him there and it turned into an utterly confused mess of plunging, screaming eagles, shotgun blasts, clouds of airborne sulfur, and Rufus rolling to and fro. Inevitably gravity had its way and he fell off the side of the track—which, here, turned into a little trestle on steel I-beams—and into the pit below. But the floor of the pit was no more than eight feet below the track, and it was half full of sulfur, so he didn't fall far and he landed on something with a little bit of give. A cloud of yellow powder went up and got into his lungs. He coughed, gagged, and pulled the earthsuit's spandex neck gaiter up over his mouth and nose. During those moments a drone came into view and lined up to take a shot at him. He rolled and drew his legs up, instinctively going into a fetal position, felt an ice-cold knitting needle pass through one calf and graze the other. He'd let go of the shotgun during all this; it was half buried in sulfur an arm's length away. He scooped up a handful of the stuff and flung it at the drone. Then he pushed himself up on one knee, banged his head on the underside of the railroad tracks above him, got his pistol out of its holster, and just blasted away at the thing until it splintered.

Vaulting out of this pit wasn't an option with his leg messed up. The obvious escape route was the conveyor. This was not moving. It consisted of a broad band of flexible rubbery stuff, maybe six feet wide, running over rollers that folded it into a U-shaped cross section to contain the powder. From his point of view right now it was just a ruler-straight yellow brick road to the sky. He had only one decent option, which was to go up the thing until the pile was beneath him, providing a surface—soft and yielding, he hoped— that would cushion his fall. Breaking very much out into the open, he began climbing the conveyor, taking long strides with his one semi-good leg and then toppling into the flume of sulfur in the belt as his other knee came down. No drones came after him. Either they were running low on those, or his move onto the conveyor had surprised them and they needed to re-vector the ones they had.

He just kept gaining altitude as best he could. As he did he gained a better view. Finally the end of the conveyor approached. From it sulfur simply fell off onto the apex of the pile and avalanched down its slopes. The drop was maybe ten feet. Rufus just dove right off and plunged belly first into the top of the cone. He was half buried in the stuff now. He kicked his legs free while elbow-crawling forward. The more he moved, the more he sank into the powder. Some of that was good if the stuff could slow bullets. Too much could be very bad. He pulled his rifle free, upended it to dump sulfur out of the barrel, then popped the dust caps off the scope and shouldered it. He blew sulfur away from the bolt and chambered a round. A drone was headed up the slope toward him, manifesting as a yellow whirlwind. No time to switch weapons. He obliterated it with a rifle shot, then worked the bolt and chambered another round. An eagle screamed overhead. He hoped the birds would look after him while he ended this. He centered the crosshairs on the elevator doors, then swung the sight picture down and back until Big Fish was centered in his view, moving pretty badly now as it seemed the one leg was completely disabled. And the pack on his back wasn't helping. Piet hadn't been wrong. It was heavy. Big Fish was maybe fifty feet from the elevator doors, partly in profile but showing his back to Rufus. Rufus made a small adjustment to his sight, centered his crosshairs on the briefcase strapped to Big Fish's backpack, had it all lined up for a second, then lost it. At any point he could have hit Big Fish, hurt him at least, maybe killed him. But he had really hoped to get through the day without murdering someone. That briefcase was the real target. But it was strapped to Big Fish, who was moving. Not in a steady way but lurching on a bad leg across broken ground.

But then all of a sudden he just stopped. Big Fish straightened up and just stood there stock-still.

Rufus put his crosshairs on the target and pulled the trigger.

Halfway to the head frame, Laks had an insight about how over-reliance on technology could lull you into a dangerous complacency. Sadly, what triggered this realization was his looking down to see that a diamondback rattlesnake had plunged its fangs into his right leg just above the knee.

They did not have such things on the coast of British Columbia, which enjoyed an Ireland-like immunity from venomous serpents. He had heard of them inland, where Uncle Dharmender lived, but had never seen one. Having spent some time in India he was not an absolute stranger to poisonous snakes. But the sheer size of this creature was appalling. Three meters if it was an inch, and *meaty*. You could feed a family with this thing.

As soon as he understood the nature of what was going on, he kicked it away. The weight of the pack pulled him off balance and sent him tumbling. The snake coiled up and rattled its tail as Laks scooted away on his butt. When he had got well clear, he climbed to his feet and put a little more distance between him and the snake, now scanning the ground more carefully in case there were others.

He sat down, took out his knife, and slit the leg of his earthsuit just above the right knee, where the fangs had gone in. It didn't look like much: two neat little punctures, the skin around them getting red and beginning to swell. He had a vague recollection that you were supposed to suck out the poison. Which might have been possible if it were lower on his leg, but only a contortionist could have got his lips onto this wound. He tried squeezing the area around the bite and got some blood to leak out of the holes but he hadn't a clue whether that was going to help him.

The only thing for it now was to keep going. The head frame was all of a thousand meters away. There was nothing between him and it but flat, albeit rough, terrain. On the far side of it was a freight train, its cars laden with yellow powder, feeding a big pile of the same, which was not too far from his destination. He'd got close enough now, and was low enough, that he had a view beneath all those stretched nets that covered the complex. He glimpsed steel buildings, systems of pipes and conveyors, parked forklifts.

When he got back to his feet he knew right away that walking to Mexico wasn't going to happen. After he completed the mission, he was going to have to come out with his hands up and surrender. Hopefully there'd be someone to surrender *to*; right now the complex seemed deserted. The only thing that kept it from being a total ghost town was some kind of activity along that row of train cars, involving sporadic gunfire and screaming birds.

The sooner he got this done, the sooner he could surrender and request medical attention. People around these parts would have snakebite kits and antivenom. They'd know what to do. Unless this thing on his back was a bomb, in which case he'd be dead anyway.

Limping along, just forcing himself to keep going, he bent his neck and looked up, trying not to be blinded by the sun, which had become brutal, like a sun on some godforsaken science fiction planet. He was looking for drones. It was no longer about the protection they afforded him. It was about Pippa. The stuff Pippa thought about. How the story was captured, how the tale was told. More important in the big scheme of things than what actually happened. He wished it was her flying those things, cutting the footage together, telling his story her way. He wished she had stuck around. He would have liked to be with her. Maybe after all this was done he could look her up. Los Angeles couldn't be too far away. He would go to the City of Angels and find her and tell her the true story.

He was so close to the Climate Weapon that he could have thrown a rock and hit it. The whole place was eerily quiet. All he had to do was drag himself another few yards. Then he could throw this monstrous weight down the shaft and be done with it. He was close enough now that he could see into the steel framework that enclosed the gun barrels and the elevator shaft and all the rest. He was looking for the right place to drop the briefcase down the hole.

But then he saw movement. Someone was moving in the middle of the structure. Climbing up from below on a ladder. He emerged into full view and stood there in plain sight on the top of the elevator enclosure. He looked around and immediately focused on Laks. A young man with long reddish-yellow hair. He reached into his pocket and pulled something out. Laks thought it must be a gun until light gleamed through it and he saw it was nothing more than a plastic water bottle. The man leaned back and dropped it. Then, after a last look back toward Laks, he turned away and dropped out of sight.

The man had gone back down the shaft.

There were people down there. At least one. Maybe more.

Whatever this device on Laks's back was, he was about to drop it down a hole where people were taking shelter.

He stopped. This wasn't part of the plan. Or was it? People weren't supposed to be down there.

Something jerked him around, shifting his weight to his bad leg, causing him to spin down onto his ass. A moment later he heard the report of a rifle. Someone had shot him! No, not him. The bullet had struck his backpack. It had scored a hit on the briefcase.

He couldn't get up as long as the weight of the pack was strapped to his back. He loosened the shoulder straps and shrugged free, undid the waist belt, got on all fours, then used his arms and his good leg to stand up.

Immediately the pack spun away from him and he heard a second shot. Then a third. The pack got a little farther away from him each time. The briefcase was getting more and more mangled. It was leaking some kind of silvery powder onto the ground.

The heat was terrific. He felt sunburned all over.

No, not all over. On his front. The side facing the mangled briefcase and the trail of silver dust it was leaking across the ground.

The horizon swung round and a rock smashed into his shoulder. He knew what this was. He'd just fallen down. Used to happen all the time after his inner ear had got messed up, before they'd fixed it. Something must have gone wrong with the equipment in his head.

He couldn't get up now. He didn't know what up was. He just lay there on his side, feeling the pressure of the world on his body. His right arm was extended on the ground in front of him, exposed skin turning red with sunburn, the steel bracelet—not a speck of rust on it—cool and pure against the blistered skin. A reminder that he should always use his strong right hand to do the right thing. He was pretty sure he had.

COMBUSTION CHAMBER

Coke," T.R. said, drawing his finger along the wall of the combustion chamber. It came away black. For the wall, indeed all the interior surfaces of the place, were as black as black could be. And not shiny black. This had a coarse, matte texture that swallowed all light.

"I was going to guess carbon," Saskia said. When she'd last seen the place, everything had been gleaming new polished steel.

"Same diff," T.R. said. "Coke is just one of those weird old English words. An old-timer word. When you take coal and bake it, drive off all the random volatile shit left over from the dead dinosaurs, eventually you end up with basically pure carbon. A very high-quality fuel."

"What's it doing all over the walls of your combustion chamber?"

"When a hydrocarbon fuel burns, some of the carbon gets deposited as a residue," T.R. said. "Builds up over time. My daddy used to take his Cadillac out on a long stretch of highway and put the pedal to the metal for a spell. Claimed he was blowing the carbon out of the cylinders. A routine maintenance procedure. Not sure if it really did anything but hoo-ee! It was a thrill to us kids in the back seat. Mom hated it. Anyway, an engineer would say this thing is getting coked up."

Saskia didn't want to get "coked up," so she spread an emergency blanket on the floor of the combustion chamber. This was bowl-shaped, no part of it really vertical or horizontal, and so when she sat on the blanket she had to pick a position somewhere between sitting up and lying down. The bottom of the bowl was occupied by a little heap of supplies, including the battery-powered flashlight that was their sole illumination. Somewhere in there was a box of emergency candles and some matches, for when the battery ran out.

Above they heard footsteps—two pairs of them, she judged—and then the profound thump of the Minus Four hatch being closed. A few moments after that, two crisp taps reverberated through the piston that served as their ceiling and the pump chamber's floor. A signal that both Conor and Jules had taken refuge up there.

"I wonder what Jules saw that made him drop the bottle," Saskia said.

"If only I could remember my Morse code from Boy Scouts, we could find out," T.R. said. He sat down on the opposite side of the bowl and looked across at Saskia. The beam of the light went straight up and basically disappeared, swallowed by the coke. T.R.'s face was a barely discernible oval on the other side of it.

"At this point," he said, "you gotta be asking yourself why the hell you came back to the Flying S Ranch."

Saskia eased herself down the slope of the bowl until she was squatting on her haunches next to the pile of supplies. She groped around and found the box of candles, then opened the lid. Next to it was a box of safety matches. She sparked one off and let it flare, then got a candle going.

"Thank you for conducting that free stress test of our gas management system," T.R. said. "If there'd been methane or hydrogen in here—"

"I know why I came back," Saskia said. She lit a second candle from the first one, then melted some wax to make a puddle on the floor and stuck a candle into it.

"And why's that?" T.R. asked, staring into the flame. Saskia was looking at it too; like all fire it drew the eye and hypnotized. Which in a way was how the world had got into this mess in the first place. She handed him the second candle.

"Someone I met wanted to send you a message. Presumably the Mossad."

"Oh? What's the ol' Mossad wanting to share with me?"

So much had happened that Saskia could barely remember it. While she was thinking about it she lit another candle and planted it on the floor. "It sounded to me as though they had picked up some chatter to the effect that China was planning something."

T.R. chuckled.

"Something in response specifically to your geoengineering activities," Saskia continued.

"They were right," T.R. said.

"That's why I asked Willem to pay you a visit."

"Much obliged."

"I have no idea whether India was also on their radar. But it was a very general sort of warning, so who knows?" She lit another candle.

"What would you say was the overall gist of this warning, then?" T.R. asked, watching—a bit nervously—as Saskia lit yet another candle.

"Tunnel vision," Saskia said. She couldn't resist tilting her head back to gaze straight up toward the coked ceiling. She knew it was up there, but no amount of candlelight was going to make it visible. "Perhaps mine shaft would have been more apt than tunnel."

"I stood right here a couple years ago, after this shaft was dug, but before we'd put anything in," T.R. said. "It was the middle of the night, totally dark. Way up above me I could see a tiny disk of sky, with a star in it. One star, all by itself. I thought to myself, 'Well, there it is! Heard about it all my life! Now I'm looking right at it!'"

"Which star was it?" Saskia asked. She was lighting another candle.

"Hell if I know. It was a lone star, is the point."

Saskia looked at him quizzically over the candle flame.

"This is the Lone Star State," T.R. explained.

"Ah, I see, so you took it as an omen."

"You know, Your Royal Highness, it's a funny thing about candles. They're real purty and all, especially when you get a lot of 'em going at once—"

"But they produce carbon dioxide."

"Yup."

"They are raising the CO_2 level of the atmosphere we depend on," Saskia said.

"Yup, I knew you'd make the connection."

"And yet, what's the harm in lighting one more candle? It's only a tiny contribution to the problem."

"You do it anyway," T.R. said, "because you can tell yourself a story about how this is going to end."

"Oh?"

"Either terrorists are gonna come down here and blow us up, or we're gonna be rescued by the good guys. Either way you can probably light all the candles you want, Saskia. We probably won't run out of 'em and find ourselves in the dark. We probably won't asphyxiate on CO_2. 'Cause something bad or good's gonna happen before we get to that point. Someone out there is gonna take some kind of action, while we sit on our butts and wait and have learned conversations about how bad these candles are. And I just hate being that guy."

"You want to be the guy up there, taking action."

"Someone's gotta."

"But then China, India, the Saudis . . . when powers like that get involved, you're helpless."

"They're gonna do what's in their national interest. Always have, always will. You think China didn't have its eye on that copper mine before I started building a gun there? The gun was a pretext, that's all. Does that mean I oughta do *nothing*? When I got the means to do *something*?"

"All that stuff you told us about raising the value of Houston real estate was just bullshit," Saskia said.

"Not exactly. That was me making sure it penciled out. But was it my only reason? 'Course not."

"We're stuck down here because India is pissed off at you," Saskia said. "I've talked to people with connections in the Punjab. I've seen climate models suggesting that this thing"—she slapped the combustion chamber wall, and her palm came away black with carbon—"this thing right *here* could reduce crop yields *there*! Is it any wonder they've sent people to blow it up? Perfectly reasonable, if you ask me."

"If they'd bothered to ask," T.R. said, "I'd have showed them Vadan. Sneeuwberg. Showed 'em the simulations my boys put together of how we can make it all work. Punjab's gonna be fine."

"But you have to tell them that."

"They have to *give a shit*. They don't. They just want to pull off a PR stunt, get votes in the next election."

"I understand how democracies work," Saskia said. "Believe me, I do. But their PR stunt might kill us. Isn't that an indication that you might have made a mistake?"

"I don't deny things have gotten a little out of hand," T.R. admitted.

Saskia laughed out loud.

"But you gotta start somewhere. Sometimes you drill a well and you get a gusher. Makes quite a mess. But you just gotta deal with it. Get it under control, cap it off."

Saskia just shook her head. They sat there in silence for a minute. Not perfect silence; it might have been her imagination, but through her back, which was leaning against the hard floor of the dome, she thought she could feel faint thumps. Footsteps, maybe.

"That's why I need you," T.R. said.

Saskia sighed.

"Sorry," T.R. added. He seemed puzzled by her reaction.

"Oh, not at all," Saskia said. "It's just that there's a lot of that kind of thing going around. I'm the Queen of Netherworld, did you hear?"

"I was so informed."

"A prince gave me a jet."

T.R. shrugged. "You crash a jet, someone gives you a jet, things even out over time."

"You can't just admit you need me and pretend that makes a difference," Saskia said. *"You have to listen."*

A blinding bright crescent appeared on the wall of the combustion chamber. Someone had opened the latch a crack. Silhouetted was the head of a person wearing some kind of getup that completely covered their head. They were breathing through a respirator. Visible just behind this person was a wall of plastic sheeting that had apparently been taped into place to create a barrier between the area surrounding the hatch and the rest of the mine shaft. They tossed a pair of bundles in and then closed the door.

Saskia was closest. She pushed herself up to her feet and carried a candle over to investigate. Each of the bundles was sealed in clear plastic: a coverall, neatly folded up, and a respirator.

Taped to one of them was a sheet of printer paper on which someone had written with a marker: RADIATION HAZARD! PUT THESE ON, THEN KNOCK.

"The cavalry, I guess," T.R. remarked.

"There must be some kind of contamination up there," Saskia said. One of the suits was a medium, the other a large. She tossed the large to T.R.

"I refuse to be the mom in the Cadillac," she said, and ripped the packet open.

"Beg pardon?"

"Your story about Daddy blowing the carbon out of the cylinders, blasting down some Texas highway in the Cadillac, made it all sound very amusing for the kids in the back and the man behind the wheel. But all you said of your mother was that she hated it. I won't be her."

"Point taken," T.R. said. "You won't be."

QUEEN OF THE NETHERWORLD

Frederika Mathilde Louisa Saskia's new plane didn't fly as high as the old one. The stratosphere was out of reach for her now; it was a realm where other people carried out wild schemes to change the climate, but not a place she would go. So the journey from Houston back to the Flying S Ranch took a little longer than doing it in a bizjet. But if she was going to take this Queen of Netherworld thing seriously she couldn't keep doing things the old way. And it gave her that much more time to get acquainted with Mohinder. She'd met him briefly last year, when she and the other guests had lunched on brisket at his T.R. Mick's Mobility Center. But they hadn't really talked, of course. So during the flight now across the endless rangeland of West Texas he was able to acquaint her with some of his people's traditions around funerals and mourning. And she was able to explain some of the practical challenges to him.

The case on Laks's back, she explained, turned out to contain a small cylinder of Cobalt-60 dust wrapped around an explosive charge. Just enough to have rendered the Pina2bo gun unusable, if everything had gone according to plan. T.R. would have been forced to fill the hole with concrete. Instead of which, a small area on the surface, near the head frame, had been contaminated and would have to be buried and capped before anyone could go near the place.

Unfortunately Laks's body was in the middle of it, and there was no way to stop buzzards and other scavengers from getting to it. Out of respect for the dead, and to prevent animals from spreading the contamination, the army had already covered the site in the only material that was near to hand in sufficient quantity: sulfur. Gravel and concrete were en route to finish the job.

By the time they were lining up the approach to the airstrip at the Flying S Ranch, Saskia had sat in the co-pilot's seat during a dozen landings. Like a lot of modern planes, the thing practically flew itself. Ervin felt comfortable having her at the controls during the landing. He could take over at a moment's notice. Or just let the thing land itself on Flying S's long, dry, and swine-free runway.

> Down safe. Go to bed!

> Good luck and good night Mama

> Same to you, Your Majesty

> LOL

Their approach had swung well clear of the big gun. Part of that was just the usual precautions taken by pilots who didn't want to get punched out of the air by supersonic bullets full of molten sulfur. There were no bullets in the air today, but there were other reasons to stay clear of that area. Still, they'd been able to view it from a distance. A lake of yellow sulfur had begun to form near the head frame, marking the extent of the contamination. Huge khaki-colored machines were moving around on tank treads. Those were the only impressions Saskia was able to take in, glancing out the side window during the preparation for landing.

The end of the airstrip closest to the terminal had become a little military hub. Several army planes and choppers were parked there instead of the usual lineup of bizjets. They'd stretched nets everywhere and set up defensive emplacements that Saskia recognized as being special transmitters that would supposedly knock drones out of the air by shooting out beams that would jam their electronics. And as a last line of defense, there were just a lot of soldiers cradling shotguns. But it was all precautionary; T.R.'s people, who had been feeding them status reports, were saying that no hostile drones had been sighted on the property since about noon yesterday, when the government of India had announced formal cessation of their Climate Peacekeeping action in the lawless, war-torn tribal region of West Texas.

She parked the plane where she was told to and thanked Ervin. He'd now have his hands full trying to figure out how to get a hydrogen truck through the military cordon. But she didn't plan on going anywhere soon. She deployed the plane's stairway and looked down the steps to see Amelia waiting for her.

Amelia raised her arms tentatively as if to inquire whether it would be altogether unprofessional for her to hug Her Royal Highness. Saskia came down off the last step and all but body-slammed her, knowing that she could take it. The hug was a long one. And by the time it was over, and they parted, so much had been said in that wordless clinch that Saskia felt no compunction about getting straight to business.

"You'll remember Mr. Singh, from last year's luncheon," Saskia said.

Mohinder had paused at the top of the steps while Saskia and Amelia greeted each other, but now descended to shake hands and exchange pleasantries.

"Do I smell barbecue?" Saskia asked.

"As Mr. Singh can probably explain," Amelia said, "it turns out that this is called *grilling*. Barbecue is different—takes longer. Red only lit the fire half an hour ago."

Saskia had instinctively made for the door of the terminal, but Amelia waved her around the side. "Unusable," she explained, "no power, no air-conditioning."

They could now peek around the corner of the building to the point where Saskia could see T.R. talking to a tall slender girl with auburn hair, who reminded her a bit of Lotte. "Who's she?"

"Pippa. A friend of the deceased." Amelia turned to Mohinder. "She's been shooting some video, but she'll leave you out of it if you prefer."

"Video of what?"

"Of the conversation you're about to have. How to show respect to the remains."

"Happy to offer some pointers," Mohinder said, "but it's really a question for the family. What's their status? I heard they got held up crossing the border?"

Amelia nodded, with just a trace of an eye roll. "American CBP is freaking out about anyone who has connections to India. We're working the problem. But they won't be here until tomorrow, best-case scenario."

Amelia led them all the way around the corner, revealing a little encampment. Tarps had been anchored to the side of the terminal building and stretched with ropes and poles to shade a little patch of level desert. But the sun was getting low enough that it was cutting under and making everyone look like they'd been dipped in honey. Picnic tables were scattered around. At one of them Saskia recognized Piet and Thordis, whom she had met during their work at Schiphol, as well as two other women whom she could guess were the other falconers she'd heard about. They were busy tending to a golden eagle, working on one of its feet. Thordis glanced up and saw Saskia. She and Piet stood up. Saskia waved at them and they smiled back.

T.R. was striding their way. "Howdy, Mr. Singh. So grateful you could make the journey."

"Evening, boss. My new friend here made it very easy. How may I be of service?"

"I am informed that priests don't exist in your faith. Very wise, if you ask me. Not that anyone's asking me."

"Until the family arrives," Mohinder said, "I am more than happy to consult on how to show proper respect for the young man's remains."

"That is indeed our chief concern," T.R. said, "now that the site has been locked down and covered up. The army boys have some maps and photos and so on if you'd like to come over and take a look."

T.R. led Mohinder toward another table where an army officer was putting rocks on documents to keep them from fluttering in the breeze.

In the middle of the little encampment, Rufus was sitting on a cooler tending a grill. He was wearing a Flying S swag T-shirt, a little too small for him, but Saskia didn't mind. A pair of cargo shorts showed a heavily bandaged lower leg, which he had propped up on a footstool improvised from two cases of Mexican beer. He gave her an understated nod as she approached.

Amelia had silently peeled away.

His eyes swiveled calmly over the scene, taking inventory, as she could guess, of who was watching.

Not wanting to make him uncomfortable, Saskia slowed as she approached.

"Are you radioactive?"

"Been checked out," he said. "Answer's apparently no. But I guess it really depends on what you mean by that."

"You aren't, in my book."

"Good to know. Welcome to Texas." He pulled a plastic plate from a stack and used his fingers to snatch a sizzling morsel of steak onto it, then handed it to her. The grill was crowded with pieces of chicken, beef, and sausages that were swelling up and beginning to split open to show chunks of red and green pepper and orange cheese inside. Saskia, who had been subsisting on granola bars for twenty-four hours, could have eaten everything there. She accepted the plate and tried not to just shove her face into it.

"Get you a beer?"

"I'm fine for now, thanks." She knew everything about this was terrible: burning wood to cook meat from methane-farting cows and serving it on throwaway petrochemical plates.

"Bison," he said, as if reading her mind. "Supposedly better."

"It's really good to see you, Red."

"Pleasure's all mine."

"Tell me about what happened."

"You want the full version? Or—"

"There'll be time for that later, I hope."

"You know about what was on his back."

"Just enough Cobalt-60 to make the site unusable for a hundred years."

Rufus nodded.

"But other than that—there would be no collateral damage."

He nodded. "That was the idea. Minimal casualties. But enough of a mess to stop geoengineering activities here until T.R. could build a new gun—at least a couple of years."

"And send a message."

"Messages ain't my area of specialization," he said.

"Shutting down the gun would cause a termination shock."

"Chance they were willing to take, I guess." He sighed. "Anyway, I didn't know what it was."

"Of course not."

"Thought it was a bomb. Thought I could disable it. Maybe give him a chance to get out of this in one piece." Rufus stared off across the desert, replaying it in his mind's eye. He stuck out his tongue, then, after a few seconds, pulled it back in. "He stopped."

"What?"

"Yeah. When he saw Jules, apparently. That's how Jules tells the story. I didn't see nothing but the device, through the sights of my rifle, so Jules had to tell me that later."

Saskia nodded.

"He stopped," Rufus repeated. "Like he realized, at that instant, that people were taking shelter down in the bottom of the shaft."

"He understood that he was about to take our lives," Saskia said, nodding.

"I hit it three times. Just to be sure. Tore it wide open. But because of what was inside of it, he got a lethal dose of the gamma rays. Something was wrong with his leg before, he wasn't moving right. Anyway. Down he went. In the army I learned enough about NBC—"

"NBC?"

"Nuclear-biological-chemical warfare. I didn't want to come near any of that shit. Soon as I seen him go down I scooted down the pile into the pit under the hopper cars and sheltered in place. Drones stopped coming. I heard the sheriff driving up from Bunkhouse. Hopped down the railroad tracks, keeping the boxcars between me and any radiation, and waved 'em off. Told 'em to call in the NBC guys from Fort Bliss. White Sands. All of that. But they'd already picked up the gamma rays from the air. So NBC was already on-site."

"The people who came and rescued us."

"Yeah."

"I saw the lake of yellow from the plane—"

Rufus nodded. "Sulfur's what they got in abundance, it's what they're using for the first layer. Army had rad-hardened bulldozers. They brought 'em in on trains overnight."

"Amazing."

"What?"

"That they have such things."

"This country is a mess," Rufus allowed, "but it's still one of the only outfits that can pull a fleet of lead-lined bulldozers out of its ass on short notice. They got started at first light, moving the pile over to cover the contaminated area and keep that shit from spreading on the wind. Gravel's on its way. Later they'll cap it with concrete."

"The dead man?"

"Still there. Will be forever." Rufus looked toward the table where T.R. had been talking to Mohinder and the army officer. They were looking down at maps and aerial photos, talking it over.

"Let's talk later," Saskia said. "I'm so glad you're safe."

"You enjoy horseback riding?"

"Love it."

"Western style?"

"English, I'm afraid."

"We'll put you on Patch," he said, "he's as easygoing as they come."

"I am very much looking forward to you taking me on a ride, Red," she said as she was turning away. But she wasn't sure that double entendres were his cup of tea. There was a stratum of society in which she had lived most of her life where that kind of persiflage was something you were expected to know how to do, just as you were expected to know how to shoot pheasants and use a finger bowl. She felt a bit stupid, just for a moment, that she'd used that sort of conversational gambit on this man who'd lived his life on the opposite pole of the world from all that. It wasn't quite fair of her. She hesitated, thinking she really ought to just say what was on her mind in a more plainspoken way.

While she was dithering over how to phrase it, Rufus had turned his attention back to his grill. "Woo-eee!" he exclaimed, "I got a hot sausage here that's about to bust open from the heat if I don't take good care."

She spun away to hide a blush and nearly collided with Pippa. There was a brief awkward moment. The Kiwi bent her long legs in a passable curtsy. "Your Majesty."

"Royal Highness, if you're going to be that way."

"Royal Highness it is."

"Pippa, is it? Short for Philippa?"

"Yes."

"Saskia." They shook hands. "I'm told you were a friend of the deceased. I'm terribly sorry."

The low afternoon sun on Pippa's freckled face made it obvious she'd been crying. But she wasn't crying now. "Talking to the family will be difficult," she said. "Not looking forward to that. Hope they don't blame me."

"Why ever would they?"

"I had some role in telling his story. Making him famous. Could be that I egged him on."

"But surely you had no hand in *this*."

"Oh, no, ma'am. Not at all. I drove out from L.A. when Red told me what was happening. Was hoping I could talk him out of it. But I got here too late."

"Well . . . now you can tell the rest of his story," Saskia suggested. "Even if it is a sad one."

Pippa nodded. "Ma'am—to the extent *you're* becoming part of that story now—I was wondering—"

"Go right ahead, dear," Saskia said. "This is what I do now."

Pippa gave a grateful nod and stepped out of her way.

"Gentlemen!" Saskia exclaimed, striding toward the picnic table. "Can anything be done? What's that I see on that laptop?" It looked like a picture of some kind of obelisk or spire.

Mohinder turned his head to look back at it. "Oh, I was showing T.R. some monuments that exist in the Punjab. Built to honor the heroes of our past. Saint-soldiers who fell in battle defending our homeland"—he looked significantly between T.R. and Saskia—"from foreigners who would seek to deprive us of the Breadbasket."

"Let's have a talk about that, shall we?" Saskia suggested, stepping between the two men and taking each of them by an arm. They turned to follow and began walking into the most magnificent sunset Saskia had ever seen. Amelia cut in front of them to look for rattlesnakes. Pippa, flanked by a couple of video drones, fell in behind as they strolled out into the desert. "I don't know if you've heard," she said, "but I just took a new job and it's time I got started."

ACKNOWLEDGMENTS

The author is grateful to the following persons who (in some cases inadvertently) helped him in large and small ways. Note, however, that the author conceived and wrote the book himself, and so a person's appearance on the following list should not be interpreted to suggest that they hold any position one way or the other on topics mentioned in these pages. Some of the relevant interactions happened long before I even considered writing this book!

Jacques Bergman, Nocona Burgess, Jennifer Chayes, William Collins, Craig Danner, Carolyn Dwyer, George Dyson, Beth Epstein, staff and ownership of the Figure 2 Ranch, Tony Halmos, Marco Kaltofen, David Keith, Frank Keutsch, Janno Lanjouw, Karen Laur, Jascha Little, Scott Little, Mark Long, Michael Mainelli, Charles Mann, Ravi Mirchandani, Oliver Morton, Nathan Myhrvold, Marla Nauni, Jan-Peter Onstwedder, Lennert van Oorschot, Gordon Roy, Lynn Schonchin, Tom Standage, Zoe Stephenson, Benny Tahmahkera, Troy, William Voelker, Steven Weber, Lowell Wood.

Lists such as the above can sometimes overstate the importance of casual or fleeting interactions. Books, and to a lesser extent Internet resources, are frequently more important even though I may never have interacted personally with the people who wrote them. It feels wrong to leave such persons off the list and so here are people whose writings, or in some cases digital content on the Internet, have made a difference:

I. Lehr Brisbin Jr.; Ken Caldeira; Tan Chee-Beng; the Comanche Language and Cultural Preservation Committee; Steve Cottrell; T.R. Fehrenbach; Stuart Gilbert; S. C. Gynne; Kyle Harper; Ray Horner; Theodora Kleisma; Jan A. Krancher; David LaVere; Thomas F. Madden; John J. Mayer; George A. Mealey; Leslie H. Palmier; Neil Price; D. S. Saggu; Khushwant Singh; Nikky Guninder Kaur Singh; Sargun Singh; the originators, compilers, and translators of the

Shri Guru Granth Sahib; Paul Chaat Smith; Doug J. Swanson; Jean Gelman Taylor; Forbes Wilson.

As of this writing (June 2021) the author earnestly intends to post a bibliography that curious readers might use to track down relevant links and references; if that ever happens it will most likely show up at nealstephenson.com.